TRACIE PETERSON

Desert Roses

TRACIE PETERSON

Desert Roses

BETHANYHOUSE
Minneapolis, Minnesota

Desert Roses
Copyright © 2002, 2003
Tracie Peterson
Previously published in three separate volumes:
    Shadows of the Canyon © 2002 by Tracie Peterson
    Across the Years © 2003 by Tracie Peterson
    Beneath a Harvest Sky © 2003 by Tracie Peterson

Cover design by Eric Walljasper

Scripture quotations are from the King James Version of the Bible.

Published by Bethany House Publishers
11400 Hampshire Avenue South
Bloomington, Minnesota 55438

Bethany House Publishers is a division of
Baker Publishing Group, Grand Rapids, Michigan.

Printed in the United States of America

ISBN-13: 978-0-7642-0292-6
ISBN-10: 0-7642-0292-8

Library of Congress Cataloging-in-Publication Data has been applied for

TRACIE PETERSON is the bestselling, award-winning author of more than seventy historical and contemporary novels. Her books make regular appearances on CBA bestseller lists. For more information on Tracie, visit her Web site at *www.traciepeterson.com*. She and her family live in Belgrade, Montana.

BOOKS *by* TRACIE PETERSON

www.traciepeterson.com

The Long-Awaited Child • A Slender Thread
What She Left for Me • I Can't Do It All!

ALASKAN QUEST
Summer of the Midnight Sun
Under the Northern Lights
Whispers of Winter

BELLS OF LOWELL*
Daughter of the Loom • A Fragile Design
These Tangled Threads

LIGHTS OF LOWELL*
A Tapestry of Hope • A Love Woven True
The Pattern of Her Heart

DESERT ROSES
Shadows of the Canyon • Across the Years
Beneath a Harvest Sky

HEIRS OF MONTANA
Land of My Heart • The Coming Storm
To Dream Anew • The Hope Within

WESTWARD CHRONICLES
A Shelter of Hope • Hidden in a Whisper
A Veiled Reflection

RIBBONS OF STEEL†
Distant Dreams • A Promise for Tomorrow

RIBBONS WEST†
Westward the Dream

SHANNON SAGA‡
City of Angels • Angels Flight
Angel of Mercy

YUKON QUEST
Treasures of the North • Ashes and Ice
Rivers of Gold

*with Judith Miller   †with Judith Pella   ‡with James Scott Bell

Shadows of the Canyon

"And in here," Alexandria Keegan announced, "are the bulk refrigerator storage areas." Alex stepped past the new Harvey House recruit and opened the door to the unit. "We keep all manner of fresh produce, fish, and . . ." She fell silent as she heard the new girl gasp.

"Oh, Miss Keegan," the girl said, blushing red and turning away.

Alex couldn't imagine what the problem was, for the girl looked positively mortified. Turning to look into the unit, Alex fully expected to see a dead rat on the floor. Such a distasteful occurrence didn't happen often, but there was that rare occasion when something unpleasant marred the Harvey restaurant's otherwise impeccable reputation.

Alex grimaced at the scene. It was a rat, all right. But this rat was the two-legged type. Worse still, this rat was her father.

Rufus Keegan, well-known for his philandering ways, was at it once again. Pressed into a compromising position in the corner of the room, one of the newer Harvey Girls appeared to be enjoying Rufus Keegan's lack of discretion.

Alex felt her cheeks grow hot as embarrassment washed over her. How many times would she have to endure this shame upon her family? How could her father just go on humiliating her mother like this, never concerning himself with the pain he caused? Alex felt tears come to her eyes at the thought of all her mother had endured.

"Bernice, please go to the main dining room and bring Mrs. Godfrey." Alex steadied her emotions. She knew it would be better to have the dining room manager and housemother take charge of the situation.

Bernice, whose face was nearly as red as her bobbed hair, hurried off down the corridor. Alex turned to find her father smoothing the wrinkles in his clothing.

"Do you never tire of bringing shame to our family?" Alex asked, her voice a deadly calm.

"There needn't be any shame if you keep your mouth shut. Honestly, Alexandria, I don't see why you concern yourself with matters that have little to do with you."

Alex forced herself to remain silent and looked past her father to Melina Page. The girl was clearly embarrassed, but she didn't appear overly worried as she adjusted her black Harvey uniform.

"You should gather your things, Melina. I'm certain Mrs. Godfrey will have no further use for you," Alex said, staring hard at the girl.

"But you said you'd keep me from getting fired," Melina said, turning to Rufus. He only shrugged and chuckled. "But you promised!" Melina's voice raised an octave.

"He promised my mother a great many things, as well," Alex said. "But so far, he doesn't seem to honor any of those promises, either." Without conscious thought, Alex reached for the closest object—a plump, ripe, California tomato. "You are without a doubt everything the newspapers say about you and more. I'm ashamed to call you Father."

"Then don't. And don't take that tone with me. You don't have to call me Father or even acknowledge me as such, but I won't take a dressing down by the likes of you or anyone else. I don't take that tone of voice from the governor of this state! What makes you think I'll take it from my daughter?"

Shame was quickly overcome by anger, as years of betrayal seemed to culminate in this one act. Without warning, Alex threw the tomato. She picked up another tomato and then another. Hurling them mindlessly at her father, she shouted a tirade of disapproval.

"You don't care anything about my mother. You've caused her nothing but shame and anguish. Her health suffers because of you and she has no friends because you can't even give the pretense of discretion."

The ripe tomatoes splattered against the wall, against Melina's dress, and against the stun-faced Keegan.

Uncaring about the mess she was making or the vegetables she might destroy, Alex only knew that she wanted to hurt her father as badly as he'd hurt her mother. "We've suffered so much because of you. Mother can't even go to church for fear of what will be said to her!"

"Miss Keegan!"

The voice of Mrs. Godfrey caused Alex to pause. She looked momentarily at the confused woman, then picked up an apple. "My father and Melina chose to make this their trysting place." She hurled the apple, which her father barely managed to dodge before it hit the back wall with a dull thud.

Mrs. Godfrey reached out to Alex. Her grasp on Alex's left hand did nothing to waylay her from securing another apple with her right. This time she aimed for Melina.

"He doesn't deserve to get away with this." Alex nearly screamed the words, not caring who heard.

"Hey, what's happening? I heard the hollering going on all the way down the . . ."

Alex turned, catching sight of Luke Toland. The tall, lanky cowboy had his hat pushed back on his head, his sandy-colored hair hanging down over his left brow. He appeared shocked to say the least, but Alex could take no more of her father's indiscretion.

She jerked away from Mrs. Godfrey and reached again for the nearest object. It just happened to be a large stalk of celery. Before she could throw it, however, Luke stepped in and took hold of her.

"I don't know what's happening here, but I'm sure throwing this celery isn't going to remedy the matter." He spoke softly and eyed Alex with grave concern. His gentleness was her undoing, and her tears overflowed as she collapsed against his chest and began to cry.

"He doesn't care how much he hurts us," she sobbed.

"Miss Page, please pick up your apron and follow me," Mrs. Godfrey commanded. "Your services will no longer be required by the Fred Harvey Company."

"But Mr. Keegan said . . ."

Alex lifted her gaze as Mrs. Godfrey frowned disapprovingly. "It doesn't matter what Mr. Keegan said. You are in my charge, and we do not tolerate this kind of behavior."

Melina began to cry as she passed by Alex, apron in hand. "But I need this job. I—"

"You should have thought about that before you lowered your standards of decency," Mrs. Godfrey said, leading the weeping girl from the room and down the hall.

"Perhaps if everyone lowered their standards a bit," Rufus Keegan suggested in a loud voice, "we wouldn't find ourselves answering to uptight virgins and sour old biddies."

Alex twisted in Luke's arms and started to charge for her father, wanting only to scratch the smug look off his face and clean the air of his vile words. Luke held her tight, however, and no matter how she tried to fight his hold, her actions were futile.

"Alex," Luke whispered against her ear, "it won't do any good. He doesn't care."

Alex grew still in his arms. She looked over her shoulder, his face so close it nearly touched her own. Turning back to her father, she felt her rage further ignite at the expression on his face.

"I see this wrangler knows how to handle you. Good for you, son." Keegan smoothed the sides of his mustache and trailed the stroke down to his chin. "You know, maybe if you'd spend more time keeping hold of her, teaching her the more pertinent things of life," he grinned and approached Alex and Luke with confident strides, "she'd be a whole lot happier and maybe even more cooperative." He paused as he passed by the couple. "See, I've always found that women were fairly easy to control so long as you handled them just right. Handle her with a tighter rein, cowboy. Show her who's the boss. It's about time she learned what the right man could do for her."

Alex drew back as though slapped. She could feel Luke tighten his hold on her arms, but it was the way Luke ground his teeth together that told her he'd reached his own limits with this conversation.

Reaching up to touch Luke's hand, Alex watched her father saunter down the hallway. "Like you said, Luke, he doesn't care."

"I want to put my fist through his face," Luke growled, his grasp becoming painful to Alex.

"You're hurting me, Luke," she said, patting his hand. He released her immediately. Alex turned and looked at her dearest friend in all the world. "Thanks for keeping me from making too big of a spectacle."

Luke's expression seemed to soften as he turned to look Alex in the face. "Your pitching arm needs some work," he said with a grin. Gone was the look of rage that had just been there. Alex could see his shoulders relax.

Turning back to look at the mess she'd created, Alex shook her head. "I couldn't help myself. I saw him doing those unspeakable things and shaming my mother, and all I wanted to do was hurt him." She looked back at Luke. "I wanted to hurt him like he was hurting me . . . hurting her."

Alex felt the tears smart her eyes again. "I try so hard to be a good Christian—to keep an attitude that would be pleasing to God—but then something like this happens. Oh, Luke, I can't take much more. How can I respect a man who so clearly does not deserve such honor? My mother has been hurt so much. What if she finds out what Father has done here today? Now her health has been suffering. I want to take her away from all of this, but she won't go."

"Why not?"

Alex shrugged. "She says she could never make it on her own—that Father would strip her of everything but the clothes on her back. She won't saddle her daughters with this, either. My sister, Audra, has offered to have Mother come live with her and her family in Wyoming, but Mother says it isn't right. But, Luke, it isn't right that she suffer this humiliation every time Father decides to chase after the newest Harvey Girl or hotel maid. It seems he's exhausted his possibilities in Williams, so now he's come here to the canyon and El Tovar. Soon there won't be a skirt in Arizona he hasn't tried to claim for his own. The management here is livid that Father would besmirch their good name."

"Why don't they forbid him entry?" Luke questioned. "After all, this is a luxury resort with plenty of important people. It's not like your father owns the place."

"No, but his political power and money keeps everyone hopping from here to Phoenix. He can pay off those who don't like his actions and cajole everyone else into doing things his way. Only the newspaper editor in Williams gives him a hard time, and that's because the owner has just as much clout as Father."

"I'm sorry, Alex."

She looked up at him, knowing he was sincere. He'd always treated her kindly in the four years since she'd come to work as a Harvey Girl at El Tovar. "I don't know what I'd do without you, Luke. Thank you for keeping me from making a complete fool of myself."

Luke grinned. "Need some help cleaning up?"

She shook her head. "No. I think the time alone will help me to cool off."

"That and closing the door," Luke motioned.

Alex had completely forgotten that they were allowing all the cold air to escape. "I should have never opened the door to begin with. Poor Bernice. She's the new girl. I was showing her around and . . . Well, the rest is pretty apparent. Anyway, I'd better get back to work. Seems like I'm always cleaning up my father's garbage."

"I really would be happy to help you. I'm done for the day and was just coming in to get a bite to eat." He seemed so eager to please her and the look on his face suggested a hopefulness that Alex couldn't ignore.

Alex patted his arm. "No. You've done more than anyone should have to do. Go eat your supper. You're a good friend, Luke." The look of pleasure left his face and was replaced with an expression of disappointment.

"Fine," he said and walked away without another word.

Alex shook her head at the hangdog manner in which he departed. Why should he be disappointed? She was saving him a great deal of messy work. Men! They were impossible to understand.

CHAPTER TWO

Luke wasn't in the mood for supper, still disgusted by the scene he'd stumbled upon in the back rooms of El Tovar's kitchen. He was also more than a little disturbed by Alex's continual use of the word *friend*.

He wanted to be more than Alex's friend. Four years of friendship had taught him that, if nothing else. He'd fallen in love with her somewhere along the way, but he couldn't put his finger on when that had exactly happened. Leaving the hotel, Luke headed down the rim path and sought solace in privacy. He ambled along just a little ways past the Lookout, a rustic creation where they offered telescopes to better view the scenic gorge.

Having spent the last ten years of his life wrangling horses and leading mule teams on various trips in the area, Luke knew the Grand Canyon like the back of his hand. He loved the canyon, and now, as he often did, Luke stared out across the vast wasteland and wondered at the glory of it all.

The sun was just starting to set in the western skies, sending slivers of orange and gold into the turquoise blue sky. The sky reminded him of Alex's eyes—eyes just the perfect shade of turquoise, with long dark lashes that, at times, gave her face a doll-like appearance. He'd memorized every inch, every feature of her face—from the high cheekbones and dark brows, to the straight nose that seemed to turn up just a bit at the tip. Her lips were full and touched with a natural blush of rosy pink that no cosmetic could ever match.

"If I ain't the lovesick cowboy," he muttered, kicking a stone over the edge. He watched the rock zigzag first this way and then that as it bounced off the rocky sentinels below.

The shadows stretched out and played games with the appearance of the canyon. The colors changed before his eyes, and only the laughter and voices from tourists strolling El Tovar's grounds reminded Luke he was not alone.

It was 1923 and this national park was getting more than its fair share of attention. Trains came twice a day, and sometimes more than that on special occasions. The cars were always filled with curious passengers who longed to see what the canyon could offer them. Few ever realized the true gift of such a majestic sight—the way the solitude could speak to their soul on a starry night, how the rush of the wind and the hum of the canyon bottom river combined to make a haunting calliope sound, or the way the scent of piñon and juniper joined with the fresh western breeze after a welcome rain.

Luke sighed. Those were the things that made this home to him. They were the wonders that made this part of Arizona a mystery to most and a heartwarming pleasure to others.

Taking off his hat, Luke wiped his brow and thought of all the changes in his life since coming to the canyon. He'd been a scrawny kid of twenty when he'd shown up looking for a job. He'd heard great things about this place all the way down in Tucson, where he'd been working as a ranch hand. He had been told the opportunity could net a man a great deal of money—enough money to start his own ranch after a year or two of work.

Luke hadn't found it quite that easy, but he had managed to set aside a good portion of his pay. While some of the other men went to Williams to spend their pay anytime they were given time off, Luke had spent his free hours at the canyon. He'd studied and educated himself on the flora and wildlife. He knew the area so well he could tell his way around in the dark . . . Well, almost.

The unmistakable sound of Alex's voice filtered through the air to reach his ears. Replacing his hat, Luke looked up to find Alex pointing the way toward El Tovar and saying something to the tourists who had stopped her. No doubt her shift had ended, and she was taking a walk to forget the scene in the cooler.

Luke deliberated for a moment. He wanted very much to ask Alex to walk with him, to spend the quiet of the evening at his side. He'd wanted that for a long time now, but he felt completely at odds as to how he could take their relationship past the point of friendship and into love. If he could just come out with the words—just tell her face-to-face that he was in love with her and wanted to spend the rest of his life with her.

Alex bid the tourists good-bye and headed toward the place where Luke stood indecisively. "I thought that was you," she said, smiling as she came to stand before him. She held a small covered basket. "Did you ever get some supper?"

"No. I just figured to get some fresh air and think a spell."

She smiled, and Luke felt the joy of it spill over him like the water at Deer Creek Falls. "Good. Then we can share my picnic."

"What?"

She held up the basket. "I packed a chicken salad sandwich, Camembert cheese, and sliced apples—instead of the applesauce that I made against the wall of the cooler." She smiled and continued. "And I have a jar of rather tart lemonade, but we'll have to share."

He smiled, knowing there was nothing in the world he wouldn't happily share with her. "Sounds wonderful."

"I thought so, too," she said, glancing around. "Where shall we share this feast?"

A great idea sprang to Luke's mind. "Let's borrow a car and get away from the area. Better yet, I'll get us a couple of horses and we can ride to this wonderful little spot I know."

Alex frowned, looking down at her uniform. "I'm hardly dressed for horseback riding. The Harvey Company hasn't seen their way to outfitting us with split skirts or trousers."

"Then we'll borrow Clancy's car," Luke said, knowing his right-hand man wouldn't begrudge him a few moments of privacy with Alex.

Alex laughed and nodded, handing the basket to Luke. "I think that sounds marvelous. My feet are sore from working tables all day long, anyway. I'm glad people love the canyon, but I do wish the management would staff more girls to help out."

They walked in companionable silence to where Luke knew he'd find Clancy feeding the mules. "Hey, Clancy, can I borrow your car? Alex thinks we need to have a picnic."

She playfully poked his ribs with her elbow. "It was his idea to borrow the car, Clancy. I had nothing to do with it. You know I've never been fond of the smelly things."

Clancy looked up and smiled, revealing a missing tooth. Just last month he'd taken a kick in the face from his favorite mule. He'd been black-and-blue for weeks, and even now the yellowed bruises were still visible in a few places.

"You can take her, just make sure you bring her back," Clancy said, straightening from where he'd been bent over the feed trough.

Luke gave his solemn promise, then ushered Alex to the car. He took them east and down a narrow road. "I know this place where we can sit and watch the sunset," he told Alex.

She said nothing but reached up to take the hairpins from her hair to let the breeze blow through her long brown curls. Luke had seen her like this once or twice before, and always it left him with a strange flutter in his stomach. She looked so very alluring with her hair down. He knew she had no idea of how her appearance affected him, and he wasn't about to tell her for fear she'd stop taking such casual liberties when she was in his presence.

Luke forced his gaze to stay on the road. In his mind he wrestled with his thoughts. *I could tell her how I feel,* he reasoned. *I could just say that she's come to mean the world to me and I'd like to court her formal-like.* Luke stole a glance and found Alex watching the road ahead. She didn't appear to have a clue as to how he felt.

Glancing at his watch, Luke pulled the car over and parked not far from the place he had in mind. "Come on. We'll walk just a bit, and if your feet are too tired, I'll carry you."

Alex laughed. "Oh, I'm sure after handling mules all day, I'd be a real treat."

"More than you know," Luke muttered under his breath.

"What did you say?"

He looked across the car at Alex and shook his head. "Nothing. Come on, we'd better get a move on if we're going to see all the colors. It's almost seven-thirty."

"That late already?" Alex questioned. "I suppose I lost track of time. Glad I got away when I did." She started to pull her hair back into a knot, but Luke grabbed up the basket and headed toward the trail.

"You haven't got time for that," he called over his shoulder. "Just leave your hair down."

His voice trembled just a bit. *Old boy, you've got it bad. Better keep quiet or you'll be making a complete idiot of yourself.*

They made their way down a narrow rocky path, angling ever closer to the rim of the canyon. Luke had a special place he liked to visit, and he knew Alex would appreciate the view, as well as the solitude. Visitors had long since headed back to the hotel and campgrounds, and they'd have the area to themselves, if Luke had judged the situation correctly. Besides, he'd never yet come across anyone who'd happened upon his secret place.

"Over here," Luke commanded. "We have to take this path."

"There's a path?" Alex teased. "Looks like a few boulders and some scrub brush."

Luke laughed. He appreciated her good mood. "See the ledge to the left?"

"You don't mean to tell me *that's* the path."

"I do." He paused and looked back at her. "You aren't going to go skittering back to the car, are you? Lost your nerve?"

Alex folded her arms against her chest. "I certainly haven't. You have the food and I'm starving. I'll follow you anywhere."

Her words hit Luke's lovesick heart like an arrow flying at full speed. "Come on, then."

He helped her around the rocks and down the last little bit of trail. Spread out before them was the Grand Canyon in all her colorful splendor. Alex gasped in surprise.

"This is incredible. How come you haven't told me about this place before?"

"It's always been here," Luke replied, taking a seat on a rocky outcropping.

Alex joined him, her gaze still fixed on the canyon below. "I've been in this area a hundred times, but I've never been down this trail."

"My own secret haunt," he said, taking the cloth from atop the basket. "You want to serve, or shall I?"

"Let's ask the blessing first and then I'll serve you." Alex bowed her head and began to pray. "Father, thank you so much for calming my spirit with the glory of your handiwork. Thank you for Luke's friendship and his wisdom in dealing with my father. And, thank you, Father, for this food and time together."

"Amen," Luke offered, trying not to think of her reference once again to their friendship. Surely married folks needed to be friends with each other. He'd try to keep it all in proper perspective.

Alex handed him half a sandwich and added, "I meant what I said. Your wisdom probably kept me from making a poor situation worse today. I prayed a great deal while I cleaned the storage area."

Luke had never been much for prayer or Christian matters until Alex had come into his life. His mother had lived a life full of faith and love of God, but her death when Luke had been only twelve had left him doubting the hope she found in such things. For years he had listened to his older brother and sister espouse their Christian beliefs and faith. Even his father, who died only two years after his mother, kept the family Bible by the bed stand and read it religiously every night before bed. But Luke had felt God a cruel master—a strict judge who stole mothers away from children.

Alex had changed Luke's heart—or rather, God had changed it because of Alex's persistent belief in His goodness and mercy. Even now, after what had transpired with her father, Alex would no doubt speak of God's goodness. It was a faith that Luke had great admiration for and had been strengthened by.

"I found it easy to react when I saw my father with Melina, but I didn't find it so easy to pray. I'm ashamed to have acted that way in front of Mrs. Godfrey," Alex admitted. She bowed her head to take a bite of her sandwich.

"Most folks would have done worse."

Alex shrugged. "But I wasn't a good witness. I didn't show myself to be guided by God's spirit. Rather I reacted like—"

Luke interrupted. "Like anyone else would have, given the circumstance. You were hurt, Alex. There's no shame in that. Sure, you could have walked away."

"Should have walked away."

"Or you could have locked them in the refrigerator." He grinned at her and waited for her reaction. She looked up and smiled. "I see the thought crossed your mind," he added.

"Anyway, thanks for understanding. You're good at knowing what to say to me and just how to help me through a tough moment."

Luke wondered if this wasn't just as good a time as any to share how he'd been feeling. He started to comment, then held back. If she wasn't of a mind to see their relationship head toward courtship and marriage, it would ruin the best friendship he'd ever had. Was he willing to let that happen?

"Oh, look," Alex said excitedly, "the entire canyon looks like it's on fire."

Luke turned from Alex and studied the horizon. "I knew you'd like it. See the way the shadows turn all purple and gray?"

"Almost the color of lilacs in spring," she murmured.

Luke nodded. The last bit of golden sun trailed out across the landscape, touching the rocky towers and outcroppings with a light that seemed to shimmer and glow. Orange-and-red rock below transformed to hues of muted brown, while farther in the canyon the shadows grew dark, swallowing up the last bits of color.

Glancing back at Alex, Luke felt himself mesmerized by her intent study of the canyon. Her dark brown curls rippled gently in the breeze.

Her turquoise eyes seemed to search for some missing piece—some subtle clue as to how it all began, how this canyon should find itself in this place, at this time. Luke leaned closer. Perhaps he'd simply kiss her and let his actions speak for his heart. He took a deep breath to steady his nerves.

She broke the spell of the moment. "I almost forgot the lemonade. Are you thirsty?"

"Huh?" He'd barely heard her words.

"I asked if you were thirsty. Do you want some lemonade?"

"Sure." Luke straightened and tried not to appear flustered. "That'd be nice."

Alex handed him a Mason jar. "Be warned, it's a bit sour."

"I like it that way," Luke said, taking a drink.

Alex picked up the conversation again. "Poor Melina was still crying when I left for the day. I don't know why women like that get caught up in the actions of men like my father. Mrs. Godfrey was clearly as uncomfortable as I was; yet she handled the matter with such grace and refinement. I guess that's what I wish I could do. Control my temper and keep a ladylike comportment about me."

"I don't see anything unladylike about the way you reacted. You were acting on your feelings and the love you have for your mother."

Alex turned to face Luke. "I feel particularly bad for the way Father treated you." She paused as her cheeks reddened. "Those lewd comments about . . . well, I won't repeat them," Alex said, paying strict attention to her sandwich. "I'm sorry he made suggestions about you and me."

Luke nearly choked. He didn't know what to say. Clearly he couldn't speak of his love for her on the tail of her father's obviously inappropriate comments. She might get the wrong idea. Worse yet, she might think Luke felt sorry for her and was only trying to make her feel better.

"Father can't understand what you and I have together."

What do we have? Luke wanted so much to voice the question aloud. Instead, he turned his attention to the food and let Alex do the talking.

"I was serious about wanting to take mother away from here. I've been saving my money. The wages, the tips . . . all of it. Tips are always good at the canyon, so I've got a good bit set aside. Even so, it wouldn't take us far. I can transfer anywhere on the Santa Fe line. The Harvey Company would find a dozen girls happy to come to the Grand Canyon and work in my place. But . . ."

"But?" Luke questioned.

"But my father would take everything from her. He'd never allow her a single dime. I could never hope to support us both," Alex said with a sigh. "There has to be an answer."

"There always is." Luke handed the jar of lemonade back to her.

"If she'd just go stay with Audra, at least it would put her out of the reach of the humiliating comments. She can't even go to church without someone approaching her in regard to father's behavior. I try my best to encourage her, but it's just too much for her to bear. And now her health is diminishing. She's lost so much weight that nothing fits her anymore.

"If Father only cared. If he cared about her and how she feels, he could never carry on with these affairs. I've tried to explain that to him, but he's not concerned. Politics and money. That's all he wants to focus on. Not my mother. And certainly not God. He has his friends, and their political power often benefits him financially. He lies. He cheats. He destroys. It's his legacy."

"I guess just about anyone without God in his life would have a similar legacy," Luke offered.

"He and his friends find cheating so completely acceptable. I've witnessed their tomfoolery with my own eyes. It's the reason I came to the Grand Canyon from Williams. I'd worked as a Harvey Girl at the restaurant in Williams, but Father was always coming there causing problems for me. Worse yet, his friends started behaving improperly toward me."

Luke hadn't heard her talk about this before, and it angered him to think of other men treating her without the respect she deserved.

Alex shook her head. "That's why I'll never marry. I'll never trust any man to be faithful and honest. I'm not sure it's possible."

"Whoa now," Luke said, waggling his finger at her. "You can't go throwing us all in the same pot."

Alex seemed to consider his comment for a moment. "Well, I suppose present company is excluded. You'll make someone a wonderful husband . . . at least I hope you will."

"Why do you take that tone with me? Do you doubt my ability to be faithful?"

Alex shrugged and nibbled at a piece of the cheese. "I'm not doubting your ability so much as my own. I doubt my judgment of people. I've been hurt one too many times, believing someone to be genuine and honest only to find out that they're self-serving and deceitful. I remember the first time a man actually asked to court me. He was all sweet talk and flowers. He doted on me like nothing you've ever seen.

Then I found out he was far more interested in doting on Father's ledgers. He figured to marry their fortunes together through me. He admitted that he didn't really love me, but rather knew it would be a beneficial union. He'd lied to me, and I caught him red-handed."

"And you think I would lie to you?"

"I don't know what to think," Alex said, her voice full of irritation. "That's the problem. That's why I'll never let my heart get caught up in such matters. I'm a poor judge of such things. Given the past, if I gave in to my heart, I'd probably end up with a man no better in his actions than my father."

"Too bad God isn't powerful enough to protect you from such a thing," Luke said sarcastically. He didn't like her attitude or the way it defeated his plans to offer her courtship and marriage.

Alex frowned and began gathering up her things. "He didn't protect my mother, so why should I think I deserve any different? It isn't that I think God incapable—it's simply that sinful man will do sinful things and good people will suffer. My desire is to help my mother—to see her through this matter. She may not be willing to impose herself in the life of my married sister, but she doesn't have that same excuse with me. I'll make her see reason. We'll go to Kansas City or Topeka or even California. We'll go far enough away that we won't have to witness my father's escapades firsthand."

She got to her feet and stared down at Luke with an expression that wavered between hurt and doubt. "I need to get back. Will you drive me or shall I walk?"

Luke got up and dusted off his jeans. "I'll drive you—that is, if you can trust me to keep my word."

"Luke, don't be like that. I didn't mean to include you. I was just talking about the men I've known in the past. I know you're not like them. I don't think of you like that." She reached out and gently touched his shoulder. "I've never seen you be cruel to anyone. I'm sorry I hurt your feelings. Please don't be angry with me."

Luke couldn't stay mad. He smiled. "Come on. Let's get you back before they send out a search party."

CHAPTER THREE

S enator Winthrop, how marvelous you could come to El Tovar!"

The stocky man smiled in greeting. "Chester Laird, as I live and breathe. If you aren't a welcome sight for these old eyes."

Alex took in the revelry with little interest as she poured glasses of ice water. She was used to parties of the rich and influential. El Tovar seemed the perfect place for their gatherings—a respite in a luxurious setting. Not only the grandeur of the canyon beyond the walls, but the hotel itself had been a masterpiece of design. Styled in the manner of a massive Swiss chalet, the Harvey Company had spared no expense to ensure its beauty and splendor.

"How do you like our little Waldorf of the west?" Laird questioned.

"I must say, this resort is far better equipped than I had figured. My aide mentioned it was quite the popular place, very European in nature. Still, when I mentioned to my daughter, Valerie, that we were spending a month in Arizona, you would have thought I'd suggested she sell her jewels and live on the street."

"I was sorry to hear about your wife's passing," Laird said, sobering rather quickly.

"Thank you, Chester. The dear woman simply gave out. Life in the political arena was much too difficult. But Valerie does a good job— well, decidedly that! She does a superior job acting as my hostess. Speaking of which, here she comes now with my aide, Joel Harper."

Alex didn't know why, but she lifted her gaze to meet the approaching couple. Valerie Winthrop greatly resembled the actress Lillian Gish. She wore an iced blue satin gown that clung to her in a most revealing way. Typical of the elaborate evening gowns Alex had witnessed on other occasions, the neckline plunged. A choker of diamonds and pearls graced her slender throat, while a feathered stole barely covered the bare skin above the décolletage.

"Hello, Daddy," she said, leaning over to give the pretense of kissing her father's cheek. Alex knew full well her lips hadn't touched the man's face because the woman's bright red lipstick would have left its mark.

"My darling, do you remember Mr. Laird? He's an attorney in California. A powerful ally, if I do say so myself."

"Miss Winthrop, it's a pleasure," Laird said, taking hold of her extended hand. He bowed over her hand, again offering a pretense of a kiss. Alex was so mesmerized by the charade that she actually paused in her work to watch. The lengths to which the wealthy played their games never failed to amaze her. Everyone appeared to know their parts in this strange little play, yet no one was overly worried about appearing realistic or sincere.

"The pleasure is mine," Valerie Winthrop said, dripping sweetness.

"And this is my aide, Joel Harper," Winthrop announced, turning to give Harper a mighty pat on the back.

"Harper? That's a name I know quite well," Laird replied. "I once kept company with Barrington Harper of Boston."

Alex lowered her gaze only momentarily to ensure that she'd properly tended to the table. At the rich baritone of Joel's reply, she was again drawn into the lives of her wealthy charges.

"Mr. Laird, I've heard great things about you. In fact, we met once many years ago, but of course, I was just a boy. Barrington Harper is my uncle and you were a guest in his home. As I recall, you beat him quite soundly at an especially challenging game of chess."

Laird laughed. "We've played many a challenging game over the years. Sometimes I win, sometimes he does, but always we enjoy the game. What of you, son? Do you play?"

Joel caught Alex watching him and winked before he replied. "Only to win."

Alex felt her cheeks grow hot and quickly looked away. She turned abruptly and almost ran over Bernice King, her newest trainee. "Oh, sorry, Bernice. I wasn't watching where I was going."

"That's all right, Miss Keegan." The girl shook her head and gazed around the room. "There are so many beautiful people here, I'm not sure that I'm doing anything right."

"You'll get used to it," Alex told her. "Sometimes it gets a bit overwhelming, but you have to keep your sights on what's real and important. Focus your attention on being the best Harvey Girl in the room and you'll benefit your customers as well as yourself. You might even make a tidy tip in the process."

"Oh, I hope so, Miss Keegan. I have six brothers and four sisters at home. My ma and pa need me to send home as much money as possible."

Alex's heart went out to the younger woman. Bernice was barely eighteen and as green and inexperienced as any girl Alex had worked with. Six years Alex's junior, the poor girl had never traveled out of Missouri before going to work for the Fred Harvey Company.

"Miss, might I trouble you for a moment?"

It was the same voice Alex had heard only minutes ago. Bernice hurried away, leaving Alex with the sensation of being deserted. She turned and found Joel Harper only inches away. He stood so close, in fact, that Alex felt the need to whisper, lest she shout directly in his face.

"Yes?"

Joel smiled a very pleasant smile. He cut a dashing figure in his black tuxedo, even if his bow tie was a bit crooked. "I couldn't help but notice you watching me," he said, lowering his voice. "I believe destiny has brought us together tonight."

Alex immediately grew uncomfortable. She took a step back. "I think you're mistaken, sir. I'm the Harvey Girl who will be seeing to your table. I was merely checking to see if your party was complete. I'll be serving the salads momentarily." *Keep it professional,* she told herself. Reserved formality did more to quench ardent fires among her customers than anything else.

"Ah, but you were particularly taken when I entered the room. I felt it."

Alex had heard all she was going to take. "I thought your girlfriend looked like Lillian Gish. In fact, Miss Gish has been our guest here before, and I wasn't certain but what she had returned. I assure you, I did not mean to stare, but it was for that reason and no other. Now, if you'll excuse me . . ."

Joel took hold of Alex's arm. She stared down at his finely manicured hand in contrast to her black sleeve. Returning her gaze to meet his, Alex felt overwhelmed with the assurance that this was a man used to getting whatever he wanted. Rich and good-looking, he no doubt played the room with great expertise.

"Don't be so quick to dismiss me. I'll speak to you more about this after dinner." He let her go and turned abruptly to rejoin his dinner party.

He's just like every other man, Alex thought. *I'll have to watch myself around him. No doubt he's used to having women fall at his feet.* Smiling, Alex went about her work and saw to the needs of her other tables before forcing herself back to the Winthrop party.

Dining at El Tovar was a much more relaxed event than diners experienced at other Harvey restaurants. So many of the Harvey House Restaurants were set up with the sole purpose of feeding large quantities of train passengers in an elegant, but rapid-paced, manner. Alex had experienced an entirely different kind of work routine from the one here at El Tovar while training and serving at the Harvey House in Williams. There, the train had come in and, within thirty minutes, the Harvey Girls would feed and water the train passengers, sending no one away hungry, unless by choice. Town folk came in for meals as well, but the pacing was always set by the railroad and those passengers who paid to ride the rails. El Tovar, however, was designed for pure pleasure and leisurely enjoyment.

The evening passed in relative ease for Alex. At two of her tables, the guests ate rather hastily and hurried off to stroll the canyon rim. They tipped well, so she didn't care that they had little interest in her attention. Her other tables had minor problems or needs, but nothing out of the ordinary. Years of serving in a Harvey uniform had taught her that very little couldn't be handled with a smile and soft word.

She had anticipated trouble from Joel Harper but found him to be a perfect gentleman. He took her service and politely responded when she offered drinks or additional courses.

But while Joel had treated her with respect, Valerie Winthrop was an entirely different matter.

"Miss, this fish is cold. Take it back and bring me something else."

"Miss, I don't care for the blend of this coffee, bring me English tea."

It went on and on. Always she complained, and always Alex tried her best to pleasantly anticipate Miss Winthrop's needs.

Alex decided she was going to escape without anything too uncomfortable as the party concluded their dinner amidst conversation regarding the retired senator's return to politics. The men seemed anxious to be outside strolling and smoking and Miss Winthrop seemed somewhat bored and ready to retire to more exciting places, although where that would be, Alex was not entirely sure.

"Winston, we need a man like you for president," Laird stated as Alex began to clear away the dishes.

"Daddy will make the perfect president," Valerie added. "He's so considerate and smart. He'll know exactly what to do to keep the country strong, and with his experience and backing, he ought to easily be able to defeat President Harding."

"President Harding would no doubt find you more appealing than Mr. Harper or your father," Laird said, leering rather suggestively at Valerie's daring neckline. The feather boa had long since eased its way up around the young woman's neck, leaving her rather exposed to view.

"That's true, Val dear," Joel said rather snidely. "You know the rumors regarding Mr. Harding and his love of female companionship."

Valerie laughed and leaned forward as if to entice Laird further. "Is it true they've created a secret tunnel into the White House so that he can get his women in and out without the public knowing about them?"

"I'm sure it's well traveled if they have," Laird replied. "Perhaps if he got the Secretary of the Interior to put in a toll booth, we could write off the debts from the Great War." Laughter erupted and Alex did her level best to ignore the conversation. She'd actually heard good things about the president, and she hated to have anyone bad-mouth the country's leader. She remembered her father laughing at a quote President Harding had made. Several years earlier Harding had stated, "It is my conviction that the fundamental trouble with the people of the United States is that they have gotten too far away from Almighty God." Alex had admired him for that. Of course, she hadn't known of his philandering ways, but it didn't surprise her if such a thing were true. She only hoped that Mrs. Harding didn't suffer to the extent Alex's mother did.

Alex was so lost in thought that she missed the next round of comments. Apparently the subject had been amusing because once again they were all laughing quite boisterously.

"Excuse me," Alex murmured, reaching to retrieve an empty dessert plate.

"And if I won't?" Joel Harper questioned, reaching out to still Alex's hand. He gripped her wrist and grinned up boyishly, as if she might be impressed by his sudden attention.

"I'm afraid I must insist," Alex said, trying hard to maintain her calm. "I have a great deal of work to do."

"That's the black and white of it, Mr. Harper," Senator Winthrop said, looking as though he thought himself quite clever.

Everyone laughed with the exception of Joel. He appeared intent on keeping Alex from her duties. "Say, Val, you'd look smashing dressed as a Harvey Girl. What do you say?"

"I think they look like nuns," Valerie Winthrop replied disgustedly. "So chaste and pure."

"Well, that would leave you out, wouldn't it, darling?" Joel said, leaning toward Valerie.

Alex happened to be standing between them and found Joel's presence much too invading. Jerking away and stepping back, she picked up the last of the dinner plates and added them to her stack. Alex had just turned to head back to the kitchen when Joel reached out and pinched her backside. Whirling around to meet her assailant, Alex lost control of her tray and sent china and crystal plummeting to the floor.

Everyone at the Winthrop table broke into laughter. Alex fixed Joel with what she hoped was an icy stare. She didn't even bother to apologize. Everyone in the dining room looked up to see what had caused the disturbance.

"Is there a problem here?" Mrs. Godfrey questioned, coming up from behind Alex.

"I'm afraid I startled your girl," Joel replied before Alex could speak. "The damage is my fault. Put it on my bill."

"Nonsense," Mrs. Godfrey said with a smile. "Accidents happen. Miss Keegan, see that this is cleaned up."

"Yes, I will." Alex tried not to appear flustered as she picked up her tray and squatted down to gather the broken pieces.

Joel leaned over to help and smiled in his dangerous way. "I'm truly sorry. I only meant to get your attention."

"Well, my name is Miss Keegan. Try that next time." Alex straightened as she picked up the last piece of china. "It generally works better than your way."

"Mine's more fun," Joel replied with a wink. "Say, why don't you meet me at the rim just beyond the rock porch. I'd like to find a better way to apologize."

Everyone watched Alex, as if to anticipate her answer. Alex shifted the tray and shook her head. With a smile she replied. "I'm afraid that would be a bad idea. I might be arrested if I joined you out there."

"But whatever for?" Joel asked, his voice lowering.

"For pushing you over the edge," Alex replied matter-of-factly before turning to head back to the kitchen. Of all the arrogant and self-absorbed men, Joel Harper had to take the prize.

Laughter rang out from the members of the Winthrop party, and Alex could hear even Joel chuckle at her response. *Let them laugh,* Alex thought. *They're too unaware of the rest of the world. All they know is their wealth and power.*

*E*l Tovar held the honor of being the prize of Harvey Hotels. The company had seen to it that every comfort could be offered. Poised not more than twenty feet from the rim of the canyon at one corner, the hotel blended rustic beauty with European refinement. The porches and supports were native stone to match the area scenery, while the bulk of El Tovar was constructed from Douglas fir logs brought in from Oregon. The four-story structure boasted nearly one hundred guest rooms—some with private baths—as well as steamed heat, hot and cold running water, electric lights, and of course, the wonderful Harvey House meals.

El Tovar was a community unto itself, with its lounges, art galleries, large elegantly set dining room, and rooftop garden. There were club-rooms, recreation rooms, music rooms—it even had its own power plant and fire safety system. The cost of construction was rumored to be upwards of $250,000, but no one seemed to question the expense. It benefited the rich, who could come and stay quite happily for about six dollars a day.

Alex felt privileged to be a part of such a fascinating place. Most of the Harvey Girls worked from around Easter until the end of summer. But some, like Alex, worked year round. There was good money to be made, especially in tips. The bulk of their customers were rich and, for the most part, liked to share the wealth. Alex's good friend Michaela Benson had managed to set aside so much money that she'd taken an extended leave of absence to travel the country. Alex knew, however, the minute Michaela wanted to come back, the Harvey Company would hire her back. It was that way with most of the experienced, popular staff.

That was also why Alex didn't worry about getting a transfer to another part of the country. Having a job, and even arranging for quarters, would be the easy part of solving her dilemma. Convincing her mother that it was the best alternative would be the difficult part. However, looking at the newly arrived Williams newspaper, she wondered if her task had just gotten easier. There on the editorial page, a cartoon once again poked fun at her family and exposed their shame.

Keegan Chooses Wrong Mount, the caption read, while a caricature of her father had been drawn alongside a mule with the branding GC, for Grand Canyon. He was running his hand over the mule's backside, while in the opposite corner, a thoroughbred mare, marked KK for Katherine Keegan, stood with her head in a haystack. The mare was contentedly ignorant of the injustice. Alex's mother would not have that luxury.

"This makes me so mad!" Alex said, flinging the paper down on Mrs. Godfrey's desk.

"I know you're not pleased to see yet another example of the paper's lack of propriety, but perhaps—"

"I'm sorry, Mrs. Godfrey," Alex interrupted, "but the paper is only drawing attention to my father's indiscretion. It's hardly their lack of propriety that disturbs me as much as everyone's lack of concern for my mother's feelings."

The older woman nodded. "I simply thought you should know about it before you had to serve luncheon. Your father is among the Winthrop party today, so I put Bernice on that table and freed you to work elsewhere. I'm sorry for the awkwardness of this situation."

"I'm the one who should apologize," Alex said, pausing at last to collapse in the chair opposite her mentor. "I have asked Father to stay away, but he refuses. Says his money is just as good as the next man's and that he helped to popularize this place. He avidly supports Winthrop's desire for the Democratic nomination for president and hopes to land himself a nice comfortable job in Washington."

"Oh, my."

Alex nodded. "Exactly. I have no desire for my mother to bear any more pain, so I must tell you that I've contemplated the idea of putting in for a transfer so that I might take her away from this."

Mrs. Godfrey didn't appear surprised. Instead, she smiled. "But, Alex, dear, you wouldn't want to rush into anything. After all, if your father is given a position in Washington, that would solve your dilemma. Perhaps he could go and your mother could remain here in Arizona."

"But that's over a year away." Alex shook her head. She'd thought all of this through more than once. "I'll just have to keep praying that God will help me to keep my temper under control in the meanwhile. I'd hate to run El Tovar short on tomatoes."

Mrs. Godfrey chuckled. "Alex, you're my best worker. You're my number one girl, and I don't want to lose you as I have Michaela. We're already two girls short. I've put in a request for at least four additional girls, especially since the Winthrop party has announced intentions to put on quite a round of entertainment and festivities. They'll be here at least a month."

"Somehow that figures." The last thing Alex wanted to have to endure was a month of Joel Harper and her father. *Two peas in a pod,* she thought.

"Though why they chose July and August to spend at the canyon is beyond me," Mrs. Godfrey continued. "They're used to the warmth of the south, I suppose. I understand they own a plantation in South Carolina."

Alex no longer cared to hear any more about the Winthrop entourage. "Perhaps they came for the air," she said, getting to her feet. "Look, I know I'm only filling in for lunch, but I can stay and do supper as well. Just because my father is here is no reason to shelter me like a child."

"Nonsense. This was your day off. Had we not fired Melina, it would still be your day off. No, I only need the help with lunch. Then go and take some time for yourself. You need to relax. There will be enough of a burden on you in the weeks to come. With the Winthrop plans, I'm sure we'll all be working extra hours. And while I hesitate to mention it, I must say this." Mrs. Godfrey paused and fixed Alex with a sympathetic expression. "The Winthrop party has specifically asked that you be assigned them on a regular basis—especially for dinners. They're paying a premium price for a private dining room and feel you are the best on staff. I couldn't argue with them there."

"Wonderful." Alex's tone of voice left little doubt as to how she felt.

"If it helps at all, they've already given me a large sum to entice you. This is half your tip money for the month if you will continue to at least be their dinner server when you are on duty."

Alex looked at the money, then raised her gaze to Mrs. Godfrey. "There's at least twenty dollars there."

"Twenty-five, to be exact."

Alex swallowed hard. Her tips from the Winthrop table would come to more than her monthly salary at this rate. The money could help her get her mother away from Arizona that much sooner.

Alex sighed and nodded. "I'd better get to it, then."

She left Mrs. Godfrey and made her way to the kitchen. Why had the Winthrops asked for her? No doubt Joel Harper was behind all of this. Why did the world have to be filled with Joel Harpers and men like her father?

The thought of her father left a sour taste in her mouth. For years she had fought a spiritual battle as to what she owed him. She was supposed to honor him—love him. But how? How could she respect and honor a man who did nothing but dishonor his family and reputation?

Why couldn't he just disappear and leave her and her mother alone? In fact, perhaps she'd take the train to Williams and visit her mother. Maybe Mrs. Godfrey could give her the next morning off and Alex could spend the night.

Alex busied herself with her customers. She served wonderful Harvey creations, including salmon-and-celery salads and spiced herring with potato salad. Most of her fares were interested in the light lunches. The day was already warming up, making some of the customers uncomfortable, and Alex did her best to cool them down. She suggested melon platters and cold roast beef and cream cheese sandwiches. Iced tea was served in abundance, as was lemonade.

By the time her father strolled into the dining room, comfortably settled between Valerie Winthrop and the senator, Alex had nearly forgotten the scandal of the editorial cartoon. Seeing him brought it all back in a flash, however. Alex thought she might escape unscathed, but her father motioned her to come to him and, rather than cause a scene, Alex did just that.

"May I help you?" she asked in a formal tone.

"This is my daughter, Alexandria," her father announced. "Is she the one you were telling me about?"

Joel joined them just then and grinned from ear to ear. His slicked-back black hair glistened under the casual lighting of the dining room. "That's the one. Mr. Keegan, you certainly have a charming daughter." He turned to Valerie and added, "And you thought I'd lowered my standards by falling for one of the help. Why, Miss Keegan is very nearly as well-off as you are, Val darling."

"Hardly that," Valerie said, looking at Alex as if anticipating some kind of counter reply.

"If that will be all," Alex said, looking back to her tables, "I need to finish my work."

"Well, that's *not* all," her father replied. "Joel would like you to join us this evening for dinner. I'll expect you promptly at six."

"I have plans and will not be in the area. You must pardon me now." She turned to go, but her father took hold of her and twisted her arm ever so slightly. "Don't disappoint the Winthrops, Alex. They're important to my career," he muttered for only her ears to hear.

"Father, I cannot join you," Alex replied. To the others she offered the hint of a smile and said, "I do apologize. I have a very busy schedule and my plans are already made."

"You aren't still sore because of last night are you?" Joel questioned. "I left you a handsome tip to assure you of my sincerity."

Alex nodded. "Yes, I found your tip and was most assured of your intentions." She met his gaze and nodded, knowing at a glance that he understood her meaning.

"It takes more than cold cash to assure that girl of anything," Rufus Keegan threw in. "She prides herself in her lofty expectations. Keeps a Bible by her bed and all such nonsense. She could make a convent look impure."

"Father!" Alex exclaimed. "I will speak to you later."

She turned to go and once again found her progress halted. This time Joel was the culprit. "I beg you, Miss Keegan. Please reconsider. I'd love to have you . . ." he paused for effect, "as a guest for dinner."

Alex wasn't the least bit enticed. "Thank you, but no. Good day."

Her fists were balled by the time she got to the kitchen. To her surprise she found Luke waiting for her there. He smiled and twirled his hat in his hand. "I have the afternoon and evening off. Thought you might like to take a ride or something."

"I'd *like* to throw my father across the room," she said angrily. Pacing back and forth in front of him, Alex couldn't seem to calm her angry spirit. *Oh, Lord,* she prayed, *why do I have to let him take this kind of control over my heart and soul?*

"Alex?" Luke questioned, stepping forward. "Are you all right?"

She sighed. "No. I'm angry and on the verge of doing something stupid."

"Should I have the chef hide the tomatoes?"

She smiled and felt the tension ease a bit. "No, but I'm not entirely certain the coconut cream pie is safe. I just may throw it."

"Don't do that—it's my favorite," Luke said, reaching out to take hold of her. "Look, forget about the problem and just come with me when your shift is done."

Alex nodded. "I suppose I could get away for a little while. I was thinking of visiting my mother in Williams. I'm worried that she's seen the morning paper."

Luke frowned. "Yeah, I heard about it."

"Well, I saw it firsthand," Alex said, trying her best to control her anger. "It just isn't fair." She stepped aside to allow the pastry chef to pass. His tray held several pies and Alex looked up to meet Luke's bemused grin. "I'll leave them alone . . . this time."

An hour later, Alex had changed into a riding skirt and allowed Luke to help her atop a lovely bay mare. She enjoyed riding and hadn't had a chance to do so in some time. She knew she might well be sore in the morning, but for now she wanted nothing more than to be free of El Tovar and her father.

"Is your father still in the dining room?" Luke asked.

"Yes, and he's responding rather excitedly to Mr. Winthrop's politics and Miss Winthrop's flirtations. It's shocking how openly they talk about inappropriate topics. I know it's part of this rather wild age, but honestly, Luke, what about modesty?"

"I'm really sorry, Alex."

Alex nodded. "I know you are. You've been very kind to me—to my mother. She thinks highly of you. She wrote me a note some weeks ago and mentioned you."

Luke eyed her curiously. "What did she say?" He climbed into the saddle and waited for her to respond.

Alex felt her cheeks grow hot and looked away rather quickly. She could hardly explain that her mother had thought he'd make a good husband and that Alex should marry and leave the area as her sister had done. Better that her daughters be able to rid themselves of their father's shame than to have the entire family continue to suffer. But Alex didn't see it that way. Luke was a nice man, but he wasn't for her.

"She just indicated that she thought well of you."

"So are you still planning to go see her?"

"No. Mrs. Godfrey can't spare me in the morning. She's not yet received any replacement staff to help out, and apparently the Winthrops are holding some kind of brunch. I'll be working all day, so I need to stay here tonight."

"Good. We won't have to hurry our ride in order for you to catch the train."

Alex nodded. "I suppose that is good."

They rode side by side, past gamble oak and pine. An ambitious gopher snake startled the horses as it left its cooler place in the shade of a rock and skirted out across the trail after a pocket mouse. The tiny mammal sensed danger, however, and disappeared into the sage.

Alex tried to calm her skittish mare, but it took Luke's strong hold to finally control the horse.

"Whoa, there. Easy, girl," he said in his soothing way.

Alex thought how very gentle, yet strong this man was. He could display such a wondrous prowess for things of nature and yet remain concerned and compassionate when it came to her feelings.

"What are you planning to do . . . I mean, will you work here for the rest of your life?" she asked without thinking.

Luke looked up, as if startled by her question. She thought he almost looked embarrassed. "I've been saving some money. Guess I'm thinking it might be nice to buy a ranch somewhere."

Alex had never considered that Luke might actually have plans to leave. The thought distressed her, and yet hadn't she made her own plans for just such an escape? "I really love it here," Alex murmured, enjoying the quiet pleasure of their ride. "I'll hate to leave because of the beauty, but I'll happily go if it means never having to see my father again."

"Don't hate him, Alex. He's wrong, no doubt about it, but don't hate him. That will just eat away at your spirit. Remember what you used to tell me when you first started talking to me about God?"

Alex smiled. She remembered the angry cowboy from four years earlier. Luke Toland seemed mad at the world, but especially at God. "I told you what my mother always told me. 'Whoever angers you, owns you.' "

"That's right. You don't want your father to own you, now, do you?" He smiled and the warmth of it spread throughout Alex in an unexpected way.

"No, I don't want anything from that man."

"Just be a good daughter and honor him as best you can," Luke suggested.

Alex felt bile rise in her throat. "I've tried to be obedient to him, but . . . well . . . there just came a time when I could no longer follow his instructions." She remembered the times her father would come to the Harvey House in Williams. He'd come with a friend or two, and they often expressed an interest in Alex. Her father seemed unconcerned about their lewd comments, sometimes even encouraged them.

Luke halted his horse and took hold of the mare's reins to stop Alex as well. "I don't know what he did or didn't do, but he doesn't have the power to do anything to you anymore. You're independent and free of his control. You gave up a lot—the comforts of home, money, your mother's company. He doesn't have to keep hurting you."

Alex met Luke's gaze. His eyes were a rich, deep hazel color that seemed to glitter green and gold when the sunlight touched them at just the right angle. "So long as he hurts my mother, he's hurting me. It doesn't matter that he speaks lewdly or suggestively when I'm in the company of his friends. It doesn't even matter that he thinks so little of me that he encourages his friends' actions toward me. It only matters that she goes on suffering and there's nothing I can do to make it any better. I wish he . . . were dead." Tears trickled down her cheek.

Luke drew a handkerchief from his pocket and handed it to Alex. "Don't let him own you like that, Alex. You'll never know a moment's peace if you do."

"I'm trying to pray through it," she admitted, wiping her face. She folded the cloth back into a neat little square and handed it back to Luke. Smiling, she apologized. "Forgive me. I seem to be so teary these days. I'll do my best not to do this again."

"Alex, we're friends, remember? If you can't cry on my shoulder, whose shoulder can you cry on?"

Alex felt a trembling course through her. She wanted to reach out and touch Luke's face—just to thank him, just to let him know how much he meant to her. Suddenly she felt very awkward. Her feelings were getting the best of her and, rather than let the conversation continue in this intimate vein, she straightened and took up her reins. She nudged the horse forward and didn't even bother to look back at Luke when she called over her shoulder, "I didn't know coconut cream pie was your favorite."

CHAPTER FIVE

Joel Harper knew the game of politics as well as he knew the exclusive brothels of Charleston. At age thirty-six, he easily recognized Rufus Keegan's interest as being one of a man obsessed. The man wanted power and glory. It was all right with him if Keegan wanted to tag along on the coattails of Winthrop's victory, but it wasn't all right if Keegan thought he was going to replace Joel as Winthrop's right-hand man. He was a man to be watched, Joel reasoned. Keegan could either be a dangerous adversary or a powerful ally. The question was, which would he be?

"The current administration has made a mess of things to say the least," Keegan stated in a critical manner. "Just look at the problems the attorney general has made over the German alien properties. Then there's that whole question of what's happening with the federal oil reserves."

"Yes, we're watching that one closely. It appears, if my spies are correct," Winston Winthrop offered, "Secretary of the Interior, Albert Fall, is headed for just that. A fall. The man has so many underhanded dealings, he doesn't know which is which. The conservationists hate him, which is precisely why Joel thought it would do the Democratic Party well to play that ticket to the hilt. We'll show the conservationists that we care about the federal land—that we're just as appalled as they are at what's been happening in Wyoming and California. We'll promote the national parks, supporting the idea of preserving the land for posterity."

"Are you certain this will matter enough to remove Harding from office? After all, he may not have any knowledge of what Fall's been up to," Keegan replied. "It will be most important to relate the two men together."

"More importantly," Joel interjected, "we relate Winthrop to Woodrow Wilson. They were old friends and saw eye to eye on most everything. We'll focus the attention of the country on the fact that Harding rejected Wilson's League of Nations, ensuring its failure. We'll remind them that Harding did this, not to mention other things . . . things that will not bode well in the south, where we have strong support."

Keegan eyed Joel intently. The idea of scandal seemed to ignite the man's excitement. "Things such as?"

Joel wasn't about to give away all of his strategies and secrets, so he drew on one of the plans that was well-known from the previous election. No doubt it would feed the older man just enough to whet his appetite. "Southern gentlemen do not take kindly to the idea of Negroes filling positions of importance—such as the presidency."

"I seem to recall that controversy," Keegan said, stroking his chin. "Someone issued statements that suggested the president was part Negro. But then there was some sort of proof offered to nix that idea, wasn't there? Wasn't the attorney general a part of that problem as well?"

Joel nodded. "Harry Daughtery was then Mr. Harding's campaign manager. He issued public statements declaring there was no truth to the rumor of Harding's questionable lineage."

"But you have proof to suggest otherwise?" Keegan questioned.

Joel smiled. "What need do we have of proof? If the issue is brought up at the appropriate moment, with the most damaging slant, it matters very little if we have to recant our words after the election. People will remember the problem from 1920. If given in the right manner, it will eat at them, wear away their trust in the administration. This, added to other issues of trust, will soon destroy their faith in Harding."

"Gentlemen, politics is a dirty little game," Winthrop drawled in a slow, southern manner. "I do despise the use of such tactics, but sometimes these things are necessary. After all, the end results are all that matter."

"Agreed," Keegan said, nodding enthusiastically.

Joel thought the man rather ridiculous and dull. He was no different than any of the other men of means who sought to better themselves by aligning their name to that of a powerful senator or governor. But Joel couldn't fault him too much. Joel himself had come into the game by the same means. His own father had long ago disowned him for his gambling and questionable behavior. When trouble came knocking, Joel had a penchant for not only opening the door, but for making it his bedfellow as well.

"You would dance with the devil himself," his father had declared on the night he'd sent Joel from the family home.

"Only if he let me lead," Joel had called back, acting for all the world as if this dismissal from his family meant nothing at all. However, it had meant more than he'd ever allowed his father to know. More than he ever would let anyone know.

Leaving his childhood home in 1913, Joel had quickly learned the meaning of friendship, both assumed and real. He settled himself near Washington, D.C., and made fast friends with the politicians of the area. He cut back on his gambling, or rather, he became more selective with the places he frequented. Early on, Joel realized he needed money to maintain his pretense of a wealthy Virginia son. The scheme had paid off, and Winston Winthrop found him to be a kindred spirit. Hiring the intelligent, quick-learning Joel at the age of twenty-seven, Winthrop had made no secret of the fact that he considered Joel as a potential husband for his daughter, Valerie.

Joel saw this as the ultimate revenge against his father. The Winthrops were worth millions in old money, while the Harpers were new industrial money and didn't come anywhere near the same income association. Joel's father would never let the truth of their parting be known, so for all the rest of the world, it seemed Joel was simply an independent, headstrong young man, out to further the good of the family name. And that was just as Joel wanted it.

When the time was right, when everything was in its place and Joel was the one holding all the cards, he'd make his voice known. He let the world know exactly what had happened. Joel fully intended to return to his father one day, wealthy and powerful. And then he would crush the man, just as he'd crushed Joel on that night so long ago.

"Ah, Valerie has chosen to join us," Winthrop declared, bringing their attention to the young woman across the room.

As women went, Valerie was a beauty—there was no doubt about that. But to Joel she was cold and unfeeling. She knew her father intended them to wed, but she made her own demands in order to condition her cooperation. She wanted her freedom until she was twenty-five years old. Freedom to play the field, to travel, and to do what her socialite friends were doing. Joel was a patient man. He kept close to Winthrop, protecting him from unwanted attention, while biding his time for Valerie to turn twenty-five. Now his time of waiting was over— her birthday had been last month and the day marked his victory.

He watched her cross the room, working it as she came. She stopped to talk to the older women who commented or called to her as she passed. She presented a lovely picture of health and beauty in her cream-colored dress. Joel had no notion of who the designer had been, but his ability to tuck and mold a dress to Valerie's willowy frame was sheer genius. He loved it that she chose expensive clothes and jewels. He loved it because it told every other woman in the room how much she had to waste on babbles and gowns. In turn, those very jealous matrons would tell their husbands, and they would quickly realize how very powerful and wealthy the Winthrops truly were.

Still, there was something more to his feelings for Valerie than simply her ability to show off a pricey piece of fashion ware. He wouldn't say he loved her, but he loved her possessions, and that was close enough. Not only that, but she held great sway over her father. The senator listened to his daughter, trusting her instincts and wisdom. Joel needed her to be his ally at best, or at worst to be so afraid of him that she did as she was told. He'd be satisfied either way.

Valerie appeared oblivious to his study. Her bobbed brown-black hair gave her face a waiflike quality that suggested helplessness and innocence. But Joel knew she was neither helpless nor innocent. The men got to their feet as she approached the table.

"Daddy," she said, leaning close to kiss the old man, "I do hope you didn't wait supper on account of me."

She smiled sweetly at Rufus Keegan and then turned her charms on Joel. "My, but don't you look handsome tonight, Mr. Harper." Her southern belle simper was perfect.

"Might I return the compliment, Val darling," he said with an emphatically possessive tone.

"We're soon to announce their engagement, don't you know," Winthrop told Keegan with great pride. "I've found Joel a most beneficial man to have in my corner, and now I'll make him family as well."

"Relatives can be dangerous to trust," Keegan said, taking his seat with the others. He eyed Joel with a serious expression. "Besides, I thought you had an eye for my daughter."

"We're very progressive, Mr. Keegan," Valerie said, batting her eyelashes coyly. "No sense in settling for one pair of shoes until you've tried several pairs."

Keegan grinned and leaned forward. "And even after you've bought the shoes, there's no sense in wearing the same old pair day in and day out, eh?"

"Exactly," she said as if to encourage him further.

Joel had seen the editorial cartoon with Keegan's likeness, and it was apparent he believed in having full range of the playing field. It seemed he thought this might extend to Valerie as well, but Joel had no intention of being made the fool at their table.

"Men make the rules and, therefore, men may break them," Joel said, looking to Valerie. As if to emphasize his point, he reached under the table and put his hand casually on her thigh. She did nothing but smile sweetly and look to Joel as if waiting for him to finish his thought.

Just then Chester Laird crossed the room to join them. He brought with him two men who were obviously reporters. One man held a camera, while the other pulled a pencil from behind his ear with one hand and notebook from his coat pocket with the other.

"Senator Winthrop, I want to introduce you to two good ol' boys. These men hail from Los Angeles. They're reporters. I thought perhaps we'd have some pictures taken and a story written up for the morning edition. How about it?"

"I'm always happy to speak with the press," Winthrop replied.

Joel watched as the experienced senator went into his routine. With the other men occupied, Joel took advantage of the moment to secure Valerie's attention. Squeezing her leg, he murmured, "Where have you been?"

"Miss me?" she asked, keeping up the appearance of complete joy.

"If I find out you've been playing the field with those stable hands, I won't be easy to deal with."

"You'll do exactly what I want you to do, or Daddy will find out about the money you've been stealing from his campaign fund."

Joel eyed her seriously and drew away. "Shall we take a walk while the press interviews your father?"

"Why not."

He got to his feet and helped her with her chair. Extending his arm, he waited until Valerie put her gloved hand in his before leading her out of the room.

"We'll be back in a blink, Daddy," she called over her shoulder. Then, gritting her teeth, she said under her breath, "as soon as I can get rid of this headache."

"You may think of me as a headache now, but I assure you, if you ever so much as open that pretty little mouth of yours to speak out against me in any way, I'll make sure more than your head hurts."

"Threatening me—again? How innovative. How thoroughly original."

He pulled her through the lobby of the hotel and out onto the porch of El Tovar. Grateful to see the place void of visitors, Joel whirled

Valerie around and pulled her into his arms. Kissing her without any feeling of love, he released her just as abruptly and smiled.

"Just the same, I mean what I say. Don't test me. Your father and I have discussed this. Our engagement will be announced the night he announces his candidacy for president. You will wear that silver number with the modest neckline and blush at the appropriate times and appear nothing but the loving and doting fiancée."

"I'm tired of the Poiret gown. I plan to wear my new Caret. It's red and has the most delightful draping. You do want me to be properly draped, don't you?"

"The silver gown is what I want and that's what you'll give me," he insisted.

"And if I don't, you'll beat me? Is that it? Not very good for politics, Joel dear."

"There are ways to make people suffer without ever laying a hand on them," Joel replied, his eyes narrowing.

"Don't I know it," Valerie answered snidely. "You make me suffer every moment of every day. If I had my way about it, I would expose your little games and put an end to this engagement."

"But then Daddy would find out about your less-than-chaste evenings in New York. And maybe he'd even learn about your little drinking problem."

"You wouldn't!" Valerie said, taking hold of Joel's arm. "You wouldn't ruin his chance at the presidency."

"But telling him the truth about you wouldn't ruin his chances," Joel replied very softly. "There are a lot of parties and moments of public exposure. There are also a fair number of sanitariums in the northeast. I doubt they'd care much whether your gown was Poiret or Caret. If you want to keep this situation under control, you'll stop flirting with everything in pants and pay more attention to your devoted fiancé."

"Does that mean you'll give up chasing after the Keegan girl?" Valerie asked snidely. "After all, she appears quite disinterested in your amorous attention."

"I'll do as I please. I'm a man, and a man has a right to do whatever he likes." Joel pointed the way back toward the lobby. "I'll expect your cooperation and public affection."

"Expect whatever you like," Valerie said, seeming to have regained her confidence, "but I have just as much dirt on you as you have on me. You'd better rethink your plans, Mr. Harper. You aren't packing me off to a madhouse, so just get past that notion. I'm not as naïve as you play me to be. I can bite when you least expect it."

*A*lex secured a black bow tie at the V of her white collar. Having spilled soup on her uniform during the lunch cleanup, she was required to put on a clean uniform before going about her afternoon duties. Pulling the starched white apron on over her black uniform, she sighed. The outfit was hot and the day had grown quite warm. Someone told her the temperature was nearing eighty degrees. Luke mentioned they were due for a thunderstorm, but it couldn't be any worse than the storm that was brewing at the hotel.

For days now she had waited on the Winthrop group. She'd endured Mr. Harper's undesired attention, Miss Winthrop's snobbery, and her own father's deplorable comments. Still, she worked as best as she could, putting a smile on her face and praying fervently for a kindness she did not feel.

Without warning the door to her bedroom opened up, causing Alex to whirl on her heel. "Michaela!" she exclaimed at the sight of her old friend.

"Well, if you aren't a sight for sore eyes," Michaela responded in turn. The women embraced as if they were long lost sisters.

Alex didn't know when she'd been happier to see someone. Pulling away, she wiped tears from her eyes and exclaimed, "Oh, your hair!"

Michaela put her hand up to the short bob and gave it a pat. "Do you like it?"

"It's charming, but I would never have expected you, above all people, to cut your hair. Your black curls were the envy of everyone on staff."

Michaela shrugged and tossed her bags to the bed on the opposite side of the room. "I found New York living to be a bit more expensive than I had accounted for. I ended up selling my hair to put together enough traveling money to come back to the canyon. I wired headquarters, and they told me they were desperate to have me return, so here I am."

"I'm so glad," Alex replied. Nothing else could have made her feel quite the same way. "Oh, Michaela, things have been really bad here. My father has been up to his old tricks, my mother is suffering terribly, and I've been singled out by my father and his cronies to be their private Harvey waitress. It's just madness."

"Sounds like it." Michaela instantly began changing out of her street clothes. "I told Mrs. Godfrey I'd get started right away. She told me on your day off I could fill in with the Winthrop group."

"So you already know about them?"

Michaela nodded and tossed her pink dress over the back of a chair and went to the closet. "Mrs. Godfrey told me my uniforms are still here."

"We didn't have time to worry about what to do with them. Although," Alex admitted, "it seems like you've been gone forever."

Michaela quickly retrieved the needed garments. "Oh, I wish we had cooler uniforms. Do you know there are places along the line where the girls wear colorful skirts and peasant blouses like the Mexican girls?"

"No, but how marvelous."

"Indeed. I think we should talk to the management and suggest we have a similar uniform. Wouldn't that be grand?"

Michaela chattered on and on as if she'd only been away a few hours instead of months. Alex felt the tension drain from her shoulders and neck as her friend entertained her with stories of her trip.

"I went to Niagara Falls," Michaela said as she pulled on her black cotton stockings. "What a place. You wouldn't believe it. It was simply marvelous. You have this lovely river that moves along quite rapidly. Pretty soon there are boulders and rocks and rapids, and then the water just seems to disappear from sight and there it goes! Over the rocks and down to the river below. It was incredible."

Alex laughed. "I can tell. You sound as though the trip did you a world of good. How is your family? Did you get a chance to visit with them in Boston?"

"We had a chance to argue and screech at each other," Michaela replied, tying her shoes. "That's as close to visiting as we get."

Alex knew from past discussions that Michaela's three older sisters, all married with children, had no understanding of their younger sister's desire to be footloose and fancy-free. Her father, an elder in the church, felt that his daughter was committing a terrible sin by heading west to become a Harvey Girl. For years, the family hadn't even spoken to Michaela. Only during the last year and a half had they finally come around to being civil.

"Don't get me wrong," Michaela said, standing up ready for work, "I'm glad we had some time together. I got to see my nieces and nephews, and my mother was actually quite interested in what I do here and what the canyon looked like."

"That's a real change," Alex commented.

"But I'm ready to get back in the saddle, so to speak," her friend replied. "I'm glad you didn't rent out the room."

Alex laughed. She'd told Mrs. Godfrey from the very start of Michaela's vacation that she hated the idea of rooming with anyone else. Mrs. Godfrey had been good to put the replacement girls elsewhere. It had worked out that Alex had kept the room to herself, a sort of perk for being Mrs. Godfrey's top waitress.

"No one else would want to room with me," Alex said laughing. "That's the only reason the room is empty."

"I can bet there's one poor cowboy who'd like to share your room," Michaela teased.

"What are you talking about?"

"Luke Toland," Michaela replied. "He's been sweet on you for years. Is he still here?"

"Yes, he's still here, but we're just good friends. You know that."

Michaela shrugged and headed out the door. "You may be just good friends, but I'm thinking Luke would like to be more than friends."

Alex shook her head and pulled the door closed behind her. "If Luke felt that way, he'd just tell me."

————

Harvey Girls always had more chores than just serving the customers, and one of the chores Alex enjoyed the most was polishing the silver. She usually found a quiet corner and went to work without interruption. Here, she could take time to think through her problems and spend time in prayer.

Rubbing the cloth against a large silver serving tray, Alex tried not to be overcome by her father's infidelity and her mother's misery. She couldn't fix this problem or make it go away, and knowing that made it all that much harder to deal with.

"You look lonely."

Alex looked up in annoyance. Joel Harper had sought her out in her moment of solitude.

"I assure you, I'm not," she answered with a smile.

"Miss Keegan, I get the distinct impression that you're avoiding me."

"How could that be, Mr. Harper? I'm in your company each and every day."

"Yes, but you won't come away with me so that I might get to know you better."

Alex put down the polishing cloth momentarily. "I'm sure my father has told you all about me. Let that suffice. Now, if you'll excuse me . . ."

"But I can't do that," Joel said, reaching out to take hold of her gloved hand. "Come walk with me."

"Now I'm the one who must refuse. I have duties to perform and in a few short hours I will be serving your party in the private dining room. So you see, there is no time for such distractions."

Joel eyed her seriously for a moment, then let go of her. "I'm sorry for the way your father has treated you."

Alex wasn't expecting this change of topic. She wasn't about to let Joel Harper quiz her on the intimate details of her life. "I'm sorry about it too." She took up the polishing cloth and went back to work on the tray.

"I know he's hurt you greatly." His voice was smooth and low; his manner was all charm and concern.

"It's not my feelings I'm concerned with, Mr. Harper. It's my mother." Alex didn't know why she'd shared that bit of information. Now the man would no doubt take her comment as an invitation to discuss the matter more thoroughly.

"I've been concerned for her—the senator has too. In fact, he had me wire her a dozen roses with his compliments."

"How kind."

"You say that like you don't believe me."

Alex sighed. "I believe you, Mr. Harper. I simply do not trust you, nor do I care."

"How can you be so heartless and cold? Your father told me you fancied yourself a Christian woman."

Guilty as charged, Alex thought. "Mr. Harper . . ."

"Please call me Joel."

"That would be inappropriate. You are a guest in this hotel and I am a staff member. I would be reprimanded by my superiors if I were to call you by your first name."

"I won't tell a soul," Joel teased.

"Mr. Harper, I'm sorry that my demeanor appears heartless and cold. I hold certain values dear, and among those are my beliefs in Christianity. My father, however, does not hold such beliefs and in fact mocks me at every turn. To trust someone in his company is difficult, especially when you've proven that your values are no different than his."

"How so?" he asked, moving closer.

Alex turned the tray over to continue her work. "You are engaged to Miss Winthrop, are you not? Yet you pursue me. How is that?"

"Val and I are very progressive. Surely you've noticed the turn of the world toward more liberty and freedom between men and women. It's no longer the 1800s, Miss Keegan. We needn't surround ourselves with outdated values and restrictions. Women have the vote and may make their choices. Val is exercising her rights, as am I. We may be promised to each other, but it doesn't mean we can't entertain ourselves for the moment."

"So you want to entertain yourself with me? Is that it?" Alex asked.

"Of course. You're a beautiful woman with an amazing charm. I'd find it a sheer delight to spend time with you. And I believe you'd feel the same in regard to me."

Alex finished polishing the tray and got to her feet. Clutching the heavy silver close, she shook her head. "I find you rather despicable and quite undesirable. You are no different than my father or any other man, for that matter."

Joel stood and reached out to take hold of Alex. The action surprised her—so much so that she froze in place.

"You don't know me well enough to call me undesirable. I think once you've tasted of my charms, you'll be glad for my company." Without warning he pulled her against him in a steel-like embrace. He held her head tight and kissed her hard. As he attempted to deepen the kiss, Alex dropped the silver tray on his highly polished shoes.

Joel let out a yell as he jumped away from Alex. "You did that on purpose."

Alex narrowed her eyes. "Just as you did. I would advise you to never attempt that again. I don't appreciate being manhandled, and I certainly have no interest in a man who would force himself upon a woman."

She took that moment to hurry away, barely stopping long enough to retrieve the tray. She hoped the heavy silver had broken his foot.

Joel watched Alexandria Keegan flee his presence, even as fiery pain shot up his leg. "Devil woman!" he muttered.

Limping out of the hotel, Joel glanced at his watch. He'd nearly let the time get away from him. He had a meeting in less than ten minutes.

Hurrying down the path as best he could, Joel pushed Alex from his mind. He'd deal with her later, for now he had plans to arrange. There was nothing and no one he would let come between himself and success. Right now his success depended on seeing Winston Winthrop in the White House.

Spying his man ahead, Joel slowed his pace. The man pushed his hat back and nodded as Joel approached.

"What's the news?"

"He's going to be heading to San Francisco and plans to stay at the Palace Hotel. I have a friend who works there. I can get in . . . no problem."

"Good," Joel said, trying to organize his thoughts. "The sooner we eliminate the competition, the better."

"It shouldn't be all that hard. I'll send you a wire when it's done."

"No! No further contact." Joel reached into his coat, glancing around him as he did. "Drop your hat."

"What?"

"Just do it. Drop your hat on the ground and I'll pick it up."

The man did as Joel instructed and watched in confusion as Joel bent to retrieve it. "This is the second third of your payment. The last third will be wired to your account upon my hearing the news. The papers will cover it, and that will let me know without any threat of our being discovered. There can be nothing—understand me—nothing that links us together."

The man nodded. "I know that."

Joel slipped the envelope into the hat and handed the hat back to him. "If I need you again, I'll know where to find you."

The man slipped the envelope from the hat and into his pocket. "Yeah, sure. I'll be around."

Joel watched him walk away as if bored with the entire affair. Hired assassins always seemed so easily distracted when killing wasn't the actual focus of their actions.

Glancing back toward El Tovar, Joel smiled. With any luck at all, he'd have Winthrop at the forefront of the race for president by the end of the week. And with that accomplished, he could turn his attention to more pleasurable things.

Alex's image came to mind. Perhaps he'd handled her all wrong. Perhaps there was another way to get to her. She'd obviously do anything for her mother. Maybe that was the way to a woman's heart.

———

Alex ignored Joel's knowing glances as she served braised duck on fine china. Risotto and buttered asparagus rounded out the entrée, and the aroma was simply heaven. Alex worried her stomach's rumblings of protest could be heard as she worked the room. She hadn't eaten supper after her upsetting scene with Joel Harper and now she regretted her decision.

The minutes ticked by amidst discussions of Washington, D.C.'s political arena. Alex listened as her father made suggestions for how he might benefit the senator. It was disgusting the way he played the room.

"I can offer a great deal to the right man," her father droned on. "I have resources to benefit the party, that will in turn benefit me."

Alex saw the men nod knowingly as if her father had spoken some great truth.

Valerie Winthrop, dressed in a gown of silver and blue, was the only female, other than Alex, present. Alex had a feeling this was probably the way things usually were laid out, whether at the Grand Canyon or elsewhere. Miss Winthrop liked being the belle of the ball and tonight was no exception. She wore her bobbed hair slicked back under a headband of rhinestones. At least Alex presumed they were rhinestones. For all she knew, they could be real jewels. Miss Winthrop certainly wore an abundance of those, as well. Tonight her throat dripped with diamonds and emeralds and her ears were sparkling with smaller settings of the same. The glittering of her rhinestone-encrusted spaghetti straps and neckline reflected with the other stones off the highly polished paneling of the private dining room.

The room was said to have been a favorite of Teddy Roosevelt. Like other Harvey dining rooms, the furnishings were elaborate and expensive. The table, set for six this evening, could be extended to seat twelve. The fine Irish linens, glistening crystal, and polished silver would have pleased even the most discriminating taste. Even so, Valerie Winthrop appeared unimpressed.

Alex began her routine of collecting the empty plates. She thought of the extra money she was making by working exclusively with the Winthrops and wondered if it was really worth the effort. Inevitably she had to see her father on a regular basis, as well as endure Joel Harper's attention, so it seemed the money was rather hard earned.

"Bring clean glasses," her father instructed, "we're going to have a drink."

Alex said nothing but quickly retrieved six wine goblets. As she began placing them in front of each person, her father popped the cork on what appeared to be some kind of alcohol.

"No prohibition here," Joel said, rubbing his hands together. "That's the first thing we get changed when you're in the White House, Senator."

"These are wine glasses," Valerie said, holding hers up to Alex. "We're drinking champagne."

"I'm sorry, but . . ."

"There are fine, Val dear," Joel interceded with a wink. "They're bigger, after all."

Everyone laughed with exception to Alex. She longed only to be rid of the entire bunch. It wasn't that they were the first ones to imbibe in spite of alcohol being illegal, but they clearly held little regard for any rules or laws. She'd heard the lawyers who sat on either side of Senator Winthrop advise him on ways to skirt the regulations and rules of politics. She'd heard Joel agree to underhanded plans that would disgrace the opposition. Her own father had agreed to do whatever he could to discredit the senator's rivals.

They were just starting to toast their plans when Alex turned to exit the room. She would serve their desserts and coffee and hopefully leave them to discuss their futures.

"Wait, Miss Keegan," Joel said, reaching out to stop her retreat. "Share a toast with us. We're drinking to the senator's health and future."

"I don't drink champagne," she said matter-of-factly. Her father eyed her with contempt.

"Surely you can drink one small glass," Joel encouraged.

"Of course she can," her father joined in. "If she knows what's good for her."

Alex caught the meaning of his words, but stood her ground. "Senator Winthrop, I pray you will have great health and happiness."

The older man smiled. "Why, thank you, Miss Keegan," he drawled. "I know you are a woman of prayer, given your father's descriptions. I will expect that prayer to be offered up."

Alex shifted the tray of dishes. "You can count on it, sir." She cast one last glance at her father, who appeared rather confused by the exchange, before leaving the room. Pausing just outside the dining room, Alex took a deep breath and prayed.

Thank you, Lord. Thank you for getting me out of there.

"We really aren't that bad of a bunch, you know," Joel said, following her out of the room.

Alex turned with the dishes and gave Harper what she hoped was a disinterested stare. "Did you need something?"

"I need a moonlight stroll on the rim with the prettiest girl in Arizona . . . I need you."

Alex backed up a step. "I have no interest in helping you out, Mr. Harper. Now, I must go and prepare your desserts."

"I could make you happy, Miss Keegan. If you'll just give me a chance."

"I am happy. I don't need you or any other man to help me along that path."

Joel stepped forward, backing Alex against the wall. He reached out and took the tray from her hands. "I have no desire to see this dropped on my feet."

"Then mind your distance," Alex said, hurrying down the hall the moment Joel turned to put the tray on a nearby chair.

"You can't escape me," he called after her. "I'm used to getting what I want."

*L*uke was in no mood for the Winthrop party's nonsense. He'd been hired to take them by mule to the bottom of the canyon for an overnight stay at Phantom Ranch. Like other groups of visitors to the canyon, the Winthrop party heard of the tourist attraction and wanted to experience it. At least Joel Harper and Valerie Winthrop wanted to experience it. The stocky senator and Rufus Keegan declined, declaring no desire to spend their day aback a mule.

As best as Luke could tell, a constant gathering of supporters for the senator's presidential campaign had been pouring in throughout the week, and it was a collection of those men and women who took his time and attention now.

Luke gave his routine speech cautioning the riders of the arduous task ahead of them. "There are places," he warned, "where the narrowness of the path allows no room for error. The mules know their jobs and heed my commands. I'll expect no less from you."

A few of the party nodded solemnly, but Joel Harper chuckled and Valerie Winthrop merely batted her eyes in a flirting manner.

"The mules are generally good-natured with our guests," Luke stated, bringing his speech to a close, "but if you'll take a look at Clancy Franklin here, you'll understand that they can be dangerous." Clancy smiled broadly for the group while Luke continued. "About a month ago, Clancy's favorite mule gave him a swift kick in the face. The blow could have killed a lesser man—but Clancy here is hardheaded." Some of the group laughed. Luke shook his head and slapped Clancy on the back. "Clancy just lost a tooth and had his nose broke. Unless you want to follow his example, I'd suggest you do exactly as you're instructed."

With that, Luke ordered his crew to assist the travelers to their mounts. He gave a cautious glance to the entire group, for Alex had implied there had been difficulties with the Winthrop party, and Luke took that very seriously. She told him that Joel Harper pinched her backside, and then last night she'd mentioned ever so casually that Joel had been demanding her attention and seeking her for private walks. Clancy had been among the group when Alex shared her woes. He'd laughed and said that someone as pretty as Alex should expect that kind of thing. The group had teased Clancy about being sweet on Alex, and the blond-haired man had blushed a fiery red.

Luke tried not to give it a second thought, for Clancy didn't seem like competition for Alex's affections. And Alex had never implied or mentioned an interest in Clancy. Luke figured that if she had thoughts in that direction, she would have enlisted Luke's help. No, Luke was more worried about Joel Harper. He worried that there was more to this than Alex was saying. He could tell she'd been greatly disturbed by the entire matter. It wasn't like her to get her nose out of joint over a little attention, but since her father was tied to the group, Luke put it off to her distaste of Rufus Keegan. After all, she'd shared with him often enough for Luke to know that Keegan was the low-life type of scum who would sell his daughter out to the highest bidder.

He gripped the reins hard and realized his attention wasn't focused where it needed to be. His mule was surefooted and knew the trail well, but Luke knew the folly in brooding or daydreaming over Alex. He needed to keep his attention fixed to the path ahead.

"Let's head out," he called and signaled the trip to begin.

At their first rest stop, Luke waited until the entire group had stretched and gotten a drink from their canteens before giving them a bit of canyon history.

"We left temperatures of around eighty-two degrees up on the rim," Luke began. "We'll find the canyon floor to be as hot as one hundred ten degrees, and that's why it's important to keep drinking."

"Drinking is always important, eh, Val?" Harper teased.

"I meant water," Luke threw out sarcastically. The group laughed, with exception to Joel. Valerie grinned and left Joel's side to come to Luke.

"Please ignore him, Mr. Toland, he can be a bit of a bore." She lowered her head just a bit. Looking up at him with huge green eyes, she smiled prettily and batted her lashes.

Luke ignored her and continued to speak to the group. "You'll see for yourself as we descend, the canyon is a series of layers. With each layer you'll see a good many changes. The canyon is a blend of lime-stone to sandstone to shale and so on. The plant life changes with the layers, as does the animal population. On the rim you might have seen gambel oaks, piñon, sagebrush, and juniper. As we head down into the canyon, this is going to change, and you'll see more yucca and mes-quite, and down by the river you'll even have cottonwood and desert willow."

Luke loved the canyon for its variety and beauty. He loved to share the information he'd learned in his years at the Grand Canyon, but he could also read a group of tourists like a book. This book was clearly bored with the information. They were city folk who were used to fast-paced lives and nonstop entertainment. Asking them to slow down to the point of recognizing the differences between sagebrush and snake-weed was expecting too much.

Valerie Winthrop took hold of his arm. "So what's the ranch like?"

Luke nodded and tried to disentangle himself from her hold, but Valerie would have none of that. Giving up so as not to make a scene, Luke looked to the group.

"Phantom Ranch is a real treat. It's going to be as welcome a sight as your own home, especially after a day on mule back. We'll have a good meal for you and cabins for your comfort. The night ends up being pretty short, given how tired you're going to feel."

"Oh, surely you cowboys don't get tired," Valerie whispered.

Luke looked to her and nodded. "Even cowboys get tired, Miss Win-throp."

The rest of the trip was much the same. Luke found that anytime he stopped the group to rest, Valerie was right beside him. Harper scowled from a distance, as if trying to assess the threat and deciding what needed to be done.

"You simply must come to New York sometime," Valerie insisted. "Have you ever been there?"

"No. I've never been there."

"Then you don't know what you're missing," she gushed.

Luke continued checking the cinches on the mules. "I thought you were from South Carolina."

"I am, but I prefer the fun to be had in New York. The parties there are so incredible—why, you'd positively think you'd died and gone to heaven. And this nonsense of prohibiting liquor is hardly a bother at all. In fact, it can be quite exciting. Sometimes the police come and we all scramble like madmen out the secret passages. They have false fronts for the bar and everything. It's truly marvelous—you'd love it.''

Luke looked up and studied her for a moment. "I don't think you know me well enough to know what I might love or detest. Because of this, I have to tell you you're very wrong. I wouldn't love it. I detest drinking—and drunks.''

The look on Valerie's face suggested complete and utter surprise. Having finally rendered her speechless, Luke took the opportunity to move away from her to talk to Clancy.

"Well, my dear, you don't seem to be making much progress with our cowboy leader," Joel said snidely. "Good thing, too, as I specifically remember telling you to leave his type alone.''

Valerie turned to meet Joel's gaze. "I'll do as I please. I don't need you telling me what to do or offering unsolicited advice.''

"The only advice I've come to give is to remind you that I'll not brook this nonsense any longer. Your father agrees with me. You're much too flighty and out of control. We've been discussing your possible liability to his campaign.''

"I beg your pardon?" Valerie was stunned. How could this man make her so completely miserable and still expect her to feel passion for their union?

"You heard me," Joel said, taking hold of her. He led her away from the others, tightening his grip on her arm as he did. "Don't cause a scene with Toland," Joel continued. "If you do, you'll be sorry.''

"I couldn't be more sorry than I am now," Valerie snapped.

"That's where you're wrong.''

"You wouldn't risk everything you have with Daddy." She worked hard to keep her voice steady, for Joel absolutely terrified her, especially after she heard of how he had beat up a Washington prostitute. Her father's secretary had told her all the gory details, ending the tirade by telling Valerie it wasn't the first time Joel had committed such an act. She worried that it would be only a matter of time until he tried the same heavy-handed manner with her. She'd tried to talk to her father about the situation, but he'd assured her that Harper was harmless.

"Let him take out his aggressions elsewhere," her father had said, which was maddening and very much unlike her father.

That was when Valerie had begun to dig for as much dirt on Joel Harper as she could possibly find. She'd learned a little about his past, although his present was much easier to figure. Either way, she'd use it all to threaten his future.

"You don't know what I'll risk and what I won't. But I'm telling you here and now: Stay away from the men. You need to start appearing the docile little darling that everyone needs you to be. That means no more booze, no more wild parties, and no more men."

"Time to mount up," Luke called.

Valerie walked toward the group with Joel on her heel. "We haven't concluded our discussion on this matter," he whispered. "We'll talk about this more tonight."

"I have plans tonight," Valerie said with a candied sweetness she didn't feel. "They don't include you."

She hurried away from him without giving him so much as a backward glance. Once she was ready to tell Joel everything she knew about him and put her cards on the table, so to speak, he'd back away quick enough. There was no way he'd want to marry a woman who could put him in prison. Or worse yet, see him get the electric chair.

———————

Luke finished caring for the mules and yawned. He was glad they'd made it to the canyon floor without any mishaps. Given Miss Winthrop's interest in him, Luke had feared she might well endanger them both. She insisted on being next to him whenever possible, boring him with her tales of New York or other big cities. She clearly had designs on him, but for what purpose, Luke wasn't entirely sure. He'd thought midway through the day that her actions were nothing more than a scheme to make Harper jealous, but that didn't appear to be the case.

The crisp chill of the night air revived Luke momentarily, but it only served to remind him of his dilemma. He loved his life in the canyon, but he longed for something more—to make a life with Alex, to own his own land, and support his family working for himself. Luke looked upward to the heavens. The sky seemed a million miles away down here.

Lord, I don't know what to do with my life. I want to be a credit to you, but there are a lot of things that I don't understand. He thought of Alex and her mother. He wouldn't mind having Mrs. Keegan move in with him after he and Alex married. She was a good woman—kind, considerate, even tempered. Still, it wasn't the most perfect way to think of starting married life.

If taking Mrs. Keegan into his home was the price for getting Alex as a wife, Luke knew he'd gladly pay it. The only problem was convincing Alex they were right for each other.

Deciding to call it a night, Luke headed back to the cabin he'd share with Clancy. It was smaller and less fashionable than the tourist cabins, but it was a roof over their heads. What he really wanted was a hot bath, but he figured that would have to wait until he was back on the rim.

Phantom Ranch had been designed by Mary Colter at the request of the Harvey Company. The company had been bringing tourists to the canyon floor for years, but they needed proper accommodations for overnight stays. Miss Colter had seen to that. Luke had honestly never met a feistier woman than Mary Elizabeth Jane Colter. The woman had more energy than six grown men and worked with details like an artist might when creating a painting. And in some ways, that's exactly what she'd done. She'd created an artist's rendering of a canyon ranch, with a large native-stone building and smaller cabins. There was a wonderful dining hall where folks could share a meal and their tales of the trail. There was even a recreational hall for those who still had energy to spend after the ride down. The cabins were designed with two beds, a desk and chair, and a fireplace. The finishing touch on the cabin was a large Indian rug on the floor in front of the fireplace. It was simple, yet stately, in a rustic fashion.

Mary Colter had been very particular about her design, as she was with anything she put her hand to. Luke had to admire that. He admired even more that she'd made the journey down on mule back for the opening celebration the previous year. At the age of fifty-three, Miss Colter had maintained a grace and dignity that many women half her age failed to show. Nevertheless, if she found any flaw with her creation, she was scathing and ruthless until the matter was resolved to the satisfaction of her perfectionist nature.

Yawning again, Luke opened the door to his cabin and found that someone, probably Clancy, had started a fire. The days could feel like a furnace on the floor of the canyon, but nights were chilly, often cold. Flames danced on the logs in the fireplace, warming the room and bathing it in a cheery glow. Luke fully expected to see Clancy sound asleep in his bed, but he wasn't there. In fact, the bed hadn't been touched.

Tossing his hat onto the peg behind the door, Luke stretched and went to where a pitcher of water and a bowl awaited him on a small stand. He took up a washcloth, poured a bit of water into the bowl, and began to strip away the dust of the day. Bending over the bowl, he poured more water atop his head and scrubbed momentarily to free his hair of the dust and sweat. He finished washing, stripping off his shirt and neckerchief. He rinsed out the neckerchief, but merely shook out the shirt and hung it over the back of the chair. The Harvey Company expected their employees to be well groomed, no matter the setting.

Sitting on his bed, Luke pulled off his boots and stretched his toes. He couldn't decide whether to wash out his socks in the already dirty water or just let them go. It wasn't like anyone was going to see them.

"It'll keep," he told the room and reached down to move his boots to the end of the bed. Standing, Luke had just started to unbuckle his belt when he froze in motion at the sound of a woman's scream.

The first scream sounded like a cross between laughter and hysteria. The second scream, however, flooded his cabin as a scantily gowned Valerie Winthrop burst into his room as if the devil himself were after her.

*A*lex knew a deep sense of satisfaction at the end of her workday. With Joel Harper and Valerie Winthrop off on an expedition to the bottom of the canyon, she had been reprieved from dealing with the party. Her father had taken the remains of their group, including the senator, into Williams for a night of entertainment. Whatever that meant. Alex found herself simply thankful to have them gone from the canyon.

Relieved of her Winthrop duties, Alex was able to work the dining room and spend more time with Michaela. Throughout the evening, they crossed paths, making comments and laughing at situations that seemed comical. Table five had a psychic who, by tasting everyone's food, could tell them in turn whether there was good fortune or bad in their future. It also saved the psychic from having to buy a meal. Table three had a honeymooning couple who seemed to hardly notice the food on their plates. Alex found it very amusing when she asked the husband if he'd like dessert and he made eyes at his wife and said he already had the sweetest confection in the world.

Surprisingly energized and happy when her shift was over, Alex made her way to her room and peeled the hot uniform from her body. She chose a simple day dress of light blue cotton for the uniform's replacement. The dress was well-worn, although not embarrassingly so. Alex was reluctant to spend money on clothes. "I live most of my day in uniform anyway," she told her reflection as she studied the dress for any unacceptable signs of wear.

The outfit passed scrutiny, although Alex noticed that the white piping around the neckline and elbow-length sleeves had dulled considerably over the years. She wondered if she might be able to take a toothbrush and bluing to the material and lighten it.

Forgetting about her clothing for the time, Alex changed shoes and stockings and decided an evening stroll was in order. The evening was settling into a pleasantly cool temperature with barely a glow of sun still available to see by. She liked this time of night and wished Luke might be around to walk with her to discuss the events of the day and share thoughts on the days to come. The days when Luke led the two-day, overnight tours down to Phantom Ranch were her loneliest. Of course, now that Michaela was back things wouldn't seem quite so lonely.

Alex moved through the lobby, smiling at the visitors, eavesdropping on their comments. So many people marveled at the canyon's beauty. The very wealthy always seemed to come in two brands—those who had started with nothing and those who were born with everything. Those who had made their own way to financial security often seemed to care more about the things around them. They seemed to remember their origins and respected life. Those born to wealth often didn't appreciate what they had or the beauty around them. Of course, there were exceptions in each group.

People from both walks often told her that coming here had made them feel closer to God. Alex knew what they meant. She had fallen in love with the place from the first moment she'd set her gaze upon the multicolored landscape. But she'd also found a deeper commune with God as she spent days walking alone, along well-defined paths. She thought of verses in the Bible where it was noted that Jesus withdrew to lonely places. And even with its throngs of visitors, the canyon bore a certain loneliness to it.

Taking the short hike to Mary Colter's Lookout, Alex was relieved to see the place void of visitors. Most everyone had gone back to El Tovar to prepare for the next day.

With its rustic fireplace alcove and art room, the Lookout was a popular gathering place. The place had been designed to provide the viewer a good place to take photographs or make sketches of the canyon below. There were several levels for viewing, giving the visitor the best vantage for sight-seeing. There were even high-powered telescopes atop this scenic overlook that allowed the visitor to look out in more detail across the wide expanse. Alex had tried the telescopes a few times but didn't like the view as much as watching the scene with the naked eye. She could take in more sights and enjoy the play of the light and shadows—something that seemed greatly inhibited by the telescope.

Heading down the path to the lower viewing station, Alex relished the quiet and took advantage of the moment to pray. *I don't know what*

*the answers are for the future, Lord. Sometimes the answers seem almost clear—
as if I can make out the truth through a veil. But the meaning is just shrouded
enough that I can neither move forward nor back. What am I to do?*

The wind picked up, moaning slightly through the trees and rock.
Alex thought of Luke. He'd once taken her, along with several other
Harvey Girls and employees, to the canyon floor on a mule ride. They'd
had enormous amounts of fun, but Alex had enjoyed the walk she and
Luke had taken that evening even more than the adventurous ride to
Phantom Ranch.

As they wandered ancient paths, Luke had told her of Indian legends and folklore. How the Havasupai Indians believed the center of the
world was the San Francisco Peaks, just north of Flagstaff. They believed
the first people lived near a pool of water under the ground. They also
had a flood story, not unlike the Bible's account of Noah and the ark.

Alex found the stories fascinating. She found Luke even more
intriguing. She'd never had a male friend before. Men were liabilities
in her life, and she'd never sought after their affections. Luke just
seemed to sort of appear in her life and remain.

Funny, she thought, *I don't think there's anything in his nature that puts
me ill at ease. If I were to seek a husband, I would want him to be just like Luke
Toland.* The thought startled her. What was this nonsense about a husband? She wasn't usually given to such whimsy—why now?

"Yoo-hoo! Alex!"

Alex looked back up the rocky path. There was hardly any light to
see by, save a bit of a glow from the interior of the Lookout, but Alex
recognized Bernice's voice as she called, "May I join you?"

Alex smiled. "Sure, come ahead."

Bernice still wore her Harvey uniform, the white apron bearing tell-
tale signs of dinner. "I saw you head this way and . . . well. . . ."

"Is there a problem?" Alex questioned.

"No, not really. Well, maybe. Your father is looking for you. I
thought maybe I'd better warn you."

Alex felt her entire body tense. So much for a restful night. "I
thought he was spending the night in Williams. Did he say what he
wanted?"

Bernice came down the trail, her red hair bobbing in the breeze.
"No, he didn't say anything much at all. Just wanted to know where you
were and demanded that we find you and tell you that he wanted to
speak with you. Said he'd be on the north porch for an hour or so."

"Too bad," Alex muttered. "He can be there all night for all I care."

"I didn't mean to cause you pain," Bernice replied. "I only hoped to help you avoid confrontation. I thought if you knew where he was, you could keep away from that place."

Alex had lost all joy in the evening. To the west, storm clouds flickered with hints of lightning. She wondered if it would rain or simply be a dry thunderstorm. Sighing, she shook her head. "I'll not walk on eggshells just because of my father."

The wind picked up, moaning again through the rock and trees. Bernice startled at the sound. "Isn't that just awful?"

Alex lifted her head to catch the sound. "I kind of like it myself. Luke says that on the canyon floor the wind and the river make music almost like a calliope. I've never really heard it myself, but I don't travel to the bottom all the time like he does."

Bernice nodded and eyed the western skies. "Looks like we're in for a rain."

"This is our wettest month. This and August. Keeps the cycle of life going, I'm sure. I suppose we'd better head back. This thing could roll in rather quickly and we'd be drenched."

They started back up the rock-walled path to the lighted walkway above. Chattering about the day and nothing in particular, Alex realized she liked Bernice's gentle, sweet spirit. The girl was only eighteen, but with a huge family at home, she'd had to grow up quickly.

"The tips have been so much better than I could have imagined," Bernice said, beaming. "I've managed to send several dollars home to my folks, and tonight I made at least four dollars!"

"Yes, the patrons are usually quite generous," Alex agreed.

"Oh, dear," Bernice said, her voice lowering.

Alex looked to her as they came to the top of the rim walk. "What's wrong? Are you ill?"

Bernice shook her head. "It's your father. He sees you and he's coming this way."

Alex looked up the lighted path toward El Tovar. Sure enough, there he was. Striding in his anger, Rufus Keegan looked to be a man with something on his mind. Alex shivered.

"I'll stay with you," Bernice promised.

"No, I can handle him. You don't need to be in the middle of this."

Bernice looked thoughtfully at Alex. "But if I'm here, he might hold his tongue."

Alex laughed bitterly. "You don't know my father very well. He doesn't hold his tongue for anyone."

"Alexandria!"

Alex said nothing and refused to move. *Let him come to me if he needs to talk so badly.*

Rufus was slightly out of breath as he joined the two women. "I'd have a word with you—alone."

"I'll be going now, Miss Keegan," Bernice said in a voice barely above a whisper. "Unless you want me to stay."

"She does not. Be gone with you, girl," Alex's father said without giving Alex a chance to speak for herself.

"Yes, Bernice, just as I told you a few seconds ago, you needn't stay."

Her father looked miffed that she should interject her own authority in the matter, but he said nothing.

Bernice hesitantly took off in the direction of El Tovar, glancing back over her shoulder as if to make certain Rufus Keegan wouldn't rise up as some legendary monster and eat Alex alive. Alex waited until Bernice was well up the path before she turned her gaze upon her father. She knew her expression couldn't help but reveal the anger she felt inside, still she tried to keep her temper under control. "What do you want? Why aren't you in Williams, living the good life?"

Keegan leaned closer. "I'm not here to answer your questions. I'm here to give you an order. Play the game in a more cooperative manner, or pay the price."

"I'm sure I don't understand."

"And I'm just as certain you do." He leaned in closer. "You're going out of your way to embarrass me in front of the Winthrops, and I'll not have it."

"Me? Embarrass you?" She laughed and moved to walk away. "That's a bit like the pot calling the kettle black." She held up her hand. "And please don't further degrade yourself by making a pretense that you don't know what I'm talking about."

"I know all about the wrongs you suppose I've done you," her father replied, keeping pace with her for a ways. "What's happened is my business, not that of my daughter. A man does not give life to a child only to be ordered about and condemned by that same child twenty-four years later."

"I'm surprised you even know my age. The knowledge certainly doesn't come from your devoted presence in my life."

Her father reached out and stopped her. "Don't meddle in this, Alexandria. You cannot hope to win. I, on the other hand, am very good at bucking the odds. I will have my appointment in Washington with the Winthrop administration. I will have the prestige and fame accorded me."

"Wear laurels in your hair for all I care," Alex said stepping away from her father's touch. "Have your fame and glory, but leave Mother and me alone."

"You have no right to order me around. I'm here to tell you that, from now on, if anyone in the Winthrop party so much as asks you to jump—you jump."

Alex could take no more. "Why do you do this? Why not divorce my mother and let us go about our lives in an orderly and pleasant fashion? You don't need either one of us. We have no political ties to anyone and therefore merit very little of your attention. A divorce would be the simple solution."

"That's how much you know," Keegan replied, his face reddening as if he'd reached the limits of his patience.

Alex didn't care. Let him rant and rage.

"I'll never divorce her," he said flatly. "Your mother is my property and my responsibility. She'll stay at my side when I want her there and remain at home when I do not."

"But a divorce would give you the freedom—"

"No divorce!" He reached out again as if to take hold of her shoulders, but Alex was too quick for him. Shrugging, he repeated. "No divorce."

"What if mother divorces you?"

"She wouldn't dare. I'd never allow her to bring such a scandal upon us."

"Her? Bring scandal? What about you? What about 'Keegan Chooses Wrong Mount'? Everyone from here to the capital knows what you're doing and with whom. I hardly see Mother seeking a divorce to be much of a scandal."

"If you encourage her to try such a thing, I'll see that both of you suffer."

"What do you suppose we're doing now?" Alex questioned. "Do you realize I don't remember a time when I felt you truly loved me? Do you have any idea what it's like to grow up seeing other children share close relationships with their fathers, knowing you will never have the same thing?"

"Spare me your sob stories. Great men of power seldom have time for such nonsense."

"But that's the truly funny part," Alex countered. "You are neither a great man, nor a man of power. You fancy that because your bank account shows a tidy sum that you have somehow earned the respect and honor of your fellow citizens, but it isn't so. You're the laughingstock of this resort. The only reason you're even allowed here is that your money spends as well as the next man's. You were the laughingstock of Williams and probably still are, and the only reason anyone tolerates your antics is the fact that you have money, along with their insane love for a juicy piece of gossip."

"Enough! I won't be talked to in this manner. You need to remember what I've said. You may not care for the harm I cause you, but I think you'll agree that your mother is hardly strong enough to endure my wrath should I find it necessary to punish you through her."

"You had better not hurt her."

"That, my dear, will be entirely up to you," he said, sounding as though he'd regained his composure.

Alex realized the impasse. There was no way to deal with this now. She would simply have to make her plans and steal her mother away when her father least expected it.

"Do you understand me?"

"Yes. I understand you perfectly," Alex replied. She met his dark gaze and feared for her mother's life. Would he go so far as to kill her?

"Good. There will be no divorce. Not now—nor ever."

CHAPTER NINE

*W*earing nothing but a thin satin nightgown, Valerie Winthrop threw herself into Luke's cabin, screaming as she entered.

Luke stared at her in surprise, not having a clue about what to say or do.

"There's something out there," she said, backing against the wall. "I heard it. It was chasing me."

Luke went to the open door and looked out. The wind blew gently, while thunder rumbled in the distance. "I don't see anything."

He looked back to Valerie and shook his head as if to confirm it. "There's nothing out there."

"I know something or someone was out there. I could hear them saying my name—low and mournful." She rubbed her bare upper arms, the action causing the deep cut of her neckline to reveal more cleavage. She batted her lashes and pouted. "Don't send me back out there."

Luke shook his head and reached for his shirt. "I'll go check things out." He'd barely pulled the shirt on when Valerie threw herself against him. Her momentum nearly sent Luke off-balance, causing him to reach involuntarily out to Valerie. As he grasped hold of her, she tightened her grip on him as well.

"Don't leave me," she whispered. "I'm afraid." She looked up into his face, appearing absolutely terror stricken.

"I'm sure it's all right," Luke said, trying to put her away from him as he regained his stance.

Valerie would have no part of his action and tightened her hold on him. "No! I know what I heard."

"Then someone's just playing a game with you."

Forcing her away from him, Luke pushed her back toward the bed.

Pulling on his boots, he said, "Stay here and I'll go scout things out."

He headed out of the cabin, uncertain of what to do once he confirmed the safety of the area. Thunder sounded overhead. Luke wondered if they'd have rain and if that rain would make the trip back to the rim more difficult.

Seeing and hearing nothing out of the ordinary, Luke walked back to the cabin, buttoning his shirt as he went. He didn't have time to tuck it back into his jeans before he re-entered the cabin to find Valerie stretched out across his bed.

Striking a seductive pose she said, "Did you chase away the boogeyman?"

"I saw no evidence that he was out there. Now come on, I'll walk you back to your place."

"Why not let me stay here with you? I won't be missed. Besides, you have two beds," she said. Then giggling she added, "But this one looks big enough for both of us."

Luke was starting to feel angry. "Ma'am, I haven't the least bit of interest in accommodating you."

"You don't like me?"

"Frankly, no." Luke motioned to the door. "Come on."

"Why don't you like me?"

"I've never cared for fast women."

"I'm not fast," she said, laughing. "I'm just purposeful. When I see something I like, I go after it."

"Well, I don't care for that kind of woman either."

"Is there someone else? Is that what this is really about? Do you have a sweetheart?"

"I wouldn't exactly say that," Luke responded, not even sure why he was bothering.

"There is someone!" Valerie sat up in the middle of the bed. "What's her name?"

"None of your business. Now get out of my bed, and let me walk you back to your cabin."

"Not until you tell me her name."

Luke had taken all he was going to take. Marching to the bed, he lifted Valerie from the mattress and set her on the floor. Again her grip on him was almost painful.

"Don't be mad at me. You and I could have a great time together. I know it."

Just then, Clancy walked through the open door. "Hey, why's the door . . ." He paused, taking in the sight.

"Miss Winthrop was sure that something was chasing her," Luke said, forcing her once again away from him. "Would you walk her back to her cabin, Clancy?"

Clancy eyed the barely clothed Valerie and then turned his gaze to Luke again. There were a dozen unspoken questions in his expression, but thankfully he didn't vocalize a single one.

"Sure thing, boss."

Luke breathed a sigh of relief, but it was short-lived. Valerie Winthrop was not a happy woman. She'd been scorned and denied, and as a rich socialite, she was probably not used to either one.

She frowned at him, her eyes narrowing as her brows came together ever so slightly. "This isn't settled between us," she whispered.

"Yes, it is," Luke replied. "Keep your distance. I don't have time for these games, and I'll not allow you to put the party in jeopardy tomorrow when we make our ascent. Keep that in mind. At the first sign of trouble, I'll separate you from the group and have Clancy escort you alone."

Valerie grew hateful then. "I can't tell you how much you've offended me. All I wanted was a little fun in this hideous place. You've made a terrible mistake."

"The error is on your part, Miss Winthrop. Good night." He hoped his firm tone would assure her of his purpose. Turning away from her, he went to the far side of the room and pretended to busy himself with poking up the fire.

"Come on, Miss Winthrop. I'll see to it that you get back safe and sound."

Luke heard Clancy's gentle tone and hoped that Valerie wouldn't take out her anger on him. Clancy was a sweet, gentle-natured fellow— Luke hated the thought of Miss Winthrop sinking her claws in him.

It wasn't until Luke heard the door close behind them that he stood and replaced the fire poker. He looked at the closed door for a long time. Why in the world had she singled him out? With the exception of two other women, both older and both obviously married, Miss Winthrop was the only female in their group. She was the obvious interest of the dozen or more men who had joined their party into the canyon.

"So why come after me?" he questioned aloud. He pulled off his shirt and draped it back over the chair. Sitting on the edge of the bed, his gaze still fixed on the door as if Valerie Winthrop might somehow rematerialize, Luke pulled off his boots and shook his head. "Why?"

Clancy returned about that time and Luke couldn't help but feel a wash of embarrassment over the episode. Clancy looked at him, as if awaiting an explanation. Luke shrugged. "She just burst in here unannounced and threw herself at me. I'm telling you, I've never seen anything like it."

Clancy smiled. "She smells good, I've got to give her that." He closed the door and walked to his own side of the room. "She isn't very happy with you."

"I don't care," Luke said, standing to take off his jeans. He thought better of it and decided to sleep with them on. Just because Clancy was here didn't mean she might not sneak back, and if that happened, Luke intended to be at least partially clothed.

"She was crying and telling me that nobody cared about her," Clancy said, tossing his hat to a hook. "I felt sorry for her."

"Don't," Luke said angrily. "She has an entire entourage of men who would be more than happy to entertain and care for her. She's just playing games with me. The problem is, I don't know why."

"Maybe she has some kind of bet with that Mr. Harper character. They seem a strange bunch. Someone said she's engaged to Harper. If that's the case, why is she here with you?"

"Exactly," Luke said in complete exasperation. He trusted Clancy not to make a big deal out of the situation, but he felt he needed to say something. "Clancy, I'd appreciate it if you'd keep what happened here tonight just between us."

"Sure, boss."

"I don't need my reputation ruined."

"Some of the guys wouldn't see it that way," Clancy said, smiling. "They'd see you as quite the man."

"Yes, but I worry more about the truth of the matter and what God thinks." Luke sat down on the bed and rubbed his chin. "I know God knows what happened here tonight, but a Christian needs to work to be above reproach."

"What's that mean—reproach?"

"Disgrace—shame—blame. It means you live your life in such a fashion that no one can hold you accountable for things you didn't do. You keep out of situations that even look like they might be a problem."

"Like before prohibition," Clancy said, "when the guys wanted you to go to the bar in Williams. They'd tease you and say you didn't have to drink whiskey or beer."

"Exactly. I could go sit in the bar and drink nothing but water—be completely innocent—but someone might see me and believe the worst. I wouldn't be guilty of drinking, but I sure would be guilty of giving someone reason to believe falsely of me."

"But you can't be held to account for what people think," Clancy said. "Surely God doesn't expect that. I mean, you can't very well control other people's lives—especially their thoughts."

Clancy eyed him seriously, as if his words were just too incredible to believe. Luke realized that Clancy had never taken much interest in talk of the Christian walk, prior to this. Luke was aware that what he said now might very well send Clancy away from God or draw him closer. He whispered a prayer for the right words.

"You can't control other people's lives or thoughts—but you can control your own," Luke replied. "Self-control is an important part of living a Christian life. But you don't have to do it on your own. God gives you a lot of help along the way. When you're tempted to do the wrong thing, go the wrong direction, He's there for you. Just like tonight."

"How so, boss?"

"I wasn't tempted to do anything wrong with Miss Winthrop, but if I had been, this would have been a bad situation for me. It would have been hard to resist a barely clothed woman who obviously was looking for a good time. But my heart was fixed on doing the right thing. It was fixed that way because I turned my desires over to God a long time ago. Since then, I've been praying and reading the Bible, and I know a little better everyday what I should and shouldn't let myself get into."

Clancy pulled off his boots and nodded. "So because you were thinking about God, you weren't thinking about what Miss Winthrop had to offer?"

"That's partially it. It's because of my relationship with God that I also respect the people in my life. I try to treat each person as I would want to be treated—with respect and kindness. It doesn't always come out that way. I have a mean streak, as you well know."

Clancy laughed. "I've seen it a time or two."

"Well, I try to control that as well. See, a man who can control his tongue can control just about anything else. And what a man says comes up out of his heart. The Bible says so."

"I ain't never heard this religion stuff put quite this way. It makes a heap more sense than what I've known in the past."

"That's because I don't care much for religion myself. I care about God and what He wants for my life. Religions can just cause a man grief.

They scatter him in all sorts of directions looking for answers to one thing and then another." Luke walked over to his saddlebag and pulled out his Bible. "This is what counts, Clancy. The Bible has all the answers we'll ever need. It's all laid out in here."

Clancy scratched his chest and looked rather embarrassed. "I don't . . . well . . . I don't have one of those. Never saw the need, so I ain't never bought me one."

"Then have this one," Luke said, bringing the Bible to his friend. "But let me share just one passage with you first."

"Sure," Clancy said, looking at the book as though Luke were offering him gold.

Luke turned to the third chapter of John. "See here, this is Jesus talking to a man named Nicodemus—he was a ruler of the Jewish people. He tells Nicodemus, 'For God so loved the world, that he gave his only begotten Son, that whosoever believeth in him should not perish, but have everlasting life.' "

"Everlasting life? You mean, you never die?"

"Your body dies eventually—everybody's does. But when you accept Jesus as your Savior—when you believe on Him and repent of your sins—you're given eternal life for your spirit. When your body dies, your spirit will live on with Jesus in heaven."

"Seems simple enough," Clancy said, looking at the words for himself. "Is there more I have to do?"

"There are things we do out of obedience and respect to God—baptism and service, tithing and fellowship—but first and foremost, we accept that Jesus is the Son of God and we accept that He died for us sinners so that we wouldn't have to face death alone. We repent of our sins and work to never repeat our old ways. It's a new life, Clancy."

"Them are powerful words, Luke," Clancy said, looking up with an expression that suggested awe. "So what do I have to do to repent? I mean, how do I know if I did something that God considers a sin?"

"God knows your heart, Clancy. If you tell Him you're sorry for the past wrongs you've committed—if you ask Him to forgive you and to come into your heart, He will. He'll help you to understand what's right and wrong in His sight. You'll learn it by reading the Bible and you'll see, too, the deep love He has for you."

"I just talk to Him—like I'm talking to you?"

"Just so. Most folks like to bow their heads and close their eyes, but you can pray with your eyes wide open sitting atop a mule. You can pray in your sickbed and pray over dinner. It doesn't matter where you pray, it's just important that you do pray."

Clancy took the Bible in his hands and nodded. "I'd like to pray. I've been real impressed with the way you handle yourself, Luke. And like tonight, I knew in my heart you'd done no wrong with that woman. I knew it 'cause of the way you live your life the rest of the time."

"I only live my life that way because God gives me the strength to do so. I'm nothing special on my own, Clancy, but with God, nothing's impossible. He gives me the strength I need for everything."

"Then I want that too. I know you wouldn't steer me wrong."

"It's not me doing the steering, Clancy. It's God."

Clancy nodded. "That's good enough for me."

Luke smiled and slapped Clancy on the back in a hearty manner. "Then let's get down to business."

So they're planning all these parties," Michaela told a group of gathered wranglers and Harvey Girls. "I've even heard it said that reporters are coming in from as far as Washington, D.C., to watch these rich ninnies fall all over themselves to see who'll be most favored to get the Democratic nomination for president."

"This is just the start. I heard they are all headed on to Los Angeles after this, and then New York," someone else threw in.

"It's all a lot of fuss for nothing, if you ask me," Luke said, eyeing Alex as she joined the little group.

"Didn't look like you minded the fuss too much last night," one of Luke's crew said snidely. "I saw that Miss Winthrop over at your cabin. Didn't look like she was fussin' much about being fully clothed. Was she campaigning?" Laughter rose up from some of Luke's crew.

"Bet she got the boss's vote for sure."

Luke had never suspected that anyone else might have seen Valerie's visit. He knew he had a confidant in Clancy, but he'd never thought to ward off this topic with the others. Looking up, he caught Alex looking at him with an expression of disbelief and betrayal. Her cheeks reddened as she realized he'd caught her watching him. She walked away from the group and headed up to the hotel without another word.

"That's not a good way to keep friends, Luke," Michaela offered without condemnation. "Come on, Bernice, we'd better get to work."

Clancy came to Luke's rescue, but not in time to help him with Alex. "Miss Winthrop got herself spooked. I took her back to her cabin. That's all that was about."

Everyone looked to Luke as if for confirmation, but all he could think of was Alex. Now she no doubt figured he'd been having some kind of clandestine arrangement with Miss Winthrop.

"Never you mind, Luke," a redheaded crew member spoke up. "There's something about the canyon that just makes women throw themselves at men."

As if to prove his point, Bernice tripped over her feet and fell into Clancy's lap. Everyone laughed in amusement at the situation. Everyone but Luke.

"If that don't beat all," Clancy murmured, helping to right Bernice. Her face turned a deep crimson, but she smiled and thanked Clancy before taking her seat in silence.

"Getting back to the parties," another Harvey Girl picked up, "I heard it said there will be a big to-do every night. The Winthrops are spending a wagonload of money on the affair. They've hired the Harvey Company to put on their best show. That means we'll be working overtime, but we'll be well compensated."

"Well, I heard . . ."

Luke only listened halfheartedly as the comments droned on about the coming events. He knew if he'd gotten up to go after Alex, everyone would have had something to say about it. As it was, it seemed wise to stay in his seat and try to catch a moment to talk to her when they could be alone.

I'm innocent here, Lord, he prayed. *I don't know why things like this have to happen to interfere in a guy's life. Alex has a hard enough time with men, and now this. It just doesn't seem fair.* He glanced across the table to where the others still carried on about the upcoming events. *Help me, Lord. Help me to find a time and place to talk to Alex. Just a quiet moment to explain.*

That moment, however, didn't come until hours later. Luke had just returned from taking a group of visitors on a rim-side trail when he spotted Alex polishing silver. She sat quietly in the most isolated corner of the room, completely lost in her thoughts

"Looks like you're gonna wear a hole in the coffeepot," he said as he came up from behind her.

Alex looked up and nodded. "It's a good task for taking out aggressions."

"And would those aggressions have anything to do with what you overheard this morning?" Alex's cheeks reddened, but she said nothing. Luke pulled off his hat and sat down at the table.

"Look, Alex, nothing happened. Miss Winthrop showed up at my cabin screaming her head off about something or someone being outside following her. She was just spooked and . . ."

"Honestly, Luke, you don't owe me an explanation. I may be naïve about some things, but I know how it is when men and women find each other attractive."

No, you don't, or you'd see how I feel about you, Luke thought to himself. He shook off the thought and instead said, "I may not owe you an explanation, but I'd like to give you one. I don't want you thinking badly of me."

Alex finally met his gaze, and Luke warmed at the sight of her turquoise blue eyes. She pierced his heart, however, with her next statement. "I don't think anything about it at all," she said. "I've seen how it can be for men, especially when a woman throws herself at them. I don't approve, and I never will, but it isn't my business or my concern how you choose to entertain yourself."

"But that's just it!" Now he was getting mad. "I wasn't entertaining myself with anything or anyone. She just burst into my cabin claiming something was after her. I checked it out and then . . ." he paused, not entirely sure how much he wanted to say.

Alex looked at him suspiciously, watching and waiting for how he would conclude the statement.

"She wanted me to let her stay, but I said no. I'm not interested in her. She threw herself at me, but I refused to be persuaded. Clancy came in about that time and I asked him to take her home. The good news in all of this is that when Clancy came back, we talked and Clancy accepted Christ as his savior."

Alex smiled ever so slightly. "That is good news."

"Especially since you're the one who helped put me back on the straight and narrow. If you hadn't given me a reason to believe again, I wouldn't have been able to share the Bible with Clancy."

"I didn't give you a reason to believe—God did that."

"Well, you let Him use you as the messenger. When I think of how much I'd hardened my heart against Him after my ma died, well, I know it wasn't easy to get through to me. I blamed God for taking her away, never thinking about the consequences of distancing myself from Him. You changed that for me. You let me see the truth."

"I just try to live out my faith," Alex said, looking embarrassed. She turned her attention back on the pot.

"Alex, I don't want you thinking poorly of me."

"I don't. If you want a . . . friendship with Miss Winthrop, you have my blessing. I promise to be civil about it. It won't affect our friendship."

"Haven't you heard a word I've said?" Luke asked, getting to his feet. He took up his hat and shook his head in anger. "I don't want a friendship with Miss Winthrop. I don't care about her. I care about . . ."

Alex looked up, waiting for him to finish his confession.

"Oh, just forget it."

He stormed out of the room to keep from saying something out of anger that he'd only regret later. He wanted to tell Alex how he felt, but if he told her in the middle of this mess, she might think he was only saying the words to get her mind off of Valerie Winthrop. Why was it his timing was always off?

Crossing the lawn, Luke stalked down the rim path, not at all certain where he was headed.

"Oh, Mr. Toland! Luke!" Valerie Winthrop called to him from where she strolled at her father's side. "Do come meet my father."

Luke felt like bolting and running in the opposite direction. Instead, he knew he needed to be amiable with the guests.

"Miss Winthrop," Luke said, tipping his hat.

"Daddy, this is Luke Toland. He was the man who led the mule trip yesterday. He's worked here for about ten years. Isn't that right, Luke?"

Luke nodded and shook the senator's hand.

"So what do you think of this park, Mr. Toland?" the senator questioned. "My daughter finds it dull and lifeless."

"Oh, Daddy, that wasn't very nice to say."

"Maybe not, but it was the truth."

Luke wanted to put an end to the conversation as quickly as he could. "I love it. The canyon is home to me. There's a great deal of peace and serenity here."

"Maybe that's why Valerie doesn't like it," Senator Winthrop replied. "She's never cared much for peace and quiet. Even as a child she enjoyed the more rambunctious games of the neighborhood boys. Could never understand why a young lady would prefer the company of ruffian boys. Still, this park is decent enough. She ought to be able to find something that catches her attention."

Valerie laughed and nudged her father. "Now, don't be boring Mr. Toland with stories about me. He knows so very much about this park that I'm sure he could really tell you a thing or two."

"I rather you tell me what your political view of the day might be." The senator appeared capable of changing subjects as fast as Clancy could change a saddle. He eyed Luke critically, as if the next words out of Luke's mouth might make or break his political career.

Luke shrugged. The conversation wasn't one he wanted to get into. "I can't say that I have a political view."

"Nonsense. We men all have views of the situation around us. This park you love so much was an act of government."

"No, sir, I beg to differ with you. This park was an act of God. The government might have set it aside as a national park, but God put it together."

"Of course, boy, but what about those groups who want to come and destroy this fine place? The Harding administration would just as soon drill her for oil as to not."

"I put my concerns in God's hands," Luke told Mr. Winthrop. "Then I don't have to worry about it, and I can get a whole lot more done with the time I might have spent in worry."

"Sounds like you're burying your head in the sand."

"Maybe, but at least I earn my money instead of begging or demanding it, and I don't trade it for favors. Say what you will, but I see your kind of life as a real bondage."

"Yes, I'm sure your kind of folk would."

Luke felt his anger stirred. "What is that supposed to mean?"

"A lowly cowboy such as yourself can't have much interest in the things of educated men. I'm sure most of it goes way beyond your comprehension." The senator hooked his thumbs in his vest pocket and rested his hands against his portly belly. Striking such a pose, he continued. "The common man doesn't always realize that he suffers because of the decisions other people are making for him. A president should take into account that the common man most likely doesn't know what he wants or needs. In turn, the right president would choose for such people and help them to better understand their needs."

"I understand my needs fully," Luke replied, barely speaking through clenched teeth.

"But you can't. Not really. For instance, you probably believe prohibition is a good thing. Prohibition is supposed to sober the country and bring back morality and sobriety. Instead, more people than ever before are drinking. And do you know why, Mr. Toland? Poor management of this country. It's a sad and depressing event."

"Now, Daddy, there's no need to get yourself all worked up. You'll be able to make speeches later."

"Yes, I really must excuse myself. I have work to do," Luke said with as much graciousness as he could muster. He tipped his hat ever so slightly, then turned to hurry across the grounds toward the stables.

"But, Luke, we had hoped you'd join us for dinner," Valerie called. Luke just kept going.

First Alex, and now this Winthrop character. Life at the canyon wasn't nearly the pleasant respite Luke had once found it to be. When had things gotten so crazy?

I don't have to stay. The thought came from the darker recesses of his brain. That had always been the plan. Come to the canyon, make enough money, then buy a place of his own. But he wanted to share that place with Alex, and now she thought he was just as bad as her father. Oh, she hadn't said it, but he could tell by the look in her eyes.

"She thinks I'm a no-good womanizer," Luke muttered, coming to the stable yards. He opened the gate and moved into the corral, determined to get some work done before the day was completely lost.

"She thinks I'm of such low moral character that I'd forsake my faith and fall into the arms of some city-bred flirt." He kicked at the dirt, startling the mules. Mindless of what he was doing, Luke managed to spook one of the newest recruits—a thin-faced mule with a bit of a temper.

To prove his attitude would brook little nonsense from the likes of Luke, the mule reared forward and kicked out with his hind legs.

Luke had no time to respond. He took the full blow in his left wrist, and he felt the bone snap almost instantly. Knocked backward, Luke quickly regained his footing, clutching his arm in desperate pain.

"Oh, all the stupid . . . lousy . . . things."

"Luke! You okay?" Clancy called, coming from the barn.

"I think this no good mule just broke my wrist," Luke said, gingerly feeling his forearm and hand. "Yeah, I'm sure that's what he did. Hurts like nothing I've ever had before."

"Let's get you to the doc," Clancy said, moving between Luke and the new mule. "Here," he added, taking the oversized bandana from around his neck. "Let's make you a sling."

Luke winced as Clancy maneuvered the bandana around the arm. The pain, so intense, shot up his arm and spread throughout his body. He felt sick to his stomach and light-headed.

"Boss, don't you go passin' out on me," Clancy said, reaching out to steady Luke.

"I won't mean it if I do," Luke said, fighting the pain. "Just keep me walking—get me to the doc and I'll be fine."

"Sure. I can see that for myself. You look like you're ready to lead another group of riders to Phantom Ranch."

"I'll be all right," Luke said, biting his tongue to keep from screaming out in pain.

By this time some of the other members of his crew showed up. They watched Clancy and Luke with a curiosity that made Luke uneasy. He wasn't a sideshow at the county fair.

"Get back to work you all. Can't a man break his arm without half the state turning out to see what's going on?"

The collection of men murmured responses among themselves, but Luke couldn't hear what they were saying. It was just as well. He needed to focus his attention on keeping his feet moving down the path. He needed to keep his mind off the pain in his arm . . . and in his heart.

"Alex!" Bernice came running into the kitchen, sliding on the still-wet floor. The boy who'd just mopped the area scowled and muttered something inaudible.

Alex looked up from the salads she'd been arranging and smiled at Bernice's enthusiasm. "What is it, Bernice? You look as if the circus has come to town."

"It's Mr. Toland!"

Alex gave Bernice her full attention, noting the look of worry in Bernice's expression. "What's happened?"

"He got kicked by a mule. He's over at the doctor's, but I heard one of his men say he's broken his arm."

"Here, take care of these salads," Alex said, not caring that it was strictly against the rules to leave her station without permission. She raced out the door and made her way to the infirmary. Visions of Clancy's broken nose and bruised face came to mind. She felt her chest tighten with worry. *Oh, God, please let him be all right.*

The doctor had finished casting Luke's wrist and hand by the time Alex arrived. A small collection of people was waiting as Luke emerged from the back room. "Well, I'm going to live," he told Clancy. He looked past Clancy and noticed Alex. He smiled.

"What happened, Luke?" Alex asked, coming from behind Clancy. "I just got here and didn't have time to ask."

Luke's brow furrowed. "I wasn't keeping my mind on my work. I backed right into one of the new mules and the crazy thing kicked me. Clancy was right there and got me up here to the doctor. I'm going to be fine. Just a few weeks in a cast and I'll be as good as new."

"No horses or mules, however," the doctor said, coming up behind Luke. "You'll need to rest for a few days and take it easy. It was a clean enough break, but there's no sense in taking chances. You'll not be able to ride for a while."

Alex saw Luke wince at that statement. Luke had grown up in a saddle. She knew riding was an important part of his life. "We'll take good care of him," she promised the doctor, taking Luke in hand. "Come on. We'll get you back to your cabin and settle you in. Then I'll get your supper and see that you have what you need for the night."

Luke grinned. "Like a mother hen, eh?"

"This is serious business, Luke," Alex chided. She didn't care how it looked or sounded to anyone else. She cared too much for Luke to let someone else take charge of him.

They walked quietly back to Luke's cabin on the far side of the stables. Alex worried about the pain he must be feeling, all the while wondering at her own feelings, which seemed much too protective and deep for mere friendship. "Does it hurt?"

"Yeah, you could say that." Now that they were alone, Luke wasn't trying to sound like his normal cheerful self.

She stumbled slightly on the uneven ground. Luke reached out to steady her, sending electrical charges up her arm and straight to the heart. She saw him grimace, however, and couldn't bear that he was hurt. Not Luke. Strong, virile, capable Luke. Why couldn't it have happened to someone else? "Did the doctor give you anything to take for the pain?"

"Yeah, but it only helps a little. He said it should stop hurting in a day or two."

"I'm really sorry," Alex said, as if somehow this had all been her fault.

"You don't need to be sorry. It was my own fool inattentiveness that brought this on. I've told my crew a thousand times, if I've told them once, you can't be daydreaming or stewing over other things while you're working with the animals. Now I'll be in this cast for six weeks, and it's going to wreak havoc with my job."

"You're in charge. Your men can get the heavy work done and you can do all the paper work and set things up for the guests. You'll see; it won't be so bad. Maybe Clancy would even let us borrow his car from time to time and we could get you out away from the hotel."

"I can't very well drive like this," he grumbled.

"Well, then I can drive us," Alex said. "It can't be that hard to learn."

Luke laughed out loud, causing Alex to halt in mid-step. "What?"

she questioned as he continued to laugh. "You don't think I can learn to drive? Is that it?"

"I just don't want the rest of me broken up," Luke said, managing to contain his mirth.

"You got yourself broken up all on your own," Alex reminded him. "I have yet to break a single thing you own."

Luke sobered at this and turned away. Alex thought his attitude very strange, but said nothing. No doubt the pain and the medication given him by the doctor was enough to alter his mood.

Approaching his cabin, Luke climbed the porch steps, opened the door, and stepped inside. Alex marched in right behind him. She knew her actions would cause eyebrows to rise and tongues to wag, but she didn't care. Luke was her best friend and he needed her. *That's what friends are for,* she told herself. *They bear all things and endure all things.* Funny, that sounded vaguely familiar. Somewhere in the back of her mind she was certain she'd heard those phrases before.

She looked around the simple three-room cabin. There was a living area with a fireplace and two small windows. Luke had a worn-out sofa that Alex thought she recognized from having been in the hotel at one time. There was a desk and chair in the corner. Stacks of papers and ledgers were neatly arranged on the desktop—the organization of it surprised Alex.

On the opposite wall from the front door was another door that Alex presumed went to the bedroom or the bath. "Where's your room?"

Luke pointed to the door, and Alex nodded and asked matter-of-factly, "And the bath?"

Luke grinned. "We're already pressing propriety here. I don't think the Harvey Company would find it at all acceptable for you to see to my cleaning up."

"I wasn't suggesting that at all," Alex replied, feeling her cheeks grow hot. "I merely wanted to know where everything was. The doctor wants you to rest. I wanted to help by making the place as conducive to your recovery as possible. If I need to move things around to make it easier for you, then I have to know where everything is to begin with."

Luke yawned and Alex wondered if the medicine was making him sleepy. "I think I will lie down for a time," he said, rubbing the upper portion of his left forearm.

"I think that would be wise. I need to get back to my shift. I'll bring supper in an hour or two."

"You'll be taking care of the Winthrops tonight, won't you?"

Alex nodded. "I suppose so."

Luke seemed less than pleased with the news. "That's going to keep you longer than an hour or two, won't it?"

"I'll just do what I can to hurry them along. They love their politics," Alex said, moving to take Luke's hat from him. "Do you need help with your boots?"

"I hadn't even thought of that. Yeah, I suppose I do."

Alex motioned him to the bedroom. "Go ahead and sit down on the bed. I'll help you get them off."

Luke did as he was told, and Alex followed him into the simple bedroom. She was surprised that this rough and rugged cowboy could be such an orderly person. The bed was made, the nightstand was clear of clutter. Without a word, Alex turned down the bed for Luke, then pointed to his boots.

Luke cradled his arm and sat down on the edge of the bed. He lifted first one foot and then the other, while Alex wrestled the boots from his feet and placed them beside the nightstand. "Do you need anything else before I go?"

"No, I'm fine. I'll look forward to seeing you tonight. Might be wise to bring someone along with you. Wouldn't look good to have you visiting my cabin like this on a regular basis."

"I don't care what other people think. They already believe the worst about my family anyway."

"Yes, but they don't believe the worst about you," Luke replied. "I don't want your reputation damaged on account of me. You heard the sport they made of me over what Miss Winthrop did. I don't want them making sport of you too."

Alex appreciated his concern. "I see what you mean. I'll do what I can. Maybe Bernice will walk with me."

Luke nodded. "Now go on back to work. I'll be just fine. Clancy is going to check in on me."

Alex was surprised at her reluctance to leave. She cared about Luke's condition and hated to think of him needing something and being unable to get to it. But it wasn't as if his legs were broken. She sighed and headed back to the hotel.

———

The next couple of days passed rather quickly, and as word of Luke's injury spread, he found himself pampered and spoiled in a way that he'd never have imagined. The hotel management offered him a room at the hotel, in spite of their huge influx of guests, but Luke preferred the cabin and declined the offer. Next, they suggested he allow them to bring meals to him at the cabin rather than him having to come to the hotel. This, Luke thought perfectly acceptable—especially if Alex was the one doing the delivery. Unfortunately, it wasn't always Alex. Still, she came as often as anyone else, and it always afforded them a few minutes of conversation. Sometimes she would even massage his neck and shoulders, easing the tension caused by the weight of the cast on his arm.

Clancy was a good man, hardworking and dependable, and seemed to be able to keep good enough order with the men and the tourists. Luke knew that, if and when the day came that Clancy was put in charge, he would make a good leader. The thought gave Luke a certain peace. Especially when he thought about buying a ranch of his own and leaving the Grand Canyon.

And that was the biggest trouble with being laid up. Luke had entirely too much time to think. He thought about the ranch he'd like to own. He thought about the kind of house he'd like to build. He even thought of how he'd like his wedding to be, and all of those thoughts brought him back to Alex. He was determined to talk to her as soon as she showed up with his lunch. He knew she wouldn't have much time, but then, he didn't need much time to explain his heart.

A knock on the door brought Luke to attention. That was probably her now. A little early, but nevertheless, it was a good time to talk. He threw open the door, but instead of Alex, he found Valerie Winthrop.

"Why, Mr. Toland, I nearly died when I heard what had happened."

Luke didn't know what to say. He felt so completely taken aback at her appearance that he could only shrug. Valerie seemed not to notice, however, and continued her conversation without difficulty.

"I told Daddy I was coming down here to see how you were. You positively must let us take care of you. We have an entire wing of rooms at the hotel and you would heal much faster there than here."

"Why do you suppose that?"

"Well, because I could take perfect care of you," she said, nearly purring the words. In fact, she rather reminded Luke of a cat in her white dress and formfitting bonnet. The hat was white with strips of black that stuck out away from the hat at strange intervals—almost like ears. "Well, aren't you going to ask me in?"

Luke cleared his voice and refused to move from the door. "I don't think that would be appropriate, Miss Winthrop."

"Please, call me Valerie. After all, if I'm to take care of you—"

"But you aren't," Luke affirmed. "I'm doing just fine by myself. I have good friends who come and see to my needs. It wouldn't be right for a guest to be a part of that."

"But I want to be a part of it. You're very special to me." She looked heavenward and put her gloved left hand over her heart. "When I heard what had happened, I just knew this was the fates bringing us to a more intimate relationship."

"Miss Winthrop, I'm not sure where you got the idea from me that such a thing was of interest, but I assure you it's not. I would rather you not come back here, if you don't mind."

Valerie frowned. "You're obviously still distraught from the accident. Maybe I'll come back later."

Luke heard the chatter of approaching visitors. It was no doubt Alex and maybe Michaela or Bernice. Alex was good to bring someone with her, just as he'd suggested. They always sat outside, away from the porch to afford Alex and Luke some privacy, while at the same time acting as chaperone.

Luke figured Miss Winthrop would have no choice but to leave now. "They're bringing me my lunch," he said, motioning toward the two approaching women.

Valerie leaned closer to Luke. "I could just as easily do that job."

"You have a campaign to help run and an election that will come up entirely sooner than you expect. Why not just go on back?"

Valerie leaned even closer, making Luke very uncomfortable. "I could make you very happy. I'm a rich woman and I have friends in high places."

"I doubt they're as high as my friend—God. He's the only one I need."

Valerie leaned forward and kissed him hard on the mouth. "I need you," she whispered. Her breath smelled of mint and whiskey. "Couldn't you reconsider?"

Luke pulled away from her but not before Alex noticed what was going on. He saw her cheerful countenance change in the blink of an eye. Valerie made no further scene, except for the kiss she blew back toward Luke when she was halfway up the path.

Uncertain what to say, Luke said nothing at all. What could he say? Alex had seen it all.

Bernice held back while Alex brought the tray. "I've brought your lunch," she said in a rather curt tone.

"Smells good. I'm nigh on to starving."

Alex said nothing. She put the tray on the porch table and turned to leave.

"Wait. Sit for a minute, I have something to say."

Alex looked extremely uncomfortable. In fact, she almost looked mad. The expression gave Luke cause to hope. Could it be she was jealous of Valerie Winthrop? "Why don't you send Bernice back and I'll just eat here on the porch and you and I can talk?"

"No, that's all right. I don't want to take you away from your . . . friends."

"Bernice," he called out, "why don't you go on back up to the hotel? I need to talk to Alex for a few minutes."

"Stay where you are, Bernice. I'm coming back with you."

Luke took hold of Alex. "Please stay. I need to talk to you."

Bernice had gotten to her feet. Her look of uncertainty spoke for itself. Leaning closer to Alex, Luke whispered, "Send her back so that we can talk. You aren't going to like this one bit if she overhears what I have to say."

Alex studied him for a moment, then nodded. "Very well. Bernice, go ahead to the hotel."

Luke let her go and motioned to the table. "Just put the tray there and then sit down with me, if you would be so kind."

"Very well, but I don't know what this is about."

She remained haughty and distant, causing Luke to smile all the more. "You're jealous. You're jealous of Valerie Winthrop and the fact that she kissed me."

"And you've gone completely daffy. Have you been hitting some bootlegged bottle of whiskey?"

Her words sounded convincingly indifferent, but her expression was one of sheer misery. "Tell me why you're jealous." He sat down and looked up at her, "Please sit first."

Alex pulled out the chair and sat down. "I'm not jealous, and no matter how many times you say that, it won't make it true."

"That's all I want . . . the truth," Luke said, eyeing her quite seriously. "Why not tell me the truth?"

Alex felt her mouth go dry. The truth was, she didn't like seeing Valerie so capably handle her dear friend. She especially didn't like the fact that the woman was so wanton with her kisses. To be exact, she didn't like Valerie Winthrop.

"I . . . well . . . I had just hoped for time to talk to you. When I saw her here, I knew it would be of no use."

"But she's gone. She can't be a problem now. Why not just admit you're feeling jealous." Luke grinned. "Maybe you wish you were the one blowing me kisses."

Alex shook her head and lowered her gaze. Strangely enough, he wasn't that far from the mark. Her problem was that she didn't understand where these feelings were coming from. She wasn't even sure she could express her feelings in words. And, even if she could, she wasn't at all certain she wanted Luke to know how she felt. After all, it was rather embarrassing.

"I just don't think Miss Winthrop would understand the kind of friendship we have," Alex finally answered flatly.

"I'm not sure I understand it either," Luke admitted, his tone sounding rather defeated.

Alex felt the words slam against her. What did he mean, saying he wasn't sure he understood their friendship? Was he trying to tell her that he preferred the likes of Valerie Winthrop—beautiful, glamorous Valerie Winthrop?

"Look, Alex, all I'm trying to say is that my feelings for you have changed."

Alex swallowed hard and felt her breath catch in her throat. How could she lose his friendship now? Now, when she needed it most of all.

"I . . . I . . ."

"Alex!" Bernice came running in a most unladylike manner down the path. "Alex!"

Alex immediately got to her feet. Bernice had been the news bearer of nearly every bad tiding Alex had received of late. What could it possibly be this time? Refusing to look at Luke in case she broke into tears, she moved down the steps of the porch. "What is it, Bernice?" She barely managed to keep her voice from cracking.

"It's your mother!"

Alex gripped her hands together tightly. If anything had happened to her mother, Alex didn't know what she was going to do. "What's happened? What's wrong?"

"Nothing's wrong. It's just that . . . well . . . she's here. She's come to the Grand Canyon."

CHAPTER TWELVE

*M*other!" Alex exclaimed, entering the lobby of El Tovar. "I didn't know you were coming."

"I scarcely knew it myself," the petite woman replied. At fifty-two, Katherine Keegan was starting to show her age. Tiny bits of gray danced throughout her dark chocolate hair, which was stylishly arranged atop her head.

"I was just escorting Mrs. Keegan to her room," a bellboy told Alex.

"That's fine. I'll come along with you."

They walked down the hall amidst the other tourists. Alex had a million questions she wanted to ask her mother, but she wanted to wait until they had the privacy of a quiet room.

The bellboy led them to a second-floor room, handling Mrs. Keegan's four bags as though they weighed nothing at all. Escorting them into the room, the boy went about his duties, securing the bags and opening the draperies. Alex watched in silence as her mother tipped him and waited until he'd gone to remove her gloves.

"So why are you here? You do know that Father is here as well."

"Yes, I know. I plan to talk to him when the time is right."

Alex came to her mother and hugged her tightly. "I've missed you," she said impulsively. And it was so true. She'd not seen her mother in weeks and her heart had grown quite lonely for the sight of her.

"I've missed you as well," her mother said, pulling away. "Let me rid myself of this hat and jacket. It's not as warm here as it was in Williams, but the temperature is more bearable without all of this on."

Alex helped her mother out of the jacket before daring her next question. "So what is it you've come to talk to Father about?"

Her mother draped the jacket to her navy blue traveling suit across the back of the desk chair. Turning to face her daughter, she stated rather stoically, "I'm leaving him."

"What?"

"I'm getting a divorce, Alex." Suddenly it seemed her mother's strength left her. Taking a seat on the edge of her bed, she buried her face in her hands and wept softly.

Alex went to her mother and embraced her in a tight hug. "You're doing the right thing."

Her mother looked up. "Do you really think so? Oh, Alex, I'm so afraid. God hates divorce—the Bible says so. Will He also hate me?"

"No, I don't believe He will. Adultery stands as grounds for a divorce, even in the Bible."

"I just can't take any more. Rufus parades his women around me like trophies from some unnamed battle. I know I've not been the best wife to him, but his treatment of me has left me completely defeated. I'm scarcely even welcome in church, and I'm always the topic of conversation. I can't bear it any longer."

"Of course not. Don't worry about a thing. You can stay here until we figure what's to be done. I've saved a bit of money. It's not a lot, but we'll use it to set you up elsewhere."

"I have money as well," Katherine said rather sheepishly.

Alex released her hold as her mother reached for her purse. "How?" she asked.

The older woman opened her purse to reveal a great deal of cash. "I went to the bank and withdrew a good portion of our shared account."

"Father will be livid when he finds out."

"He'll be angry no matter what," her mother replied.

"That's true," Alex answered, remembering what her father had said. "He's going to be quite ugly about this—you do know that, don't you?"

"He can't hurt me any worse than he already has."

Alex studied her mother as if seeing her for the first time. She'd lost a great deal of weight, leaving her face gaunt and strained. Her clothes actually hung loose around her shoulders and waist. Alex shook her head. How many youthful dreams had been crushed and broken on the altar of Rufus Keegan's infidelity?

"Mother, Father plans to win himself an appointment to Washington. He's here to lay the foundation for that, and he won't allow us to interfere with it. Maybe it would be best if we just leave without saying a word to him."

"No, I'll have to talk to him sooner or later." She closed her purse and looked to her daughter. "I just need to know that you don't think badly of me."

"Honestly, Mother, I've thought you should leave him for ages. Father has brought shame upon this family, and now the shame should rest upon his shoulders alone. Let him suffer as we have."

"I don't want to seek revenge, Alex. I've prayed that God might just take me—pull me out of this misery so that I wouldn't have to make any choice at all—but that's not happening. I just want to be released from the pain. That alone would be enough for me."

Alex wondered if it would truly be enough. She'd like to see her father called to account for his actions. She'd like to see him stripped of the things he held dear—just as her mother had been. Her mother had little choice but to stand by and watch her dignity and social standing diminish. She could say nothing as her husband cavorted with one woman after another, all within the eyesight of the town's biggest gossips. No, Alex wasn't at all sure that merely having the pain removed was enough.

"I just need to know that God won't hold this against me," her mother continued. Getting to her feet, she paced a space at the end of the bed. "I want to be a good Christian, to be a good wife, but it's so hard. When he brought liquor into the house, breaking the law, I said nothing." Her voice broke and a little sob escaped as she continued. "When he dealt in underhanded manners with his businesses and cheated others of what is rightfully theirs, I did not condemn him. I knew God would eventually deal with him on all this and more. But if I walk away and divorce Rufus, then the blame will be mine."

Alex could sense her mother nearing hysteria. "Look, why don't you just let things lie for a time. There is nothing that says you must divorce immediately. Just take a holiday. You've come to El Tovar, so let that be the start. Tell Father you need a rest and that you're going to visit Audra. You could go there and see her and the family, while I square things away with the Harvey Company and find us a new location to live."

"Yes, but once your father learns the truth about the money . . ."

"We'll deal with that when it happens," Alex interjected. "Father is not going to immediately concern himself with such things. He's with friends—powerful friends—who can give him exactly what he wants. He won't think about banking matters for a single moment. Today, just rest. Let's just concentrate on getting through one day at a time and give the rest to God."

"I'd like that—truly I would."

A heavy knock sounded at the door, causing Katherine to jump back. "I'll get it," Alex offered. "Why don't you just freshen up a bit?" She didn't wait for a response but went to the door.

Her father pushed her back as soon as the door opened a few inches. "What are you doing here?" he demanded of his wife. He came in rather like a bull moose stomping and snorting, ready to take on his adversary.

Alex tried to think how she might intercede for her mother and create a story her father might accept, but nothing came to mind. She opened her mouth to comment, but already her mother was pulling something from her purse. With a smile on her face and a cheerfulness Alex knew her mother did not feel, Katherine Keegan handed the card to her husband.

"I came here because the Winthrops invited me to join you here. It seems they have a series of special dinners and gatherings and thought I might like to be a part of their celebration. I even purchased a new gown for the main gala. I knew you wouldn't want me to look shabby next to you."

Rufus Keegan grunted as he pulled the invitation from her hand. "You should have stayed home where you belong." He considered the card for a moment, then glared back at his wife. "*I* didn't invite you here."

Alex stepped forward. "She's here and to send her back to Williams now would only disgrace you—the Winthrops issued the invitation personally."

Her father turned on her. "You'd better remember what I told you—I won't brook any nonsense from either one of you. I intend to see myself in Washington, D.C., working with the new president, and perhaps one day even enjoying that office myself." He turned back to his wife. "I won't tolerate your interference or scenes. If you so much as open your mouth to say the wrong thing, you'll regret it. Do you understand me?"

Alex moved between her father and mother. "Don't threaten her. She's put up with enough of your embarrassing games."

"This is no game, Alexandria. You'd do well to learn that here and now. Your mother knows her place most generally, and it isn't until she talks to you that she feels compelled to create a fuss. If you want to keep your job here, I'd suggest you learn your place as well."

Alex straightened her shoulders and leaned toward her father's face. "You have no power over me here. Of that I have absolute confidence. You cannot see me hired or fired, and that's the truth of it, so do not pretend to threaten me."

"It's not a pretense, and the threat is very real." His brows drew together as his eyes narrowed. "I fully intend to see my plan through to completion."

"Please don't argue," Alex's mother said, coming to stand beside them. "Someone might overhear."

Crumbling the invitation in his hand, Keegan threw it at Alex and stomped to the door. "You mark my words and mark them well. I won't be kept from my dreams by the likes of either one of you. I have a plan to get me where I want to be, and you'd better stay out of my way. Or else!"

"Or else what?" Alex questioned, unable to keep her mouth closed. "To what extent will you go to silence us?"

At this her father calmed, almost unnaturally so. He rubbed his mustache and actually smiled. The sinister expression on his face left Alex cold and weak-kneed.

"People die all the time, don't they?"

With that he opened the door and left the room. Alex felt frozen in place, while her mother crossed the room and quickly shut and locked the door.

"Oh, what are we to do?" she questioned. Her pale face contorted in fear and anguish.

Alex barely felt able to draw a breath. "I don't know. I wouldn't have believed him to say something so . . . so . . ." She left the words unspoken.

Her mother reached out and took hold of her. "I'm terrified, Alex. I've never seen him like this, not even when he's hit me in anger."

"He's hit you—and you stayed with him?" Alex questioned.

Her mother released her grip on Alex and walked to the window. "Alex, a married woman makes many a choice that seems irrational to others. I've done what I had to do, just as I'm doing what I have to do now."

"But, Mother, this has to stop. He must be stopped."

Her mother nodded. "I know."

CHAPTER THIRTEEN

Valerie Winthrop had never known a man she couldn't conquer. Generally all she had to do was bat her eyelashes, smile coyly, and show a spark of interest and the men came running. But in the case of Luke Toland, that simply wasn't so. Luke had no interest in her, and that could only mean one thing—another woman.

He had said as much, but Valerie couldn't find out from Luke who that woman might be. Watching him, however, she'd been able to pretty much ascertain that Luke was in love with Alex Keegan, the dowdy little Harvey Girl. Worse still, the Keegan woman also appeared to have feelings for Luke—although Valerie wasn't entirely sure the woman knew it yet. Women were such queer creatures at times, and Alex Keegan seemed the strangest of them all. For all Valerie could tell, Miss Keegan was not at all interested in the men around her, in spite of numerous comments of praise and adoration. Although why anyone would praise the creature was beyond Val. She found Miss Keegan quite boring with her spiritual interests and Biblical restrictions.

As she dressed for dinner, Valerie took special care to wear something sensually appealing. She hoped later to slip away to Luke's cabin. Poor, dear man. His broken wrist was making him quite miserable. Valerie knew just the right medicine to help him heal, and perhaps by wearing this gown, she might actually take his mind off the homely Miss Keegan.

But along with her interest in Luke, Valerie longed to have everyone's attention fixed on her. She loved the way men came to attention when she entered a room—loved the look of admiration, of longing in their eyes. She was like a prized jewel that everyone wanted, and she enjoyed the position. Her life—on her terms.

Too bad she had to contend with Joel Harper. She had grown

bored and weary of his attention. He only wanted the money and power her status could afford him, and he was a bitter man with an agenda to right the wrongs done to him. Had he been even the slightest bit attentive, Valerie might have found him worthy of her affections. After all, he was handsome. He had a sort of Fred Astaire look to him.

She'd even told him so when they'd been in London earlier in the summer and had seen Astaire dance with his sister Adele. Joel had been flattered, unnecessarily so. He'd pressed for her affection after that, seeing her comment as some open door to become more intimate. But her comments had been nothing more than passing thoughts, certainly nothing to suggest she was ready for physical romance with her father's lackey.

Smoothing down the satin of her Poiret dinner gown, Valerie tried not to think about her fate with Joel. She still had her freedom for a time. A freedom that might see her happily entangled with a certain cowboy, if she could only find a way to capture his attention.

Looking at her reflection in the mirror, Valerie knew she looked rather scandalous. The pale green satin clung to her in a most daring way, while the draped neckline scarcely hid the fact that she'd chosen to wear very little under the gown. Just let Luke Toland try to ignore her now.

She rubbed her favorite scent on her bare upper arms. It had been her experience that this was most effective in drawing a man's attention. Lastly, she touched up her makeup and hair.

"Perfect," she murmured, noting her reflection one last time.

The evening had cooled considerably, but Valerie refused to take a wrap. The look she wanted would be ruined if she were to add so much as a scarf to the ensemble. Making her way to the rooftop garden, where they'd all agreed to meet prior to dinner, Valerie drew appreciative stares from every man she passed along the way. She smiled to herself. It was good to feel their approval—to sense their longing. It gave her a sensation of power.

Reaching the roof, she immediately spotted her father's stocky frame. Dressed rather uncomfortably in the tuxedo he hated, her father was already playing the room. A consummate politician, Winston Winthrop knew very well how to work the crowd to his advantage. The best thing he had going for him was his ability to listen—really listen. He could pick up details in a conversation that everyone else tended to miss. Using these details, the good senator managed to align himself with the common man. It had worked to his advantage and had seen him through thirty-some years of public office.

"The common man," he would say to Valerie, *"holds the key to success. For the common man, once influenced for you, will eagerly share what he knows with his neighbors. And, once they are convinced, they will share their opinion with their neighbor and so on. The wealthy not only care little for such matters, but rarely are willing to share their news with each other for fear of their powerful friends becoming even more powerful."* And Valerie knew this to be true, for her father rarely spoke of important matters unless it was to press someone into service on his behalf.

"Daddy," she said softly, coming up beside the portly senator. She leaned in to kiss his cheek, stopping just before reaching face. She'd learned long ago that her father's cheek was hardly the place for her lipstick.

Joel stood just to the right of her father. His perusal of her costume seemed to come in a mix of emotions. He liked what he saw, she was sure of that. But she was just as sure that he didn't like everyone else seeing her that way.

"Sweetheart, you'll catch your death. Perhaps I should escort you back downstairs so that you can get something to put about your shoulders," Joel suggested.

Valerie loved that he was disturbed by her appearance. *Let him fret and fuss,* she thought. *I will never let him own me.*

"I'm perfectly warm, thank you." She turned away from him then and met the man at her right. "I'm Valerie Winthrop."

The man was of no special account. He was just one of the many who followed her father around like a faithful dog. Valerie pitied these men. They were like pack animals seeking out the strongest among them. Sometimes that strength came in the form of intelligence and sometimes in physical stamina, but always they sought it out and aligned themselves accordingly.

When it was time for dinner, they adjourned from the gardens and made their way to the private dining room. There were twelve of them tonight, Valerie noted. Her father had brought in several additional players, including Rufus Keegan's wife, Katherine. The petite woman was absolutely no threat to anyone. Nor was she of any interest. Mr. Keegan did nothing to hide his open admiration for Valerie, breaking away to whisper obscenities in her ear, promising her things he couldn't possibly make good on. Valerie knew him to be the worst of philanderers. Several times he had cornered her to suggest they slip away to his suite. She'd never given him serious thought, however. He was old.

Much too old. And not nearly as wealthy or powerful as he liked to think. Why, she could have her pick of wealthy men from New York to Los Angeles. There was no reason to settle for the likes of Rufus Keegan.

With the additional people to serve, Valerie found that there were two Harvey waitresses at their disposal. She did her best to keep them both working. Miss Keegan seemed to realize her game, while the stocky little redhead who assisted her seemed as naïve as a schoolgirl.

"This tea is tepid," Valerie complained to the redhead. "Bring me another cup."

"Yes, ma'am."

Valerie watched Alex Keegan with a particular curiosity. What was it about her that Luke Toland should find so appealing? She wore no makeup, yet Valerie had to admit her skin was the color of peaches and cream. Her cheeks blushed naturally and her dark lashes needed no paint to make them more appealing. Even her hair, which was dark brown and wavy, had been pinned into a rather attractive style atop her head. Valerie almost envied the fact that Alex had long hair. In the city you seldom saw any woman their age still sporting long hair. Yet, Valerie had seen the men admire those few remaining souls who kept their locks long, almost as if these were the last vestiges of true womanhood. Men could be so peculiar.

Still, Alexandria Keegan couldn't match Valerie's beauty. Valerie's classic looks had been praised from London to Madrid and all across Europe. She had been toasted in New York and New Orleans. She knew the power her looks gave her. So why hadn't they yet given her the elusive Mr. Toland?

Then it dawned on her. Somewhere between the pear salad and the filet mignon, Valerie suddenly realized the attraction. Luke Toland felt sorry for Alex. His supposed love was born out of pity. The idea churned in her head as she made small talk with her father's dinner guests, and by the time éclairs and chocolate russe were served, Valerie had it all figured out.

Luke doesn't really love her, she told herself. *He sees how poorly her father behaves and knows the shame she's endured. He no doubt has befriended her thinking her a sweet, naïve young woman who would never do anyone harm. But I can change that.* After all, Valerie already knew of Joel's interest in adding the elusive Miss Keegan to his list of conquests.

As the dishes were cleared away and the coffee served, Valerie excused herself, mindless of Joel's scowl, and left the room. She had told her father she needed to powder her nose, but in truth, she knew this would be her chance to visit Luke.

Her strapped heels were hardly the proper footwear for the rocky and uneven path to the cabin, but Valerie guarded her steps. Her thoughts, however, ran away with her, suggesting all sorts of scenarios.

"First, I'll tell him I was worried about his recovery," Valerie mused. She wished she'd thought to bring him one of the chocolate-glazed éclairs. Her mother had often told her that a man's affection could often be roused with food.

She neared the cabin and smiled at the hint of light coming from behind the pulled curtains. *Then I'll pace a bit in front of him, letting him see every curve and line. That should warm his blood considerably.*

Reaching the cabin porch, Valerie slipped off her shoes and placed them on the top step. She wanted her approach to be quiet, because as a final thought she decided she wouldn't so much as knock. She'd simply walk in on him and catch him unaware.

Reaching for the doorknob, she smiled when it turned easily in her hand. She pushed open the door and found Luke rather stunned, sitting on the couch.

"What are you doing here?" he asked gruffly.

"I thought you could use some company."

"No, I'm afraid not. Clancy's coming back in a minute—he's gone to get a chessboard. We have a game to play."

"I'd be more fun to play with than Clancy."

"I doubt it. Clancy is pretty good at chess," Luke said rather dryly.

Valerie knew she'd have to act fast. Crossing the small room, she positioned herself between Luke and the fire. The warmth felt amazingly good. "That's not what I mean and you know it."

"I'm never sure what you mean, Miss Winthrop. I've never been able to figure women out. Seems to me they play a lot of games, and chess just isn't one of them."

Valerie smiled, hoping the coy look she'd perfected would give Luke reason to send Clancy packing. "I can learn to play whatever game you'd like."

"I'd like for you to leave," Luke said, getting to his feet. His broken wrist seemed to be of no consequence, and he seemed completely capable of fending for himself.

Valerie backed up a step, suddenly feeling uncertain of her plan. Luke took hold of her arm and practically dragged her to the door. "I don't know why you came here, but don't come back. I have no interest in your kind."

Anger rose up in Valerie. "What do you mean, my kind?"

"You know exactly what I mean," Luke replied. "You know exactly what you're doing and what you're planning on getting, but you won't be getting it here—with me. Good night."

With that he shoved her out the door and locked it behind her. Valerie stood in dumfounded shock for several moments. How dare he treat her like a common trollop? Dismissing her like one of his crew members.

"You'll wish you'd played the game with me, Mr. Toland."

Valerie picked up her shoes and made her way back to the hotel. Her confidence was slightly damaged by Luke's rejection, but she pushed her feelings aside. Pausing to put her shoes back on, Valerie was taken aback when Alex Keegan came out the door.

"Good evening, Miss Keegan," Valerie said, straightening.

"Oh, hello." Alex started to walk past, but Valerie reached out and stopped her. "I'm so glad we have had a moment alone. I must tell you that despite substandard food from time to time, your performance has been remarkable."

Alex eyed her suspiciously, but Valerie knew very well how to lull her into a false sense of security. "I'm simply amazed," Valerie continued, "that you can remember what everyone has ordered and keep it all straight. You must be a very smart woman."

Alex shook her head. "No, I credit the training. Having been here for four years, the job is second nature."

"Four years? My, but that's a long time. I know when Luke told us he'd worked here for over ten years, I found it hard to believe. Of course, Daddy has great new plans for Luke, and I'm sure it is only a matter of time before his years at the Grand Canyon are behind him."

This got Alex's attention. Valerie nearly laughed out loud as the woman froze in her steps. "What do you mean?"

"Why, Daddy has offered him a position. Once he's president, Daddy won't have time to mind all his interests."

Alex's demeanor relaxed a bit as she smiled. "Luke would never take a job in the city. He hates them. Hates the noise and hubbub. And he hates politics."

"Oh, I know all of that," Valerie simpered. "He's just the dearest thing, isn't he? Anyway, Daddy has a ranching interest he's just purchased in Wyoming. He's offered Luke the job to run it as if it were his own. And who knows, if he plays his cards right—it just might be his own someday. After all, Daddy says Luke would make a wonderful husband and father."

Valerie noted the defeat in Alex's expression. Feeling good about what she'd accomplished in such a brief conversation, Valerie turned to leave. Calling back over her shoulder, she plunged the knife in a little deeper. "I'm sure Luke will be glad to leave this place. There's nothing here he'd want to stay for. He told me as much."

Alex watched Valerie Winthrop leave. For several moments, Alex felt as if her legs were made of lead. Unable to move, Alex remembered every detail of their conversation. Luke was going to work for the senator? It just didn't make sense. *He hates politics and can't abide the men who pursue such power. Why would he do this?* Then a sinking thought came to her. *He's always wanted his own ranch. Maybe he sees this as an easy way to make that come true. But at what cost?*

Making her way to the Lookout, Alex tried to rein in her thoughts. In spite of the party going on in the main dining room, her duties for the evening had concluded. She would go to the Lookout and escape the noise and party spirit of the tourists. Hopefully, there would be very few people around.

The upper level appeared to have one or two people milling about, so Alex chose the lower level station for her respite. Hiding in the shadows under the overhead balcony, Alex tried to regain her composure. Surely Miss Winthrop was lying.

"But how do you propose to eliminate the competition?" A voice sounded from overhead, and Alex recognized it as her father's.

"By doing exactly that. Eliminating the competition," Joel Harper said snidely.

Alex pulled back even farther into the dark recesses of her hiding place. Apparently her father and Joel had left the party in order to consider their plans.

"You don't mean kill them?" her father questioned.

"I mean exactly that."

Alex put her hand over her mouth to muffle the gasp that escaped. Joel apparently talked of death as easily as someone else might talk of the weather.

"But how?

"I have some people already on the job."

"Truly?" Her father sounded completely fascinated, and Alex

cringed, remembering his threats to her and her mother.

"I've been working on this for nearly a year. We do whatever we can to buy off the competition or otherwise entice them to give up the race. Those who won't be bought or put off have to be dealt with in, shall we say, more permanent manners?"

Alex felt her breathing quicken. She had to get out of here before they discovered her overhearing the conversation. She tried to think clearly, but her heart was pounding in her ears.

"Do you see yourself eliminating the likes of John Davis and Bradley Jastrow?" her father questioned.

"It's already being worked out. Why, Davis has even decided against coming to the canyon for the celebration this week and next. We've managed to create a little problem with the American Bar Association that he must attend to. After all, he's the president of that dear organization."

"Fascinating."

Alex heard a shuffling, as if the men were moving from one side of the balcony to the other. "Look," her father continued, "I'll do what I can to aid your cause. I have no desire to be the man in the presidential chair—I'd rather be one of those who puts him there and helps to keep him there."

Liar! Alex thought. She could have called it out, too, except for what she'd already overheard.

"Good," Joel answered as they moved inside. "I knew I could count on you. Things will really start to get ugly in the days to come. As we move toward the convention in New York City next June, we need to have a solid following. That's where I'll need people like you. You will be called upon to influence your circle of friends, as well as your enemies."

"My enemies know better than to cross me, they only have . . ."

Their voices faded away as they moved indoors. Alex tried to steady her nerves as she got to her feet. "I can't let them know I was here," she whispered, her worries turning into a prayer. "Oh, God, help me to do the right thing. I wish I could talk to Luke."

In a rush of emotion, however, she realized she couldn't talk to Luke. If she could believe Valerie, he was one of them. He was going to work for the senator. But even if it was true, her heart argued, Luke would never abide killing. She knew him well enough to realize that much. Maybe she could dissuade him from going to work for the Winthrops. Maybe if he knew the kind of things they advocated, he'd reject their offer.

Alex heard the men move out onto the rim path and head back to El Tovar. They were laughing and enjoying some great joke as they went. After a few moments of silence, feeling confident she could slip back to her room unnoticed, Alex came out from the shadows and moved up the rocky path to the top of the rim.

"Where do you think you're going?"

Joel Harper came out from the darkness of the Lookout doorway. Alex swallowed hard and tried to smile. Not that he could really see her face.

"I'm sorry, I didn't know anyone was here."

"You lie rather calmly," Joel said, standing only inches from her. "Now tell me what you overheard."

Alex knew lying was no good. He already knew the truth of the matter. "I heard it all."

"That's what I figured." He reached out and gripped her arms tightly. "If you say a word—so much as a single hint of a word about any of this—I'll see you dead."

This threat, coupled with her father's, and added to Valerie's announcement about Luke, left Alex in a state of near hysteria. Laughing, she shook her head from side to side as if to shake away the image of her nightmare. Joel pulled her down the path away from the Lookout. The area afforded them a bit more privacy.

"I'm serious. I'll kill you."

"It seems you'll have to stand in line, Mr. Harper." Alex managed to sober herself a bit. "I've been threatened all day long—all week, in fact."

"Those were most likely idle threats, my dear." He pulled her close against him and held her fast. "But my words are more than that. I'd hate to harm you—you're so lovely, so pure. We could make a great team if you'd just give me a chance."

His breath against her face reeked of whiskey, and his hands fondled her back and neck in a much too familiar way. Alex pushed against him, but he didn't release her. She began to fight in earnest and tried to scream, but he clamped his mouth upon hers without warning. The sickening taste of whiskey touched her lips as he forced himself upon her. Alex feared not only for her life, but for her innocence. She brought her foot down on top of Joel's, all while struggling to pull away.

"Fighting me is no good. I have the ability to break your neck right here and now," Joel said in panting breaths. "You need to stay on my good side."

Alex laughed bitterly and with all her strength managed to push him slightly off balance. As he let go of her to right himself, Alex hurried away. "You have no good side, Mr. Harper," she called back, not waiting to hear if there might be a reply.

As Alex neared the hotel, she tried to appear self-confident and self-assured. She wouldn't run. She'd walk very quickly and put herself near people. Surely Mr. Harper wouldn't cause a scene in front of others. She pushed aside her first reaction, which was to go to Luke. She felt safe with Luke, in spite of her anger at men in general. Luke had been trustworthy.

But Luke had said his feelings had changed, and the thought of facing Joel Harper and the Winthrops without him left her with an aching loneliness.

Oh, God, what am I to do?

*L*uke watched from a distance as Alex and Mr. Harper appeared to share an intimate moment. He watched Harper embrace Alex and pull her close. With his stomach churning, Luke looked away. He didn't want to wait and see if Harper and Alex kissed. The intimacy of the scene suggested it just might happen, and the image that flooded his head sickened him.

How had his life suddenly become so complicated? The woman he cared about was in the arms of another man. The job he loved was off limits to him because of his broken wrist. It was so frustrating.

Walking back to his cabin in the cool night air, Luke fought the need to rush back to Alex and force her away from Harper. *She can't possibly be attracted to him,* Luke reasoned. *She hates men who act as Harper acts. She despises infidelity.* He paused, stopping behind El Tovar, wondering if he had misjudged the situation. Perhaps Alex wasn't all that willing to be alone with Harper.

"Hey, Luke, I was just lookin' for you," Clancy said, coming upon him. "Your boss wants to see you. Something about coordinating several mule trips."

Luke nodded, pushing aside his concerns about Alex. "Thanks, Clancy. I didn't figure anyone would be looking for me this late."

Clancy shrugged. "Guess they've got a full party going in there and one thing led to another. You know how money talks. Someone mentioned how much fun it had been to take the ride down to Phantom Ranch, and the next thing you know everybody wants to go. This whole political thing is bringing in some real dillies, let me tell you."

Luke knew only too well. He thought of Alex with Harper. Maybe she'd aligned herself with him because of her mother. Alex was rather desperate to see her mother away from the humiliation caused by

Rufus Keegan. Maybe she'd gone to Harper for help. The idea irritated
him, almost more than the thought of Alex being involved romantically.
Emotions could carry a gal away, making her do stupid things she'd
later regret. But helping her mother was something Alex would think
out—plan out. If she'd gone to Harper for help, it would be because
she'd calculated the risk and the result.

"Guess I'll go see what we can figure out. You boys are going to have
your work cut out for you," Luke muttered. "Wish that mule hadn't
broken my arm."

"You've said that at least fifty times since it happened," Clancy
grinned. "It's still broke. Wishin' it wasn't doesn't make it so."

"Tell me about it."

———

"God, help me to do the right thing," Alex murmured as she continued toward El Tovar. A hot bath and quiet night of rest was all she
wanted. She wondered about her mother and whether she should go
and check on her, but decided against it. No doubt her father had man-
dated that her mother not be allowed out of his sight for long. Of this,
Alex felt confident.

With her mind on these things, Alex refused to give Joel Harper any
further consideration. His threat was very real, but if Alex dwelled on
it, she wouldn't be able to think clearly.

"I'm not done with you," Harper declared in a menacing tone.

Alex had thought herself rid of Joel Harper for the night, but
instead she found him back on her heel, his anger only piqued by her
attitude. He took hold of her arm and turned her back to face him.
The rage in his expression was quite evident.

"I said, I'm not done with you," he growled.

"Well, I was through with you. I have no desire to be manhandled
by you or anyone else. You think very highly of yourself and your effect
on women, Mr. Harper, but your flattery and attention would be better
shared with someone who finds such things appealing."

Joel seemed to regain control of his temper. His face relaxed just a
bit, but not so his hold. "I can give you many good things."

"I have all I need."

"You could have more. I can make your life very comfortable."

"I thought you were to marry Miss Winthrop."

Joel nodded. "I am, but it needn't concern us. I find your innocence and purity quite refreshing." He tightened his hold and pulled

her close. "You must have some kind of feelings for me."

Alex struggled but to no avail. "Oh, I do have feelings, Mr. Harper, but they aren't at all the kind of feelings you'd like to hear about. Now let me go."

"Just give me a chance," he said, lowering his voice to a husky whisper. He leaned closer to Alex's ear. "I have a way with women."

Alex stopped fighting against him. Her voice was flat and void of emotion. "Let me go."

"Not until you understand. I can't have you threatening our plans—my plans. But I think you can realize that much. I can make life very good for you—or very bad."

"So your purpose for this is to overwhelm me with your romantic passion so that I'll remain silent about your plans to eliminate the competition, is that it?" She asked the question very matter-of-factly, as if the answer were of no concern to her. In truth, however, she felt dizzy, almost near to fainting from fear.

"We could have a wonderful time together. And your father might even get that appointment to Washington he so badly desires. You wouldn't want to stand in the way of that, now would you?"

"So if I cooperate with you, become your mistress, you'll ensure my father's appointment? Is that it?"

"Something like that," Joel said, grinning. "I see you're beginning to think like one of us. Threats aren't always the way to get things done. Sometimes promising benefits can be much more productive."

"I don't want your promises. I prefer your threats to your sweet talk and promises, any day. You hold absolutely no appeal to me whatsoever."

"Maybe not, but you're going to have to promise me your cooperation, one way or another. I'm just saying it can either be a whole lot of fun for both of us, or it can be a misery that makes you wish you'd never met me."

"I realize the validity of your threat, Mr. Harper. I can't make promises as to what I'll do or say, however. Lives are at stake."

Joel's expression hardened again. "You are so very right, Miss Keegan, and the very first life at stake . . ."

"I know. I know. The first life at stake is mine. Go ahead and threaten me." Alex hoped she sounded bored with the entire matter, when in truth she was praying someone would come along and interrupt this affair.

"That's not what I was going to say," Joel said, his whiskey breath hot upon her face. "The first life at stake will be your mother's."

"What?"

"I'm telling you that if you refuse to cooperate with me, I'll see your mother dead. I have many people who are willing to help me. I have men here who are at my every beck and call. They will willingly do anything for money."

"You would kill an innocent woman to have your way?"

"I will do whatever is necessary to win this election."

Alex felt her knees weaken. A trembling started in her legs and wound its way up her entire body. She had to get away from this evil man. She saw the pleasure he took in speaking of death and destruction. She could feel the cold, heartlessness of his soul in his very touch.

She tried to pull away. "Let me go."

"Stay with me," he encouraged. "I have a wonderful room and I think you and I could very much enjoy the night together."

Alex fought harder. This time, she dug her fingernails into his arm. "I said, let me go. Let me go or I'll scream." Her voice grew louder.

"Miss Alex? Are you okay?"

It was Clancy. Alex breathed a sigh of relief. Joel instantly unhanded her and stepped back a pace.

"Clancy, would you walk me back to the hotel?" she asked, looking at the ground rather than let Clancy see in the dim lighting how upset she really was.

"Sure thing, Miss Alex."

Alex said nothing more to Joel. She knew there was nothing she could say. He wouldn't listen to her, nor would he pledge to leave her mother out of the situation. Walking in silence with Clancy, Alex felt tears come to her eyes. Things had gone from bad to worse in just a matter of days. What was she to do?

"I hope I didn't interrupt anything important," Clancy said softly, almost hesitantly.

"No, Clancy, you did exactly right. Mr. Harper was out of line." She paused momentarily and reached out to touch Clancy's arm. "Please don't tell anyone what happened. It's rather embarrassing."

"I'm not sure I know just what did happen, but I won't say a word, Miss Alex. I know how things can get misunderstood. That's the way it was with the boss and that Winthrop gal. She just don't seem to like taking no for an answer. Guess her boyfriend feels the same way, eh?"

"Yes." Alex felt an overwhelming regret that she'd believed Luke might actually have encouraged Valerie Winthrop's actions. Hearing

Clancy speak of it now, in the aftermath of her own forced encounter, Alex knew that Luke was innocent. Sometimes hindsight wasn't all that comforting.

Back in her room, Alex felt overwhelmed with her fears. Michaela had already made her way to bed but wasn't asleep, so Alex took the opportunity to try to better understand her own turbulent emotions by talking.

"Do you think people always mean what they say? Like when they threaten people or talk about threatening people?"

Michaela sat up and pushed her pillow behind her. Leaning back against the headboard she shrugged. "I guess that would depend on who they are and what they have planned. Why do you ask?"

Alex took off her apron and tossed it aside. She wanted to tell Michaela everything—the talk she had with Valerie Winthrop, Joel's threats, even her confusion over Luke. Instead, when she opened her mouth she said, "My mother wants a divorce."

"Well, I would too, if I were her. The way your father treats her is abominable."

Alex undressed and pulled on a robe. "I know. He's threatened us both if we cause him trouble."

"Never mind the fact he's caused you both more trouble than you deserve," Michaela threw in.

"Exactly," Alex continued. "He's pressing for a presidential appointment, so he's sidling up to Senator Winthrop. He's probably bribing and threatening him as well." She sat down on the chair beside Michaela's bed. "Then tonight, Mr. Harper took liberties with me."

"No! What did he do?"

Alex felt the disgust well up inside. "I'd overheard him saying some things that were rather incriminating. He was talking to my father, and after my father had gone, he realized I'd overheard the conversation. He forced me to a secluded place, threatened me, then tried to woo me by touching me and kissing me. I tried to fight him off, but of course he was much too strong." She shuddered. "I just wish I'd never heard what he told my father."

Michaela leaned forward. "What did he say that was so bad?"

"He plans to eliminate the competition for Senator Winthrop."

Michaela laughed and eased back against the headboard. "Is that all? Of course he wants to eliminate them. The fewer people running against his man, the better."

"No," Alex countered. "He really wants to eliminate them—kill them if necessary."

Michaela's eyes grew wide but she said nothing, so Alex continued. "But don't you breathe a word of this to anyone." She grew silent for a moment as she contemplated the situation. "I don't know what to do."

"In what way? I mean, what is there that you have to do?"

"That's just it, I don't know. If Mr. Harper is being truthful, then someone should notify the authorities. But how can I be certain of the truth? I don't know if he's just talking big, trying to scare me and everyone else into cooperating with his plans. Then I guess I want to be helpful to my mother, but at the same time . . . well . . . I guess I'm afraid for her and for me. While I don't know what Mr. Harper is able to do, I fully understand what my father is capable of. It just scares me that I won't do the right thing . . . that someone I love will suffer because of my poor choice."

Michaela shook her head. "That doesn't sound like you. Why be afraid? God's big enough to handle this, isn't he?"

"I guess it's just a real test of my faith. I feel like crying, but I know I'd be better off praying."

"Then pray."

Alex nodded. "I guess you're right. It's just that . . . there are other things too."

"Like Luke?"

Alex looked at her friend—hesitant to reply. "I suppose he's a part of it as well. Miss Winthrop told me something tonight that didn't sit well."

"And you believed her? Goodness, Alex, you've grown into a ninny while I was gone."

Alex smiled at her friend's good-natured teasing. "Well, she said that her father was offering him quite a deal. A ranch of his own to run in Wyoming and plenty of money, and . . ."

"And?"

"And I guess he's even offering Miss Winthrop, at least that's how it sounded."

"I thought she was engaged to that Mr. Harper menace."

"She is, but she implied . . ."

"Oh, Alex, just listen to yourself. Why should you give anything the woman says a second thought? She's out there wearing next to nothing for clothes, dressing more scandalously than anyone I saw on my travels, and playing games of romance with every man she meets. Obviously she's just come to realize you're in love with Luke and wants to put a stop to that while she decides how to deal with it. Only problem is she didn't count on the fact that Luke's in love with you."

"That's crazy talk. You've said as much before, but Luke and I are just friends."

Michaela laughed. "Sure you are and I'm going to get the nomination for presidency. First woman president. Makes about as much sense as you and Luke being just friends."

Alex got up and began to pace. "I don't know how I feel about anything. I don't understand half of what's happening around me, and with my mother and father at odds the way they are, I certainly have no desire for love or romance."

"Why not? Your mother and father are no example of what happens in romance. By your own admission, you've told me about your parents and their history. Your mother was of a good family with money. Your father knew that, as an only child, she'd inherit everything and, if they married, then he'd be wealthy. And so he is. And that's the basis of their relationship. But none of that has anything to do with what you and Luke share."

"But that's just it. Luke and I don't share anything—not really—unless you count friendship."

"Friendship's a good place to start. But you and Luke have gone beyond mere friendship—and I think if you look deep into your heart and forget about everybody else's problems for a few minutes, you'll see what I mean."

————

Luke looked at the advertisement his brother had sent in his last letter. The notice was about a ranch for sale in Wyoming, just north of Laramie. The Broken T Ranch was well within a price Luke could afford. It wouldn't have many provisions to start with, but there was a small house and a few outbuildings and corrals. A very small starter herd was included in the price, but it would take some time to build the herd into a productive and profitable business. Of course, Luke hardly expected to walk right into a well-established business. These things took time and money.

His brother's letter explained that the man who owned the ranch had taken ill and had never been one who managed things well to begin with. His vast herd had dwindled over the years as the man battled his illness. Now, knowing his days to be numbered, the man simply wanted to sell the property and be done with it. The rest of the letter told of the family and of his brother's interest in moving to California.

Putting the letter and advertisement back in the envelope, Luke contemplated what he should do. The answer seemed so hazy in his mind. If he left the canyon and bought the ranch without Alex as his wife, he might never see her again. Yet the ranch was a good offer, probably better than what he could get elsewhere. And if he could convince Alex of his love and commitment, he'd be able to provide her a home near to her sister. That way she'd have family close, and her mother would probably be able to travel between the two families with relative ease.

Luke pulled out his Bible to consider some of the Scripture from last Sunday's church service. He prayed there might be an answer to his dilemma, but his mind wasn't on it. Again he thought of what he had seen.

Why had Alex been with Joel Harper? What did she think to accomplish by enlisting his help? Harper was nothing but trouble, and she'd already mentioned a deep dislike of the man.

His wrist irritated him, causing Luke to leave his desk and seek the comfort of his sofa. There didn't seem to be easy answers tonight. Just frustration and misery. Why, Lord? Why did that mule have to kick me? Why do I have to be laid up like this? Why did I fall in love with a woman who has absolutely no interest in loving me back?

The questions flooded his conscious mind. If he fell asleep, no doubt they'd pester his unconscious mind as well. Why couldn't things be simple?

He thought about the advertisement. *I want a ranch for Alex and me together,* he reasoned. I want to settle down and start a family. He glanced to the ceiling. "I thought you wanted that for me, God. I mean, it sure seemed like something you were leading me to. Lord, if this isn't supposed to be the way I'm to go, then why can't you take the desire from my heart? If I'm not supposed to marry Alex, then why don't you send me the woman I am supposed to marry?"

He mentally ran down a list of the current Harvey Girls. There wasn't a single one, except Alex, who had ever struck his fancy. He could see himself having fun with any number of women, but with Alex, he had completely different visions. He saw himself marrying and living happily with a lifelong companion. He saw himself fathering children and raising them with Alex. No matter what scenario he dreamed up, he always saw Alex in the middle of it.

"This is crazy," he said, getting up off the sofa, ignoring the ache in his arm. He crossed to the desk and took up his brother's letter. Sitting down, Luke reached for pencil and paper. He'd send a letter to the Broken T and let the owner know his interest. It couldn't hurt to just let him know. Then if it were meant to be, God would work out the details. Including Alex.

The morning train brought the arrival of additional political supporters and adversaries. The front contender, John Davis, had been unable to attend the party at the Grand Canyon due to complications with the American Bar Association. The reporters noted that one of the Bar's board members had somehow been charged with bootlegging and Davis himself was called to answer in regard to the matter. Joel smiled to himself to see his plans come into play.

Bradley Jastrow, a solid citizen with a war hero record and brief state representative experience in Alabama, was also a contender for the Democratic nomination for president. His appearance at the Grand Canyon sent reporters scurrying to get information and pictures for their papers. Joel thought it all rather amusing. They were like dogs running from person to person, begging scraps as they went.

Jastrow cut a rather dashing figure with his red, wavy hair and piercing blue eyes. As a lieutenant in the army during the Great War, Jastrow had led his troops against a German trench, resulting in its capture. Later he was severely wounded while single-handedly taking out a machine gun position. His wounds resulted in a lengthy hospital stay, a battlefield promotion to captain, and, if Joel's research proved correct, an addiction to morphine.

Jastrow, the eldest son of a wealthy shipping magnate in Alabama, maintained his bachelorhood at thirty-six and seemed to draw more than his fair share of feminine attention. Since women now had the right to vote, Joel needed to take his appeal seriously. Appearance had always had a certain amount of importance, but that usually lent itself to the image of the "older, wiser" contender. The man who convinced the nation of his experience and knowledge of certain matters, showing his patriotism and ability to connect to the general public, always made a strong showing. The country had always looked for father figures—a strong, steady man to stand at the helm.

Eyeing Jastrow, with his winning smile, broad shoulders, and classic looks, Joel reconsidered the matter. Women would change the political arena. Their desires and views would matter. Jastrow would appeal to the emotional, feminine voter, especially those who were single. Valerie had pointed this out, noting he had a certain charisma, especially in light of his hero status. Still, Joel felt confident that he could arrange to have the man taken care of if the need arose. There was always the possibility that Jastrow's popularity had been underestimated. Not only this, but the tide of support could easily turn from one candidate to another, depending on the mood of things across the nation.

Jastrow was very much against prohibition, unlike many of his other Democratic contenders. The attitude won him friends among those in southern society and big cities, but elsewhere he was seen with contempt. He was also very supportive of the Ku Klux Klan, which again split his support.

"So what do you think of the news that President Harding has . . . food poisoning?" Senator Winthrop asked Joel in a low, rather hesitant tone.

Joel smiled. "Food poisoning, eh? Well, life is sometimes hard on all of us. The president certainly is no exception to that rule. The trip he made to Alaska was quite arduous. I'm of the mind that this adventure was probably too difficult. The man has heart troubles, or so I've heard." Joel wasn't about to tell the senator everything he knew. After all, there might come a time when they would be called upon to deny any knowledge of certain . . . affairs. Better the senator have no knowledge of those unpleasant matters.

"I find it more of a concern to us that Bradley Jastrow and John Davis should still have a large following of supporters," Joel added. "The others are hardly worth our time, but those two need to be watched. They will be a challenge to be sure."

The senator hooked his thumbs in his vest pocket as he was wont to do. "I welcome the challenge. I have nothing to hide and a positive record to support me. Davis was nothing more than a minor candidate in 1920. He'll be nothing but a minor candidate in '24."

Joel smiled. Winthrop could be very naïve, but it worked to Joel's advantage. "I'm sure you're right."

"Now, Jastrow's father is a well-known friend of the south," the senator continued. "We have many of the same friends. There will be supporters who will find themselves torn right down the middle. What shall we do about that?"

"I have some thoughts on the matter. I think in the long run, we won't need to worry about Jastrow. His health isn't all that great."

"But of course not. He was wounded in the Great War," Senator Winthrop added.

"Yes, but his war wounds aren't causing near the problem his addiction to morphine is creating."

"I didn't know about this."

"And you really don't need to know more than that. I have it under control. I don't believe Jastrow will be a problem. Addictions have a way of resolving themselves," Joel said, just then seeing Rufus Keegan enter the room with Valerie at his side. He wanted to get the senator's blessing once and for all on announcing the news of their engagement, so he quickly put the issue of Jastrow aside. "Senator, I'm grateful that you would share the limelight with your daughter and announce our engagement at the main gala. I think many people will be swayed to vote for you because of the family image you'll portray."

"Nothing's too good for Val. She's my pride and joy. My life."

Joel nodded. "Yes, and the public will find that heartwarming." He watched Valerie simper over Rufus Keegan. "If you'll excuse me, Senator, I have some plans to discuss with Valerie. I see she's just come in with Rufus Keegan."

"Good man, that Keegan. He's offered me the support of all of Arizona and part of California."

"Let us hope he has the ability to deliver on such a promise."

"We should find something for him to do once the election is won. I'll need people like him. After all, when you and Valerie marry, I know your time will be divided."

Joel started to frown, then caught himself. "Nonsense, Senator. Valerie knows very well how time-consuming politics can be. She'll understand my allegiance to you."

The senator nodded, smiling. "She's a good woman. Always looking after my interests."

Joel could see Valerie toying with Keegan's tie and felt a surge of jealousy. "Indeed," he managed to say.

Joel left the senator to his own devices and crossed the room to greet Keegan and his reluctant fiancée. "Good to see you, Mr. Keegan," Joel lied. He had so little use for the man. His overinflated sense of self-worth was an irritation to Joel. More worrisome was Winthrop's apparent belief that the man was of value. Joel would have to deal with that soon. "Hello, darling," he added, turning to Valerie. He kissed her on the cheek, surprising her momentarily. "You look positively radiant."

Valerie eyed him suspiciously but said nothing. Joel smiled and continued as if nothing were amiss. "I hope you're looking forward to tonight's party," he said to Keegan. "The senator is eager to discuss his plans for the campaign."

"I wouldn't miss it. I'm eager to hear his plans and know his mind."

Yes, I'm sure you are, Joel thought. He took hold of Valerie, however, without comment. "Val, darling, we need to discuss our plans for announcing our engagement."

"I thought you'd worked that all out with Daddy," she said rather sarcastically.

Joel laughed. "You're such a goose, Val. Of course we've worked it all out. I simply need to tell you what's expected of you."

Keegan laughed out loud at this. "Good man. Put her in her place and tell her what to do. That's the way to groom them. If you don't catch them early, they'll turn out like my daughter. Headstrong and inconsiderate of the men in her life."

"Now, Mr. Keegan, I find your daughter quite delightful. Quite . . . delightful," Joel said, emphasizing the words. "I'll look forward to her being close by in Washington should you accept the senator's position once he's installed as president."

Joel watched the man's face contort from an expression of anger and disgust to the realization that someone was actually mentioning a position for him. Joel loved to throw crumbs to the dogs that way. If nothing else, it often proved entertaining just to watch them fight amongst themselves. Of course, this time, he wanted to make clear that he considered Alex a part of the package. Keegan seemed to understand rather quickly and, as that understanding dawned on him, he nodded.

"I'm sure Alexandria would love Washington."

Valerie frowned and tried to pull away from Joel but he held her fast. "Perhaps Val and she can be great friends." Joel tightened his grip on Valerie's arm. "Ah, here comes your lovely wife, Mr. Keegan. I'm sure you'll have things to discuss with her, so if you'll excuse us . . ."

"Of course," Keegan said, giving Valerie a wicked smile. "I enjoyed our time together."

Valerie smiled in return. "As did I. Perhaps we can spend time together later. I'll expect to dance with you this evening." Her voice dripped honey, and Joel felt as though she purposefully worked to humiliate him.

"You may count on it," Keegan replied.

Joel yanked Valerie away from Keegan with the briefest acknowledgment of Mrs. Keegan. The woman looked haggard, so he offered nothing more than his greeting before forcing Valerie into a quiet corner.

"Your father's campaign is dependent upon you playing your part, my dear. I have plans for you that do not include playing the tramp with Rufus Keegan."

"What do you want from me?"

"You know very well what I want," Joel said, lowering his voice. "And one of these days I'll tire of waiting for what I want and simply take it."

"Are you threatening me?"

"Actually, yes. I am. Now, will you be a good girl and cooperate with me?"

"I'll never cooperate with you. I'm going to speak with Daddy and see that this ridiculous farce is brought to an end. I don't love you and I have no desire to marry you. I only agreed to the matter to shut you both up for the time. Daddy may adore you, but you know only too well how I feel about you." She squared her shoulders and seemed to strengthen her resolve. "Besides that, I know things about you. Things that could see you sent to prison for a long time—if not put to death."

She adjusted her hat and turned as if to go. Joel refused to be dismissed in such a manner, and he refused to allow her to ruin his plans. "You think to threaten me and walk away? I've worked too hard for you to spoil this. What makes you think I'd ever allow you to cause me the slightest bit of trouble? I can see you put in your place rather quickly, Val. A place that would be far more frightening and worrisome than the one you're in now."

"You talk big, but you're nothing more than my father's flunky."

"If we were alone, I would slap you across the face," Joel said, clenching his teeth.

"Well, rest assured we will never be alone. I could end up like that poor prostitute in Washington." She smiled. "See? You aren't the only one capable of learning secrets."

Joel's gaze narrowed. "You think me incapable of accomplishing whatever I set my mind to, but I'd ask you to reflect back on that banker's son you made such a fuss over last year."

Valerie grew still. "Leave Andrew out of this. You know his death hurt me greatly."

"Yes, I do. That's why I arranged it."

Valerie's face drained of color. "What are you saying?"

"I'm saying you were getting out of control. People were beginning to talk. It seemed the sensible thing to do." Joel prided himself on his stoic tone and rigid stance. He loved the power he felt over Valerie. Loved the complete disbelief and heartache written in her look.

"But . . . he . . . he . . . drowned," Valerie offered weakly.

"Yes, I know. I was there." Joel loosened his hold on her arm and smiled rather contentedly. "The man was a nuisance to me. Just as you are beginning to be. Just remember, Val dear, I seldom tolerate irritations for long." He reached up and rubbed her cheek with his thumb. "Poor darling. Here you thought you could scare me with your knowledge of past events, when it's you who should be terrified. Those two deaths are just a pittance. When people annoy me, I make them go away. It's that simple. Keep it in mind, my dear. Once we're married and your fortune is mine, you'll want to be particularly well-behaved."

"I'm not afraid of you. Kill me. This misery is worse than death," she said, jerking away from his touch.

"Oh, but, my dear, I wasn't speaking of your death," he said, giving her a cold smile. "I was speaking of your dear father, our next president. It would truly be a pity if he were to die so soon after our marriage. Why, we might never know what a truly wonderful president he might make."

She stared at him openmouthed for a moment, tears forming in her eyes as she searched his face. Turning abruptly, she hurried away from him as if he'd suddenly grown horns atop his head. Joel drew a deep breath and stood awash in a sensation of nervous excitement. He'd never told anyone of his deed. It seemed risqué, bold, even adventurous. Of course, she'd say nothing about it. She'd be too afraid of how it might appear to other people. There was one thing about Valerie that Joel knew he could count on: She adored her father. And that adoration ensured his control.

Seeing the Keegans standing outside on the veranda, Joel made his way to join them. He wanted to press home his point regarding Alex. Walking outside, Joel found the warmth of the day uncomfortable, but the shade afforded them on El Tovar's porch was welcome.

As he approached the Keegans, Rufus pulled his wife behind one of the stone archway supports. Joel thought it rather strange. It looked as if Keegan was trying to hide away from the other guests. Joel smiled to himself. The Keegans apparently had things they'd rather not discuss with an audience, but that was exactly what Joel was going to give them. Stepping from the porch, Joel positioned himself just beneath the arch and well out of sight of Keegan.

"What do you suppose to gain by this?" Keegan asked his wife.

"Rufus, I have no desire to fight with you. I have simply come to tell you that I'm leaving. I want a divorce, and I mean to have one."

Joel started at this news. He pressed closer to the porch. He had to hear every word, for this could prove very beneficial.

"There will be no divorce," Keegan growled out. "You are my wife and you'll stay that way."

"You're mistaken, Rufus. I've endured a great deal because of your escapades, but no more. Alex and I will quietly leave. There needn't be any public show."

"Ah, so Alexandria is in this. I should have known. I warned her . . ."

"Alex did nothing," Katherine Keegan interjected. "I simply came here because it seemed a good way to tell her good-bye and inform you at the same time. She has insisted I allow her to come with me, and frankly, I'm glad for her company."

"There will be no divorce! I won't tolerate it. I won't bear such public humiliation when I'm attempting to better myself with a position in Washington."

"I've borne your public humiliation for years. In fact, the final straw arrived at my door just before coming here."

"What do you mean?" Keegan asked, his rage apparent in his tone.

"I mean your child. Your illegitimate son. One of your conquests, a Miss Gloria Scott, has given birth to your son and has made it clear to me that she'll make this quite public if we do not pay her well. I have no desire to be a part of this. Divorce me and marry her, but do not expect me to stand by idly and bear even more disgrace." Her voice broke and she began to cry. "I cannot take this anymore. You must understand."

Joel thought the news rather tasty. There was a great deal he could do with something like this. Already the plans were churning in his head. He'd have to get one of his men to go check out this Gloria Scott woman.

"No divorce. I'll see you dead first." Keegan's low, ominous tone struck a chord in Joel. He recognized his own determination in Keegan's temperament.

"Do you hear me, Katherine? I'll see you dead before I let you do this."

"Then kill me," she sobbed. "Kill me and release me from this unholy bond."

Keegan laughed. "You miserable wretch. What a waste of my time. Stay out of my way. Go hide yourself in your room and leave me to work my plan."

"Please, Rufus. Please. Not just for my sake, but for Alex. She deserves happiness, even if that's impossible for us."

"It's not impossible for us, woman. I'm living it daily. You're the only one who is unhappy. But trust me, it could be much worse."

The crying grew louder and Joel backed away a bit to avoid being seen. He'd heard enough. Rufus Keegan had fathered an illegitimate child. Katherine Keegan wanted a divorce. This was rich fodder for the purposes of controlling a man—or a woman. He immediately thought of Alex. He licked his lips, anxious to pick up where he'd left off with her. Valerie would be his wife and with her would come fortune and status, but Alexandria Keegan would be his as well. It was just a matter of coordinating the details. Something Joel was very, very good at.

I brought you some supper, Luke," Michaela said after he'd opened the door to his cabin. "Looks like a pretty night for a party, don't you think?"

"I guess so." Luke wasn't in the mood for small talk. "Thanks for the grub."

She put the tray on the table and turned to look Luke straight in the eye. "Are you in pain?"

"Not really. Why do you ask?"

"Because you look like you're in pain, and I just wondered if it was your arm or Alex that's causing you the most grief."

Luke felt his stomach tighten. What did she know about his feelings for Alex? Why should she even suggest such a thing as Alex causing him pain?

"Look, I know this is none of my business, Luke, but I think you probably need to talk to someone, and since I know the situation probably better than most, you can talk to me."

"Talk to you about what?" he asked, turning away.

"About being in love with Alex. About Alex being in love with you."

He turned back around at this. "Alex said that?"

Michaela laughed. "You've got it bad for her, don't you?"

"Just answer my question."

"No, Alex didn't say that she was in love with you. But I'm with her more hours of the day than not. I can tell how she feels. I can tell how you feel as well."

"How?" He watched her as she considered his question. She seemed completely at ease.

"It's the way you look at her. The way you touch her fingers when she hands you something. It's the way you speak to her. Everything about you sings it loud and clear."

"Very well. I do love Alex, but that stays right here between you and me. You may have figured me out, but I don't think you know Alex very well at all. I saw her in Joel Harper's arms last night. She can't be that much in love with me if she's carrying on like that with him."

"You don't honestly think she was in his arms because she wanted to be, do you? He forced his attentions on her, and she had to fight him off to get away."

"What? She told you this?" Luke felt sick to his stomach imagining that Alex had needed him—that she'd been in trouble no more than fifty yards away—and he'd done nothing about it.

"Luke, Alex is going through a lot right now. I can't give you all the details, but you have to understand that things aren't at all good. She's going to need you now more than ever, and I felt like I needed to speak my mind. You need to tell her how you feel about her. Don't let the days get away from you—tell her tonight."

———————

As the sun set and a riot of color splayed out across the western horizon, the first of the Winthrop parties began on the lawns outside El Tovar. Alex had no idea where all of these people were being housed. There were no fewer than three hundred guests gathered on the south rim of the canyon.

It appeared that the Winthrops were the perfect hosts. They had arranged the finest foods from the hotel, paid for lavish tables and decorations, and spent hundreds of dollars to orchestrate every detail. And this was only one of several parties. The main gala was not scheduled to occur for another two days.

Valerie Winthrop seemed in her element. She glided comfortably across the lawn in a flowing creation of silver and black. The look was lavish and opulent in a way that Alex could never hope to know—not that she'd want to. Yet it was amazing just the same.

A kind of silver spider's web was molded to Miss Winthrop's slicked-back hair, while long silver-and-diamond earrings hung from her ears. Diamonds were also draped, almost haphazardly it seemed, around her neck and bodice. She looked the epitome of the modern woman—seductive and alluring, tempting and mysterious.

Alex watched Valerie with a strange sort of interest. The debutante had no apparent modesty when it came to dealing with the opposite sex. She openly flirted, moving from man to man like a bee gathering pollen. The only man she seemed to completely ignore was Joel Harper, a fact that didn't appear to set too well with Mr. Harper. There was trouble in his expression, and Alex felt certain there would be a confrontation before the night was over. This thought was only compounded when Valerie attached herself rather openly to Alex's father.

Laughing in a manner that seemed much too loud, Valerie appeared for all the world to be completely taken with Rufus Keegan. Alex's father loved the extra attention. Alex couldn't help but wonder rather crudely if her father had made Miss Winthrop his latest conquest.

Surely he wouldn't risk the possibility of losing a position in the White House. Alex stared hard at her father, willing him to see her and know what she thought of the entire matter. When he finally did look her way, however, Alex was immediately sorry. His foreboding expression said more to her than any words. Not only had he threatened her more than once, but he also had aligned himself with Joel Harper and his talk of eliminating the competition. Whether Harper had been serious or not—and Alex was becoming more and more confident that he had been—her father apparently believed such actions were necessary to gain entry to the White House. He might even be involved with the man to act on those plans, taking the life of an innocent person in order to win an election. The thought sickened Alex and made her more determined than ever to expose them both and let the law deal with them.

Moving across the well-manicured lawn to offer refreshments to the guests, Alex immediately spotted Bradley Jastrow. The handsome politician from Alabama stood near Hopi House, where guests could buy handmade Indian crafts. The Winthrops had arranged for the Indian dances to be performed during their lawn party, and Jastrow seemed quite interested in those who would dance for the event.

Alex couldn't be sure what Joel Harper and her father had planned for Jastrow, but she was desperate to warn him. Still, what could she say? *Hello, Mr. Jastrow, my father and his new friends plan to eliminate you from the race for president? Even if it means killing you?*

Maybe I could just tell him that there are rumors going around that someone plans to harm him, she reasoned. *I wouldn't have to say who told me this.*

Offering hors d'oeuvres to those she passed, Alex tried to make an inconspicuous attempt to reach the popular man. There were at least a dozen beautifully attired women who stood in a circle around him.

They simpered and pouted and vied for the man's attention, all the while appearing to size up each other. It was a most unusual game they played.

Alex's only intention, however, was to warn Jastrow of the impending danger. And there was another candidate, although she'd not been told his name, who'd arrived at El Tovar for the party. Both were in danger.

First things first, she thought. *I'll tell Mr. Jastrow and then I'll seek out the other candidate.* But even as she drew near enough to hear Jastrow denounce the illegal actions of those who opposed prohibition, Alex caught sight of Joel Harper watching her.

Sweat trickled down her back. How could she possibly warn Mr. Jastrow and not arouse Mr. Harper's suspicions?

Alex looked across the crowded lawn and found her mother in conversation with Senator Winthrop. The conversation appeared all one-sided on the part of the senator, but nevertheless her mother looked every bit the captive audience. Alex couldn't help but feel proud. Her mother was a pillar of strength and managed to give a pretense at happiness that Alex would have found impossible.

Dressed in a crepe de chine gown of dark burgundy, Katherine Keegan looked almost regal—queenly in her stature and deportment. Why couldn't her father see her beauty and grace and be content with her rather than chasing after so many other women?

Jastrow moved across the lawn with several people at his side, drawn into conversations Alex had no business in. She looked back to where she'd seen Joel Harper and found him watching her. The hair on her neck stood up, and a prickling sensation climbed her spine. Harper smiled and nodded, as if knowing his effect.

Alex looked away, wishing desperately she could talk to Luke. Luke would know what to do, or at least he could give her a clearer idea of what wouldn't work. Right now Alex would settle for that alone. If she could just figure out what not to do, then maybe the proper action would present itself.

Her desperation mounted as the third contender for the Democratic nomination made his appearance. Laughter loud and shrill broke out from this new group of visitors. No one seemed to mind, however. Alex wondered if they had any idea the danger they were in. Surely not, she mused; they wouldn't be here otherwise.

Seeing her tray was nearly empty, Alex moved across the grounds, her thoughts whirling around her. Perhaps if I appeal to Mr. Harper, maybe talk to him about the importance of . . . of what? She faltered in her step, nearly falling. She turned to see if Harper was watching her, but he'd disappeared.

Frantic, Alex scanned the crowd. What if he was already putting into play some plan to eliminate the competition? She saw nothing of the man. The orchestra began to play a popular tune and people gathered onto a makeshift dance floor.

Alex's heart raced and the beat of it pounded a rhythm in her ears, threatening to leave her deaf. Hurrying from the scene, she prayed. *God, you're the only one who knows what is happening. You know the corruption here. You know what Joel Harper plans to do. Please intercede on behalf of these people.*

She picked up a full tray of lobster canapés and returned to the lawn, hoping, praying that nothing would go amiss. Scanning the grounds once again, Alex felt momentarily relieved. Mr. Jastrow seemed to be enjoying himself. Still surrounded by beautiful women, the handsome man appeared oblivious to any hint of danger. The other opponent to the senator's campaign seemed equally entertained as he helped himself to a glass of punch from Bernice King's tray.

Maybe I'm overreacting, Alex thought. *After all, nothing seems amiss. Everyone is laughing and having a good time. Maybe Mr. Harper's plans would take place only if things don't appear to be going the senator's way.* She tried to comfort herself with this idea. Surely she was making too much out of Harper's threats.

But even as she reasoned with herself, other thoughts crowded in to take away her comfort. His threats were serious. *He and my father plan to eliminate whoever gets in their way—whether it's the opposition, my mother, or me.*

Thinking of her mother, Alex quickly searched through the guests to find her. Feeling a bit panicked when her first cursory glance didn't yield her mother's location, Alex gave a more dedicated study to each area of the lawn. All the while people took food from her tray, ignorant of her growing concern.

A petite woman in burgundy could easily be swallowed up among the hundreds of guests, and Alex found herself catching a glimpse of color matching her mother's gown only to lose it in the throngs.

There were too many people. People dancing. People talking. People eating and strolling. But Katherine Keegan was nowhere to be found. *Where could she have gone?* Alex trembled, knowing her mother intended to speak about her desires for a divorce. Alex had tried to talk her out of it, but her mother was convinced that this was the way it should be. Now she feared her mother had said something and was now having to face the wrath of the man she'd borne so patiently for so many years.

Lord, I know you hate divorce, but my mother is suffering greatly. She's so frail, even sick from the worry and pain. Please help her now. Let me find her and know that she's safe.

As the skies grew darker, lights especially strung to provide a magical effect, shone down upon the crowds. Forcing herself to remain calm, Alex picked up her step as she moved through the mingling guests. *I'm getting upset for no good reason. I need to see things as they are. Mother is probably nearby or maybe she's gone back to her room. Perhaps she had a head-ache and retired early.* Continuing to search, Alex quickly realized her father was also missing. Was he with Joel Harper? Or was he in a con-frontation with her mother? The nagging doubts resurfaced. Would he really make good on his threats?

Alex's breathing quickened. What should she do? *Oh, Luke, I wish you were here. I need you.*

Realizing how much she'd come to depend on Luke was of no com-fort to her. She had prided herself on needing no one, save God. Espe-cially no man. But right now, with every nerve in her body tingling from head to toe, Alex knew the only person in the world who could help stave off her hysteria was the one person she'd pushed away and kept at arm's length.

The orchestra ended one song and had just begun the opening strains of another when a woman's scream tore through the air. Every-thing stopped. The orchestra conductor put down his baton and looked to the crowd as if for a cue. Alex stared at the faces around her, frozen in time with her companions. Faces filled with fear, curiosity, and con-fusion stared back at her.

The woman screamed again and then there was silence.

Alex couldn't move. No matter how hard she tried. She looked at the tray in her hands, then looked to the orchestra and the people who'd been dancing. Everyone remained fixed in place, as though a photograph had been snapped of the entire group.

"Where did that come from?" someone finally questioned among a growing hum of murmured questions.

"Do you suppose it was just someone having a good time?"

"Didn't sound like a good time to me," another guest answered.

The murmurings grew to a cacophony of questioning and reasoning. Confusion settled over the crowd as they began to move again. Some moved in the direction of the scream, others went back to the food table as if to bolster their strength with refreshments.

A woman next to Alex agreed. "That woman sounded terrified, if you ask me."

This seemed to be the only encouragement Alex needed. Shoving the half empty tray into the stunned woman's hands, Alex ran at full speed across the lawn. The sound had come from the rim path, yet how far away, Alex couldn't be sure. The canyon had an eerie way of distorting sounds. Sometimes it was quite confusing.

Many of the party guests had already begun moving in the direction of the rim. Those that pushed ahead at a rapid pace were mainly the newspaper reporters.

"Someone's fallen into the canyon!" came the call.

Alex felt sickened and stopped to catch her breath. There was a part of her that suddenly didn't want to know the truth.

Oh, God, please help me. I'm so scared. She repeated the prayer like a mantra. Forcing herself forward, she regained her momentum and pushed through the crowd.

"Someone has fallen off the edge," murmured a woman to her companion.

"No one could live to tell about that," he replied. "I took that mule ride down—that canyon's a mile into the ground. No, there won't be much left of them—whoever they are."

Alex glared at them but pressed on. The hotel had positioned additional lighting here, which seemed to only create more shadows.

"Excuse me," she said, over and over. An air of excitement enveloped the crowd, and people weren't always of a mind to move out of Alex's way. Her patience wore thin and she found herself becoming quite demanding. "I work for the hotel—get out of my way."

Finally, she cleared past the last of the onlookers and found two people standing about ten feet away. The man turned out to be Luke. Alex could see the cast on his left arm in the dim light. The woman he held was sobbing. Her face was buried against his chest, but from the look of her build and the color of her gown, Alex felt confident that it was her mother.

Two men came to stand beside Luke. One wore a park ranger uniform, while the other was dressed in a tuxedo. They were speaking in hushed tones with Luke.

Alex's legs felt weighted with lead as she pressed closer. In a hoarse whisper she asked, "Luke, what's happened?"

Luke looked up and met her gaze. She could see his expression, although shadowed. His look told her that nothing would ever be the same after tonight.

"What is it?" she pleaded. "Tell me."

Her mother pulled away and looked at Alex with tear-filled eyes. Luke released his hold on her and the ranger sympathetically took Mrs. Keegan's hand and led her to a nearby bench. Luke then turned to Alex and looked into her eyes. "I'm sorry, Alex. It's your father. He's gone over the edge."

I can't believe he's really dead," Alex said in disbelief nearly two hours later. Numb from the news, she hadn't cried a single tear. She wondered if Luke thought her cold and unfeeling.

Luke reached out and took hold of her hand. "If he'd only fallen to the first ledge, he might have made it."

"What could have happened?"

"I don't know. I came upon your mother after it'd happened. She crumpled to the ground crying. She's the only one who saw anything, and she's not talking," Luke replied, gazing at her with such tenderness. "I'm sorry you have to endure this. It's never easy to lose a loved one."

The words "loved one" slammed up against her like the time she'd stepped on the prongs of a rake, bringing the wooden handle full force against her face. She didn't consider her father a loved one. She didn't even mind the idea that he was gone—forever. Except . . . She shook her head. Except nothing. She didn't care.

Shock washed through her veins, leaving her cold. *This is your father,* she chided herself. *He's dead and you must care.* A sense of guilt crept in where the stunning news had first left her without feeling.

She tried not to think of her father, focusing instead on her mother. The poor woman had cried enough tears for both of them. Katherine Keegan now slept sedated in her suite with a ranger guarding the door outside. The canyon physician worried about her mental state and general health. There was talk, murmurings and whisperings about the accident. People were beginning to say that Katherine Keegan had killed her husband. It was all too much for Alex to take in.

"I know this is difficult for you. In spite of the way your father behaved, I know you didn't wish him dead."

Alex couldn't even look at Luke, for too many times she'd wished just that. Well, maybe not that he'd be murdered. She'd wished often enough that he'd die in his sleep and free her mother from her misery. Or that he'd die on one of his many trips to the capital. Did that make her a horrible person? Was she less of a Christian because she was glad her father had died instead of her mother? She couldn't keep from trembling.

"The rangers want to talk to you," Luke said softly. "I told them you were too upset—that they'd have to wait. But you can't hold them off forever."

She looked blankly at the wall, not seeing a thing. "I understand."

But in truth, Alex didn't understand anything at all. Joel had threatened her mother's life, but was this what he'd meant? Alex had feared he might kill her mother, but perhaps this was even worse. Had Joel Harper somehow arranged her father's death and allowed the blame to rest on her mother's shoulders? But if that were the case, if there was another person involved, then surely her mother would tell them.

Luke rubbed her hand. His warmth seemed to permeate the icy feeling that ran the full length of her body. How could it be that her father was dead? How could it be that her mother appeared to be the prime suspect?

"What's going to happen, Luke?" She looked deep into his green eyes, praying she'd find an answer she could cope with. "Are they going to blame my mother—arrest her?"

"I don't know. I wish I did—then I might feel more capable of helping you through this." He continued to hold her hand, and Alex found that she liked his touch very much.

"She's been through so much already. I don't know how she'll ever manage to get through this."

"God will give you both the strength to endure it."

She studied his face for a moment. "I need to ask you something," she said, knowing that she would know in his expression if he lied to her.

"What is it?"

"Do you think my mother killed him?"

Luke didn't hesitate. "No. I don't. She doesn't seem capable of such a thing."

"But she had plenty of motive," Alex argued, needing to hear him dispel her fears.

"True, but she's had motive for years. Why wait until now?"

"I suppose that's true. Nothing new has happened to make her act any differently."

"Are you sure nothing has happened recently?" Luke questioned. "Not that I think it would result in your mother killing him, but someone has. Perhaps a business deal went bad. Or maybe it's this whole political thing. Do you know if someone wanted to see him dead?"

Alex immediately thought of Joel Harper but dismissed the thought. Joel and her father were like-minded. They were working together. Joel hardly seemed likely to kill off a man who was happy to do his bidding in return for an appointment in the White House.

"Miss Keegan?" a ranger questioned from the door.

"Yes, I'm Miss Keegan." Alex knew a lot of the rangers, but this man was a complete stranger. Standing picture perfect in his pressed uniform, the older man held a sympathetic expression on his face.

"I know this is a difficult time, but I need to ask you a few questions," he said rather apologetically. "It's just routine when something like this happens."

Alex looked to Luke once more. He nodded and Alex looked back to the ranger. "I suppose now is as good a time as any."

Luke got to his feet. "Do you mind if I stay here with her?"

"Yes, please," Alex said.

"I have no objection. This won't take long." The man pulled up a chair in front of Alex. "First of all, you have my sympathies. I know you must be quite taken in your grief."

Alex looked to the floor. "I'm still so shocked."

"I'm sure that's true," the ranger replied. "I understand you were working at the time of the incident."

The incident? Alex thought. How silly to call someone's death an "incident."

"Yes. I'm a Harvey employee. I work in the restaurant, and this evening I was serving at the lawn party hosted by the Winthrops."

"I understand both your mother and father were guests of the Winthrops."

"Yes. My father has been a part of the Winthrops' party since they arrived. My mother only just arrived." Alex felt as though she were sorting through facts in her mind, trying to offer them back to the ranger in order to make sense of a much bigger puzzle.

"Why did she come to the Grand Canyon?"

"The Winthrops sent an invitation. She showed it to me. They were paying for her suite," Alex said, trying to remember everything.

"It was mentioned that Mrs. Keegan came here to confront her husband."

Alex had no intention of giving them information that they could use against her mother. "She told me she came because of the invitation." That wasn't a lie. She held her breath for a moment, trying to still her rapid breathing.

"Then you aren't aware of any problems between your mother and father?"

Alex let out her breath and shifted uneasily. Glancing to Luke, Alex felt she had no choice but to admit what everyone was already talking about. "My father was a philanderer. He had . . . ah . . . many other women in his life."

"So there were problems?"

"Yes." She bit her lower lip and prayed he wouldn't ask her to explain the fight she'd witnessed, nor tell of her father's threats. She wasn't ready to divulge this information. She first needed to talk to her mother. Tears flooded Alex's eyes and she lowered her head. She began to rub her temples where the throbbing was becoming unbearable.

"Look, why don't you wait to finish this up later?" Luke asked. "You can see she's clearly distraught. She did just lose her father."

"Yes, I understand. I suppose this can wait until morning." The ranger got to his feet and walked to the door. "Miss Keegan, I realize this is difficult, but I'll need to speak with you first thing tomorrow."

Alex sniffed back her tears and nodded. "I'll be here."

After he'd gone, Luke moved back to sit beside her on the sofa. They were in Mrs. Godfrey's private quarters, as it seemed the only place to get away from the reporters and other busybodies.

"Alex, I'm sorry for all of this. I don't know what I can do to help, but I feel I have to offer to try."

"Luke, she couldn't have done it. My mother isn't like that. She was unhappy with my father—she has been for years. I've never known a time when he was faithful. Even when I was young he had his lady friends. I've never understood it, but Mother told me it was just the way things were. She bore it all with grace and determination. And even with all his threats . . ."

"What kind of threats?"

Alex bristled. Had she said too much? She looked to Luke and his image blurred behind her tears. How she longed to trust him with what she knew. "My father wasn't very happy that my mother had come to El

Tovar. He really wanted to gain a position in Washington and he feared she might make trouble."

"How so? Everyone knew what he was doing," Luke stated matter-of-factly.

Alex got to her feet and paced the small space. "I don't know. He threatened us both."

At this Luke got up and came to her. "He threatened you? Why didn't you tell me?" He studied her a moment before reaching up to push back an errant strand of wavy brown hair. "Oh, Alex, don't you know I would have protected you? I would have talked to him at least."

His tenderness touched something deep within her. "I . . . well . . . you were busy and then you got hurt."

Luke gently touched her wet cheek. "Alex, don't you understand? I'm never too busy to care about what happens to you."

Alex could recognize the sincerity in his expression. His generally good-natured temperament had been transformed into a much more serious, more intense attitude. There was nothing casual about this cowboy. This man was all concern and . . . something else. Something Alex couldn't quite put her finger on.

His touch sent charges of electricity down her body. His gaze, so intense—demanded an intimacy from her that Alex had never shared with anyone. When he took hold of her shoulder, Alex lost herself in the moment.

"Alex, I won't let them hurt you, and if I can do anything about it, I won't let them hurt your mother."

"How did you come to be with her?"

"My arm was bothering me, so I went for a walk. I'd been walking around, trying to pray through some difficult decisions. I was headed back to my cabin when I heard her scream. I was just the first one there—the closest one to the rim."

"And you didn't see anything? No other person?"

"No. There didn't appear to be anyone else. Your mother had collapsed to her knees in complete shock by the time I got to her."

Alex began to cry in earnest. Her voice broke as she declared, "She couldn't have pushed him over. She couldn't have done it. As discouraged and betrayed as she was, she might have jumped off the ledge to take her own life, but she wouldn't hurt my father. Even if he wouldn't divorce her. . . ."

"She wanted a divorce? I thought you said she wouldn't leave him."

"I know, but . . ." Alex knew she had to tell him the truth. At least about this. "She came here . . . to . . . to tell him she was leaving him. She'd withdrawn a great deal of money from their account and had come to tell him good-bye."

"Alex, that doesn't help her situation very much. Do you suppose they fought over this?"

"Of course they fought over it," Alex replied in near hysteria. "They always fought. Father never had a civil word for Mother, and Mother had made up her mind. I'm sure they argued about it, since she had her mind set to leave."

"You'll have to tell the ranger tomorrow," he said matter-of-factly.

"I can't tell him. It would make her look bad—the wife scorned. The wife who depleted the bank account and made plans to run away and divorce her husband. None of that will help her case."

"But you have to tell the truth."

"The truth is, my mother could never have pushed my father over the edge."

"Be that as it may," Luke said gently, but insistently, "you have to tell him."

Silence fell between them as Alex tried to compose herself. The hole she'd dug herself into seemed to be collapsing around her.

"Where did she plan to go—I mean, after she left him and El Tovar?" Luke asked.

Alex drew a deep breath to steady her nerves. "We weren't sure. I was planning on asking Mrs. Godfrey to transfer me as soon as she could."

"You were going to leave with her—leave El Tovar? Were you planning on talking to me about this?"

"I wanted to talk to you." Alex tried to compose herself, but her efforts weren't amounting to much. Her world was falling apart piece by piece and now she had to confront the possibility of another woman in Luke's life. "You were . . . were . . . busy. And Valerie Winthrop said . . ." Alex buried her face in her hands and sobbed. With his good right arm, Luke pulled her against him and held her safe. She could feel his cast, rock solid, against her side as he tried his best to pull her closer.

"Shhh, you don't have to go on. There's plenty of time to talk about this later."

Alex relished the warmth of his embrace. Luke smelled of hay and burnt wood—earthy smells that served to calm Alex's soul. Luke was her mainstay. Luke was the one she could count on when things went bad. God would always reign supreme in her life, but Luke had come to mean more to her than any other human being. Was this love? Was this, in honesty and truth, what she had hoped existed but never dared to believe in?

He stroked her hair, then gently rubbed the back of her neck. "It's going to be all right. You'll see. God is bigger than this. He'll let the truth win out."

Alex pulled away just enough to see Luke's face. "But, Luke, what if the truth is more than I can bear?"

He gently cupped her chin. "Alex, no matter what the truth is, God will see you through. Remember, you've shared those very words with me. Bad things happen, but God is still there for you. He still loves you."

"I just don't know what to do anymore," she cried.

His face was only inches from hers and, looking up, Alex found herself wondering what it would be like to kiss him. She didn't have to wonder for long. Lowering his mouth to hers, Luke kissed her long and passionately. The warmth of his touch and the depth of his kiss were enough for Alex to completely forget the moment. She put her hand up to feel the stubble on his jaw, her heart racing madly. This felt so right.

As he tightened his hold on her, Alex melted against him. They fit so well together, as if they'd always been intended for each other. If only this moment could go on forever. But like everything that offered comfort to Alex, this too had its end.

"Alex," Luke whispered, "there's something I need to tell you." This time, he was the one to pull away.

His words were like a slap in the face. Alex immediately realized what they'd just done and stepped back. What had she been thinking? "I . . . I . . . don't know what came over me."

She continued to back away as images of Luke and Valerie crept into her memory. She had to let go of her feelings for him. Even if those feelings were . . . very possibly . . . love.

"You're upset," Luke said, moving toward her. "I didn't mean to take advantage of that. I don't want you to think badly of me, but I have to tell you why I . . ." He stopped when he saw her intense gaze.

"Luke, I heard all about the ranch in Wyoming."

"How could you possibly know about that?" He seemed confused, speechless.

It was true—everything Valerie had said. He was turning his back on everything she had thought he stood for. Alex felt sick.

"I can't say," she replied. "I just do."

"Well, that's part of what I want to talk to you about."

Alex didn't want to hear about his plans with Valerie Winthrop. Not now. Not after what they had shared. "I can't stay here anymore. I need to see if they'll let me see my mother. I can't just leave her to their mercy." Alex reached for the door handle.

"Wait. We need to talk."

"Not now, Luke. I just couldn't bear it." She opened the door and stepped into the hall. Walking toward the stairs, she was immediately set upon by reporters.

"Is it true your mother killed your father because of his affairs?" one man questioned.

"No!" Alex replied. They were like wolves circling prey.

"Is it true your father sired an illegitimate child and that the woman was making demands on your mother?"

"No! How can you say such things?"

"Did your mother confess to pushing your father into the canyon?"

Alex tried to move away from them, but it wasn't until Luke pushed his way through the crowd that she had any success.

"Miss Keegan has been through a lot this evening. She's not up to answering any more questions."

"Say, aren't you the cowboy who found her?"

"Yeah, that's him, he's got a broken arm."

"Did you see what happened when Mrs. Keegan pushed her husband into the canyon?"

Luke fairly growled as he pushed Alex ahead of him. "I said, no more questions."

Taking hold of Alex, Luke maneuvered her down the hall. When they came to her mother's room, he paused momentarily. Alex thought he seemed reluctant to let go of her, but finally he released his hold. "Alex, I have to talk to you. I won't press you tonight, but tomorrow, we need to talk—it's important."

Alex faced the idea with sheer dread. Nevertheless, she nodded. "All right. Tomorrow."

Tomorrow her world would further unravel, but tonight . . . tonight she would force a stay of execution in the memory of his kiss.

———

That night in his cabin, Luke poked up the fire and stared absentmindedly into the flames. Nothing in his life had prepared him for the experience of kissing Alex Keegan. He felt weak and powerful all at the same time. He knew in that moment, sharing their kiss, that she cared for him as he did for her. She wouldn't admit it, but he knew it just the same.

The night had brought about more than one revelation, however. Luke couldn't help but remember Katherine Keegan's sobbing hysteria and the words, "Rufus went over the edge."

Luke had been helpless to do much more than get Katherine to her feet. He held her against him while she cried, much as he had with Alex, but no other word from her was forthcoming. When the crowd arrived and others had taken over so that he could comfort Alex, Luke wondered quite seriously if they would simply haul Katherine to jail. She was the only one there when he arrived. She was the prime suspect, and yet Luke felt certain she hadn't done the deed herself.

Still, who else would want Rufus Keegan dead?

The mood of the hotel guests the following morning was more than somber—it was very nearly mournful. Luke ate his breakfast in haste, anxious to get away from El Tovar and back to the stables. He had told Mrs. Godfrey that he'd take his meals at the hotel from this point on, eating with his men in the employee dining area. She'd assured him that it was no trouble to have the girls bring meals to his cabin, but Luke felt otherwise.

Walking through the lobby of El Tovar, Luke's only desire was to talk to Alex. When he reached her mother's room the ranger told him that Alex and her mother were not taking visitors. He'd insisted the man ask Alex to step outside to speak to Luke, but when the ranger returned, he reiterated that Miss Keegan was speaking to no one.

Feeling a deep sense of frustration, Luke headed downstairs. If he couldn't talk to Alex, maybe he could find Michaela. Instead, he found himself face-to-face with Joel Harper. The man stared at him with an expression that suggested contempt, and Luke wondered if his own face revealed his intense dislike for the man. Ever since talking with Michaela, Luke had wanted to put Harper in his place.

"Mr. Toland." Harper's greeting was low, almost inaudible.

"Harper," Luke replied. "I'd like a word with you."

"Oh? I heard about your involvement in last night's affair. Are you in some kind of trouble?"

"No, but you will be if you don't stay away from Alex Keegan."

Joel Harper's upper lip curled and his expression took on a decidedly sinister quality. "And since when do employees make demands of hotel guests?"

"Since you found it acceptable to force yourself on hotel employees. I know all about your actions with Alex, and I won't tolerate it. If you doubt me, we can take this outside right now."

"Are you threatening me, Mr. Toland?"

"It's not a threat—it's a promise. If you don't leave Alex alone, I'll take the matter into my own hands."

"Is that what you did with her father?"

Luke's eyes narrowed. He'd never wanted to hit a man more than he wanted to hit Joel Harper. "I don't know what you're implying, but I've got no interest in discussing Keegan's death. I want to make clear that you understand you aren't to touch Alex again. Do you understand?"

"I think that mule must have kicked more than your arm. Are you sure you haven't loosened something in your head? Really, Mr. Toland, you should watch what you say to powerful men."

Luke stepped away lest he be tempted to give the man a sound beating. "If I see a powerful man, I'll do just that."

"You don't want to be on my bad side, Toland. You truly don't."

"I don't see that there's any other side when it comes to you, Harper. Just remember what I said."

Luke stalked off in anger. He'd never intended to let the man get the best of him, but still, he had. Why was it so hard to remain calm and rational when dealing with the matter of Harper? *It's because he keeps bothering Alex,* Luke reasoned. Michaela said he forced himself on Alex, and that was reason enough to resent him.

The worst of it was that he wasn't half as frustrated with Harper as he was Alex. Why wouldn't she talk to him? After last night, he felt there was so much he needed to say. He couldn't help but wonder if she didn't feel the same way.

Luke wondered if the rangers had talked to her again. They would need to get all their information together in order to figure out what had happened. Alex had nothing to do with her father's death, of that he was certain, but he also felt she wasn't telling the full truth. Luke believed she was holding back more than the fact her mother wanted a divorce, but he didn't know what it could be. It wasn't like Alex to lie, even to protect someone she loved. Still, nothing like this—nothing this horrible—had ever happened to her before.

Walking along the rim path, Luke tried to make sense of everything that had happened. Keegan's death. The kiss he'd shared with Alex. Her unwillingness to talk to him. *How did she know about the ranch I want to buy? And why should it upset her so much?*

The park seemed uncommonly quiet. He saw a few visitors walking the pathways around the rim, but they made special effort to stay away from the edge. Where yesterday people had joked and teased each other by standing as close to the edge as possible, today they were guarded and sober. Keegan's death had reminded them of their own mortality. Reality had once again set in.

Another thing Luke noticed was an almost morbid curiosity to go to the place where Keegan had fallen. Not that there was much to see. There were no railings along the edge at this point, so it would have been very easy for a person to be pushed over. But could Katherine Keegan have done the deed? Luke seriously doubted it.

Rufus Keegan was a good-sized man. He probably outweighed his wife by at least a hundred pounds. He could have easily fended her off, even if she'd thrown her full body weight against him. No, Luke didn't believe for a moment that Mrs. Keegan had killed her husband. But if not her, then who? Someone wanted Rufus Keegan dead and Katherine, having been with him until the end, had to know who it was.

Luke studied the shadows on the canyon walls. Someone must have killed Keegan. He was too ambitious to have risked his own life by dallying on the edge. Rufus Keegan was no one's favorite character. He'd hurt people, stolen their livelihoods away, carried on affairs with women both single and married. Perhaps an irate father or husband had caught up with him. And the man's business dealings, by Alex's account, were far from fair or aboveboard. His death was probably a relief rather than a tragedy for most people. It would feel that way especially to Alex.

Alex. Luke felt better just knowing that Alex had been busy with her duties last night and had witnesses to prove her whereabouts. As much as she despised her father's actions, she would never plan out his murder—she wasn't capable of that. But he'd also seen Keegan get the best of Alex's gentle nature. Especially when the man insulted or hurt her mother.

If Alex had come to him saying that she'd fought with her father and pushed him over the edge, it wouldn't really have shocked Luke all that much. Keegan had long ago killed off any affection Alex had for him. His infidelity had left her doubtful of all men—even men who didn't deserve the same reputation, like himself.

Luke kicked at the dirt. *Alex did not kill her father,* he reminded himself. Though she might have wanted to as she labored with her anger and hate, she didn't do the job. She didn't want him dead—just out of her life. Luke only wished he knew who had wanted the man dead. If he could figure that out, he could save them all a whole lot of grief.

Luke walked back to the hotel, lost in his thoughts. He'd not gone far from the place where Keegan had died when he heard his name being called.

"Mr. Toland—Luke!"

Luke looked away from the canyon and found Valerie approaching from the hotel.

"I was hoping we might talk. Do you have some time?"

"Not really," Luke said, feeling uncomfortable as she closed the distance between them. He crossed his arms against his chest as if to put a wall between them. Valerie Winthrop knew no walls, however. She gently touched his arm.

"Please. Last night was . . . so . . ." Tears filled her eyes and her voice broke.

Luke felt sorry for her, but not enough to offer any physical comfort. He hesitated to send her away, however. "I suppose I can talk for a minute."

She sniffed daintily and dried her eyes with a lacy handkerchief. Luke thought for a moment that her tears were just put on, but she seemed genuinely upset.

"What is it you wanted to talk about?" Luke questioned. The flowery scent of her perfume assailed him, and her nearness bothered him. He wasn't attracted to her in the least, but he feared what other people might begin to think if they found him alone with her, standing so close, appearing so intimate.

"I'm afraid," she finally said. "Last night . . . it proved to me that life is definitely unpredictable."

"True enough," Luke replied. "That's why a person needs to know where he stands with the Lord. You could be talking to a person one minute and the next minute find they're gone."

Valerie nodded. "That's exactly what happened. Mr. Keegan and I were talking at the party. We were laughing and making plans for the future. Daddy had invited him to South Carolina—to our home. He was to come and bring his family and share our southern hospitality. The next thing I know, he's dead." She paled a bit and turned away from Luke to gaze at the canyon. "What a terrible place." She rubbed her bare arms as if the sun had suddenly gone out of sight and the day had turned cold.

"It isn't the *place* that killed Rufus Keegan."

"I know, but if that big canyon hadn't been there, he might yet be alive. Not only that," she paused, looking around to make certain she wasn't overheard, "my father . . . well . . . I fear for him."

Luke didn't make the connection. "But why? He seems healthy enough. Safe enough."

Valerie drew close again. "I think someone may want to kill him. This campaign is so ugly. There are things going on that you can't begin to know about. I just want to keep Daddy from harm."

"He's going into a business that hardly allows for that. You can't keep people from disliking his politics and him. He'll be in one type of danger or another for the rest of his life."

"My point exactly," Valerie said, taking hold of Luke's hand. "You must help me."

"I don't understand."

"I want to hire you. I want you to be Daddy's bodyguard."

"Why me?" Luke asked, pulling away. He didn't want to appear rude, but her touch was making him very uncomfortable. "I've got a busted wrist. I'm hardly going to be able to fight off ruthless attacks."

"You won't be in that cast forever. You don't even need a sling anymore, so I know it must be healing fast. You're a good man, Luke. You have scruples. That's not something you often see, especially in political arenas. If I hired you to watch over Daddy, I know you'd do the job without reservation. You'd give it your all."

Luke managed to move away from her enough to raise his casted left arm. "I'll be wearing this for weeks. I'm telling you, even if I wanted the job, I wouldn't be of any use to you or your father."

"Don't say that. You're still strong and capable," she gushed, moving toward him again. This time she threw herself against him and wrapped him in her embrace. "Please, Luke. I need you to do this for me. I couldn't bear it if something happened to Daddy."

Luke pushed her back none too gently. "That's hardly called for, Miss Winthrop."

She started to cry again. "Don't be cruel. I'm not trying to make a scene, I simply don't want anything to happen to my father." She paused and looked at him quite soberly. "I thought you were a Christian. Aren't Christians supposed to be kind to people? Aren't they supposed to lend a helping hand and offer comfort?"

"I suppose they are," Luke said, feeling caught between the canyon and her wiles. "But that doesn't mean I must sacrifice a job I love simply because you ask me to. I'm trying to show you Christian charity just by talking with you and listening to your concerns. But you're making this really difficult. People in my world don't just throw themselves all over another person. You seem to make a practice of it, and I don't like it."

"You just don't care," she said, sobbing into her handkerchief. "I have no one who cares."

"What about Mr. Harper? You two are supposed to marry, aren't you?"

Valerie shook her head. "I don't want to marry him. I don't trust him. Joel is deceptive and devious. He does all sorts of underhanded things and threatens me all the time. I don't dare talk to him about this, for he might very well be in on the plan to harm my father."

Luke's eyes narrowed. He looked at the woman in front of him, praying to discern if she lied. "There's a plan? Do you have proof?"

Valerie wiped her eyes once again. "No, but I know something's going on nevertheless."

"How?"

"There have been people in and around my father—around his room—who have no purpose being there. Daddy is always drawing the coattail crowd."

"The coattail crowd?" Luke questioned.

"You know, those people who plan to make it big or get rich by riding his coattails to the top. Daddy is so giving, so generous, he never sees harm until it's too late. I've heard rumors and—"

"Look, you can't go acting on rumors," Luke interjected. "If you don't have proof, the authorities aren't going to be able to help you."

"But I'm not going to the authorities. I've come to you."

Luke shook his head and started back up the path. "You need to talk to the authorities. If there is a problem, they're the ones who can help keep your father out of trouble. They can even post a guard on him while he's here at the canyon."

"Please don't leave me, Luke. Please don't say no. Don't leave me all alone in this."

Luke stopped and looked at her for a moment. She seemed so delicate, so vulnerable and lost. "Miss Winthrop, if you would turn to God, you would find you're never alone. Pray about this and ask His guidance. God will surely show you what to do."

"I don't need religion—I need you."

"No, you don't. You hardly even know me," Luke replied firmly.

"But I'd like to."

"Miss Winthrop, I can't help you, except to pray for you." He didn't know if it was God's stirring or his own personal discomfort, but Luke felt an overwhelming need to escape. "Good day," he added rather abruptly.

Luke walked away, leaving the crying woman to her own devices. He wasn't interested in anything she had to offer, and the pricking of his conscience seemed a foreboding of things to come.

The Winthrops were bad news for the entire area. He didn't want to get involved with them on any business or personal level, yet they seemed to impose themselves on people. They represented everything Luke disliked: power, money, fame, and politics. They were of the world. They were the world.

The Winthrops and their kind used people. Used them no matter the cost. If a person proved useful, they were brought in as the best of friends. Once they'd served their purpose, however, and that person was no longer needed, they were disposed of as neatly as . . . Luke stopped in his thoughts.

"As neatly as Rufus Keegan was pushed over the edge," he murmured.

The slender build of Valerie Winthrop came to mind. She'd admitted to spending part of the evening with Keegan. Maybe she knew something. After all, it was entirely possible that, short of the confrontation that sent Keegan to his death, Valerie Winthrop was the last person to speak to him.

"But she'd probably only lie," Luke surmised. He hated to judge her harshly, but each encounter with her seemed to bring trouble.

Luke contrasted her to Alexandria Keegan. Alex's gentle spirit and quiet, unassuming manners made Luke feel protective and loving. Valerie Winthrop just irritated him.

The need to see Alex, to hold her and tell her how he felt, grew stronger with each passing moment. Luke knew it was poor timing given the situation, but each time he had put off telling her of his love, things only seemed to get worse.

"I'd like a few words with you, Mr. Toland."

Luke looked up to greet the stern expression of the ranger who'd tried to talk to Alex the night before. His counterparts had already asked Luke a couple dozen questions related to Rufus Keegan's death, but he had figured they were far from done.

"Sure," Luke said nodding. "What do you want to know?"

The man's eyes narrowed. "Did you have any reason to want Rufus Keegan dead?"

Valerie Winthrop had never felt more alone in her life. She watched Luke walk away and hook up with another man. No doubt another friend—a part of his life at the Grand Canyon.

It seemed everyone had someone they could trust—but she had no one. Even her own father was so focused on his campaign and his desire for the presidency that he couldn't see anything else. Oh, she knew he loved her, but she was something more ornamental than useful in his eyes. Her father trusted her to host his dinner parties, but not to pick her own husband. Her father had never denied her anything, but on the issue of Joel Harper he seemed blind and deaf.

Drying her eyes, Valerie looked out over the canyon. It would be easy enough to jump to her death. Die in the flash of a moment—like Rufus Keegan. The thought of him dying sent chills up her spine. She remembered his suggestions the night before during their walk along the rim. She could almost recollect the feel of his hands upon her—touching her, demanding things of her she didn't want to give. She shuddered and refused to think about it. There was nothing she could do about it now.

She had thought her lie about someone trying to kill her father would cause Luke to care about her. She'd thought that if her looks couldn't bring him to his knees, then perhaps the idea of being her rescuer and protector would. But Luke hadn't been interested in this role either. He puzzled her like no other man ever had. Usually all she had to do was bat her eyelashes or wave her money and men were at her beck and call.

Even as she thought this, the idea left her more lonely than ever. Would anyone ever love and care about her—for herself? She'd played so many games acting the coquette, the wild rebel, the sweet, attentive daughter. She wasn't even sure who she was anymore. Her life in Charleston was one of privilege and elegance. She was a daughter of the South—highly respected, belonging to that elite world of modern southern belles.

She'd been born to this, taking her mother's place in society, serving as she had served. Valerie generally saved her wild behavior for times when she was away from her home. New Yorkers didn't care how she conducted herself. They didn't mind her wearing scandalous clothes and being seen entering speakeasies. They turned a blind eye to her flirtations and drinking.

Valerie only wished she could turn a blind eye to herself. She didn't like herself very much. For all the confidence of her position, somewhere along the way Valerie had lost sight of the truth.

"I have no clue as to what the truth is anymore," she whispered.

Luke had said she needed God, but Valerie had tried church and religion. It left her hopeless and burdened with its many rules and regulations. She could never hope to be the pure and innocent person that religion demanded. She could never be good enough—not with her problems and life-style.

There has to be something else, she thought. *Something more than this emptiness.* The vast emptiness of the canyon seemed to mirror how she felt inside. It would take an awful lot to fill up the Grand Canyon, but surely that would be simple compared to Valerie trying to fill the hole in her heart.

God would be big enough to fill that space, she thought, then quickly pushed the thought aside.

Ignoring the acquaintances who looked her way, Valerie went back to her suite on the third floor of El Tovar. She had no desire to mingle and make small talk. Luke's words continued to haunt her—his talk about how a person needed to know where they stood with God. But how was a person to know something so vast as that? It wasn't as if God would come down and speak to a person face-to-face. Was it?

She thought of the whiskey she'd hidden in her dresser. The idea of drinking herself into oblivion appealed to her greatly. Let them all dine and party without her. She wasn't feeling well. Her father or Joel could make her excuses. The alcohol wouldn't solve her problems, but it would make them go away for at least a few hours. Or rather, it would make her no longer care about their existence.

Entering her room, she immediately locked the door behind her. She wanted no one to disturb her.

"I saw you with Toland," Joel stated.

Valerie turned with a start, her hand clasping the collar of her dress. "How did you get in here?"

"That's unimportant," he said, getting up from the bedside chair. "What is important is that I saw you with Toland just now."

"So what?" Valerie said, trying hard to be brave. "I happened upon him while I was walking and we talked."

"Is that what you call it when you wrap yourself around someone?"

Valerie recognized his jealousy. It was almost enough to make her laugh. Almost. But the anger in his expression drew her up short. "I've been greatly upset since last night's events. Not that I would expect you to understand."

Joel watched her with an odd sort of expression, one which Valerie found completely unnerving. He wore his dark brown suit, the one she'd helped him pick out in Charleston. The tie was also one she'd helped him choose. His entire appearance, quality through and through, should have pleased her, but instead it left her feeling cold and disinterested. Next to a man like Luke Toland, Joel seemed boring and lifeless.

"Things have gotten out of control," Joel announced, crossing the room to look out her window. "Unscheduled events are taking place, and it's causing me a great deal of trouble."

"I'm sure I don't know what you mean," Valerie said, taking off her straw hat. She wished Joel would simply leave her alone but knew full well he'd come with something or someone on his mind. The sooner he got it out for her consideration, the better off they'd both be. "Maybe you should explain," she finally added, coming hesitantly to sit on the edge of her bed. She hoped her calm approach would soothe him.

"This election means everything to me. To your father as well," he said, turning from the window. "There is a great deal at stake, and no one will be allowed to ruin that. Not the Keegans. Not John Davis or Bradley Jastrow. Not even you." He lowered his voice a bit before adding, "Especially not you."

Fear washed over her, and the loneliness she'd felt earlier seemed to magnify. "Why don't we go downstairs for a bit of lunch?" she suggested. "You can tell me all about this over one of those lovely salads." She got to her feet, but Joel quickly crossed the room and stood between her and the door.

"You aren't going anywhere, my dear. There is much we need to consider—to take charge of. I'm going to need your help in order to see my plans to completion. You do want to see your father elected as president, don't you?"

Valerie bit her lower lip and backed up a step. "It's hardly proper for us to discuss it here."

"Why not? I'm sure you've had many other men here for . . . discussions."

"That's not true," Valerie countered. "You shouldn't be here."

"But we're engaged, my dear. Tomorrow night we'll make it official.

Surely there can be no harm." He smiled in that self-confident manner she'd come to hate.

"It's not proper. People will talk."

"People are already talking, Val. They're saying things like, 'How is it that Miss Winthrop should act so freely with other men?' Or 'Didn't I hear that she's engaged? What must her fiancé think?' Those are the kind of things people are saying. You're making me the laughingstock of our social circles."

"It hasn't been intentional. You and I both agreed that we should enjoy ourselves with other people," Valerie protested in her defense.

"I believe we had both agreed to be discreet. You have obviously given no regard to that agreement. All last night you hung on one man's arm or another. I believe you made the circle to include every-one—everyone but me, that is." His eyes narrowed as he stepped toward her. "I would certainly hate to have people believe my soon-to-be wife was a woman of loose moral character."

"You've never cared what anyone thought," Valerie said, backing away from him. "Why concern yourself now?"

"Because I intend to win this election for your father. I intend to see us married and my future secured." He paused. "I intend to have access to the Winthrop fortune—that's all I care about."

He reached out to her and Valerie cringed and closed her eyes. When his touch didn't come, Valerie opened her eyes and noted his expression. It seemed a mix of frustration, disgust, and maybe even hurt.

"Please go," she whispered, barely able to get the words out.

Joel shook his head. "No. I intend to have what you so freely give to everyone else. Your days of denying me are over."

"Don't do this, Joel. You'll regret it, I promise."

He took hold of her dress at the neckline and tore the material down the bodice. "The only regret I have is that I didn't do this sooner."

"It's not what you think," she pleaded. "Joel, I've never been with a man. I swear it. You may have all your jealous thoughts, you may imag-ine the worst—but I swear it's true."

He stopped, looking at her oddly. "I don't believe you."

Panic swept through her like a fire. "I'm not lying. I'm a virgin. I may not act the part, but I've always remained that way—I do have my scruples."

"Saving yourself for marriage, eh?" His voice took on a sarcastic tone. "Well, consider this your wedding day."

———

Hours later, Joel left Valerie's room in a sense of euphoria. Who would have believed the woman was chaste? Not that it mattered now. She was his. Now she'd have to marry him or face the embarrassment of her ruined reputation. He might have even managed to get her pregnant. What a delight that would be. She'd have to marry him in a hurry or lose her precious social standing in Charleston. Perhaps Joel would push for a Christmas wedding. That would give them enough time to finish this trip and settle back into a more normal routine.

He could see it all now—a beautiful Charleston wedding with all the right people in attendance. He would never be fully accepted as one of them because he was a Yankee and there still existed long, wounded memories of the War Between the States. Still, with Winthrop backing him, society would play their part. They might talk about him behind his back, but to his face they would be the epitome of graciousness.

Smiling to himself, Joel felt as though he could move a mountain. Rufus Keegan had proved a rather unpleasant inconvenience, but that was behind him now. Keegan could no longer cause him trouble or make threats. He shook his head and frowned, remembering the man's audacity. Keegan had said he would relay damaging information to the senator should Joel not bring him into their folds immediately instead of waiting for the election. Foolish man. No one threatened Joel Harper and got away with it.

Systematically, Joel would take care of each problem and see his life put in order. Tomorrow night would bring him victory—sure and sweet. He had Valerie where he wanted her. He had the senator eating out of his hand. And now Keegan was out of his way.

He paused at the top of the steps to glance back at the door to Valerie's room. He thought he might feel some small measure of regret, but none came. He'd only taken what was rightfully his to take. There'll be no more Luke Tolands or Rufus Keegans or Andrew . . . what was his name? Shrugging, Joel smiled. It didn't matter what his name had been. He wasn't a problem anymore.

CHAPTER NINETEEN

alerie stared up at the ceiling and wondered how her life had ever come to such a tragic place. She had no idea how long she'd lain there. Minutes? Hours? Days? Still too stunned to move, she nevertheless felt the pain and misery of her encounter with Joel. Closing her eyes against the images, Valerie wished herself dead.

How could anyone be so hateful and cruel? Joel had taken her innocence with hardly any more concern than if he'd been stepping on a bug. He'd appeared only momentarily stunned to realize she had been truthful about her claims of purity. But it didn't stop him. He'd laughed then, and she could still hear the sound ringing in her ears.

He had told her, even as he raped her, that she was a worthless and stupid woman. He told her that he only placed himself in her life in order to get what he wanted from her father. Then he threatened her with worse if she dared to breathe a word of his admission.

Valerie was used to using others, used to moving them like pawns in her game, but this time she'd been on the receiving end. And it wasn't at all the innocent act she'd thought it to be.

For years, she had convinced herself that the goal justified her poor behavior. Now she knew that wasn't true. It had taken Joel's attack to make her see the lie, however.

Rolling to her side, Valerie simply wanted to hide away in her room until her father decided it was time to leave the Grand Canyon. How she hated this place! Her entire life had ended here—nothing would ever matter again. The parties no longer offered her their magical illusions. Those wonderful moneyed people she often kept company with were of no interest. They couldn't make things right again—not that a single one of them would ever care.

She wept softly into her pillow. A parade of faces came to mind—

Andrew, Luke, and so many others. She'd played with them, teasing them with her flirtations. She'd visited Luke in his cabin—knowing full well he'd never take advantage of her. She'd known she could take the game as far as she wanted with him, and that he'd stop when she told him to. Unlike Joel.

She cringed, still feeling his breath upon her. Sometime during his attack he'd had the audacity to tell her that she needed him.

"You'll see it in time, my dear," he had whispered against her ear. *"You'll see how much you need me."*

But she didn't need Joel or anything he had to offer. Luke had said she needed God, but she was certain God didn't need her. Especially not now.

"You've brought this on yourself," Joel had said as he dressed to leave her. *"I might have reconsidered if I'd truly believed in your innocence. Of course, there's nothing to be done now, but when you look in the mirror, you'll see exactly who brought this to pass."*

For all her flirtations and wild encounters, Valerie had always managed to get away from difficult situations just in time. There was a certain thrill to her game. She would take herself almost to the point of no return, then turn and flee before life and its mongers could take from her what they would. Now all of that had changed. Joel was right. She'd brought this on herself, and now she had to live with the consequences. Or die with them.

She dozed off and on, refusing to get out of bed. The shadows of the day shifted, changing as the hours passed. Nightmares robbed her of any peaceful sleep. She couldn't close her eyes without seeing Joel Harper staring back at her.

Hearing someone at the door to her room, Valerie held her breath and stifled her sobs. The door opened and the image of her nightmare took shape. Had he come to hurt her again?

"What are you doing just lying there? Have you been there ever since I left?" Joel questioned, turning on a light. "You're hosting a party in less than an hour's time. Get up and make yourself presentable."

"I'm not going," she answered flatly. There was nothing else he could do to her. She wasn't about to cower in fear.

"Oh yes, you are," he said, coming to the bed. Reaching out, he grabbed her arm and pulled her from the bed. She collapsed on the floor at his feet, clutching at the tattered remains of her dress. "Get up!" he commanded. "Get up and stop acting like a child."

Valerie could hardly think, much less make sense of his purpose.

"Why are you here? Haven't you caused enough damage?"

"I haven't begun to cause damage," Joel said with a laugh. He crossed the room to her wardrobe and pulled open the doors with great flourish. "Oh, here, wear the scarlet gown. That suits you perfectly."

"I'm not going."

"Yes, you are. You aren't going to give me any more trouble," Joel stated, walking to where she sat on the floor. "You think I've done the worst thing to you—worse than anything else I could do—but let me assure you, my dear, that's hardly the case."

She looked up at him and met his hateful gaze. "I despise you."

"And I despise you. You're a willful, spoiled child who's had everything handed to you on a silver platter. You may have Daddy wrapped around your little finger, but you don't have me in such a position."

Valerie felt anger surface where numbness had been only moments before. Surprising them both, she leaped to her feet and raised her hands to Joel's face. She would have scratched his eyes out, but he took hold of her wrists.

"Good to see you back among the living."

"I wish it had been you who'd died instead of Mr. Keegan," she said, trying to pull away from his hold.

"No doubt that is true. It certainly would make your life less complicated, eh?" He narrowed his eyes, his brows pulling together. "Now get ready for the party. You have exactly half an hour and then I drag you out, dressed or not."

"I need a bath."

"Then take one, but be quick about it," he said, releasing her and pushing her away from him. "Oh, and one other thing, Val darling," he said sarcastically, "I know I mentioned it earlier, but I'm concerned that you might not have been paying attention. Say nothing about what happened here today."

Valerie lifted her chin defiantly. "Why? Are you afraid Daddy might send you packing if I tell him the truth?"

"I'm afraid something might well happen to *you*. You see, we mustn't let anything upset this campaign. We must keep your father in the forefront as the most positive and beneficial candidate for the job of the presidency. Having a lunatic daughter won't help his cause. Although having a dead daughter just might."

Valerie tried to keep the fear from her voice as she replied, "I suppose having a raped daughter would only cause problems for the rapist. Perhaps Daddy could receive public sympathy over the fact that his aide not only raped his campaign treasury, but his daughter as well."

"And who would believe such fabrications? After all, most everyone here, as well as elsewhere, knows full well that the daughter in question has lived life in a most provocative manner. You're already known to do as you please, with whatever man you please to do it with."

"I was a virgin. You stole that from me," she managed to say.

"And who would believe that?" he questioned. "You dress in such a manner to suggest yourself quite free and easy with your favors. You hang on the arm of every man who shows you attention—you let them handle you in ways that make decent people turn in disgust. Who would ever believe such a nonsensical declaration?"

She shook her head, tears forming in her eyes. "You know it's true."

He grinned in wicked delight. "Yes, of course, but I'm the only one who does know it for sure. And if pressed, I'll certainly say nothing of the fact—rather, I'll take the public's admiration and even sympathy for agreeing to marry such a promiscuous woman. I can manage to produce a dozen witnesses who will all swear to having been your lovers.

"No one will ever believe you, Val. If you declare me to be a rapist, I'll merely speak to the issues of your sanity and bring in my friends to declare you quite the liar. Were sexual freedoms not already a somewhat socially acceptable thing in certain circles, you might already be facing four walls in a sanitarium—or perhaps some quiet little convent in Europe. Just remember that. Remember, too, I can produce enough information on you to prove whatever I need to prove. Even to give reason, after your father's successful election to the office, for why his darling only child should end up miserably taking her own life."

Valerie shuddered. "You're mad. You've caused the death of people and you have no remorse whatsoever."

Joel shrugged. "It's rather like being hired to remove vermin. I do the job and eliminate unpleasant and nonproductive people from the world. Generally people don't want to know the details of what I do, and neither do they care. They simply want the job done. I'm needed, my dear, for there will always be vermin."

"Too bad you can't eliminate yourself," she muttered in reply.

"Now, Val, you don't mean that." He smiled at her as though he thought himself to have some special power over her.

"I hate you," she blurted.

"The feeling is mutual. I've never loved you and probably never will," Joel said matter-of-factly. "You've been nothing more than a stepping-stone to what I want. If I could kill you and still have what I want, nothing would give me greater pleasure."

Val felt as though he'd struck her. She'd never believed him to really care, but she'd never anticipated such hate. "You'll be sorry."

"Not nearly like you will be if you dare to interfere with me again." Joel took a step toward her, and Val, still clutching her torn dress, backed up against the wardrobe. "After all, you forget I know all of your little secrets. *All* of them. Do we understand each other?"

Valerie trembled from head to toe. "I understand. Better than you can imagine."

Joel smiled. "Good. Then we should get along famously."

Val took up her toiletry items and headed into the private bath, defeated. It was more than the rape. It was the knowledge that she would have to face every day of her life with this monster as her master.

Closing the door between them, Valerie began to cry anew. There was no hope. Everything was gone. Everything had suddenly become very ugly. Death would be so much easier.

————

Alex looked at her mother in exasperation. "Why can't you tell me what happened?"

Her mother looked back toward the window. Her petite form seemed swallowed up in the nearly floor-length gray dress she wore. "I don't want to talk about any of it."

Alex had pleaded with her mother for answers all day long, and always, it was the same answer. Alex tried to stress the urgency of the situation once again. "But, Mother, they could put you in jail for murdering Father. If you continue to refuse to tell them what they need to know, they'll send you away from me."

Katherine Keegan looked back to her daughter. "I can't talk about it. Please don't ask me to."

Alex went to her mother and hugged her close. "I'm sorry, Mother. It's just that there is so much that needs to be explained. No one understands what happened. I know you didn't push Father over the edge. I know that within my heart. But if you won't talk to them and tell them the truth of who did murder Father, they'll presume you guilty. You could even face death yourself." She pulled back and looked into her mother's face.

"There are worse things than death," her mother replied. She moved away from Alex and turned back again to the window.

"I love you, Mother. It hurts so much to see you suffer. Just like it hurt all those years watching Father—"

"Don't speak ill of the dead, child. He can't hurt anyone any more."

Her words were cold, almost emotionless. Alex felt a shiver run up her spine. "Mother, how can I help?"

"There's nothing anyone can do now. I'm a prisoner here, I'm sure."

"But if you weren't?"

"Then I'd rather be away from all this fuss."

"I'll arrange it then," Alex said, suddenly getting an idea. "We'll hide you away while the entire matter is investigated. I know of a cabin—it's been closed for repairs so none of the staff is living there. It doesn't have electricity, but there is a small bathroom. We'd have to put up thick blankets at the windows so that you could light a candle or lamp, and I could bring you food."

Her mother turned around to face her. "Do you really think that's possible?" It was the first real interest she'd shown all day. "I'm weary of the reporters."

"I'll arrange everything," Alex replied, hoping she wouldn't regret her words and get her mother in more trouble for her exploits. Perhaps Alex could even speak with those in charge of the investigation. "I'll go now and see what I can manage." She kissed her mother on the cheek and hurried to find the ranger who'd questioned her the night before.

———

"I can pretty well guess who gave you the idea that I might have something to do with Keegan's death," Luke said, barely keeping his temper under control. "Joel Harper feels that I've overstepped my bounds by telling him to stay away from Alex Keegan. He imposed himself upon her, and I put him in his place."

"It doesn't matter who brought the accusation to our attention," the stiff-backed ranger said. "The fact is you've always been a suspect because you were there when the others arrived. With Mrs. Keegan refusing to cooperate, you are next in line."

"I didn't kill Keegan," Luke said flatly. He stretched his jean-clad legs out in front of him and tried to relax. He had nothing to hide. He needed only to rest in the Lord and wait for the truth to be revealed. "If anything, I think you should seriously consider Joel Harper."

"Why?"

"Because he seems the type to eliminate obstacles. Keegan might very well have been giving him trouble."

"If that's the case, why would Mrs. Keegan remain silent on the matter?"

Luke shrugged. "I have no idea. I would imagine the woman is pretty lost in her grief and shock. This wouldn't be the kind of thing a person would get over easily."

"Was Rufus Keegan alive when you came to the canyon rim last night?"

"I don't know. He wasn't there, if that's what you're asking. I heard the screams and came to see what the trouble was. When I got to the rim, I found Mrs. Keegan alone. She'd collapsed to the ground and was crying. I helped her up and she told me, 'Rufus has gone over the edge.' Then she said nothing more—she just cried."

"How is it that you know her so well? Well enough that she'd allow you to comfort her?"

Luke leaned forward again at this. "She was in shock. She'd just seen her husband fall off the edge into the Grand Canyon. I doubt seriously she would have cared who held her while she cried. Nevertheless, she knew me through her daughter Alex. We're good friends and have worked together for the last four years."

"Did you have any reason to want Rufus Keegan dead?" The man narrowed his eyes as if to ascertain the truth in what Luke was about to say.

"No. I hardly knew the man."

"I understand you'd had an encounter with him some time back. An encounter that revealed him in a compromising situation with one of El Tovar's Harvey Girls."

"I did." Luke refused to offer any more information. If the man was going somewhere with this line of questioning, then Luke would let him do the leading.

"Did he threaten you then?"

"I don't recall that Mr. Keegan has ever threatened me."

"What did he say to you?"

Luke shook his head. "I don't recall word for word. He made some suggestive comments about his daughter and me."

The ranger seemed to perk up at this. "Comments that made you mad?"

"They certainly didn't make me happy."

"Were you mad enough to kill him?"

"No." Luke had reached the end of his patience. "You know, I've willingly answered all your questions. I'm not of the habit of lying and, while I realize you know very little about me, there are plenty of people here who can vouch for my character—many of them wear ranger uniforms." He got to his feet. "I wouldn't see killing a man as the solution to anything. Human life is valuable in the eyes of God—no matter who that human life belongs to. Therefore, I value it as well. Now, if you'll excuse me, I need to get back to work."

"As long as you're a suspect in this investigation, I'll need to advise you that you cannot leave the area."

Luke turned and frowned. "What did I do to deserve that mandate?"

"You were in the right place at the wrong time," the ranger said matter-of-factly. "And right now things aren't looking all that favorable for you—after all, as you pointed out, Mrs. Keegan is a small woman hardly capable of manhandling her husband. You, on the other hand—"

"I have a broken wrist," Luke interrupted, holding it up as if to offer evidence.

"It wouldn't keep you all that encumbered, Mr. Toland. Besides, Mrs. Keegan could have helped you as well."

"This is outrageous," Luke said. "You may have a job to do, but I'm innocent and expect you to treat me as such. The real killer is out there. That's where your focus needs to be."

"Just the same, you need to keep me apprised of your whereabouts. You aren't to leave the South Rim."

———

"I don't like the idea of moving her," the ranger told Alex. "I can't see why it should matter."

"It matters because she's withdrawing from everyone. She feels as though everyone is watching her every movement. The reporters are hounding her in spite of your men's efforts to keep them at bay. Why, this afternoon one of the men from Los Angeles threw rocks at her window until we were sure he'd break the pane."

The older man looked sternly at Alex. "Where would you move her?"

Alex quickly told him of the cabin. "You could post a guard in a discreet location. Somewhere in the trees where no one would see him watching the cabin. He could even be posted inside the cabin for that matter. Don't you understand? She's not about to leave without permission. She's a delicate old woman in a fragile state of health."

"I realize that. It's the only reason she hasn't been sent to the jail in Williams. By her own admission, she was alone with your father at the time of his death."

Alex felt her stomach tense at this reference. "Look, I don't care what the situation looks like, I know my mother didn't kill my father."

"She's not telling us who did," the man replied.

"I know," Alex said, feeling defeat wash over her. Perhaps it was a bad idea to suggest moving her mother. Maybe she would have been better off if they had taken her to Williams. At least in jail the reporters wouldn't have as much of a chance to pester her.

"I just want to protect her. Not from having to provide the truth, but from accusation and unnecessary grief. She's mourning my father's death and the reporters will not let her be. She's become a tourist attraction. If you need to move her to Williams, then do so. Either way, I just want to give her some peace."

The man studied her for a moment. "She'd have to have a guard. The sheriff is on his way and until we conclude our investigation or additional proof is given to refute what currently appears to be true, she's our prime suspect."

"I understand, but she's not guilty. I promise you that much. Please . . . please, just help her."

He sat in silence for several minutes. His gaze never left Alex's face. Finally he cleared his throat. "Look, I'm going to let you do this," the ranger announced, "but only because the reporters are making my life just as miserable. How do you propose to move her without the press knowing her whereabouts?"

Alex could hardly believe her ears. "I've got an idea."

After explaining her plan to the ranger, Alex went in search of Michaela. Within the hour Alex, Michaela, and Bernice had managed to arrange everything. Taking Bernice with her while Michaela kept watch on the back stairs, Alex put her plan into action.

"What is this?" her mother asked as Bernice came into the room carrying a Harvey uniform.

"We're going to sneak you out of here," Alex said. "I've even managed to get the ranger's permission."

"You what?" Katherine questioned, a look of hope filling her expression.

"I told them how difficult it's been for you here. They've agreed to let you move to a secluded cabin. A guard will be posted in the cabin with you, but otherwise they will endeavor to leave you alone until they decide what's to be done."

Katherine looked to Bernice and then back to Alex before sitting on the edge of her bed. Just as quickly as the hope had come, it seemed to flee. "What do you suppose is to be done?"

Alex went to her mother and knelt on the floor in front of her. "Mother, you have the public's sympathy. People are even protective of you. The mayor of Williams is here and stated publicly that you could not possibly have caused your husband harm—that you're a pillar of the community. The entire staff of El Tovar believes in your innocence, and I've heard it rumored that the Winthrops are even hiring a private investigator."

"No!" Katherine exclaimed. "No more investigators."

Alex studied her mother's face. She seemed almost panicked. "Mother, what is it that you aren't telling me?"

In spite of Bernice's presence, Katherine reached out to take hold of Alex's shoulder. "There are things that are better left unsaid. I can't talk about this. Please try to understand."

"But I don't," Alex said flatly. "You are suspected of causing Father's death. It's only because of your friends and public opinion that they haven't already whisked you away to Williams and jail."

"Alex, whatever happens, you must understand that I've done what I felt best. Just trust me, please."

It was then that Alex knew for certain her mother was hiding the truth. Before, Alex had told herself the moments of the murder were just too horrific for her mother to face. Better still, that her mother hadn't even been there when the murder had happened. She'd tried to convince her heart that her mother had said nothing to the officials because she had nothing to tell. But now she could see for herself that wasn't the case.

Nodding slowly, Alex spoke. "I'll try to do as you ask, but if it all begins to turn against you, you must tell them the truth. God would want no less from you."

"I know," her mother answered sadly.

Alex helped her mother dress in a Harvey uniform and planted a large straw hat upon her head.

"Keep your face down and stay in the middle of us. If we pass other people, just keep looking to the ground. Hopefully they won't be able to tell the difference."

When the coast was clear, they hurried down the back stairs. The guard had just forced several newspapermen to the top of the stairs and was to follow later in order to throw off any suspicions about the women.

Alex heard the ranger reprimand the press for interfering in his job. The men protested loudly demanding their rights to report the truth. Alex pushed her mother past the stairs, laughing and murmuring something inaudible to Bernice.

Michaela joined them outside, giving the appearance of a friendly group of co-workers out for a stroll. It was a scene often observed at El Tovar, and they figured this to be the best way to avoid suspicion. Whenever they passed by hotel guests or reporters, they giggled like schoolgirls and put their heads close together, as if telling secrets. Alex saw the fear in her mother's eyes, but she kept moving forward.

It was agreed between the three Harvey Girls that each one would take turns bringing food and supplies to Katherine Keegan and her guard. Alex could only pray they wouldn't need to leave her there for long. The place was positively dingy, and Alex feared it would only add to her mother's depressed spirits.

"I have to go work at the party the Winthrops are giving now," she told her mother. "In fact, I'm already late. You remain here and I'll come to you as often as I think it safe."

"There's no need to fuss over me, dear. I'm not running away or going anywhere. I don't wish for anyone to worry after me. I'm sorry for the trouble," she stated, saying more than she had since Alex's father had died.

Alex hugged her mother, wishing to herself that she could turn back time and spare her mother this misery. Yet at the same time, Alex felt guilty because she wasn't all that sorry her father was gone. She was sorry he'd died without Jesus in his life. She was sorry he'd been so mean and adulterous. And she was sorry that she'd never known a time when she felt her father had really cared about her. But she wasn't sorry he was dead.

Leaving her mother safe and secure, Alex headed back up to the hotel at a run. She knew she needed to get back to the matters at hand. She needed to make an appearance at the party and assure people that all was well. She needed . . .

"Whoa, there!" Luke said, reaching out to steady Alex with his one good arm. "I don't think I've ever seen you run like that."

"Sorry . . . I . . . didn't see . . . you there," Alex panted.

He continued to touch her, rubbing his fingers along her upper arm. "I'm glad we ran into each other." He grinned. "I've needed to talk to you."

"I know, but things have been so crazy. I'm late for the party," she said, her voice steadied a bit.

"Surely they don't expect you to work—your father just died."

"Mrs. Godfrey tried to force me to take time off, but I can't. I'd go mad sitting there thinking of everything that has happened."

"They might see you as unfeeling—maybe even involved in the murder if you don't show some sorrow in his passing," Luke suggested. "I don't want them to get the wrong idea about you, Alex." He reached up and gently touched her cheek.

Alex's breathing and heartbeat continued to race. Luke's touch ignited feelings in her that she had never thought herself capable of. All she could remember was his kiss, his touch, his scent.

She dared herself to look into his eyes. What was happening to her? Why were all these feelings coming to the surface now, after he said his feelings had changed? Would he go away with Valerie Winthrop? Was there no hope of a future for them?

"I don't care what anyone else thinks," she managed to whisper.

"But you should. You don't want to give them cause to turn the light on you."

"Let them!" Alex declared, finding her voice. "I haven't done anything wrong. I may not show all the proper etiquette of mourning, but I've done nothing I should be ashamed of."

"They think I'm a suspect," Luke threw out.

This instantly sobered Alex. "But why?"

"Because I was there."

"But you didn't come until after the screams. Just like the rest of us."

"But it's my word against theirs."

Alex shook her head. "You can't be serious."

"I am. Joel Harper—at least I'm pretty sure it was him—suggested that I might have reason to want your father dead."

"No!" Alex gasped. She saw Joel Harper disbanding her support of friends and family, piece by piece. Had the world gone suddenly mad? *God, where are you in all of this?* First her mother, now Luke. How many more would have to suffer before the truth was brought to light?

*O*n the horizon, storm clouds brewed and churned in the early morning light. Alex noticed the ugly blackness from her window and silently prayed it would rain all day and night. Tonight the gala party to end all parties was planned by the Winthrops, and already the idea wearied her to the bone. The events the night before were sedate and small, compared to what she would face tonight. Tonight, the candidates would each announce their desire to receive the nomination for president, and their cronies would expound on their capabilities and positive qualities.

Even more guests were pouring in on special trains, and Alex knew it would be impossible to pause for a moment's rest once her workday began. Not that she wanted to rest. The night had been impossibly long, and knowing her mother was the prime suspect in her father's murder, with Luke a close second, did nothing to offer her comfort. Once again her father was ruining her life.

Father. Alex had tried not to think of her father, for it was a painful chore she'd tried to avoid. She had so long wished him out of her life—out of her mother's life—but now that he was, she felt rather confused. What plans should they make? Would her mother be freed to go about her business and live out the rest of her life, or would they assume her guilt and jail her? If freed, would her mother want to remain in Williams or go elsewhere? And always in the midst of these thoughts, Alex felt guilt overcome her peace. She'd never cared enough to share the Gospel with her father. Never cared enough to approach him with anything but her anger.

"You can't hand your daughter over to your vulgar friends and expect anything but anger," she said to the room. Her words reverberated off the windowpane right back at her, even as thunder rumbled in the distance.

Turning from the window, Alex felt a sense of loss. Her spiritual peace felt ripped to shreds. The truths she'd known and honored for most of her life seemed little comfort. Her father had wounded her so often that Alex had lost count. He didn't deserve to be mourned or cared about. He didn't deserve her love or sorrow.

She sat down at her writing desk and brought her hands together in her lap. She tried hard to muster up some feeling other than anger, but short of bitterness and regret, she found nothing she could give in the wake of her father's passing. Mrs. Godfrey had offered her time away from her job to tend to her mother and deal with her father's death, but Alex had declined. Her father's death still seemed unreal. She had hardly known anything of the man.

"God, I don't mean to be so hardhearted," she whispered. "You know that has never been my desire. Every time I had an encounter with Father, I tried so hard to remain at peace with him. I tried to respect his position in my life, even if I found it nearly impossible to respect the man himself.

"I wanted to have a close family. I wanted to believe he could change and remain faithful to my mother, but instead he only grew worse." She blinked back tears. "He hurt my mother so much, Lord. How do I forgive that? How do I put this to rest and let go of my hatred and bitterness? How?"

———

Alex joined her co-workers as they met to discuss the day's events and the evening party. Mrs. Godfrey seemed rather frazzled, even though the hour was still quite early.

"We have a few additional staff coming from along the Santa Fe line here in Arizona. The girls will act as hostesses on the lawn," Mrs. Godfrey explained. "Michaela and Alex will be in charge of the lawn teams. There will be five girls in each group. A supper is to be given, as well as refreshments after the speeches. As I understand it, there will be festivities until well past midnight."

Several of the girls groaned, Alex included. Her job required she get up at five every morning as it was. Now they were suggesting she work until midnight or one and still have enough sleep to pull a full shift the following morning. Politicians and their madness had corrupted the gentle beauty and peace of her canyon park. The entire thing only served as one more incident to deeper harden Alex's resentment toward the Winthrops and Mr. Harper.

"You'll all help with breakfast here in a few minutes," Mrs. Godfrey announced, "then after the morning rush, Michaela and Alex, along with whomever they choose to help them, will see to the lawn tables. I have lists of necessary articles," she said, leaning forward to hand Alex a piece of paper. "This entire event will run smoothly and without problems, if you adhere to the list."

When the meeting broke up, Alex went to the private dining room and made certain her table was set properly for breakfast. She adjusted pieces of silverware and replaced a chipped plate before leaving the room to retrieve steaming pots of coffee. This was the routine with the Winthrop party. They would no doubt want the same thing today as they had on all the other days.

True to habit, the Winthrop party, this time minus Valerie, showed up at exactly seven o'clock. Joel Harper seemed to be in particularly good spirits, talking in rapid-fire to the man on his left, laughing and gesturing as they took their seat at the table. Alex wondered what could have the man so gleeful at this hour, but she didn't care enough to position herself close enough to overhear the conversation.

"Miss Keegan," the senator said, taking her aside, "I am so very sorry about your father. He seemed a good man, and I would have enjoyed having him on my staff."

"I'm sure he would have enjoyed that as well," Alex said, feeling hard-pressed as to how she should reply.

"I'm also sorry about the nonsense with your mother being held suspect. I'm certain such a dear sweet woman could have had nothing to do with such an ugly act." His drawled words were soothing.

"Thank you, Senator Winthrop. I'm certain of her innocence as well."

"I've decided to help the matter as best I can. I've hired a trustworthy man I know to do a private investigation for us. He lives in Dallas, but he should arrive by train this afternoon."

She was touched that a stranger should care so much about her mother's innocence as to spend his own money on seeing her name cleared. She also remembered her mother's panic at the thought of additional investigators. It didn't make sense to Alex, but she wouldn't say anything about it. Her mother wasn't thinking clearly—that was all. "That's kind of you, Senator," Alex replied.

"Not at all. Not at all." He hooked his thumbs in his vest pockets and smiled. "The real interest here is truth. We want the truth to be told so that we can lay your father to rest without this stain upon your family's good name."

Alex nodded and excused herself to begin taking the breakfast orders. Most everyone stuck to a routine of the same type foods. One man always ordered dry toast and iced, poached eggs. Another wanted three grapefruits and a banana. They were as eccentric in their food orders as they were in their choices of companionship.

The meal ran smoothly, without so much as a raised voice until a panic-stricken man in a wrinkled blue suit appeared at the door to the dining room. "I'm ... sorry ... to interrupt," he said, gasping for breath. "I just got the news and knew the senator would want to know."

"What is it?" the senator asked, while everyone grew silent to see what the trouble was. The scene mesmerized even Alex. She stood frozen, a pot of coffee suspended from her hand.

"It's President Harding," the man said, his breathing coming in a steadier pace. "He's dead."

"What!" several men called out in unison.

The murmuring between them started out low and built quickly into loudly expressed comments of disbelief. Only Joel sat in silence, a smile touching the corners of his mouth, and in that moment Alex knew that he'd somehow had something to do with the president's death. His gaze met hers and refused to let her go. Alex felt the malice of his soul reach across the table as if to take hold of her.

"Do they say what killed him?" Winthrop asked, pushing back from the table.

"They aren't certain. He grew ill several days ago. They thought food poisoning might be to blame. It was rumored he'd eaten cherries and milk on his journey down from Alaska."

The senator nodded solemnly. "A deadly combination to be sure. Still, it seems unlikely that the president of the United States would have no one to warn him of such matters." The senator looked to his comrades in the room. "I suggest we adjourn and see to this news. If this proves to be true, we will need to postpone our announcements and party until another night."

Alex watched as the men filed out one by one, following after the senator as though they were sheep to a shepherd. Joel got up from the table at a leisurely pace, but instead of following the entourage, he moved toward Alex with a smug expression of satisfaction.

"You see, I told you I had ways of dealing with troublesome situations. You should have no doubt about the harm I could cause you, should you bring even the tiniest hint of trouble my way."

A thought suddenly came to Alex. She put down the coffeepot and braved her question. "Did you murder my father?"

Joel laughed, then moved closer and lowered his voice. "I wish I could take credit for that. I had planned to push Jastrow over the edge of the canyon—but then, you probably overheard that mentioned when I spoke to your father that night. Keegan's death ruined my plans, for you can hardly have two people fall within days of each other—especially from the same gathering of politicians.

"Besides, what do you care? You hated the man. Even now I see the contempt you hold for him written in your expression. Why should you care who did the deed so long as it's done? You could just as easily have pushed him over the edge as your mother."

"My mother is innocent. She had nothing to do with Father's death!" Alex protested loudly.

Joel put his finger to her mouth and pressed against her lips. "Shhh, darling, you don't want to raise the suspicions of others. If they hear you speaking of death, those ink slingers will hardly care what the truth is. They're after a story—the more sensational, the better."

Alex stepped back and pushed his hand away. "They're hardly going to care about my father's death, now that they have the president to contend with."

"But then, you hardly care about his death either," Joel said snidely. "Funny thing, you hated the man, made clear your utter and complete distaste for him, yet the two of you were so much alike. Dealing with you was like dealing with a younger version of him. Ruthless. Cold. Calculating."

Alex slapped Joel hard across the face, then backed away. "Don't *ever* compare me to him again." She started to leave, but Joel took hold of her and pulled her close.

"You're really disgusted by such a comparison, aren't you? Poor Alex. Didn't you ever see the truth for yourself? You're just like him. You're strong, just like he was. You're opinionated and bold, just like he was. You're ruthless and care little for things that don't concern you, and you rush to judgment about anything that doesn't fit in your perfectly ordered little world."

His words hit her hard. The truth of them scared Alex in a way that she'd never experienced. *I am like him,* she thought. *I am as horrible and awful a person as my father.*

"Let me go," she said, not even bothering to fight back.

Joel seemed surprised by her reaction and released her. "You think that I've just insulted you, but frankly, it's a compliment. I'd like to win you over to my side. There's a great deal I could do with a woman like you. Let me move you to Washington once we've won the election, and I'll show you just what I'm talking about."

Alex shook her head. "You sicken me. You arrange the death of the president, then talk of making me your mistress? Have you no soul?"

"None that I'm aware of—thankfully," Joel mused.

Alex felt a cold shiver rise up the back of her neck. "Leave me alone, Mr. Harper. I have no desire to even speak with you. Light has no communion with darkness."

"But what of shadows and shade?" he questioned. "Might those two compliment each other? The contrast of such brings beauty and grandeur to the canyon—might it not do the same for a man and woman?"

Alex felt sickened. She picked up her tray and left the dining room without another word. Harper stayed where he was, not following her for once. But it didn't matter. His words followed Alex, and they were enough to haunt her throughout the day.

————

The parties were canceled, and within an hour after breakfast, a storm moved in and poured monsoonal rains on the canyon park. Alex busied herself helping with lunch and then found other odd jobs that needed her attention. By the time the storm moved out in the late afternoon, leaving the canyon and El Tovar washed clean, Alex still struggled to find peace. Approaching the kitchen a few minutes before she was scheduled to work the evening shift, Alex heard Mrs. Godfrey call her name.

"Miss Keegan, would you please join me in the office?"

Alex put down the tray, her hands trembling as she moved to join her supervisor. Joel's comments rang over and over in her head. *"You're just like him."*

"Miss Keegan, this is Mr. Stokes, the investigator hired by Senator Winthrop, and Sheriff Bingham. They've come to ask you some questions about your father."

If I were given to fainting, now would be the time, she thought. The stern expressions of the men standing before her, coupled with Joel's startling revelation and added to the events of the last few days, were enough to send anyone into a faint. But Alex stood firm, though she now found herself full of doubts.

"Whatever I can do to help," Alex replied, "but my shift is about to start."

"Don't worry, Alexandria. I have someone taking your place. You're to have the remainder of the day off. You may use my office as long as necessary, gentlemen," Mrs. Godfrey said, moving to the still-open door. "I'll be seeing to my girls. If you need anything, just ask Miss Keegan for help. She knows the place nearly as well as I do."

"Thank you for your hospitality," Mr. Stokes said.

His frame reminded Alex of one of the tall cactuses she'd seen near Phoenix. Slender of build and rather gangly of limb, the man maintained a gentle countenance that put her at ease. The sheriff, on the other hand, seemed so tense and observant that he made Alex feel as though she were under a magnifying glass. He frowned at her as if she'd just done something rather disgusting. The expression reminded her of a time when she'd been a young girl of twelve. She'd taken an interest in a boy at church. Her mother thought it amusing, but her father was put out by the entire matter. He'd looked at her just as the sheriff did now, declaring the boy and his family far beneath the Keegans. Worse still, he'd caused the boy's father to lose his job and the family eventually had to move away.

"Please have a seat, Miss Keegan. We know you're no doubt mourning your father's loss, but if you would be so kind as to help us for a few moments, I assure you it would be to your benefit."

"I don't mind helping you. I am anxious to clear my mother of any suspicions."

"And you wouldn't help us if it didn't clear her name?" the sheriff asked.

"I didn't say that," Alex replied coolly. If they thought to catch her in lies, they might as well save their breath. With the shock of her father's death still wearing on her and her mother's unwillingness to cooperate, Alex felt she had no other choice but to be open and honest. At least to the best of her ability.

She took a seat in one of three chairs that had been arranged in front of Mrs. Godfrey's desk. The sheriff surprised her by walking to the chair behind the desk rather than taking one of the other two chairs beside her.

"Miss Keegan, I understand you were working the night your father died," Mr. Stokes began. He took the chair beside her, turning it so that they faced each other, more or less.

"Yes. I was serving in the capacity of hostess to the Winthrop lawn party and dance."

"And your hours of service for this event?"

"We were called to the kitchen by five-thirty and began arranging tables for the affair within the hour. The party was set to begin at eight o'clock and I was either on the grounds or in the kitchen the rest of the evening."

"And of course there were witnesses to verify this?" Stokes asked.

"Yes."

"And at any time did you leave your post to meet in private with your father?" the sheriff questioned.

Alex turned to the man. "No. My father and I did not get along, and I had no desire to seek him out."

"Why was it you didn't get along?" Stokes interjected the question in his calm, soothing tone before the sheriff could react.

"My father was a womanizer. He was also a cheat and liar. He scoffed at the beliefs held by my mother and I—beliefs of faith and high morals. He had little use for either one of us or our ideals and, in turn, I had little to do with him."

"Did you want him dead?" the sheriff asked, not to be outdone by Stokes.

Alex thought for a moment, searching her heart for the truth. She slowly shook her head. "No, not really. I wished him to be out of my life and out of my mother's life. But in all honesty, I didn't want him to die in order to accomplish that."

Stokes picked up the interrogation again. "Did your mother feel the same way?"

"I don't really know. My mother is a very private person. Whenever I tried to encourage her to leave him, she refused. She always held on to the hope that he would change. When she came here to El Tovar, I knew something was different. She was now telling me that she wanted a divorce."

"I see. And what was your father's response?"

"He didn't want one," Alex replied, feeling that she had to tell them the entire truth of their encounter. "What he did want was a post in Washington. He supported Senator Winthrop's nomination for the presidency and planned to ride along on his success. He didn't want anything to hinder that, and a divorce would have cost him an unwelcome scandal. He threatened my mother and me and told us to let the matter drop."

"Threatened you? How?"

"He didn't really say. I threw out a comment, asked what he would do to keep us silent, and he said that people were likely to die every day or something like that. It was the first time he'd threatened my life, and it stunned me."

"You and your mother are very close, aren't you?" Stokes asked gently.

"Yes, we are. I care a great deal about her welfare."

"Which is why you asked the rangers here to let you move her to an undisclosed location?"

"Yes."

Stokes nodded. "I suppose the attention from the reporters and such was starting to be a problem."

Alex had no idea what the man wanted from her. She didn't appreciate his around-the-bush questions and said so. "Look, if you want to ask me questions, then please just ask them. If you want to know if I think my mother pushed my father into the canyon, then the answer is no. My mother weighs all of ninety pounds and my father must have weighed at least two hundred, maybe more. She's frail and unhealthy and there is no way she could have caused him that kind of harm."

"But she did have a motive," the sheriff said flatly.

"We all had a motive," Alex answered angrily. "My mother had motive. I had a motive. Half the people here at El Tovar—forget that— half the people of Arizona had a motive for wanting my father dead. But someone is responsible and I cannot tell you who that person is. I'm not even convinced my mother can give you that name. She and I have talked, and she hasn't divulged anything beyond the pain she's enduring."

"Is that because she can't or because she won't?" the sheriff asked, his eyes narrowing as if he might scrutinize the answer from her.

Alex shrugged. "I honestly don't know." She remembered Joel and her father conspiring and, although the Winthrops had paid for this investigation, she hoped the sheriff was impartial enough to want to hear the truth. "I do know, however, because I overheard the conversation myself, that Joel Harper and my father were plotting and planning against the senator's competition. Mr. Harper talked of eliminating the competition in whatever manner necessary. My father agreed. Mr. Harper has since implied to me that he has caused problems for other candidates and will stop at nothing to get his man elected."

Instead of getting angry, both men smiled at her. "Miss Keegan, that certainly doesn't imply murder," Stokes said. "I can understand you're filled with worry over your mother's situation. So much so, no doubt, that you would say anything to keep her from going to jail for your father's murder."

At this Alex decided she'd had enough. She'd hoped they might listen, but she could see that they believed her to be nothing more than a faithful daughter lying for her guilty mother. Getting to her feet, Alex looked first to the sheriff and then to Mr. Stokes. "I'm a Christian woman. I am not in the habit of lying. I've answered your questions as best I can. Good day." She crossed to the door and opened it.

"Miss Keegan, please sit down. We're not finished with you yet," Stokes said sternly.

Alex felt the room close in as the sheriff got to his feet. "There are some important questions that we, as of yet, do not have answers for."

"Such as?"

"Well, for starts, it's been suggested that you or your mother might have hired someone to kill your father."

*A*lex froze in place, unspoken words stuck permanently in her throat. She looked at Mr. Stokes, unable to read from his expression whether or not he took the comment seriously.

"Please sit down, Miss Keegan, you look rather pale."

She shook her head, almost afraid that if she did as she was told, they might actually find a way to accuse her and judge her guilty.

"Someone remembered you threatening Mr. Harper," the sheriff threw in. "You said something about pushing him over the edge. Do you remember that?"

Alex thought back to her first encounter with Joel Harper. The night he'd pinched her and caused her to break a tray full of dishes. He'd wanted her to join him at the rim after dinner, and she'd said . . . The memory sickened her. She'd joked about pushing him over the edge. Someone in Winthrop's party had obviously shared that little story with the sheriff and Mr. Stokes. No doubt that someone was Joel Harper or Valerie Winthrop. Both had reasons to implicate her.

"Miss Keegan, you must admit it looks rather suspicious that you would suggest such a thing in regard to Mr. Harper, only to have it later happen to your father," Stokes said softly. "Given the things your father did to bring embarrassment and disgrace on you and your mother, perhaps you felt you needed to take matters in your own hands, eh?"

"I can't believe this," Alex said, finally finding the words. "I would never hurt anyone. I can't even imagine resolving my problems in such a manner."

The sheriff laughed in a humorless manner. "You imagined it quick enough when putting Mr. Harper in his place."

"People have fallen over the edge before. The canyon is full of dangers and it is something often spoken about amongst the workers here. After all, we live with this danger on a daily basis. I wasn't serious about what I implied, I was trying to defuse a rather testy moment. Mr. Harper was being too free with his hands and needed to be put in his place. As for the similarities, hear me once and for all. I didn't kill my father, nor did I hire it done. I resent that you would question my character when you know nothing of me."

"We can only go on what we've been told in our investigation. Do you have someone who can vouch for your character?"

Alex could scarcely believe this line of questioning.

"I, for one, can vouch for the character of this woman," Luke Toland said, joining the party uninvited. "But since I'm also a suspect in this whole sordid affair, that probably doesn't hold much weight. I'm sure Mrs. Godfrey and at least a dozen other people, however, could vouch for Miss Keegan. I heard what you just said, and I can tell you from my knowledge of her over the past four years, there's no way in the world she'd even consider such a thing. Now, I'd personally like to talk to whoever is telling such lies."

Luke took a protective stand at Alex's side. In spite of his casted forearm, he looked for all purposes like a lion about to spring should anyone threaten his lair.

"Now, mister, don't go getting all uppity and stickin' your nose in where it don't belong," the sheriff said, coming from around the desk. "This is a private matter."

"Hardly," Luke replied, the anger building. "I'm Lucas Toland. I was summoned here to speak to a Mr. Stokes, and I'm supposing that's one of the two of you."

"I'm Stokes."

"Yeah, well, I'm not impressed. Is it your plan to badger my friend and her mother? Because if it is, I'm going to have to put a stop to it."

"I'm sorry, but this young woman and her mother are suspects in this investigation. By your own acknowledgment, you are also a suspect, Mr. Toland. After all, you were with Mrs. Keegan when the murder was discovered. For all I know, you and Mrs. Keegan were lovers and you did the old man in so that you could run away together. Or perhaps you were paid by Miss Keegan and her mother to kill Rufus Keegan."

"Of all the low down . . ." Luke stepped forward, grabbing Stokes by the lapels of his suit. His broken wrist seemed to cause him little trouble in getting his point across. "You have no right to talk in such a vulgar manner—especially in front of a lady."

"You seem awfully upset and defensive for someone who is claiming innocence," the sheriff said, reaching out to push Luke back.

"I ought to deck the both of you, and were I not a Christian, I might do just that."

"And you'd go to jail too," the sheriff said. "I'm Sheriff Bingham, and I won't tolerate any cowboys coming between me and truth. I've dealt with your kind before, and I can see to it that you're no trouble to me at all."

Alex felt as though she were watching a play. Worse yet, she felt she had been pulled from the audience and forced into a part she didn't know. She waited for someone to tell her what her lines should be—where she should stand—but no one said a word.

Without warning her eyes filled with tears and a sob broke from somewhere deep in her chest. Her breath came in ragged gasps. "Stop!" she screamed. "Stop it now!"

She turned and ran down the hall and out the hotel. She didn't stop running until she was well down the rim path, past the Lookout, past the studios. She was nearly to the Bright Angel Trailhead when Luke caught up with her and took hold of her. Spinning her around, he pulled her into his arms with such force that he nearly knocked the wind out of her as she slammed against his chest.

Spending her tears against his well-worn shirt, Alex didn't fight his hold. She felt such hopelessness, such despair. Luke was keeping her from throwing herself over the edge—maybe not literally, but certainly figuratively.

"I can't believe this is happening," she said, clinging to him tightly, almost afraid he'd push her away.

"I know, darlin', and I'm sorry."

"It's just too much, given everything else."

Luke gently tipped her chin up so she was forced to look into his eyes. "As much as I love holding you, why don't we sit down and talk this out? I want you to tell me everything. I want to talk about us."

His words brought back her biggest fears. Fears of Luke going away. Fears of him siding with the Winthrops. She loosened her hold and her words tumbled out. "I don't know if I can. I don't know that it would be a good idea. I know you have plans. Plans that will take you away from here—from me."

"They don't have to, Alex."

She looked up and met his warm expression. "But I know about the ranch—about Valerie Winthrop and her father."

"What are you talking about?"

Alex shook her head. "You don't have to hide it. You don't have to worry about my feelings. I already know. Miss Winthrop told me everything."

"Then maybe somebody better tell me, because I don't have a clue as to what you're talking about."

Alex had never known Luke to lie to her. She studied him for a moment, then raised her apron to dry her eyes. Swallowing hard, she drew a deep breath. "Miss Winthrop told me her father had offered you a ranch in Wyoming—a ranch that you would manage as your own. She said the senator thought you would make a good husband and . . . father. . . . I just figured . . ."

"You figured wrong," Luke said. He reached out and took her face in his hands.

The hardness of the cast's molding around his left hand rubbed against her cheek, but she didn't care.

"Alex, you figured this all wrong. I should have straightened this out weeks ago when I had the chance. Maybe even months ago."

Alex felt her heart race, and a tingling started where he had touched her cheeks. The sensation edged along her neck and spread throughout her body. *What's happening to me? Is this love? Am I in love with Luke Toland?*

She moaned slightly at the thought. *I can't be falling in love—not now.* "But you said . . . I mean when I mentioned the ranch you didn't deny it."

"I'm buying my own ranch," Luke replied. "My brother sent me an advertisement about a ranch in Wyoming. It was just about the right size and already had a place to live and outbuildings. It had nothing to do with the Winthrops."

"But Miss Winthrop said . . ."

"Miss Winthrop is a liar," Luke said firmly.

He continued to rub his thumbs against her cheeks. Alex felt as if her face were on fire. "But you're still going away."

"Not without you," he replied, lowering his mouth to hers. "Not ever."

His kiss was slow and sweet. He pressed his right hand against the back of her head as if to pull her more deeply into the experience. Alex felt herself yield to the warmth and sensation of falling. Nothing like this had ever happened to her, not in all her life.

He lingered over the kiss, then pressed his lips against her cheek, her nose, her eyes. "Ah, Alex, do you know how long I've waited to do this? How much I've longed for this . . ." His voice trailed off as his mouth came back to hers. He kissed her again, then pulled away.

Alex, lost in the feeling of free falling, felt as though she'd landed rather abruptly. Opening her eyes, she looked at Luke, struggling to regain control of her breathing.

"Alex, I'm buying the ranch in order to offer you a home. You and your mother, if she'll join us."

"I don't think that would . . . I think . . ." She shook her head. "I can't think."

Luke laughed and wrapped her in his embrace. "You don't need to think right now. Just say yes."

"Yes? Yes to what?"

He laughed even harder. "I guess I never did ask you, did I?"

She shook her head again, not at all sure she understood what was happening.

"I'm asking you to marry me, Alex."

Her thoughts cleared with those few words. Suddenly ugly memories of her father's infidelity came rushing back. Other images came too. Valerie Winthrop with her arms wrapped around Luke. Joel Harper's unwelcome advances. It was too much, and Alex pushed Luke away and started to walk up the path.

"Wait! What are you doing?"

"I don't know," she said, refusing to stop or even look at him.

"Then come back here and talk to me."

"I don't think I can."

Luke took hold of her arm and drew her back around. "I think you'd better."

"It's just that . . . oh, Luke, you've been a dear friend to me. You've been the only man I could talk to and feel safe with."

"So what's the problem?" Luke asked, his brows knitting together in worry.

"Marriage is built on trust and love. I don't know that I could ever trust any man. That's why I've always avoided any kind of relationship. Any kind except the friendship I have with you."

Luke grinned. "Let's deal with one thing at a time. First, you said marriage is built on trust and you struggle with that. But I notice you didn't say anything about struggling with the love part."

Alex felt her cheeks grow hot. "I can't talk about love when I can't figure out the trust issue. I mean, what about the past? What about my father and people like him?"

"Do you think I'm like him?" Luke asked seriously.

"I . . . never . . ." She looked away. "I don't think you're like him, but you're a man. Flesh and blood. Men have been unfaithful since the beginning of time. There are all kinds of examples in the Bible."

"Alex, I don't deserve your distrust based on the actions of someone else. If that were the case, I could say that you were just like Miss Winthrop or those trollops your father dallied with. I saw you in Joel Harper's arms the other night. I could accuse you of throwing yourself at him, and in fact, I did worry that maybe you'd gone to him for help, but Michaela set me straight."

"You'd really think me capable of—"

He put his finger to her lips. "I was wrong to suspect without any basis for the truth. I let presumption push me to suspicion. Just as you're doing with me."

His statement struck a nerve and hit her heart straight on. She'd never considered how it might be if someone perceived her on the same scale. She suddenly felt very ashamed of her attitude. Every man deserved to be dealt with as an individual. They weren't all men like her father . . . or Joel Harper.

"Oh, Luke, I'm sorry. Of course you're right. I never thought of it that way. It's just that I've been so surrounded with men who—"

"The past is not important, Alex. I'm asking you to put the past behind you and build a future . . . with me."

She looked into Luke's eyes and saw the love reflected there—love for her. It wasn't fair to believe him to be like her father or his cronies. It wasn't right to anticipate that he would cheat on her should she marry him. But the problem wasn't with Luke, she realized. The problem was with herself.

"I'm sorry, Luke. I've been so unfair to you. I don't deserve your kindness or your . . . your . . ."

"Love?" he asked, reaching up to touch her cheek. He gently stroked the smooth skin of her face, mesmerizing her with gentleness.

"Yes," she whispered.

"Alex, I don't love you because you deserve it, although you do. I love you because of who you are and who I am with you. I'm a different man with you, a man I can live with. My heart used to be all hard and bitter before you came into my life. Now I know God really cares about me, and I believe He's brought us together for a reason."

He moved to draw her into his arms once again. The cast felt cold against her shoulder, but his embrace warmed her to the core. How could she possibly walk away and never experience this warmth again?

"Alex, give me a chance to prove to you that I can be worthy of your trust. Give me a chance to show you that not all men do the things your father did. Please . . . give us a chance. Please trust me."

Alex thought of all the misery she'd endured since coming to the Grand Canyon. It was always Luke who transformed her day from bad to good. She thought of the way he'd kept her secrets—he deserved her trust.

She took a deep breath. "I overheard my father talking with Joel Harper. I think Mr. Harper has schemed to kill Mr. Jastrow, along with anyone else who plans to compete against Senator Winthrop—including President Harding."

He looked at her in disbelief. "You truly believe Harper has had something to do with the president's death? That seems unlikely. He's been here all along."

"They accused me of hiring someone to kill my father. Why does it seem so farfetched that Mr. Harper could hire someone to kill the president? After all, he has plenty of money to use for whatever he needs." Alex felt better for having told Luke the truth, for trusting him, but she had no idea where her words would lead them.

Luke pulled away, the expression on his face betraying his concern. "If this is true—if he's not just trying to sound threatening to you and the others—this is a whole lot worse than I'd imagined."

"I would guess that Mr. Harper does nothing to merely sound threatening, Luke. I think he's very dangerous, and it wouldn't surprise me at all if he was the one responsible for my father's death."

"But your mother was there when it happened. She surely wouldn't try to protect Harper."

"Not unless he was threatening her," Alex countered. "But I don't honestly know what he could use against her. He might have known about the fact that she wanted a divorce, but everyone would have found out about that sooner or later. No, if my mother had witnessed Mr. Harper killing my father, she wouldn't have a single reason to keep it from the authorities."

"That's not true," Luke said, looking even more worried than he had before. "She'd have one very good reason . . . you."

Nothing was going right for Joel Harper. The grand gala to announce Senator Winthrop's candidacy for president and Joel's engagement to Valerie was to have been the culmination of everything he had worked for, but now all that had changed.

"I think for the benefit of the nation and for our good name, we should return to South Carolina," the senator told his group over breakfast. "The death of our president should be properly mourned."

Joel couldn't repress a laugh. "Two days ago we were talking about how incompetent the man was. Now we're going to pretend to care about his death?"

"No pretense, Joel. I do care about his death. I care about his family and the pain this loss will cause them. I care about the vast number of supporters who will be devastated at this news," the senator replied.

"The immoral women of Washington, D.C., are the supporters who will miss him most," Joel said with a sneer. "No doubt those wretched creatures will have to find some other means of support."

"That's enough, Joel. There's nothing to be gained by such talk," the senator commanded. "We'd be seen as worse than opportunists if we were to continue with a party and politics as usual. It would ruin our campaign."

"I agree," Laird said. "I never cared for the man one whit, but I won't be accused of refusing him the respect due the office. My secretary is securing our train passage at this very moment."

"As is my daughter," Winthrop replied.

So that's where she is, Joel thought. He'd figured her to be hiding in her room, cowering away, avoiding him. The thought had given him great pleasure.

"I instructed her to get us tickets for the first available train," Winthrop added.

Joel wasted little time asserting his views. "It will take time to gather our things, pay the bills, see to our entourage."

"Exactly so," the senator replied. "We'll leave someone here to see to it all."

Joel shook his head, trying desperately to think of a way to buy time. "It will be difficult to bring everyone together in one place again. This is a prime opportunity, and we'll be less than responsible to our supporters if we walk away from the campaign now."

"No one is walking away from the campaign," the senator said firmly. "There are plans to be in Los Angeles in October and, of course, we can always reschedule our own event either here or back in South Carolina."

"But it's not the same. The momentum will be lost," Joel said, fearing his plans would completely unravel. He wanted to eliminate Jastrow before leaving the canyon, but he could hardly explain that to this group.

"The momentum is already lost," one man at the table threw in.

Joel narrowed his gaze, marking the man as an enemy. "The people are shocked, naturally. But this is the time to move forward and remind them that Calvin Coolidge will take the office of president and that we need to—"

"No, Joel. I generally agree wholeheartedly with you," the senator interjected, "but this time, I must object. Proper etiquette demands we show our respect."

"But you can't leave without letting the people know your intentions," Joel said, quickly trying to think of how he might convince the senator to at least give one last party. "You may desire to save your official announcement for the presidency, but the people who've come here deserve to hear you say something about this entire matter."

Joel could see the senator's expression grow thoughtful and felt a small twinge of victory. "Remember," he added, "the people are rather like sheep waiting to be herded and told what to do. You've instructed them to come, and come they have. Now you want to just leave them to their own devices. That would certainly spell disaster for you."

"Well, I suppose you have a point, Joel. When I discussed this with Valerie, she said we should head for home immediately," the senator drawled in his slow southern manner. "But I suppose she wouldn't object to a brief gathering, one in which we could share our condolences with our supporters. Maybe even give them some idea of our future arrangements."

Joel began to breathe a little easier. He'd deal with Valerie later—punish her for attempting to thwart his plans with her influence over her father. But for now he'd help the senator decide what was to be done, and then he'd step up his plans for Jastrow.

Two Harvey Girls entered the room to serve breakfast and Joel immediately noticed neither one was Alexandria Keegan. It was as if the entire world was attempting to foul up his day. His feelings of elation over what he'd managed to accomplish with the president were fading fast in the face of these minor defeats. He toyed with a fork while waiting for the dark-haired Harvey waitress to serve his plate.

"Where is Miss Keegan?" he questioned.

The woman eyed him with a look of disbelief. "Her father was murdered."

"Yes, I know that. She was about her business yesterday, so I presumed she was attempting to keep busy."

"I believe she and her mother are planning the funeral," the girl offered and said nothing more.

"Remind me to send her an extra bonus," the senator told Joel. "Her work was exemplary, and I want to reward her."

Joel nodded but said nothing. He pushed the food around on his plate and tried to calculate what needed to be done to control the most damage and return order to his plans.

With the others talking amongst themselves, the senator leaned over to talk in a hushed whisper. "Joel, I know you're disappointed, but there are several factors we must consider. Our public will expect us to offer them comfort and hope. You see, what happened to President Harding could just as easily happen to the next president. We must be prepared to show them our strength, without looking as though we have no feelings for the situation at hand."

Winthrop drew a deep breath and continued. "There are also matters we need to discuss privately, between the two of us."

"You and me?" Joel questioned, not liking the idea.

"Yes. You see, I'm concerned about Valerie. She's not feeling well—in fact, the last few days she's been most unhappy. I'm not at all comfortable with forcing her to announce her engagement when she's feeling so poorly."

His words came as a blow to Joel's ego. "She's just succumbing to the heat and excitement. She might even be struggling with the tragedy that has occurred here."

"Nevertheless, we'll wait a week or two and let her recover."

The words were given without room for protest. The senator didn't even wait for a response as he turned back to his companions to offer his ideas for the evening's event. Joel felt his temper rise, but there was no way he could let it become evident.

"If you'll excuse me," Joel said, putting his napkin aside, "I believe I could use some air."

He exited the room, narrowly missing the Harvey Girl who entered bringing coffee. He pushed back several tourists and made his way through the hall and up the stairs. Taking the steps two at a time, he made his way to Valerie's floor and proceeded to her room. Taking the key he'd managed to buy off one of the bellboys, Joel opened the door to find the room completely deserted. The bed stood pristine, in freshly made order. The nightstand was void of Valerie's book and other accessories.

A search of the wardrobe and bath revealed the same. She had removed all evidence of her presence. Where had she gone? What kind of game did she think she was playing?

He slammed the door behind him and stood in the hall momentarily. His own room was at the end of the corridor, with Winthrop's suite situated between his room and Valerie's. He walked toward the senator's door, thinking to knock and see if Valerie had hidden herself in her father's room, but just as he approached a maid came out from the room.

"Excuse me," Joel said, smiling and putting on his best display of charm. "Could you tell me if Miss Winthrop is inside?"

"No, sir. There's no one in there."

"Do you mind if I look for myself?"

The woman shook her head. "I can't let another guest inside the senator's suite."

Joel pulled several bills from his wallet. "Not even for this?"

––––––––

Luke knew he had no conclusive evidence to prove Joel Harper's plans, but armed with Alex's information and his own suspicions, he intended to meet with the rangers. Most of these men knew him well after ten years at the canyon. They knew his character and the way he conducted business. If they were going to learn the truth about Harper, someone was going to have to listen to reason.

He had nearly reached El Tovar when he spotted Valerie Winthrop coming back from the direction of the train depot. Luke thought momentarily to hide from sight, but then reconsidered. The woman might very well be willing to offer up information vital to his task. After all, who would know Joel Harper better than the woman he intended to marry?

She spotted him and smiled. Gone was the enthusiastic greeting and flirtatious temperament Luke had been forced to deal with on so many occasions.

"Hello, Mr. Toland," she said softly. She actually looked past him, rather than at him.

Luke noted that she had dressed conservatively in a brown tweed skirt and jacket. A peek of a turquoise-colored blouse could be seen at the top of the jacket, but otherwise there was no other hint of color. It was a far cry from the flamboyant and daring fashions she'd worn before.

"How are you today, Miss Winthrop?"

She surprised him by refusing to meet his gaze. It was almost as if she was embarrassed. "I suppose I'm as well as one can be, given the news."

"Yes, it's quite a blow to hear about the president."

She finally turned her gaze upon him. "You know, I've been thinking about the things you said."

Luke started at the change of subject. "What things?" He knew his tone sounded suspicious, but Valerie Winthrop had been a real thorn in his side.

"The things about God. I suppose hearing about the president's death and, of course, Mr. Keegan's . . ." She shuddered. "Well . . . I guess . . . I just wondered about what you'd said. You talked about turning to God and never being alone."

"That's right." Luke pushed aside his suspicions. If she wanted to know about a relationship with God, he needed to be open to that.

"Well, it just seems that my life is rather . . . well . . ." She sighed and looked past him to the canyon. "I feel like nothing is going right. I feel alone, and yet there are so many people who play a part in my life." She shook her head. "I know none of this probably makes any sense to you."

"It makes perfect sense, Miss Winthrop." Luke prayed for the right words. "Without a rightness to God, nothing is ever really put in order.

We're just going through the motions. We get up in the morning and go about our affairs, meet with our friends and deal with business, but something is always missing."

She looked rather shocked and nodded. "Yes. Yes. It's exactly that. I know I've been rather outspoken and the manner in which I've treated you has been inappropriate, but I really want to better understand what you're talking about. My mother—she was religious. I know she spoke about God, but I never listened. My father insists we go to church every Sunday, but I'm not sure that it's for God's sake so much as for the sake of public approval. After all, everyone goes to church."

"Not everyone, Miss Winthrop. But even so, going to church isn't enough. It's not about being religious, either."

"Then what?"

He kicked at the dirt and chose his words carefully. "It's about putting your trust in God. It's about letting Him take control—putting the past behind you and seeking a newness in Him."

Several guests approached, talking in animated conversation about the death of the president. Luke stepped aside in order for them to pass by. He tipped his hat at the ladies and received their nods, while the men in the party did likewise for Valerie Winthrop. Luke was surprised to watch her acknowledge them briefly, then turn away. Gone was any hint of a desire to flirt and be the center of attention. In fact, if Luke hadn't known better, he'd have believed she would just as soon have been swallowed up by the earth.

Once the visitors had passed, Valerie let out a long breath. Luke could see she was relaxed to be once again alone with him. What did it all mean?

"Can God care about someone like me, Luke?" she asked, forgetting her earlier formality of calling him Mr. Toland.

"Of course He can. You aren't the worst sinner to ever walk the earth, neither are you the least. We're all just sinners to God, and He deals with each one of us as an individual child."

"Yes, but I've done things in my life, things that will have lasting consequence." Her lower lip quivered and tears came to her eyes. "You know how I've acted. Does God know too?"

Luke felt sorry for the lost woman. "He does, Miss Winthrop. He knows how you've acted and He knew how you would need Him. He knew it long before you were even born."

"That's hard to believe."

"But true."

She looked him square in the face. "But aren't there times when you feel lonely? When you feel like the rest of the world has deserted you and you're all alone?"

At one time Luke might have perceived such questions as a come-on, but not now. He realized she was searching, nearly crying out for understanding.

"I used to feel that way. I felt like I was all alone after my mother died. I didn't understand why God would take away someone I needed and loved. But you know, over the years, now that I've put things right between God and me, I don't feel that way. I might feel a sense of being by myself and maybe want to be with other people, but I'm never lonely. I know God is there for me. I know He's walking right beside me."

"But there are so many people I've wronged. You included."

Luke smiled and pushed back his hat. "I forgive you."

"You do?" she questioned. Her tone was one of disbelief.

"I do," Luke assured.

"But I lied to your . . . to Miss Keegan. I made her believe . . ."

"I already know about all of that," Luke admitted. "And I still forgive you."

She looked at him with an expression of wonder. "And God does the same thing?"

"When you ask Him to, and you're truly sorry, then God forgives you. You can ask Him to help you not make the same mistakes again."

Additional groups of tourists were on the lawn now, some heading down the path toward them. Valerie grew noticeably uncomfortable, and Luke couldn't help but glance over his shoulder to note Joel Harper was heading down the rim path toward the Lookout studios.

"I have to go," she whispered. She moved toward the hotel.

"Sure." Luke didn't try to stop her. "I'll be praying for you, Miss Winthrop."

She stopped and turned around at this. "Would you, please? Will you truly pray for me?"

Luke felt awful inside at the realization that he should have thought of this a whole lot earlier. "Of course I will. Alex will too."

Valerie bit her lip and nodded. "Thank you." She started to turn, then surprised Luke by coming back to him. "Might I further impose?"

"I suppose that depends on what you need." He smiled, trying to appear lighthearted about the whole thing.

"Would you mind meeting me this evening? I'd like to talk to you more about these God matters."

Luke shook his head. "I don't think it would be appropriate for us to meet alone."

Valerie nodded. "I wasn't suggesting that. I'm not entirely sure what my father plans. We were to head home today, but the trains are booked. We can't head out until tomorrow morning. With the cancellation of the gala, there doesn't seem to be much purpose in continuing our stay. At least that's what he and I decided this morning. Hopefully Mr. Harper hasn't changed Daddy's mind. I think it would be in the poorest of taste if we were to continue campaigning in the wake of the current president's death."

"I can see what you mean."

"Anyway, if there is to be some sort of gathering, I'll send you word. I'd like you to be my guest. Otherwise, let's simply meet after supper in the lobby. There should be plenty of people there."

"All right," he said, hoping it was the right thing to do.

"Thank you."

She seems sincere enough, Luke thought. He watched her enter the hotel quickly and disappear from sight. *Lord, I don't know what's gotten into her, but I'm sure it's for her good. Let her understand the truth about you. Let her desire to know you more.* His prayer seemed such a pittance. *I should have been praying for her all along. Instead of being angry with her or worried about my relationship with Alex, I should have concerned myself with Miss Winthrop's eternal soul.*

Realizing he'd forgotten his meeting with the rangers, Luke refocused his energies. He would continue to pray for Miss Winthrop, but for now he needed to speak with the authorities and see what could be done to figure out the murder of Rufus Keegan and what, if anything, Joel Harper might have had to do with it. If the man had a hand in killing the president of the United States, surely he'd have no problem at all in eliminating a man such as Keegan.

*M*other, you must tell them what you know. If not them, then tell me and I'll tell them," Alex pleaded. "You can't let the responsible party get away with murdering Father." Alex had just been given the word that the authorities were going to take her mother to Williams and formally charge her with the murder of Rufus Keegan. The fact that they were giving up on the investigation simply because there were no other viable options or suspects was tearing Alex apart.

"You don't know what you're asking, Alexandria," her mother replied.

Alex felt only a marginal sense of achievement. At least her mother hadn't dismissed the matter completely.

"I know they're talking about moving you to the jail in Williams. You're the prime suspect and they mean to charge you with Father's murder if you can't prove otherwise."

Alex took ahold of her mother's hand. "Please, Mama, don't let them send you to jail for something I know you didn't do. If Joel Harper is responsible for this, then you must tell the authorities. If he's threatened you or me, you must ignore it and let the law deal with him."

Her mother shook her head and looked down at the floor. "Mr. Harper is in no way to blame for what happened."

"How can you be sure? If it was another man who pushed Father, then perhaps Mr. Harper hired it done. The man is ruthless. He would stop at nothing to see his precious campaign won."

"It wasn't Mr. Harper's doing," her mother insisted. "Please, just let it be."

Alex stepped away from her mother and tried to figure another path of reasoning. "There was someone else there that night, wasn't there? You weren't alone."

Her mother said nothing but turned uncomfortably, glancing at the door. The ranger had agreed to wait outside while they talked, but his presence was very evident.

Determined to have an answer, Alex confronted her mother. "Who are you protecting?" Alex questioned.

Katherine Keegan put her hand to her mouth as if to keep the words from flowing out. Alex's knees trembled. Her mother really was protecting someone. All this time, Alex had only guessed that it could be one of many possibilities. She feared that her mother had been threatened and that this was the reason for her silence.

"Mother, please."

Her mother lowered her hands, twisting them together anxiously. "I can't. Now that you've guessed this much, please understand. I can't say anything more."

Alex walked the rocky path back to El Tovar, more frustrated and worried than ever. Her mother was protecting someone, but whom? Why would her mother be willing to go to jail for a murderer? There were few people—Luke and Clancy, Mrs. Godfrey, Michaela, and a few other Harvey Girls—who showed her mother the slightest bit of respect or courtesy. It just didn't make sense for her mother's loyalty to run so deep. Alex knew she wouldn't rest until the truth came out for everyone to see.

Then Alex began to let her imagination run wild, and for just a moment Luke's image came to mind. Was her mother protecting him? Could it be possible he had taken Alex's frustrations and pain and decided to put an end to her father's life?

"No," she said, shaking her head vigorously as she entered the kitchen.

"What did you say?" Michaela questioned.

Alex looked up and realized several Harvey Girls as well as two of the kitchen staff were watching her as if she were about to impart some great truth to them.

"Nothing. I'm just muttering to myself."

"Well, when you get done with your own company," Michaela teased, "Mrs. Godfrey has asked to see you in her office."

Alex nodded and took off down the hall to see what Mrs. Godfrey required. Knocking on the open door, Alex peeked her head inside. "You wanted to see me?"

Mrs. Godfrey nodded. "Come in and close the door."

Alex eyed her curiously for a moment, then nodded. Closing the door behind her, Alex walked to the desk. "What's this all about?"

Mrs. Godfrey handed her an envelope. "Senator Winthrop brought this by earlier."

Alex took the envelope and opened it. "Oh my." She counted at least a hundred dollars more than she'd been promised from the Winthrop group. "What's this all about?"

"The senator praised your work, sympathized with your circumstances, and said he wanted you to have this. He was very complimentary and said that in spite of knowing you often faced difficulty with his group, you were the epitome of graciousness and charm."

Alex sat down opposite Mrs. Godfrey and shook her head. "I've never hated working with a group of people more than I have the Winthrops. It was only the love of God that kept me on the job."

"Perhaps the senator understood your misery."

"Maybe. I don't know that he could really focus on anything other than his campaign and his plans for the presidency."

"People are often deluded, blinded even, by the goals they set," Mrs. Godfrey said in agreement.

The words went straight to Alex's heart. "I know I've been guilty of that, but hopefully no more."

"Alex, I wanted to talk to you without anyone else around. I know you're struggling with a great many issues right now. I realize there is pressure to find out exactly what happened that night with your father. Given this and everything else, I feel I must require you to take a few days off. I know you wanted to keep working. I know, too, that there was no real love lost between you and your father, but I see a weariness in you—a state of mind that would benefit from rest."

Alex eased back in the chair and considered Mrs. Godfrey's words. "I suppose you would know better than I would." The idea of a rest didn't seem so bad. "I thought keeping busy would help, but it hasn't."

"I presumed as much. Do you feel like talking about it?"

Alex appreciated her motherly concern. "I've tried to talk with my mother, but she's not of a mind to listen right now."

Mrs. Godfrey nodded, her tightly curled gray hair barely moving with the motion. "She's no doubt consumed with her own emotions. I'd like to help if I can. You girls are like daughters to me. I never had children, and after my husband passed on, I always longed for a daughter to give me companionship. Now I have a dozen or more at times and I find I love the camaraderie."

Alex smiled. "You've been a good friend to all of us. And believe me, if I knew how to put my feelings into words, I would. But I find myself a mix of emotions—from guilt to frustration to sorrow."

Mrs. Godfrey's sympathetic expression put Alex at ease. Where her mother had clearly closed the door to communication, Mrs. Godfrey seemed eager to help. "I've been praying for your peace of mind. I know that your father was less than helpful in your life. I know he grieved you on many occasions. But he's gone now. He can't hurt you anymore."

"But that's just it. He is hurting me. His death is unresolved and my mother stands at the center of controversy once again. It's almost as if he's still determined to torment and torture her further."

"Have you spoken with your mother about what happened?"

Alex sighed and cast her gaze to the ceiling. "I've asked, I've cajoled, I've begged, and I've pleaded. She won't talk to me about what happened. She knows full well what occurred. Of this, I'm convinced.

"We were planning Father's funeral this morning and I tried to reason with her. They'll take her to jail in Williams if they can't find any conclusive proof to show she's not responsible for this." Alex brushed aside the tears that came unbidden. "She's going to go to jail, Mrs. Godfrey. And all because she's protecting someone else."

"But who?"

"That's just it. I have no idea." Alex met her supervisor's gaze. "I have no idea and because of that, I am helpless. Besides those involved, God alone knows what happened that night. And He sure isn't saying a word about it to me."

"I understand. Just know that I'm here to talk to," Mrs. Godfrey encouraged. "I care a great deal about you, Alex. I know your days here are probably numbered. Your mother will need you now, no matter the outcome of this matter. You'll go your way . . . but just know how much I care."

Alex smiled in spite of her tears. "I do know, and I very much appreciate it."

That evening, Alex milled about the grounds, her spirit restless in her idleness. She'd worked so hard over the past four years, she'd scarcely taken time for herself. There were occasional outings with Luke or some of the other girls, along with trips home from time to time, but over all, she'd chosen to work.

"I worked because I wanted to free my mother from her misery, and now . . ." She let the words trail off as she suddenly realized she was speaking them aloud. "My goal blinded me to so much."

Looking out over the canyon, Alex wondered silently about the days to come. Everyone here at the canyon, including the rangers, seemed very protective of her mother. They'd certainly gone the extra mile by allowing Alex to seclude her mother away from the crowd. They'd spoken to the reporters, who had reluctantly agreed to leave the woman alone. The matter had only been helped by the death of President Harding. The smaller news of her father's death paled in comparison to the pain of the nation.

Turning to gaze back on the structure she'd called home for four years, Alex sighed. Her life here at El Tovar had been a good one overall. She'd made friends and she'd always felt safe, unlike her life at home.

People were gathering in front of the steps of El Tovar's main entrance. Alex had learned that Mr. Jastrow and Senator Winthrop were going to announce an end to their festivities and a postponement of their bids for the Democratic nomination for president. She was surprised, but pleasantly so. She reached into the pocket of her skirt and lightly fingered the envelope from Senator Winthrop. Perhaps they weren't all such bad people. Maybe Valerie was spoiled and self-centered, but she was only portraying what had probably been acceptable behavior for all of her life. Alex felt her heart soften a bit in her thoughts of the entourage. The only exception was Joel Harper. She knew him to be the snake he appeared to be. She could only pray he'd be caught red-handed at his schemes. She knew no one would ever believe her if she told them what she knew. After all, she'd tried and the investigator and sheriff had merely laughed her off.

Then there was the issue of her father. She could still hear Joel's comments on how much she was like him. *I am headstrong and determined. Although,* she reasoned, *those could be good qualities if used properly.* Her father's actions, however, always bordered on cruelty.

Oh, God, I don't want to be like him. He broke my mother's heart, and mine as well. When other girls were strolling hand in hand with their fathers, when they played together at picnics or went to the fair—oh, how I envied them! She looked back at the canyon and let the colors blur together, not really seeing anything in particular. *I know I have you, Father, but was it wrong to desire an earthly father too?*

"Penny for your thoughts."

She turned and met Luke's smiling face. Just seeing him here, all dressed up in his finest suit of brown serge, gave her heart a start.

"Why are you dressed to the nines?" she asked, trying to put her introspective thoughts aside.

"I was invited to attend the gathering tonight. I wanted to find you first, however."

"Why?"

"The invitation came from Miss Winthrop." Alex frowned but said nothing as Luke continued. "She's been asking me about God, Alex, and I think she's sincerely seeking."

Alex put aside her twinges of jealousy and smiled. "I hope she is."

"Besides that," Luke continued, "I want to talk to her about Harper. I figure if anyone can help us to figure out his part in your father's death, it will be Valerie. I also want to watch Harper. I had a long talk with my ranger friends this afternoon. I told them what you'd shared with me and that I thought there was merit in checking it out."

"And did they listen?" Alex asked hopefully.

"To a point. They said they'd keep on the lookout for anything unusual, but that just because Harper spoke in such a manner didn't mean he meant to act on it. He might have been trying to impress your father."

"I know what I heard. It wasn't a matter of impressing anyone."

"I believe you," Luke said, reaching out for Alex's arm. "Now, I want you to believe me when I say you have nothing to worry about in regard to Miss Winthrop." He pulled her toward him and began to walk along the rim path. "I'm not the least bit interested in what she has to offer, but I am interested in you. Have you been thinking about us?"

"A little," she answered honestly. "Frankly, the events of the past few days have rather overwhelmed me. I can scarcely think of anything but the fact my mother is protecting someone with her silence."

Luke stopped and looked at her long and hard. "Keep praying about it, Alex. The truth is bound to come out."

"I know. I just hope I can bear it when it does."

He smiled. "God won't ever give you more than you can bear. Just remember that. You once told me the same. Now I'm going to join Miss Winthrop, but my main desire is to keep track of Joel Harper. I don't want you in any danger, but perhaps you could keep focused on Jastrow and where he is at all times."

"That should be simple enough."

"Good. I'm confident we can figure this out together," Luke said, then surprised her by leaning over to kiss her forehead. "This will have to do for now."

Alex felt a ripple of excitement course through her as his lips touched her skin. She longed for a real kiss but knew such a public display would be uncalled for. Especially at such a time as this.

Alex watched Luke stalk off across the lawn, wishing he would remain at her side. She understood his plan, but nevertheless, his absence was sorely felt.

"Alex!"

It was Michaela, and the look on her face told Alex something was wrong. "What is it?"

"Your mother is gone. She's not at the cabin and neither is her guard."

"What? How can that be?"

"I went there to take them some supper, but they're gone. I asked the first ranger I caught sight of, but he didn't have any idea what had happened either."

Alex went cold inside. Surely they wouldn't have taken her mother to Williams without telling her first. Convinced that something more sinister was afoot, Alex insisted, "We must search for her."

Michaela nodded. "I'll let the others know."

Alex was frantic to reach Luke, but the speeches had already begun and Bradley Jastrow was expressing his regret over the death of President Harding. Alex moved toward where Luke stood with Valerie Winthrop when she found herself halted by Joel Harper.

"Miss Keegan, I'd hoped I might run into you. You see, there's a matter I think we should discuss."

"I haven't the time or desire, Mr. Harper." She tried to jerk away from his ironclad grip, but he held her fast.

"It would be most beneficial if you were to speak with me," he said in a whisper. "Beneficial to you and to your mother."

Alex felt her eyes widen, fear raced through her body like a wildfire. "Where is she? Where have you taken her? If you've hurt her . . ."

"Hush," he said, motioning toward Hopi House across the street from the gathering.

Alex allowed him to lead her to a more secluded spot but made sure they were still in sight of the crowd. In spite of their isolation, Joel leaned in close. "Now, my dear, what did you say to the sheriff about me?"

"I don't know what you're talking about," Alex replied nervously.

"You said something to him because he's hinted at it. He's told me he wants to speak to me about threats I made. You're the only one who knows about any such threats."

"I seriously doubt that," Alex said, trying hard to stand her ground. "Your Miss Winthrop knows plenty, I'm sure. Not only that, but there are also those lackeys you hire to do your dirty work."

"Nevertheless, they've not spoken to the sheriff and investigator hired by the senator. You have."

"I have nothing to tell you, Mr. Harper. I simply want to know what you've done with my mother."

Harper laughed softly. "I'm sure you do."

Luke could barely concentrate on the speeches, for he'd seen Harper approach Alex and then drag her off to Hopi House. He'd almost gone after them when Harper stopped abruptly, still within Luke's range of vision, and began talking intently to Alex. So long as he could see her, Luke decided against going after them.

The speeches concluded and people were encouraged to linger and talk if they desired. Jastrow was immediately surrounded by a throng of supporters, as was Winston Winthrop.

"It was hard on Daddy to hear of the president's death," Valerie said. "He loves a good competition, but he always wants a fair fight."

"And this one isn't a fair fight, is it?"

She paled and began to stammer. "I . . . don't . . . well, that is . . . I can't . . ."

Luke took hold of her elbow and led her away from the others. "I just want to ask you one thing, and I need an honest answer."

Her eyes widened in fear and Luke felt sorry for her. He knew he sounded gruff, but their time was running out. "Is Joel Harper capable of murder?"

"You shouldn't speak of such things," Valerie said, lowering her gaze. "You mustn't."

"I'll do whatever I can to protect you, but you have to tell me the truth."

She returned her gaze to his face. "It's too late to protect me."

Luke shook his head. He had to find a way to reach her. He felt the urgency of it even as he glanced over his shoulder to find Harper still with Alex. "What about your father, then? What about protection for him? You told me you wanted to hire me as a bodyguard for him. Are you still extending that offer?"

Valerie began to sob softly. "I don't want him hurt. He's a good man. He knows nothing of Joel's scheming."

"Then tell me about it so we can put a stop to it."

She looked at him, her face blotchy and tear streaked. She seemed to be sizing up the situation, reasoning within her mind what was to be done.

"If I tell you everything and he finds out . . . he'll kill us both."

CHAPTER TWENTY-FOUR

*J*oel thought to further grieve Alex Keegan when he spotted Luke and Valerie in a close-knit conversation. Rage welled up within him. She'd been after Toland since they'd arrived at the canyon.

"It would seem your friend doesn't know when to leave well enough alone," he muttered.

Alex moved away from him and turned to look back at the crowd. "They're talking."

Joel laughed bitterly. "For now. But knowing Valerie as I do, they'll soon be involved in much more."

"Well, knowing Luke as I do, she won't get that far with him."

He turned to Alex and shook his head. "For one so beautiful, you're quite naïve. Money, power, and charm can get whatever it desires."

"It didn't buy you what you wanted," Alex replied brazenly. "It didn't buy me."

"Ah, but you'll come around in time. I'm not used to having to battle women of virtue, you see. I find those steeped in their religious nonsense to generally be avoided, but with you, I couldn't help myself. Now you're a challenge."

"A challenge you cannot hope to win," Alex answered. "You disgust me. Your money and power are false gods that give you deceptive confidence in what can be had. Not everyone can be bought at a price."

Just then Joel saw Luke put his arm around Valerie and actually pull her into an embrace. "Of all the nerve. So your cowboy won't succumb to her charms, eh? Just have a look."

Joel watched Alex as she scanned the crowd to again take note of Luke and Valerie. There was none of the jealousy or anger he anticipated, however. Her countenance remained calm, almost tranquil. But just as quickly, she turned back to him and frowned. "Luke can take care of himself, just as I'm sure Miss Winthrop can. I want to know where you've taken my mother. If you don't tell me, I'm going to the authorities."

"You won't go to the authorities," Joel said snidely. "You won't go to them because I have proof of what really happened the night of your father's murder. Your mother killed him just as sure as we're standing here. I heard them argue, you see. A little matter of an illegitimate child born to your father and one of his many women."

He watched the color drain from Alex's face. *Good,* he thought. *Let her be shocked and dismayed. Let her believe the worst—that I have the power to put her mother away forever. Let her see me as her salvation—then she'll be mine.*

"I don't believe you." Her voice was considerably less brazen than it had been only moments ago.

Joel smiled. "I don't suppose it really matters. The truth is the truth. The woman and her child were the final straw for your mother. She came here for a divorce because she could no longer deal with the matter. She argued with your father and told him to marry the woman if he chose, but to give her a divorce and let her be free. I believe she wanted to go away with you—to live elsewhere, just the two of you. At least I heard something to that matter."

"My mother didn't kill my father."

"Poor thing. The truth is really just too much to bear, isn't it?"

"I won't stand here and listen to your lies for another moment." Surprising him, Alex set off across the lawn.

This action, in turn, brought Joel's attention back to Luke and Valerie. They were still together, she still in his supportive embrace. Enraged at the public humiliation she continued to bring upon him, Joel marched across the grounds to take his fiancée back in hand.

They watched him approach, and Valerie appeared to have the good sense to pull away from Luke's hold. Joel seethed. He would teach her a lesson once and for all.

"What is the meaning of this?" Joel hissed in a low, menacing voice.

"Mr. Toland and I were merely talking. I got rather emotional and he comforted me," she offered.

"I need to speak with you alone," Joel said, reaching out to take hold of Valerie's arm. "Now."

Luke surprisingly said nothing. Joel had been prepared to do battle with the man, but he remained silent as he pulled Valerie away.

"Didn't I warn you? Didn't I tell you that I wouldn't tolerate your flirtations? I would think, given what happened between us in your room, you wouldn't risk annoying me further."

"He was merely comforting me," Valerie protested. "There was nothing flirtatious about it. Good grief, Joel, look around you. People are weeping and miserable over the news of the president. They may not have liked the man, but the shock and sadness of it is overwhelming. Have you no feelings whatsoever?"

"The feelings I have or don't have are really of no concern to you. What does matter is that we have a job to do and I intend for you to uphold your part. Otherwise, some very unpleasant things are bound to happen."

"You don't scare me anymore. You've already done your worst," she said hatefully.

"You'd like to believe that, I'm sure. But, as I've told you, there are far worse things to come if you fail to cooperate."

She shook her head, as if uncertain. He could sense her apprehension and smiled. Sometimes the less said the better. The imagination was a powerful weapon. Given a chance to think about it, she would imagine far worse arrangements than he could dream up. Well, maybe not worse, but just as bad.

Luke watched the couple, wondering momentarily what had happened to Alex. She seemed to be nowhere in sight. The thought worried him, but so long as he had Harper in his sights, surely Alex would be safe.

He tried to appear interested in the conversation of those around him, while watching Joel Harper. He talked in rapid-fire to Miss Winthrop. She shook her head ever so slightly; he said something else, and this time she fervently shook her head. Whatever he was saying, Luke felt certain it had to do with Harper's plans to eliminate his competition.

Finally he saw Valerie acquiesce. She nodded and dried her eyes on a handkerchief given her by Harper. With this done, she moved away to join her father. The senator smiled broadly and welcomed her with a hearty embrace. There was no doubt in Luke's mind that the man loved her a great deal.

Continuing to watch, Luke saw Valerie lean toward her father's ear. She appeared to be whispering something that met with his approval because the senator nodded enthusiastically and allowed her to take hold of his arm.

Senator Winthrop and his daughter mingled through the crowd of well-wishers and stun-faced supporters. They didn't stop until they reached Bradley Jastrow. For several moments they talked, just the three of them, and then the senator took his leave and it was just Valerie and Jastrow. Several times, other supporters came up to them, but Jastrow dismissed them. At one point, he led Valerie to the rim walk and pointed something out across the canyon.

Every nerve in Luke's body grew taut. It would be a simple matter to push the man over the edge. Perhaps Harper had threatened Valerie into doing just that. Scanning the crowd for Harper, Luke discovered he was nowhere to be found. Neither was Alex. His heart began to pound an anxious rhythm. *Help me, Lord,* he prayed. *Help me do what must be done.*

Luke moved away from the crowd to both search for Harper and try to keep track of Valerie and Jastrow as they moved down the rim walk.

"Mr. Toland, I would have a word with you."

Luke looked up to find Valerie's father making his way across the lawn. "I don't really have time right now, sir."

"Nonsense. This is important." The senator planted himself between Luke and the walkway. "I want to discuss the canyon with you. Valerie said you were quite knowledgeable."

Luke had no desire to discuss such things with the man. Not when the lives of so many might well be on the line. Luke narrowed his eyes. "Did Valerie also tell you that your campaign aide is systematically killing off your competition?"

Winthrop looked completely shocked at the suggestion. "My good man, how dare you slander one of my staff?"

"I dare to because it's true, and right now you're detaining me from preventing him from killing again."

"I don't believe you."

"I don't much care. The fact of the matter is, your daughter filled me in on a great deal."

"I believe she's just suffering from the heat and the news of the president. I'm sure she didn't mean anything by it."

"She's suffering all right," Luke said, resolving to give the man whatever truth he needed in order to get the job done. "She's suffering because Joel is threatening her with your downfall and even death if she doesn't remain silent and cooperate with his schemes."

Winthrop looked stunned, his face contorting and changing colors until it remained a mottled purple. "You lie!"

"I actually wish I were," Luke said sadly. "Valerie needs you to prevent any more of this from happening. Apparently Harper has killed before and plans to kill again. She believes he even masterminded a plot that resulted in President Harding's death."

Winthrop began slowly shaking his head from side to side. "This can't be."

"What proof can I offer you? I only have your daughter's word and the word of another who overheard Harper plotting."

"It's just unheard of. Why would Joel resort to such things? I'm a popular candidate. I have a strong backing of supporters." He hooked his thumbs into his vest pocket and tried to appear under control, but Luke could sense he was anything but. "I believe you're making this up."

"Listen to yourself, Senator. This is your daughter we're talking about. Would she lie about such a thing? What would she have to gain from that?"

Winthrop considered the question for a moment. "She doesn't wish to marry Joel Harper. She would probably do anything within her power to keep that from happening."

"Then she's lied about the death of a dear friend named Andrew, as well."

"The banker's son? The boy drowned."

"Yes, I know. Valerie told me that Joel admitted to arranging the entire thing. Now we sit here with Keegan and the president dead, while Bradley Jastrow walks the south rim path with your daughter."

Winthrop's expression took on one of complete defeat. "You must save her."

"I'll do what I can," Luke replied. "You go to the authorities and tell them where we've gone. I've no idea what Harper has in mind, but my guess is he plans to eliminate Jastrow—and even Valerie if she's too much trouble."

———

Alex had no idea where Luke had gotten off to, but seeing Valerie move down the rim path with Bradley Jastrow on her arm, Alex knew she had to follow. She pushed aside Mr. Harper's threats to her mother and herself, pushed aside her fears of what she might actually bear witness to. She had to keep Joel Harper from reaping more harm. If that meant she put herself in an uncomfortable position, then so be it.

Following at a discreet distance and using the hotel to hide her movements, Alex observed Valerie and Jastrow as they talked and walked at the canyon's edge. They appeared to be moving in the direction of the Lookout. Alex wondered if they would go there or perhaps move on past to the more secluded studio cabin to the west. There were trees and a good deal of cover for someone who might wish to be left alone.

As they moved past the Lookout, Alex knew she could no longer stay under cover. She hurried away from the hotel and toward the patch of trees to the south. If she could make it there unnoticed, she could hide and move through the shadows until she reached a place where she could watch the path or even the studio.

Gasping for breath as she pushed herself to run faster, Alex nearly collapsed as she reached the first tree. The heady scent of pine and juniper filled the air. She leaned against the trunk of one tree, hoping to catch her breath before pursuing the couple. She had no idea how she might stop the turn of events, but she had to try. Visions of her father going over the edge haunted her imagination. It was such an awful way to die—to know for those last few moments that you couldn't stop the motion of events that would take your life. To endure seconds that would seemingly last an eternity.

She pushed away from the tree and pressed through the underbrush. She had to reach them—had to save the innocent.

Without warning, however, someone reached out to take hold of her. One hand clamped firmly on her arm and another went over her mouth and pulled her backward against a rock-hard chest. She screamed, but the sound was lost in the smothering hold.

*A*lex met Luke's warning glance as he turned her in his arms. She'd been almost certain she would find herself face-to-face with Joel Harper, and she fell against Luke in relief.

"I thought . . . I . . ."

"Shhh. Look," he whispered and pointed to the rim path. Harper walked at a rapid clip along the narrow path. Luke pulled her close to him and added, "I saw a rough-looking character give him something. I've no idea what it was, but I'm figuring it has something to do with putting an end to Jastrow's life, and maybe even Valerie's."

"What can we do?" Alex questioned, pushing away from Luke to better see where Jastrow was headed.

"I'm not sure. I guess we follow him."

"He's not stopping at the Lookout, so maybe he's going to the art studio. It would be deserted at this hour."

Luke nodded. "Come on, but stay quiet."

They pushed through the trees as quietly as possible, Alex clinging tightly to Luke's hand. She thanked God silently for the support of Luke's presence. No one else in the entire world could give her the feeling of strength and security that Luke gave her. Yet what did it mean? Was this another sign that she was really in love with Luke?

"There they are," Luke said, pulling Alex to his side. His arms about her felt warm and protective and Alex had no desire to resist him. Instead, she looked through the brush to see what was happening.

She could see for herself that the trio stood just outside the studio. Joel pulled something out of his pocket and waved it in front of Jastrow. Alex put her hand to her mouth, realizing Joel held a gun.

"Shhh," Luke warned. They watched in silence for several

moments before Luke motioned to the right. "We need to get closer."

Alex knew they could do nothing from this distance, but she didn't want to see Luke risk his life. There was a part of her that wanted to beg Luke to stay where he was or even turn back, yet at the same time, Alex felt overwhelmed with the need to know the truth.

They cautiously moved nearer, almost behind the three, stopping no more than eight feet from where Valerie stood.

"Please, Joel. Please don't do this." Alex could easily hear Valerie Winthrop's pleading.

"We agreed this was for the best. You don't want to see something else go wrong, do you, Val dear?"

Jastrow's expression looked like he was sizing up the situation. For a moment, Alex thought he might jump Harper, but Joel apparently realized his intentions and waved the man back. "Sit down on that rock. Now! You may have held the Huns at bay, but you'll find it another story dealing with an American."

"Mr. Harper, I fail to see . . ." Jastrow tried to speak in protest, but Harper pushed him back.

"Sit!" Joel commanded again.

Jastrow did as he was told while Joel Harper fished something out of his pocket and handed it to Valerie. "Take this syringe and load it."

"I don't know how," Valerie protested.

"It's simple enough. Even you can do it."

Alex watched Val take the vial in hand. "You do it, Joel."

"Pop the cork on the vial," Joel commanded. She looked at the bottle, then slowly pulled the cork from the top.

"Just put the needle down in there and pull the back on the top. It will suck the contents right up into the syringe," Joel said, smiling. "As for you, Mr. Jastrow, well, let's just say that by this time tomorrow, the nation will be mourning more than just the president's passing. We shall also be mourning the passing of a great war hero."

"And how is it you plan to kill me?" Jastrow questioned calmly.

"Haven't you figured it out?" Joel questioned, sounding almost indignant. "You're going to take an overdose of morphine. The pain you're suffering has become unbearable, coupled with your horrid memories of the war. It's just too much for you to endure. Death will be a welcome release."

"No one is ever going to believe it," Jastrow said quite seriously. "I've never been the type to give up."

Valerie began to cry. "Please don't do this, Joel."

She reached out to touch his arm. He pushed her back. "Don't whine at me. You know what I'm capable of."

"But Mr. Jastrow doesn't have to die. You could just threaten him and get his promise to drop out of the race for president. You'd do that wouldn't you, Mr. Jastrow?"

The man looked intently at Valerie and then Joel. "Is that what this is all about?"

Joel laughed. "You're a liability in my boss's campaign. You're young, handsome, popular with the women—a war hero, for pity's sake. It's difficult for the senator to contend with such things."

"My father knows nothing about this," Valerie assured Jastrow, then turned to Joel. "You know Father would never want this. He's a man of honor."

"He doesn't know how things get done in this business. When he first ran for the senate in South Carolina, people still remembered the Civil War. He could appeal to other southern gentlemen who'd suffered as his family had suffered. That's not the case with the presidency."

"If that's all this is about, you should know that I've already reached a decision to pull out of the race," Jastrow said. "I had a talk with my staff this morning. I've decided to get back in the family business."

"I thought you weren't the type to give up," Joel said sarcastically.

"It's not a matter of giving up. I was merely testing the waters regarding the presidency. In weighing the situation, I simply made a logical choice to put off my candidacy until another time."

Joel frowned and Alex thought for a moment that he'd change his mind. He lowered the gun and bit his lower lip. Alex had never seen him quite this indecisive. Perhaps he would put aside his plan and let Jastrow go.

"See there, Joel," Valerie said, her tears still flowing. "He doesn't even plan to continue the race against Daddy."

Joel squared his shoulders and raised the gun again. "It doesn't matter. He knows too much now. Get that syringe loaded. Do it now!"

"Please, Joel," she began to sob in earnest, her hands trembling as she held the syringe and bottle. "Please just stop before it's too late."

"If you don't do as you're told, you'll end up like Mr. Keegan, over the edge without so much as a prayer."

Valerie paled and shook her head. Alex nearly gasped aloud at this, feeling certain Joel was the one responsible for her father's death.

"So you did kill him," Valerie cried.

Joel smiled. "No. I actually wish I could take credit for it. The man was a dense-headed bore who held an overinflated image of his own self-importance. He deserved to die." He looked to Jastrow. "Unlike you, our most heralded war hero. You're simply in the wrong place at the wrong time. Or from my point of view, the right time. Your death will be mourned by thousands—maybe even millions. I sincerely doubt Keegan has so much as his wife to shed a tear over him. It's for certain his daughter won't."

Alex felt something move beneath her feet. A deer mouse skittered across the toe of her shoe, causing Alex to shriek without thinking. She looked to Luke, knowing the damage she'd done, and unable to utter so much as a whispered apology before Joel Harper demanded they show themselves.

———

Katherine Keegan stood before the men who held her life in their hands. They looked at her with skepticism and a hint of confusion. Looking to the man who'd been her guard for the last few hours, she nodded. The man handed her a basket, then reached into his pocket and handed his superior a folded piece of paper.

The ranger in charge took the paper and read the contents. "What's the meaning of this?"

Katherine Keegan reached into the basket and pulled back a cover to reveal a very small infant. "This is my husband's son. My husband's and Gloria Scott's. The woman whose letter you now hold."

The sheriff eyed her suspiciously. "What does this have to do with anything? Your message to us said that you were ready to talk about your husband's death."

Katherine nodded. "And so I am."

"Then what's with the kid?" he asked gruffly.

"The baby is the reason I came to Grand Canyon to ask my husband for a divorce. I'd just learned from Miss Scott that she'd had an affair with my husband, and this baby was the result. She had come to me seeking help. She had actually threatened me with public humiliation, but of course I assured her that was already a daily fact for me."

Katherine looked down at the sleeping infant. Her heart ached for the suffering and misery her husband had caused this child and his mother. It seemed most unfair that even one more innocent person should pay the price for her husband's indiscretions.

"I still fail to understand what any of this has to do with your husband's death," the sheriff replied.

"I must admit, Mrs. Keegan," Winthrop's private investigator, Mr. Stokes, said. "I am rather confused, as well."

Katherine looked back to the men who eyed her as if she might disappear from their sight at any given moment.

"I was very angry when I came here," she admitted. "I confronted Rufus about the baby and about his affair with Gloria Scott."

"And?" the sheriff demanded impatiently.

"And he laughed it off. Said there would be no divorce. Threatened me and our daughter if we should so much as hint at my desire to leave him."

"So he was mad and threatening, and you felt that you had no other choice but to kill him," the sheriff announced. "Is that what you're trying to tell us?"

Katherine shook her head. "No. That's not at all what happened. But if you'll bear with me, I'll tell you what did take place that evening."

*W*ell, this is quite a mess, isn't it?" Joel stated, more than questioned, as he motioned Alex and Luke to come out from the clearing. He was careful to keep Jastrow and Valerie in his sight the entire time. Waving his gun, he motioned to Luke. "You, over there with Jastrow." He reached out and grabbed hold of Alex. Putting the revolver to her head, he smiled. "And you stay here with me."

"Let her go, Harper!" Luke demanded, taking a step forward.

"If you want to keep her alive, you'll do what I say and stay there. I've no desire to end the life of one so sweet," he said, pulling Alex backward against him, "but I'll do what I must."

Alex fought against his hold until Joel put his arm around her neck and pulled back hard. For a terrifying moment he cut off her air. Alex became still, knowing he meant business.

"Why not fight this out like a man?" Luke questioned.

Alex could see the anger in Luke's expression. The tick in his cheek, his clenched teeth, and the narrowing of his eyes were sure signs he was beyond mere fear and annoyance. Now he was enraged. She wanted to keep the situation under control, and her mind raced for something she might offer to neutralize the sparking emotions.

"Mr. Harper, this isn't the way to accomplish anything. You know the authorities have already been notified. They're on their way, even now."

"I don't believe you, my dear. They didn't believe a word you said to them. The sheriff had a good laugh when he told me that you'd suggested I might have murdered your father."

"You seemed a logical suspect," Alex said, hoping if she kept Joel talking and preoccupied with their conversation, someone else might actually think of something to do. "After all, my father was causing you some discomfort."

"How do you know that?" Joel questioned.

"Because my father caused everyone discomfort," Alex said, trying hard not to move lest Joel tighten his hold around her neck.

Luke shifted from one foot to the other, immediately catching Joel's attention. "Sit down next to Jastrow," he commanded. "I want you both where I can see you."

Luke studied him for a moment as if to ascertain the seriousness of his demand. Joel drew the revolver level with Alex's head. While his right hand steadied the gun, his left tightened against Alex's throat. For a moment, Alex panicked. She feared he'd kill her, if for no other reason than to lessen the odds against him.

"Joel, please stop this. You must stop now," Valerie pleaded. "These people have done you no wrong. They've shown only kindness to Daddy and I, and we've sorely misused them. Let them go."

"You simpleton. Don't you see?" he questioned. "They plan to destroy us. To destroy me. I've worked too hard, Val. I've worked my fingers to the bone for your father. I've rearranged too many affairs to go down without a fight. Your father must be the president, and I must be at his side."

Valerie stepped toward him. "But if you kill us all, Daddy will never continue to run. He wouldn't run if I were dead. He would despair of even living."

"I won't have to kill you in order to keep you cooperative."

Valerie shook her head. "That's where you're wrong. I won't cooperate with you anymore. You've left a trail of death and sorrow behind you, and no matter where you go, those demons of the past will follow. I won't let you go through with this. I won't."

Alex thought Valerie Winthrop had never looked more determined. Not when pursuing Luke. Not when trying to bring a room full of strangers to their knees. No, this time Miss Winthrop knew she was playing a life-and-death game.

"Shut up, Val, and load the syringe."

She looked down at the items in her hands and Alex strained to watch. Moving even that small bit, caused Joel to tighten his hold once again. Alex had to press back against him to keep from losing consciousness. The idea intrigued her as Joel loosened his hold. If she pushed back against him with all her might, she could very well knock them both to the ground. It would be a risk as to whether or not the gun would go off, but it might be a risk worth taking.

She looked to Luke, who seemed to sense what she was thinking. He shook his head ever so slightly and Alex got the distinct impression he was telling her not to do anything at all.

"Put the needle into the vial and pull back on the top of the syringe. When you've managed to empty the contents of the bottle, I want you to take the syringe and inject Jastrow."

"Why?" Alex couldn't help but ask. It seemed such a logical question.

Joel laughed and pressed his lips against her ear. "Because, my dear, that's the way this plan works." He kissed Alex playfully on the lobe of her ear, causing Luke to take a step forward.

"As much as I would hate to bring any attention upon us, I will use this gun if necessary. Given this setting, I could most likely shoot the three of you, and Valerie and I could be well away before anyone figured out where the shots were fired from."

Valerie began to cry again. Alex could see that she'd done as instructed and now stood with the full syringe, looking for all the world as if she were frozen in place. Except for her tears, she didn't move. She scarcely even appeared to be breathing.

Joel turned slightly, nearly sending Alex off-balance. "You see, Mr. Toland, Valerie has morphine, Mr. Jastrow's dearest friend—his constant companion since the Great War. When Jastrow overdoses on the very drug he uses on a daily basis to control his pain, people will automatically assume he was unable to deal with the pain any longer and took his own life."

"Out here? Wouldn't it make more sense to seek the privacy of his room?"

Joel seemed to consider this for a moment. His hold on Alex loosened considerably. "It would have been more ideal. I had hoped that Valerie would work her wiles on the man and get him to take her back to his room, but it didn't work out that way. People seem to always be thwarting my plans."

"No one is ever going to believe the man came out here to take an overdose of morphine," Luke said, pushing his hair back ever so slowly. "You have to rethink this, Harper. His murder is going to be very evident."

"No. No, it won't. Valerie will tell them all how he told her he wished to die."

"No, I won't," Valerie said, coming toward Joel. "I won't do it. I'll tell them all exactly what has happened here."

"You wouldn't dare," Joel said, laughing nervously. "You're the one who will administer the deadly dose. You'll be guilty of murder."

"Then so be it," Valerie said, looking Joel dead in the eye.

Alex could feel Joel tense. "I think I'm going to faint," Alex said softly. She could only hope that Joel might be taken by surprise enough to forget the gun momentarily. Faking the faint, her knees buckled and she started to slide down to the ground.

"No!" he declared, trying to pull her back up by the hair.

"I'm sorry," Alex murmured, even as Joel tried to steady her. She landed on her knees, kneeling on the hard rock path.

Joel took hold of her by the hair and at the same time pointed the gun at Luke. "Don't take a single step. Valerie, do what I told you to do. We've got to be done with this before someone comes looking for us." Alex felt a grave sense of urgency. Her ploy had failed. What could she do to help now?

Valerie stepped forward, but at the last minute she turned and lunged for Joel with the syringe held like a dagger. He dropped his hold on Alex and managed to narrowly avoid the needle.

"You traitor!" he screamed, slapping her back. Whether she let go on her own accord or had no choice due to the force of Harper's blow, Valerie dropped her hold on the syringe and let it fall. Hitting hard against the stones, the syringe shattered and the contents spilled out.

"No!" Joel screamed, pushing Alex aside.

Luke sprung into action like a mountain lion to the kill. He rushed Joel and sent him sprawling backward. Alex hurriedly got to her feet, determined to help Luke in whatever way she could, but instead found Jastrow at her side, pulling her and Valerie back up the path.

"You ladies must get out of harm's way," he told them.

"But he has a gun," Alex protested. "We have to help Luke."

"I'll do what I can, but first I must see you safely away from this area. Go for help."

Alex looked to Valerie, who nodded. "We can get help," Valerie said as if to assure Alex it was for the best.

She looked back at the men who were fighting. "Please help him," she said, turning to go up the path with Valerie. They'd only gone a couple of feet, however, when the sheriff, followed by several rangers, Mr. Stokes, and Senator Winthrop, appeared on the trail.

"Down here!" she called. "Help us—Mr. Harper has a gun." Just then a shot was fired. Alex gasped for breath and turned on her heel, her hand at her throat. *Dear God, don't let Luke be hurt,* she prayed.

The sheriff and rangers rushed past her to take the matter in hand. Valerie began to cry anew and Alex thought for a moment she might join her.

"Neither one is shot!" the sheriff called out.

Alex watched Luke get up and dust off his clothes. She longed to go to him, to feel his arms around her.

"Alexandria? Are you all right?"

She looked behind her to see her mother coming behind the senator and nodded as the senator hurried to take Valerie in his arms.

"What of you? Are you hurt?" he asked his daughter.

"Oh, Daddy, I'm fine now. Now that I know he can't hurt you."

The senator's expression grew stony. He put Valerie at arm's length and looked her over. "I'm so sorry for what I've put you through."

Alex's mother took hold of her and hugged her close. "Oh, my darling, I feared the worst."

"You had good reason to," Alex admitted. "Harper planned the worst." Then remembering she'd confronted Joel only a short time earlier about her mother's whereabouts, she questioned. "Where did he take you? He didn't hurt you, did he?"

"Who?" Katherine looked confused.

"Joel Harper. Didn't he find you in the cabin and take you from there? Michaela came and told me you were missing. I was afraid, and when Mr. Harper made some comments to me this evening, I presumed he was the one responsible."

"No," her mother replied, shaking her head. "Not at all. Something came up, and with the help of my guard, we settled the matter quite readily. No, Joel Harper had nothing to do with me leaving the cabin."

"I'm so glad, Mother. I've only wanted your safety—your happiness."

Katherine Keegan reached up and gently touched her daughter's cheek. "I've wanted no less for you, child. You're safe now. That's all that matters."

Valerie began to sob loudly. The senator stepped back, appearing uncertain as to what he should do. Alex saw her mother's expression and knew the compassion she felt for the younger woman.

"Maybe you could talk with her, Mother. Her own mother died, and I can speak from experience—you never outgrow the need for your mother."

Her mother smiled and nodded. "I'll see what I can do." Katherine went to Valerie and embraced her. The debutante seemed to fall apart at the motherly touch.

The senator went to Bradley Jastrow and shook his head. "I can't begin to extend my apologies for what my aide perceived as acceptable politics."

Alex heard little else. Luke approached her with a look of grave concern. "Are you all right?"

"I am now," she said in a barely audible voice.

Luke pulled her close, wrapping his arms around her. "I thought he would kill you."

"He would have. There's no doubt about that." She looked up to meet his gaze. "I thought he would kill you. I could hardly pray."

"He can't hurt anyone now." He held her tight and Alex realized she loved this man more than life.

"I couldn't have endured it if he'd killed you," Alex said softly. "I . . ."

"You don't understand! They have to die. They know too much!" Joel screamed as the sheriff and one burly ranger forced him back up the path. "It's too late now. Too late. They have to die."

Alex pulled away enough to see Joel's crazed expression as he came to a halt in front of the senator and Bradley Jastrow. "You don't know how hard I've worked," he said to the senator. "I've done all of this for you—for us. We must go to the White House. We must be president!"

The senator shook his head. "No, Joel. All that's over with. I'm resigning from the election. My daughter needs me now."

"You can't! I've done too much to make this happen. I've . . . I've even . . ." His expression grew wild and he lunged forward as if to harm the senator, but the sheriff and rangers held him fast.

Half dragging, half carrying Joel Harper, they moved off toward the hotel. The remaining ranger turned to the party. "I'll need to talk to you all."

A loud commotion could be heard at the top of the walkway. Alex strained to see what was happening, but when flashes of light exploded in the dimming evening light, she knew full well the newspaper reporters had found out the truth. Or at least their version of it.

Several of them came rushing down the path toward where the senator stood beside Bradley Jastrow.

"Senator! We need a statement. Is it true that your aide tried to murder Mr. Jastrow?"

"Did he also kill Rufus Keegan?"

They seemed to momentarily forget Alex and Luke. Valerie went protectively to her father's side, as if bolstering her own strength in order to protect him.

"Leave my father alone," she demanded.

Katherine came to Alex and Luke. "There something I need to speak with you about. Something you must see for yourselves."

"What is it, Mother?"

Alex looked to Luke, but he shrugged. "Yes, what is it?"

Katherine drew a deep breath. "Let's go to Mrs. Godfrey's office. I can tell you all about it there."

*A*lex settled into step beside Luke, while her mother took the initiative and led the way back to El Tovar. Alex felt Luke reach for her hand and she smiled. Looking up to meet his gaze, her smile broadened. How right it felt to hold hands with her best friend in all the world—to love him and care about him as she did. She looked away, wondering what had caused her mother to suddenly take leave of her protective cabin.

"Do you know what this is about?" Alex asked Luke softly.

"No, I was about to ask you the same question."

Alex shrugged. "Guess we'll find out soon enough."

She looked up at El Tovar in all its glory. The chalet-styling looked foreign against the canyon setting. With the sunlight all but gone, the place loomed like a brooding hulk. *I'm tired*, Alex thought. *I'm tired of this place and this job. I'm tired of the things that Arizona represents to me.* She had never thought it possible that she'd feel this way. She'd loved the canyon since she was a child and now she only wanted to leave.

Luke's giving me a way out, she thought as she continued her self-reflection. Marriage . . . a home . . . a family of her own. She could have it all with this man, if only she'd put aside her fears. Luke wasn't like her father. He wasn't like Joel Harper. In fact, Luke was unlike any man she'd ever known. She looked to where her mother stood waiting at the porch entry to the hotel.

She smiled at the approaching couple, and Alex wondered what her mother might say to her concerns. Perhaps she'd get the chance to ask her later.

"Can't you just tell us what's happened?" Alex questioned.

"You'd better see for yourself," her mother replied. "I think such a monumental moment merits a face-to-face experience."

Alex couldn't begin to imagine what her mother had planned. She could see her mother's peaceful countenance, however, and knew that whatever the news, it must be good.

They made their way down the employee hallway and turned toward Mrs. Godfrey's office. Just then, Alex heard the unmistakable cry of a baby. Her mother opened the door before she could question the matter and revealed Michaela holding a squalling infant.

At first, Alex wondered if this had been the real reason Michaela had gone away on vacation. She'd left rather abruptly, surprising everyone with her temporary resignation. She'd been gone long enough to have given birth.

"Oh, Mrs. Keegan," Michaela declared, "I'm so glad you're back. He won't settle down. I tried feeding him as you suggested, but he just isn't interested."

Katherine smiled. "Alexandria, I know this will come as a shock to you, but this is your little brother."

Alex felt her mouth drop open. Her eyes widened as she looked to Luke. He appeared just as shocked as she was. "How . . . I mean who . . ." She let her question trail off as she searched her mother's face for an answer.

"Sit down," her mother instructed. "I need to tell you the whole story."

Michaela got up. "Here, sit here. You can hold him. I think if I live to be a hundred, I'll never want a child of my own."

Alex took Michaela's chair and, without even knowing why, did just as Michaela directed. As her friend placed the baby in her arms, Alex couldn't help but smile. "He's so tiny."

"Tiny, but loud," Michaela said, heading quickly to the door. "If you need help with him, maybe it would be better to call Bernice. She has a whole collection of brothers and sisters and probably knows better what to do than I would." She hurried from the room, pulling the door closed behind her before anyone could offer a comment.

But there was no need for comment. The baby had calmed in Alex's arms. He looked up at her with deep blue eyes, warming Alex to the bottom of her heart.

"I think he likes you," Luke said, coming to stand beside her.

"What's his name?" Alex asked her mother.

Katherine took a seat directly across from Alex. "His name is Brock. Brock Scott. His mother was Gloria Scott."

"Was?" Alex asked. "Is she dead?"

"Yes, I'm afraid so," Katherine replied. "But I'm getting ahead of myself. Let me start at the beginning. You see, shortly before I came to El Tovar to tell your father I wanted a divorce, Miss Scott showed up at the house in Williams, with Brock in tow. I didn't know who she was, but it was dreadfully hot that day so I invited her in. Once we sat down, she informed me that Brock was Rufus's son and that she had come to insist we help her out financially."

"Oh my," Alex said, knowing how much this woman's appearance must have wounded her mother.

"I'd never had to confront one of your father's women, and I'd certainly never had one of them share such news. I was stunned to say the least."

"And hurt," Alex said, feeling for her mother.

"Yes," Katherine nodded. "I was hurt as well. This revelation was the final straw. It was as if my eyes were suddenly opened to the truth. There was no hope for Rufus and me. Here was a young woman with a new baby and the need for a husband and father for her son. I figured Rufus might as well divorce me and marry the poor woman and give the child a name."

"Oh, Mother, I'm so sorry." Alex met her mother's gaze and saw the pain reflected there. Her expression pierced Alex's heart, reminding her yet again of her father's cruelty. Without thinking she said, "I'm glad he's dead."

"Alex, don't be bitter about the past. Your father was a lost soul. He never knew what was missing in his life because he was so certain his money and power could fill all those empty places. When it didn't, he tried to fill it with women. When that didn't work, he just became angry and hateful. You don't want to be like him."

"But I am like him," Alex said, shaking her head. She looked back to the baby who was falling asleep. "Joel Harper reminded me of that very fact. He said I had my father's independent nature, his determination, and his judgmental attitude."

"I disagree," Luke said softly. "You may have an independent nature and determination. You may even be a bit quick at times to assess a situation and see it in the wrong light—but you are nothing like him."

"I agree," Katherine replied. "Rufus did everything out of selfish need. He wanted the best—not for his family, but for himself. You've been patiently working this job for four years and during this time you've told me off and on that you were saving your money in order to take me away from my misery. That isn't the act of a selfish woman."

Alex felt a tear slide down her cheek. "I wanted to be a good Christian where Father was concerned. And how I wanted to respect him and honor him as the Bible said. But I feel I can't mourn his passing now because I've mourned his absence all my life. I watched him with one woman or another since I was a small girl. I always envied those women because they were laughing and having such a marvelous time and Father was laughing too. I always wondered why he didn't laugh with me?"

"Oh, my darling, I know. I know your pain so well. I tried hard to shield you from his actions. I knew you longed for him to care—to just once tell you that he loved you."

"And now he never will."

"No. He never will. But neither will he ever hurt us again." Katherine's words were firm. "I mourn the man I first married. The man I loved. But like you, I mourned that man's passing a long time ago. Losing the ugliness and sin of the man who'd become Rufus Keegan is not a sorrowful parting. Still, I won't speak ill of him. He was a troubled man who was hopelessly lost without God. He has condemned himself. Therefore, I don't need to, and neither do you."

Luke offered Alex a handkerchief. His expression was sympathetic, understanding. Alex felt certain he knew full well how confused her heart and head were over the entire matter.

"I know you're right," Alex said, cradling the baby close.

They sat in silence for several moments before her mother picked the story back up. "Gloria told me she would bring the baby to the newspaper office and tell her story if I refused to help her. I told her I had no idea of where Rufus had taken himself off to and had no way of dealing with the matter myself. I gave her a small bit of money, just what I had in the drawer for household expenses. I told her I would find Rufus and discuss the matter and see what was to be done. She left and shortly after that the invitation to join your father here at the Grand Canyon came from the Winthrops. I knew what I had to do.

"When I confronted your father about the matter, he would hear nothing of it. I tried to talk to him on several occasions, and always he'd either laugh it off or dismiss my concerns. I told him it was unfair for the child to suffer simply because its parents had been less than prudent. He told me to stay out of it, that he would deal with Miss Scott when the time came."

Katherine folded her hands and sighed. "Only the time came much sooner than he expected."

Alex noted the change in her mother's spirit. "What happened?"

"I hadn't realized it at the time, but Miss Scott had followed me to El Tovar. She lost no time in seeking us out. Rufus was livid. He threatened her and the child, then seeing that was getting him nowhere, offered to meet her later to discuss an arrangement."

Alex began to get a sick feeling in the pit of her stomach. "Gloria was the one on the rim that night, wasn't she?"

Katherine met her daughter's eyes and nodded. "I wasn't to go there. I wasn't to share in this meeting, but I felt compelled to be there. I talked to your father prior to the meeting. I begged him to divorce me and marry Gloria, but he was still adamant. He was sure it would ruin his chances with the Winthrops, and he was probably right. Nevertheless, I told him the child was more important than a lifetime of appointments in Washington. He only laughed at that.

"I had planned to remain in my room, but your father insisted I come to the lawn party. He felt I could boost his chances for appointment with the senator. I argued with him about it but finally agreed. He went down ahead of me and after I dressed, I joined him. He'd been drinking, there was no doubt about that. Someone had managed to get him exactly what he needed to bolster his courage." She shook her head. "Would that he could have turned to God the way he did to drink." She sighed again.

"But I digress. I went to the party and then, when he slipped away to meet Gloria, I couldn't help but follow him. I stayed hidden, not wanting to further anger him. I watched as they met on the canyon rim. She didn't have the baby with her and this seemed to make Rufus quite enraged. I heard him telling her to go get the infant immediately and meet him back there, but she refused. I believe now he intended to push them both over the edge and eliminate his problem."

"But why? Why would he act in such an irrational manner? Father never worried about his affairs. Why now?" Alex asked, shuddering at the thought of her father being a murderer.

"I don't know. When Gloria refused to go get the baby, Rufus slapped her hard. He lunged for her as if to send her over the edge but Miss Scott was prepared for this. She sidestepped him and pushed him away. Unfortunately, she pushed him off-balance and he stumbled backward into the canyon."

Alex sat in shocked silence. The clock on the wall ticked away the seconds, but she found no words to speak. The picture in her mind filled in all the missing pieces. Luke tenderly squeezed her shoulder, causing Alex to raise her gaze to his. The look she found there gave her hope and filled her heart with the assurance that no matter what else happened, she would always have Luke.

"I screamed and ran to where Rufus had gone over," her mother continued. "Gloria screamed when she saw me and ran for the hotel. Moments later Luke appeared. I collapsed on the path, unable to even comprehend what I knew must be true. I knew Rufus was dead, but I just couldn't believe what I'd witnessed."

"Oh, Mother, I'm so sorry. I knew you hadn't pushed Father. I knew you would never do such a thing, but I couldn't understand why you'd protect the person who had. I feared the guilty party was threatening you or threatening me. I was so afraid you were protecting someone else so that they wouldn't hurt me. I couldn't have lived with it if you'd gone to jail to protect Gloria Scott."

"I wasn't protecting her," her mother replied. "I was protecting him. He didn't deserve to end up orphaned."

"But what of his mother?" Alex said, gently stroking the baby's dark hair. "You said his mother ran for the hotel. What happened?"

"After everyone learned Rufus had died, I figured I'd heard the last of Gloria Scott. I knew I couldn't prove what had happened and I honestly thought that if it kept mother and child together, it would be better for me to be blamed for Rufus's death. I prayed about the matter and decided it would be best to keep my mouth shut. No one knew about Gloria except me. I mean, I figured someone on the train might have remembered her, but I had no idea where she was staying, and it would have been very difficult to prove what had happened."

"But it was an accident," Alex said, realizing for the first time that her father hadn't been murdered at all. "The poor woman was simply defending herself."

"Yes, but no one but me knew that, and Gloria had disappeared. She wasn't registered at El Tovar, and I had no way of locating her without exposing her part in the matter."

Luke shifted beside Alex and asked, "So what happened?"

"Alex arranged for me to be moved, as you know. I felt better knowing the reporters wouldn't be hounding me and trying to break down my door to get answers. I also felt that the privacy would allow me a chance to actually find Gloria. I wasn't sure how, but I knew my guard would have to sleep sometime. But instead, Gloria left a note and the baby at the front desk. The note only said that this child should be delivered to me and that I would know what to do. The people there knew the rangers had me under their protection, so they delivered the baby to the rangers and they in turn brought the baby to me. What no one knew, until I'd taken the baby out of the basket, was that there was another letter under the baby's blanket."

"What did it say?" Alex asked anxiously.

"Gloria told me she couldn't live with the guilt of what she'd done. She knew she was responsible for Rufus's death and figured no one would believe it was an accident. She feared for the child and begged me to make a home for him so that he wouldn't end up in an asylum somewhere. She concluded the letter by stating that she planned to end her life. She gave directions as to where the rangers could find her, and sure enough, she had committed suicide."

"Oh, how awful." Alex continued to stroke the baby's head, saddened to think of his mother deserting him at such a tender age. "And now he's orphaned."

"He doesn't have to be."

Alex looked to her mother. "What do you mean?"

"I mean you could raise him. It's obvious you have a way with him."

"But, I know nothing of raising a child. I'm not even married." She looked to Luke as if he could verify that one detail.

He smiled and reached down to touch her hand where it rested on the baby's head. "You could give me an answer to my question and sew things up rather neatly."

Alex felt overwhelmed by the moment. She knew she loved him. Knew that she didn't want to lose him. So why couldn't she give him the answer he wanted to hear?

She got to her feet and handed him the baby. "I need to think and to pray. I need time to sort this out."

Luke said nothing as Alex walked from the room. He looked down at the sleeping baby and then to Katherine Keegan.

"She'll do the right thing," Katherine said softly. "Not only by him, but by you as well. She loves you, of that I'm certain."

"I know it too," Luke admitted, "but she's scared."

"Of what?" Katherine asked, seeming surprised by his statement.

"She's afraid all men are like her father and his friends. She's afraid that fidelity isn't a possibility for any man. She's afraid to love and afraid to trust. And until she can come to terms with that, I know she can't marry me."

Katherine nodded. "Rufus hurt her badly. While other little girls had fathers to be proud of, Alex hid her parentage at every turn."

Luke took the seat Alex had just vacated and eased the baby onto his shoulder. Brock didn't so much as stir. "He's so tiny," Luke commented.

"Yes. He's only a few weeks old. Far too young to be without a mother and father."

Luke nodded. "I'm buying a ranch in Wyoming. It's a small place, but large enough for all of us. If Alex will marry me, I'd like you to consider coming with us."

"I appreciate that, Luke. You've been more than kind to me. I've always been reassured to know you were there for Alex. I know at first it was only in friendship, but I think that's what will make your marriage work. You were friends before the idea of falling in love ever came to either one of you. Maybe then, if the feelings fade, you'll still be friends and still have a foundation for your marriage to grow on."

"I'll never stop loving her," he said softly. "Even if she says no to my proposal. I'll never love anyone but Alex."

CHAPTER TWENTY-EIGHT

Valerie Winthrop looked to her father in complete dismay. "But, Daddy, everyone knows this affair was all Joel's fault. No one blames you. Why are you withdrawing from the campaign?"

The senator, looking older than his years, cast a sorrowful gaze upon his daughter. "I can hardly ask the country to allow me to keep their affairs when I can't keep my own in order."

"But Joel was underhanded and conniving," she protested. "He never let any of us know what was going on until it was too late. Why, I didn't even know about some of it until just a week or so ago."

"Exactly my point, Valerie. I had no idea what was going on under my own nose. I should have seen it. I shouldn't have had my sights so fixed on the presidency that I missed what was happening right in my own office—my own house. I will always blame myself for how Joel treated you. I can overlook his greed and ambition, but I will never forgive him for hurting you."

Valerie reached out and touched her father's hand. "There is no merit in holding anger toward him. Mrs. Keegan told me that such things will only fester and allow for a hard and embittered heart. And she should know, given what she had to endure with Mr. Keegan."

"She's a lovely woman, gracious and soft-spoken. Just like your mother."

Valerie nodded. "She reminded me very much of Mother when she comforted me. I think her advice is most beneficial. She speaks as one who knows, and that will help others to listen and heed her word."

He looked to her and Valerie could see the tears form in his eyes. "I've been very wrong to subject you to all of this. Will you forgive a silly old man his ambitions?"

"Oh, Daddy, you didn't hurt me. I wanted you to run for president. I thought it would be marvelously exciting to play hostess in the White House."

"That will never happen now. The papers are running rampant with the scandal. Even Jastrow is backing out of the race. No doubt we'll be left with that rascal John Davis for a Democratic contender." He paused and shook his head. "No, by the time this scandal subsides, it will be too late for me to consider running for anything, much less president."

Valerie picked up her fork and toyed with her breakfast. "Perhaps you could write a book about all of this. Since scandal sells so well, maybe you should share with the public how you were a victim to Joel Harper, just as much as the next man. I wouldn't be surprised if you didn't have publishers clamoring to print it."

"It's a thought, I suppose," her father said, picking up his cup of coffee.

They were alone in the private dining room, tolerant only of each other's company. The press had hounded her father morning and night for exclusive interviews and always the senator declined. Valerie saw the toll it had taken on him, and she was secretly glad he'd decided to call off the campaign plans. He needed to rest. He needed to know she was well and safe and that Joel hadn't harmed her beyond her ability to recover.

"I know it would go over big. Why, we could even contact this one publisher in New York. I'm friends with the owner's daughter. I would be willing to wager money they would come all the way to South Carolina to talk it over with you."

The senator took a long drink and seemed to perk up a bit. "There are a lot of details that could benefit those in the business of politics."

She smiled. "Of course. There are businessmen who would most likely benefit as well. Then, if told in the right manner, you might even attract quite a few women readers."

"I could start with my early days in business and move into the political arena," he said, nodding. He looked to her and smiled. "You're good medicine for this old heart. Just like your mother used to be. I miss her a lot, you know."

"Yes," Valerie said, reaching out to cover her father's hand. "I miss her too. She made us both feel very loved."

"Indeed," he replied with a sigh.

Valerie gave his hand a squeeze and then picked up her fork again. With a forkful of eggs halfway to her mouth she said, "I would want to help you with the book, but there is something else I'd like to help with first. Maybe you'd like to be involved as well. It's a very good cause."

Her father seemed surprised. "Do tell. What has caught your attention this time?"

————

"Mother, I really need to talk to you," Alex said as her mother cuddled Brock and talked to him in animated tones.

"You know you can discuss anything with me." She looked up to meet Alex's gaze.

"You're so kind to him," Alex said, motioning to the baby. "How can you abide him? I mean, surely he reminds you of your bad times with Father."

Katherine looked taken aback. "Well, it's hardly his fault that his parents had no concern for their actions. This baby is innocent. Completely and totally innocent. He must be allowed a fresh start."

"I agree. I'm just not sure that start should begin with us."

"But why?"

Alex sat down on the foot of the bed. "It's just that I wouldn't want this baby to be a reminder of all you suffered, a living memory of the things that happened the night Father died."

"Alex, you're worrying for nothing. I look forward to grandmothering this infant. I don't have the stamina to raise him, but you do. You would make a good mother for this child. He's flesh of your flesh. He's your father's son. We can't let him go to strangers. Could you really abide that? Knowing that your little brother was out there somewhere with someone not of your choosing to raise him?"

"No, absolutely not!" Alex declared, feeling a fierce protective nature toward the baby. "But you are uppermost in my thoughts. I'd hate to see you hurt again. We'll be burying Father in four days' time. I'd like to be able to bury the pain of his actions as well."

"This baby will always be with us," Katherine stated matter-of-factly. "You can't bury everything about your father's indiscretions. But God can make smooth the rough places. He can bring sunlight to the shadows and change night into day. A God who can do all of that can surely heal the hearts of two women."

Alex smiled. "Luke once accused me of thinking God couldn't handle everything. That some things were just too big."

"And was he right? Did you feel that way?" her mother asked softly.

Alex chewed on her lip for a moment before responding. The way she'd felt only weeks ago seemed so very different than the way she felt now. "I suppose I did in some ways," she finally said. "I didn't mean it in the literal sense, because I know nothing is too big for God. But it seemed too big."

"And now?"

"Now I feel confused by the sudden change of many of my feelings."

Her mother smiled and gently laid the baby on the bed. "Luke?"

"For one," Alex admitted. "I love him."

"Yes, I know."

"And he loves me."

"Again, this is not news to me." Her mother reached across the baby to touch Alex's knee. "What are you going to do about it?"

"He wants an answer to his proposal of marriage. He's bought a ranch in Wyoming and would have us live there with him. All of us. Me, the baby, and you."

"He said as much."

Surprised, Alex rose from the bed. "When? When did he tell you about this?"

"Yesterday, after you left to go think and pray."

Alex paced the floor at the end of the bed. "Mother, it's so hard to know what's right. My heart tells me one thing, but my mind . . ."

"Reminds you of the past and of the bad things done to you," her mother interjected.

"Yes. Yes, the past is haunting me. I couldn't face Luke if he took lovers as Father did."

"He won't."

Her mother's voice held such certainty, but still Alex wasn't convinced. "He's just a man, Mother. He's flesh and blood. He'll be tempted."

"Maybe tempted, but he won't cheat on you as Rufus did with me. I feel confident of that."

Alex shook her head and stopped directly in front of her mother. She wanted to believe her words, but fear bound her in a way that nearly choked all hope from her. "How can you be so sure? What guarantee can you offer me?"

"Alexandria Keegan, you know full well that life comes without guarantees. However, you also know that God has promised to be with us through the thick and thin of it. How can you doubt that He would protect you and help keep Luke faithful?"

"But God didn't keep Father faithful."

"Your father didn't desire to be faithful. Not to me, nor to God. Your father had his own plan and always at the center of it was Rufus Keegan. Luke loves God."

"I know he loves God, Mama," Alex said, falling to her knees in front of her mother. "But he's only human."

"As are you. What makes you so sure you won't be tempted to cheat on Luke? After all, you'll be stuck out in the middle of nowhere on a ranch without too many other people around. Those who are around will most likely be men—ranch hands."

"That's silly. I could never look at another man as I do . . . Luke."

Realization began to sink in. Why should the same not be true for Luke? Why couldn't he be just as faithful as she? Why couldn't Alex trust that he would push aside any seemingly tempting moments in favor of his love for Alex?

"I'm being really ignorant, aren't I?" she asked her mother.

Katherine reached out and gently stroked her daughter's wavy brown hair. "It's the first time you've been in love. You're entitled to not have all the answers."

"I really do love him. When I wake up in the morning, he's the first person I think of. When I go to sleep at night, I always do so with something he said on my mind. He makes me laugh—he makes me feel safe and protected."

"And he loves God," her mother added. "What more could you possibly want?"

Alex shook her head. "Nothing. He's everything."

"So what are you going to tell him?"

Alex smiled. "I think you already know the answer to that. But what about you? Will you come live with us?"

Katherine looked to the baby and shook her head. "No. I have plans."

Alex pulled back. "Plans? What plans?"

"I want to sell the house in Williams and dissolve all of your father's business dealings. When this is completed, I want to move to a larger city—I'm not sure exactly which one. Maybe Denver, so that I could be close to you."

"What would you do there?" Alex got to her feet and pulled a chair up close to her mother's bedside. Sitting down, she waited for her mother to explain, seeing a light in her eyes that she'd not seen before.

"I want to buy a big house with lots of rooms. I want to open a home to women who have suffered as I have—as Valerie has."

"Valerie Winthrop?" Alex still prickled at the name. "I'm still working on my feelings toward her. She was always flirting with Luke and
lying to me."

"Don't blame her, darling. She has suffered unimaginable horrors
in her life. You two have more in common than you would imagine.
While her father thought she hung the moon and stars, he was always
busy. Too busy to guide her actions. She was spoiled and encouraged to
be flirtatious and do whatever she had to in order to get the attention
she wanted."

"But at least her father loved her."

"Yes, but an absent father is still an absent father, and a child growing up without the loving guidance of such a parent will still suffer. Just
as you did, but for entirely different reasons."

Alex felt overwhelmed with guilt. "I'm sorry I've judged her
harshly."

"I hope you will put the past aside," her mother said gently. "Valerie
decided to trust the Lord and follow His will—just last night. She and I
had a long talk."

"Really? Well, that is good news," Alex said, not exactly sure how to
deal with the issue. It was hard to just automatically switch from feeling
a measure of contempt to joy, yet this new information really did
change everything. *Oh, God, forgive me for my hardheartedness. I thank you
that Valerie Winthrop came to you. I'm glad you're there for each and every person, not just the ones I think deserve your mercy.* She felt deeply ashamed of
her attitude. "Oh, Mother, I have so much to learn—so far to go."

"But we all do. As long as we're still here walking this earth, there
are things the good Lord is teaching us—showing us—bringing us
through. Valerie is no different. She just needed help to see the way."

Alex felt tears come to her eyes. She sniffed and nodded. "I'm so
glad you were there for her. I'll make a special point to offer her my
apology and my congratulations."

"You'll have ample opportunity. You see, Valerie wants to help me
with my idea for the home to help needy women."

Alex was truly surprised by this. The Valerie Winthrop she knew was
self-centered and . . . *I'm doing it again,* she thought. *I'm judging her by
her old nature, not the new creation she is in Christ.* Meekly Alex questioned,
"She does?"

"Yes. Not only that, but she's going to talk to her father about putting some of the Winthrop money into the effort. With that kind of

backing, we can do something truly wonderful. We'll be able to buy a very large place, furnish it nicely, and even bring in some staff to help keep it up. Maybe we can offer programs to teach women various things that can help them to be more self-sufficient."

Alex laughed as she wiped away her tears. "You have this all figured out, don't you?"

Her mother smiled and nodded. "I've had a lot of time to think. Ever since your Father's indiscretions became more frequent, I wished there might be something out there for me. Then when he died and I was left alone while the investigation went on, I began to pray in earnest for how I might make a difference. I knew Rufus couldn't atone for his sins, but perhaps I could atone for mine, as well as serve other hurting women."

"I think it's a grand idea, Mother. If anyone can make such a thing happen, you'll be the woman for the job."

"I'm glad you approve."

Alex saw the joy in her mother's expression and it warmed her to the innermost part of her being. "How could I not? I only want happiness for you. You deserve it."

"So do you. So are you going to go find that cowboy and tell him how you feel?"

Alex smiled. "I think he's waited long enough for an answer—and for my complete trust."

"I think you're right."

As Alex got to her feet, her mother did likewise. Embracing her daughter, Katherine Keegan said, "Trust God first and foremost. The world will always disappoint you, but God never will. His love is never ending. He will see you through, even when things seem grim and dark. Even when the morning seems as though it will never come, He is your light. Don't put that job off onto Luke. He'll never be able to live up to it, and you'll be disappointed in him. Just remember, it's not his duty. As you said, he's only human."

Alex hugged her mother tight. She could only pray that she might gain insight and maturity from her mother's words.

A knock on the door interrupted their moment, but Alex knew she would carry their conversation in her heart for the rest of her life. Allowing her mother to answer the door, Alex finished wiping her eyes.

"Ah, here's where my best gals are held up," Luke announced as he came in. His loud voice woke the baby, causing Brock to whimper and fuss. Without a word to the ladies, Luke strode across the floor and picked the infant up and rocked him back and forth. "Guess I'm going to have to learn to be a little more quiet when I enter a room, eh, Mrs. Keegan?" He grinned at Alex's mother.

"When you have a baby in the house there are all kinds of concessions to be made," her mother answered.

Alex thought it rather amazing that Luke should feel so at ease with the child. Alex felt her cheeks grow hot when Luke looked up to catch her watching him. He winked and gave her a smile.

"We were just talking over our plans for the future," Katherine told Luke.

Alex nodded and tried to steer the conversation away from anything too personal. She wanted to wait until she and Luke were alone in order to discuss their own plans. "Mother plans to open a home for women who've been hurt or abandoned. She might move to Denver, and Valerie Winthrop is going to help her."

"Miss Winthrop? Really?" Luke seemed just as surprised as Alex had been.

"Yes," Alex replied. "Last night Mother helped Miss Winthrop see her need for the Lord."

"Well, I'll be," Luke said, nodding in approval. "Just goes to show those folks I would have given up on, God has a plan for. Good thing I'm not in charge."

Katherine smiled, looking more youthful in her appearance than Alex could ever remember. "I think we would all fail miserably at His job."

"Well, I know I don't have a big house yet, Mrs. Keegan, but you'd be welcomed to come live on our ranch and bring your wounded women too." He chuckled softly. "Hey, I might even put them all to work. After all, I'm going to need ranch hands."

Katherine and Alex shared a smile before Katherine crossed the room to take the baby from Luke. "You watch out, Luke Toland. I just might take you up on the offer." She rocked the sleeping child a moment before looking back up to Luke. "You know, you're quite good with children. I hope you'll give me lots of grandchildren. You'll no doubt be a wonderful father. We'll have to work on that Mrs. Keegan thing, however. I don't think I'd want you calling me that if we're to be family."

This time Luke blushed a deep crimson. Alex watched the color climb from the collar of his shirt and fan out across his cheeks. Even his nose turned red. "Well . . . uh . . . you know, I haven't had an answer from your daughter regarding that matter."

Alex knew the time had come to talk to Luke about her feelings. Looking to his broken wrist, she questioned, "Luke, do you suppose you could handle a horse? I mean for a ride?"

Luke looked at her with a bemused expression, seeming to forget his embarrassment. "Handle a horse? Can I handle a horse?" He looked to her mother. "Did you hear what she asked me?"

Katherine laughed and Alex reached out and grasped Luke's arm. Pulling him toward the door, Alex called back over her shoulder. "We're going for a ride, Mother. We shouldn't be gone long."

She could still hear her mother's gentle laughter in the hall as she led Luke toward the stairs.

"Can I handle a horse? What kind of question was that, Alex?"

"Better mind your manners, Mr. Toland, or you won't get an answer to the question you've been pestering me with of late."

Luke stopped short, and Alex couldn't help but laugh at the serious expression on his face. "Yes, ma'am," he said with the briefest nod. "I surely wouldn't want to jeopardize that."

"I didn't think so," Alex said with a smile.

CHAPTER TWENTY-NINE

*A*lex finished with her horse, slipping three fingers between the cinch strap and the horse's belly to make certain it was tight enough. Satisfied with her job, she couldn't help but smile at the memory of Luke first teaching her to saddle a horse. She was just about as green as a girl could be when it came to dealing with livestock. She'd lived a sheltered city life, and the idea of having to deal with a horse was not only foreign to her, but scared her as well.

"What's that smile all about?" Luke questioned.

"I was just remembering when you first taught me to do this."

"You haven't done it all that much even in the four years since you've been here. I'd better inspect your work." He took his horse's reins in hand and wrapped them around the fence post. He went to Alex, looked over her work, and nodded. "You always were a quick learner."

"I had a good teacher," she threw back.

Alex raised the split skirt just enough to bring her booted foot to the stirrup. This accomplished, she grabbed for the horn and gave a couple of bounces to hoist herself into the saddle. Luke helped by giving her a push. He adjusted her stirrups to the proper length, making certain she was comfortable.

Handing her the reins, Luke let his hand linger on hers. "See, I told you I could handle a horse."

She grinned. "We haven't even started the ride yet. I wouldn't be boasting until after we return."

He laughed, gathered up his own reins, and vaulted into the saddle. Alex thought he made it look so easy. She always felt as though she were raising her leg straight up in the air just to put her foot in the stirrup.

They moved away from the stable at a leisurely pace. Alex eyed Luke's cast and thought again of his injury. "So how is the arm? Is it hurting much these days?"

"Nah, it's mostly just an inconvenience now. I can't believe I have to wear this cast for another few weeks. Seems like bones ought to knit faster than that."

"Too bad your patience suffers just as long in coming," she teased.

"I have more patience than you know of. I've been mooning over you all spring and you didn't even notice me."

Alex felt her stomach do a flip. "I noticed you, but I didn't notice you like that. I thought you were just—"

"A good friend," Luke interrupted. "I know. I came to hate those words."

She laughed and took the lead on the trail as it narrowed. They rode for some distance, neither one talking. Alex knew Luke was waiting for her to speak up and tell him what he wanted to hear, but frankly she was nervous. Her hands were shaking even as she gripped the reins. Her horse whinnied softly, sensing her state of mind. *It was probably not a good idea to suggest the ride,* Alex thought. She knew horses were very sensitive to their rider's dispositions.

The trail widened again when they reached the place where it headed into the canyon, but the widening was brief. The path quickly narrowed as it dipped at an incline. The canyon spread out below like a rich tapestry of browns and golds, greens and reds. It was God's handiwork and God's alone.

Instead of going into the canyon as Alex had suggested earlier, she reined back on the horse. Luke came even with her and frowned.

"What's wrong?"

"I think I'd like to talk to you here. My hands are shaking so hard I can hardly hold on to the reins."

Luke grinned. "Shaky hands make it sound like things just might be going in my favor."

She cast a gaze toward the skies above. "Doesn't everything go in your favor?"

"I sure hope so—especially in this case."

He dismounted and Alex did the same without waiting for his help. Kicking free of her stirrups, she slid over the side of the horse and landed with a thud on the rocky path. She was going to have to get a whole lot better at this kind of thing if she was to become a rancher's wife.

She pulled the horse along and went to stand not far from the path. "So what's wrong with being friends?"

The question took Luke off guard. In a flash she saw his expression change from humored to very serious. "There's nothing wrong with being friends, unless you want more." He came to stand beside her. "And I want more."

His horse whinnied and bobbed his head up and down against Luke's hold. They couldn't help but laugh at his antics.

"See," Luke said. "He agrees."

"So do I," Alex said softly. "About that and so much more."

Luke reached out and pushed back an errant strand of brown hair. "I love it when you wear your hair down. Did you know that?"

"No, I don't guess I did," Alex replied, feeling her heart pick up its beat. Her breath caught in her throat.

Luke gently stroked her cheek. "So what more do you want?"

"Hmm?" she asked, feeling a million miles away, mesmerized by his touch.

"You said you wanted so much more."

She nodded and looked back to the canyon. This piece of ground, this phenomenon of nature had played such an intricate role in her life. Even now, it was the scale on which she measured her next words.

"I want to receive enough love to fill up this canyon. I want to give that much love in return." She turned to see Luke's thoughtful expression. This time she was the one who reached out. She touched Luke's cheek, feeling the warmth of his skin beneath her fingers. She rubbed her thumb along his jawline, the stubble scratching against her touch. Luke said nothing, although she could feel him tremble.

"I want to wake up every morning with my best friend at my side. I want your smile to be the first thing I see every day."

"I'm kind of a bear in the morning," he admitted. "You might not get a full smile out of me."

Alex laughed. "Well, if Daniel can brave the lion's den, then I suppose I can brave a bear in my bed." She raised a brow as if considering something important, then added, "And if it becomes too difficult, I'll simply have one of our children wake you up."

Luke reached for her and pulled her close. The reins of his horse slapped gently against her arm. "I like the sound of 'our children.' I like even better the idea of waking up next to you every morning."

"Oh, Luke, I love you more than I thought possible. The idea of giving my heart to someone has frightened me for so long that I couldn't imagine ever getting beyond that hurdle. I truly figured to be alone for the rest of my life—or at best to be living with my mother."

"Ah, darlin', I could never have let that happen. My life isn't worth a plug nickel without you. Spending most every day seeing you here at the canyon proved that to me. Every time you went away, I felt like a big chunk of my heart went too. I love you, Alex. I'll never love another woman. I told your mother that, and now I'm pledging it to you."

"What about Brock?"

Luke's brows drew together. "What about him?"

"What about us keeping him and raising him? It won't allow us to go into marriage on our own. We'll have a ready-made family."

"I don't mind one bit so long as you're a part of the arrangement. That baby doesn't appear to have anyone else standing in line to make him a home."

"But can you love him?"

"Can you?"

Alex nodded. "I wouldn't have asked if I didn't already have it in my heart to love him."

"Then give me credit for feeling the same way."

"You truly are a treasure of a man," she said, wrapping her arms around him. Lifting her face to him, Alex remembered the thrill of his kiss and hoped he'd seal the deal with another just like the first.

"So are you saying yes to me?" he asked, his mouth just an inch or so above hers.

"Yes," she breathed. "I'll marry you."

"When?"

She laughed. "Are you going to kiss me or not?"

He grinned at her playfully. "First answer my question. When are we getting married?"

"Probably sometime after my father's funeral. Knowing my mother, she's already planning the wedding. Will next week be soon enough?"

"I suppose if I have to wait until then, it'll have to do."

Alex tightened her hold on him. "Now kiss me."

"Yes, ma'am." Luke pulled her tight and lowered his mouth to hers. As his lips claimed her, Alex thought she might burst from the sheer joy of the moment. The emotion from their kiss warmed her from head to toe. Life with Luke Toland was going to be quite the adventure, she decided.

"Is this part of the park's new attractions?" a familiar voice called out.

Luke and Alex separated and pulled back to find Clancy leading a small group of mules and riders. He motioned to the group. "We're going to have to charge extra if this is going to be a regular show."

Luke kept his hold on Alex and nodded. "This is going to be a regular thing, but not here at the canyon. We're getting married and moving to Wyoming, just as soon as I get the details sorted out on the ranch I'm buying."

"That's why it's particularly fortunate that we've run across you here," another man called out. Bradley Jastrow dismounted from his mule and came to where Alex and Luke stood. "I was hoping to speak to you before I left the canyon tomorrow, and here you are."

"I didn't know you were still here, Mr. Jastrow," Alex commented. "I'd heard your party had pulled out."

"Most of them have," the handsome man admitted. "I dismissed my staff as soon as I gave the press the word that I was pulling out of the race for president. But I stayed on because I wanted to arrange something special. I haven't gotten all the details worked out, but I want you to have this." He reached into his pocket and pulled out an envelope. "Consider it thanks for saving my life."

Luke took the envelope, but shook his head. "No thanks are needed. Like I told you before, Alex is the one who had most of this figured out. I just kind of followed her lead."

"I'm grateful to you both. And in speaking with Miss Keegan's mother, I understand there might be reason to celebrate soon."

"That's right," Luke said, loud enough for Clancy to hear. "She just accepted my proposal of marriage."

"Well, pardon my sayin' so, Miss Keegan, but it's about time. I figured him a goner if you didn't give in soon."

Alex laughed, watching the grin broaden on Luke's face.

"I might say the same about you and a certain red-headed Harvey Girl," Alex teased Clancy. "I've seen the way you two look at each other, so don't think you're fooling me."

Clancy turned scarlet and looked away, muttering, "A fella has to think these things through."

Alex and Luke laughed, knowing that Bernice just might have her work cut out for her with Clancy Franklin.

"You both have my congratulations," Jastrow said, bringing their attention back to him. "Please consider this a wedding gift if you figure my thanks to be otherwise unnecessary."

Luke opened the envelope and studied the paper for a moment. "I can't accept this."

"Mr. Toland, please understand, I'm a wealthy man and this is one way I can show my appreciation. I know that there is no amount of money that could equal my life, but rest assured when I say this is but a pittance, and I truly want you to have it."

Alex couldn't wait any longer. "What is it, Luke?"

Luke handed her the paper. "Mr. Jastrow is arranging for us to take ownership of a nine-hundred-acre ranch, complete with herd and house."

"What!" Alex couldn't believe it. "Mr. Jastrow, that's much too generous. We could never accept this."

"Please. You saved my life, and I have it in my means to help you with your new start in life. I know you didn't save me because of what you could get out of me. That makes it all the more important that you let me do this. You helped me out of the goodness of your heart—out of a belief that life is sacred and that people should stop injustice where they find it. You were a blessing to me, now let me bless you in return. This entire matter has given me a new outlook on life. It's really changed everything for the better."

Alex looked to Luke and shrugged. "We've had worse thrust on us."

He laughed out loud at this. "Indeed we have. Well, Mr. Jastrow, I suppose we could allow you to impose on us just this once. But there must be a provision."

"And what would that be?" Jastrow asked.

"That you come out and visit us sometime. I know Wyoming is a long ways from Alabama, but a man of your means shouldn't find it too difficult."

Jastrow smiled and when he did, his entire face lit up. "I should say not. I would be most honored to visit you and your new bride in Wyoming. We'll set up the arrangements in a few months—after you've had time to settle into a routine."

"Oh, there will never be anything routine about living with her," Luke said in a teasing tone. "That's what I like the best."

———

Alex finished with her packing and made her way to the kitchen to say good-bye to everyone. It wouldn't be easy to say farewell to Michaela or Mrs. Godfrey, or even Bernice. Alex had come to care a great deal about each and every one of the girls, but especially those three people.

The plan was to return to Williams with her mother and to hold the funeral for Rufus Keegan on Friday. The fact that her father was truly dead still didn't register or ring true. Alex kept waiting for him to walk through the doors of El Tovar with his latest conquest at his side.

"I wish you weren't going," Michaela told her as she approached the salad preparation area.

"I know. I'm going to miss you all so much. But you'll come visit me on your vacations, won't you? I plan to have a big house with lots of guest rooms," Alex said enthusiastically. "I want lots of visitors, especially at first, because I know nothing of being a rancher's wife and everyone tells me it's very hard and very lonely."

Michaela laughed and tweaked Alex's cheek. "You'll never be lonely with that cowboy of yours."

Alex knew she spoke the truth. She couldn't begin to imagine herself lonely with Luke in the same house. "Then there's Brock. We're adopting him, you know."

"I'd heard that, but to tell you the truth, I thought you were crazy."

"But he's my brother—he's family. I couldn't send him out to be taken in by strangers. What if they failed to teach him about God? What if they were mean and heartless people?"

Michaela patted her arm and nodded. "I know. I know. I completely understand. I only thought you were crazy because you'll have no time to be alone, just you and Luke."

"We'll make up for that," Alex said confidently.

"Alex!" Bernice called, bringing in a tray of dirty dishes. "Are you leaving now?"

"On the evening train," Alex replied. "My father's funeral is Friday and my mother wants to prepare the house in case people stop by."

"But of course they'll stop by," Bernice said, taking Alex's hands in her own. "I wish we'd had more time to know each other. I already feel we're the best of friends."

Alex felt a special warmth toward the girl. They'd shared the horrible scene of Rufus Keegan's indiscretion, yet Alex had never known a gossipy word to come from Bernice on the matter. She valued and trusted the girl.

"We are the best of friends," Alex agreed, "and as I was telling Michaela, you must come and visit me soon. I'll send Mrs. Godfrey my Wyoming address."

"I've already checked into it," Bernice admitted. "We can take the train from here to Williams and head to New Mexico and up through

Colorado. We have to change trains a couple of times, but then we head to Cheyenne and over to Laramie. It's really quite easy."

Alex laughed. "It sounds like you have it pretty well figured out."

Bernice nodded. "I don't have too many friends, so I'm not about to lose the ones I do have."

Alex left them to go in search of Mrs. Godfrey and found the woman in her office. "I've come to say good-bye. We take the evening train to Williams."

"Yes, I know," Mrs. Godfrey replied. "I'm going to miss having you here. You're my number one girl. In the four years since you came to El Tovar, I've never had a moment's trouble with you."

"Until the last month," Alex teased.

"No, even then the problems weren't of your making. You were merely caught up in the games that were played out around you. You were never to blame." Mrs. Godfrey extended an envelope. "Here is the pay owed you."

Alex took the envelope and tucked it in the pocket of the green skirt she wore. "Thank you."

"And this is a little something from the girls and me," Mrs. Godfrey said, pushing forward another envelope. "We all wrote a little note to you so that when you feel the need for company you can open this letter and have all of us with you."

"Thank you," Alex whispered, her voice cracking. Tears slid down her cheeks. "I'll cherish this. You truly were my family here."

"How is your mother taking all of this?"

"She's doing remarkably well. Who would have guessed that there was such a bold, adventurous woman buried beneath that tiny frame? She's already contacted a real estate company in Denver. She's to look at four estates the week after next."

"When do you plan to marry?"

Alex grew thoughtful. "I didn't want to do anything that seemed disrespectful to my father. I figured to wait several weeks, but my mother insisted we go forward with the wedding as soon as possible. We'll probably marry in Denver, although I wish it could be here with all of you. What a very special ceremony that would be."

"It will be special no matter where you have it," Mrs. Godfrey insisted. "We'll all be with you in spirit, if nothing else."

The clock on the wall chimed and Alex realized the hour was getting away from her. "I'd better go. I need to find Luke and make sure he knows how to find us in Williams. He won't be able to join us until tomorrow."

Mrs. Godfrey got to her feet and came around the desk to give Alex a hug. "God be with you, child, and if you ever want to come back to work for Fred Harvey Company, you know you have a job."

"I'll remember that," Alex said, kissing the older woman's cheek. "Thank you. For everything."

CHAPTER THIRTY

*G*oodness, Mother, I've never seen you so worried about catching the train," Alex said as her mother bustled around the room. "Where is my traveling dress? I laid it out before I went downstairs."

"I packed it away. I have a special dress for you to wear," her mother said, pulling a box from under the bed.

"Mother, is this new?" Alex questioned. She opened the box to reveal a beautiful creation in crepe. Pulling the dress out, Alex gasped. "Mother, this is incredible. Where did you get it?"

"I have my sources," she said smiling. "I just think it would be to our benefit to look our best when we return to Williams. We've lived in shame for too long. Now we can return with our heads held high."

"But what about Father and mourning? This gown is the palest lavender I've ever seen. It's almost white. And silk hose and matching shoes! I can't believe it. This is far too rich for the likes of me."

"Nonsense. You're a Keegan, and your financial situation is not such that you should dress as a pauper. Now, hurry. I want to be ready to leave in exactly half an hour."

"But, Mother, that will put us waiting at the station for at least an extra thirty minutes."

"I don't care. That's the way I want it. Now you dress. I need to finish with my jewelry. Brock is sleeping, so he shouldn't be a problem for either of us."

Alex nodded. There was nothing else she could do. Her mother had made up her mind and Alex hadn't seen her this animated in a long, long time. Maybe never. Putting the gown back into the box and taking it with her into the private bath, Alex began the transformation.

Peeling off her old blouse and skirt, Alex took up the new dress and marveled again at the silky feel. The delicate handkerchief hemline was scalloped and trimmed with a fine lace. Alex pulled the dress on over her head and marveled at the feel of it against her skin. She adjusted the top and smoothed the low waistband across her hips. Looking in the mirror, Alex thought the color was marvelous. The pale lavender reminded her of the orchids that sometimes were brought in to grace the Harvey tables.

"Arrive in style, eh, Mother? Well, we will certainly be doing that."

Alex added the hose and shoes of the same color, then wondered about what she should do with her hair. Pinning it carefully, she looped and twisted her wavy curls until she had managed to pile it all atop her head. She would have to wear a hat, of course. No decent woman would travel with her hair bare, and this style would allow her to wear even the closest-fitting hat. Then it dawned on Alex that she didn't have a hat worthy of this dress.

Running her hand down the material of the long sleeve, Alex smiled. She had planned to locate Luke and tell him good-bye. He would be so surprised to see her in this. The smile stayed on her face even as she came into the bedroom. "Well, how do I look?"

Her mother turned from where she was fussing with the baby. "Oh my!" She put her hand to her mouth.

Alex twirled around in a circle. "I don't know how you managed this, Mother, but thank you. It's lovely."

"Well, actually, I did have some help. I hope you don't mind. The dress has never been worn, but it did belong to someone else—Valerie Winthrop."

Alex paused a moment and waited for some ill feeling to surface. But there was none. Smiling, she shook her head. "I don't mind at all. I hold Valerie no malice. Especially now that she will be working with you on the house in Denver. No, my only regret is that I don't own a decent hat to wear with it."

Her mother went to the far side of the bed and held up a hatbox. "You do now." She smiled. "I hope you don't think me silly, but I really wanted things to be perfect."

Alex laughed and pulled out the cloche hat of the same pale color. It dipped low on one side and flared out ever so slightly on the other. "Oh, it's charming." She hurried back to the bath where she tried the hat on while looking in the mirror. "It's perfect, Mother."

"Wonderful. Now we really must hurry. I have the baby ready to go. I've asked Michaela to come and help us." A knock sounded at the door and her mother hurried to answer it, even as Alex came from the bath. "And here she is."

Michaela took one look at Alex and began to clap. "My, but don't you look marvelous. The picture of grace and elegance."

"My mother gave me this wonderful outfit. Believe it or not, it's one of Valerie Winthrop's. Apparently she purchased it, but changed her mind." Alex twirled in girlish delight. "Mother said it's never been worn."

"Until now," Michaela replied. "And worn quite well. Luke's eyes will pop out when he sees you."

"Well, that's provided I can find him. I looked all over for him earlier. He promised to come to the station with us."

"Then I'm sure he will," Michaela declared. "Here, Mrs. Keegan, I'll take baby Brock." She took the baby in her arms and cooed at him. Brock seemed captivated with her murmurings and watched her silently.

"I can carry him," Alex said, reaching out for the baby.

"You'll get to play with and carry him all the time," Michaela replied. "It's my turn for now."

Alex laughed. "I thought you weren't interested in children."

Michaela jostled the baby in her arms and replied quite seriously, "I can't imagine what you're talking about. I'll probably have at least ten." She giggled then and stuck her tongue out at Alex. "Oh, you're right. I'll probably never have any, but I don't mind carrying Brock just now."

"What of the luggage, Mother?" Alex asked.

"The bellboy was coming up right behind me," Michaela replied. "So we needn't worry about that. Come on. I'll walk with you."

Alex chatted with Michaela and her mother about the days to come. Michaela promised to come to the funeral and offer her support, and Alex blessed her for her concern. They descended the stairs, Alex knowing in her heart it would probably be the last time that she'd do this. She looked around her as if to memorize every feature.

"Funny," she told her companions, "I've lived here for four years and never really thought about the day I'd leave."

"Will you be sad?" her mother asked, her tone quite serious.

Alex shook her head. "No. Not at all. I'll have Luke and the baby, and one day we'll have children of our own. I'm bound and determined to prove myself a good rancher's wife. I'll buy books or take lessons or whatever it takes so that I'm just as useful to Luke as I can be."

Michaela laughed. "Oh, you'll be useful to him. On those bitterly cold Wyoming nights, he won't even need to take a hot water bottle to bed with him."

They laughed at this and proceeded through the lobby to the porch. "Well, this is it," Alex said as they descended the steps. She turned to say something else and forgot her words as she gazed across the lawn to the south rim and found Luke and a multitude of others gathered.

"We wanted to surprise you," her mother said when Alex turned a questioning gaze upon them. "I didn't want you to have to wait for a funeral in order to have a wedding."

"I don't understand," Alex said, looking from her mother to Michaela.

Michaela laughed and shifted the baby. "This is your wedding, silly. We hope you don't mind that we took liberties, but what's done is done. You can't leave the man waiting at the altar, so pick up the pace."

Alex looked across the lawn again and met Luke's gaze. He was dressed impeccably in a dark blue suit that she didn't recognize. Maybe it, too, was compliments of the Winthrops.

Her hands trembled as she turned to her mother once again. "You planned all of this for me?"

"I'm sorry if I've overstepped my bounds. A woman should plan such things for herself, but I couldn't bear the idea of a hurried wedding in Denver. Your friends are here. Why not have it here?"

"I'm delighted. Stunned. But nevertheless, delighted."

They made their way across the lawn, and Alex found Mrs. Godfrey nodding in approval and wiping tears from her eyes as Alex joined Luke before the preacher.

"You look . . . well . . . there aren't words," Luke said as he took hold of her hand. "I'm completely captivated."

Alex smiled. "I'm rather taken aback, myself. You cut quite the figure in that suit."

Luke pushed back his sandy hair and grinned. "The collar itches. I can't wait to get out of it. It's sure not what I'm used to."

Alex giggled. "Me neither. The Harvey uniform was good enough for me."

"Shall we begin?" the preacher asked.

"Yes, we have to hurry," her mother said, coming to stand beside her daughter. "The train leaves in thirty minutes."

Alex looked to Luke. "It's not what we planned, but do you mind?"

"I don't mind at all. This way I know you're mine—I know you won't change your mind before I can join you in Williams."

"I wouldn't change my mind anyway, Luke Toland. You're stuck with me through thick and thin."

"Just the way I want it."

The sun had moved to the west, but it still shone across the canyon in a glory of color. Alex marveled at the wonder of it all. The way the clouds played across the blue skies, the way the shadows below danced in and out of the crevices. Alex knew that as long as she lived, she would always stand amazed at what God had done here.

"Are you ready to do this?" Luke asked. She nodded, feeling the thrill of his smile go clear to her toes. He turned to the preacher. "Let's get to it."

Twenty minutes later Alex was announced as Mrs. Luke Toland. Everyone pelted them with rice as the first warning whistle sounded from the train in the station.

The party moved en masse toward the station but held back, giving their good-byes before reaching the platform. When only Luke remained, he took Brock from Michaela and crossed the platform with Alex at his side. Katherine took the baby from his arms and moved to board the train.

"I'm blessed to have you for a son," she told him as he helped her aboard the train.

"I'm blessed to have you for a mother," Luke replied in turn. "Mine has been gone for a very long time, and I think it will be pretty nice to have you around from time to time. Are you sure you don't want to come and stay with us for a while?"

"Not just yet. There's so much work to be done. I want to stand before the Lord and feel I did my best for Him."

"That's all any of us want," Luke agreed. "I have a feeling you'll more than satisfy the Lord in your love for others."

Katherine smiled. "I have no doubt the same will be true for you. I know what you did for Valerie. She told me about your kindness to her, talking to her about God despite her brazen actions toward you. You have a good heart, Luke." She smiled at Alex, who stood only a few feet away, listening to their exchange. "Now, you go give your wife a proper good-bye and we'll see you on Friday."

Luke nodded. "Yes, ma'am." He tipped his hat and waited until Katherine had disappeared before turning to Alex.

"You said some very sweet things to my mother," she told him as he took her in his arms. As he pulled her close, Alex put her hands on his chest. "Behave yourself—we're in public, Mr. Toland."

"Yes, Mrs. Toland, but I'm a newly married man and I won't be able to hold my wife again until . . . well, it seems like it will be forever. As soon as I finish showing the new crew the ropes, I'll be back, and then I'll never have to let you go."

She smiled and lifted her hand to touch his face. "I know. I feel the same way, even if it is only until tomorrow."

He kissed her sweetly on the mouth, then trailed kisses on her cheek and nose and eyes. "Don't forget me," he whispered just before he kissed her mouth again.

Alex pulled back and smiled. "I could sooner forget to breathe."

The train whistle blasted and the conductor called the final board.

"I have to go," Alex said, pulling away from Luke's protective hold. "I'll pick you up at the station tomorrow. Don't miss the train."

"I won't. I'll be there before you know it. You'll see."

He walked her to the train and let the conductor help her aboard. "I love you," he whispered.

She replied in like manner, but the train whistle blocked out her words. They laughed and Alex found herself pushed up the stairs by the insistent conductor. She waved as the train pulled out, joyous in her newfound feelings of love and contentment. There was no fear of whether he'd come back to her. No fear of what might happen in her absence. God had melted away her fears—He had taken away the shadows and put sunshine and hope in their place.

*A*lex laughed at the antics of two-year-old Brock as he toddled around the corral where his father worked to pick out the horse stock he would sell in Laramie.

"He'll be climbing that fence before you know it," Luke called out as Alex pulled Brock away from the fence.

"Don't I know it. He already climbs everything else. I'm always finding him up on the table," Alex replied.

It was their second-year anniversary, and Alex couldn't help but wonder if her husband would remember. She had a very special gift for him, but she hated to mention it for fear he had forgotten. She certainly didn't want to make him feel bad.

Luke continued with the stock, pointing out this one and that one among some thirty horses. Clancy, who'd joined them from the canyon recently, marked the horses in order to separate them out later.

Brock fussed in Alex's arms. "What's the matter, little man?"

"Wanna horsey. Wanna ride horsey."

"You can't go riding just now. Papa will take you later," she said softly and kissed his dirty cheek. The boy squirmed and fussed until she put him on the ground. "Why don't you go play with the puppies?"

"Pubbies!" Brock clapped his hands and headed to the porch where their collie dog, Mollie, kept her rapidly growing brood of six pups.

Two years of marriage to Luke. Two marvelous, love-filled years, she thought as she dusted the dirt from her apron. She'd been happier than she'd ever dreamed possible. Happier still when Clancy showed up to hire on with the announcement that he and Bernice would be getting married the following October. They had all agreed that

Clancy and Bernice would need their own little house, so he and Luke had begun immediately to put something together. Alex was delighted with the news that Bernice would soon be her ranch companion. The company of other women was generally reserved for church on Sunday or those rare occasions of visiting.

The men came from the corral and Clancy nodded and took the paper from Luke. "I'll see to this, boss. Don't you worry a thing about it."

"With you on the job, Clancy, I never do."

Luke crossed the yard to where Alex stood. "I have a surprise for you. Will Brock be all right for a few minutes?"

"Oh, sure. He's with Mollie now." She pointed to where Brock patted the mother collie on top of the head with rather strong-handed pats. "Be gentle, Brock. Don't hurt Mollie."

"I see pubbies," he said, moving from Mollie to the babies.

"He'll be busy for a few minutes—but only a few. He'll soon figure out that he needs to be off doing other things."

Luke laughed. "Then come with me to the barn. I want to show you something."

"All right."

Alex looped her arm through his. "So what's the occasion, Mr. Toland?"

"You know full well the occasion, Mrs. Toland. It's the same occasion that caused you to bake a cake this morning." He looked at her and laughed. "You thought I'd forgotten our anniversary, didn't you?"

"I didn't think that at all. I just didn't want you to feel bad if you had."

"Well, I didn't forget. In fact, I've been thinking about it for weeks. I got Clancy to help me with your gift."

"Really? What is it?"

"You have to wait and see. Now close your eyes and I'll lead you."

She laughed and did as he bid her. Leading her into the barn, Alex felt the warmth of the sun diminish and the shadow of the interior fall upon them. It was a bit cooler here, but only marginally. But instead of stopping and having her open her eyes, Luke led her back outside. Alex could only imagine that he'd taken her completely through the barn.

"Okay, you can open your eyes now."

Alex did so and found herself standing in front of a car. "You bought this for me?"

"Well, for us, but I figured it was time you learned to drive. You never know when you'll need to take yourself to town when I'm too busy to drive you."

"Oh, Luke, you're a very thoughtful husband."

He turned and studied her for a moment. "Do you really like it? I know you've never been all that fond of automobiles, but they really are the way of the future. The horse and buggy days are all but behind us. Especially in the cities. I figure the day may even come when we want to drive to Denver and visit your mother."

"I'd like that," she admitted. "Yes, it's the perfect gift."

He smiled and kicked at the dirt. "Glad you like it." He paused for a moment. "So what did you get me?"

"Well," Alex began, "you can't have it just yet."

He frowned. "Why not?"

"Because it won't arrive here until about six months from now." She grinned and felt overwhelmed with the joy of her news. "We're going to have a baby."

He stared at her in disbelief. "We're what? Are you serious?"

She giggled. "Yes, I'm quite serious."

Without warning he lifted her in the air and circled her around and around. Putting her back on the ground, Luke pulled her into a crushing embrace. "I couldn't be happier. This is the most wonderful news I've had since you agreed to marry me."

"I thought you'd be pleased," she said, seeing the pure joy in his expression. "I know I am. I'm completely in love with the idea of having your babies."

He set her away from him just a few inches and put his hand to her stomach. "Do we really have to wait so very long?"

"Good things take time. You worked for four years to get me," she reminded him.

"I know, and it seemed to take forever."

"Well, this baby will be with us before you know it."

"God has been so very good to us," Luke said, putting his arm around her shoulder. Together they walked back to the house where Brock was still consumed with his puppy visit. "Brock will be excited, that's for sure. He sometimes seems kind of lonely."

Alex nodded. "I know, but soon he'll be patting the baby on the head instead of Molly." She smiled and leaned against Luke, her head nestling against his shoulder and neck. She had never wanted anything more than what she had with Luke. Gone were the nightmares of the past, her anger with her father. Yielding it to God seemed the only way to have true happiness.

"I wanna ride horsey!" Brock declared, seeing them standing there watching him.

Alex smiled and turned to her husband. "Well, I suppose you and the boy should take your daily ride."

"I suppose we should," he said as Brock came plowing across the porch and jumped off the edge. Luke caught him and lifted him high in the air before settling him on his shoulders. "The boy is fearless."

"So are you," Alex said with great pride.

"That goes the same for you, my darlin'. I think you're probably the bravest one of us all."

"It comes with knowing where to place your trust," Alex said, knowing Luke would appreciate her meaning.

He leaned over and kissed her forehead. "I couldn't have said it better."

Across the Years

CHAPTER ONE
Winslow, Arizona, September 1929

a'am, my train leaves in less than ten minutes," an irritated passenger complained.

Ashley Reynolds pulled a slip of paper from her apron and handed it to the man. "Sir, there's plenty of time. Here's the check, and I'll have those sandwiches ready for you to take momentarily." She sighed. The life of a Harvey Girl was not all it was cracked up to be. Especially when working the lunchroom counter. Ashley much preferred her regular duties in the dining room. It always seemed the lunchroom counters of Fred Harvey's restaurants were frantic-paced battlegrounds where a girl's only weapons were her charm and quick wit.

In another hour it was all behind her—at least the work was behind her. The worst was yet to come. With feelings of trepidation, Ashley finished straightening her station and headed to the back room.

"Are you going home?" one of her co-workers questioned.

Ashley didn't feel like chatting. "Yes," she answered in a rather curt manner. "See you tomorrow." But even as she said the words, Ashley realized that wasn't true. She wouldn't be back to work tomorrow or the day after. Maybe never.

Turning in her resignation was the hardest thing Ashley had ever done. After working nearly ten years for the Harvey Company, Ashley was quite comfortable in her routine. Now everything was changing—and not for the better.

A hot desert wind whipped across Ashley's skirt as she made her way home from work. Worn and perspiring from her long hours waiting on customers, the dry breeze created the tiniest sensation of cooling, and Ashley cherished it. A weariness unlike any she'd ever known, however, sapped all remaining strength. How was she ever to find solace when she would soon become the bearer of such bad tidings?

Walking past the construction of the new Harvey hotel resort, Ashley couldn't help wondering if the throngs of tourists would come as they had predicted at the onset of this proposed high-dollar dream. Vast gardens, orchards, and lavish furnishings were to beckon the wealthy to come and take their rest—and spend their money.

Having worked for nine years at the established Harvey House to the west, Ashley thought the new resort a waste of money and time. She found it impossible to believe people would actually spend a small fortune to come and bask in the desert heat. Not that she didn't love Winslow and all it had to offer. This had been, after all, home for the last ten years, and she'd grown rather attached to its idiosyncrasies and lovable characters.

"Mama!"

Ashley glanced up the street. The animated movements of the skipping girl brought a smile to Ashley's face. Despite the warmth of the day, her daughter fairly danced along the brick sidewalk.

"What are you doing this afternoon, my little miss?" Ashley questioned.

"I took over that mending you did for Mrs. Taylor at the boardinghouse. She said to tell you that you sure do fine work." Natalie beamed her mother a smile. "She also gave me a nickel for being such a good delivery girl."

Ashley couldn't help grinning and shaking her head. The child positively owned Winslow, Arizona. She was everybody's darling. Everyone from the train yards to the downtown businesses knew Natalie Reynolds. Knew her and loved her.

"Well, that was kind of Mrs. Taylor."

Natalie fished into the pocket of her cotton dress. "She said to give you this." She handed a dollar bill to her mother. "She said this was for last week's mending too."

Ashley tucked the bill into the skirt of her Harvey apron and pulled out a nickel. "Why don't you go get an ice-cream cone. I need to talk to Grandpa, and dinner won't be for hours yet. You might well feel done in before then."

"I already have the nickel Mrs. Taylor gave me."

"Yes, but you may need that later for some other treasure. This time the treat's on me."

"Thanks, Mama." Natalie took the money. She leaned up on tiptoe as Ashley bent down, then kissed her mother soundly on the cheek before making a beeline for her favorite ice-cream parlor.

Ashley sighed as she watched Natalie's gleeful exit. She was such an easy child to care for, but Ashley worried about her. Being loved by the town regulars, Natalie held a loving attitude toward most everyone she met. With the trains that came and went at a constant pace, there were always strangers in town, yet Natalie knew no stranger. She would just as soon strike up a conversation with someone she'd never met as to talk with a friend. Soon she'd come to an age where that could be misconstrued as flirting—or worse yet, it could become very dangerous.

She's growing up so fast, Ashley thought as she continued her journey home. Had it really been ten years since Natalie had come into the world? Ashley remembered the easy delivery with fondness and regret. She had been alone, except for Grandpa Whitman. Her own parents had exiled her, rejecting her for marrying without their permission. Worse still, she'd married a man of no real means or status, something absolutely vital to her social-climbing mother and father.

Ethan . . . her beloved. The pain that had one time been a stabbing, white-hot torture was now a dull ache. Expecting Natalie had given her a will to go on after receiving notice that her war-hero husband had been killed. Ethan had never even known about the baby they'd created. They'd married in a whirlwind in March of 1918, and before either one knew what had happened, Ethan had gone to war and had given his life for his country. There was no time for letters to tell of the pregnancy. No time for letters telling him how much she loved him. No time for letters saying good-bye.

Ashley paused at the iron gate and stared at the brick house she'd called home. The two-story house was quite simple, but it suited her and Natalie and Grandpa Whitman just fine. They'd had a great life there— just the three of them. Together they never felt isolated. They had each other . . . and loved each other and it was that love that helped them through each difficult event.

But with the doctor's visit at the Harvey House today, Ashley knew all of that was about to change. She'd been serving at the lunch counter when he'd come in and asked to talk to her privately. The news was not good, and now she would have to break it to Grandpa. But how? How could she tell him that he was going to die—and quickly?

Cancer of the liver was the culprit, and like an unseen evil that had crept in while everyone slept, Ashley felt the burden of this horror wrap around her and threaten to squeeze the life out of her.

She pushed open the gate, her legs heavy—weighted, barely moving.

She trudged toward the front door and sighed. A person should never have a duty like this befall them, she thought. Ashley had been the one to make her grandfather go to the doctor, and upon completing the exam, Grandpa had flippantly told the doc to just let Ashley know the results of his tests. Grandpa had strolled out of the office as if he owned the world, in spite of the pain he'd been suffering.

Now the tests and examinations were complete, and the doctor felt confident that her grandfather would rather hear the truth from her than from him. He'd offered to accompany Ashley, but she knew her grandfather would resent the intrusion. He hadn't wanted to go to the doctor in the first place, but the pain had become nearly unbearable, and he could no longer ignore his weakness and loss of weight.

"Grandpa?" Ashley called out as she pulled open the screen door.

"I'm here." His voice lacked its usual firmness.

She entered the room, pausing momentarily to allow her eyes to adjust to the shaded room. Grandpa sat slumped at the dining room table, a newspaper laid out before him.

"We need to talk," Ashley stated matter-of-factly.

Russell Whitman looked up at her, appearing to gauge the importance of the matter without being told. "Sit down and tell me what's wrong."

Ashley pulled out the simple wooden ladder-back chair and sat. It felt so good to be off of her feet. She stretched her legs out under the table before looking up to meet her grandfather's intense stare.

"I talked to the doctor today."

Grandpa nodded, seeming to understand. "It's not good, is it?"

Ashley fought back the urge to cry. "No. It's very bad. You have a cancer in your liver."

"Can anything be done?" the eighty-two-year-old asked as he straightened in the chair.

Ashley longed to give him better news. She wanted so much for the entire matter to be a mistake. She bowed her head. "No. They can't do anything to eliminate it. The doctor did say he could give you morphine for the pain, but otherwise . . . well . . . it's just a matter of time."

"How much time, Ashley?"

His tone was almost childlike, causing Ashley to immediately seek his face. She saw the acceptance in his expression but also something akin to concern, even worry. "The doctor said it could be weeks, maybe even months."

"Not much time, then," he said, growing thoughtful.

Ashley reached out her hand and covered his bony fingers. "Not nearly enough." Again, she forced back the tears. His gruff, weathered face appeared so thin and pale. Just months ago he'd seemed vibrant and alive and now . . .

"Well, we need to make plans." He got to his feet slowly, grimacing in pain. "We have to see to everything right away. I can't be taking medicine like morphine and think clearheaded. I saw what it did to old Jefferson Dawson." He paused and looked at Ashley. "You remember him, don't you? Used to work at odd jobs around town."

"I remember."

"As I recall, he took up with using morphine after he'd had that scaffolding accident. Never was the same after that. I don't need that kind of confusion."

"But you also don't need to live in anguish," Ashley said, getting to her feet and coming to his side. "I don't want you hurting anymore."

He patted her hand. "Sweetheart, soon there will be no more pain. I reckon I can bear up just a little while longer. But the truth is, you and Natalie need for me to make some good choices and decisions now. I don't intend to see you left without provision."

With those words Ashley allowed the tears to come. A sob broke from her throat. Even with this terrible news, the old man was more concerned for her well-being than his own. "I can't lose you."

Grandpa pulled her close and gently patted her shoulder. "There, there. You're not losing me. You know that. I'll go to a better place. A place with no pain or sorrow. Would you deny me that?"

Ashley shook her head. "But I'll still be here with the pain. I know that sounds selfish, and I was really determined to be brave and strong for you. But, Grandpa, what will I do without you?"

"You'll survive. You'll live for Natalie, and you'll work to see her happy and healthy. It's just as it should be. I've lived longer than most. I've had some very good years." He chuckled weakly and added, "And some not so good years. But you'll see. It's all going to work—"

"I know. I know. '. . . together for good to them that love God.' But this is serious."

"So is that. God didn't give us His Word just to have us ignore it or take it lightly. I know you don't hold much stock in such matters. God knows I've tried to help you see the truth of it for yourself, but maybe this is one way you'll finally come to know the truth."

Ashley pulled away. Her grandfather had been after her for over ten years to join him and Natalie at church on Sundays and Wednesdays.

But Ashley couldn't understand a god who would let a woman fall in love with the man of her dreams, only to kill him off and leave her alone to raise a child her husband never even knew existed. That wasn't the kind of god she wanted to serve. So she always made sure she had to work whenever church was in session. She also made sure her heart was closed off to any of Grandpa's suggestions regarding God's love.

"Please, let's not make this about me. I want to know how I can best help you. The doctor said you'd need round-the-clock care before long. I've put in for a leave of absence from the Harvey House. I intend to take care of you."

Russell Whitman looked at her with an expression that suggested he just might put forth an argument about her actions, then nodded slowly. "I'd like for you to be with me. It won't seem nearly so tiresome or lonely with you by my side. You've been like a daughter to me."

Ashley hugged him, careful not to hurt his fragile body. "When my world fell apart, you were the one who was there to pick it back up for me. When Mother and Father turned me away . . . when Ethan died . . . when I found out I was expecting Natalie, you were the one who stood by me. Now there will be no one." She pulled away and swiped at her tears with the back of her hand.

"I'm sorry. Here I am a thirty-two-year-old woman, and I'm acting like a ten-year-old. Not even that. I know Natalie will handle this better than I am."

"You mustn't fret. I've got a plan," Russell Whitman said, going to the door. He took up his hat from the peg there and grabbed his cane. "I'm going for a walk just now."

"I'll start supper," Ashley offered.

"Nothing for me," he said as he often did of late. Ashley wondered how he'd managed to stay alive this long with the little he ate.

"I'll just fix something light. You might be hungry when you get back."

He nodded but said nothing more.

Russell Whitman took himself off toward the depot. He liked to sit and think while watching the trains come and go. The rhythmic rumblings as the wheels rolled over the tracks seemed to block out the rest of the world.

Lord, he prayed, *this is a hard one to face.* He continued ambling toward the tracks, mindful of the pain in his right side. *I always knew the day would come when you'd call me home, but there's so much I've left undone—*

so much I thought I'd have time to see to.

He lifted his snowy head to the heavens. White wisps of cloud hung like gossamer veils to the west. The land needed rain, but it probably wouldn't come.

"Hey, Russ!" a brakeman called. The man's face bore the same grease and grit that marred his overalls.

Russell waved his cane briefly. His steps slowed to accommodate the lack of support. "How are you doing, Bob?"

The man pulled his billed cap from his head and wiped his forehead. "Doing good. Doing good. The missus told me to invite you over for dinner next time I saw you. Said she'd make your favorite."

Russell smiled and leaned heavily on the cane as he paused beside the boxcar the man had just jumped from. "She makes the best Swedish meatballs I've ever had."

"That's 'cause she *is* Swedish," the man said with a laugh. "God bless Fred Harvey for bringing those girls west. My Inga was the best waitress he ever had and now she's mine."

"She's a keeper, that's for sure," Russell replied.

"You'll come, then?"

Russell thought of his situation and all the work that was yet to be done. Still, it might be one of the last times he'd have the opportunity to share a meal with his friends. "I'll come. Just tell me when."

"How about tomorrow about seven?"

Russell shifted his weight and began walking toward the depot bench. "Tomorrow it is."

He left the man behind and nodded to other workers as he crossed over the tracks. He liked the life here. It was so much more peaceful than Los Angeles, where he'd spent a good deal of his adult life.

He approached the depot and spotted yet another friend of his. Sam Spurgeon got to his feet and waved to the bench he'd just vacated. "I was keepin' it warm for ya."

Russell chuckled and shuffled toward the respite. "Good of you, Sam. Are you heading home?"

"Yup. Been here too long as it is. My daughter's gonna be wonderin' where I got off to." He laughed. "Like she wouldn't know where to find me. I tell her, 'Sissy, I go to watch the trains or to the cemetery to talk with your mother.' Never go anywhere else—no need." He shrugged. "Be seein' ya, Russ."

Russell smiled and took a seat, then sighed in relief. The pain dulled a bit. How long had he ignored it? Two, maybe three months? And now the doctor could only say that it was too late—that there wasn't much time. Maybe he'd known it all along—down deep inside. Maybe that was the reason he'd put off going to the doctor. It wasn't until Ashley had insisted that Russell had finally gone for an examination. Now the truth was known. Cancer.

Russ leaned forward on his cane and sighed again. This time it wasn't from relief. There was a dull ache deep in his heart for Ashley and what she would bear in the days to come. No doubt his care would be extensive.

It's not fair for her to have to care for me. She's had enough to see to. The thought bothered him more than he could say.

She's walled herself up, Lord. She thinks she's safe that way. Safe from the hurt and the people who would rob her of her joy. But we know that's not true. Lord, I worry about her, and the facts are, I don't hardly see how I can come home to you when she's so lost.

A Baldwin 4-6-2 pulling a long line of freight cars signaled down the track. Russell felt the ground quiver under the massive monster's approach. Such power and energy—and all from a man-made machine.

I've seen a lot in my time, Lord. I've seen powerful machines like this. I've watched contraptions take to the skies. I've lived through the War Between the States, the Spanish-American conflict, and the Great War. I've been blessed to not have to take up arms against any man, and for that I am grateful.

The train stopped—not at the depot, but down the line nearer the shops. The ground stilled, but not so Russell's heart.

I've seen a lot, Lord, but I've made a mess of a lot as well. You know the troubles I've caused and been a part of. You know I've not spoken to my own dear daughters in eleven-some years. Not of my choosing, but still it's something I've endured because of my actions.

And there's poor Ashley. Her sorrow has made her heart hard. She's lonely, yet she won't even turn to you for strength. What do I do, Lord? How can I leave now—just when it appears she needs me most?

———

Ashley climbed the stairs to her bedroom. She longed for a cool bath but knew there wasn't really time. She still needed to work on sewing Natalie's new dress; then there were the new curtains for Mrs. Simpson. Ashley thought of all the bits and pieces of sewing she'd taken on. It gave them a little extra money and that was always nice. They weren't paupers by any means, but they lived cautiously and conservatively. It suited them both after years of wealth and extravagance.

Sponging the heat from her body, Ashley finished by completely dampening her hair. With the short, bobbed cut, she wouldn't have much to worry with. She'd comb it out and maybe later put in a few well-placed bobby pins to add curl. This accomplished, she put her apron to soak and added her uniform to the growing pile of laundry.

"Well, there's going to be more time for the house chores at least," she murmured as she pulled a lightweight cotton dress over her head. "More time to spend with Natalie too." This bonus did nothing to mend her frayed spirit. A weariness and hopelessness—like she'd known the day the news came of Ethan's death—washed over her. Ashley sunk to the floor beside her cedar chest. "What are we going to do?" she whispered. She leaned against the chest for support and buried her face in her hands. Tears came again, but this time they seemed to stretch across the years to that day when hope had died.

She could remember exactly what she'd been doing—what she'd been wearing when word came of Ethan's sacrifice and bravery. That morning she had donned her two-piece salmon-colored dress—the one she'd worn when they'd married. The skirt fell just about eight inches off the floor, allowing her to show off the sweet little button-up boots Ethan had bought her just before he'd gone off to war. She liked to wear this outfit because it made her feel close to Ethan, and she always dreamed of wearing it when he arrived back home.

But, of course, he hadn't come home.

That August in Baltimore had been very warm, but a cold chill had permeated the house after word of Ethan's death. Only the news that she carried Ethan's unborn child had kept Ashley from throwing herself into the harbor. For days she had refused to see anyone, barely dragging herself from bed each morning.

Her mother, a socialite who valued her position and status more than her daughter, had cut off all communication with Ashley when news had arrived of her marriage to Ethan Reynolds. The man was of no account as far as her mother was concerned. As a student of architectural studies, he could hardly hope to go far; besides, his parents were common factory workers.

After Ethan had joined the army, Leticia Murphy had fought to get her daughter to annul the marriage but without any luck. When this failed, she made one final threat. The words still rang in Ashley's ears.

"Annul this farce of a marriage or you'll never again have anything to do with our family. The choice is yours. It's either him or us."

Ashley hadn't concerned herself overmuch with her mother's

threat. After all, her mother was always creating tirades, storming around for days in order to get her own way. Ashley had thought of simply going to stay with Ethan's parents. They lived just outside of Baltimore, and she knew they'd be delighted to take her in until their son returned.

Then the influenza epidemics began sweeping the larger East Coast cities. People were advised to stay inside, to wear a mask if they went outside—though the very smell of death necessitated one anyway. This made Ashley all the more determined to leave town and stay in the country with her in-laws, but then word came that both of Ethan's parents had succumbed to the flu themselves. Ashley was devastated. She would have to write Ethan with the news, and she knew his heart would break.

But before she could send him word, she was notified of Ethan's death. Shocked beyond words, Ashley had sat around in a stupor for days afterward. Her entire world had changed.

Somewhere, someone had told Leticia of Ethan's death. No doubt she knew full well Ashley couldn't afford the expenses that would come. Despite her grief, Ashley had already taken a mental tally of her assets and knew they were sorely lacking. No doubt her mother knew this too.

Leticia Murphy came to the little house Ethan and Ashley had rented and demanded entry. Ashley had no strength to deal with her mother, but rather than order her to leave, Ashley waited to hear what her mother had to say. A thin ribbon of hope still existed that her mother, seeing Ashley's grief, would find it in her heart to comfort her daughter. But that wasn't the case at all.

"You look positively ill—you don't have the influenza, do you?" Ashley's mother demanded to know.

"No, Mother. I do not have the influenza." Ashley wasn't sure how to break the news that her look of ill health came from morning sickness rather than the epidemic.

"Good. Look, I've heard of his death." Ashley burned at the thought her mother wouldn't even call Ethan by name. "We can still annul the marriage. You surely can't protest it now. The man is dead and hardly cares what you do. You'll forget about him, and in the meantime, you'll marry that nice Manchester boy your father and I have picked out for you. He's willing to overlook your indiscretion in marrying that Reynolds man."

"Will he also overlook the fact I will never love him?" Ashley threw back, feeling a bit of her determination return.

"Love has very little to do with a lucrative marriage. This is what your father and I want."

"I can't marry Mr. Manchester. Neither can I annul my marriage." Ashley had been about to tell her mother of her pregnancy when the woman began a tirade that didn't end until half an hour later. Ashley had been unable to even offer a word of protest or explanation. When her mother had finished insulting and demeaning Ashley and her choice of husband, Leticia Murphy had picked up her things and headed for the door.

"You are dead to me—just like my father," she decreed like a queen calling down a traitor. She had stormed from the room, but the mention of her father, Ashley's dear Grandpa Whitman, had given birth to an idea. Her mother had turned away from him, just as she had turned away from Ashley. And all because the man had become religious. He'd sold off a successful business to his partner and settled huge sums of money on his two daughters. But that had only proven to Ashley's mother that her father had lost all sense of reason. She refused to have anything more to do with the man because she believed he was a fool. Never mind that he was trying to put his life in order with his new spiritual beliefs. Never mind that the real estate ventures he'd made a fortune from were underhanded and oftentimes illegal. They'd made money for the family. Money which Grandpa Whitman quite generously lavished upon them all. Now that would stop, and Ashley's mother had been beside herself with the thought of what this would mean.

There had been a trip to Los Angeles for her mother and father. Ashley remembered it well because she'd not yet met Ethan and was still living at home. Her mother had said very little except that she and her sister Lavelle would straighten their father out or have him committed. When her parents had returned from Los Angeles, Ashley had been stunned to hear her mother say that they would no longer have any association with the crazed old man.

Ashley had tried to at least get her father to relay what had happened, but something had changed in him. It was almost as if her father's entire demeanor had taken on a different personality. He was no longer the man she could talk to.

Feeling isolated from her family and tired of dealing with her mother's misery, Ashley had been easily won over by Ethan Reynolds's winning charm. Within weeks of meeting, Ashley had married Ethan, furthering the disorder of her mother's once perfectly ordered world. Then Ethan died, and Ashley had wanted to die as well.

Natalie and Grandpa had given her a will to live—they'd made her happy in spite of her loss. And until now, life had been as close to perfect as it could be.

Ashley raised her head and drew a deep breath. She blew it out rather quickly and drew another. The action seemed to calm her a bit.

"Why can't things go on as they always have?" she asked in the silence of her room. "Why must I lose the people I love?"

CHAPTER TWO

A week later Ashley sat across the table from her grandfather. She
listened to him read from a list of wishes he had for his funeral. It
wasn't at all what she wanted to hear. In fact, Grandpa had been feeling better the last few days, and Ashley liked to believe the doctor was
wrong and that he had nothing more terminally wrong than a bout of
old age.

"I don't want a lot of fancy flowers," Russell Whitman said firmly.
"Never could abide that kind of nonsense. If you want to give me flowers, do it now. That's my motto." He looked up and grinned at Ashley,
his gray mustache twitching in boyish charm. "Frankly, I'd rather have
candy than flowers any day."

Ashley smiled. He had a way about him that always managed to
make her see the hope in every situation. He was just that kind of
man. His spiritual walk made him that way, she supposed.

"All right, so when I go shopping, I'll bring you a box of the best
chocolates," Ashley finally answered, attempting to change the topic.

"Make sure they have nuts in them," her grandfather said with a
wink before turning his attention back to the list. "Now, about the
burial."

So much for giving reality the slip.

"I want to be buried next to your grandma back in Los Angeles.
The lawyer will have all the information about that and make the
arrangements. Don't be thinking you have to have a service here and
there. Just have one here, put me in a box on the train, and ship me
off."

"I wish you wouldn't talk so casually about such things," Ashley
said, feeling a chill run along her spine.

Russell reached out and patted Ashley's folded hands. "But such things only deserve casual reference. I won't be in that box—you know that, don't you, child?"

Ashley knew he'd speak to her again of Jesus and heaven, but for once she didn't mind. Maybe she'd have some peace about her grandfather's dying if only she could make herself believe that God really cared—that He understood her pain. But if He understood, truly knew how she felt and yet did nothing, then that made it even worse.

"I don't know what I believe," she said frankly. "I think it rather cruel of God to give me the man of my dreams—the one great love of my life—and then take him away. Take him before his own child could ever get to know him—before he could get to know her. I think God is merciless at worst, or indifferent at best, to take you away now."

"So God is cruel and awful because He allows for death? Is that it?"

Ashley considered his words for a moment, then met her grandfather's hazel-eyed stare with determination. "Yes. I suppose that's exactly what I mean."

"But what if one person's death means other people live?" he asked softly. "And what if those who live go on to do profound and wondrous things—things that reach out to the rest of the world and inspire them to do something even better?"

"I've heard all this before," Ashley protested. "I know what's preached—that Jesus died to save us from our sins. One man's sacrifice for the masses. Which just proves my point. God let His own Son die a brutal death."

"I wasn't thinking of Jesus just then," her grandfather said softly. "I was thinking of your Ethan."

Ashley felt the wind go out of her. "Ethan?"

Russell nodded. "Ethan gave his life, throwing himself into the path of certain death, in order to save a unit of men. That much you know. But what you don't know is where it went from there. These things always have a rippling action, like a stone thrown into the water. Ethan saved lives, and perhaps those men in turn went on to save other lives and so on. Perhaps Ethan's sacrifice was the very turning point of the war. You have no way of knowing. Perhaps your daughter is living safe and free from the horrors that we heard about during the war because of Ethan and what he did."

Ashley said nothing. She had always seen her husband as a hero, had taught her daughter the same, but in truth she'd never considered how it might affect anyone else. In her own self-focused pain, she'd never really cared about the benefit to others.

"You're right, child, about Jesus sacrificing His life for the multitudes. But God wasn't cruel in sending His Son. He was generous and self-sacrificing. We believe God the Father, the Son, and the Holy Spirit are one. God gave of himself—don't you see? Jesus' death and resurrection continue to ripple out amongst the masses and make profound changes in lives everywhere. He came to serve—to be a sin offering in order that those who deserved to die might live. Jesus gave His life, and in turn, I accepted His gift. He saved my life as clearly as Ethan saved those men in the war. Because Jesus saved me, I became a different person, and because of that, I was available to help you when your time of need came. Ripples—don't you see? Jesus gave us a gift of eternal life. Ethan gave a gift of life to his men. Why can you accept one sacrifice and not the other?"

Ashley had no answer. The words pricked her conscience as they never had before. Grandpa had never used Ethan in an illustration about salvation. *It's not the same,* she told herself. *Ethan did his duty. He went where he was sent and followed the orders given him. He had no choice.*

But as soon as the thought came to light, she chided herself, knowing full well that this wasn't true. He had a choice. A choice to stay in his trench or to go after the enemy who was killing his friends and comrades.

"I need to get to work on the laundry," Ashley said, getting to her feet. "You should rest for now."

"I can't rest. The pain is too great," he admitted.

"I have the morphine powder," Ashley offered. "I can mix some up."

"That won't help this pain," her grandfather said, folding his papers. "My pain is over you, and I won't be able to rest until I know you have come to an understanding of the Lord and how much He loves you." He stood, folded the papers into his pocket, then shuffled across the room in a slow, determined manner. "You think on what I've said."

Ashley did think on his words, but if her grandfather had known exactly why she'd chosen to do so, he wouldn't have liked it. Ashley knew Grandpa held great store in his faith and the issues that came out of that faith. He wanted very much for her to believe—to accept the things he'd come to accept.

"Maybe I can do this for his sake," she said softly as she put another dress through the washer wringer. Squeezing the water from the material, Ashley contemplated what she should do.

"Maybe I could just tell him that I've accepted Jesus and repented of my sins and then he'll be happy," she murmured. What could be wrong in that? God would know the truth, so it wouldn't be like she was fooling Him. And Grandpa would die in peace.

Still, lying about something so important to Grandpa didn't seem right. Grandpa had always been able to pretty much read her like a book. Ashley couldn't abide that he was hurting and suffering because of her pride, but should she go to such extremes to make him feel better? Wiping her brow, she sighed. "I just don't know how to deal with this."

———

Natalie fiddled with her food, glancing from time to time down the hall to Grandpa Whitman's closed bedroom door. "He never eats with us anymore," she murmured.

Ashley poured some milk into Natalie's glass and took a seat opposite her daughter at the small oak table. "I know. He doesn't feel well enough to eat."

"But wouldn't food make him feel stronger? Doesn't he want to get well?"

Ashley knew the time had come to tell her daughter about the illness that would soon take her beloved great-grandfather. "Natalie, you know that Grandpa isn't a young man anymore. The doctor says that this sickness is too strong for an old man to fight. Grandpa probably isn't going to get well." She threw in the word *probably*, hoping to soften the blow.

Natalie put down her fork and stared down the hall. "He's going to die?"

Sorrow gripped Ashley's heart. "Yes."

"When . . . when will he . . . die?" Her voice quivered.

Ashley steadied herself with a deep breath. "Soon. The doctor said it wouldn't be very long."

Natalie's face contorted as she appeared to fight her emotions. "Does it hurt?"

Ashley saw her daughter's eyes dampen with unshed tears. "He's in some pain, but the doctor has given me medicine to help Grandpa. It should help keep the pain down."

"Will it hurt to die?"

Ashley hadn't anticipated the question. "I don't know. I don't think so."

"I wish he didn't have to die." The tears streamed down her cheeks. "I wish the people we loved didn't have to die . . . like Daddy and now Grandpa."

The mention of Ethan only served to multiply Ashley's pain. Why did it still have to hurt so much after all this time? It seemed that Grandpa's dying only served to reopen those old wounds. "We will miss him. Probably more than we realize."

Natalie scooted out of her chair and came to her mother. Ashley hugged her close and then drew Natalie onto her lap. "I wish you didn't have to hurt, sweet pea. I wish neither one of us had to hurt ever again."

"I try to be strong, Mama. I try to remember that God loves all of us and that He knows best. Grandpa said that just last week."

Ashley knew her daughter shared Grandpa Whitman's faith. She'd watched Natalie get baptized in Clear Creek just last year. The child seemed to have a profound grasp of the spiritual and yet, here she was, just a little girl saddened by the events of her life. Ashley wished she could kiss away the hurt and make it better.

Ashley smoothed back her daughter's light brown hair. How baby fine and soft it was, even now after years of rough-and-tumble play. "At least by knowing that Grandpa is going to die, we can say all the things that are really important. Some people never get to do that," Ashley offered.

"Like with you and Daddy?" Natalie questioned, rising up. "You never got to tell him about me."

A tightness formed in Ashley's throat and seemed to settle down over her chest. She strained to breathe and found it nearly painful. "Yes. That's true."

"Then I suppose it's better this way," Natalie said, sounding very adult. She hugged Ashley's neck once more, then hopped up and went back to her chair. The child sat in silence for a few minutes. She dried her eyes with the linen napkin, then questioned her mother. "Does Grandpa know?"

Ashley nodded. "Yes. He's probably suspected for a lot longer than any of us figured, but he knows the truth of it now."

"Is he afraid?"

"I don't think so, Natalie. I think he trusts that God has it all under control."

"Do you think that's true?" Natalie asked, her dark brown eyes wide with wonder.

Ashley felt trapped. She didn't want to discourage the one thing she knew Natalie would find solace in—her faith. Real or imagined, Ashley wanted her daughter to know the comfort and peace that Grandpa Whitman seemed to have. "Yes, Natalie. I'm sure God has it all under control. We just don't always understand why God does things the way He does." That much was true, Ashley realized. She did think God was in control. She just didn't think He was very fair or kind.

"Will you go to church with me after Grandpa is gone to heaven?" Natalie questioned.

Ashley studied the hopeful look on her daughter's face. It seemed she hung all her hopes on that one question. "I might even go with you before then," Ashley said, making up her mind that she would do whatever was necessary to put both her daughter and grandfather at peace through this dying process.

Natalie smiled. "I know that would make Grandpa feel better. Every Sunday we pray you'll come with us."

The wonder of that statement buried itself deep into Ashley's heart. "You do?"

Natalie nodded and picked up her fork. "Grandpa said if we prayed long and hard, God would bring it to pass." She looked rather thoughtfully at the food on her plate before raising her gaze again to her mother. "Do you think it's wrong for me to pray that God would send me a daddy?"

The statement completely stunned Ashley, who had never heard her daughter make such a comment. "I . . . well . . . I don't know."

Natalie smiled. "Well, I'm going to pray about it, and I'm going to talk to Grandpa too. He'll know. He might be sick, but he'll know if it's okay to pray about it."

Ashley pushed away from the table. She couldn't take any more of the religious battle that raged inside of her. One minute she was convinced of the validity of such thinking. The next minute she questioned everything she believed. And now Natalie wanted a father. It was all just too much.

"Would you like dessert? I have some fresh berries and cream," Ashley offered.

"Yes, please. Oh, and Mama, can we make a bowl for Grandpa? And can I take them back to his room and eat with him?"

Ashley smiled down at the child. With her hair tied back and a few wispy strands escaping the hold of her ribbon, her face held an elfish charm. Her delicate little upturned nose and finely arched brows made

Natalie seem almost doll-like in appearance.

"I'm sure Grandpa would like that. I'll fix the berries."

Ashley produced the bowls of dessert and watched as Natalie care-fully balanced them on a tray. She heard Natalie call out, then was glad to see that apparently the child's request had been met with acceptance. Natalie disappeared inside the room, leaving Ashley to clean the table and contemplate the future.

Russell perked up at the sight of his great-granddaughter. He'd often wondered if there'd been other great-grandchildren. Ashley had three brothers, after all. They had been headstrong businessmen when Ashley had left Baltimore. Family seemed unimportant to them at the time.

"Grandpa, I brought some berries and cream."

Russell scooted up in the bed and swung his legs over the side. "Sounds delicious." It did sound good, even if he had no appetite.

Natalie put the tray down and brought him a bowl and a spoon. "Mama said I could eat my berries back here with you."

He thought she sounded sad. She looked up at him as he took the bowl and added, "Is that okay with you?"

"You know it is." Russell pushed back an errant lock of hair, the same trademark lock his own mother and wife had spent a lifetime pushing back.

Natalie took up her bowl and sat in the chair beside the bed. "I . . . um . . . well, I was hoping we could talk."

"What about?"

She glanced up momentarily, then lowered her gaze to the bowl. "Mama says you're real sick."

Russell heard her voice tremble. Ashley must have told her that he was dying. He'd wondered how long she would wait until telling the child the truth. He'd only mentioned it once before, but Ashley hadn't been ready yet to deal with facing the truth herself, and sharing that knowledge with Natalie seemed impossibly hard.

Russell knew Natalie would need help dealing with this and so he asked, "And you wanted to talk about it?"

"Uh-huh," she said, her crossed legs swinging back and forth as she toyed with the berries.

"I'm sure the news has made you sad," Russell said. He ate a spoon-ful of the berries and waited for her to respond.

"Grandpa, I don't understand why God would do this." She looked up, and Russell could see the glistening of tears in her dark brown eyes. "We need you here. What will we do when you're gone?"

"Well, child, would it hurt any less if you understood the whys and hows?"

"I don't know. I just don't want you to die." She sniffed back her tears and put aside her bowl.

Russell put his bowl aside as well and opened his arms to her. "Come here, Natalie."

She did so and fell against him, sobbing. The pain in his side ripped through him, but Russell said nothing. He held her close and stroked her head, knowing there were no words that would make her understand or feel better.

After several minutes he said, "You know, God has His own way of doing things, Natalie. We don't always see them as reasonable or understandable. We don't always know what He has in mind, but it's been my experience over the years that God never closes a door without opening a window."

Natalie rose up, wiping at her eyes. "What does that mean?"

"It means that God may be calling me home, but at the same time He could be sending someone else into your life to help you in my place."

"They could never take your place," Natalie said, her lower lip quivering.

"I didn't say they would. I was merely suggesting they would come to help in place of me. You never know what God has in mind, but it's always better than what we have in mind for ourselves."

"But even if someone else comes, Grandpa, I'll miss you. Who will go for walks with me and tell me stories about the old days?"

Russell laughed. "Child, there's always someone around who will share stories about the old days. Look, we still have a bit of time. Only God knows the hours of man's life. You have to trust that He knows best."

"I do trust Him. I just wish that Mama trusted Him too."

Russell nodded. Nothing would make him happier. "We'll have to keep praying for her, Natalie. We'll have to pray and wait for God to act. Maybe my sickness will make her realize what's missing in her life."

"Like getting married again?"

"Could be," Russell said with a grin. "You just never know what God has in mind."

"I want a new daddy," Natalie said, her tears gone. She went back to her chair and picked up the bowl of dessert. "I'm still praying for one."

Russell picked up his own bowl, not wanting the child to think he didn't appreciate her efforts. He ate some more of the berries and pondered her desires. A father for Natalie and a husband for Ashley did seem like an answer to many problems. Of course, it still wouldn't bring Ashley to an understanding of God. No, that was something God would have to do himself. No human could do it for her.

————

The food on Ashley's plate served as a reminder that she'd eaten very little at supper. It was hard to think of eating when her world seemed to be falling apart. Ashley scraped the food into the garbage pail, then put the plate in the sink before going back for Natalie's dishes. A knock on the door interrupted her duties, and Ashley glanced at the clock on the mantel. Seven o'clock. Perhaps someone had come to visit.

Exiling the remaining dirty dishes to the kitchen sink, Ashley pulled her apron off and went to see who had come to call. Opening the door, she found Pastor McGuire, her grandfather's minister.

"Good evening, Mrs. Reynolds. I'm wondering if your grandfather is up to receiving a visitor?"

"I'm sure he'd be glad to see you," Ashley said, adding, "Won't you come in?"

The tall redheaded man removed his hat as he stepped through the doorway. His compassionate expression preceded his next question. "And how are you holding up? I know this news can't have been easy on you."

"No, it hasn't been easy," Ashley admitted. She took the man's hat and hung it on a peg by the door, then motioned him toward the small living room. "My daughter is sharing dessert with Grandpa just now. He so seldom eats that I'm hoping her enthusiasm and company will at least get a few spoonfuls down him. If you don't mind waiting just a little while, we can visit here." Ashley led him through an arched opening to the living room. She really had no desire to answer the pastor's questions or, worse still, to be preached to, but she knew she needed to put her own comfort aside and think of Grandpa.

"That would be fine. I so seldom get to share your company." He unbuttoned the lower button on his suit coat and smiled.

"Would you like a cup of coffee?" Ashley offered.

"No, nothing just now. I've just come from our supper table."

He waited for Ashley to lower herself into the rocker before he seated himself in the overstuffed chair. Stroking the patterned red fabric, he sighed. "Ah, this is so comfortable I just might not get back up." He threw her a smile that seemed to light up his entire face.

Ashley nodded. "That's Grandpa's chair. He's always said that a man who works hard all day deserves a good soft chair for the evening."

"And he's so right." McGuire shifted as if to get even more comfortable. Stretching out his legs, he crossed them at the knees and looked quite casual and comfortable.

The action put Ashley at ease for some reason. Maybe it was that he looked less threatening—less likely to start preaching hellfire and brimstone. Looking at her hands, Ashley searched for something to talk about. "So it looks like they're making good progress on the new Harvey resort." That topic seemed harmless enough.

"Yes, I do believe they are. Should be quite the place. I'm told the food will be even grander, if that's possible. Are you still working at the Harvey House?"

"No, I took a leave so that I could be with Grandpa. The doctor said . . ." She let her words trail off. She really hadn't wanted to get into this conversation, and now that she had, she didn't seem to be able to stop it. "The doctor said his time would be very short. The cancer is quite progressed and very . . . aggressive." Her heart ached to have to acknowledge this truth, yet it was undeniable. She'd watched the old man fail a little more each day.

"It's hard to lose the people we love," the pastor said, nodding. "I'm going to miss your grandfather greatly. Even the promise of heaven isn't much of a comfort at times."

Shocked by his words, Ashley looked at him for a moment and tried to gather her courage to question him. "How can you say that? You're a man . . . of God. You believe that a Christian person goes to heaven."

"True enough, but as you stated, I'm a man first and very human with my feelings. My spirit is at peace because I know Grandpa Whitman is going to heaven. I feel confident of what God has done in his life and what God holds in store for his future—after death. But I'll miss my time with your grandfather. I'll miss our checker games and coffee at the café. I'll miss our talks. I've learned a lot from him."

Ashley felt a warmth in the pastor's loving words. "I'll miss his company for sure. He's so long been a staple in my life. I really have no one else, besides Natalie, of course."

"Well, just know you're welcome at our table anytime. My wife, Essie, would love to have you and Natalie over for supper sometime. She adores your daughter, and every time we've had her and Grandpa Whitman to our house for lunch after church, Natalie has always been such a help."

"I suppose I didn't realize that they'd ever come to lunch at your place." Ashley felt guilty for admitting that, but it was the truth. "I generally work on Sundays at the Harvey House. People have to eat and travel just the same on Sunday as other days," she added, almost defensively.

"Well, you're always welcome to come to service when you can. I know your work has kept you away." He leaned forward and his expression grew quite serious. "Ashley, I'm not of the mind to make this uncomfortable for you, if that's what you're worried about. People have to make their own decisions and choices. Grandpa's told me some of the issues you've faced. Frankly, given your youth back then and the responsibilities of a new baby, I completely admire your ability to overcome your widowhood. Just know that we care about you, and we'd be glad for you to join us when you can."

There was nothing condemning in his tone. Nothing that suggested he knew Ashley for the heathen she thought herself to be. And yet she didn't doubt that Grandpa had spoken the truth to the man on more than one occasion. No doubt he'd even asked the pastor to pray for Ashley.

About that time Natalie came skipping down the hall carrying two empty dishes. "Look!" she exclaimed. "Grandpa ate his berries and cream."

Ashley saw the look of triumph on her daughter's face. "Good for you, Natalie. I think that's the first thing he's eaten all day."

"Oh, hello, Pastor McGuire," Natalie said, catching sight of the man. "Are you here to visit Grandpa?"

"I sure am," Pastor McGuire said, getting to his feet. "Would you like to let him know I'm here?"

Ashley got up quickly and took the empty bowls from her daughter's hands. "I'll see to these. You go ahead and take Pastor McGuire on back."

Ashley set the bowls to soak with the other dishes. She still needed to take down the laundry from the line, and it needed to be done before the light was completely gone. The dishes could wait.

Taking up her basket, Ashley slipped out the back door. Her mind reflected back to what the pastor had said. It somehow comforted her to know he'd miss her grandfather nearly as much as she would. She had been so afraid he'd come at her with all sorts of religious nonsense about how much better off Grandpa would be in heaven and how life up there couldn't compare to life down here.

"That may well be true," she muttered, "but it doesn't mean our lives will be better." She knew the sentiment was selfish, but she couldn't help it. She didn't want him to die. She didn't want God taking away yet one more person she loved.

E. J. Carson studied the blueprints before him as if they were battle plans for an invasion. Helping with the many architectural designs created by Mary Elizabeth Jane Colter, architect and interior designer for the Fred Harvey Company, gave his life purpose and occupied his mind. This project in particular gave E. J. the opportunity to utilize the training and interest he had in Spanish architecture.

Mary Colter worked for the Harvey Company, having been hired at the turn of the century to help invent a personality and vision for the Fred Harvey hotels, restaurants, and tourist attractions. She was a diligent, demanding woman, but she was also brilliant. At least in E. J. Carson's opinion.

Colter's ability to look at the raw bones of a project and breathe life into it amazed E. J. every single time. Too bad she couldn't breathe life into him as well.

He frowned at the thought and forced his attention back to the blueprints. They were building what was to be the cream of Harvey's hotels. A grand resort that would draw in the rich and famous from far and wide. A resort so magnificent that people would have to book months in advance just to take lodging. The project was ambitious to be sure, but certainly no more so than the dynamite little woman who planned and arranged it all.

Mary Colter was undaunted by the prospects of taking a piece of land where a roundhouse had once existed and turning it into a lush and exotic playground for the wealthy. Considering Mary's vision for landscaping and construction, E. J. had to admit the woman was positively inspired. Her plan was to raise up a resort hotel to look as if it had been there for hundreds of years. She even created her own myths and legends to surround it—giving history to what had just months ago been nothing.

The task wouldn't be easy. It would take more than average attention to detail to build this hacienda-style hotel. It would demand a tremendous amount of work and the highest quality of craftsmanship. It was easy to slap together a square of bricks and windows but something entirely different to fashion a dream.

And it was harder still when your ability to dream had been destroyed in the wake of man's fury.

E. J. pulled his wire-rimmed glasses off and rubbed his closed eyes momentarily. The haunting images of his past were never further away than a thought. The nightmarish vision of men dying was always with him. Blood and decay filled his thoughts as permanent reminders of all that he'd lost. For most Americans, the Great War was over and done with. They seldom gave it consideration. But for E. J., he truly wondered if the war would ever end. Would the ghostly faces of his dying friends ever fade?

He opened his eyes and replaced the glasses once again. *How can I see the vision of a beautiful creation when all of my thoughts are consumed with the ugliness of such an evil?*

For a time after the war he'd immersed himself in studying Spanish architecture and furnishings. He found the dark woods and extensive carving to be a fascination all its own. The buildings, however, were what had truly captured his imagination. Tiled roofs and stucco walls, stone floors and brightly painted tiles—all of it was different and exciting. There was a taste of the exotic in such masterpieces, and it was this interest that eventually brought him to work with Mary Colter.

"Hello."

E. J. looked up to find a sweet-faced little pixie watching as he pored over his drawings. E. J. hadn't expected to find a child on the construction site.

"Hello," he said, trying hard to sound stern. "This isn't really a safe place to play."

"I didn't come to play. I want to build places like this someday. I came to see how it's done."

E. J. smiled. "Oh, you did, now." Her innocent comment pushed away his previous darkness.

The little girl nodded, her two long braids bobbing as she did. "I like to draw. My daddy was an architect. He was going to build all sorts of buildings and now I want to. Do you like to build things too?"

"I do indeed." He rolled up his blueprints and glanced around at the busy construction crew. "Would you like a look around?"

"Oh, very much," the girl answered. She came closer and extended her hand in greeting. "I'm Natalie."

"And I'm E. J. I work with Miss Colter. She's the one who planned all of this." He waved at the framework that would one day become a grand resort. "I would think Miss Colter would very much like to meet you. See, she has been working in this business for many years and can tell you all about how it is for a woman to work in a job that's usually performed by men."

Natalie smiled, but her gaze was fixed on the construction crew. She watched without concern to her own safety as the men moved through the open room carrying impressive loads of mortar, lumber, and tools. As they marched dirty boots across lovely carpets of intricately woven patterns, Natalie looked to E. J. in question.

"Won't they ruin those pretty rugs?"

E. J. laughed. "That's the idea," he said rather conspiratorially. "Miss Colter thought they looked too nice—too new. She's done this before. She likes to have the workers walk on them and make them look old and used."

"But why?" Natalie questioned, scrunching up her face and cocking her head to one side.

The puzzled look on the child's face gave E. J. a feeling of delight he'd not known in years. "It's her way," he answered. "She likes things to look like they've been in a place forever. She says it's a way of making the new look comfortably old and welcoming."

Natalie seemed to consider this for a moment, then took her attention elsewhere. "What are they building back there?" She pointed past E. J.

"That's to be the dining room. Come on, I'll show you around." E. J. picked up his drawings and tucked them under his arm. Natalie quickly followed as he led the way. "See, overhead we have log-beamed ceilings to make it look very Spanish."

"Why?"

"Miss Colter wants the entire place to look like one of the old Spanish haciendas. She wants it to look like it belongs here instead of something that was just picked up elsewhere and plopped down here. Do you understand?"

Natalie nodded. "She doesn't want it to be out of place."

"Right," E. J. replied. "She has a dream to make this a lovely resort where people will come and feel as though they're visiting one of the ancient Spanish ranchos from the early eighteen hundreds."

"Will people like that?" Natalie asked, looking toward the arched windows.

"People are always looking for something different from what they are used to. So I think they'll like it very much. Besides, they already love Fred Harvey's hotels and restaurants."

Natalie smiled. "I know. My mama works at the Harvey House. At least, she did. She's quit for now to take care of my grandpa. He's dying."

E. J. frowned. "I'm sorry to hear that."

"I was too," Natalie said, digging the toe of her leather shoe against the stone floor. "Grandpa's been like my best friend. He's always telling me stories and helping me learn about things."

E. J. had no idea what to say, his own losses fresh in his memory. So many people he'd cared about had died tragically. Friends in the Great War. His parents and wife to influenza. How he missed them all.

"So will they have a lunch counter too?" Natalie suddenly asked, taking E. J. out of his sorrowful memories.

"Yes," he nodded. "It will be over this way." As they walked, E. J. explained, "They plan to use the most beautiful Spanish tile on the counters. It's really going to look impressive."

"My mama doesn't like to work the lunch counter. She says it's a more frantic pace of life than working in the dining room."

E. J. couldn't help smiling at this bit of insight. "I can well imagine that's right. I'm staying over at the present Harvey hotel, and I eat in the restaurant every day. The lunch counter *is* more frantic," he said with a wink.

Natalie grinned. "My mama says people come storming in there shouting their orders, calling out for more attention than the next person. She said it's like they think being louder will make things go faster."

E. J. nodded. "The world is full of those kinds of folks."

They walked around the building site, E. J. pointing out the workers and what they were doing. Finally, they ended up outside.

"What are those people doing?" Natalie questioned.

E. J. looked to where she was focused. "There's going to be a sunken garden over there with all sorts of hidden shrines and fountains. Miss Colter has this wonderful plan, and I know it will be spectacular. Everything she creates is wonderful."

"But why does she worry about the garden part? I thought architects only worried about building things."

E. J. motioned with his arm. "But all of this is just an extension of the building. Don't you see? It's like a giant canvas, and we're the artists who are painting upon it. You wouldn't just paint the building and leave the rest of the canvas blank—now, would you?"

Natalie's face lit up and E. J. was certain she understood. "No," she replied. "You have to make it all work together. Just like Miss Colter wants it to look like it belongs."

"Exactly. We don't want the guests to show up when the building's all done to find that the grounds are still cluttered with building materials and tools. We want to extend the beauty beyond the walls of the hotel. We want it to be a lovely place to come share a quiet moment— a peaceful rest."

"I want to do things like this when I grow up," Natalie announced confidently. "I want to build pretty places where people will be happy. That way my daddy's dreams can come true."

"Your daddy's dreams? What about yours?" E. J. questioned. He found it odd that the little girl should want to fulfill someone else's plan. "Can't your daddy make his own dreams come true?"

"My daddy died in the war. He was an architect like you. He wanted to build wonderful things, and my mama says he was very good." She smiled at E. J., melting his heart. "My daddy was a hero in the war."

"Was he, now?" E. J. found Natalie's adoration of her father quite charming, but talk of the war made him uncomfortable. This little girl had a way about her that took him back to 1918. And it wasn't only the talk of the war. It was also rather disconcerting that the little girl, with her huge brown eyes and dark lashes, made E. J. think of his own beloved wife, now dead and gone. He sighed but tried to maintain his composure. One could never tell when the past would catch up with the present.

Natalie seemed oblivious to his momentary sorrow. "I never got to know my daddy, but everyone has told me what a hero he was. He saved a whole bunch of men in the war. Whenever we have a parade, I get to ride with the veterans in honor of my daddy. I get to help decorate the graves too, and last year a man came from the newspaper in Phoenix and talked to me about my daddy and took my picture with the veterans."

Her expression completely told the story. She practically worshiped the memory of a man she couldn't possibly have known. After all, she was such a little thing, E. J. would never even have imagined she was old enough to have been conceived prior to the Great War.

"How old are you, Natalie?"

She twirled in her yellow cotton sundress and laughed. "I'm ten and I'm going to be eleven next January. How old are you?"

Her question caught him off guard but made him chuckle nevertheless. He stroked his bearded chin as if he had to remember all the years and tally them up. "I'm thirty-two. Kind of old, huh?"

"No," Natalie replied, shaking her head. "That's not old at all. My mama is thirty-two and she's very young, but she works too hard. At least that's what Grandpa says. He says she's trying to keep busy so that she doesn't get too sad."

E. J. had no idea how to respond. The warmth of the afternoon gave him an idea. "Would you like a cold drink? I think we have some lemonade and tea."

"Sure. I like lemonade."

E. J. smiled. "I do too." He was surprised when Natalie danced off ahead of him. He ambled after her, realizing suddenly that she was like a balm to his chafed and wounded spirit. In spite of her comments of the war, her sweetness and girlish delight in everything she saw made E. J. most aware of one thing. Life. She was a tribute to the living—joyous, blooming, shining with an inner light that somehow permeated the darkness of his soul.

Once inside, E. J. arranged two glasses of lemonade, then directed Natalie to a reasonably quiet corner of the area where they'd first met. He offered her a glass, then sat down opposite her. He'd hoped that Mary would return before long, which was the real reason, he told himself, that he delayed Natalie's departure.

"Have you been working here for a long time?" Natalie asked.

"No, I've only been here this last week," E. J. admitted. "I finished up some final details on a hotel over in Santa Fe, New Mexico. It's called La Fonda. It's a very beautiful hotel, but I think this one will be even nicer."

Natalie took a sip of the lemonade and asked, "Did you build that hotel too?"

"No. The hotel was already there. The railroad bought it and asked Miss Colter to come in and make some changes and improvements." Natalie nodded as if she were a company employee well versed in the routine. E. J. smiled. "You should have seen some of the things she did."

"Like what?" Natalie appeared to be his captive audience.

"Well, she designed furniture and special light fixtures. She had murals painted in some of the rooms and redecorated the walls in other parts of the hotel."

"But that's not architect work," Natalie argued.

"She's an interior architect as well as exterior," E. J. explained. "Miss Colter is equally talented in interior decorating as well as creating the actual building and landscape. Remember what I told you about painting the whole canvas? Miss Colter believes that canvas is inside the building as well. Like I said, I think you'd like her a lot."

"So will she make furniture here too?"

"She's hiring it done. She's designed some very nice pieces. There will also be some that are simpler. Miss Colter likes the contrast. She's bringing in beautiful china and copper pots from Europe and Asia. This hotel will even have a patron saint—San Ysidro."

"We don't have any saints at my house. We aren't Catholic," Natalie said, putting her lemonade aside. "We don't pray to saints; we just pray to God directly."

E. J. found himself amazed at her bold yet easy manner in speaking of her faith. "So where do you go to church, Miss Natalie?"

"We go to Faith Mission Church. Would you like to come with us? My mama plans to come to church tomorrow and you could come and meet her. She's real pretty."

E. J. grinned. "If she looks anything like you, I'm sure she's beautiful."

Natalie's brown eyes seemed to flash with an inner light of joy at this comment. "So will you come?"

"I'm afraid I can't. I'm taking the train to Santa Fe tonight. I won't be back here until next Wednesday. Maybe another time."

Natalie fairly bounced in her seat. "Good. I'll come see you again when you get back. You can tell me about your drawings." She pointed to the papers he'd been carrying around since she'd first shown up.

"I'd be happy to do that, but right now," he said, glancing at his watch, "I have to go. I have a meeting. When you come back, I'll see if I can introduce you to Miss Colter. You'd like her a lot. She sometimes seems mean and gruff, but she's really a very nice lady."

"I'll come after school on Thursday if it's okay with Mama," Natalie promised. "Will you be here?"

E. J. thought about his workweek and nodded. "I should be. Sometimes we have to go scout up workers or supplies, but otherwise, I should be around."

"Then I'll come back. Thanks for the lemonade."

She got up and skipped off, weaving in and out of the construction workers until she'd disappeared. E. J. thought it rather strange and delightful at the same time that a young girl should be so captivated by the architecture and building of this marvelous resort. Some of the local boys stopped by from time to time, but Natalie was the first girl to show interest. He sighed and gathered up his things. The afternoon promised to be long, and then there would be the ride back to Santa Fe. He smiled to himself as he made his way across the lobby floor. Silly as it sounded, he would have much rather spent time talking with the girl than dealing with meetings and contract issues.

––––––––

That night after Natalie and Grandpa had gone to bed, Ashley finished ironing her good dress in preparation for the next morning. She'd promised Natalie she'd go to church, and she intended to see it through. Grandpa had been surprised at the news, and when Ashley had taken some lunch to him he'd told her how much it pleased him.

Ashley remembered the look of delight on his face and knew he really meant it. Grandpa was never a man of false words. At least not since finding Jesus. She thought back to the things he'd told her about his past. Things he was deeply ashamed of. It was the reason he'd left Los Angeles and a lucrative partnership in the land business. Her grandfather had been a great salesman—and con man. He had a knack for convincing people of what they needed and then producing that exact thing. Even in getting Ashley to church, he'd been very persuasive. Had she not been so angry for the past, she might well have gone before now.

A sound from upstairs caught her attention. She strained to hear.

Nothing.

Maybe it was just my imagination. She finished the dress and put the iron aside to cool. Checking to make sure that Grandpa was asleep and didn't need anything, Ashley picked up the dress and made her way upstairs.

Natalie's room was closest to the stairs, and then next there was a small room that doubled as a sewing and guest room. At the end of the hall on the opposite side was Ashley's room and next to it was their bathroom. It was all very compact and neatly ordered. Exactly as Ashley liked it.

Reaching her door, Ashley heard the noise again. She quickly hung her dress in the wardrobe, then made her way back to Natalie's room. Through the closed door, she could hear her child sobbing softly.

Ashley entered the room quietly and went to Natalie's bed. Sinking onto the mattress, she lifted Natalie into her arms and rocked her back and forth. "Did you have a bad dream?" Ashley asked.

"No. I just got sad," Natalie admitted. She pulled away and pushed back her hair.

"Is this about Grandpa?"

Natalie nodded. "I tried to stay quiet."

Ashley shook her head and smoothed back the errant strands of hair that Natalie had missed. The light from the hallway spilled into the room, casting a soft glow across them. "Darling girl, you never have to hide your tears from me. I love you, and what's more, I understand the hurt you're feeling."

"But you grew up with your daddy. My daddy is gone and Grandpa is the only daddy I've ever had. Now he's going away too." Natalie's lower lip quivered as her emotions overtook her once again.

Ashley held her close and kissed the top of her head. "Shh, it's all right. I know how important he is to you, but you mustn't mourn him yet. He's not even gone. Grandpa is still with us. We mustn't make him feel bad these last few days."

Natalie jerked away. "He's going to die in a few days?"

Ashley shook her head. "No one knows when he's going to die, Natalie. I only said that to mean whatever time Grandpa has left should be spent in as much comfort and happiness as we can give him. When he's gone, we can cry all we want, and then it won't hurt him."

"Will he see us from heaven? Won't it hurt him to see us cry then?"

Ashley shrugged. "I don't know if he will be able to see us from heaven. I don't know a lot about heaven, but I remember Grandpa saying there's no pain there. So if that's the case, then maybe he'll only see the good things down here on earth and never be sad again."

Natalie hugged her close. "Will you stay with me till I fall asleep?"

Ashley didn't normally indulge the child, but this time it seemed appropriate. "All right. How about I sit right here beside the bed?" Ashley got up and pulled a chair over to the bedside.

"Would you read to me?"

Ashley smiled and turned on the bedside light. "Just for ten minutes. Then you really need to go to sleep. What do you want me to read?"

"Would you read the Bible?"

Ashley tried to hide her grimace, but apparently she wasn't successful.

"Please, Mama?"

Ashley reached for the black book on Natalie's nightstand. "All right. Where do you want me to read? The beginning?"

"No. Just open at the marker. That's where I was reading earlier."

Ashley opened the Bible and found herself in the Psalms. "Psalm sixty-three?" Natalie nodded and Ashley continued. " 'O God, thou art my God; early will I seek thee: my soul thirsteth for thee, my flesh longeth for thee in a dry and thirsty land, where no water is.' " She smiled. "Sounds like the desert, eh?"

"It's one of Grandpa's favorite chapters. He told me about it," Natalie said, yawning. "He told me there's another verse in the Bible that talks about how God makes rivers in the desert." She snuggled down and closed her eyes. "God can do anything."

Ashley nodded and continued. " 'To see thy power and thy glory, so as I have seen thee in the sanctuary. Because thy lovingkindness is better than life, my lips shall praise thee. Thus will I bless thee while I live.' " Ashley paused, uneasy at the reminder of her grandfather's fleeting days. She looked over the last line. *Thus will I bless thee while I live.* It was such a simple statement. She drew a deep breath and read on. " 'I will lift up my hands in thy name. My soul shall be satisfied as with marrow and fatness; and my mouth shall praise thee with joyful lips: When I remember thee upon my bed, and meditate on thee in the night watches.' "

She glanced over to see that Natalie had fallen back to sleep. Her even breathing left no doubt that she had found her comfort and peace once again. Ashley replaced the marker and closed the Bible. She turned off the lamp and left the Bible on the nightstand before leaving the room. A strange peace was upon her. A peace she hadn't known for some time. Could it really be that simple? she wondered. Could merely reading the Bible—God's Word—give that kind of comfort to her soul?

CHAPTER FOUR

Ashley sat beside Natalie in church, hoping her nervousness wouldn't show. Grandpa sat on the other side of Natalie, and both were beaming from ear to ear because of her attendance. This only served to make Ashley more edgy. What if she said or did something that embarrassed them—made them sorry she'd come?

They picked up hymnals as directed by Pastor McGuire and turned to the page he directed. Ashley looked at the words to the song while the organ introduced the melody. When the singing began, Ashley followed the words in silence, mesmerized by their powerful effect.

"Oft my heart has bled with sorrow. Not a friend my grief to share." *How very true,* Ashley thought. She listened to her daughter sing the words with great enthusiasm and conviction.

The congregation moved to the second verse. "Once I sighed for peace and pleasure, felt a painful void within." Oh, the words were like affirmation to her soul, and Ashley couldn't help but eagerly seek the next refrain. "Life was gloomy, death a terror." *Oh yes,* she thought. *Yes. Death is a terror. It threatens to steal away all the joy I've worked so hard to own.*

The chorus interrupted her thoughts. "Is there here a soul in trouble—whosoever needs a friend? Jesus' love your heart will gladden, bless and keep you to the end."

Could it really be that simple? Could turning your heart over to Jesus—accepting His love—really be the key? If so, why didn't everybody do it? Ashley teetered between complete confusion and an intense desire to understand. God had seemed so distant to her when Ethan died. She'd attended church most of her life—her mother had insisted. After all, they'd purchased an entire pew at the front of the grand cathedral and no one was ever allowed there but the Murphy family. It was important to be seen in church. It lent an image of worthiness and respectability, her mother had said. This time, however, church seemed different.

The congregation concluded the song and Pastor McGuire began to pray. He prayed for peace for each individual and then prayed for God to speak through his words. Ashley could hardly concentrate. Her thoughts were still lost in the words of the song. Had she missed something all those years ago?

Throughout Pastor McGuire's sermon, Ashley kept coming back to the words of the hymn. *Is there here a soul in trouble—whosoever needs a friend?* That could certainly describe her, but could she accept that the solution was in seeking God? God, who had taken away her husband and turned her parents against her? What kind of friend would that make God?

"Why do we suppose when bad things come that God is the only one to bring them?"

Ashley heard Pastor McGuire's question and snapped to attention. She looked up to meet the older man's gaze. It was almost as if he'd been waiting for her acknowledgment.

"Sometimes the trials we bear are the consequences of our own actions. We know better than to touch a hot stove. Should we put God to a foolish test and touch it anyway? We know that standing on the railroad tracks in defiance of a speeding locomotive is sure to bring us death. Do we stand there anyway, just to see if God is powerful enough to keep us from harm? Of course not.

"If we put ourselves in harm's way, purposefully seeking our own pleasure and benefit, and then find ourselves in danger, how does this become the fault of our Lord and Savior?" He paused for a moment and studied the faces of his congregation. His expression softened as he continued. "Of course, there are those things that are thrust upon us that are not of our doing." Again he looked directly at Ashley. She warmed under his stare and shifted uncomfortably in her seat. Why had Grandpa and Natalie insisted on sitting so close to the front?

"Sometimes we suffer the consequences of other people's sin. A man is murdered by a thief. He leaves behind a wife and several children. They will bear the consequences of the murderer's actions. Are they to blame? No, of course not, but suffer they will, nevertheless. Does this make God unjust? Does this make God an uncaring bystander who leaves His children to fend for themselves?"

Ashley swallowed hard and leaned forward ever so slightly to hear the answer. Surely this man knew her heart—knew the questions and misery that lived there.

"God is not unjust—nor uncaring," Pastor McGuire continued. "He has offered us shelter in His love. The world will do as it will. Sin will abound and the curse of sin will follow from generation to generation. We will neither go untouched nor unscathed. However, we have but to draw nearer to God in order to be healed of the wounds. We have only to rest in Him and find comfort from the pains of this world. Jesus himself said we would have these trials and pains. He said family members would turn against each other because of Him. He said the way would be difficult. . . . However, He promised we would never face it alone."

But I feel alone, Ashley whispered in the depths of her soul. *I feel terribly alone—especially now that Grandpa is dying. How will I make a good home for Natalie once he's gone? How can I be both father and mother to this child?*

She missed the pastor's final comments but stood with the others as they sang another song. This time she paid little attention to the words or music. Ashley knew there was no sense in trying to focus on anything at this point. Her mind was awash in questions without hope of answers.

———

The days that followed were peaceful ones despite Ashley's worries. Grandpa, although weakened greatly, seemed as alert as ever. The pastor came and played checkers twice, and Natalie read to the older man every evening after supper. The routine seemed comfortable, almost easy.

But by Thursday Grandpa's pain had grown almost unbearable. Ashley offered him the morphine the doctor had given her, but Grandpa was still not yet ready to succumb to the medicated stupor that it promised.

"I need you to go bring my lawyer here. He's been processing some papers for me—some things we have to tend to before I start taking the medicine," Grandpa told her that afternoon.

"I'll go right away," Ashley promised. "Will you be all right alone? I could wait until Natalie comes home from school." It was only after the words were out of her mouth that Ashley remembered Natalie's request to go to the Harvey building site after school.

"No, I'm fine. Just go ahead. I'm going to try to sleep while you're gone," Grandpa replied.

Ashley reached out and gently stroked the old man's snowy white hair. "Grandpa, I love you. I wish I could take this sickness from you."

He smiled up at her, the weariness evident in his expression. "To every man is appointed a time to die."

"I wish it could be otherwise." She took hold of his hand and squeezed it gently. "It's so unfair."

"You're troubled. I can see that," he said, surprising her. "Sit here with me for a minute. The lawyer can wait. Tell me what's on your mind. This is more than just me and my situation."

Ashley carefully sat on the bedside. She knew any movement at all only caused Grandpa greater pain. "I just don't know what to do," she admitted.

"About what?"

She shrugged. "Everything, I guess. I want so much to give Natalie a good home, but I can't be both mother and father to her. I've relied on you for so much over the years, and I don't know how to make it all work."

"You could remarry," Grandpa suggested rather hesitantly.

"That's what Natalie wants," Ashley admitted. "But I could never love another man the way I did Ethan."

"Who's asking you to? Why don't you just love another man for himself?"

"I'm afraid I would always be comparing a new husband to Ethan."

"Child, you only knew Ethan for a short time. Please don't misunderstand me, but can you truly have that much to compare with, or are you living in the memory of what you've created over the long, lonely years?"

Ashley felt as if he'd slapped her. She opened her mouth to speak in anger, then closed it again. Convicted in her own heart, she knew his words held an element of truth. "I suppose there are certain things I've created in my mind. We had so little time together, and I didn't want to lose a single memory. But, Grandpa, he was the love of my life. He made my life seem complete."

"But he's dead and gone. His suffering is over, but yours goes on. Maybe Natalie wants a new father as much for you as for herself. Maybe she realizes how lonely and miserable you are—how much you need a companion."

There was no need to deny it. Ashley knew her grandfather would figure out the truth whether she tried to conceal it or not. "I just don't know if I can open my heart up to someone again. The people I loved so dearly have hurt me so deeply."

"Like your own mother and father?"

"Yes. And my brothers."

"You need to mend that fence."

Ashley jerked upward, bristling at the thought. "Why should I? They care nothing for me. They're the ones who sent me away without another word—without a cent to my name."

"True enough, but they may have had a change of heart. In fact, your brothers and father may never have agreed with your mother's actions at all. You never gave them a chance to voice an opinion. You never let them know where you were, and because you were with me and pleaded for me not to tell them, they don't know how to reach either of us."

"Which is exactly how I want it." Ashley got to her feet. "I can't imagine that they'd care to know where I am—even now."

"But you can't assume that. You need to turn this over to the Lord and work through it, because, frankly, I'd like to see your mama—your aunt Lavelle too before I die."

Ashley had never considered this for even a moment. Up until now, Grandpa had said very little about his daughters. "After the way they treated you, Grandpa, how can you want to see them? They were cruel. They forced you to divide up your property and live without the wealth and possessions you'd collected over the years."

"Those things meant very little to me in light of my children's happiness. I knew the money and things couldn't make them happy," Grandpa admitted, "but I also knew that they would have to come to their own understanding of that. I forgive them for what they said and did, and I want to put the past to rest."

His expression took on a faraway look, as though he were drawn back in time. "I know there's a possibility they still feel as angry and hateful as they did when I first told them I was leaving the real estate business in Los Angeles. Still, there's the possibility God has done a work in their lives and they've changed." He looked back at Ashley. "I wouldn't want to die and not at least try to make things right. Besides, your mother and father might very well want to be a part of your life— your brothers too. Once I'm gone, you might want them in your life as well. Ashley, at least promise me you'll think about it."

Ashley's breathing quickened with the tightening in her chest. "I'll think about it, but that's all I can promise at this point." But even as she said the words, Ashley knew there wasn't all that much time to think about anything. With the doctor's last visit, she knew there was little time left.

Grandpa smiled. "That's enough. For now."

Ashley thought about his words as she readied herself for town. Running a comb through her bobbed brown hair, she wondered if there was even the slimmest chance that he was right. Maybe her parents had felt bad for the way they'd done things. Perhaps her father, upon hearing what her mother had done, had come to speak with Ashley only to find she'd already gone. It was possible. But did that change things for her? Her mother had still chosen money over love and made it clear that Ashley had no place in her life unless she did likewise. Even if they showed up on the doorstep tomorrow—could she forgive them?

Russell heard the door close and knew Ashley had left the house. He moaned softly as he settled into the mattress.

"Lord, the pain is so great. Please ease it—send me comfort."

He thought of the morphine. It was there for his benefit, and yet he refused to take it. How often in life had there been other things he'd refused—things that might well have made the way easier, less painful?

"I just don't want my head clouded. There's still too much to tend to. I want to see my daughters, Lord. Please bring them to me—please give me time."

Russell had spoken to his lawyer about notifying the women and then stopped short of having the man actually do the deed. Ashley wanted nothing to do with her mother. When he'd moved here to Winslow with Ashley, it had been with the promise that he'd never do anything to give away her whereabouts. Now he needed to ask her to release him from that promise before it was too late.

"She won't like the idea, Lord, but I'm hoping to cushion the blow. Surely once she sees how she doesn't have to worry about where she'll live or the money . . . maybe then she won't mind her mother knowing where she is. Maybe too she'll consider putting the past behind her as I've asked."

———

"Hello again!" Natalie called to E. J. as she crossed the lobby.

E. J. turned from the older woman and motioned Natalie to join them. "Natalie, I want you to meet Miss Colter."

Natalie came to a halt in front of the woman and extended her hand. "I'm Natalie, and I want to build things like you do."

Mary Colter nodded and shook Natalie's hand. "It's not an easy job for a woman. Men seldom listen to you, yet they're the ones who generally carry out the actual construction work."

Natalie looked at E. J. and commented, "Mr. Carson says you're the very best. He doesn't mind working for you."

"Yes, well, E. J. is the exception. He seems quite willing to follow instructions."

E. J. laughed. "I wouldn't dare do otherwise. Everyone knows it's better to do what Miss Colter says than to question her. Besides"—he leaned down and whispered conspiratorially—"I think Miss Colter is one terrific lady."

This brought a bit of a chuckle from Mary Colter. "Well, not everyone feels that way, but I'm working on them. Oh, I'll have to talk with you more tomorrow, E. J. I see one of my boys making a mess of the ironwork." She pushed past Natalie without another word.

"Her boys are working here?" Natalie questioned.

E. J. shook his head. "No, she calls all of us 'her boys.' Most of the men hate it, but I find it rather endearing. My own mother is dead and gone, so I don't mind it at all."

"I think she's very nice," Natalie said, watching as Mary Colter waggled her finger at the ironworker.

"Come on, I was just finishing for the day. We can go look at the garden if you like."

"I really want to get an ice-cream cone. I have enough money to buy you one too," Natalie offered. "Would you like to go with me?"

E. J. considered the matter for a moment. "Wouldn't it seem rather strange for you to go there with a grown man who isn't a member of your family? I wouldn't want your mother to worry."

Natalie whirled around and gazed at the ceiling overhead. "I go have ice creams with lots of grown-ups. People are really nice around here. I don't have to worry 'cause they're all good people. Grandpa says you can always tell good people, and I know you're one of them."

E. J. rubbed his chin. Having had a good portion of his lower face ripped to shreds by the explosion of an enemy potato masher, his jaw periodically ached and caused him pain even after all these years. Today had been one of those days when the dull ache seemed more intense.

"I suppose some ice cream might very well hit the spot," he finally answered. "But it will be my treat."

Natalie shrugged. "If you want to."

They ambled out of the building and headed toward town. "So tell me about your family, Natalie," E. J. said, still not exactly certain that he should be making this trip with the girl.

"My mama and I live here with my grandpa. She moved here before I was even born." Natalie waved to a couple of older men as they ambled along on the opposite side of the street. "Hello, Mr. Braxton, Mr. Lynn." She looked back at E. J. and smiled. "They always walk down to the Harvey House and have supper at exactly five o'clock. My mama says they're always very punctual."

"So you were telling me about your mother. Where did she live before coming here?" E. J. asked innocently.

"Baltimore. She lived there with my daddy before he went to the war. My grandma and grandpa didn't like my daddy, so they were real mean to my mama."

E. J. looked down at the child as if she'd spoken Greek. "Why didn't they like your daddy?"

"He wasn't rich. They wanted Mama to marry a rich man, but Mama said she only loved my daddy and would never love anyone else. And you know what, she never has," Natalie said, looking quite serious. "She says that's what it's like with true love."

E. J. felt his mouth go dry. The child was giving an uncanny account of his own life. How could this be?

"Here's the store I like," Natalie said, rushing into the ice-cream parlor and drugstore without waiting for E. J.

"Hi, Mrs. Nelson," Natalie called as she came to the counter. "I've come for ice cream."

A plump woman stood behind the counter. She put her hands on her hips and smiled. "I suppose you'll be wanting the regular, eh?"

Natalie giggled and nodded. "Chocolate."

The woman then looked to E. J. "Is this man a friend of yours, Natalie?" She eyed him suspiciously.

"Yup. He's working over at the new Harvey House. His name is E. J. Carson and he's an architect like my daddy was. Mr. Carson has been showing me all around the Harvey hotel and he even introduced me to Miss Colter. She's the one who designed the entire place."

The woman's expression relaxed. She smiled, revealing crooked teeth. "Well, it's a pleasure to meet you, Mr. Carson. Any friend of Natalie's is always welcome here."

"Thank you, ma'am," E. J. replied uncomfortably. He hated to be under anyone's scrutiny, but worse yet, he couldn't stop thinking of what Natalie had shared with him only moments earlier.

E. J.'s mind moved in a hundred different directions. It's just coincidence, he told himself. Just one of those flukes of time and nature.

That Natalie's mother should have lived in Baltimore and married against her parents' wishes was just ironic. It wasn't so very extraordinary. E. J. ordered a vanilla cone and paid for the purchase before following Natalie to a small table for two.

"I love to come here. I like to watch the big fans go round and round," she said, pointing overhead. "On a hot day, it's the best place in the world to be."

E. J. nodded and ate absentmindedly. He pulled himself out of his thoughts and looked hard at the child sitting opposite him. Dark brown eyes gazed back at him. Eyes so much like . . .

"My mama likes to come here too, but she's usually too busy," Natalie stated, happily devouring her cone.

"Your mama sounds like a very nice lady," E. J. said, his voice trembling.

"She is. She's the best in the world."

E. J. forced himself to ask the question that wouldn't let him be. "What . . . what is your mother's name?"

"Ashley," Natalie replied. "Ashley Murphy Reynolds."

E. J. stared at the child for a moment, then quickly got to his feet. "I need to get back. I'm sorry."

"I'll go with you," Natalie said, following him to the door.

"No, that's all right. I forgot something at work."

"There you are!" a familiar voice called out.

E. J. forced himself to look up. It was her. She was alive. His wife was alive.

Ashley moved toward them and smiled. "I figured I'd find you here, Natalie. Who's your friend?"

She didn't recognize him. But why should she? He wore glasses, had a full beard and mustache, and had endured multiple surgeries to set his jaw and lower face in order. There was no reason she should see him for the boyish man who'd gone off to war only a few weeks after their wedding.

"This is Mr. Carson," Natalie told her mother.

"E. J. Carson," he said, extending his hand. He didn't know what else to say. How could he simply introduce himself as her long-dead husband? Furthermore, why did she believe he was dead? Who had told her that? Anger burned inside. Perhaps the same person who had told him she was dead had masterminded a scheme to make her believe he'd perished upon the battlefield.

Ashley's smile was just as he remembered. "It's nice to meet you, Mr. Carson."

"Mr. Carson works building the Harvey hotel," Natalie explained, finishing her ice-cream cone. "He was just going back to work."

"Well, don't let us keep you, Mr. Carson," Ashley said sweetly. "Come along, Natalie, I've been on business for Grandpa and we should get right home. I hate to leave him alone too long."

Natalie nodded and took hold of her mother's hand. "Can Mr. Carson come have dinner with us sometime?"

E. J. cleared his throat uncomfortably. He knew the little minx was playing matchmaker. But he was the only one of the trio who knew there was no need. He was already married to the woman.

Ashley met his gaze and replied, "Of course he can, but not tonight. We have too many things to take care of."

E. J. breathed a sigh of relief. He could barely stand to be this close to her and not pull her into his arms and declare his identity. The only thing that stopped him was the past. A sickening sensation crept over him; the images of his nightmares came to rest on his heart. He was of no good to this woman and her child. *Her child.* Was she also his? His mind reeled. A child? Could he be a father? It was all too much to fathom.

"I really have to go. It was good to meet you, Mrs. Reynolds."

He hurried away, not giving either one of them a chance to reply. With his world crashing down around him, E. J. felt rather like Pandora. He'd opened a box that he'd thought long ago sealed and forever closed to him. His heart begged him to look back over his shoulder— to catch a glimpse of her face once more. But the demons of the past would not let him. How could he saddle a wife and child with the horrors that lived inside him now? He wasn't Ethan Reynolds anymore. In many ways, Ethan Reynolds *had* died on the battlefields of France, just as they presumed he had.

E. J. stretched out across his bed and stared up at the ceiling in his hotel room. He'd isolated himself from everyone after learning the truth about Ashley. How could she be alive?

He thought back on every word Natalie had told him. Her grandfather was dying. Would that be Ashley's father? E. J. had never had much to do with the man, but the image of the man's wife, Leticia Murphy, was clearly etched in his memories. As were so many other images.

"She didn't recognize me," he murmured. *But why should she?* He took off his glasses and laid them aside. He looked completely different now. He even shocked himself sometimes when he looked in the mirror. Of course, there was also the fact he'd changed his name. Ashley was introduced to E. J. Carson—not to Ethan Reynolds.

He'd changed his name shortly after learning Ashley was dead. The journalists were hounding him for comments and interviews, for he was heralded as a hero and everyone seemed to want the intimate details of his experiences. When he was stuck in the hospital, there was little he could do to escape the attention. But once he was out, he wanted only to be free from the memories that were stirred every time someone mentioned his deeds. Pity that changing his name hadn't also altered the dark images in his mind.

So he had become E. J. Carson, using the initials of his first and middle names, Ethan James. Carson came compliments of his mother's maiden name. And now he was here in Winslow, where the woman he had long believed to be dead had lived her life for the last decade.

Ashley. He moaned softly and covered his eyes with his hand as if to block out the picture of her standing there in the afternoon sun.

"How can this be happening?" He'd given up hope so long ago. She was dead, they had told him. Dead to influenza. It was reasonable to believe; after all, his own parents had succumbed to the illness, as had vast numbers of other victims. He'd managed to catch it himself after coming home that winter of 1918. Weakened from his injuries, he'd nearly died—so many times he'd wished he had.

He sighed and folded his hands together behind his head and again looked at the ceiling as though it might offer some answers for the questions in his mind.

Ashley's mother must have lied to him. She hated him from the very beginning.

He remembered the night Ashley had first brought him to meet her folks. They were having a celebration of sorts. Ashley's oldest brother had just been made a partner at the bank where he worked. Friends and family had gathered to wish him well and applaud his good fortune. Ashley had insisted on bringing Ethan to the party. Her parents were clearly not pleased, although they had not made a public scene over the matter.

That wasn't true, however, of the next visit he made to their plush Baltimore home. Ashley's mother had made little effort to hide her displeasure. In fact, she'd made more than one comment alluding to Ashley being spoken for—of their plans for her to marry well.

By the time Ashley brought him around for a third visit, Leticia Murphy was willing to speak quite frankly and tell him that he was to leave her daughter alone. When Ashley had gone upstairs to change her clothes, her mother had even offered him money to never see Ashley again. He'd been deeply offended; so much so, in fact, that he'd told Ashley what had happened. Shortly after that incident, Ashley agreed to marry him and on March twentieth they had done exactly that.

Ethan had never known such happiness. He could still see Ashley standing there, her beautiful chocolate brown hair done up in a loose bun. . . .

"She's cut her hair," he murmured, recalling how her hair was bobbed in a fashionable cut. He had never wanted her to cut her hair, but he had to admit the cropping did nothing to take away from her beauty. If anything, it only enhanced her delicate features. No wonder Natalie had appealed to him so much. She looked just like her mother.

Sweat trickled down the side of his face. He wasn't perspiring from the heat, however—it was more a nervous energy that had built inside him since seeing Ashley again. Now, in the quiet of the night, he could scarcely believe the events of the day.

Why hadn't he just told her who he was? Why hadn't he taken her in his arms and . . .

Because you're a coward, that's why, he told himself.

But it wasn't that simple. If it were, that would be easy. Ethan had always found ways to muster up his courage for the moment. No, this was much more difficult and so very complicated.

First there was the obvious problem of letting Ashley know he was alive and well. But then, perhaps she knew that already. Perhaps she had agreed with her parents that Ethan was no good for her and had annulled the marriage. But if that were the case, why had she raised Natalie to believe her father had died in the war?

But was he Natalie's father?

The questions poured in around him like sand through a sieve. What possible good would it do to come back into Ashley's life after all these years? Even if he were Natalie's father, wouldn't it be more harmful than helpful to suddenly make that announcement?

As the night wore on, sleep overcame him and with it came the nightmares that always haunted him. Tossing fitfully, E. J. fought the war all over again. The smell of death permeated the air around him and blended with the heady scent of raw earth. The battle raged and Ethan, with his Springfield rifle, bayonet fixed, waited for the whistle signal that would send him over the top of the trench and into the embrace of eternity.

Suddenly the artillery barrage that had begun at seven that morning stopped. The silence was uncanny, almost deafening. Then without warning, the shrill metallic scream of their advancing signal rent the air. A battle cry rose up from a hundred soon-to-be-dead men as the forces moved up and out of their protective trenches.

Ethan looked to the man on his right—John O'Malley from Boston. They had bonded easily because of an interest they shared in architectural studies. Ethan saw the sheer terror on John's face—and it was as if Ethan stared into a mirror. The man's expression reflected his own heart. They stalked the no-man's-land together, and although hundreds of other uniformed men did likewise, it was almost as if they were alone.

Ethan felt the sweat run down his back and chill him to the bone. The anticipation of enemy fire . . . waiting for the adversary to move from their bunkers to the machine guns . . . waiting for that first spray of deadly rain. It was like a madness—an insanity. How was it that they should find themselves here, like this? How was it that farmers, painters, teachers, and architects were now bearing arms against one another—fighting a war of kings?

Ethan forced himself to keep stride with John and the others as they moved out across the crater-ridden landscape. Someone had mentioned how beautiful the landscape had once been, but Ethan saw only the scars and ugliness. This was the third major battle the area had hosted, and the damage from the artillery had left a desolate and barren land. Even the grass was gone and what trees had existed were now charred, wraithlike figures that rose in ominous fashion—almost as if they were skeletal guards of what had been left behind.

And then the machine guns began their staccato symphony. Bullets zipped past their heads, and the men dove into the nearest crater. All around them soldiers did likewise, some making it without harm, others crying out in pain as the bullets ripped into their flesh.

"For sure it's gonna be a long day," John called over his shoulder. Already he was heading out over the top of the crater. Digging his elbows into the ground, he crawled away from Ethan, pausing only momentarily to raise up his rifle and fire.

Ethan followed, all thoughts of patriotism and bravery faded. All around him men were dying, dropping to the ground with stun-faced expressions. It was almost as if they hadn't expected the possibility of death.

"Help me," one soldier, looking to be only a boy, cried out. He reached out to Ethan in sheer misery. Then his expression changed, the pain vanishing in the noiseless sigh of his last breath. Ethan pushed back the boy's arm and pressed on. The haunting expression stayed with him, however. What had the boy seen on the brink of death? Ethan and his buddies often sat around discussing their lives back home, and every once in a while someone would bring the topic back to the war and the possibility that they would be killed.

John had voiced the question just the night before. "Do you suppose you hear the bullet coming when it's for you?"

Ethan wondered that also as bullets shot past his head.

The danger grew as they closed the gap between their trenches and those of the enemy. The air was thick with smoke and cries of wounded men. With more of the desolate stretch of empty no-man's-land behind them than in front, the men of Ethan's unit and others pushed forward. A charred scarecrow of a tree offered them the tiniest defense. They paused to catch their breath, then saw their comrades moving out.

A sudden *thud* caused the hair on Ethan's neck to rise. He tasted blood and realized he'd bit his own lip. Then, as if time stood still, Ethan froze in place. A potato masher landed only a few feet away. There was no time to yell out a warning. No time to seek cover or turn away. The explosion blasted, sending shrapnel ripping through the lower half of Ethan's face. For a moment there was nothing but the searing heat and sensation of something gone terribly wrong. Then the pain radiated throughout his entire body.

Ethan rolled to his side and touched his face. His hand came away wet with blood. Looking across to his friends, he saw one man's hand torn away. Another man suffered a leg wound. The agony of their pain rose up like a banshee cry on the winds. John was nowhere in sight.

"Oh, God, help us," moaned the man with the leg wound. "Oh, help us, Jesus." The man groped around him for his rifle.

Someone screamed in the distance as another explosion of machine-gun fire cut the air. The scene was unreal; slowed in motion, it seemed to take forever for the unit to move even a few feet.

Ethan struggled to sit up. The rapid-fire barrage of bullets poured over and around him. Across the field, men were struggling to advance, struggling to stay alive. The sight caused something to snap inside him. He was tired of being afraid. Tired of spending his nights in trenches. Tired of this war. Without warning or even stopping to see if he could help his friends, Ethan got to his feet and stormed across the remaining distance to the machine-gun nest.

He could hardly see out of his right eye; blood and debris barred his sight and made his depth perception questionable at best. But it didn't matter. Staggering as his foot hit a hole, Ethan still refused to stop. Pain shot up his leg and he didn't know if it was from the misstep or a bullet. It didn't matter. Either way, he had a mission to complete.

Pushing past the barrier of sandbags and logs, he fired as he jumped into the enemy trench. The stunned faces of the German soldiers would always haunt him. He shot the gunners first, then bayoneted them even as they cried out in their misery. One man took off down the line and Ethan, in a blood haze that overcame common sense, followed the man.

He couldn't say how many men he killed that day, but he could remember the looks on their faces and the feel of his bayonet stealing the life from them. A dozen or more men dropped their weapons and raised their arms in surrender. Yelling, *"Kamerad! Kamerad!"* But Ethan didn't care that they now wanted to be his friend—that they were willing to give themselves up. He wanted them all dead. He raised his Springfield once again and fired into their pleading expressions.

"Ethan!"

He looked up through the haze and saw John, along with several other men he didn't know. A dizzying sensation overcame him. John and the others pointed their rifles at the enemy just as Ethan felt himself beginning to fall. Helpless, he reached for the open air as if to find something to hold on to, but there was nothing.

E. J. awoke with a start and a cry as he always did. Looking around the darkened room, his mind refused to accept the safety offered there. He got to his feet and turned on a light. The rapid pounding of his heart left him lightheaded and breathless.

"It's all right. It's over," he said aloud.

But would it ever really be over?

He sat down on the edge of the bed, panting for breath. "Oh, God, where are you? Why do you hide yourself from me? Why must this torment go on and on?"

*A*shley sat crocheting a sweater for Natalie, marveling at how much her daughter had grown over the last year. The sweaters she'd made last fall no longer fit and had been given away to friends in the neighborhood. Hooking the red yarn in and out of the loops, Ashley knew in the blink of an eye Natalie would be grown. And then what?

She had tried to save money in order to send Natalie to college, if she desired to go. Right now Natalie wanted very much to train as an architect, but Ashley had no way of knowing if that passion would follow her into adulthood. Natalie would most likely marry, whether or not she went to school. It was just the way of most women. A girl would be frowned upon if she remained single for too long. Even a widow became the object of ridicule if she refused to remarry. Many fellow Harvey workers urged Ashley to consider settling down with one of the railroad men. But Ashley couldn't bring herself to do such a thing. The men, while kind and attentive and often very handsome, were simply not appealing. She'd given her heart to Ethan, and everyone else paled in comparison.

Still, one day Natalie would make a life for herself. Once Natalie did marry, she would probably move away—maybe far away. She'd have a family of her own.

Ashley shuddered at the thought of being alone. *Maybe I should remarry,* she thought. *I could never love anyone as much as I loved Ethan, but that doesn't mean I couldn't have a good companion. A lot of people marry without love,* she told herself. But what kind of life was that? Would there ever be satisfaction, contentment in such an arrangement?

She was still considering this when the lawyer, Simon Watson, showed up to finalize all of Grandpa's final requests. Ashley put aside her crocheting and opened the door to admit the man.

"Good morning, Mr. Watson," she greeted, reaching out to take his gray fedora.

"Good morning." He smiled ever so slightly and nodded. "Is your grandfather awake?"

"I'm not sure, but I know he'll want to see you. He's weakened considerably since you saw him last week. I'm glad you could make these arrangements quickly because, frankly, he needs the pain medication and he won't take it until his affairs are in order."

The middle-aged lawyer nodded. "He's said as much to me."

Ashley knew there was nothing else to be said. She'd wanted to make certain the lawyer understood Grandpa's plight and apparently he did. "I'll go make sure he's awake," she finally said. "Why don't you have a seat in the living room?"

"Thank you. I'll do just that."

Ashley hurried to Grandpa's room and knocked lightly. "Grandpa? Are you awake?"

"I'm awake. I was just reading." His voice sounded weak and worn.

Ashley came into the room and gave it a cursory examination. Grandpa lay with his Bible in hand. He had asked for several of his favorite books, and they now were stacked beside the iron-framed bed. Beside this, a nightstand of intricately carved oak bore a pitcher of water, a glass, and his pocket watch. Grandpa always liked to keep track of the time.

Ashley went to him and straightened his covers. "Mr. Watson is here to see you."

"Oh, good." Grandpa struggled to sit up.

"Here, let me help you," Ashley said, taking hold of his arm. She carefully helped him to sit, although she could tell his pain was excruciating. Plumping the pillows behind him, she eased him back against them. "How's that?"

"As good as it's going to get," he declared. "Go ahead now and show Simon in."

Ashley fussed with the covers for another moment, then smiled. "Would you like me to bring you something to eat? I could set a tray for you both—a little midmorning brunch."

"No, nothing. I don't think this will take long. In fact, I need you to stay and hear what Simon has to say."

Ashley had never been included in any of Grandpa's discussions with the lawyer. She nodded slowly. "If that's what you want me to do."

"It is. I have instructions for you, and they need to be carried out immediately."

"Let me go fetch Mr. Watson, then," she said, curious now as to what Grandpa needed her to accomplish.

Ashley bit at her lower lip as she made her way to the living room. The stocky lawyer sat at attention on the sofa. He appeared to be lost in thought momentarily. Ashley stopped and cleared her throat. "Grandpa said he'd see you now. He wants me to come as well."

Watson nodded. "I presumed he would." He picked up his satchel and nodded. "I'll follow you."

Once they were settled back in Grandpa's room, the lawyer turned to open the briefcase he'd brought. "Russell, I believe I've handled everything you asked me to take care of. You'll see that I've sold off the stocks you held and have put the money into a bank account in your granddaughter's name. Here are the figures on these statements." He handed the old man several pieces of paper.

Ashley felt her eyes widen at this news. She had no idea Grandpa even had stocks. She looked to her grandfather for some sign of confirmation, but the old man was intent on studying the papers given him.

"What about the house?" he asked.

Watson nodded. "I've arranged it all. The deed is now in Mrs. Reynolds's name. She owns the house free and clear."

"What's this all about, Grandpa?" Ashley questioned, feeling mild shock at the lawyer's words.

"I've put my affairs in order," Russell Whitman stated simply. He lowered the papers and looked at Ashley with a serious expression. "I paid cash for this house; there are no bank liens on it, so now it's yours without restriction. I don't have long, child. We both know that. The last thing I want to do is have you fretting and stewing over how you'll manage once I'm gone."

Ashley felt her cheeks grow hot. She had been fretting over that very thing, but not because of the money or her home. She knew she'd get good wages at the Harvey House and besides, she'd already set aside a good portion in savings. She had hoped to make it a college fund for Natalie but knew they could easily use the money to live on if necessary.

"There are conditions, however," Mr. Watson stated in his lawyerly way. He looked to Grandpa to take it from there.

"That's right," Grandpa said. His gaze never left her. "I want to see your mother and her sister Lavelle before I die." Ashley stiffened but said nothing. He continued. "All these years I've abided by your wish that we have no contact with them, but now I need to break that agreement. And I need your help."

Grandpa looked at her with an expression of mixed emotions. "Your job is to contact them both and bring them here. If they need money to make the trip, then tell them it will be provided."

Ashley swallowed hard. The thought of having to deal with her mother at a time like this was more than she wanted to endure. She twisted her hands together. "But what if they don't want to come?"

"That's a chance I must take." Grandpa's voice took on a saddened tone. "I must account for that possibility, but if we don't at least try, we won't know. After all, we've been here for all this time without letting anyone know where we'd disappeared to. Your mother and aunt could be half sick wondering where we are."

Ashley folded her arms against her chest. "Like they would ever care. They didn't care then; why should they care now?"

Grandpa's expression grew pained. Ashley felt terrible for destroying his hopes and immediately tried to turn the tables on her own question. "On the other hand," she hurried to continue, "they could be sorry for the way they acted. They could possibly want to see us both."

The lawyer nodded. "Exactly. There's a good chance that all has been forgiven and forgotten. You must at least give them the chance to refuse."

"I can telegram them at the last known addresses," Ashley added. "Would that be sufficient for a start?"

Grandpa smiled. "I think it would be a good way to begin." He seemed to recover a bit of his positive spirit. "Ashley, I know you have been deeply hurt by your mother and father. I was hurt by them as well. But I want you to know that there is nothing to be gained in holding a grudge. There's also Natalie to consider. Do you want to teach her the same kind of hatred and anger?"

Ashley was rather startled by his words. She'd never wanted Natalie to feel the same hurt and anger she felt. In fact, she'd avoided telling Natalie much of anything about her grandma and grandpa Murphy in order to avoid speaking ill of them. Still, even while she'd tried hard not to show her animosity toward her mother and father, Natalie was no dummy. She knew there were problems, and true to her gentle and compassionate nature, she never pressed Ashley for answers.

"You don't want to teach Natalie to hate her family. If they reject her or cause her grief, then let her decide for herself. Either way, I need to see my daughters—and I need you to help me."

Ashley met his pleading eyes. "All right."

"Good. Now that we have that matter resolved," Mr. Watson interjected, "I want to discuss the sale of your stocks. The result was quite lucrative. I've also been told that there is a buyer for your property east of town. That is, if you are of a mind to sell."

Grandpa looked at Ashley as if for an answer, but she felt she could be of no help. She didn't even realize Grandpa owned stocks, much less property. "What property is Mr. Watson speaking of, Grandpa?"

"Oh, it's just some acreage I picked up a few years past. I was helping out a friend who needed the money," Grandpa replied.

Ashley realized she'd paid very little attention to her grandfather's business dealings over the years. She supposed it shouldn't be that surprising that Grandpa should have found a way to turn a dollar. Everyone was always saying he had a golden touch. Suddenly her curiosity got the better of her.

"Grandpa, what kind of money are we talking about in regard to the sale of these stocks?"

Russell looked to his lawyer for this information. The lawyer looked down at his own copy of notes. "It would appear once funeral expenses and transportation to Los Angeles are subtracted that you would realize the sum of around $82,370 and some odd change. Of course, that doesn't include the sale of the land."

Ashley sat back feeling as though the wind had been knocked out of her. Nearly one hundred thousand dollars! How could this be?

"What's wrong?" Grandpa asked. His tone revealed his concern for her.

"I can't believe . . . well . . . we're rich."

Grandpa winced as he chuckled. "I'm full of surprises. I wanted you and Natalie to be provided for. It was important to me to see that you had what you needed after I was gone."

"But so much? I'm just . . . well . . ." She looked at the lawyer. "I'm shocked."

"Well, I hope it's a pleasant shock. You deserve to be happy, Ashley. You've worked hard all these years to provide for your child. I let you work because it was easier than arguing with you. Besides, in the early days I feared your sorrow would overcome you. You had Natalie, but sometimes I feared she only added to your pain. Then, too, I wanted you to have a sense of self-worth. You know you're capable of doing what needs to be done now. You know that God will provide in any circumstance."

Ashley shook her head. "I suppose if I didn't know that before, I know that now."

Grandpa reached out his hand and Ashley quickly came to his side. Grasping his bony hand, Ashley leaned down to kiss his fingers. The man had once weighed just over two hundred pounds, but the cancer had reduced that number by at least fifty.

All at once, Ashley began to feel very guilty. Did Grandpa feel he had to give her the money and house just to convince her to contact her mother and Lavelle? She felt very ashamed. *I've kept him from his daughters all these years. What if he's right? What if they've changed?*

"I'll do what I can to please you, Grandpa. I'll send the telegrams and encourage Mother and Aunt Lavelle to come, but you don't have to give your money to me. I'd do it anyway—because it's what you want. Besides, if I know Mother, at least, she'll expect the money and house to go to her."

Russell frowned at this. "I gave her an inheritance long ago. Her sister too. They've had what's coming to them. This is for you and Natalie. I took what I had left after settling on them both and came here to start a new life with you. I bought the house free and clear and took the remaining money and invested it. I did so only with the thought that you and Natalie might be provided for. And that's why I've asked Simon to take care of all this business today. There will be no misunderstanding when my time comes. In fact, you needn't even answer any of your mother's or Aunt Lavelle's questions regarding any money. Send them to Simon. There are issues and details that you needn't worry yourself with, that Simon is fully knowledgeable of. He can handle them if they decide to get greedy."

The lawyer nodded. "I've dealt with harder cases than theirs," he said. "You refer them to me if there is any question at all about the settlement of this estate."

"That's the beauty of this arrangement," Grandpa added. "There is no estate. As far as they're to know, the place is yours and everything in it. Because now, thanks to Simon, that's the truth of it. They don't need to know where you came by it or how."

"It means more to me than you'll ever know to have a home for Natalie. She loves it here. And I know the memories of our time here together will keep her from . . . from . . ." Ashley's words halted as she tried to think of a way to say what she needed to without bringing up Grandpa's death.

He smiled as if knowing. "She'll be fine, you know. When I'm gone, she'll be sad for a time, but she'll know where I am and that we'll meet again." He drew a breath that seemed to pain him more than ever.

"You should rest now."

"No, there's one more thing I want to say. Our Natalie wants you to remarry. She's mentioned it in prayer so often that I'm beginning to expect an announcement most every time you come into the room."

Ashley shook her head. "Natalie dreams big."

"You should too. God has a plan for each one of us. You have a child to raise, and I can hardly believe God wants you to do that alone. You need to at least think about remarrying so that Natalie can have a father."

Ashley straightened. She bit back a retort that Natalie *had* a father and although he was dead, he was nevertheless irreplaceable. "I'm thinking on it," was all she could manage to say.

"Well, if there is no further business, I must be getting back to my office," Mr. Watson said, getting to his feet. He tucked his copy of the papers back into the satchel. "I know my way out, Mrs. Reynolds. There's no need for you to accompany me. When you are ready for the details of the bank account and other information, feel free to come see me."

"I will," Ashley replied. "Thank you." She waited until she'd heard the front door close before turning to Grandpa. "I'm going to compose the telegrams for Mother and Lavelle. Is there anything in particular you want me to say to them?"

Russell Whitman closed his eyes and grimaced. "Tell them to hurry."

CHAPTER SEVEN

S o your grandfather has provided for you?" a young blond-haired woman asked, leaning across the Fred Harvey lunch counter.

Ashley nodded to her friend Glenda. "He has and he's done so very generously. I won't even have to come back to work here if I don't want to."

"By the time you're ready to come back to work," Glenda said, straightening up to smooth the white apron of her Harvey uniform, "we'll have moved to the new place." She pushed a piece of pie in front of Ashley and smiled. "The resort is supposed to be the bee's knees. All beautiful blue and yellow tile in the lunch room, and the dining room will be better than ever."

"I've heard all that too," Ashley said, picking up a fork. She cut into the apple pie and took a bite. As always, Harvey food was sheer perfection. She smiled and leaned back to contemplate her future. "The new place sounds really nice. I've been watching them put it up as I walk by to come here. Of course, I don't get out as much as I used to." Ashley continued eating the pie.

"I was going to ask you about that. Is Grandpa Whitman home alone?"

Ashley shook her head and swallowed. "No, I had some things to do, so I asked Mrs. Breck to come over. She lives a few blocks away but always needs to earn an extra dime or two. I feel sorry for her, so when I get extra sewing money, I let her come do a few chores for me."

"You'll be able to hire her full-time now. Goodness, you won't even need to stay in Winslow if you're of a mind to move away," Glenda commented. "You could even get a transfer to one of the Harvey Houses in California. I'd sure love to go to California."

Ashley knew she spoke the truth, but as much as her memories of

Los Angeles caused her to want to revisit the sights from time to time, she never really wanted to leave Winslow. "I've no desire to go away from here. I like Arizona, and I like the way the people are here. Besides, Natalie's been here all her life and she's happy here."

"Well, I know that's important, but maybe you'd both be happier in a bigger town." A distant train whistle perked Glenda's attention. "Well, we're bound to get busy now. I'd better stop gabbing. You know how maddening the pace can get at the lunch counter."

Ashley nodded. "I'll finish up here and be on my way. There was trouble with the telegraph lines. They told me to come back later, but I still need to write out what I want to say to my mother and Aunt Lavelle."

"What *are* you going to say?" Glenda asked, her blue eyes seeking Ashley's face for an answer.

Ashley didn't mind her probing question. Glenda had been as close of a friend as Ashley wanted. They didn't do a lot of running around or going places. Many times Glenda had tried to talk Ashley into side trips on the train or just sightseeing to places like the nearby meteor crater, but Ashley generally declined because of Natalie. She hated leaving Natalie behind for any reason, and a group of single adults really had no use for a child.

Eating the last of her pie, Ashley shrugged and wiped her mouth with a napkin. "Grandpa said to tell them to hurry. Otherwise, I don't know what to say. I mean, how do I just open up the lines of communication after ten years of separation?"

Glenda took up the plate and fork. "I can't imagine not talking to my mama for over ten years."

Ashley felt the cynicism streak up her spine. "If my mother were your mother, you could imagine it well enough."

The rumble of the train drew their attention as the passenger service slowed to a stop outside. "Talk to you later," Ashley said, giving Glenda a little wave. She hurried across the room and out the side door before the crowds could pour in.

She couldn't help smiling at the ruckus behind her. Life in the Harvey House was always exciting. Especially in this town, where the passenger trains came through at regular intervals. Ashley missed the commotion and urgency. She loved being home with Grandpa and Natalie, but Natalie was at school all day and Grandpa slept a good portion of the time. The old man was unable to bear up under the pain, and now that he had finally allowed Ashley to give him doses of the morphine, he slept more than ever. Already she had begun to mourn him—the one thing she'd promised herself she wouldn't do until he was actually gone.

Stepping outside into the comfortable warmth of the late afternoon, Ashley pulled the brim of her straw hat down to avoid freckling from the sun. Consumed with thoughts of the job she had to do, Ashley's steps were slow and methodical.

How do I write to Mother when she swore she'd never speak to me again— never hear a word I had to say? What makes me think she'll even read a telegram that I send? Then it dawned on Ashley that perhaps the best thing to do would be to send the telegram in her grandfather's name. She could send the news that he was gravely ill, not expected to live, and that he desired to see his daughters again. Ashley could even mention that she was now living with Grandpa—Natalie too. But sign the entire message from Russell Whitman instead of Ashley Reynolds.

It seemed reasonable. It also seemed to lessen the feeling that Ashley was betraying herself and Ethan's memory. She had sworn she'd never again talk to her mother or father or have any communication with them as to her whereabouts. Somehow it seemed an honorable thing to do for Ethan.

"Oh, excuse me."

Ashley looked up at the sound of a familiar voice. Strange how thinking of Ethan had caused the stranger's tone to sound so similar. She looked into the face of E. J. Carson and blinked against the glare. "I'm sorry, did I nearly run you over?" she questioned, realizing she hadn't been paying attention to where she was going.

"It's as much my fault," E. J. replied. "I wasn't paying attention either." His voice sounded shaky, almost as if they'd nearly fallen off the edge of a cliff rather than simply bumping into each other on the street.

The silence between them seemed quite awkward, and with nothing else to say, Ashley smiled and excused herself. "Well, I'll be on my way."

E. J. blurted out, "I think you have a very remarkable daughter. She's been here several times to study the architecture of the hotel."

Ashley paused in midstep. "Yes. She loves it. She's quite good at drawing her own designs."

E. J. nodded and a lock of wavy brown hair fell over his forehead, touching his gold-rimmed glasses. Ethan's hair had been wavy and brown as well. He wore it shorter and fashioned just a little different, but nevertheless, Mr. Carson's hair reminded her of her husband. For just a moment, Ashley almost reached up to push it back. She stopped herself just in time and shook her head. "Natalie speaks quite highly of you. I know she enjoys learning about the hotel. It's kind of you to be so patient with her."

He looked at the ground, seeming most uncomfortable. "I enjoy it myself. I haven't had the opportunity to be around many children in my day, but Natalie is so much like a little adult that I scarcely notice the difference."

"She is like that," Ashley admitted. "She is probably far too much like that for her own good." Ashley could clearly see that E. J. wasn't at ease with her. She thought it strange, given the fact he'd started the conversation to begin with, but took that moment to put an end to their talk.

"I must be going. My grandfather is ill and I need to return home."

Mr. Carson nodded. "I am sorry about that. Natalie mentioned her grandfather was ill."

"Actually, it's her great-grandfather, but he's known by most everyone around here as Grandpa Whitman, so she just calls him that too." E. J. looked up and Ashley added, "I hope things go well for you. I'm sure we'll meet again."

"To be sure," Carson replied.

That evening Ashley thought back to her encounter with E. J. Carson while Natalie sat playing jacks on the floor of their living room. He seemed so eager to share his admiration of Natalie, yet so uncomfortable in speaking to Ashley.

Picking up her crochet work, Ashley wondered about Natalie and her artistic talent. She came by it naturally, that was for sure. Ethan had been a master at drawing. He'd won several awards and the esteem of his teachers. Perhaps Glenda's thoughts of their moving away weren't quite so out of line. Maybe Natalie could benefit by moving closer to a school that had classes for architects. It bore some consideration.

Her thoughts quickly moved from Natalie and school, however, to the task of notifying her mother and aunt of Grandpa's illness. The telegraph office had remained closed and it seemed like a respite to Ashley. She supposed it might be prudent to check into telephoning, for her mother and father had put in a telephone in the years prior to Ashley leaving home. But she no longer recalled the number. Maybe they didn't even have the same number, and if that were the case, how would she find out how to reach them?

This is so hard, she thought. *I don't know anything about Mother and Father these days. They could be dead for all I know.* Ashley thought of that for a moment and wondered if it would grieve her to know they'd passed from this life without resolving the differences between them.

Then even as she thought of this, she looked at Natalie and knew how awful it would feel if Natalie rejected her the way Ashley had rejected her mother. *But my mother brought it on herself,* Ashley reminded herself. *I wasn't the one to say I'd never have anything more to do with them, until it was demanded of me that I never return—never write—never contact them at all.*

And for what? Because her mother's pride had been damaged? Because they couldn't seal the deal with their wealthy, politically-minded friends? Because Ashley wouldn't marry into the upper crust of Baltimore society?

She remembered her mother's anger and rage upon learning of Ashley's marriage to Ethan. The conversation had been so ugly and hurtful. Her mother accused Ashley of trying to destroy everything her father had worked for. Leticia Murphy had slapped her daughter hard across the face, telling her that she hoped to "knock some sense" into her wayward child.

Staring down at her crocheting, Ashley realized she'd messed up several stitches and had to pull out the thread and go back. She wished it could be that easy to unravel the mistakes of the past. Maybe her mother was sorry for what had transpired. Maybe she wished over and over that she'd never acted the way she had.

Ashley looked at her daughter once again. Her mother and father didn't even know about Natalie. Ashley had never been given a chance to explain. They only knew that their daughter had defied them and their wishes for her life. They only knew that their bank accounts would not be quite so large because Ashley had married a lowly architect.

"Are Grandma and Grandpa Murphy going to visit us?" Natalie asked, as if she could read her mother's thoughts.

Ashley continued working, paying closer attention to the stitches. "I don't know, Nat. They might. Grandpa wants them to come, so I hope they will," she said, though she really didn't want them to come. She looked down at Natalie, hoping her daughter would just drop the subject.

"I hope they will too," Natalie said, pushing her jacks aside and stretching out on the floor. She leaned up on one elbow. "Grandpa says he's just holding on for the day he can seek their forgiveness and see the family brought back together. Do you think Grandma Murphy and her sister will forgive Grandpa?"

Probably not, Ashley thought to herself. *Not if my mother is still the self-centered, bitter woman she was when I left.* Ashley shrugged. "You know, I don't see that Grandpa has anything to be forgiven for. Frankly, your grandpa is one of the most giving and loving men I've ever known. If Grandma Murphy and Aunt Lavelle can't understand that, then it's their loss."

"Grandpa hopes they'll come to know Jesus before he dies. He hopes that for you too," Natalie said, smiling. "He says you'll all be much happier if you know the source of life."

Ashley bit her tongue. How dare Grandpa put her in the same category as her mother and aunt? They'd deserted him and done nothing but hurt him. *I'm not like that,* Ashley told herself, feeling a frustration she couldn't begin to explain.

"Look, you need to get ready for bed. Have you put your clothes out for tomorrow?"

Natalie moaned. "Yes, but can't I stay up? It's just eight o'clock."

"If you want to read in your bed for half an hour, then you need to get headed that way. By the time you get your jacks cleaned up, make sure your clothes are ready for tomorrow, brush your teeth, and actually get into bed, it will be eight-thirty. Then if you read for half an hour, it will be nine. So you need to scoot." She smiled at Natalie, trying hard not to take out her frustration on the child.

Natalie yawned and picked up her jacks. "Okay." She pushed the jacks into a little drawstring bag that Ashley had made for her, then came to give her mother a hug and kiss. "I love you, Mama."

"I love you too, Natalie. Always remember that, no matter what happens. We have each other."

"We've got Jesus too," Natalie insisted.

Ashley nodded. "I'm sure we do."

"Mama, what are we going to do after Grandpa is gone?" Natalie asked as she pulled away from the embrace.

"What do you mean?"

"Well, where are we going to live and who will take care of us?"

"We'll live right here. Grandpa made sure of that. The house is ours. As for who will take care of us—well, I'll take care of us. I have some money and we've always gotten by without any trouble before."

"Sure, but we had Grandpa. When he's gone we won't have a man of the house. That worries Grandpa and it worries me. I think you should get married again."

If a noose had tightened around her neck, it couldn't have caused

Ashley more discomfort. The very idea of sharing her life with a stranger was more than she wanted to imagine. She'd given cursory thought to remarrying. She'd acknowledged that she didn't want to be alone for the rest of her life, but marrying again was a fearful thought.

Natalie continued before Ashley could respond. "Mr. Carson is very nice. He's handsome too, don't you think?"

Ashley was even more taken aback by her daughter's reference to E. J. Carson's appearance. "I don't think that's something a little girl should be thinking about."

Natalie shrugged. "His wife died, so he knows how it feels to lose someone you love. He knows a lot about building things too, and he likes the desert. He might like to stay here once the hotel is built, and maybe he'd even like to have a family."

"Where do you get these wild ideas?" Ashley said, shaking her head. "Go on, now, and go to bed. Your imagination will wear you out if you don't."

Natalie turned to go but paused by the arched entry. "I want a daddy. Someone who will teach me things and who will keep you from being too lonely." She didn't wait for Ashley's reply but instead headed off for her room.

Ashley contemplated her daughter's words and felt tears form in her eyes. "Have I so deprived her by not remarrying? I thought I'd done a good job of raising her. I thought having Grandpa here would make the loss of her father easier—more acceptable," Ashley whispered to the empty room. "Was I blind to her need—to mine?"

Russell Whitman stared into the darkness of his bedroom. He'd found it impossible to sleep, although he'd dozed from time to time when the pain hadn't been too much. He wondered if his daughters would come to see him. He wondered, too, if they would be willing to make some sort of peace with him—and with Ashley.

Pastor McGuire had said that God only expected him to do the things that were up to him to do. He couldn't force Lavelle and Leticia to care about him or his beliefs.

"But I want them to love you, Lord," he whispered.

Weary from the battle, Russell drew a ragged breath. "I want them to love me again as well. Is that so wrong?"

He remembered a time when the girls had been very small. They were such giggle boxes, as he affectionately called them. Work kept him away from home much of the time, but when he could, he arranged picnics or outings to show them how much he loved them.

"Ah, Peg, do you remember it?" He spoke to his dead wife as though she might answer. "You would dress in those lovely silk gowns. You always looked like a billowing cloud. The girls would wear pink ribbons in their hair, and you would don one of those extravagant hats that had become so fashionable."

He smiled at the memory. In his mind he could see his little girls playing ball or hopscotch. Once he had made them a kite and they'd gone to the beach to fly it. It had crashed after only a few short tours in the air, but they'd had a marvelous time.

What had happened to change all of that?

Russell knew he'd taken up with the wrong people and had worried about the wrong things. Money had become increasingly important, and the more he made, the more he needed. It was a vicious circle that robbed him of time and of his children.

I can't change that now, he reasoned, *but if only they'll come and see me, then maybe I can die in peace.*

But there was always the chance they wouldn't come. Streaks of pain shot out across his body, but the pain in his heart was still more intense. If they wouldn't come—wouldn't even acknowledge his need—it would surely kill him quicker than the cancer.

————

E. J. Carson sat across from Mary Colter at the impeccably dressed dinner table in the Winslow Harvey House. Fine linen tablecloths and napkins lent elegance to the patterned china and silver. The traditional settings of the Fred Harvey table were not to be ignored. Coming into the room, E. J. had immediately been transported from the tiny desert town to one of the better East Coast supper clubs. And that was just as Fred Harvey, the creator of this experience, would have had it. It was good to see that in spite of the man having died over twenty years earlier, his sons were still looking to fulfill and carry out their father's dream.

E. J. glanced to Mary's right, where Earl Altaire, an artist who'd been hired to do paintings on the stucco walls, sat trying to explain a pattern he intended to use. He was sketching on a torn scrap of paper with a piece of charcoal he'd taken from his pocket. Mary nodded and from time to time commented, although E. J. couldn't tell what was being said. To Mary's left was E. V. Birt, master carpenter, who would take

Mary's furnishing ideas and recreate an antique look. The man had a true gift for working with his hands, and E. J. had thought to question him about some benches that were being designed for the lobby when the man on his right began to tap on his water glass.

"I'd like to make an introduction."

E. J. recognized the man who spoke. He held some sort of position with the Winslow Chamber of Commerce. However, the man's name totally eluded him.

E. J. paid attention as the older man motioned to a tall, lanky fellow on his right. The man had a good-natured look about him, rather casual and almost out of place at the elegantly set table.

"This man is responsible for designing our airport. Of course, that is but one of his many accomplishments. He was the first to cross the Atlantic, and he sealed Winslow's prosperity when he made her a part of the new Transcontinental Air Transport service. I give you Charles Lindbergh."

E. J. nodded in acknowledgment but said nothing. He didn't really have a chance. Other people began to talk around him, asking Lindbergh questions and listening to the somewhat shy man speak about his exploits.

"What was it like to fly across the Atlantic?" one rather enthusiastic man questioned. E. J. recognized the man as one who assisted Mary in her scheduling.

"It was long," Lindbergh replied with a grin.

The conversation went on, but E. J. found himself bored. Flying was a fascinating thing but much too expensive for the common man to really take note of. There was discussion of how flying would soon put train service out of business, but E. J. found that hard to believe. Trains were more accessible. Trains could be routed via spurs to every city in America—even very small towns could have train service. Planes would never have that kind of accessibility. Besides, he didn't know many people who would trust themselves to such contraptions. Hanging high above the ground was hardly his idea of sensible.

As the conversation at the opposite end of the table continued in the direction of flight, Mary Colter focused on the hotel. "I'm wondering if you found those swatches of material for me to examine, Mr. Birt."

The man perked up at the sound of his name. "I have the silk velour in mulberry, mauve, and plum. Each varies a little from the other, but I think it will give you a nice selection to choose from."

Mary nodded. "I want it for seat padding on the horseshoe chairs," she said, looking to E. J. as if he'd asked a question. "The wood is a lovely walnut, and I believe the cushions will be just as vital as the rest of the chair." She turned to Birt. "I'll see them in the morning."

"I'll have them ready. Also . . ." He hesitated momentarily. "I have some questions regarding the chandeliers you wanted carved. The wood isn't the quality I'd like to see."

They continued to talk about the light fixtures while E. J.'s thoughts wandered back to his own dilemma. Ashley and Natalie were never far from his mind. He toyed with the prime rib he'd ordered for dinner, pushing the pink meat around his plate to give the appearance of actually eating. From time to time he put a piece of the tender beef in his mouth, grateful it wasn't tough like some meat he'd endured. Ever since his jaw had been damaged in the war, his ability to chew had suffered. Funny how something so simple and commonplace could sometimes cause him great pain.

"Mr. Carson, you've not said more than two words this evening. Is there a problem?" Mary Colter demanded.

E. J. smiled. Mary brooked no nonsense from "her boys." "No, ma'am. I'm just reflecting on personal matters."

She nodded, her probing gaze bringing him a moment of discomfort. "Are you able to come with me to that old Mormon fort tomorrow? I want to bring in more of that stone for the west wall. It's perfect for landscaping and giving the grounds an antique appearance. The more we utilize the natural resources at hand, the better off we are."

E. J. had heard it all before. "I can come with you if you need me to. There is still the matter of seeing to that list of issues you had with the west wing."

Mary considered this for a moment then waved her fork at him. "Stay here. I need those things taken care of. I'll take a couple of my boys to help me. If you talk to any of the locals, see if you can round up some old relics that might make pleasant *objets d'art*." She didn't even wait for E. J.'s reply but turned to the man beside her. "Now, Mr. Altaire, we need to discuss the designs for the hall. I have in mind a vining leaf and flower."

E. J. let his thoughts recede to Ashley and Natalie. It felt strange to realize and truly accept that he had a wife and child to consider. Even if he couldn't be sure Natalie was his child, he knew if he took Ashley back into his life, Natalie would naturally come along too.

Memories of his short whirlwind romance with Ashley Murphy came to mind. He'd first set his gaze upon her in the park. She was there with friends, laughing as she seemed wont to do. She appealed to him because of her vivacious spirit and her simplistic elegance. She'd worn a plain white muslin dress, pleated in the bodice and layered in the skirt. The sunlight gave her face a delightful glow, but her eyes seemed to sparkle with a light all their own. Ethan had been mesmerized.

He'd spied a couple of his college classmates talking with Ashley and her girlfriends. They seemed to be enjoying a leisurely game of croquet and the afternoon air. Ethan knew their social circles separated them, but as a college student he felt he could cross some barriers better than others. He longed to be included in that group, and barrier or no, the next time he saw them gathered, he made certain someone introduced him to the young beauty.

The opportunity came at a war-relief rally. Americans were doing their part to aid their European brothers, and if it presented a reason to have a celebration at the same time, people seemed all in favor of that. Ethan worried that the war would soon spread to engulf the Americans, and he wondered if he would go and fight or avoid taking up arms. He was still contemplating this matter when his classmate introduced him to Ashley Murphy.

He could still picture her warm chocolate brown eyes. She looked at him with such intensity, almost as if he were a piece of art she would study in detail.

"Ethan is an architect," his friend announced.

"Well, at least I'm in training to be one," Ethan corrected. "So far, no one's hired me on."

"It's just a matter of time," his friend interjected. "Ethan is top in the class."

"I'm glad to meet you," Ashley said, reaching out to shake Ethan's hand.

The moment their hands touched, Ethan felt the overwhelming sensation of electricity that moved between them. He wouldn't say it was exactly love at first sight, but it was certainly fascination at first sight.

From that point on, they began a conversation that didn't seem to end until three weeks later, when they agreed on a whim to get married.

E. J. shook the memories from his mind. *I was a different man then. She barely knew me, and what little she knew was completely lost in the trenches of France.*

He nodded as a Harvey waitress in her pristine black and white offered him coffee. The hot liquid helped warm the chill left by the memories of what had been.

Glancing across the room, E. J. noticed a man watching him most intently. The man was just a bit stocky in build, with a head full of curly brown hair. He wasn't at all familiar to E. J., but he stared in his direction as if he knew him. An uneasiness crept along E. J.'s spine. What did the man want? Who was he?

You're just being paranoid, he told himself. He drank from the cup and tried to steady his nerves long enough to take a second glance. The man was still watching.

Then it dawned on E. J. Charles Lindbergh sat at their table. The man was a notable public figure. No doubt the watcher had in mind that he might meet the famous flyer.

E. J. stole another glance and felt his heart pick up its pace. He'd so long hidden himself away from the press and anyone at all who knew him for who he'd been when he called himself Ethan Reynolds. He'd grown weary of his hero status, feeling that people were always trying to claim a piece of him. One woman had even snipped his hair, proclaiming she would have good fortune for the rest of her life because she had a locket of Ethan Reynolds's hair. Now there were Ashley and Natalie to consider, and until he was ready to let them know his identity, he certainly didn't need someone else spilling the news.

E. J. forced himself to go through the motions of drinking his coffee and eating his peach shortcake. It had to be Lindbergh the man was watching. No one knew he was really Ethan Reynolds. Even his wife didn't know, and she'd spoken to him twice now.

He'd convinced himself that his identity was safe, until the man got up from his table and moved across the room. E. J. tensed, fighting the urge to flee. *This is stupid,* he told himself. *It's been ten years. No one knows what I look like or where I've gone.*

"I wonder if I might be so bold as to introduce myself," the man said, standing just to the right of E. J. "I'm Marcus Greeley. I'm a journalist and author by trade. I saw Mr. Lindbergh here and I couldn't help myself."

E. J. breathed a sigh of relief. He didn't even bother to look up as the conversation continued at the other end of the table and introductions were made.

"Miss Colter," E. J. said, putting his fork aside, "I'm afraid a headache is keeping me from being any real use to you. I'm going to make it an early night."

Mary Colter nodded. "I'll speak to you in the morning before I head out. Why don't we meet here and talk over breakfast?"

"I'll be here," E. J. promised.

He moved past Mr. Greeley, only to have the man extend his hand. "The name's Greeley. Marcus Greeley."

E. J. didn't look up but nodded. "E. J. Carson." He shook the man's hand rather abruptly, then turned without another word. The man might think him rude, but he'd never guess his true identity if E. J. had anything to say about it.

The last thing I need, E. J. thought, *is for someone to declare that the famous Hun killer, Ethan Reynolds, is in town.*

*J*need to send two telegrams," Ashley announced as she approached the telegraph operator's counter. She'd only learned a few minutes ago that the wires were finally up and running. Grandpa was fading fast, and she knew that time was of the essence.

"What do you want to say?" the man asked, taking up a pencil and pad.

Ashley opened the first of the two missives. "This goes to Mrs. Lavelle Guzman. 'Please come to Winslow, Arizona, immediately. I am dying and wish to see you. If money is a concern, please advise. Father.' "

Ashley gave the man the Los Angeles address for her aunt, then folded the piece of paper away and opened the second. "The other telegram is for Mrs. Leticia Murphy." The message read the same, but Ashley added, " 'Please be aware I currently reside with Ashley and her daughter.' " She again had him sign the missive, "Father."

"These are urgent," she told the man. "My grandfather hasn't got long to live, and he wants to see his daughters before he dies."

"I'll do what I can from this end," the man assured her. He figured the cost and Ashley paid him before he asked, "If there's a reply, where should it be delivered?"

Ashley hadn't thought of a reply. She wrote her address down for the man and pushed it across the highly polished counter. "Just bring any response here."

She hurried to leave before she could change her mind. She knew the telegrams had to be delivered—knew that Grandpa was only holding on in order to see his daughters again. But Ashley could imagine the conflict ahead and it caused her stomach to ache just thinking about it.

Pushing open the door, she stumbled into the brilliance of the morning sun. Stubbing her toe, she sucked in her breath and fought to keep from crying. Then suddenly it wasn't her toe at all that brought the tears.

"What if Mother refuses to come because of me?" she murmured, wiping her eyes. She tried to straighten and regain her composure. *Then it will be my fault that Grandpa dies without feeling he's made his peace with her. I'll never be able to live with myself if that happens.*

There was a bit of chill to the air. It was well into September and the dry hot days of summer were behind them. Ashley had heard Mrs. Taylor mention the possibility of rain, but the clear skies overhead suggested nothing of the kind. Instead, as the wind whipped up, Ashley tasted the desert grit against her teeth and lips. It only served to make her more uncomfortable.

"Are you all right?"

She looked up into the face of E. J. Carson. Funny how he always seemed to turn up when she least expected it. She drew a deep breath and quickly looked away. "I'm fine." She choked back a sob and shook her head. "No, I'm not fine. I'm sorry."

"Would you like to take a walk, maybe talk it out?" The compassion in his tone became her undoing.

Ashley bit her lower lip as her tears spilled. "I'm afraid I would be a poor conversationalist."

"Never mind talking, then. We can simply walk, and if you feel you can share the burden with me, I'll be here ready and able to listen."

She nodded ever so slightly and allowed E. J. to lead her away from the busyness of town.

E. J. had no idea what had gotten into him. How in the world did he find himself walking along Second Street with his wife? He stared at the ground, trying to think of something to say. A tiny green lizard darted across the tip of his shoe, causing E. J. to make a bit of a side step. Ashley didn't appear to notice, however. Her sorrow, for whatever reason, seemed more than she could bear at the moment.

"Did you have more bad news?" he asked, hoping his tone wasn't too prying.

"No," Ashley replied, using her handkerchief to dab at her eyes. "I just had a difficult job to do."

"I see."

She shook her head. "No, you can't possibly understand. I'm sorry.

You really don't have to walk with me." She looked around as if to figure out how she might escape.

E. J. didn't want her to get away just yet. He longed to comfort her, but even more, he longed for her company. He wanted to know the kind of woman she'd become. They'd married so young and so quickly that neither one really knew the other one at all.

He reached out to touch her arm gently, cautiously. "Please tell me what happened."

Ashley looked at the sky and then lowered her gaze to his face. "I had to send a telegram to my mother. She needs to come see my grandfather before he dies. It was very hard to send the message."

"Oh, because she'll be so upset about his situation?"

Ashley laughed bitterly. The sound chilled E. J. to the bone. "Hardly that. She'll be upset because we've dared to disturb her peace. After all, she warned us both."

"What do you mean?"

"She wanted nothing to do with either of us," Ashley explained. "My grandfather took away her financial support when he became a Christian and decided to follow the Bible's teachings. She swore she'd never speak to him again."

"Because he turned to God?" E. J. vaguely remembered something from the past. Hadn't the old man been doing something illegal—but financially beneficial? He rubbed his jaw, trying to remember.

"It's a long story," Ashley said with a sigh in her voice.

"I have the time if you do." He looked at her face and saw the need there. Her dark eyes, still glistening with tears, seemed to consider him momentarily as if to ascertain his worthiness.

"My grandfather was not concerned with business ethics when he was younger. He made a lot of money and in turn he gave generously to his children—my mother and her sister. When his dealings caught up with him—or rather, when God caught up with him—Grandpa knew he had to give up his life of crime and turn over a new leaf."

E. J. nodded and stared ahead at the sandy, rock-laden landscape. How desolate and lonely it all seemed. The barren wasteland made him ache to create something beautiful and lovely to put in its empty space. But wasn't that why he'd come in the first place? He was here to help with the Harvey resort—beauty amid the ancient, inhospitable land. And somewhere in the midst of that aspiration, God had brought him face-to-face with the past.

Ashley halted rather abruptly, causing E. J. to walk past her. He stopped and turned to look back at her. She stared off to the south, past the railroad tracks. He wondered what she saw there.

"I know it sounds completely ridiculous," she began, "but I'm terrified of my mother coming here." She glanced at E. J. "I'm afraid of her and what she'll do. I'm afraid of myself and who I'll become when she's around."

"What can she possibly do to hurt you?"

Ashley shook her head back and forth slowly. "I'm not sure, but if there's a way, she'll find it. She doesn't know I'm here—well, once she gets the telegram she'll know. But for a very long time, she's had no idea of my whereabouts. She doesn't even know about Natalie."

"But why?"

A train whistle blew, signaling a Santa Fe freighter coming in from the east. Ashley watched the train momentarily, then turned back to E. J. and began walking again.

"My mother is a difficult woman. She wasn't pleased with my choice of husbands. When he was killed in the Great War, I figured she would end her tirade about my choice and leave well enough alone. After all, I was in mourning."

"But she didn't?"

"No. She made matters worse, demanding I annul the marriage, telling me it wouldn't matter to my husband because he was dead."

"Annul the marriage? But if your husband was supposed to be dead . . ."

Ashley seemed to understand his confusion. "She wanted the slate cleaned, as though the marriage had never happened. That's how they do it in high society when they want to pretend things are different than they really are. She wanted me to marry a very wealthy man who could benefit the family name." Ashley's voice lowered to an almost inaudible tone. "But she didn't understand the situation at all."

"You mean Natalie?" E. J. asked, hoping to learn once and for all if the child was his.

"No," Ashley said, leaving him disappointed. "She didn't understand that I could never love another man. I loved my husband and would continue to love him until I was in the grave beside him."

Then, as if realizing she'd become much too personal in her revelations, Ashley stopped again. "Look, I'm sorry. This is too much of a burden to put on anyone, much less a stranger." She gave him a tight smile. "Natalie said you were easy to talk to."

She began to walk back in the direction they'd come, and E. J. had no choice but to accompany her. "So you haven't seen your mother in all this time?" he questioned, hoping she'd not worry about the intimacy of the topic.

"No. I've not seen her or had any form of communication. She wanted it that way and I wanted it that way even more. I figured someone that meanspirited and hateful did not deserve to be a part of my life or that of my child. Now Grandpa wants to see her before he dies, and I find my life turned upside down."

"Will she come here now?"

"I have no idea. I know Grandpa is praying she will, and he seems to have God's ear."

E. J. laughed. "He does, does he?"

Ashley smiled, as if realizing how silly she sounded. "Well, let me put it this way. When Grandpa gets to praying about a matter, things start happening."

"And your grandpa is praying for this reconciliation?" E. J. questioned.

Ashley nodded. "That among other things."

"That's not enough, eh? What else could possibly be as important to him now that he's ready to meet his maker?"

Ashley tucked her handkerchief away. "Grandpa and Natalie want me to remarry." She laughed nervously and shrugged it off. "It's silly, I know. But when those two put their minds to something, well, it's best to get off the track and let the train come on through."

E. J. felt a tightening in his chest. He followed after her, struggling to figure out how to reply. What could he say? He could hardly tell her that she couldn't remarry because she was already married—to him.

"What do *you* want?" he asked instead. They'd come back to where the new Harvey resort was being built. He stopped and asked again. "What do you want?"

Ashley looked so forlorn and sad. "What I want doesn't matter. I have to think of what Natalie needs."

"And what does she need?" E. J. asked, struggling to know how to deal with the emotions she was evoking.

"She needs a daddy. Someone who can teach her things and keep me from being too lonely," Ashley whispered. Then, drawing a deep breath, she smiled. "At least, that's what Natalie says."

"But what do you say?"

Ashley considered his question for a moment, then came back at him with a question of her own. "Mr. Carson, are you a God-fearing man—are you a Christian?"

He cleared his throat and looked to the ground. "I . . . well . . . yes."

"Why do you hesitate with your answer?"

E. J. looked up and met her curious but beautiful expression. Her dark eyes seemed to study him intently. "I suppose that's a long story on my part. I came to God during the Great War."

"Why?"

He chuckled. "Because I was terrified. Death was all around me and I was all alone."

"Is fear an acceptable reason to take Christ as your eternal savior?"

"Well, I see it as being one way to come to God," E. J. replied. He shoved his hands in his trouser pockets and immediately fisted his hands against his legs.

"Grandpa wants me to come to God," Ashley offered in a surprisingly strong manner. She straightened her shoulders as if she'd suddenly regained her second wind. "But I can't."

"Why?"

"I just don't know that fear is a good enough reason to accept something so serious. You see, it's not that I don't believe in God. I believe in Him quite well, thank you. But I have to question whether He cares about me and what difference it would make whether or not I come to Him. He'll do to me and with me what He wants anyway. It won't much matter that I plead with Him for help."

"I've felt that way too," E. J. admitted. "In the war, things seemed so . . ." He shook away the brutal images. "God seemed so distant, yet at the same time He seemed so close. I wanted to believe that He cared about me there in the trenches. I wanted to believe that He would be with me as we advanced on the enemy."

"And what happened?"

E. J. shuddered. "He allowed the enemy to blow me up."

Ashley's expression went blank and her face paled. "You were . . . were wounded?"

E. J. realized he'd said too much. "Yes, but my point is, I felt betrayed by God. I'd come to Him, pleaded with Him for protection, and then I was suddenly fighting to live. I watched friends die and saw others who wished they had."

"It's just one more thing that makes me question whether God really cares," Ashley interjected, staring past his shoulder. "And why should I put my trust in Him if He doesn't really care? If He's just out there—somewhere—watching and allowing life to go on as it does, why does it even matter to Him if I repent of my sins?"

"Or maybe it matters, but your sins are too great," E. J. murmured.

Ashley frowned. "I'm sorry. I should never have gotten this maudlin. I'm afraid my mother brings out the worst in me. Thank you for the walk."

She turned on her heel, her blue print dress swirling around her knees as she walked away. E. J. watched her for several minutes, completely captivated by the rhythmic way she sauntered up the walkway. *I've driven her away with my talk of war and sins,* he thought. But truth was always painful when it wasn't what you wanted to hear. And his truth—the very essence of who he now was—could never match what she needed him to be. It made his choices and decisions even more difficult.

She doesn't need a wounded war vet who still feels the breath of the enemy on his neck. She doesn't need a man who is afraid of the future and what it might hold.

E. J. looked to the heavens, wishing some great revelation might be revealed. Instead, he felt worse than when he'd set out to walk with his wife. He knew her a little better—that much had been accomplished. But in knowing her better, he also knew without a doubt that he wasn't what she needed. She needed Ethan Reynolds, and that man had died—at least in spirit—on a pockmarked battlefield in France.

*F*aith Mission Church gave an annual autumn party, and with this excuse the regular members of the congregation and some not-so-regular members had reason to gather that mild October day on the banks of Clear Creek. There was to be plenty of food and games, as well as preaching and baptizing.

Natalie had made certain E. J. received an invitation to the gathering. She'd even gone a step further and showed up at the hotel on Sunday morning to remind him.

"Mr. Carson, are you coming this afternoon?" she'd questioned, nearly breathless from running.

E. J. couldn't turn her down. He felt so captivated by her love of life and the expectancy of her expression that he could only nod.

"Now, don't forget," she told him as she moved toward the door. "We're eating lunch there and then we'll have games. Come to the church by noon and you can drive out with the rest of us. Oh, and don't worry about your tableware. Mama will pack you a plate and silverware."

E. J. had nodded and waved, and two hours later, with some goodies he'd purchased at the Harvey restaurant, he joined the festivities.

Clear Creek ran to the east of town, but the picnic location where they gathered was nearly five miles to the southeast of Winslow proper. E. J. thought it a marvelous respite. After driving out across the sandy red desert dotted only with scrub and cactus, the barren land gave way to natural rock platforms and sandstone outcroppings. Between this framework ran the most beautiful, inviting blue water—Clear Creek. It was easy to see why the location was such a popular gathering place. It was truly an oasis.

E. J. liked it best because it looked nothing like the wartorn lands of his nightmares. Here, in spite of the appearance of being desolate and barren, life sprang up seemingly out of nothing. There were all manner of insects, reptiles, and birds. From time to time a variety of mice, jackrabbits, and even coyotes and mule deer could be seen skittering across the sandy desert floor. In France the only things that had marched on the land were men and death—hand in hand like bizarre players of the same game. The thought chilled E. J. to the bone.

"Why, Mr. Carson, I'm so glad you could come," a matronly woman looking to have enjoyed quite a few picnics commented. "Do you know my husband, Mr. Willis?"

"He's on the town council, is he not?"

"But of course he is," the older woman stated as if to suggest otherwise was simply ludicrous. "I'll have to make sure you're better acquainted. My husband is quite knowledgeable about Winslow and has played a prominent role in seeing that the Harvey Company chose our town for their new resort. He promises it will bring in millions."

"Let's hope he's right," E. J. replied.

"But of course he is," the woman said, looking down her nose at him. "My husband is never wrong. Why, he predicted the strength of our economy years ago. Put Hoover in the office of president, he said, and we'll see nothing but prosperity. Of course, we could hardly elect that Catholic Mr. Smith or the Indian Charles Curtis. What tragedy would have befallen this great nation then," she declared, as though she were making a speech for some great occasion.

Ethan longed to get away from the woman, but instead he found himself hopelessly entangled as she continued. "So, Mr. Carson, tell me what the railroad is doing to entice tourists to the new resort. I do hope we'll get good, solid citizens to come. I've nothing against the flamboyant celebrities of the movie industry, but Mr. Willis says there's really no future there. And, of course, we don't want to see nothing but consumptive patients. My word, but we've had our share of people coming to this great state to take the cure for their disease-filled lungs."

Ethan struggled to figure out what he could say in regard to her question, then just as quickly realized that she'd probably never give him a chance to reply.

"Mr. Carson!" He looked behind him to find Natalie skipping up the trail with her mother at her side. How wonderful Ashley looked. Her soft pink suit seemed just casual enough for a picnic, while at the same time it gave her a clearly feminine, almost elegant appearance. With her face raised to the sun, he thought her radiant.

"Hello, Natalie," he called out, waving at the child. He cast a quick glance back to Mrs. Willis, who by this time was frowning. "Natalie invited me here today," he said as if the woman had questioned him.

"Poor child. Her mother's a heathen, don't you know." The woman leaned toward E. J. to whisper this, but her voice somehow carried on the breeze. E. J. tried to keep the shock from his face but wasn't very good with the cover-up. "Oh, it's true," Mrs. Willis said, leaning in closer. "Why, the woman has only been attending church services the past few Sundays. I think her grandfather's impending death has given her reason to consider the status of her soul."

"Mr. Carson, do you remember my mama?" Natalie asked as they approached.

E. J. didn't know whether to acknowledge Mrs. Willis's comments or the child's. Finally he dismissed himself from the older woman's company, much to her dismay. "If you'll excuse me."

Mrs. Willis *harrumphed* and marched away, as if he'd verbalized that he didn't mind the company of heathens. He couldn't help but smile at the thought of what she'd tell her friends.

"I remember your mama," E. J. said as Natalie grinned up at him. "My, but don't you ladies look nice."

"Mama's wearing a new hat, but the dress is just an old one."

"Natalie!" Ashley's embarrassment was apparent.

E. J. laughed to lighten the moment. "I think both pieces of apparel are quite fetching. But I must say, Miss Natalie, your dress is even nicer." The child, clutching a small basket to her chest, whirled to make the skirt of the lemon-colored dress swirl out around her tiny legs. How very small and delicate she looked.

"Mama made it. She's a good sewer. That's something a wife should know how to do, don't you think?"

E. J. looked past the girl to find Ashley gazing at the skies. "I'll bet she's a great cook too," he said, noting the picnic basket in Ashley's hands.

"She is a good cook. She makes the best fried chicken and—"

"Natalie, that's enough. Why don't you take our basket and set out the things we've brought to share?"

"I could help," E. J. offered. "I just delivered some Harvey pies to the dessert table. I managed to sneak a peak at the main table and it looks quite promising."

Natalie put her own basket down in order to take up her mother's. "I'll leave the dishes here," she announced, and Ashley nodded.

Natalie took hold of the handles on her mother's basket, but E. J. could see she struggled with the weight of it. "Why don't I carry it and you can lead the way? It's just over there," he said, pointing.

Natalie nodded and let him carry the basket. "I can show you what Mama made and you can decide for yourself if she's a good enough cook."

Ashley opened her mouth as if to chide her daughter again, then closed it rather quickly. She offered E. J. an apologetic smile and turned to gaze at the crystal clear water.

E. J. would much rather have stayed with his wife, but instead he followed after Natalie, weaving in and out of congregation members, trying to tip his hat as he returned their greetings.

"I'm so glad you came today," Natalie said as they reached the table. She took hold of the basket and pulled it away from E. J. Settling it on the ground, Natalie quickly opened the latch and pulled out a platter. Removing the dish towel that covered it, she held it up and smiled. "Fried chicken."

"It certainly looks delicious."

"It is," she said confidently.

E. J. helped her find a place on the sagging makeshift table. Natalie took out several smaller containers, one of creamed peas and potatoes and one of a delicious-looking squash. He helped her arrange the food, then followed her back through the crowd to where they'd left Ashley.

"Mama wasn't going to come, but I told her we had to. I told her I'd invited you and that there wouldn't be any food for you if she didn't make some and come too."

E. J. knew from the sight of the luncheon tables that this would never have been the case, but he only smiled and nodded. The child was clearly enjoying her role as matchmaker. The thought amused E. J., and yet at the same time it seemed quite strange to be thrust into a situation where he was being set up to court his own wife.

By the time they rejoined Ashley, she had settled herself on a blanket on a flat, rocky outcropping beside the water. When she saw they'd returned, she issued a warning to her daughter. "Be careful for snakes and such." She looked at E. J. and added, "There are quite a few poisonous critters that live in the area. Rattlesnakes, scorpions, and so many other things. If you haven't been advised of this, it's a good time to take note. They like to hide in the rocks, and if you disturb them, they'll retaliate."

He looked around them, feeling a strange sense of protectiveness. "I'll keep that in mind."

"Why, Mrs. Reynolds. You're a sight for sore eyes." A stocky man strode up to share their company. He settled alongside E. J. and held out his hand. "Todd Morgan."

"Mr. Morgan," E. J. acknowledged, shaking his hand. "I'm E. J. Carson."

"You're new in town, aren't you?" He let his gaze travel up and down E. J. as if assessing him as an opponent.

"I'm here with the Harvey hotel."

"Mr. Carson is an architect," Natalie offered.

"That's nice, kiddo," Morgan answered, quickly ignoring the child. "It's good to see you, Ashley. I haven't seen you at the Harvey House lately."

E. J. bristled at the usage of his wife's first name. Who was this man to treat her so casually?

Natalie reached out and took hold of E. J.'s hand. "I want to show you my favorite place. It's over by the bridge."

E. J. looked at Natalie and then Ashley. "If it's all right with your mama."

"Can I show him around, Mama?" Natalie begged.

"Of course. Just be careful and mind your step."

E. J. hated to leave her there with the personable Mr. Morgan, but he felt he could hardly act the part of jealous husband—even if that was what he was.

Natalie pulled him along to the bridge, where she threw stones into the water below. "Isn't this the best place in the whole world?"

E. J. looked down the long meandering stream and had to admit it was truly an oasis. "It is wonderful. I can see why you like it so much."

"I'd like to build my mama a house right over there." Natalie pointed to a rise of red rock. "That way she could always see the creek and be happy."

"Why do you suppose that would make her happy?" E. J. asked, needing to know about the woman he'd married and who she'd become in the last decade.

To his surprise, Natalie shrugged. "I don't know. I just think she'd like it. My daddy was going to build her a really wonderful house, but then he died."

E. J. felt a quickening in his soul. He easily remembered the two-story house he'd designed, patterned after the early classical revival style so popular in the early eighteen hundreds. Ashley had told him of her passion for the style, pointing out several houses in the Baltimore area.

E. J. had taken the things she liked most, the portico with its lower and upper levels supported by slender Doric pillars. The second-story porch would be accessible to them through artistically carved French doors in the master bedroom. E. J. could see it all as if it were yesterday. He had sketched the house while Ashley detailed it, and before he'd left for the war, he'd given her the drawing, reminding her that when he returned they would build their home together.

Only he hadn't come home. At least not when she'd expected him to.

". . . but she really wants me to go to college first."

E. J. shook away his thoughts. "What did you say?" He looked at Natalie, who was still staring off toward the red rocks.

"I want to build my mama her house and make it just like my daddy planned it out, but she wants me to go to college first."

"Well, that's not a bad idea," E. J. replied. "After all, you'll need training to be an architect."

"I know, but I don't want to leave Mama alone. She's been so brave and strong all these years, but she's had Grandpa to help her. She's going to need someone to be with her if I go away."

E. J. glanced back to where Ashley sat. Todd Morgan had squatted down to talk with her and still remained. It looked to E. J. as though he were trying to convince Ashley of something as he waved his hands throughout the conversation.

"I think maybe we'd better head back. It won't be long till they say the blessing, and I don't want to miss a chance at your mother's fried chicken."

They walked back in companionable silence. Natalie seemed content in her efforts to walk up and down various rocks, balancing like a ballerina on tiptoes as she jumped from one boulder to another.

"We're back, Mama," Natalie announced, jumping down to land between Todd and her mother.

"Natalie, be careful," Ashley warned.

Todd rose to stand beside E. J., but his gaze was still fixed on Ashley. "So will you come with me?"

Ashley looked most uncomfortable but finally replied, "It's difficult to leave my grandfather. Besides, with his impending death, I'm really in no mood for excursions. I'm sure you understand."

Morgan looked none too happy with her reply but tipped his hat. "Well, I suppose if that's the way it is."

E. J. watched the man walk away, feeling delighted that Ashley had rejected his advances. The mood surprised him. Todd Morgan had no way of knowing he'd just propositioned E. J.'s wife. Ashley, herself, had no idea she was anything but the widow she believed herself to be. What a tangled web they'd all woven for themselves.

Plopping down on the rock across from her, E. J. smiled. "I hope we weren't gone too long."

"No, you came back just in time."

Ashley removed her brimmed straw hat and let the breeze blow through her dark hair for a few minutes. With her face raised to the clear blue skies and the wind gently rippling her hair, E. J. felt himself falling in love with her all over again. For just a moment he was twenty-one and innocent of war.

"Let's gather for the blessing, folks," Pastor McGuire declared.

E. J. jumped up and extended his hand to Ashley. She paused momentarily to replace her hat. Fixing it with her long hatpin, she smiled up at E. J. and allowed his help.

"Thank you," she murmured, not seeming to mind that E. J. still held her hand.

Natalie took hold of her mother's other hand and pulled. "Come on, Mr. Carson wants to be sure to get some of your fried chicken."

Ashley beamed him a smile. "If you miss out here, I'll fry up another batch just for you."

E. J. found himself almost praying the china platter would be empty when they reached the table. He wouldn't mind at all lingering over a private dinner of fried chicken with his beloved wife.

Pastor McGuire offered the blessing, and soon the crowds were divided into two lines, passing down both sides of the table. By the time E. J. reached Ashley's platter, all but the tiniest chicken wing had been claimed.

"Look, Mama, it's all gone," Natalie declared. "Now you'll have to fry up some more chicken for Mr. Carson."

E. J. met Ashley's face. "You don't have to, but . . ." He grinned and let his expression speak for him.

"But if I don't, I'll never hear the end of it from my daughter," Ashley replied. "I'll be happy to fix some for you—in fact, Natalie could bring it over when she visits you at work."

"No, Mama, let him come to dinner tomorrow night," Natalie

demanded, pushing matters right along. "Please?"

Ashley looked from her daughter to E. J. "That's fine with me."

E. J. nodded, finding it impossible to speak. Never in his life had he ever wanted anything more.

Later that afternoon, as the sun began to set, Pastor McGuire concluded the party with a final sermon. E. J. felt sated and happy, and for the first time since the war, he found himself looking forward to the next day.

"We've had a good day here," Pastor McGuire announced. "Now the chill of evening is upon us and we need to make our way back while there's still light to see. But before we go, I just want to say something that's been burdening my heart. I feel as if the Lord is telling me that someone here needs to hear this message."

E. J. shifted and stretched his legs out in front of him. Seated there on the banks of Clear Creek, he waited for the pastor to continue.

"We often do things in life because they are thrust upon us to do," the pastor continued. "We find ourselves feeling compromised in our beliefs and dreams. Sometimes this comes when we least expect it. Maybe through the death of someone we love. Maybe through an event that changes our lives forever.

"In times like these, God seems so distant and far removed. We convince ourselves that He's gone away because of something we've done or said. I just want you to know today that God doesn't leave. He's not the leaving kind. He's steadfast. The Word tells us that God is faithful, and because He's faithful, we can rest assured that He will never leave us."

E. J. found himself longing to hear more. The words burned in his heart like a tiny spark of hope.

"Now, that isn't to say that we won't walk away or choose to ignore God. It isn't saying that circumstances won't come up to deceive us and make us believe God has turned from us, that He doesn't care. But God's love and forgiveness are real and permanent. If you seek Him, He will be found.

"You might say, 'But, Pastor McGuire, I've done things in the past. Things that weren't pleasing to God.' And I'm here to tell you that I've been guilty of the same. Many of you have heard about my younger, wilder days. I'm not proud of the man I was back then, but with God's help, I've become a new creation."

E. J.'s discomfort grew. The pastor's words dug in deep. Still, E. J. couldn't imagine that Pastor McGuire had all that much to be ashamed of in his past. Maybe he'd been given to drink or to gambling. Maybe he was a womanizer or a con man; either way, it couldn't be as bad as what E. J. had done. He could see the faces of the men he'd killed. The looks of shock, the stunned disbelief that they were dying.

Reliving the nightmare, E. J. tried to draw a good breath but found it almost impossible. The shadows of evening began to play tricks with his mind as he looked out across the desert.

"God knows your heart and He understands your pain. He's offering you forgiveness today. But you have to be willing to take it. Don't let the hurts of the past keep you from coming into right accord with the Almighty. If you've put up a fence between you and God, now's the time to take it down. Now's the time to reach out and accept forgiveness."

Someone began singing in a clear baritone voice, and soon the entire gathering joined in—except for E. J. and Ashley. E. J. looked at Ashley, wondering if the words had disturbed her as much as they had him. Her face was a mask of indifference, however. There was no reading the emotion there, because there frankly didn't appear to be even the tiniest thread of feeling.

It dawned on E. J. then that this was how she had survived the years since his disappearance. She had carefully put aside her feelings, hidden them away so that she wouldn't have to deal with even the smallest, most insignificant emotion. She was like a beautiful china doll. Cold and hard and forever fixed in time with a painted smile and empty heart.

When he'd seen her on the street crying, that had been the exception. Her feelings had caught up with her, overwhelming her and demanding attention. She probably would never have allowed anyone to see her like that if she'd had a choice.

Still, he reminded himself, there was Natalie. Natalie meant the world to her mother and he could easily see this. But even there, it seemed that Ashley held back a part of herself. Almost suggesting that if Ashley loved Natalie too completely, she might also lose her—as she had lost her beloved Ethan.

Even thinking of his name caused E. J. pain. A part of him wanted to be Ethan Reynolds again. Ethan—the man Ashley loved. Ethan—father to Natalie. Ethan—the promising young architect who would change the world with the beauty he'd design.

But with that name and that man, he also had to remember he was Ethan—war hero. Ethan—the killer of young men who had thrown down their weapons and begged for life.

How in the world could there be forgiveness for that?

CHAPTER TEN

Ashley rose that Monday morning with a great deal on her mind. After seeing Natalie off to school, she bathed Grandpa and tried to encourage him to eat a bit of hot cereal.

"You have to eat," she said, doing up the buttons of his sweater. During the day he liked to wear his regular clothes, even though he seldom left his bed.

"I have no appetite, child," he said softly.

"I know, but you're wasting away. You need the nourishment." She picked up the cereal from the tray and extended it toward him. "It's really quite good, and I've put a dollop of brown sugar on it, just the way you like."

"I'm sure it's delicious, but there's no stopping this kind of wasting," Grandpa replied. "What I would like, however, is another pillow. Have you one?"

"Of course. I'll . . ." A knock at the front door interrupted her, and Ashley put aside the bowl of cereal. "I can't imagine who that might be." She grabbed a pillow from the closet and worked to position Grandpa comfortably before going to see who had come to call.

To her surprise she found a young Mexican man on her doorstep. "I have a telegram for Mr. Whitman."

Ashley gasped and nodded. "I'll take it." She grasped the envelope, then started to close the door. "Oh, wait." She went to the living room and found her pocketbook. Taking a dime from it, she rushed back to the door. "Here. Take this."

The young man's eyes lit up at the extravagant tip. *"Muchas gracias."* He tipped his cap to her and pocketed the coin as if it were a great treasure.

Ashley quickly forgot the man and closed the door to read the telegram. It was from her aunt Lavelle.

FATHER STOP COMING IMMEDIATELY STOP CAN'T WAIT
TO SEE YOU STOP LOVE LAVELLE

The notification was so very brief, but even so, Ashley felt encouraged by the words. Her aunt Lavelle was coming and she loved her father. Surely those were good signs.

Ashley returned to the bedroom. "Grandpa, it's a telegram from Aunt Lavelle."

The old man perked up a bit at this. "What does she say?"

"She's coming," Ashley replied. "She's coming right away and she says she can't wait to see you." She handed him the telegram, not entirely sure he could read it. "She signed it, 'Love Lavelle.' "

He clutched the paper to his chest. A tear escaped his eye, trickling down his cheek and onto the pillow. "Thank you, Lord," he whispered. "Thank you."

"I thought it very good news," Ashley said, trying hard not to grow weepy herself.

"Yes, indeed. She was no doubt stunned to hear from us after all this time," Russell said, looking again to the telegram.

Ashley felt a wave of guilt wash over her. "I'm sorry that I made you promise not to let them know where we were. It was wrong of me, but I was so hurt."

"I know that," he answered. "It's behind us now."

For several moments neither one spoke; then he turned to Ashley. "And what of your mother? Has she sent word?"

Ashley stiffened. "No. There's been no word from her." She was afraid he might see her relief in that fact, so she turned and busied herself by straightening his bedcovers. He would never understand how much she dreaded seeing her mother.

"She'll come. I know she will."

"Please don't get your hopes up, Grandpa. She had little use for either one of us."

"But neither did Lavelle," Grandpa replied. "And now she's coming."

Ashley nodded and picked up the tray with the bowl of cereal. "I know, Grandpa. I know. We have to have hope that Mother will understand the importance and put aside her differences from the past." *But can I put aside our differences? Can I welcome her here after all this time?*

Mrs. Breck came around noon to sit with Grandpa while Ashley went to shop for that evening's supper. She needed to buy another chicken to fry, and as a last thought, she decided to also make a cobbler.

In spite of her nerves about having E. J. Carson to dinner, Ashley actually found herself looking forward to the evening. E. J. had been very kind to her that day when she'd cried. He didn't make her feel as though she were silly for her tears. She remembered a time long ago when one of the neighbor men had caught her crying as she tended her garden. He had chided her to buck up and be strong, telling her that only silly females were given to fits of tears. Ashley had never forgotten the rebuke. She had worked hard to keep her emotions under control, and that day with E. J. Carson had been the first public display of emotion since being taken to task. E. J. had been compassionate and kind, listening as well as speaking. He didn't seem to mind her crying, and when they'd parted company he hadn't left her with quaint platitudes. That meant a lot to Ashley.

E. J. Carson would be a good change of pace. Grandpa had been a poor conversationalist of late. He wanted only to talk of his will and death. Ashley couldn't abide either one, so she always sought to change the topic. Then Grandpa would find a way back to it, or he'd bring up her mother and Aunt Lavelle, and that was even worse than talking of his impending departure. Ashley had come to realize at the picnic how much she longed for adult conversation. She'd not seen how she'd filled her loneliness by talking to customers at the Harvey House. Those conversations had been light-hearted and, in many ways, of no consequence. Now, however, she could see that they filled a need in her life.

The customers there kept her apprised of the world outside of Winslow. Passing salesmen would tell her of scandals in big cities far away, while well-dressed women accompanying equally stylish men would offer her some insight into the world of fashion. Sometimes the people didn't really talk to her as much as to each other, but Ashley took part as a listening bystander. How strange that it should have meant so much to her, and she'd never even known until now.

Of course, it wasn't Grandpa's fault, but Ashley could already tell his death was going to leave her more lonely than she'd ever imagined. The old man had been her mainstay—her focus along with Natalie. Those two people meant more to her than anyone else in the world, and now she was losing one of them.

"But I'll lose Natalie one day too," she murmured as she walked to the store. She felt a band tighten around her heart. The world seemed to be closing in on her. Maybe it was better not to love so deeply, she thought. Maybe it was better to cut those feelings off before you lost them to other things. Grandpa would die and his love would be taken from her, but maybe it would hurt less if Ashley buffeted her heart against the loss. Maybe she should reinforce her heart with stronger stuff than the love she felt for Grandpa. But what was stronger than love?

Moving up and down the aisles of the small grocery store, Ashley was amazed at the number of people who stopped to ask her about Grandpa.

"How is Russell?" one old woman questioned.

"He's very weak," Ashley told her, then smiled and added, "but very stubborn. He still insists on playing his weekly checkers with Pastor McGuire."

The old woman smiled. "Your grandfather is a good man. It'll be hard to see him go, but then again, I don't suppose I shall be here all that much longer myself."

Ashley didn't know what to say. The woman's casual reference to her own passing made Ashley uneasy.

She picked up the things she needed, sharing snippets of conversation with each one who engaged her. Always they asked about Grandpa. They knew him well and loved him. It gradually began to dawn on Ashley, however, that she had never really bothered to formulate any relationships with these folks. She knew the people around her from having seen them on nearly a daily basis. Some had come to the Harvey House where she worked, while others were the storeowners she did business with. Still, beyond knowing their names and occupations, Ashley really didn't know these people at all.

Somehow she had lived her life disjointed from her surroundings. Somehow she had isolated herself in the midst of her community. Like most small towns, there were some people who were only too happy to give detailed accounts of everyone and everything, but Ashley had always turned these people away. Now she almost wished she hadn't.

In the past, Grandpa always told me about people, she mused. *I didn't have to get to know them for myself.* She knew about Mr. and Mrs. Willis's business problems and their son who was training to be a doctor. She had heard accounts of Mrs. Moore's arthritis and Mrs. Morgan's bouts with various blood disorders. Why, Ashley even knew about building projects and plans for the town's expansion because of the things Grandpa had shared.

When he's gone, she thought, *I'll have to make the effort to get to know people better.*

It wouldn't just be an issue of loneliness that she could fill through her job at the Harvey House. And it wouldn't be just a matter of knowing what was going on in the community and in the lives of those whom she'd known for so many years.

I won't be able to rely on Grandpa to help me fit in—to have a place in this town. I won't be able to live vicariously through him anymore. This thought, coupled with her earlier musings of how she could keep from being lonely, made Ashley feel tired and discouraged. *How could I have lived to this age and not even realize that I'm not really living at all, but merely existing?*

Struggling with the grocery sack as she made her way home, Ashley pushed the thoughts aside and tried to regain a more positive spirit. She thought of her aunt's impending arrival. She hoped the things she'd picked up for meals would be pleasing to the woman. Ashley had become a pretty fair cook over the years, but that didn't mean it would satisfy her aunt's particular tastes. Whatever those tastes might be.

Ashley had only seen her aunt once, at least once that she could remember. It had been the summer Ashley was thirteen. Lavelle and her husband had come from California on the train. The trip had been grueling and had stripped them of all energy. Ashley remembered her aunt and uncle being tired the entire time of their visit. She also remembered Lavelle's beautiful clothes. Dresses with beautiful colors and evening gowns that shimmered in the light.

In spite of their exhaustion, the Guzmans had accompanied Ashley's parents out every evening, and Ashley remembered how magical it all seemed. Her mother's own fashion sense was keen, but where her choices were more matronly, Lavelle appeared youthful and exciting. Ashley remembered pining over one particularly lovely green gown.

Best of all, Lavelle surprised everyone by announcing that she'd brought Ashley a present. It turned out to be the most remarkable leather suitcase. The hand etchings had been painted to create a riot of colorful flowers along the upper edge of the case. Her aunt said Mexicans had created the design and that they were very good with leather crafts. Ashley saw this for herself in Winslow. Across the tracks in one of the clusters of Mexican homes, Ashley had witnessed many varying accomplishments among the workers there. The Harvey Company had even allowed the people to come and sell some of their wares to the train passengers. Everything from purses, to saddlebags, to saddles and belts had been offered to the public.

Ashley had to smile, however, as her memories took her back to Aunt Lavelle and the suitcase. The case had been most beloved to Ashley. In fact, she still had it tucked under her bed upstairs at home. It was full of Natalie's baby things now—things Ashley hoped to one day give to Natalie for her own children.

Maybe her aunt would still be kind and sweet. Maybe her attitude and reactions toward Grandpa all those years ago had been a one-time occurrence, brought on by the worry of losing the things that were important to her. Of course, there was no way to know until she actually arrived, and by then it would be too late.

Back at home, Ashley began preparing the dinner. She wanted things to be special for Mr. Carson, but at the same time she found herself growing nervous about having a stranger to dinner.

We really know nothing about him, she thought. Glancing at the clock on the wall, she realized time was getting away from her. Where was Natalie? Why hadn't she come directly home from school?

Ashley wasn't really worried, but she couldn't help wondering, since Natalie had been nearly beside herself at the thought of Mr. Carson coming to dinner. Ashley was going to have to find time to talk to the child before Mr. Carson arrived.

As if drawn there by her mother's thoughts, Natalie came bounding in through the back screen door.

"Mama, I got an A on my report about the Great War. I told them all about Daddy and all the things he did. Nobody else had any stories like it. Teacher said my stories were special because Daddy was a hero."

Ashley smiled at her daughter. Pigtails danced down her back as Natalie flitted about the room in unconfined energy. "I stopped and talked to Mr. Carson. I told him about my A too. He was really happy for me."

"I'm sure he was. You should have come straight home, however. Look at the time. We still have to set the table and get things ready for supper. He'll be here in half an hour."

"I know, that's why I hurried home," Natalie said, her eyes lighting up. She washed her hands and dried them on a dish towel before reaching up into the cupboard for the plates. "Can we use Grandma Whitman's good china?" she asked, even as she reached for the delicate white plates trimmed with posies and gold. "It's really important that things look nice."

"Natalie, about Mr. Carson. You really shouldn't try to . . . well . . . what I mean to say is, you shouldn't play matchmaker. Mr. Carson and

I aren't interested in each other that way."

"But you might be," Natalie said, looking rather perplexed.

Ashley felt sorry for her child. "Natalie, it's just not right to try to meddle in people's lives. I'm just suggesting you leave well enough alone. The man probably has no interest in being in the middle of your schemes."

"Well, I don't think he minds at all," Natalie said, balancing the plates as she headed to the table. "He told me he thinks you're beautiful."

The words made Ashley's cheeks grow hot. It also left her speechless. What could she say to make her daughter understand?

Giving up for the moment, Ashley focused her attention on the chicken, sprinkling in just a touch of paprika and cayenne pepper to the flour and salt mixture. She liked the flavor the spices added and hoped Mr. Carson would like them as well. She'd learned the trick from Mrs. Breck, who told her that often the blandest foods could become a feast with a little seasoning.

"Mama, do you think Mr. Carson would like to sit in Grandpa's chair?"

Ashley gave it little thought. "I'm sure that would be a good place for him to sit. Grandpa's chair is bigger and very sturdy." She plopped a plump chicken breast into the heated lard and watched it sizzle and pop. Putting the rest of the chicken into the cast-iron skillet, Ashley glanced again at the clock. It was time to take out the cobbler.

Reaching for the potholders, Ashley found her hands trembling. Why was she so nervous? This was just a friendly gesture—nothing more. It wasn't like Todd Morgan, who had asked her out to the picture show. His intention clearly ran along the lines of serious commitment. He'd told her more than once that he was looking for a wife.

The cobbler's crust was golden brown with blackberry juice oozing out from the sides. Ashley placed it in the warming box and leaned forward for a sniff. Natalie came alongside and did likewise.

"That smells really good. I bet Mr. Carson will like it."

Ashley nodded and deposited the pan on the cooking rack at the back of the stovetop, then turned to slice a few tomatoes for the table. After this, it was time to turn the chicken, and before she knew it, it was time for E. J. Carson to arrive.

Right on schedule, E. J. knocked on the door.

"I'll get it!" Natalie declared.

Ashley went to check on Grandpa while Natalie went to the door.

The old man slept soundly, the covers pulled up under his chin. Ashley backed out of the room so as not to disturb him. She headed back to the kitchen, pulling off her apron as she went.

"Mama, look what Mr. Carson brought us," Natalie declared.

Ashley looked up to find Natalie holding a bouquet of daisies. "Oh, they're very pretty," she said, patting Natalie on the head. "Why don't you give them to me and I'll find a vase." Natalie quickly complied and turned her attention back to Mr. Carson.

Ashley met E. J.'s steady gaze and smiled. "Thank you."

He nodded, but Natalie's animated chatter captured his attention.

"You get to sit in Grandpa's chair since he's too sick to join us," Natalie announced. "It's a nice chair. Good and strong for grown men. I used to like to sit in it when I was a little girl and pretend that I was all grown-up."

Ashley caught the conversation from just inside the kitchen door, smiling to herself, for she still considered Natalie a "little girl."

Ashley reentered the room with the vase of daisies in one hand and a platter of chicken in the other. "Natalie, we need to get the rest of the food on the table."

"May I help you?" E. J. questioned.

Ashley noted that his brown hair was still damp from washing up. Obviously he'd wanted to make a good impression. His eyes watched her every move from behind gold-rimmed glasses. She thought him a handsome man in spite of his beard and mustache. She'd never really cared for facial hair, but Mr. Carson wore it well.

"No, Natalie and I can finish up. You go ahead and have a seat. Would you like coffee to drink?" She positioned the daisies in the middle of the table, then stood back to wait for E. J.'s answer.

"Yes, thank you, that would be fine."

Ashley went back into the kitchen and poured coffee into two china cups. The china had belonged to her grandmother, and it was one of the only things Grandpa had held on to, refusing to let his daughters strip it away from him. He had told Ashley on more than one occasion that he would always remember his beloved wife sharing a cup of tea or coffee with him as they sat together over a candlelight dinner. The china was his link to her and to happier days.

They all sat down to the meal and Natalie prayed, asking God to bless the food and to let them enjoy each other's company. She prayed God would be merciful to Grandpa and not allow him to be in pain, and she prayed that her grandma Murphy and aunt Lavelle would come quickly to see him before he died. After concluding her prayer, she turned to E. J. and extended a bowl of black beans and squash.

E. J. took helpings from each of the dishes and marveled at the flavors as he sampled everything. "You were right, Natalie. Your mother is a good cook."

"I know. She makes wonderful food. She learned about cooking from Mrs. Breck and at the Harvey House. She said when she was first married she couldn't cook at all. She even had trouble making tea. She said they might have starved to death but for the fact that my daddy could boil water."

E. J. smiled and threw Ashley a glance that made her cheeks grow warm. It was almost as if he knew this to be true for himself.

"I'm sure there is something else we can talk about," Ashley encouraged. But to her surprise Natalie said very little. She wolfed down her food as if she were starving, then asked if she could take some of the black beans and squash to Grandpa.

"This is his favorite," she explained to E. J.

Ashley wanted to call her daughter back, but it seemed she could hardly do so without explaining to E. J. Carson that she was suddenly uncomfortable with the idea of being left alone to make conversation with him.

With Natalie gone, the room seemed smaller, and Ashley wondered how she would make it through the rest of the meal without making Mr. Carson bear the brunt of her discomfort.

"So will you return to work at the Harvey House once your grandfather is gone?" E. J. asked, surprising her.

Ashley picked at her chicken and nodded. "I like the work. The new resort promises to be even better. I suppose I'll work there at least during school days. I'd like to be home for Natalie, since Grandpa won't be there to keep an eye on her."

E. J. nodded. "She's a special girl."

Ashley nodded, knowing that she had to speak her mind or go on feeling completely out of sorts. "Look," she said, putting down her fork, "Natalie has it in her mind to play matchmaker with us. I don't know why, but she's now focused on finding herself a father."

"And that makes it difficult for you, doesn't it?"

Ashley straightened and looked E. J. in the eye. "Why would you say that?"

"Well, it's obvious that you are uncomfortable with the idea."

Ashley folded her hands together. "Mr. Carson . . ."

"Please call me E. J.," he interrupted softly. "Mr. Carson is much too formal."

But formal was how Ashley wished to keep things. Wasn't it? "E. J., my daughter doesn't understand how love works. My heart is forever taken. I loved my husband and will love no other. It would hardly be fair to put that off on another man. Although, I must admit, I have considered it. I know I'll be lonely when Grandpa is gone. I know Natalie needs a father. All of these things rush through my mind but refuse to be settled." She couldn't believe she was telling him all of this. She calmly picked up her fork and began eating again, hoping he'd put the topic behind them.

"It's all right. I'm not looking for another wife."

She looked up to see the sorrow in his expression. "Natalie said your wife died in the influenza epidemic. I'm very sorry."

"I wasn't with her when it happened. I'd been severely wounded in battle and by the time I made it back to the United States, the war was over and so many people at home and abroad were dead from the influenza. I caught it myself and lingered in a horrible state for weeks, but I guess I'm too tough to kill off. Just rest assured that, like you, I have no mind to marry again. I loved my wife completely and seek no other."

His tone sounded so sad to Ashley that she immediately thought to change the subject. "Are you ready for the blackberry cobbler?"

"Sounds good."

Ashley quickly put aside her fork and napkin and went to retrieve the cobbler. She felt a trembling inside at the turn of events this evening. Who would have ever thought she'd have the boldness to clearly state her position to E. J. Carson? Moreover, she was amazed to realize her heart in the matter of remarriage. For once she saw clearly that she could never marry another man. He would forever live in Ethan's shadow. Even Natalie would constantly compare the two, although she might not understand that now. It would be hard to explain to the child, and Ashley felt guilty for putting her own needs ahead of Natalie's. *She'll understand one day*, Ashley thought. *When she falls in love and marries, she'll understand why I can't have another man taking hold of my heart.*

E. J. waited in silence while Ashley moved about in the kitchen. He thought of her openness with him and how her love for her husband warmed him through and through. *She still loves me*, he thought. But then he chided himself. *No, she loves Ethan Reynolds, the happy-go-lucky architectural student who was set to change the world with his passion for build-ing great beauty. She loves Ethan Reynolds, the man who took her away from her unfeeling mother and preoccupied father. I'm not that man anymore, and I can't pretend that I can go back to being him.*

"Here we are," Ashley said, putting a bowl heaping with blackberry cobbler and cream in front of E. J. "I hope you like it."

"I'm sure I will. It smells wonderful."

Ashley took a smaller portion with her and sat opposite E. J. once again. "I do appreciate the kindness you've extended Natalie. She's quite enthusiastic about the new Harvey resort."

"Yes, I can see that. She studies it with an architect's eye." E. J. tasted the dessert and knew he'd never had anything so wonderful. Natalie's comments about Ashley's inability to cook in her early days of marriage were true. Ashley had been a pampered child, the youngest of four, if Ethan remembered correctly. She'd lived with cooks and maids prior to their marriage, never needing to arrange meals for her-self. Her early kitchen concoctions had nearly killed them. She'd even gone through several kettles, burning them one after another when she'd forget them on the stove and go off to do something else. The thought made him grin, and he quickly ducked his head so that Ashley wouldn't question him on it.

"This is really very good," he murmured. "As for Natalie, I'm sure she'll one day be a great architect herself. If that's her dream, she strikes me as the kind of person who will make it happen."

"She takes that from her father," Ashley admitted.

"She must have been very small when he died."

Ashley shook her head. "She wasn't even born. Ethan never knew about her. He was killed before I could get word to him. That hurt almost as much as losing him. I wanted very much for him to know about the baby. I know it sounds silly, but I suppose that was the roman-tic girl in me."

E. J. felt the cobbler stick in his throat. So Natalie was his daughter. But then, hadn't he known it all along? The ease with which they com-municated, their passion for building and design, her natural talent with drawing—it all made perfect sense.

He swallowed hard and lifted the coffee cup to his mouth, hoping to push the cobbler on down.

"Natalie adores her father," Ashley continued. "I've tried to keep his memory alive, but it hasn't been easy. Ethan and I had so little time prior to his going off to war. Natalie knows he was a great hero. You might even have heard about him—he saved an entire unit of men by sacrificing himself. I don't know a lot about what happened. I tried to find out, but no one talks much to young widows." She bowed her head and picked at the cobbler with her spoon.

E. J. grew uneasy. To sit there and say nothing about the truth of who he was made him the worst sort of cad. Yet he couldn't bring himself to speak. Just as Ashley had confessed her inability to love another man, E. J. knew confidently that he couldn't impose the man he'd become on this sweet woman and her child. He struggled with his emotions for several moments. Finally the urge to tell her the truth was overcome once and for all with the fear of what the truth might mean to them both.

"I'm afraid I'm going to have to go," he said, pushing the cobbler back. "This meal has been most delightful, and the food has been incredible. I thank you for having me."

Ashley seemed relieved more than upset. She got to her feet even as he did. "I'm glad we could share our meal with you."

He looked into her eyes, knowing the mistake in doing so. He wanted to lose himself in their depths but knew he had no right.

She walked behind him to the door. He could hear her light steps clicking on the hardwood floor and then silenced as she joined him on the entryway rug.

"Thank you again. I'm sure I've never had anything quite so delicious. Will you tell Natalie good-bye for me?"

He barely waited for her assuring response before opening the door. With long-legged strides, he hurried from the house and the memory of what he'd left behind. Ashley's soft voice echoed in his mind. *"I loved my husband and will love no other."*

The words were an embrace, a kiss, and a curse—all at the same time.

With Natalie in school and Mrs. Breck sitting with Grandpa, Ashley stood on the depot platform waiting for the Santa Fe eastbound passengers to disembark. Her aunt Lavelle was to be among the travelers, as stated in her last telegram. Ashley looked at the message one final time to make sure this was the right train.

When Lavelle Guzman stepped from the train, Ashley had little doubt as to her identity. Although it had been half a lifetime since Ashley had seen her, Lavelle looked strikingly similar to Ashley's mother. There was a difference, however. Lavelle smiled in greeting. Ashley couldn't remember the last time she'd seen her mother smile—if ever.

"Aunt Lavelle?" she questioned, skipping to greet the dark-haired woman. Moving closer, Ashley could see a shock of silver-streaked hair peeking out from her cloche brim.

"Ashley!" the woman gasped her name, reaching out to embrace her tightly. "I can't believe it's you." She held Ashley at arm's length. "Let me look at you."

Ashley endured her study momentarily. "I hope you had a good trip."

"It was a wonderful trip. I only wish I could have come the very moment you sent the telegram. I pray I'm not too late." She frowned and added, "Is Father . . ."

Ashley nodded. "He's still alive. Grandpa is in great pain and he's slipping away fast. I wish I could say that he was better. He takes very little of his morphine because he longs to see you and to have his head clear. He longs to renew the relationship between you."

"Oh, my poor father. How he must have suffered these long years." Lavelle looked at the ground. "I feel so awful for the past."

Ashley felt uncomfortable with the topic and looked down the track to where they were unloading the baggage. "I've arranged for a friend, Pastor McGuire, to pick up your luggage. He's going to drive us home. Usually I just walk, but I didn't want you to have to do that."

Lavelle reached out again and touched Ashley's shoulder. "Have you heard from your mother?"

Ashley shook her head. "Not a word."

Lavelle's expression hardened. "Leticia is a difficult woman. She's very opinionated and harsh. I know what she did to you. Mind you, I didn't know about it until years after the fact. She never wrote me with much of any detail. When Father disappeared from Los Angeles, I'm sorry to say I was caught up in my own problems. I never even tried to see him—and all because your mother convinced me it was for the best."

Ashley wanted nothing to do with talking about her mother, but her aunt was insistent on bringing the past to light. "Mother always seemed to believe she knew what was for the best. Frankly, I try to put it from my mind. Grandpa has been good to me, and we've had a wonderful life here."

"He's a good man," Lavelle replied. "I wish I'd seen that sooner. It might have saved me years of pain."

Ashley was surprised at her aunt's words. "I thought you hated him, as Mother did."

Lavelle's eyes narrowed. "I suppose I did at first. Leticia convinced me to do so."

The passengers around them cleared out, some heading to the Harvey restaurant to partake of lunch, while others were eager to reach their destinations.

"There's Pastor McGuire," Ashley said, spotting the man as he worked his way through the crowd. "We can continue our conversation at home where you can relax, and I'll fix us some tea or coffee."

———

With Lavelle's suitcases put in the spare bedroom, Ashley bid the pastor and Mrs. Breck good-bye, then set out some refreshments for her aunt. Grandpa was in a deep sleep, so Lavelle and Ashley both thought it best to let him rest. Ashley wondered if she would find it difficult to communicate with her aunt. The woman seemed nothing like Ashley's mother and yet she, too, had just as easily turned her back on her father.

"This is such a sweet little house," Lavelle said, coming into the kitchen where Ashley worked. "I love this flowered wallpaper. I'd like to have something like this in my kitchen. It makes everything so bright."

"It does at that. I used to have it painted a light yellow and that was nice, too, but I found this paper and thought it rather charming," Ashley admitted, studying the delicate rosebud print. She drew her thoughts back to the task at hand and smiled. "I've made some tea and have some cookies, if you'd like."

"The tea alone is fine, my dear." Lavelle smiled. "I just can't believe this is you all grown-up. What have you done with yourself all these years?"

Ashley brought the cups of tea and motioned to the dining room. "We can either sit at the table or we can go to the living room."

"Wherever you're most comfortable."

Ashley led the way to the living room, knowing she could pick up her crocheting between sips of tea. Once they were settled, Ashley answered Lavelle's question. "You wanted to know what I've done with myself. Well, I have a daughter."

"You do? Why, that's marvelous. I didn't even know you'd married. Well, I mean, I knew about the man your mother hated."

"Yes, Ethan. He's my daughter's father. He didn't know I was expecting when he went to war. He never knew."

Lavelle's expression changed to one of genuine sorrow. "Oh, my child, how awful for you."

"Mother wanted nothing to do with me, since I wouldn't cooperate with her plans. I never even had a chance to tell her about Natalie. I contacted Grandpa, knowing that you and mother had rejected him, and figured we'd make each other good company."

"So you came to Los Angeles?"

Ashley nodded. "He was just finishing the last of his business dealings. I told him my situation, and he took me under his wing. We came here to Winslow because he'd heard the climate was very good and the life-style simple. He bought this house and let me furnish it the way I wanted to. It's been a good life these eleven years."

"I can tell. You're beautiful and gracious." Lavelle sipped her tea for a moment, then asked, "Would you tell me about him?"

"Grandpa?" Ashley grinned. "I've never known anyone with a more pleasant and contented disposition. Grandpa says that becoming a Christian changed his entire outlook and that the things that seemed important to him so long ago were no longer as valuable to him."

"I know what he means."

Ashley looked at her aunt oddly. "You do? You're a believer?"

Lavelle nodded. "You see, not long after your mother forced me to break ties with our father, my husband became ill. It was only after he died that I learned he'd squandered a good portion of my inheritance. He owned several businesses, none of which was all that profitable. I sold those off. Sold the lavish home we'd built and managed to put aside what money I made in those sales. I dismissed all my servants, with exception to one dear sweet old woman, Eva, who had been with me since I'd married Bryce."

"I'm so sorry about Uncle Bryce. I had no idea he was gone."

Lavelle opened her mouth to speak, then closed it again. Ashley couldn't imagine what had stopped her from speaking her mind, but she let it go.

"I hope you don't mind if I work on this while we visit," Ashley said, picking up her crocheting. She gazed at her aunt, who looked ever so elegant and refined in her camel-colored traveling dress. Her hair, now free of the hat, was shaped in soft waves of brown with silver highlights.

"I don't mind at all," she said, offering Ashley a weary smile. She took up the tea again and grew very thoughtful. "My housemaid, Eva, led me to an understanding of what my father had found. She shared the Bible with me, and it changed my life."

Ashley nodded, not wanting her to give any detail to the matter. She was already feeling conviction enough from Natalie and Grandpa. "Grandpa will be glad to hear that. He puts great store in his faith. All of Winslow esteems him for his generosity and kindness. He's a great man—they'll be sad to see him go."

"I could have guessed that. My father was always a charismatic soul. He could have made friends with the enemy in any war," Lavelle said, laughing. Then she sobered rather suddenly. "I would give any amount of money to turn back the hands of time so that I could spend more days with him. I hope that while I'm here you'll allow me to take over his care—or at least help."

Ashley smiled and worked at the stitches of the sweater's collar. "I'm glad for the help. Frankly, it's been hard to watch him deteriorate. Some days he seems to rally a bit. He'll get out of bed and sometimes even join us for a brief time in the living room, but most of the time he stays in bed, weakened by the cancer."

"I want to spend whatever time we have together. I want to talk to him and have him talk to me. I hope your mother will feel the same way."

"Don't count on that." Ashley's snide tone drew her aunt's stare. "As I mentioned, I haven't had a response from the telegram I sent her. I sent it at the same time I sent yours."

"Well, I'll see to that. I'll send her one myself and get her to at least explain why she isn't here."

Ashley put down the crochet hook. "Have you been in touch with my mother over these years?"

Lavelle looked away as if uncomfortable with the question. "I have had some contact. Your mother and I are hardly close anymore. She doesn't share my feelings about faith or God."

"I could have guessed that," Ashley said, still unwilling to admit she didn't share them either. Tucking her hair behind her ear, Ashley picked up her cup.

"We've exchanged a few letters—a very few. Your mother seems to think that unless a person can profit her in some way, they are useless."

Ashley nodded. "I know that well enough. It's the reason I came here. But I'm not sorry I came. I've had a good life here. I've worked as a Harvey Girl at the station for most of those years. I'm the top waitress now, although I've taken a leave of absence to be here for Grandpa."

"Will you go back to it now that I'm here?" Lavelle asked.

Ashley finished her tea before answering. "I might. It couldn't hurt to have the income." She didn't want to let even her aunt know about the bank account the lawyer had set up.

"I intend to earn my keep while I'm here," Lavelle stated. "I will buy groceries as well. I'm not wealthy by my previous standards, but I'm certainly not destitute. You needn't worry about the extra mouths to feed."

"I wasn't," Ashley quickly said. "We're quite comfortable here, as I've already told you. I have preserves put up, and I know how to stretch a meal if need be. I came here hardly knowing how to boil water, but over the years I've learned to fend for myself quite nicely. We'll be just fine." A train whistle blew in the distance, and Ashley looked at her watch. "Natalie will be coming home from school soon." She looked at the sweater and picked up her hook one more time. "Before she gets here, I wonder if you would mind my asking you something."

Lavelle put down her cup and nodded. "Please do."

Ashley met her aunt's curious expression. "Why did Grandpa's choice make Mother so mad?"

"Well, that's an easy question. He threatened her comfort."

"But my father was a wealthy man. He was from old New England money."

"Yes," Lavelle admitted, "but while the prestige was there, the pocketbook didn't always match the expense ledger. Our father was a generous man who lavished us with large sums of money for no reason at all. He spoiled us terribly. As a young woman, I remember only having to ask for some bauble or trinket and Father would see to it that I had it. We wore Worth gowns and ate off of Crown Derby china. We had wonderful collections of jewels and our own carriages and teams of horses.

"Of course, we were his only family. And Father simply knew how to make money. He was quite gifted. After Mother died, he poured himself into his work even more than he had before. The only way he could feel our approval or love was to bestow his wealth upon us, and he did so with great flourish." She paused and grew misty eyed. She twisted her hands together and sighed.

"One day Father wrote us a letter. He told us he'd been in an accident. A car accident."

"Yes, I know about that—he told me. He'd broken his back and nearly died."

Lavelle drew a deep breath. "It was during that time someone shared the Gospel with him. He didn't know if he'd live or die at that point."

"I remember he said the hospital chaplain came to see him. He asked Grandpa if he were to meet God that night, would it be a good thing or a bad thing?"

"Exactly," Lavelle said and continued. "He tried hard to share with us how he felt about learning of God's love, but your mother was focused on the other parts of that letter. Father told us he'd put an end to his business dealings with his partner, Jerreth Sanders. He'd sold out his holdings and had used part of the money to try to make things right with people he'd swindled. Your mother went completely out of her mind. She said he was setting himself up to be sued or worse."

"I can't imagine her caring about that," Ashley said without thinking.

"Oh, she didn't care about Father's well-being; she only cared that the funds would be completely drained in a legal battle. I feared it, too, for your mother and I discussed our own situations and knew we needed Father's continued support. We were used to spending well beyond what our husbands gave us, and frankly, our husbands were used to the extra money as well."

"What did you do?" Ashley questioned, knowing the ultimate outcome but not understanding how they arrived at it.

"Your mother and father came to Los Angeles. It would have been that trip they made the winter before you married."

"I remember. All I knew was that they were very upset with Grandpa."

Lavelle sighed. "Yes, well, upset hardly says it all. They arrived and your mother took me aside first and discussed the situation in detail. Then our husbands joined us and finally we went as a force to meet with Father. It was ugly. We were ugly." Tears streamed down Lavelle's cheeks. "We said things that should never have been spoken."

Ashley felt sorry for the woman. She was so clearly contrite for what she'd done, and it made Ashley feel some small amount of hope that perhaps her mother had changed as well.

"Before the day was over, Father had agreed to divide his remaining estate and settle it upon Leticia and me. It was no small pittance, and he agreed he'd rather we have the benefit of his money than to see it go to some lawyer and settlement. But with that agreement, he tried to tell us of God and how much we needed to know the truth. I listened but saw the anger in Leticia and figured it couldn't be something good for either of us. I rejected his thoughts and listened to her. She said he was crazy—that he should be put away. She actually talked of locating a sanitarium where he could get help. My husband wanted no part of that. He had friends in Los Angeles who could very well make or break him. To have a crazy relative—especially a father-in-law—was hardly a glamorous calling card.

"Finally, your mother agreed we'd let it drop. Father was so hurt by us and how we acted. By then I think he was glad to see us go."

"I had no idea. He's never spoken out against either of you, even once," Ashley said, saddened by the scene she envisioned.

"Somehow that doesn't surprise me," Lavelle said, dabbing a handkerchief at her eyes. "Years later, when Father had vanished and no one seemed to know where he'd gone, I found out that Bryce had lost most of my inheritance. He suffered a heart attack and lingered for days, then finally died. Like I said, I sold off most everything and now have enough to live on until I die. Perhaps if I'd had children as your mother did, I wouldn't have done things that way. But I'm not sorry for it. I don't miss the house and the trappings. I don't miss the servants whispering behind my back. And I certainly don't miss the worry that accompanied owning more than I could ever hope to use."

The ringing of a bell brought Ashley's attention. "Grandpa's awake." She smiled. "He'll be so happy to see you."

"I hope so," Lavelle replied. "I want very much for this to be a good reunion."

Ashley got to her feet. "This is a dream come true for him, Aunt Lavelle. To find that you share his faith and have come to see him again are the only things he's longed for."

Her aunt sniffed back tears. "Thank you so much for sending me the telegram."

Ashley shook her head. "Come to think of it, I'm not even sure how it found its way to you, given the fact I sent it to the last address Grandpa had for you. That must have been the house you sold."

Lavelle smiled. "God always finds a way, even when there seems to be no chance at finding one. This is His doing, Ashley. Pure and simple."

The idea bothered Ashley in a way she couldn't understand. Trembling at the thought of God's divine intervention in matters of her life, Ashley pushed the idea aside. God didn't care about the details. He didn't care about her.

Or did He?

CHAPTER TWELVE

Russell looked up to see the face of his younger daughter. Oh, how much she favored her mother. For a moment, all he wanted to do was memorize the way she looked. It was almost like having Peg with him again.

"Papa?"

His heart swelled with pride. "Come here, child. I've so looked forward to this moment."

Lavelle left Ashley at the door and took the chair beside the bed. She reached out to grasp Russell's hands. "I can't believe it's been so long."

"I need to pick up more medicine from the doctor, so I'll leave you two to talk," Ashley said, closing the door quietly.

Lavelle looked to her father, as if awaiting some instruction on how she should comport herself. Russell felt sorry for her and immediately set out to soothe her conscience. "I've asked you here to seek your forgiveness."

"What?" Lavelle questioned, shaking her head. "You can't be serious. I'm the one who's come seeking forgiveness. You've done nothing wrong." She began to weep softly, pulling a handkerchief from her sleeve. "Oh, Papa, I can't believe it's come to this."

Russell squeezed her hand. "I'm so glad you came. I was worried that you wouldn't."

"And you had good reason, given our last encounter. Oh, I can't tell you how ashamed I am of the way I acted. I was so influenced by Leticia and Bryce, but even then, I cannot blame them for the path I chose. I could have taken a stand and told them I didn't agree with the way they wanted things to be. But I was weak and silly. Bryce had me convinced that this was the only way to ensure our survival—and he had a good reason to feel that way."

She dabbed at her eyes before continuing. "Oh, there aren't even words for all the things I want to say. That day . . . that day when you divided the money, I thought I understood life so well. I thought money was the way to be happy. Bryce certainly thought so—Leticia too. I figured if I just went along with everything, I would find that same happiness."

Russell saw the weariness in his daughter's face. She'd aged so much since he'd seen her last. Perhaps that was why she reminded him so much of her mother. "Lavelle, my sweet Lavelle. You always were such a gentle soul."

"But I wasn't then," she said, pulling back as if her presence might pain him.

"But the past is in the past. That's why I wanted you here today." Pain tore through Russell as he struggled to sit up.

"Here, let me help," Lavelle said, getting to her feet.

She gently supported his shoulders as Russell pushed up with his feet. The movement cost him all pretense of strength. He fell back against the pillows and closed his eyes, willing the pain to diminish. He knew he needed another dose of morphine, but he had no desire to spend his last days on earth in such a drugged stupor.

"I want the past to be behind us," he finally whispered. "I want your forgiveness for anything you might believe me guilty of. I know I was given over to making money—any way I could. I know I was often away from the family, and I know you probably suffered for it."

"Papa, I forgive you if it sets your mind at ease, but believe me, I feel there's nothing you need to be forgiven of. I'm the one who wronged you. I need your forgiveness. I've prayed over these last few years that if I ever had the opportunity to see you again, I wouldn't rest until I set this right between us."

Russell opened his eyes. "So you've made your peace with God?" He smiled and closed his eyes. "That's what I've always prayed for."

He breathed just a little easier, knowing that his hopes had been realized. His child had come to God. He thought of his long-departed wife and how she had pushed for the family to attend church. It was the acceptable thing to do, to be sure, but at the same time, Russell found no purpose in going other than the possible financial benefits. Many had been the time he'd made a good deal in the vestibule of the church. Never mind that he'd joined the den of thieves who robbed the focus from God and put it on money.

"I kept remembering things that you said to us that day," Lavelle began. "Things about how we wouldn't find our stability in money or possessions. Then one day Bryce took sick and died. It wasn't long after our fight."

Russell opened his eyes and looked at her sad expression. "I'm sorry, child. I had no idea."

"But of course you didn't." She shook her head. "Bryce was no good with money or numbers. He had a weakness for gambling and his gambles never paid off. When he died and I finally knew exactly where we stood, I was shocked. Most of my inheritance was gone. I had a palatial estate to show for it and a handful of other properties, but nothing like I thought I had."

"What did you do?" Russell asked.

"I sold off most everything—the house, the jewelry, the businesses, even some of the furniture. It was then that I came to realize who my true friends were. Good friends—or at least those I thought were good friends—turned away from me when my social and financial status began to drop. The more I rid myself of the trappings of wealth, the less interest I held for those in my old circle.

"Little by little I dismissed all of the servants except one. I kept my maid Eva. I don't know if you remember her or not; she was an older woman with a sweetness about her that made my days brighter. She was also a godly woman. She began sharing her Bible readings with me and eventually we started going to church together. I came to realize that the things I valued in life were not the things that would matter in death—nor in the afterlife."

Russell nodded. He could almost hear his sweet wife say the same thing. If only Leticia and Ashley would speak likewise, he could die a happy man. He bolstered his hope. He'd thought Lavelle lost too, and God obviously took care of that matter. God was big enough to see to Leticia and Ashley. But as usual, it would have to come in His timing and not Russell's.

————

Ashley hurried from the doctor's office, hoping to get home before Lavelle or Grandpa should need her. She knew Grandpa would be over-joyed to learn that Lavelle's heart had been softened over the years. He would rest easier and that made Ashley happy. She knew the mor-phine powder now secure in her purse would also make him rest easier. The doctor had increased the dosage, suggesting that Ashley not pay attention to her grandfather's request to keep the doses light.

"He needs this medicine," the doctor had told her. "He's a stubborn man, and oftentimes that means the rest of us must intercede to make choices for his good."

Ashley had agreed, but even now she wondered if she could go forward with the plan to give Grandpa a stronger dosage.

"Mama!" Natalie called, running up the street at a rapid pace. With school out, she appeared to have one purpose and goal.

"Natalie, people must think you run positively wild," Ashley said, laughing. Her daughter's wool skirt flew up in an unladylike fashion, revealing her bare knees, but Natalie didn't care. She barreled into Ashley, using her mother's body weight as a stopping block for her momentum.

"Mama, can we invite Mr. Carson to dinner again? I want to go see what they're doing with the building today, and I thought it would be fun to have him come to dinner."

"Natalie, your aunt Lavelle is here from Los Angeles. We already have one dinner guest."

"So it wouldn't be any trouble to have two—right?"

Ashley shook her head. "Natalie, you need to have some consideration for your great-aunt. She's probably not interested in meeting anyone new tonight. The train ride was very long and no doubt tiring."

"Please, Mama! He's all alone."

Natalie's pleading expression was Ashley's undoing. It wasn't as though Mr. Carson was poor company. And she had set him straight on how she felt about Natalie's matchmaking plans.

"All right, I suppose you may invite him. We'll eat around seven-thirty."

"Thanks, Mama!" Natalie called over her shoulder as she skipped away. "I'll tell him to come over at seven so I can show him my pony."

Ashley rolled her eyes heavenward, then started to head for home when she thought to tell Natalie that she might let Mr. Carson know what they were having for dinner. She spied Natalie turning the corner for Second Street, but she also saw something else as well. A man appeared to be following her daughter.

Concerned with this, Ashley carefully picked up the trail herself. She watched as the man followed Natalie at an even distance. He watched Natalie cross Second Street and waited until she closed the distance to the construction site before he did likewise.

To Ashley's relief, Natalie spotted E. J. early on. He was outside directing some work on one of the windows. Ashley held back and watched the man as he walked past them, then disappeared into the shadows.

Maybe I'm just imagining this, she thought. *Maybe it was just coincidence.* She shook her head. *No, the man had clearly been watching Natalie.* Ashley hadn't recognized the man. He seemed well enough dressed, but a long coat could hide a poor wardrobe. His coat and hat had shrouded his face and physique. Ashley had no idea what he really looked like.

She swallowed hard, feeling the uneasiness drench her in a cold sweat. *Maybe the man is a transient, one of the railroad bums. Maybe he's just trying to get back to the tracks without anyone recognizing him.*

Ashley breathed a little easier. *Yes, that's probably what it is.* From time to time the less fortunate hitched rides on the boxcars. Still, he didn't look to be that type of man. Perhaps he was a train passenger. He might have been visiting someone in town, or maybe he didn't like the crowds at the Harvey House. The man had probably come into town to get something to eat and was now headed back to catch his train. She waited a moment more, and when Natalie raced off for home and no one followed her, Ashley smiled and continued her own journey.

I'm just being silly, she thought. *Grandpa's sickness has wearied me and given rise to my imagination.*

She reached the iron gate of their yard and smiled. Natalie had forgotten to close it again. In her hurry to get changed out of her school clothes and get to her pony, she often forgot to take care of little things like open gates. Pulling the gate shut, Ashley made her way inside. She hoped her aunt had enjoyed a pleasant visit with Grandpa.

"Ashley, is that you?" Lavelle questioned, coming down the hall with a worried expression.

"Father is in a great deal of pain. Can we give him something to help?"

Ashley pulled the medicine from her purse. "I'll mix him something right now. I didn't intend to be gone so long, but I ran into Natalie."

Lavelle smiled. "I heard the door open and someone run upstairs. I thought it might be her."

"She likes to groom her pony or go for a ride on nice evenings. I'd imagine she's changing her clothes to do just that. I'll make her stop long enough for an introduction."

Ashley moved toward the kitchen. "If you want to join me, I'll show you how this is done. Then, if I'm not around, you can feel free to give him the medicine when he needs it most."

"I'd like that. I'd like to assist with Father's care. I feel it will give me the precious time I might otherwise not have had."

Ashley wasn't sure how to feel. On one hand, she had hoped to have that time for herself. On the other, she knew that Lavelle needed to have time to say good-bye to her father. Smiling, Ashley reached out and embraced her aunt. "The help will be greatly appreciated. We can relieve each other, and that way Grandpa will always be with family. The doctor said we're getting to a point where we might want to keep someone in the room with him at all times."

Lavelle nodded. "It's good he has such a nice large room on the first floor."

"It used to be his study," Ashley said. "About six years ago his knees and hips started hurting him something fierce. I suggested we convert the room at least enough to put a daybed there for him. That way on nights when he didn't feel like climbing the stairs, he'd have some place to rest." Ashley put water on the stove to heat. "The daybed gave way to a regular bed, and he's been there ever since. Oh"—she motioned to the teapot—"he likes to take the morphine in hot sweetened tea. It seems to help cut the bitterness."

Lavelle nodded. "That makes sense."

"Mama, I'm going out to brush Penny," Natalie called from the hall. "Mama, where are you?"

"I'm in the kitchen, Nat. You needn't yell," Ashley replied, shaking her head at Lavelle's grin. "Come meet your great-aunt."

Natalie came into the room, her braids and jean-clad legs bouncing to the same rhythm. Ashley had found the pair of boy's pants at the secondhand store and on a whim had bought them and altered them for her daughter. No one seemed to mind, given Natalie's status of town darling.

"Hello," Natalie said, beaming Lavelle a smile.

"You must be Natalie," Lavelle said, reaching out to touch the little girl's face. "My, but you're a pretty little thing."

"Thank you, ma'am," Natalie replied.

"Natalie, this is my aunt Lavelle. She's your great-aunt."

Natalie nodded. "Mama said you would come today. I'm glad you're here. I always wanted to meet you. Grandpa told me stories about when you and my grandma were little girls."

Ashley started at this. She hadn't realized that Grandpa had told Natalie much of anything about the family.

"Grandpa said you and Grandma got in lots of trouble one time when you decided to pick all of the neighbor's flowers for a bouquet for your mama."

"I remember that well," Lavelle said, laughing. "I was all of six or seven, but I remember to this day having to go and apologize for my wrongdoing."

"No doubt Mother put you up to it," Ashley said rather bitterly. Turning away, she tried to focus on the tea. She didn't even want to consider that her mother might have been innocent.

"Grandpa's told me lots of stories," Natalie continued. "I like hearing them. It's almost like I know you."

Lavelle chuckled. "I should like very much for us to know each other better, Miss Natalie."

"Me too. But right now I need to go take care of Penny. She's my pony. Would you like to see her?"

"We need to get Grandpa his medicine," Ashley told her daughter. "Maybe Aunt Lavelle could see Penny later."

"Yes, I'd like that, Natalie. Would you be willing to show me your pony later tonight?"

"Sure." She snagged a cookie from a plate on the counter, then hurried to the back door. "Oh, Mama, Mr. Carson said he'd be pleased to come to dinner."

With that she was gone and Ashley was left to explain to her aunt. "Mr. Carson is a man Natalie met over at the new Harvey hotel building site. She's fascinated with him because he's an architect. She's also trying to make a match, so be forewarned. She seems to be convinced that I need someone in my life."

Lavelle smiled. "She's absolutely delightful, Ashley. A sweet and loving child to be sure. How much she must love you to worry about your having someone in your life."

"It's for herself as much as me," Ashley replied, beginning to feel a bit desperate to change the conversation. But instead of bringing up something else, Ashley chose to focus on the work at hand.

They worked together in a companionable silence for several minutes. Ashley hoped she hadn't offended her aunt by suddenly going silent. It wasn't that she wanted to hide their life away from Lavelle; rather, she didn't know how much to share. Some families were very close, but obviously this one wasn't.

Finally the silence seemed stifling. Ashley strained to think of what she might talk to her aunt about. Then it came to her. "Did you have a nice talk with Grandpa?" Ashley asked, trying to sound nonchalant and hoping she wasn't being impolite. She arranged a napkin and small bowl of cottage cheese on a tray. She hoped she might get Grandpa to eat just a bite or two.

"It was wonderful," Lavelle admitted. "I'm afraid I cried a good deal." She smiled, then looked away. "We made our peace with each other, and that's what counts."

Ashley nodded. "I'm sure Grandpa was pleased."

"I know it put my heart at rest. I don't want to see him go, Ashley, but I couldn't have made it through if I'd never had the chance to seek his forgiveness. Thank you for that—for sending the telegram. I couldn't leave things as they were. The ugly memories of how I acted are not what I want him to remember of me."

Ashley put a spoon atop the napkin. "I'm sure he won't remember those things at all. He'll probably see you as a little girl in frilly calico and muslin. He'll remember the good things—he's like that."

Lavelle grasped Ashley's hand. "I pray that's the way it is. It's all I could ever really want for him."

Ashley nodded and pulled away just as the kettle began to whistle. She poured the water and said, "I just make half a cup; that way he doesn't have so much to drink. Just stir in the morphine powder while it's still hot and then add the honey." She mixed the concoction, then turned to her aunt. "Do you want to take it to him?"

Lavelle took hold of the tray. "Please."

"He may not want anything to eat, but I always try. I know if I have it with me and he asks, then he'll eat it. If I don't bring something, he won't allow me to go after it."

"I'll keep that in mind."

Lavelle went off into the dining room and down the hall. Ashley followed, watching her manage the bedroom door with ease. She felt a bit empty—almost useless—but realized it was for the best. Ashley had had the old man to herself for the last eleven years, with exception to Natalie. It was time to share him with those who also loved him.

Frowning, she couldn't help thinking of her mother. Would she be one of those who cared? Would her mother show up as Lavelle had, all sweetness and gentleness? Somehow Ashley couldn't imagine that happening.

"And even if it does, that doesn't mean I have to accept her back in my life," Ashley whispered. "Grandpa might want me to make peace, but there's a difference between that and allowing her a place in my heart."

E. J. approached Ashley's house with a sense of fatal fascination. He knew he should have told Natalie no when she'd invited him to supper that afternoon, but he couldn't. Truth was, he was only too happy to share the company of Natalie and her mother.

Lately, Ashley and Natalie had filled his thoughts. Especially Ashley. He'd thought about their days together—about their wedding and their wedding night. He couldn't help feeling a sense of elation at knowing she was still alive, but at the same time the feelings were mingled with regret of the deepest kind.

And the confusion that came from those feelings was maddening.

One minute E. J. was absolutely confident that he needed to explain his identity to Ashley. The next minute he was just as convinced that such a thing would be sheer insanity.

Now, pausing to knock at Ashley's front door, E. J. knew he'd remain silent. *Test the waters,* he thought. *See what might or might not be best. It's the reasonable thing to do.* It didn't make him a coward—it merely made him prudent.

He knocked, then felt his heart begin to race. He twisted his hands together, then pulled them apart and plunged them into his coat pockets. Would she open the door? What would she be wearing? How would she look?

But it wasn't Ashley who greeted him, it was Natalie. She smiled up at him with her endearing expression—her brown eyes huge with wonder.

"You're here!" she declared. "Come on in. We can go through the house and out the back door and I can show you my pony." She reached for his hand and pulled him along.

"Good evening to you too, Miss Natalie," E. J. said, laughing. She had such a way about her. It completely disarmed him and took away all fear of the evening.

"Mama said I should show you the pony first and give you plenty of time to clean up. But Penny's not a dirty pony. I keep her real clean. I comb her every day."

"You sound very devoted," E. J. replied.

"Mr. Carson," Ashley said as she came into the hallway. "We're glad you could make it on such short notice."

E. J. looked up and felt his breath catch in his throat. She was a vision in the butterscotch-colored gown. The most feminine of lace collars trimmed the neckline of her dress, giving her a dainty appearance in spite of the rather shapeless straight lines of her outfit. The dress was a bit longer than most fashions these days, but E. J. liked it very much.

"I appreciate the invitation. The food was so delicious last time that I felt I had to try it again."

"I hope you'll enjoy our southwest flavoring tonight. I've put together a few Mexican dishes."

"They're my favorite," Natalie chimed in.

"I'm sure to love them, then," E. J. responded.

"Mama, I'm going to show Mr. Carson my pony. Is that all right?"

Ashley smiled. "Of course." She looked at E. J. and added, "I'll introduce you to my aunt when you come back. She's with my grandfather right now."

E. J. nodded. "I'll look forward to it."

E. J. followed Natalie outside to the backyard. Living on the east edge of town had afforded them a bit more space than some. The yard was large, with an area that had been cultivated for flowers and maybe even vegetables. A small lean-to served as Natalie's stable, and around this someone had built a circular wooden fence. Inside that fence was the object of Natalie's affection.

"Penny's really friendly." Natalie whistled for the pony and sure enough, she came trotting to the gate, kicking up dust all the way.

"She's very pretty," E. J. offered as he inspected the pinto. He'd picked up a bit of horse knowledge when he'd worked for a time on a horse farm in Kentucky. The brown-, black-, and white-spotted pony seemed a perfect fit for Natalie.

"I've only had her a year," Natalie told him. "Grandpa got her for me for Christmas, and then he got me a saddle for her on my birthday."

E. J. smiled. "Seems like a very fitting present for you."

Natalie grinned up at him. "I'm going to see if my mom will get me a dog this year."

He laughed. "Are you trying to build your own farm here?"

"Nah, I just don't want Penny to be lonely. Besides," she said soberly, "after Grandpa's gone, it might be nice to have a watchdog."

E. J. didn't want her to dwell on the sadness in her life. "Well, she's a perfect horse for you. I don't think I've ever seen one prettier."

"She can go pretty fast too, but Mama doesn't like me to ride her that way."

"Your mother sounds wise. A lot of things can happen when you ride too fast." He hated the very thought of his daughter meeting injury for any reason. He stroked the pony's velvet nose, while Natalie stroked her mane.

"I called her Penny 'cause I used to have a doll named that, but I lost her," Natalie said as though he'd asked the question. "When I get a dog, I'm going to call him Duke 'cause my daddy had a dog named that when he was a boy."

E. J. drew his breath in sharply. He hadn't thought about that dog in years. "A black Lab," he murmured.

"How did you know?" Natalie asked, her eyes wide in amazement.

E. J. realized his mistake. He quickly worked to cover his tracks. "That just seems like the kind of name you'd give to a dog like a black Labrador."

Natalie nodded. "My daddy was really smart." She smiled in her girl-ish self-confident manner and went back to stroking the pony's neck. "If you were a daddy, what would you name a dog?"

The words rang in his ears and echoed in his heart. *If you were a daddy . . ." But I am your daddy and I want to be your daddy*. E. J.'s stomach knotted and he forced the thoughts away. "I don't know. I guess I like Duke well enough."

"Natalie, it's time to wash up for supper," Ashley called from the house.

E. J. rubbed his stomach. "Good thing too. I'm starved."

Natalie giggled. "Mama made lots of good food. You won't be starv-ing for long." She took hold of his hand once again. The action caused a lump to rise up in E. J.'s throat. For a moment he actually felt tears sting his eyes. This was his daughter, a child he scarcely knew. How could it be that she so easily reached out to him when she didn't know him at all? How was it that they had found each other across the years and miles that had separated them?

The question haunted E. J. all through supper. The food proved to be as delectable as Natalie had promised. He'd had three helpings of the enchilada pie before realizing he'd made such a pig of himself.

"I'll have to be the one to furnish dinner next time," he said apologetically.

"Nonsense," Ashley replied, offering him more spicy rice. "I made plenty."

The real surprise of the evening was that Grandpa had asked to join them for dessert and coffee. Ashley had already enlisted E. J. to help get the old man to the table. When E. J. waved off the rice, that seemed a signal to the group. Ashley gathered up several of the empty dishes while her aunt took up the serving dishes. Natalie collected silverware and the salt and pepper.

"Maybe you could see if Grandpa is ready to join us," Ashley told E. J. as she returned from the kitchen. "Natalie can show you the way."

He pushed back from the table and placed his napkin beside the plate. "I'd be glad to." Ashley reached for his dishes and met his gaze. The warmth there in her eyes might have given him reason to believe she held an interest in him, but E. J. knew better. That was merely a look of gratitude for his kindness to her grandfather. It was nothing more.

Natalie hurried off down the hall. "Grandpa!" she called. "Grandpa, it's time for dessert."

E. J. followed at a slower pace to give the man time to compose himself after Natalie's invasion. E. J. wondered if Russell Whitman would be angered at his appearance; after all, the man didn't know E. J. at all. They'd never met—not even in those earlier years when life seemed so charmed.

E. J. entered the dimly lit bedroom and smiled. The room was warm and inviting—a man's domain to be sure. A bookshelf with numerous volumes sat in one corner, while additional books were stacked beside the old man's bed.

Overhead, a Mexican-styled iron fixture offered light, giving the room a decidedly regional flavor. He'd seen Mary Colter use similar pieces. He turned to the old man, who was even now watching him, while Natalie fussed with finding her great-grandfather's slippers. "I'm E. J. Carson. I'm here to help you."

Russell Whitman eyed him seriously for a moment, then smiled. "Glad to know you, E. J. I'm Russell, but most folks your age call me Grandpa. You might as well."

His voice held none of the strength he must have once known, but E. J. immediately liked the old man. "I'd be honored to call you Grandpa. I've never known my own. Both my grandfathers died before I was very old."

"My grandpa is the best in the world," Natalie offered. "He's got enough love to share, so he can be your grandpa too." She put the slippers on her grandfather's feet, then stepped back.

E. J. was touched by her words. "I'd like that," he said softly, realizing how dearly he missed a sense of family. He'd been very close to his mother and father, perhaps because his younger siblings had died as toddlers or at birth. There had been a sister and two brothers, but polio had taken one brother, meningitis another, and his sister had been stillborn. It gave his parents great reason to cling to him, and because he was older and knew the pain of losing part of his family, it caused E. J. to feel the same way. Perhaps that was why it hurt so much to return home from the war only to find his parents gone.

The short walk down the hall was a strenuous effort for the old man. As they neared the table, E. J. nearly carried him in full. Helping Grandpa to take a chair, E. J. couldn't help noticing the laborious way the man strained to draw a breath. He looked at Ashley, meeting her worried expression. Grandpa's time was certainly running out. Her expression acknowledged this fact with a sorrow that seemed to permeate her entire being.

"I've made Grandpa's favorite chocolate cake," Ashley announced, appearing to recover from her sadness. E. J. watched as she put her defenses back in place, her expression masking the pain he'd seen there only moments before.

The old man looked up with a hint of gratitude. E. J. thought his eyes looked rather cloudy. Probably the medication, he reasoned. "Thank you, young man," Grandpa murmured.

E. J. took his seat and nodded. "Glad to help. I've heard so many wonderful things about you, I knew I had to meet you for myself."

Soon they were served with large pieces of what E. J. clearly knew was the best chocolate cake he'd ever tasted.

"I remember Mama made a cake similar to this," Lavelle said, sampling her dessert.

"It's the same recipe," Ashley replied, forking into her own piece.

"How in the world did you get it?" Lavelle questioned.

"Grandpa gave me a book of recipes that had belonged to Grandma. They were among the things he managed to save when . . ."

Ashley's voice trailed off. Her expression was clearly one of embarrassment.

"When we forced him to divide up the household?"

Ashley looked away, and E. J. felt most uncomfortable in this sudden baring of dirty family linen.

"I'm so sorry, Aunt Lavelle. I didn't mean to say anything hurtful."

"Nonsense, Ashley. I've caused my own hurt." Lavelle reached over and patted Ashley's hand. "Don't give it a second thought. You could, however, copy the recipes down for me." She smiled lovingly.

E. J. thought the matter closed until Grandpa spoke up. "Lavelle, I hope you and Leticia understand that I've left my remaining possessions to Ashley. There isn't much—your mother's china, some odd pieces of furniture, and a couple of photo albums."

"The things we didn't pillage in our war with you, don't you mean?" Lavelle asked softly. "Oh, Father, I'm so sorry for the past. Of course I don't mind those things going to Ashley. Who better to care for them and pass them down through the generations?"

"Mother won't like it," Ashley declared, surprising E. J.

"Have you even heard from her?" Lavelle questioned.

"No, but that doesn't mean she won't make her presence known when it comes to possessions and what she believes she has coming to her."

Lavelle reached out again to Ashley. "Darling, you have no idea how she might react. Let's give her a chance. Tomorrow I'll do what I can to locate her. I have friends in Baltimore who can help."

Ashley bowed her head, and E. J. longed to put his arm around her and offer whatever comfort he might.

"I don't care if she comes at all, except that I know it means a great deal to Grandpa."

"It does mean a lot," Grandpa managed to say. This brought Ashley's immediate attention. "It means even more to know that you'll try to put an end to this bitterness and let the past die."

Ashley nodded. "For you, I would do that."

"I hope you'll do it for yourself and for Natalie too."

The little girl smiled and leaned over to touch her head to the old man's shoulder. "Grandpa's been praying for us, Mama. It's bound to work out. And Grandpa said we don't have to be afraid, because perfect love casts out fear. That's in the Bible."

Ashley nodded. "But the only perfect love I knew was with your daddy, and he's gone."

E. J. felt as if he'd been punched in the gut. The chocolate cake, as light and succulent as any he'd ever known, suddenly felt like a lead weight in his stomach.

"Perfect love is God's love, Mama. People can't love perfectly, but God can. And He doesn't want us to be afraid. So when we love Him, we don't have to be afraid of what will happen or what other people will do."

"You should listen to the child," Grandpa said, breathing heavily. "She knows what she's talking about."

Later that night E. J. continued to think on Grandpa's and Natalie's words. Reluctantly, he took out a Bible Natalie had brought him. She had lent it to him when E. J. admitted he didn't have one of his own.

Now, turning the book over and over in his hands, E. J. felt almost afraid to open it. What if he read something there that caused him even more pain?

"But how can I not seek God's direction?" he whispered aloud. "I've long put off paying attention to what God wants in my life. I've tried to deal with the past in my own way, but still it haunts me." He ran his hands through his hair and shook his head. "Nothing is working. I still have nightmares. I still struggle with my guilt, and now I have this revelation that my wife is alive and I have a daughter. I have to at least try to figure this out—with His help."

For so long he'd held God at arm's length. He didn't feel as Ashley did, that God didn't care, but rather it was more a situation of God putting more on him than E. J. could bear. God seemed a harsh task-master, pushing E. J. to limits that were far beyond his ability—then standing back to laugh cruelly at his plight.

But the God Natalie described—the loving Father Pastor McGuire preached of—didn't seem the kind to laugh at his children's sorrows. *Perhaps I've missed something*, E. J. thought. If his little daughter could hold God in such esteem and trust the future to His care, then what was it that kept E. J. hesitant?

E. J. opened to the Psalms, remembering they offered comfort and wisdom. His gaze fell to the page where the thirty-second chapter declared, *"Blessed is he whose transgression is forgiven, whose sin is covered. Blessed is the man unto whom the Lord imputeth not iniquity, and in whose spirit there is no guile."*

E. J. read on, a prayer in his heart that the words would somehow give him strength and encouragement. Several verses later he came to a passage he could not ignore.

"I acknowledged my sin unto thee, and mine iniquity have I not hid. I said, I will confess my transgressions unto the Lord; and thou forgavest the iniquity of my sin."

E. J. took off his glasses and rubbed his eyes. "Oh, God, can you forgive me? The wrong I've done is so hideous—so destructive. I've killed men. I've watched them die, even as they pled with me for life. How can you forgive that?"

The silence did nothing to reassure him, but a quickening in his heart ignited a spark of hope. God was in the business of forgiving grave sins. He recalled a story his friend John had told him about a man in the Bible, King David. The man had been a chosen king of God—a man after God's own heart. Yet David had sinned greatly in the eyes of the Lord. He had committed adultery with another man's wife, then arranged for that man to be killed on the battlefield. David had murdered the man as sure as if he had wielded the weapon himself.

And God forgave David.

The spark ignited and his heart warmed.

"You can forgive me. If I choose to repent . . . if I give this to you and seek your forgiveness . . . if I let the past be put to rest . . . then I can have peace and maybe even be a husband and father in action as well as deed."

E. J. knew he'd never wanted anything more in his life. These past weeks of getting to know Natalie and Ashley had greatly blessed him. Even Mary had noticed the change in his attitude and temperament. Natalie and Ashley were good for him. Was it too much to ask God that he might be good for them in return?

CHAPTER FOURTEEN

The next few weeks were spent in a routine that Ashley found much to her liking. Lavelle sat with Grandpa in the morning while Ashley took care of the house chores and sent Natalie off to school. Then around noon Ashley would relieve her aunt, and Lavelle would take care of her own needs. Near to the time when Natalie was due home from school, Lavelle would take over Grandpa's care again, freeing Ashley to be there for Natalie. By evening Grandpa was usually fast asleep, completely worn-out from his efforts of trying to stay awake and communicate through the day. It was only at suppertime that he'd allow Ashley to give him a large dose of morphine, pleading with both her and Lavelle to understand that he needed to be cognizant for as long as he could stand the pain.

Near the end of the month, however, Ashley felt her neatly ordered world once again shift. A telegram arrived from her mother. After weeks abroad, her mother had finally returned to Baltimore to receive word that her father was dying. Lavelle received this information from friends who lived nearby and knew Ashley's mother.

Ashley felt the wind go out of her at the words on the telegram. WILL ARRIVE ON THE TWENTY-EIGHTH TO OVERSEE THIS MATTER.

The words pierced her heart. Her mother was making it clear she intended to take control of the situation.

"Well, we won't allow it," Lavelle said, trying to encourage Ashley. "Your mother will find us both much stronger than when she last saw us."

"Have you not had contact with Mother these last eleven years?"

Lavelle brushed lint from her already immaculate navy blue dress. "There have been letters, but I only saw your mother once in that time. It was about four years ago. She and your father came to Los Angeles on business. She was greatly disappointed in the way in which I lived. I have only a modest home, not even as big as this one. I live very comfortably, but your mother was completely put off by it. She had hoped to step into Los Angeles society through my introduction. When she found that was not to be the case, she found other ways, of course."

"Of course," Ashley said.

"She did ask me whether or not I knew where Father had gone. Of course, I didn't know. I think she might have even hired someone to find where he'd gone, but she never found out. I'm sure she went home from that trip very disappointed in me. It didn't help matters at all that I'd become a Christian."

I should become a Christian to spite Mother, if for no other reason, Ashley thought. But immediately she knew that would never work. She might lie to the world, but she couldn't very well lie to God.

"Your mother said I was weak, just like Father. I'm sure that's why she feels she must come and oversee matters now. But, Ashley, she has no power here except that which you give her. The house is yours. Father told me all about giving it over to you, and I'm quite pleased he did. I'm glad he left you the entirety of his estate, and I will support you in this one hundred percent."

"I appreciate that, Aunt Lavelle, but . . ."

Lavelle took hold of Ashley's hand. "Look, I know you've not yet put your trust in God. Father told me of his concern for you. I don't know what keeps you from doing so or why you distance yourself from God—but no matter what, He is here and wants only the best for you. It might not always come in a comfortable, easy manner. Growing is sometimes very uncomfortable—think of when you carried Natalie. I've heard many a pregnant woman complain of the discomfort."

"But don't you feel that God . . . well . . . doesn't it seem sometimes that He's forgotten you—that He doesn't care?"

Lavelle hugged her close. "Ashley, we all go through moments of time when we feel confused by the things that happen in our lives. We wonder where God is and why He allows such tragedy. There are times when we feel completely deserted. Even Jesus bore that feeling."

"He did? When?" Ashley's voice belied her disbelief.

"On the cross, dear. He said, 'My God, my God, why hast thou forsaken me?' "

The words went through Ashley's heart like a white-hot coal. They seared her mind and burned deep into her lost memories and dreams.

The words of Christ were her very own.

Lavelle seemed to understand the impact. "Ashley, God might seem silent for a season, but be assured, He is never absent. He won't leave you to bear things alone unless that's the way you choose to bear them. He leaves it up to you."

———

The next few days seemed to drag by in some ways and fly by in others. Ashley furiously cleaned the house, certain her mother's biggest criticism would be in how they lived. She beat the rugs and took down all the curtains to wash and iron. The hardwood floors were scrubbed and polished and the furniture carefully dusted and wiped. Lavelle tried to assure her the place was already spotless, but Ashley continued to find fault.

"If only I'd thought to paint the living room," Ashley reflected. She was on her knees scrubbing the baseboard when this idea came to her. She looked up at the walls, wondering if there still might be time.

Finally, Lavelle brought Ashley her sweater and demanded she go for a walk. "You haven't been out of the house since that telegram arrived. Now go."

Ashley looked up in complete surprise. "But I haven't scrubbed out the fireplace yet."

"Ashley! Your mother's arrival isn't worth this grief. We know her to be a critical woman. Do you really suppose that your efforts will matter? If she's still of the same meanspirited temperament, she won't appreciate the effort. And if she's had a change of heart, then none of this will matter."

The words made sense. Ashley slowly got up from her aching knees. "I suppose you're right. I just wanted to . . ."

Lavelle touched her face tenderly. "I know, sweetheart. I know."

Ashley put aside her sponge and bucket. "I suppose I should go to the market and pick up a few things."

"Or at least take a walk and enjoy the sunshine."

Ashley nodded and took up the sweater. Pulling it around her shoulders, she sighed. "I'd like to believe she's changed, but I have no faith in that. Not given the telegram."

"I know. But God is sufficient even in this. He'll see us through— you simply have to trust Him, Ashley."

Trust. That was the real crux of the matter.

How could she trust God when she wasn't even sure who He was?

She didn't like that her mother's impending arrival was giving her cause to act so completely out of character. She couldn't help questioning herself. *I've not cared what that woman thought in eleven years. Why is it so important that she approve now?* Just as her aunt had told her, if Leticia was the same woman whom Ashley had parted company with all those years ago, nothing Ashley did now would meet with her approval.

Walking to town, Ashley couldn't help sidetracking in order to see the Harvey hotel's progress. She hadn't talked to E. J. Carson since that night at dinner weeks ago. Natalie had asked several times to have him over, but Ashley had always refused for one reason or another. There was something there that made her uncomfortable—almost uneasy. Maybe it was the easygoing manner in which she shared E. J.'s company. Maybe it was the way he seemed to know things about her.

His tenderness toward Grandpa had nearly been her undoing that night. He was so gentle with the old man—so careful of his frail, pain-filled body. She could easily remember his expression, so concerned, so compassionate. Something in his manner reminded her of Ethan; at least she was fairly confident that the memory was true. As the years went by she had to admit that it was harder and harder to remember his mannerisms, his voice. It grieved her, but as Grandpa had suggested, it was very possible that she was also assigning things to the past that had no bearing in truth. She and Ethan had shared only a matter of weeks together. It was hardly enough to build a lifetime on. But then again, it had given her Natalie.

Natalie adored E. J. Carson. There was no doubt about that. She talked about the man from morning until night. But now that her mother was coming, she'd have ample excuses to delay his visits when Natalie insisted.

Ashley wouldn't impose her mother upon anyone. Especially if she were to have the same nature as before. No, their house and dinner table would be full. Ashley would give up her bedroom to her mother and share Natalie's bed, and while she knew the arrangement would be adequate for most anyone else in the world, Ashley was confident it wouldn't meet with her mother's approval.

"Mrs. Reynolds!"

E. J. Carson called to her from beyond a newly constructed portion of stone fence. Ashley felt her stomach flutter. Suddenly she was aware that she was quite happy he'd sought her out. *Why should this man have the power to make me feel this way?* Guilt immediately washed over her. What of Ethan?

"Hello, Mr. Carson."

He tipped his hat and smiled. "I was hoping to see you today. In fact, I had thought to come by. I have a question for you. Remember? I promised you dinner sometime."

"Yes, but that's hardly necessary," Ashley argued. The last thing in the world she wanted was to be asked out on a date with this man or any other.

"Well, I've been talking with several of the workers," he continued. "I was wondering if you've ever been to the meteor crater west of here?"

Ashley shook her head. "No. Grandpa and I talked about going, and Natalie has nagged us both about it ever since hearing about it in school, but we've never managed to make arrangements. We have no car, you see."

"Well, I do. I've just acquired the use of a vehicle, and I'd like very much to propose a picnic tomorrow. I figured since it's Saturday and I have the day off and Natalie will be out of school, we could take all day. It's about twenty-one miles to drive there, so we'd have plenty of time to explore."

The thought of spending all day in the company of this gentle-spirited man held both appeal and terror at the same time.

"I know it's short notice, but I would bring a picnic from the Harvey House," he said, his voice almost pleading.

Ashley knew Natalie would be beside herself if Ashley were to say no. How many times had she begged her mother to ask Pastor McGuire for the loan of his car for just such an adventure? The only problem was, Ashley didn't drive.

"I'm sure Natalie would enjoy the trip," Ashley began, almost confident that she would turn down E. J. Carson's offer for herself. But when it came time to speak the words, she found herself agreeing instead. "I'll need to make sure Aunt Lavelle doesn't mind taking care of Grandpa all day. Still, I wouldn't want to leave her alone for too long. We'd have to be back by dark."

E. J. smiled. "I can arrange that; just leave it to me. I'll pick you both up about nine in the morning. We'll get there in an hour or less, and that should leave us plenty of time." He tipped his hat again, then sauntered off as if he'd single-handedly won the World Series.

Ashley had to smile, until she heard him start to whistle. The tune left her cold. She could hear Ethan whistling the same song. It was his favorite ragtime melody. He'd whistled it incessantly while they'd courted.

E. J. disappeared into the construction site, but Ashley felt fixed to the spot where she stood. All at once she exhaled, not even realizing she'd been holding her breath. *Oh, Ethan, why should you be gone while E. J. Carson is here? It's not at all how I saw life when you married me.*

Her heart ached within her and the memory was more than she wanted to deal with. *How am I to spend the day with this man and not die from loneliness?*

————————

E. J. felt a sense of renewal in his spirit. He had actually taken time since last seeing Ashley to pray and seek God—and it felt marvelous. Though he still suffered the terrors of his war memories as he slept each night, the dreams seemed shorter and less violent. Perhaps true healing had begun.

Now he waited for his wife and daughter to join him on an outing to the meteor crater, and an overwhelming giddiness engulfed him. He wanted this freedom of spirit. He wanted to look forward to the day and to know that it would come around right in the evening. He wanted for once not to dread the nightfall.

Natalie came bouncing out the door as she so often did. She wore her dark hair pulled back into a high ponytail, which swung back and forth as she came down the path to the borrowed car. Her skirt jogged up and down, revealing rolled-up pants beneath.

E. J. reached out and opened the door for her. "I see you wore jeans under your dress. You must be planning for quite an adventure."

Natalie jumped up on the Packard's running board. "Mama said I had to wear the dress over them," she replied, wrinkling up her nose in distaste. "She doesn't understand that sometimes I like to climb and not worry about dresses."

Natalie climbed into the backseat and plopped down dead center. "I get all this room to myself?"

E. J. laughed. "Well, so long as you mind the picnic lunch I've put down on the floor behind my seat."

"Is this your car?" she questioned, running her hand over the seat. "This is the nicest car I've ever been in."

"This is one of the Harvey company cars. They gave it to Miss Colter to use, but since she's out of town, she told me I could borrow it for our trip."

About that time Ashley came from the house. Her face glowed from beneath a wide-brimmed straw hat. She caught him watching her and smiled hesitantly, her gaze curious, almost as if she were trying to figure out a puzzle. E. J. felt a wave of guilt for keeping his identity from her. He knew she deserved to know and make the choice for herself as to whether they'd continue their marriage or end it.

"I hope I've dressed all right," she said, breaking his thoughts. "I thought a simple skirt and blouse would be easiest."

He nodded and noticed she'd put on very sturdy walking shoes. "You look perfect. Natalie too."

"I've brought some sweaters, although I doubt we'll need them as the day seems so fair. Oh, and I've brought a couple of blankets for the ground. I didn't know whether or not you'd think to bring something to sit on."

"No, I totally forgot about that. Glad you considered the matter for me." He smiled and took the blankets from her while she handed the sweaters back to Natalie. E. J. held the door for Ashley as she stepped up on the running board and got in. He watched her gracefully arrange herself on the seat before nodding to him.

Soon they were on the road, driving west with the sun at their back, the world stretched out before them in a raw and rugged landscape that begged exploration. Cactus, scrub, and a variety of nondescript brush dotted the red, sandy soil. The dusty desert road offered nothing in the way of shade or real diversion, but E. J. hardly cared about that. He'd made up his mind. He was going to tell Ashley the truth. Once they were at the crater site and Natalie was preoccupied with her exploration, he would break the news to Ashley as gently as possible.

The anticipation of that moment was enough to keep E. J. focused and energized on the journey west. For over an hour he contemplated what he would say.

Ashley, there was a mistake about your husband dying in the war.

Ashley, I didn't know until I saw you that you were still alive.

Ashley, the government makes mistakes, and I'm not dead like you thought.

Nothing sounded exactly right, but he was certain the words would come when the time was right.

Upon finally arriving without mishap, Natalie's chatter caught up with his thoughts. "I've wanted to come here forever. We learned all about this place in school. Did you know they were trying to mine the crater for iron ore? They stopped because they couldn't find very much and they just kept striking water or having other problems. They just stopped work this year.''

E. J. smiled as he parked the car. There were only two other cars at the location, probably belonging to whoever might remain on-site to answer questions, he figured.

"My teacher said the meteorite probably weighed three hundred thousand tons but that it probably broke apart and smashed into little dust pieces when it came to earth. Isn't that hard to imagine?''

"Indeed it is,'' E. J. replied.

"This is all she has been able to talk about since yesterday,'' Ashley told him.

"It's just that it's the most amazing thing in the world, and it's not very far from home. People are going to start coming here more and more to see it, and that's going to make this area very popular.''

E. J. laughed and opened the car door. "And that's important to you?''

"Sure,'' Natalie said, jumping from the car. "The more people who come and want to live here, the more they're going to need architects to draw the plans for houses and businesses. That will give me a job.''

E. J. shook his head. She certainly had it in mind to stick to her guns regarding her dream.

The meteor crater proved to be fascinating, but E. J.'s mind couldn't completely appreciate the phenomenon. He wandered around for a time with Natalie and Ashley, listening to his daughter marvel at the impact indentation nearly a mile across in size. All the while the words of his explanation to Ashley ran through his mind.

"See down there?'' Natalie questioned E. J., pointing to the floor of the crater. "My teacher said that some of those rocks that just look like little stones to us from here are actually boulders. Isn't that amazing?''

"Indeed it is.'' He found great delight in her reactions. "Say, are you ready to eat yet?'' he asked Natalie. "I'm starving.''

"You and Mama can go ahead and eat, but I just want to explore. Please?'' She looked at her mother first and then E. J.

"I think that's perfectly acceptable,'' E. J. said, then looked at Ashley and added, "If it's all right with your mother.''

Ashley nodded and Natalie took off without another word.

"Her energy level is daunting,'' E. J. said, still watching Natalie skitter over the rocks.

"She never wears out. She's on the go constantly.'' Ashley looked up at him, her face shaded by the brim of her hat. She seemed to study him, especially his eyes. Could it be she already suspected the truth?

They walked back to the picnic basket and blankets. Ashley had placed the covers atop the basket, but before E. J. could take hold of it, she grabbed it. "We'll need to shake these out just in case something has crawled in."

E. J. took up the other blanket and followed her example, snapping it open. Once assured they were safe, they spread them on the ground. As they sat down, E. J. decided to get his confession out of the way. There was simply no telling when Natalie would return.

"Ashley, there's something I need to talk to you about."

She looked up, rather startled. Cocking her head to one side, she seemed to contemplate his expression and waited for him to speak—seeking understanding in the silence.

"Well, that is . . ." Why did this have to be so hard? She was his wife—she needed to know the truth. "Something happened a long time ago," he began again. "Something that forever changed my life."

"Ashley! Hey, Ashley!"

E. J. looked up to find a tall, slender blond woman waving. At her side, a beefy-looking man studied him with an arched brow.

"Glenda, hello!" Ashley called back and waved.

E. J. held his breath, hoping—even praying—that this would be the end of the matter. The woman moved forward, however, dashing his hopes.

"I thought that was you. How are you? Where's Natalie?"

Ashley put her hand to the brim of her hat as if to further shield the sun. "She's exploring. There she is, over there." She pointed to the north and the couple turned in unison.

"Oh, sure. I see her. Goodness, but that girl can climb like a mountain goat."

Ashley smiled and nodded. "Glenda, this is E. J. Carson. He's actually become a good friend of Natalie's and thus mine. He's working with the new Harvey House construction." She turned back to E. J. "This is Glenda and her fiancé, Marvin."

"Nice to meet you both," E. J. said, not really meaning it. It wasn't that he minded meeting Ashley's friends, but now wasn't the time.

"I see you're having a picnic. We brought some food too," Glenda said, motioning to Marvin and the basket he held.

E. J. held his breath. *Please don't ask them to join us,* he thought over and over. *I need the time to tell you the truth, Ashley.*

"Why don't you join us?" Ashley moved closer to E. J. "There's plenty of room."

"Are you sure?" Glenda asked, then looked at Marvin. "Would you like to join them?"

"You bet," he said, pushing back a rowdy shock of red hair. "I'll go anywhere you go."

Glenda laughed. "You'd better."

They joined E. J. and Ashley, laughing and talking about people they knew at the Harvey restaurant or on the railroad. Glenda asked about Grandpa Whitman, and Ashley made comments about how quickly he was fading. She also mentioned that her mother was due in town on Tuesday.

By the time Natalie was completely satisfied with her rock expedition, it was time to go. In frustrated silence, E. J. drove back to Winslow. Natalie dozed in the backseat, completely spent from her day of running and climbing. Ashley stared absentmindedly out her window, then suddenly turned to him.

"You were going to say something to me back there. You'd started to tell me something about the past."

He considered for a moment that he might break the news to her before Natalie woke up, then decided against it. There was always a chance she might awaken in the middle of his explanation. No, he'd just have to wait until another day.

She'd gone eleven years without knowing the truth. He supposed she could wait another day or two.

"It wasn't important. We'll save it for another time," he replied good-naturedly. But inside, E. J. knew a building frustration that refused to be ignored. He had to tell her—and it needed to be soon.

CHAPTER FIFTEEN

*M*onday. That dreaded day.

Ashley looked out her bedroom window, then turned to face the room itself. She'd tried to arrange it perfectly, but no doubt her mother would take displeasure with something. How was it that a person could live thousands of miles away and still heavily influence the heart and mind of another?

Ashley smoothed the chenille spread on the bed. The white ridges were dotted with tiny pink flowers and green leaves. Her mother would probably say it was too feminine or too childish. The pillows would probably be too flat and the temperature of the room too cool at night.

Checking the freshly washed and ironed curtains, Ashley inspected the material for any holes or snags. She just wanted to give her mother as little reason for criticism as possible.

Sighing, Ashley took a handful of her clothes and moved them to Natalie's closet. Hanging her dresses on the bar beside her daughter's, Ashley bit her lip to keep it from trembling.

"I'm absolutely terrified of her coming here."

Once the words were spoken, it was almost a relief. It was as if by speaking them, Ashley could finally accept them.

"She will criticize and cause me grief. Of that I can be sure."

And that was perhaps more troubling than anything else. If her mother were the same woman she'd been eleven years earlier, Ashley knew there wouldn't be a moment's peace. And that was what this house had always represented to her. Peace.

This house—this home—had been a respite and a comfort. She'd sought sanctuary here and felt warm and loved within these walls. Now her mother would come and all that would change. The house would become a battleground—no different from the other places Leticia Murphy had stormed.

"I have to get ahold of myself," Ashley said, speaking into the mirror over her daughter's desk. She saw her expression in the reflection there and it only served to further discourage her. She looked scared, and her mother would feed upon that like vultures to carrion.

———

"I know she's afraid," Russell told his daughter. "She believes her mother will come here and wreak havoc on her life. And she may have a point."

Lavelle nodded. "If Letty is the same woman she used to be, then Ashley has good reason to believe that."

Russell fought against the waves of nausea and pain. "I know, but I want her to have hope. Ashley can't change her mother, but she can change herself." His words were barely audible, but Lavelle apparently heard, for she nodded as she got to her feet.

"Papa, if I find Leticia to be as she's been in the past, I'll speak to her sternly before we arrive. She must understand that she cannot come in here and turn everything upside down. She may not like it, but she will hear me out."

Russell nodded. "I'm glad you're going for her and not Ashley."

Lavelle glanced at her watch. "The pastor will be here momentarily to escort me."

"You go ahead. I'll be praying," Russell said, shifting only the tiniest bit to see if the pain decreased. It didn't.

Lavelle had only been gone a few moments before a knock sounded on his open bedroom door. Glancing up, Russell smiled weakly and motioned Pastor McGuire to come in.

"I see you're still taking life easy," the pastor teased. "How are things today?"

"Difficult."

"A lot of pain?" Pastor questioned.

"Yes. And I find myself just wishing to slip from this body into heaven."

McGuire reached over and touched Russell's shoulder. "The time will come, my friend, soon enough. I don't desire you to live out your days in pain, but I do cherish your existence. You'll be sorely missed when you're gone."

"You're one of only a few folks I know who can talk so openly about my dying. It's a relief, you know, to be able to say the words out loud. It's not as if it is a secret."

McGuire nodded. "I know. My mom and dad both said the same thing when they were dying. People avoid speaking of it when they're with you because they're afraid of causing you more grief. Yet what they don't realize is that some things need to be said."

"Exactly."

Russell looked up to find Ashley standing in the doorway. He figured she'd heard their discussion, and he quite frankly hoped it might make a difference. Ashley was one of those people who avoided speaking the truth—as if in keeping silent, she might stave off death. It only got worse the closer he came to actually dying.

"Ashley, come on in, child."

Pastor McGuire looked over his shoulder and nodded. "Yes, do. We aren't speaking of anything that you can't be a part of."

Ashley looked most uncomfortable. "I . . . uh . . . just wanted to let you know that Aunt Lavelle is ready to go. The train is due ten minutes from now."

"Well, I suppose we should head out, then," Pastor McGuire said. He offered a quick prayer of hope and comfort, then headed to the door. "Ashley, we've certainly enjoyed having you in church when you're able to be there. I hope you know that."

Ashley smiled tentatively. "I've . . . well . . . I've enjoyed it too."

Smiling, the tall pastor nodded. "That's music to a minister's ears. I'll look forward to seeing you Sunday."

Russell could see his granddaughter's uneasiness. It was something akin to embarrassment. "Ashley, would you sit with me for a moment?"

"Sure, Grandpa." She came to his bedside and pulled a chair close.

"I wanted to talk to you before your mother got here." He bit back a cry as his side exploded in pain. The shock of it left him gasping for breath.

"Are you all right, Grandpa?"

He opened his eyes and noted her concern. "It's just this momentary trouble. Soon I'll be right as rain."

Ashley frowned. "I heard what Pastor McGuire said. I didn't know that you needed to talk about dying."

"It's not so much the actual dying, but there are things I want to say before I slip away. It's one of the reasons I don't want to take the medicine." She nodded and he continued. "You're afraid . . . aren't you?"

Ashley laughed bitterly. "I'm terrified. Of so many things."

"Tell me."

She looked toward the wall, avoiding his eyes. "I'm just not that confident of being able to handle things once you're gone. I'm afraid Mother will come in here and make a mess of everything and demand her way, and I won't have the strength to stand up to her."

"I know those things worry you, but God is with you. You've only got to reach out to Him."

"Will God keep my mother under control?" Ashley asked seriously. "If so, why didn't God do that for you all those years ago?"

Russell knew she desperately needed answers, but he had none. "God is not in the habit of explaining himself to me." He smiled and it took all his energy. "You've got to have trust, Ashley. You can trust Him to be faithful. Let your Mother rant and rave if that's why she's come. Let her talk of what money she expects to get after I'm dead. She can only hurt you if you let her. Her words may be caustic, her temperament harsh. But she cannot change the fact that this house is yours and the bank account is yours. She can't reach into your soul and separate you from what's most important—God."

"No, I suppose I've done a decent job of that myself," Ashley admitted. "Grandpa, I've been thinking of all the things you've told me. I've been listening to Pastor McGuire as well. I wish I could say I have the faith to believe it's all true, but right now I just don't."

Her lost expression and the pain in her eyes made Russell wish he could give her his own precious salvation, just in order to see her at peace—happy.

"It's all God's timing," he said, more to remind himself than her.

"I know, Grandpa. I just want you to know that I'm trying to understand it all. I want to understand. I can even honestly say that I want to trust God again."

He nodded, closing his eyes. "That's enough for a start. Just give Him a chance, Ashley. He's more than happy to prove himself to you."

"God? Prove himself to me?" Ashley asked in surprise. "But I thought it was the other way around—I thought I was supposed to prove myself to Him by trusting and believing and doing all that other stuff."

"The Bible says that we should 'Taste and see that the Lord is good: blessed is the man that trusteth in him.' See, first it says, 'Taste and see.' In other words, give God a try and see if He doesn't prove to be exactly what He said He'd be. Faith and trust don't come overnight, Ashley. They grow, and just as people need time to get to know one another, so it takes time to get to know God and grow in trusting Him. But blessed are you when you come to that place." He closed his eyes, exhaustion claiming the last bit of his strength.

He felt Ashley kiss his forehead. "You rest now, Grandpa, and I'll be thinking on what you said. I promise."

He drew a ragged breath but said nothing. *Lord, please don't let this time go wasted. Let her hear your words and take courage. Let her come to you and heal her wounded heart. I cannot rest until I know she is safe.*

––––––––

Lavelle stood on the platform waiting for her sister. She squared her shoulders and prepared for the battle to come, believing in her heart that Leticia would come off the train with guns blazing.

She's always been like that, Lavelle reasoned. *She's always been the kind to act first and think later. She never cares who she hurts or how difficult she makes life for someone else. Those things are immaterial.*

Lavelle had never really stood up to her older sister. Leticia had ruled their nursery with an iron will to match that of any adult. Lavelle had just calmly gone along with most any plan Leticia thought up. *But I can't be like that anymore. I need to be strong for Ashley, and I need to stand firm in my faith. Letty won't like it, but that's the way it will be.*

Now Lavelle fretted over the fact that she'd never found an opportunity to tell Ashley that her father had passed away some years earlier. When Lavelle had first arrived, she'd felt certain she'd have to explain it, because Ashley kept talking about her parents and wondering if Lavelle had had contact with them. But there never seemed to be the right opportunity to speak to the matter of Marcus Murphy's death, and so Lavelle had left it unsaid. Now she regretted it, knowing that Leticia would be the one to break the news. And no doubt she'd not do the telling in a gentle manner.

Lavelle knew that Leticia blamed Ashley for her father's passing. Marcus had fretted and worried over Ashley's disappearance—that much Leticia had shared with Lavelle. Letty felt he had worried himself into the grave over Ashley, and she probably held Ashley accountable for the matter. Regret washed over Lavelle. "I should have told her," she whispered.

The westbound Santa Fe passenger train blew its whistle from down the track and Lavelle held her breath. She walked out a pace from the depot and exhaled softly. *Lord, give me strength to deal with my sister. Give me love to shower upon her, even though I don't feel very loving.*

The train pulled in and groaned and ground to a halt. Porters and other railroad men moved into position to make the detrainment as simple and orderly as possible.

And then before Lavelle knew it, Leticia was stepping from the train. She looked for all the world as though she owned not only the train she'd just come from but the land upon which she'd just stepped. Overdressed in an elegant three-tiered bolero coat and dress by Chanel, Leticia demanded attention. The dark red color made Lavelle immediately think of blood, and she couldn't help wondering how her sister would stage the first lethal blow.

"Leticia," Lavelle said, going to her sister. "I'm so glad you've come."

"Is he dead yet?"

The opening thrust of the sword.

Lavelle startled at the question. "No. Our father is still alive. I think perhaps he's been holding on to see you again."

She made a huffing noise and turned to look past Lavelle. "Where is she?"

"Who?" Lavelle questioned, completely taken aback by her sister.

"You know perfectly well. Ashley. Where is she? I suppose she doesn't have the good manners to be here."

Blow number two.

"She stayed home with our father," Lavelle explained. "Someone needed to be there, and I told her I thought it best if she stayed and I came."

"I see. Well, let's not dillydally at the station," Leticia said. "I've come this far; I might as well finish it. I'm sure there's much to be done. I certainly can't count on anyone else to have managed Father's affairs. The incompetence in this family speaks for itself."

The third in what was to become a long line of plunging attacks cut Lavelle to the quick.

"Leticia, before we go, I want to say something." Lavelle lifted her chin and straightened her shoulders. "You were not asked here in order to create a scene. Our father is dying, and I do not wish to see him in any more pain than he's already enduring."

"I don't know what you're talking about." Leticia shifted her matching handbag and stared at her younger sister.

"I'm talking about you. It is my fondest hope that you will be peaceable with Father and with Ashley. They are both suffering in this, and I don't want to see them hurting more than they already are."

"Might I remind you, you are my younger sister. I did not seek your advice. Furthermore, I do not intend to stand here and be dressed down by anyone—but especially not you."

Lavelle bolstered her courage. "Leticia, you're a headstrong and often cruel woman. I won't stand for it this time. You'll either conduct yourself civilly or—"

"Or what?" Leticia laughed haughtily. "You have no power over me. You're as destitute as most of these people." She waved her arm to the departing crowd. "I have enough money to buy and sell you many times over. I'll hire a lawyer if need be, but you won't stand here and threaten me." The woman's dark eyes seemed to blaze with fire.

Lavelle remained calm. "I'm not trying to threaten you. I'm merely stating that our . . ." She paused. She'd started to reference the house as belonging to their father, but that would never do. Better to set the stage early. "Ashley's house is a peaceful one at this point. Father is much beloved in this community, and it would grieve those around him to know his own daughter cared nothing more about him than to cause him even more pain. I want to see him die in peace."

Leticia pushed past her sister. "And I'm just ready for him to die."

———————

E. J. was relieved to have the workday behind him. He had thought to go to check up on Ashley and her grandfather but remembered that her mother was coming to town today. Her mother was the one person who very well might remember him. He couldn't risk running into her—not just yet.

He whistled and made his way to his room at the Harvey House. He hoped to simply spend the night reading his Bible and praying. There was still the matter of telling Ashley the truth, and he hoped he could keep his courage to do so by drawing closer to God.

"Mr. Carson, wait up!"

He turned to find Natalie running after him. "I drew you a picture at school today." She waved the folded paper as she approached.

"Why, that was very kind. What is it? The meteorite crater?"

"Nope. This is the house I'm gonna build my mama someday."

She came to a halt in front of him, her pigtails resting down her back. He took the paper from her and opened it. There, in a very detailed manner, was the house he'd once designed for his wife. Of course, it was an amateur attempt, but he easily recognized it.

"Do you like it?"

E. J. nodded. "I like it very much, Natalie. Thank you."

"Sure," she grinned. "I think my mama likes you."

E. J. was taken aback. "Why do you say that?"

"Well, she sure never took trips with anyone else. I think she only let you take us to the meteor crater because she likes you."

"I think she likes you," E. J. teased. "I think that's the reason she allowed the trip."

"Well, she liked me before and we never let Mr. Morgan take us to the meteor crater." With that, she turned to go. "I have to get home. My grandma is coming today. I've never met her, but I sure hope she's nice."

E. J. waved good-bye. "I hope she is too, Natalie." It was a sincere wish, but remembering Leticia Murphy, E. J. wasn't at all encouraged to believe Natalie's hopes would come true.

He took the picture with him and made his way to his hotel room. He couldn't imagine what Ashley must be enduring, seeing her mother for the first time in so very long. He wished he could be there for her— to offer support and to stand ready to defend her against her mother's meanspirited blows.

"God, you're the only one who can intercede in this. Please don't leave Ashley alone."

He smoothed out the drawing on his desk and traced the lines with his index finger. Memories flooded his mind, and before he knew it, E. J. had taken up his own sketch pad. Within a few moments, he'd drawn a rough outline of the house. Standing there, hunched over the picture, E. J. realized how very much he'd missed creating beautiful things. He felt his demons leave him—at least momentarily—as he sketched out more and more detail. Perhaps this had been the answer all along. Maybe in his creativity—his passion for beauty—he could find a way to dispel the darkness in his life.

"A little light can make itself quite evident in the blackest night," he murmured.

CHAPTER SIXTEEN

*A*shley watched her mother scrutinize the house as Pastor McGuire carried her luggage upstairs.

"It's rather what I expected," her mother said, sounding very bored.

Without elaborating on her comment, Leticia turned her sights on Ashley. "I see you haven't changed much. I understand you have a child. Is she legitimate? Who's her father?"

Ashley raged inside at the question of her daughter's legitimacy. "She's Ethan's daughter, of course. I've never remarried."

"I don't recall you mentioning that you were with child when I last saw you in Baltimore."

Ashley barely held on to her anger. "I don't recall being given a chance. You were, as I recall, far more focused on getting my marriage annulled than knowing the truth of the situation."

"Well, it's of no matter. No decent man would have you now— especially with a brat." Leticia lifted her chin and looked left and then right. "This is an awfully small house. I understand from Lavelle that you're the owner?"

Ashley looked at Lavelle and then back at her mother. "That's right."

"Humph."

"Natalie should be home any minute. I do hope you'll be kind to her," Ashley said, trying hard to stand firm without resorting to her mother's nasty tactics.

"She's a darling child, Leticia," Lavelle interjected. "You'll be pleased to have her as a granddaughter." She stood close to Ashley.

Ashley narrowed her eyes, watching her mother's every change of expression. It was rather like watching a rattlesnake prepare to strike.

What would the woman do next? Where would she attack?

"Where is my father?" Leticia asked, surprising Ashley.

"His room is at the end of the hall. But before you visit him, I want you to understand something." Ashley bolstered her courage. "Grandpa has advanced liver cancer. He's in a tremendous amount of pain. You were notified to come at his request." She hoped her mother understood the implication that she had not been brought here because of Ashley's desire. "He cannot be up and about. He doesn't eat, and he has been given pain medication, though he often refuses to take it because he desires to think in a clearheaded manner.

"It's Grandpa's desire to put the past behind us. I'm willing to at least give pretense to that, for his sake," Ashley said, her voice unemotional. "I would like to know your intentions toward that matter."

Leticia looked at her daughter as if she'd suddenly grown horns. "I don't think that merits an answer. You are my child. I do not answer to you."

Ashley stepped between her mother and the hall leading to her grandfather's room. "Until I understand if you mean to cause him more pain and suffering than he's already enduring, you are not going to be allowed to visit with him."

"Of all the stupid, disrespectful—"

"I agree with her, Letty," Lavelle said. "Father is in no condition for one of your scenes. He has no money—no possessions—nothing monetary to advance your position whatsoever. If you're here for that, you might as well turn around and head back to Baltimore."

Ashley watched her mother's face contort. Her eyes blazed with anger and hatred. "Do not make me seek help from other sources in dealing with you two. As I told Lavelle, I have more money and power than either of you could ever hope to know. I will do what I have to in order to ensure that things are properly handled."

"Grandpa has already turned matters over to his lawyer, Simon Watson. If you have questions regarding the business of Grandfather's estate, then you will talk to him and not to Grandpa. That is how it will be," Ashley replied sternly. "Otherwise, I'll have you removed from this house—my house."

The battle lines were drawn.

"Mama, I'm home!" Natalie declared, coming through the front door.

Leticia turned, apparently startled at the sound of the child's voice. Ashley watched as she studied Natalie's pixielike face. She was such a delicate and tiny child, and for a moment Ashley wanted to rush between her mother and Natalie to protect her from whatever vile things Leticia Murphy might say.

"She looks just like you," Leticia commented, appearing not to realize her own words.

"Are you my grandma Murphy?" Natalie questioned.

Ashley didn't wait for her mother to comment. "Yes, Natalie. This is my mother—your grandmother."

Natalie smiled sweetly. "I'm sure glad you came to visit us, Grandma."

Leticia eyed her suspiciously, then lifted her chin. "Call me Grandmother."

Natalie frowned but only momentarily. "All right. Grandmother."

"I suppose you've had your head filled with all manner of evil when it comes to me and the rest of the family."

Natalie's expression changed to complete confusion. She looked to Ashley as if for an answer. Ashley's heart swelled with pride for her child. She went to stand beside Natalie and gently embraced her.

"I've always stood by the conviction that if you couldn't say something nice about someone, don't say anything at all. I've actually told Natalie very little about my family." Ashley knew she shouldn't speak thusly in front of Natalie, but her feelings were still smarting from the earlier exchange of words.

"She's terribly small," Leticia said, returning her attention to Natalie. "Is she sickly?"

"Not at all," Ashley said.

Lavelle laughed at this and agreed. "She has the energy of ten children her age. I've never seen anyone so in love with life."

Natalie beamed a smile in Lavelle's direction, then turned her attention back to her grandmother. "I have a pony. Her name is Penny. Would you like to meet her?"

Leticia looked rather horrified. "I should say not. I've no time for ponies."

"Your grandmother needs to be with Great-Grandpa," Ashley said, squeezing her daughter's shoulders. "Remember, I told you she would probably have very little time for us. Grandpa hasn't long, and we want her to spend as much time with him as possible."

Natalie nodded somberly. "I remember."

"Why don't you go change your clothes and then take care of

Penny? Maybe later at dinner, you and Grandmother can talk some more."

"Sure, Mama." Natalie darted off for the stairs without another word.

Ashley waited for her mother's painful comments. She didn't have long to wait.

"She doesn't look old enough to be the child of that Reynolds man."

"Well, she is," Ashley stated flatly. "I left Baltimore and went to live with Grandpa in Los Angeles and moved here shortly before Natalie was born. We've had a good life here, and the folks who know us love and adore Natalie. I don't intend to see you hurt her." Ashley hadn't meant to let the latter statement slip out, but now that it had, she intended to stand her ground.

"I'm going to check on Father," Lavelle said, looking as if she wanted Ashley and her mother to have a moment alone. She hurried down the hall.

"I know you don't want to be here. Just as I don't want you here," Ashley said flatly. Honesty, blatant and brutal, seemed to be the only way to deal with her mother. "I had hoped your attitude would have changed, but I realized even in your telegram that you had your own ideas to come here and take over. That's not at all how things will be. Grandpa, Natalie, and I have lived very comfortably these last years. I won't allow you to turn our order into chaos. Do you understand me?"

Leticia seemed taken aback but not enough to keep from commenting. "You are still the same stubborn, headstrong child you've always been. You dug your own grave eleven years ago, but you'll not dig one for my father as well. I will take charge of his estate."

"No, you won't."

Leticia's eyes narrowed. "You can't hope to win against me."

Ashley thought of something Grandpa had once told her. Something about all things being possible with God. Was that true? Could she count on God to help her if she called upon Him? *God, if you're listening, I guess I need help now.*

"I don't intend to stand by," her mother continued, "and see you take from me that which is rightfully mine."

Ashley shook her head. "There is nothing here that belongs to you. The house and its contents are mine. Grandpa settled his affairs some time back. He's arranged his own funeral here, with his body afterward being shipped for burial beside Grandma in Los Angeles. His lawyer has the details of his will. His pastor has a finalized eulogy. You may discuss this with either of them, but I will not argue it with you any further."

Ashley turned to go, but her mother seemed determined to have the last word. "You might notice," her mother began, "that your father is not here. That's because he's dead."

Ashley turned back around and drew her hands together. "I'm sorry to hear that." The statement shocked her, but she'd not allow her mother to see her weakened or made vulnerable by this news.

"You should be. You're the one who killed him. He never got over what you did. He died three years ago, his heart still broken at your disappearance."

Ashley saw her mother's face. She seemed delighted—almost expectant. It was almost as if she thrived on the telling of bad news. Shaking her head, Ashley replied, "I won't accept any blame in his death, Mother. If there is someone to blame, you might consider yourself. Your negative temperament and bitterness would be enough to kill anyone living close to you."

With that, Ashley went quickly to the kitchen and out the back door. She heard her mother's gasp of surprise but didn't care. The news of her father's death had been a shock, but nothing that she couldn't bear. Everyone died, she reminded herself. Ethan, Grandpa, and now her father. Everyone died.

————

That evening, after a most uncomfortable dinner, Ashley took up her week's worth of mending and sat down to relax in the living room. She'd laid logs in the fireplace earlier and now a fire roared in welcome from the hearth. She loved quiet evenings like this, and usually Grandpa was with her. Now there'd never be any more nights with Grandpa telling stories from his boyhood. There'd never be moments of Natalie stretched out before the fire, watching as Grandpa spoke in his animated way, her eyes wide with the wonder of his memories.

Even her mother's animosity couldn't ruin the memories of those times for Ashley. She smiled and picked up her needle and thread. With Natalie and Lavelle taking an evening stroll and her mother visiting with Grandpa, Ashley had a few moments alone to contemplate the day's events.

Her mother hadn't changed, nor had Ashley expected she would have. Ashley wanted very much to ask about her brothers and if they'd married or had families, but she couldn't yet bring herself to even attempt the questions. Somehow, she knew her mother would use it against her. She could detect weakness in Ashley through her curiosity . . . and even her caring.

Ashley loved her brothers and had always wished to have maintained communication with them. She'd been their darling little sister, much as Natalie was a darling to the people of Winslow. They had doted on her and given her much attention. No doubt her mother had corrupted their feelings toward her. They probably blamed her for their father's death as well.

Sighing, Ashley picked up one of Natalie's blouses and began to mend a tear in the sleeve. The child was always getting a tear here or there. Humming one of the hymns they'd sung at church on Sunday, Ashley felt a bit of contentment wash over her. What were the words to that song? She remembered at least the first line—it was the same as the Scripture quoted by the pastor. "Let not your weary hearts be troubled."

Her heart was weary. So weary of the load she'd had to bear alone all these years. It was hard to deal with the way her family had turned away from her . . . to bear Ethan's death . . . to raise Natalie alone.

But you were never alone, she chided herself. *Grandpa has been here all along. How very ungrateful I am acting. Yes, I wish Ethan would have been here, but he wasn't and Grandpa was, and I cannot discredit the love of that old man.*

God had made provision. The thought startled her. Grandpa was always telling her this. Always commenting that God had never left her to bear the past or the future alone. Could God truly buffer her from her mother's harsh and bitter ways?

Grandpa said the key was in forgiving. Forgiving people even when they didn't deserve to be forgiven. "It releases you," he had told her. "It sets you on a journey of freedom, and whether the other person involved desires that same freedom or not, forgiveness has a way of lifting you above the mire that weighs you down on the road of life. If the other person wants to stay back in the mud—you can't very well force them to leave it."

She thought on those words while moving the needle in and out of the blouse. She'd learned so many skills over the last decade. She was nothing like the scared girl she'd been. Was it possible that God truly had been there all along, helping her each step of the way, giving her exactly what she needed—when she needed it? Was this the next thing she needed? Forgiveness?

"You need to forgive your mother and father," Grandpa had told her. "They were wrong in the way they treated you, but you were wrong too. You went against them and dishonored them by refusing to obey. True, you were an adult, but you were still under your father's authority, and you should have sought a different way of resolution."

Ashley knew it was true. She'd married Ethan in such a whirlwind—as much from a wish to defy her parents' plans as from her own emotions and desires. She had taken great pride in putting her parents in their place and asserting her own authority. That attitude had been wrong. She knew that now.

"He's asleep," her mother stated matter-of-factly.

Ashley had been so deep in thought that she'd not even heard the woman come into the room.

"Yes, I would imagine so. It's been a big day for him," Ashley said softly. "I'm sure it pleased him greatly to have you come." *I can do this,* she thought. *I can be kind and gentle tempered. I can forgive her for Grandpa's sake.*

"He said little. He was in a drugged stupor most of the time."

"The pain is so great," Ashley said, looking at her mother's expression to gauge whether she was really listening. "He doesn't want to take the morphine, but he needs it. It clouds his thinking, however, and leaves him unable to communicate as he would like. You'll have a better time of it in the morning."

Her mother crossed the room and looked out the front window. "It's really of no matter. It's obvious the old man is not in his right mind and probably hasn't been for some time. He mentioned giving you this house. Is that true?"

Ashley straightened uncomfortably. "Yes. It's true."

"Well, that won't do. We'll sell it once he's gone. The money will be divided between Lavelle and myself." She turned to Ashley. "The same goes for the household goods. I know you had no money when you came here. You may have purchased things over the years with your waitressing salary, but you could never have afforded to do so had he not provided room and board. Therefore, everything will be sold."

"No, Mother, it won't be," Ashley said flatly. She looked at her mother, challenging her to contradict her statement.

"My lawyer will see to it. You'll have no say in the matter."

Ashley went back to her sewing as if to prove to her mother that she was unconcerned. "I'll leave it in the hands of Mr. Watson, our lawyer.

He warned us you might try something like this and he's already prepared."

"Warned you, eh? Probably because he knew of the lack of legal standing."

"Mother, you live in wealth and plenty. You have nothing to gain by spending any of your money on this matter. This house wouldn't bring even a pittance of the price it will cost you to battle for it. As for the furnishings . . . again, they are mostly secondhand or inexpensive pieces we've acquired over the years."

"I don't care. I want what is mine."

Ashley was quickly losing the ability to control her temper. "You got what was yours and then some many years ago. Grandpa told me all about it." She looked up to catch her mother's face contort in anger. "He said emphatically you were to have nothing else."

"The nerve of you both! You've done nothing but cause me pain and suffering. I received only what I deserved when that old man decided to sell out to religion. He owed me every cent he gave me."

"You had already married and married well, I might add. Grandpa owed you nothing. He wasn't in this world to cover the cost of your lifestyle. How can you be so cold and calculating in this? Your father is dying. His last wish was to have you and Aunt Lavelle come and see him, and all you can think about is whether there is some trinket or bauble you might sell. What a sad thing. What a very sad person you've become."

"I demand you be silent! You have no right to speak to me like this. You're a hateful woman, just as you were eleven years ago. I'm glad I took matters into my own hands when the truth came out."

Ashley looked at her mother's reddened face and the ugly scowl fixed on her expression. "What are you talking about?"

"Your husband."

Ashley felt her heart skip a beat. For a moment she wasn't sure she could draw enough breath to reply. "What about him?"

"He's alive. At least he was in the summer of 1919." Her mother smiled smugly. "But I told him you were dead. Told him you'd died in the epidemic."

Ashley gasped for air. "I don't believe you."

"Oh, you should. He showed up all scarred and ugly from war. He was never much to look at before, but now he was less to look at. Apparently he'd had a good portion of his face blown away."

Her mother shook her head and smiled. "I couldn't see you wanting him after that. Besides, as far as I was concerned, you were dead to me."

Ashley felt the truth of it sink in. Her mother wasn't lying—she was taking far too much satisfaction from this for it to be a lie. "He's alive?"

"I'm sure I cannot say. I certainly did nothing to keep tabs on him. I sent him packing, as you should have done in the beginning."

Ashley carefully gathered up her things and systematically put them into her sewing box. Getting to her feet, she stood trembling. "I was trying hard to do what Grandpa had suggested and forgive you for your cruelty and vicious nature." She stared at her mother's self-satisfied expression and wanted nothing more than to banish her from the house, but for Grandpa's sake she would let her stay. "But I'll never forgive you for this."

She walked to the arched doorway and turned.

"So long as you do nothing to cause harm to Natalie or Grandpa, you may stay here. But—"she paused to draw a deep breath—"do even one thing—one thing, Mother—to hurt either of them as you've hurt me, and you will rue the day you came to Winslow."

Ashley walked to the stairs in a methodical, mechanical manner. She climbed and with each step the words reverberated in her brain.

Ethan's alive.

CHAPTER SEVENTEEN

ews of the stock market crash in New York trickled in with the passing of each new train. E. J. listened to the comments of railroad officials as they spoke with Mary Colter about their thoughts on the matter.

"This is a passing problem," one man assured Mary as they moved
out to the depot platform, where everyone but E. J. expected to catch
the awaiting westbound train.

"The railroad is secure. We'll weather the storm," another man
added. "We made some very good business decisions months ago, and
it leaves us in good stead, unlike some of the other lines. We'll ride
out this problem as we have every other storm."

"So you do not see this creating a problem for the hotel we're
building?" Miss Colter questioned.

Her gaze scrutinized each man at length. E. J. almost believed the
woman to be capable of reading minds for the truth. The thought
made him smile, but he quickly lowered his face so that no one would
believe him less than serious about the situation.

"No, I don't think there is anything to worry about. We've invested
heavily in this hotel. Plans are even set in motion to move the present
Harvey House next door. It will have to be plastered and covered in
stucco to match the décor, of course. McKee Construction Company
assures me that this can be done with relative ease. Not only that, Miss
Colter, they assure me the hotel will be completed on schedule. They
still give December 15 as the completion date, despite this stock market nonsense."

"Good," Mary said, then turned to E. J. "I want you to make sure
those northern balconies are properly fitted with the wrought-iron
rails. Remember the problems we had on the west side? See that we

aren't repeating history."

E. J. nodded. "I'll see to it."

The conductor called for final boarding, and E. J. bid the trio good-bye. He turned to go back to work, relieved to be left behind. The business dealings were of very little interest to him. In fact, since sitting down to sketch out the house he'd promised to build Ashley, E. J. knew his desire lay in creating. He wanted to become more heavily involved in design work—in the actual laying out of plans. That wasn't something he was likely to get a hand at working with Miss Mary Elizabeth Jane Colter. Miss Colter let no one come between her and her creations. The intelligence, creativity, and drive of the woman was positively daunting, but she operated much like a one-man band. Oh, she had workers and assistants. She had "her boys," but she was the queen of her kingdom and that left little room for E. J.'s own creativity. Perhaps this would be the last time he worked for Mary Colter—perhaps he'd remain in Winslow and develop his own company, a company he could pass on to his daughter.

E. J. had nearly reached the Harvey hotel building site when he heard Natalie calling his name. She crossed Second Street with only the briefest pause, then hurried to where he stood. Across the street, a man rather stocky in build paused for a moment, as if watching Natalie and E. J. There was something familiar about the man, but his hat was pulled low and it was impossible to see his face. E. J. wondered what the man wanted and thought to hail him over, but as if realizing he was being watched, the man darted away, leaving E. J. feeling rather uncomfortable.

"I'm glad you stopped by. I have something for you," E. J. told Natalie. He reached into his pocket and pulled out the rolled-up drawing. "I did this from the drawing you gave me."

Natalie put her book satchel down on a nearby rock and took the drawing from E. J. She unrolled it carefully, as though she'd been given a great treasure map. "Oh, it's wonderful. It's even better than the one my mama has."

E. J. smiled. He'd embellished a few things here and there. Things he thought might work better than the original plan. Things he and Ashley had considered changing after the original drawing was made. "Do you like it?"

"I do, very much," Natalie admitted. "I'm going to keep this in a special place."

"I don't think you should show your mama just yet. Since your daddy drew the last picture, we wouldn't want to make her sad."

Natalie nodded in complete agreement. "Grandmother is making her sad enough. I wouldn't want to make Mama cry again."

"Your grandma made your mama cry?" E. J. felt a tightening in his gut. He knew how very destructive Leticia Murphy could be. After all, she was the one who had told him Ashley was dead to begin with.

"My grandmother isn't being very nice," Natalie said, frowning. "I don't know why. She talks real mean sometimes and it hurts my mama's feelings. Mama's sharing my room 'cause she gave her room to Grandmother. Mama doesn't know I heard her crying last night. She thought I was asleep. I heard her say something about never forgiving Grandmother for what she'd done. I don't know what Grandmother did, 'cause Aunt Lavelle and I took a walk, and I think whatever she did happened while we were gone."

E. J. chilled in the afternoon air. What had Leticia done to Ashley? Had she confessed the fact that she'd lied when Ashley's husband came home from the war? The thought left him cold through and through. He had to find a way to let Ashley know the truth. This had gone on entirely too long, and if Leticia was the one to break the news, it would make Ashley believe he no longer loved her—that he hadn't even cared to look for her. But maybe if Leticia had told Ashley of his showing up that day in 1919, she would also confess to telling him that Ashley was dead.

"I have to get home. Mama wants me to help her with supper. I sure wish I could invite you to come, but Mama said it was best not to have extra guests right now."

"And she's absolutely right," E. J. said. "Your mother has a great deal on her mind and an entire household of people to care for. I'm sure we'll have time to share supper in the future."

Natalie tucked the drawing into her skirt pocket and skipped away. "I'll see you tomorrow," she called over her shoulder.

She was gone from sight before E. J. realized her books still sat on the rock at his feet. He picked the satchel up and quickly crossed the street and headed down the sidewalk in the direction of Natalie's house when he noted the same stocky man from before—only this time he appeared to be slinking along in the shadows. E. J. couldn't tell if the man was watching Natalie or himself. He thought to call to the man, but just then Natalie came running from the opposite direction. When she saw E. J. she called out.

"I forgot my books!"

He smiled nervously and held up the satchel. "I know. I thought I'd bring it to you."

When he glanced over his shoulder to see if the stranger was still there, he found only an empty place in the doorway where the man had hidden himself only moments before. E. J. felt a sickening dread in the pit of his belly. It was like being stalked by the enemy, only this was an enemy he didn't know or recognize.

Worse still, what if the man had no interest in E. J. at all but rather was stalking Natalie?

"Natalie, it might not be a good idea to come by the hotel tomorrow. In fact, you might give it a few days before you do. There are some difficult jobs to be done and you might get hurt."

She looked hurt—disappointed in his obvious rejection. "You don't want to see me?"

"It isn't that, sweetheart," he said, hoping she wouldn't take his words so personally. "It's just that some dangerous things will be going on. It would just about break my heart if you were to get hurt."

She shrugged. "Okay. I'll wait until Saturday and come with my mama."

He nodded. "That would be just fine."

She took off again, while E. J. studied every doorway and shadowed corner. The man was nowhere to be found. He struggled to think who the man might be. There was something familiar about him, but E. J. hadn't been able to get a good look.

"God, please protect her," he prayed aloud. "Don't let harm come to my child or my wife."

———

Russell had refused to take any medicine that morning. The pain was excruciating but no more so than the burden he had for his eldest child. "Letty, I'm glad you came to see me. There are some things we need to set straight between us."

"Oh, I certainly agree. This whole nonsense of having given Ashley the house and furnishings is ridiculous. I'll have my lawyer on the case before—"

"Letty, my lawyer has already seen to the transfer. There is nothing for you here." He spoke with a deep pleading in his tone. "Please don't make yourself any more unwelcome than you already are."

"What's that supposed to mean?"

Russell reached out to take hold of her hand, but Leticia pulled away. "Letty, you've made yourself unwelcome in the way you treat people. All your life you've hurt folks and made them feel unimportant. That's not the way you should treat people—especially family. Especially your own child."

Leticia scowled. "You are a foolish man, and I have no intention of letting you ruin my life the way you've ruined your own. This has nothing to do with Ashley. It's only sensible and reasonable that you should settle your estate on your children."

"Which I did nearly twelve years ago. I told you then that I would yield and give you what you demanded." He paused and gasped for breath against the pain. His tone took on a gravelly sound as he continued. "You never could see that the most important, most valued thing I had to give you was my love and the knowledge of what God had done in my life."

"Nonsense!" Her eyes narrowed, and the hateful look on her face made Russell actually cringe. "Love doesn't put food on the table or furniture in the parlor. It doesn't buy the pleasures of life or pay for the problems of it. You may believe whatever you choose, but when your beliefs infringe upon my comfort, then it's time for me to look out for myself. You made choices that changed my life. That was unfair."

"Letty, you were a grown woman with a husband. A wealthy husband, I might point out. I was under no obligation to continue supporting your expensive dreams."

"Humph, and you talk of love. Wouldn't a loving parent desire for his child to have a better life than he had? Wouldn't a parent want to see his child content, comfortable, and well cared for?"

"I might ask you the same thing in regard to Ashley. She's happy here. This has been her home since before she gave birth to Natalie. Now you suggest I take that away from her. Is that love? Or is that simply your way of making clear what everyone knows—that you don't love your own daughter?"

"My daughter stopped loving me the day she went behind my back and married that no-account art student."

"He was an architectural student—soon to be employed by a well-known firm, as I recall Ashley telling me."

Leticia lifted her chin, a habit of defiance Russell had dealt with since she was an infant. "That doesn't make what she did right."

"No. No, it doesn't and I've even told Ashley that. She should have found a better way to deal with you and the problems she felt she had at home."

Leticia looked at her father in disbelief, then quickly masked her surprise. "Well, it's of little matter now. As far as I'm concerned, she made her bed and I owe her nothing."

"Just as I feel you've made your bed, Letty. You insisted on your inheritance long ago, and you received it. I owe you nothing. Fight me if you must, but you won't win. Ashley is well-known and loved in this town—Natalie too. If you bring in your lawyers and fuss about, you'll only cause yourself grief."

"People are always causing me grief. I must fight for what is mine, although I don't expect you to understand. Yes, I have wealth, but I learned a long time ago the only way to keep that wealth growing is to amass more. I've grown wiser through the years."

"I don't see greed and wisdom as the same thing," Russell replied.

Letty's eyes seemed to blaze with a fire all their own. "Call me what you will. Call me greedy—I don't care. The one thing I've learned, the wisdom that has kept me stable when others around me were floundering, is that I must put myself first. I can be of no use to my children or anyone else if I don't take care of myself."

"And has taking care of yourself in turn caused you to be more generous with your children?"

Leticia squared her shoulders. "I've taught them to be self-sufficient."

Russell shook his head. "Something I should have taught you a long time ago. Letty, I've tried to teach you the important things of life, but they've eluded you. You are selfish and greedy. I honestly thought that your reaction all those years ago was due to fear—fear of the money you would lose—fear that you might have to change your life-style." He gasped for air and closed his eyes momentarily. *God, give me strength. I have to try to make her see.* He opened his eyes slowly.

"Letty, the people in your life are far more important. You can always make more money. Even if you lose it all, you can find a way to make more."

"It didn't work that way for you. You live in poverty here," Leticia replied snidely.

"I made as much as I wanted to make," Russell replied. "We didn't need a great deal of money to be happy. We had one another."

Leticia's expression fell momentarily and she looked away. Russell felt sorry for her and tried to reach out to her. She would have no part of that, though, and crossed her arms tight against her chest.

"Happiness, Letty . . . true happiness isn't found on the pages of a bank ledger or in the number of jewels you can call your own. Possessions are temporary and never last."

"You don't know what you're talking about, old man." She eyed him with contempt. "You're only saying this hoping that I'll change my mind. Well, I won't. I intend to have what belongs to me."

Russell gave up. "You may not recall it, but you and your husband both signed certain legal documents when I gave you your inheritance."

Leticia frowned. "What documents? I don't remember any such thing."

Russell eyed her seriously. "I had papers drawn up that you signed in order to receive your bank drafts. You agreed to take your inheritance at that time and seek no further compensation from me."

"I recall nothing of the kind."

"Go see my lawyer, then. He has a copy of the agreement you signed, as well as a copy of your sister's. You should also reread the clause that states that should you seek to benefit from any additional part of my future estate, you will forfeit the original agreement—and all monies and articles given to you as inheritance, which are also listed there, will be returned within thirty days of the condition being broken."

Leticia gasped. "I . . . I would never have signed such an agreement."

Russell knew she would take such an attitude. He had expected it twelve years earlier and he expected it now. "You did sign it. In fact, you had your lawyer go over the paper and agree to the terms. Letty, it's finished. You need to let go of this madness that you can somehow milk another dime or dollar from me. What I have accumulated since then has gone to Ashley and Natalie. Try to take it from them, and my lawyer will see you fulfill the requirements of a forfeited contract."

"You conniving old man! I . . . well . . . I will see to it . . ." Her words trailed off in sputters and gasps as if she were a fish out of water.

"Letty, there is one thing I want to share with you." His voice sounded firm and clear. Russell silently thanked God for strength and now prayed for the words to share his heart.

She perked up at this and leaned forward. "What is it?"

"Jesus."

She rolled her eyes and shifted in her chair. "Do not start that drivel with me. I've lived quite well without any religious nonsense touching me. I see no need for a religious crutch to support me."

"Letty, money isn't everything. I know from experience. It can buy you some good times and some comfort—for a while. But after that, it can also be a noose around your neck, a burden. What happens when it's no longer there—when you have nothing else to turn to?"

"That isn't going to happen," she said in a smug, self-confident tone.

"Letty, I want to tell you a story. There was this man, see. He was a wealthy man and he had just about everything a guy could want. His house was full of things and his fields were full of crops. In fact, his harvest was so great that he couldn't begin to get everything in the many barns he had for storage. So instead of sharing his good fortune and blessing others with what he'd been given, he chose instead to build a bigger barn."

"That's only prudent. A wise man, indeed," Leticia responded.

Russell shook his head and tears came to his eyes. "No, Letty. He was greedy and selfish. He didn't care that he could help anyone else. He thought only of himself and how he could continue to prosper."

"Again, he was only being smart," Leticia said. "He was storing up the things he would need for his comfort later."

"Letty, that night the man's soul was required of him. He died." She looked taken aback but said nothing. "His money and stored goods could not keep him from facing the eventuality that we all have to face sooner or later—death. Letty, what will you do when that happens to you? What good will your wealth do you when you are the person lying on the sickbed, waiting to die?"

"My money will buy me a decent doctor and hospital, for one."

Russell shook his head. "Letty, everyone has to die. It's appointed to man to die once. But if you die without Jesus as your Savior, you'll die a second death."

"Listen to yourself. How ridiculous you sound. Second death. Yes, I realize everyone dies sooner or later." She got to her feet. "I never said I would live forever."

"But you can," Russell said softly, his strength giving out. "With Jesus you can live forever."

"I didn't buy into this nonsense twelve years ago, and I'm certainly not buying into it now."

Just then Russell's door flew open. Ashley stood there, looking rather stunned. "I just heard some news. Apparently something terrible has happened in New York with the stock market. Some people have lost everything, and rumor has it several banks have collapsed. There are even reports that grown men threw themselves from the windows of their buildings and killed themselves."

Russell watched the color drain from his daughter's face. "Where's the telegraph office?" she demanded. "Where's a telephone? I have to talk to your brother."

Ashley stood back as her mother rushed through the door. Russell thought Ashley looked quite alarmed. "Child, this isn't that worrisome for us. We sold our stock, remember? We'll be just fine."

Ashley came to him and offered him a drink. "I know, but I just feel this sense of dread. Like the world has come to an end."

"For some folks, it has," he said softly. "But for others, it might just be the new beginning they've been waiting for."

"What if Mother has lost all her money?"

Russell smiled. "Then maybe there will be hope for her too."

*T*hree days later, Ashley stood with Natalie at her side while Leticia read the results of the stock market crash on her holdings.

"The news is more devastating than I could have imagined. Mathias says that we might well be ruined." She looked up in disbelief. Her hand shook, causing the telegram to flutter.

Ashley thought of her brother Mathias and his work with the banks. What would this mean for him? "Does he say how this will affect his job?"

Her mother looked at her rather dumbly, then frowned. "I have no idea, and frankly, I don't care. This isn't about Mathias; it's about the family fortune. We stand to lose everything."

"I'm sure this will come around right," Lavelle said, reaching out to gently touch her sister's arm.

Leticia jerked away. "This is not going to come around right. The other telegrams from Mathias are just as bad. There were even runs on some banks. This is terrible. We must go to the bank and see what funds we can pull out."

"Perhaps it wouldn't be such a good idea to panic," Lavelle stated. "After all, the crash happened several days ago."

"Stupid hick town. If I'd stayed in Baltimore, I would have known about this. I might have been able to save my stocks, and then I wouldn't be facing ruin. Mathias probably tried to reach me prior to this but simply couldn't locate me."

Ashley had no idea what to say. She couldn't muster up a single ounce of sympathy for her mother. Over and over, the only words she could hear in her mind were the ones that spoke to Ethan being alive. Ashley still hadn't figured out what she was going to do about that situation. She needed to talk to someone—to be counseled on how to go about searching for her husband.

Her mother's ranting grew to a louder volume still. "None of you understand because you had nothing to begin with!"

Ashley thought of the money her grandfather had the lawyer deposit into the bank for her and Natalie. Were the funds still safe? She supposed she should talk to the lawyer. But on the other hand, her mother was partly right—they'd never had that much to begin with. If suddenly her money were all gone, Ashley knew she'd simply go back to work and continue to support them as best she could.

"Letty, you must calm down," Lavelle insisted. "This isn't going to do you any good."

"I can't calm down." Leticia used the telegram like a fan. "This is the worst thing that has ever happened to me."

The worst thing that ever happened to me was losing my husband, Ashley thought. But immediately that idea was canceled out. *No, it is worse knowing that he is alive and thinks I am dead.*

"Grandmother . . ." Natalie left Ashley's side and went to Leticia. "We just need to pray. God will take care of us."

Without warning the old woman slapped Natalie full across the face. The child instantly began to cry and ran to Ashley's arms. Ashley was stupefied. "How dare you? She's just a little girl."

"Oh, Leticia, you shouldn't have done that. She's only trying to help," Lavelle declared. "She's right. We must pray and trust God to take care of us."

"You and your stupid God nonsense. This is ridiculous. First Father and now all of you. God couldn't care less about me. He's proven that on more than one occasion."

Ashley cringed and pulled her sobbing child closer. The words could have been her own, and they left a bitter taste in her mouth. Stroking Natalie's head, she felt a deep offense and sense of protectiveness toward her child.

"I think you'd be wise to pack your things and move into a hotel," Ashley said. Her tone caused both her mother and aunt to look at her. She pulled Natalie with her toward the stairs. "You are unwelcome here, Mother. Aunt Lavelle, please help Mother make other arrangements. You may visit Grandfather but only with my approval."

Natalie cried all the way to her room, and it wasn't until they were safely behind the closed doors of her daughter's bedroom that Ashley, too, broke into tears. "I'm so sorry, baby. She should never have done that." Ashley felt the pain of a lifetime wash over her.

"Why is she so mean and angry?" Natalie asked, sobering at her mother's tears.

"I don't know," Ashley said as she sat down on the bed. She opened her arms to Natalie, who quickly fell into her mother's lap. Ashley saw the angry red welt on her daughter's cheek, the outline of her mother's handprint. She longed to go downstairs and pay her mother back in kind. Why should a little child have to suffer?

Natalie hugged her mother close. "I'm glad you're sending her away. She isn't nice and she makes Grandpa sad." She straightened up and looked Ashley full in the face. "Everything has been hard since she came here. Maybe you and Grandmother are right. Maybe God doesn't care."

The words pierced Ashley's heart. "No!" she exclaimed, not meaning to startle her child. "Your grandmother is wrong. God does care."

"Do you really believe that, Mama?" Natalie searched her mother's face. "I mean, God is letting Grandpa die and Grandmother's lost all her money. Nothing good is happening to us . . . just bad stuff."

Ashley thought of the news that her husband, Natalie's father, was alive. He was out there somewhere living his life without them. Maybe he'd even remarried. After all, it'd been eleven years. The idea that Ethan might have a life without her hurt Ashley so badly she couldn't even speak the words. So while it was good news, it was bad as well. Ashley certainly couldn't tell Natalie about it and give her false hope, but there had to be something positive she could tell the child.

"Natalie, I don't think our life is just bad stuff. Grandpa has given us this house and—" she looked toward the door and lowered her voice—"and a great deal of money. We will be just fine."

"But if Grandmother lost all her money, couldn't we lose all of ours?"

"I don't know, but even if we do," Ashley assured her, "God will take care of us." For once, Ashley actually believed it. She felt a quickening in her spirit that gave her a lightness she'd not felt in years. "God gave you to me in the darkest hour of my life, Natalie." She gently touched her daughter's cheek. "I know God cares for us, or He would never have done such a wonderful thing."

Natalie wrapped her arms around Ashley's neck. "I'm so glad you think God cares for us. I think He does too. I guess I was just scared, but I know God is good."

"Then don't let your grandmother's ugliness take away your hope and faith in Him. Grandmother's acting out of fear. She doesn't know how to trust God."

Natalie pulled away and looked up with an expression of expectation. "Do you know how to trust God, Mama?"

Ashley smiled and nodded. "I think I'm learning."

———————

With her mother and Lavelle out of the house, Ashley went to sit with her grandfather. The old man slept fitfully, finally waking just a few minutes after Ashley took a seat beside him. The past few days had taken their toll on him, and Ashley knew it wouldn't be long before he gave up the fight. His labored breathing seemed to echo throughout the room. Ashley found herself trying to breathe with him—for him.

"Ashley," he murmured. Gone was any pretense of strength.

"Grandpa, I know the time is short," she said, remembering what Pastor McGuire had said about needing to be open and honest with a dying person. "Grandpa, I love you. I love you so much. I don't know what I'll do without you."

"God—Ashley. God will be everything you need."

"Grandpa, I want to believe that. I think God has been working on me." Ashley thought she noted a hint of a smile on Grandpa's lips as she continued. "Grandpa, Mother told me something very painful. She lied to Ethan and it set into motion an entire lifetime of sorrows. Ethan's alive, but I don't know where. He came home from the war— apparently there had been a mistake and he hadn't died on the battle-field."

"But that's . . . good," Grandpa gasped.

"Yes and no. Mother told Ethan I was dead. She told him I'd died in the influenza epidemic. He probably thought it made sense. After all, my letters stopped because I thought he was dead."

"Oh, Ashley."

"Grandpa, I want to forgive her, but she's forever altered my life. I could have had a life with Ethan. He could have been there for Natalie—for me. I know it would have been difficult to find me here with you, but she could have at least told him I was alive." She began to cry. "I can't believe he's out there somewhere. I can't believe he's alive but not a part of our lives here. How could she be so cruel? I hate her for what she's done.

"And not only this thing with Ethan, but she slapped Natalie. She's been vicious and cruel, seeking only her own benefit. She never shows concern for anyone but herself. I look at her and see such hardness—such ill will."

"Give . . . to . . . God."

Ashley nodded. "I want to, Grandpa. I want to give it all to God. I want to do the right thing and know Him for myself."

This time Grandpa did smile. He closed his eyes, his breath rattling in his chest. "It's . . . easy. Just . . . ask."

"I remember what you told me before. Ask for forgiveness and ask Jesus to take over my life. I did that before I came in here, Grandpa. But even if I allow God to help me forgive Mother, how can I ever forget what she's done? I might never find Ethan again."

"God . . . has . . . a . . . plan."

A shadow passed across the window. Ashley straightened. Perhaps her mother and aunt were returning. She wanted to bar the door and never let her mother back in the house, but she knew she had to allow it—at least until Grandpa was gone.

"You will pray for me, won't you, Grandpa?" Ashley whispered as she looked back to where he lay.

Grandpa said nothing. His breathing slowed, his chest barely moving with each strained gasp. Ashley knew he was fading away—leaving her behind and going to his heavenly mansion, as one of those lovely church hymns spoke of.

Stroking his hand, she began to sing, remembering the words of that hymn. " 'My heavenly home is bright and fair; no pain nor death can enter there. Its glittering towers the sun outshine; that heavenly mansion shall be mine.' " Tears streamed down her cheeks, and her voice caught as she sang the chorus and Grandpa drew his final breath.

" 'I'm going home, I'm going home, I'm going home to die no more; to die no more, to die no more, I'm going home . . . to die no more.' "

She kissed his weathered cheek. "It's all right, Grandpa. You go on home."

CHAPTER NINETEEN

*A*shley was relieved to find it was not her mother who had returned to the house but rather Natalie.

"Sweetie, I have something to tell you," Ashley said as she met her daughter in the hallway.

"Is it about Grandpa?" Natalie asked, seeming to know.

"Yes. He's gone."

Natalie's lower lip quivered. "I know it's a good thing because Grandpa suffered so much, but it feels so bad here inside."

Ashley pulled her into her arms and held her tight. "I know. It hurts me too. But you know what? Grandpa died a happy man. I told him that I'd turned to God and that made him very happy."

Natalie nodded as she looked up. Tears glistened in her eyes. "That's the best news Grandpa could have had. He just wanted to be sure he'd see you again."

"I know. Look, I need a big favor from you."

"What?"

Ashley gently held her daughter's chin. "I need you to run and fetch Mr. Watson. We'll need him here when Grandmother Murphy gets back. You tell him about Grandpa. He'll also know to get the funeral home to come."

"Sure, Mama," Natalie said, straightening. "That's an important job."

"It sure is and one that only you can do for me. I can't leave and do it myself because Aunt Lavelle and Grandmother Murphy might come back and I'll have to tell them about Grandpa."

Natalie nodded somberly, the weight of responsibility combined with great pride. "It's Saturday. Will he be at his office or should I go to his house?"

"Hmm . . . start at the office, since it's so close. Then go to his house if he's not there. I think you should ride Penny," her mother encouraged. "Mr. Watson's house is clear on the other side of town, just off of Douglas."

"I remember," Natalie said. "I'll come right back so you don't have to be alone." She embraced her mother once again, then ran through the house and out the back door.

Ashley fretted that her mother and aunt would return before Mr. Watson had a chance to come and offer his support. She found herself uneasily praying.

"I know I just started turning to you, Lord. And I know I've brought more than my share to you already, but please just get Mr. Watson here before Mother and Lavelle return. I can't bear to face them alone."

With each passing moment, Ashley jumped at every sound. She set out to straighten the living room, knowing that as soon as word got out about Grandpa, people would start showing up to bring food and offer comfort to the family.

When a knock sounded at the front door, Ashley nearly came undone. She hurried to see who had come and found a stranger. The stocky man lifted his hat in greeting. There was something vaguely familiar about him, but Ashley was uncertain where she might have seen him.

"May I help you?"

"I hope so. You are Mrs. Reynolds, are you not?"

Ashley felt an uneasiness come over her. "Yes."

"And you have a little girl. I believe her name is Natalie."

It was then that Ashley remembered the man. He'd been following Natalie on the street. "Who are you and what do you want?"

"I'd just like to talk to you about your husband, Ethan Reynolds— about his war efforts and his death. See, I'm putting together a book . . ."

"I have no time for this," Ashley declared. "We've just had a loss in the family. I'm going to have to ask you to leave." She started to close the door, then pulled it back open. "Oh, and leave my child alone. I've seen you following her and if I see you again, I'll contact the police."

She closed the door and leaned against it momentarily. How could she tell this man anything about Ethan? She didn't know anything. Didn't know where he was or why he was alive instead of dead as the army had told her. Tears streamed down her face. "I can't help you, mister. I can't even help myself."

Half an hour passed and Ashley slowly recomposed herself. She heard a car pull up and stop in front of the house. Looking out the window, Ashley saw a black sedan, and behind it, another car also came to rest. Ashley recognized it as belonging to Pastor McGuire, and in the front seat Natalie sat all prim and proper. Penny was tied to the back. The scene brought a smile to Ashley's face. Natalie seemed to take life and death in stride. She didn't seem to bear any long-lasting grudge against her grandmother, and neither did she seem destined to despair over her great-grandfather's passing. Perhaps she would handle the news of her father's surviving the war as well.

Natalie jumped out and saw to Penny, while Pastor McGuire and Mr. Watson made their way past the wrought-iron gate and up the walkway. Ashley met them at the door. They took off their hats as they walked into the house.

"I'm so glad you're both here."

"Has your mother returned?" Watson asked, peering past Ashley toward the living room. Apparently Natalie had told him of the urgency involved.

"No," Ashley said, taking the men's hats. "I thought for sure she would be back by now. She and Lavelle have gone to the bank, forgetting that it's Saturday. I suppose they've tried to locate the bank president and see what can be done about all this business of last week. I've asked my mother to move out of the house. She struck Natalie, and I have no intention of letting it happen again."

"Struck her?" Watson questioned.

Ashley nodded. "Mother was upset by the telegram my brother sent. It had to do with the stock market troubles."

"Ah, I see." Watson nodded thoughtfully.

"Anyway, Natalie suggested we needed to pray about the matter, and my mother let her nerves get the best of her and she slapped Natalie. I told her to pack and get out. Perhaps that's where they are now. Maybe my aunt is helping Mother arrange to move into the Harvey House."

The men nodded. "We will just wait with you, then," Simon Watson stated matter-of-factly.

Pastor McGuire gently touched her arm. "I know Grandpa's passing is both a relief and a grief."

"Yes, to be sure," Ashley said, drawing a deep breath. "Would you like to see him?"

"Yes. Yes, I would," McGuire responded. "Simon?"

"You go ahead. I'll pay my respects later."

Ashley led Pastor McGuire back to Grandpa's room and closed the door quietly once they'd entered. "I need to tell you something," she said softly, almost reverently, as if God's spirit had settled over the room.

Pastor McGuire looked at her rather oddly. "Oh?"

"I . . . well . . . I prayed." Ashley knew it sounded silly, but she felt completely flustered. "I've taken Jesus as my Savior."

Pastor McGuire grinned. "No wonder Grandpa felt he could finally go. What a blessing that must have been to him—he did know, didn't he?"

"Yes, he knew." Ashley had a great sense of peace about being able to honestly come to God before Grandpa died. "I had thought of just telling him what he wanted to hear. After all, God would know the difference."

"So would Russell Whitman. The man was no fool."

"I'm sure you're right. Like I said, I toyed with the idea, but I could never bring myself to do it. Then I thought of coming to God merely because my mother so thoroughly rejects Him. That hardly seemed right either."

Pastor McGuire's smile broadened. "No, it would never do to come to God in order to spite someone else. It wouldn't be genuine."

"I know. It just seemed that the more trouble came, the less confidence I had in myself or anything else. It hurt to deal with the past and the present, and the future just seemed like a nightmare waiting to happen. I wanted nothing more than peace of mind and heart, but it eluded me at every turn."

"And do you know that peace now, Ashley?"

She looked into his compassionate face and smiled. "I do." She looked back to where she'd left Grandpa. She'd neatly combed his hair and pulled up the blanket to his chest. She'd carefully brought his arms together, and it looked as though he were simply taking his afternoon nap. "I can't imagine life without him."

"Nor can I," the pastor replied. "Good men like Russell are hard to find. We need to cherish them when we come across them."

For some reason Ashley thought of E. J. Carson. He seemed to be such a kind and considerate soul. Always so gentle and loving with Natalie. Perhaps that alone should have endeared him to Ashley. But then there was the issue of Ethan. Somehow she had to know the truth about him.

"Pastor McGuire, there's something else." Ashley swallowed her pride and self-reliance and explained the situation regarding Ethan. She noted the man's expression as it changed from sympathetic to intense concern. "I don't know," Ashley continued, "how to go about finding him. He may be remarried, and how awful that would be, because we're still married—I'm not dead." She knew she stated the obvious, but she needed to hear the words aloud.

Pastor McGuire put his arm around her shoulder. "I'll do what I can to help you. There are records the army keeps and people who can help in this. Don't worry. But tell me, does Natalie know?"

Ashley shook her head. "I don't want to tell her until I'm certain he's still alive. She positively worships his memory. It would be so hard for her to think he'd come back to her, only to lose him again."

"I understand, and I think you're wise. We'll take care of matters with Grandpa, and then we'll get right on this other."

The unmistakable sound of voices in the hall confirmed that her mother and Lavelle had returned. She heard her mother saying something about taking over the matter of her father's burial just before she opened the bedroom door and pushed past Ashley to Grandpa's bedside.

"So he's finally gone," she stated, then looked to Ashley and the pastor as though she'd posed a question.

The pastor maintained his hold on Ashley, and she wondered if he did so out of fear of what she might do to her mother. He gave her a gentle squeeze of support before speaking. "Your father is in a better place now. He's finally out of pain."

"Be that as it may," Leticia said, looking to them again and then to her sister and the lawyer, who had now joined them. "There are matters to be taken care of."

"All the arrangements were made by your father," Simon Watson stated.

Leticia's expression changed to one of smug assurance. "But I am here now and have my own ideas of how things will be handled."

"I'm sorry you feel that way, Mrs. Murphy. Your father stated specifically that I was not to allow you to make any changes in the arrangements. You are, of course, free to return home and not participate in the plans he made. However, there will be no changes."

"I am quite sure—"

"No changes, Mother," Ashley stated, pulling away from the pastor.

"You are in no position to dictate to me." Leticia arched her brow and squared her shoulders. She held the look of a tyrannical queen.

Ashley thought to demand that she leave, but instead she stayed her anger. She didn't know how she was supposed to act or respond as a Christian—not really, but she did know what Grandpa would want her to say, and he was a Christian. She could almost hear him saying, "Be a peacemaker, Ashley."

"Mother, you need to respect Grandpa's wishes. I think you should sit down with Mr. Watson and Pastor McGuire and listen to what they have to say. You too, Aunt Lavelle."

Lavelle nodded and agreed. "I think we should, Letty. Why don't we go out into the living room and talk about this." Lavelle led her sister toward the door.

To her great surprise, Ashley watched as her mother allowed Lavelle to direct her down the hall. Simon Watson followed, with Pastor McGuire bringing up the rear. Ashley glanced back at Grandpa's still figure.

"I wish you were still here to advise me," she murmured.

————

Ashley listened to the lawyer quietly explain the situation surrounding Russell Whitman's last requests and arrangements. Her mother often interrupted to dispute issues, but Simon Watson was no small-town lawyer to be bullied. The man had come to practice in Winslow after a long career in Chicago. Had his wife not needed the dry climate, he might be there still, he'd told Ashley previously.

Tiring of the details she already knew by heart, Ashley dismissed herself to make some refreshments for the group.

"Mama?" Natalie questioned quietly. "Oh, here you are. I thought you'd be out there with Mr. Watson."

"I'm fixing a plate of cookies for our guests. Do you want to carry it out to them and then come back and have a couple for yourself?"

"Sure. Can Penny have something too?"

Ashley took an apple and cut it into four pieces. "You may give this to Penny when you get back."

Natalie picked up the plate of cookies and started to leave. She paused, however, and turned back to Ashley. "We will be all right, won't we?" She dragged the toe of her shoe across the tiled floor.

Ashley saw the apprehension and uncertainty in her daughter's face. The moment reflected the questions in her own heart. "Grandpa said we would be just fine. He said God would take care of us. You believe that, don't you?"

Natalie looked at the floor. "I want to believe, and sometimes I feel really strong. But sometimes, like now, I just don't know. Will God be mad at me?"

Ashley had no idea what to say, but her heart was overwhelmed with love for her child. She reasoned the matter quickly. "Natalie, sometimes bad things happen, right?'' Her daughter nodded. ''And we don't always understand and sometimes they scare us.''

''Like when you found out about Daddy dying?''

Ashley stiffened. ''Well . . . yes. When bad things happen, it's easy to forget that God is there. That's what happened to me all those years. I didn't think God cared about me anymore. But I know now that I was wrong. God does care.'' She felt strength mixed with turmoil. There was no easy answer to give her child, but she wanted very much for Natalie to be at peace. ''Some of this is just as hard for me as for you. I wish I'd listened to Grandpa a long time ago. I wish I'd read my Bible and gone to church, and I wish I knew better what to expect from God. The truth is, I don't know what will happen in the future, but Grandpa told me that God has a plan for us.''

''He told me that too,'' Natalie said. ''And Grandpa never lied.''

Ashley smiled. ''And God doesn't lie either. That much I'm confident of.''

Natalie's expression changed to one of relief. ''That's true—and Grandpa said that Jesus promised to be with us always. So we'll be okay.''

Ashley could see that Natalie now had great satisfaction in this solution. Somehow her daughter's confidence gave Ashley strength. ''Exactly. So you deliver the cookies, and then you can take the apple out to Penny.''

Natalie disappeared and in a few moments she was back collecting her own cookies and Penny's apple. Ashley figured she'd dart right outside, but instead, Natalie posed another difficult question.

''Mama, is Grandma . . . I mean Grandmother . . . going back home now?''

''I suppose after Grandpa's funeral she will. She has no reason to stay here.''

''She doesn't love us, does she?''

Ashley stopped fussing with the coffeepot and looked at her daughter's curious expression. What could she say? There was no way to lie to the child. She already knew the truth of it. Kneeling down, Ashley toyed with her daughter's braid. ''Some people don't know how to love, Natalie. I think Grandmother is one of those people. I don't think she does it because she wants to be mean or hurt people. I just think she's got a lot of anger and bitterness inside and there's no room for love.''

Natalie's eyes widened. ''Just like there's no room for Jesus. Grandpa told me that God is love. He showed me a verse in the Bible that says that. If Grandmother doesn't have any love inside, it's probably because she doesn't have God inside either."

"I suppose that could very well be true," Ashley said, amazed at how insightful her daughter could be.

"Mama, after I give Penny her apple, can I go let Mr. Carson know about Grandpa?"

"Sure. Just be careful."

"Oh, I will. Today was the day we were supposed to go see him anyway. He didn't want me to come by last week because they were doing dangerous things and he didn't want me to get hurt. But when I told him I'd come today and bring you, he said that was okay."

"I can't go with you," Ashley said, almost wishing she could go along. "But you tell Mr. Carson we'll have him to dinner once Grandmother goes back to Baltimore."

"I know he'll like that," Natalie said, grinning. She gave Ashley a kiss, then burst out the back door as if the house were on fire.

Ashley laughed and went back to work on the coffee. That girl never slowed down for more than a second. She put her grandmother's posy-patterned cups and saucers on a tray, then added the sugar bowl and creamer, some napkins and spoons, and finally a china coffee server. She filled the china pot with coffee, then hoisted the heavy tray and made her way to the living room.

Seeing that Simon Watson had the situation clearly under control, Ashley felt a sense of relief. She wondered if she should begin to pour the coffee and glanced at her aunt. Lavelle waved her off and reached for the pot instead.

Sensing that the trio had her mother fairly well managed, Ashley backed out of the room. There was no point in remaining, especially when there was so much work to be done.

Thinking that she should probably get their Sunday clothes ready for the following day, Ashley went upstairs to Natalie's bedroom. She chose her plum-colored dress, knowing that it had been Grandpa's favorite. She wasn't going to wear black to church. She might very well don it for the funeral but not for church.

The thought of a black dress made her smile. *I could always wear my Harvey uniform*, she thought. *Minus the apron, of course.* And then it came to mind that she was now free to go back to work. Free to work for the Harvey Company while she tried to figure out what was to be done about Ethan. She made a mental note to contact her supervisor on Monday.

She rummaged through Natalie's dresses and found a dark green one that seemed serviceable. Ashley hoped to avoid any last-minute ironing and quickly inspected the dress for wrinkles. It appeared quite passable.

She put the dresses aside and went to make sure Natalie had clean socks to wear. Sliding open the top drawer of Natalie's dresser, Ashley noted at least three pairs. She also noted a rolled-up piece of paper. She smiled. No doubt Natalie had been drawing again.

Unrolling the paper, Ashley couldn't help but gasp aloud. There in charcoal, just as it had first been sketched, was the house she had dreamed of building with her husband. Surely Natalie hadn't drawn it. The lines were too perfect—too certain. From the columns to the French doors to the . . .

A strange feeling washed over her as her gaze caught sight of the initials in the right-hand corner. EJC.

Her breath caught in the back of her throat, then released as a low moan. Hurrying from her daughter's room, Ashley threw open the door to her own bedroom. Under the bed was the suitcase her aunt Lavelle had given her so long ago. Ashley knelt down and pulled the case out. Opening it, she searched for what she knew she'd find.

Along with Natalie's baby clothes and other cherished memorabilia was the drawing Ethan had sketched for her so very long ago. She tenderly unfolded the paper and placed it atop the bed. She pushed the suitcase back and got to her feet.

Picking up the drawing, she walked back to Natalie's room and placed the drawings side by side. She already knew they'd be nearly identical. The way the house sat amidst the imagined landscape. The same light fixtures in the portico. Only here and there did Ashley find any real differences, and even then they only served as more conclusive evidence. They were changes she and Ethan had discussed.

Closing her eyes and drawing a deep breath, Ashley prayed, "Oh, God, I'm not very good at this, but please hear me. I . . . what's happening? What does this mean?"

But even as she asked the question, she knew what it meant. She opened her eyes and looked at the initials in the corner of Natalie's drawing. Then she looked at the corner of her own drawing. EJR. Same style of writing with the "R" being the only change.

Without thinking another single thought, Ashley took up both pictures and darted from the room. She raced out of the house so fast she gave no one any indication of where she was going. The sun was setting in the southwest, the blue sky mottled with orange, pink, and yellow. It was a cold sky nevertheless. Or maybe it was just that the world seemed suddenly cold.

Ashley went to the new Harvey resort and marched into the building without slowing. She looked from side to side, seeking E. J. Carson. She found him in the dining room. Holding the drawings behind her back, she fought to steady her voice.

"I need to speak to you . . . in private."

E. J. nodded. "Is something wrong?"

Apparently Natalie hadn't caught up with him yet. Ashley nodded. "Yes. I need to talk to you."

He appeared to catch on to the urgency, for he moved across the room quickly and didn't even stop to talk to a worker who was signaling him. "Come this way. Is Natalie all right?"

"She's fine," Ashley said, the words sticking in her throat. "For now."

He looked at her oddly, but Ashley dropped her gaze. How could this be? How could this man have eaten at her table—walked beside her—and she still not know who he really was?

E. J. led her to a private office. "This is where I usually work. Now tell me what's wrong." He stood directly in front of her.

Ashley raised her head, praying for strength. She held up Natalie's picture. "I found this."

E. J. looked away. "I drew it for her from a drawing she'd given me."

Ashley held up the original. "She sketched hers from this. The drawing my husband did for me eleven years ago." She saw it then. Saw the familiarity behind the glass and wire of his spectacles. She remembered his whistling the same ragtime tune Ethan had loved.

"I don't understand," she said, her voice breaking. "I don't know how it can be that you're my husband and I didn't even recognize you."

"He's not my daddy!" Natalie cried from behind her. "He's Mr. Carson. My daddy died."

Ashley whirled around and saw the look of disbelief on her daughter's face. "Natalie, I . . ."

"No!" Natalie screamed, then ran from the room.

Ashley started to go after her but stopped. If she left now, she'd still have no answers for the child. Her heart pounded as she turned to face the truth. Leaning heavily against the open door, Ashley braced herself.

"Ethan," she breathed his name. "Please tell me how this can possibly be."

E. J. wanted nothing more than to go to his wife and embrace her. He wanted to tenderly hold her, to kiss her and breathe the scent of her hair. Instead, he calmly went to the door and gently took hold of her hand and led her to a chair. He returned to the door and closed it before pulling up a chair in front of her.

"I've only known a short time myself," he said, his voice hoarse with emotion. "Your mother told me you were dead."

"I know."

She spoke the words so softly he wasn't sure if he'd heard them or imagined them. E. J. drew a deep breath. "I was nearly killed in France. An explosion left my face hopelessly mangled, and I suffered several other injuries. They took me to the nearest hospital, where I lost consciousness. When I awoke, my face was completely bandaged, even my eyes. I was terrified. I thought I'd died and this was some sort of eternal holding place. I thought maybe all that stuff I'd been told about God was wrong. See, I'd learned to pray and to trust God during the war, but now I wasn't so sure."

Ashley said nothing. She stared at him as though he were a ghost. Her pale face only served to remind him that while he'd known for some time that she was his wife, Ashley was just now coming to understand that her husband was alive. After eleven years, it had to be more than she'd ever imagined having to deal with.

E. J. leaned forward. "I had to endure several surgeries; that's why I don't look very much like the man you knew me to be. The ordeal left me badly scarred, but at least I could grow a beard to hide most of it.

"After the surgeries, I fought infections. They thought for sure I'd die, but I kept thinking of how I would come home and find you waiting and everything would be all right. I learned the war had ended, but I was still so sick. They nursed me back to reasonable health, then shipped me back to Baltimore. I hadn't been back in the country long before I came down with influenza. Men throughout my ward died, but I kept fighting it—thinking of you—knowing I had to recover. I tried to get in touch with you. I had a couple of different people offer to take you a message, but they were unable to locate you. I figured you'd moved. I thought maybe you'd even gone back to your mother and father's house, but I couldn't really believe that you would."

"I'd moved to Los Angeles and then to Winslow, with Grandpa," Ashley explained. "I'd received word that you were dead." Her eyes filled with tears. "They told me you were dead. The army said you died in battle—that you were a hero."

She sounded desperate, almost as if she needed him to believe her. He did.

E. J. nodded. "I know. I figured that part out."

"I was going to have a baby and my mother was trying to force me to remarry. She didn't know about Natalie—just as you didn't know."

"No, I didn't," he admitted. "When I finally recovered and was released from the hospital, I went to your parents' house."

"Yes, I know." She seemed to regain a bit of strength. "Mother blurted out a confession the other night. See, I hadn't seen or talked to her since leaving Baltimore. She'd disowned me—told me to never try to communicate with her or Father. She came here for Grandpa—he wanted to see her again. Then in the middle of one of her tirades, she just spilled out the truth. She told me she had seen you after the war, that you were alive." Tears flooded Ashley's eyes. "I wanted to die and shout for joy all at the same time."

E. J. knew exactly how she felt. "When I first met you on the street, that day Natalie introduced us, I was sure there had to be some mistake. But there you were, looking so much like you did all those years ago."

"Why didn't you say something then?"

"I couldn't. I . . . well . . . you have to understand, Ashley, I'm not the same man you married."

"What do you mean? You're Ethan Reynolds, aren't you?"

"Yes. I changed my name to avoid dealing with the hero status they were awarding me. People were hounding me. Veterans' groups wanted to hear me speak of defeating the Germans. Ladies' clubs wanted to have me as the guest of honor at their teas. I couldn't handle it. I felt so ashamed of who I'd become in the war. You have no idea of the things I did." He fell silent and looked at the floor as if for answers. "I killed men—boys, really. I killed them even when I didn't have to."

"You were a soldier. You did your duty." Her words were calm and gentle.

"Yes, maybe," he said, still unable to look her in the eye. "But I did it too well."

"I still don't understand why that would delay you in telling me who you were."

E. J. looked up. "Ashley, up until a short time ago, I could hardly stand admitting to myself what the past had done to me—what I'd done to myself. Every night I still have nightmares. The torment and demonic visions that come to me in my dreams are more than I could ever subject anyone to—much less you."

"But that choice should be mine," she said, meeting his gaze. She searched his face, as if to find some scrap of evidence that he was who she knew him to be.

Finally she asked, "How did you come to be in Winslow?"

"After your mother told me you were dead, I didn't care what happened to me. I drifted for a time. I had no desire to live. My parents had died from the influenza as well and I had no home—no one."

"I'm so sorry. If I'd only stayed in Baltimore," Ashley said, looking past him to the wall. "But it was so awful. I was so alone. Mother had disowned me and I was going to have a baby."

"No, don't blame yourself. You did the right thing," E. J. said, reaching forward to take hold of her hand. "You had to think of yourself and Natalie. You thought I was dead. There was no reason to stay in Baltimore and wait around."

"I know, but I just keep thinking of all those wasted years. It was so hard." She didn't seem to notice that he continued to hold her hand. Instead she appeared lost in her memory. "I wanted to die. I wanted to join you wherever you were. I couldn't bear the idea of your being dead. Natalie was the only one to give me a reason to go on. Grandpa tried, but he just couldn't understand. Natalie was a part of you, and in a way, I guess that's why she strengthened me and gave me hope."

Ashley returned her gaze to E. J. "She's everything to me, and now with Grandpa gone . . ."

"Grandpa died?"

She nodded. "Just this afternoon. That's why Natalie was coming here. She wanted to tell you about him. But I found the picture and knew . . . the truth. I didn't even consider that she might overhear us talking."

E. J. squeezed her hand. "I had planned to tell you the day we went to the meteorite crater. I had a speech all prepared, and then your friends joined us and I couldn't tell you. I even thought about telling you on the drive home, but I worried that Natalie might wake up and overhear us."

Ashley shook her head. "I've spent the last few days since Mother told me about you wondering how in the world I'd ever find you again. I worried that you would have remarried and that in finding you I would completely ruin your life. I didn't tell Natalie because I was even afraid you might have died sometime after Mother saw you. I didn't want Natalie to lose her father all over again. She adores you."

"She adores Ethan Reynolds."

"But you are Ethan Reynolds," Ashley said firmly. "No matter what you did in the war and no matter what has happened since, you're Ethan Reynolds . . . my husband." She pulled away from him and put her hands to her cheeks and exhaled loudly. "What do we do now?"

————

The question rang over and over through Ashley's mind. *What do we do now?* Her thoughts were so jumbled—so disjointed. *Ethan is alive, but Ethan is E. J. Carson. My husband is alive, but he's not really my husband at all. We knew each other only a brief time and then he was gone. We have a child. Oh, Natalie, where have you gone off to?*

"I have to find Natalie." Ashley jumped up. "I have to try to explain this to her."

E. J. got to his feet as well. "I'll come with you."

"No, she's too upset. I need to talk to her alone—to try to explain."

But how could she rationally explain any of this to a ten-year-old girl when she could hardly begin to comprehend it herself?

"I want to help," E. J. said. "Is there anything I can do?"

Ashley shook her head. "I can't think of anything—though of course you could pray."

He looked at her with such a mix of compassion and sorrow. Ashley regretted leaving him alone just now, but she couldn't subject Natalie to even more pain. It was clear the shock had been too much for her to handle.

"I'll let you know . . . we can . . ." She fell silent. "I'll talk to you later."

Ashley hurried from the room and made her way outside. It was already growing dark and the chill of the night was upon them. The desert could get so cold at night—so very cold. Ashley felt the urge to run all the way home but fought it. She needed the time to pray and collect her thoughts. What was she going to say to her child? How was she ever going to make Natalie understand?

Making her way inside the house, Ashley found it strangely quiet. A note had been left by Lavelle. Picking it up from the dining room table, Ashley read, *We've gone with the pastor to the funeral home.*

Ashley breathed a sigh of relief. At least it would give her time to deal with Natalie alone. "Natalie!" she called as she went upstairs. She fully expected to find her daughter stretched out across her bed, crying her heart out.

"Natalie, hon," Ashley said, turning on the light. She wasn't there. The bed was still made and the green- and plum-colored dresses were laid across the end just as Ashley had left them.

She searched the rest of the upstairs, but Natalie was nowhere to be found. Flying down the stairs, Ashley searched through the rest of the house. She went to Grandpa's room first, thinking that Natalie might have found it comforting. The sight of the empty bed only served to make Ashley feel alone.

"Oh, Grandpa. If only you were still here."

Ashley thought of Penny and how much Natalie loved the pony. That had to be the answer. Natalie was with Penny. Ashley hurried through the house and out the back door. The screen slammed hard behind her as Ashley called out in the growing darkness.

"Natalie! Natalie, where are you?"

She went to Penny's little corral, but the pony was gone. Searching the stall, Ashley realized the saddle and bridle were also missing. Natalie had taken Penny and ridden off. But to where?

Ashley's heart filled with dread. She thought of all of Natalie's favorite places. Where would she go to hide out and deal with this news? She had her friends and might have gone to see one of them, Ashley thought, but even as the idea came, Ashley dismissed it. Natalie would want to be completely alone.

Surely she wouldn't head out away from town. Ashley looked past the yard off toward the open desert. Night was upon them and the desert was no place to play. Would Natalie be so foolish as to venture beyond the safety of town?

"Oh, God, help me. I don't know where she's gone. I don't know how to find her." Ashley blinked back tears. "She's everything to me, Father. Please don't take her too."

Ashley went back into the house. She had to get help, and Ethan was the only logical one to ask. How could she possibly explain the situation to anyone else? She pulled her sweater out of the closet and was just putting it on when her mother and Lavelle came through the door.

"Where are you off to at a time like this? In fact, where did you disappear to earlier?" her mother questioned.

"I have to find Natalie. She's taken the pony, and I don't know where she's gone," Ashley said, picking her words carefully. She wasn't about to tell her mother about the encounter with Ethan. At least not yet.

"That child runs positively wild. I would give her a sound spanking when she gets home," Leticia said sternly. "You've obviously raised her with little or no discipline."

"Letty, that isn't kind," Lavelle scolded. "Today has been very hard on Ashley and Natalie. No doubt Natalie has been saddened by her grandfather's death and has gone off to grieve." Lavelle looked to Ashley as if for confirmation.

"Yes," Ashley said. "She was very upset." That much was true.

"She is an inconsiderate, undisciplined child to put us through such a scene," Ashley's mother said, refusing to back down.

Ashley thought of reminding her mother that she was no longer welcome here, but she bit back the retort and instead moved to the door. "If Natalie comes home, please tell her I'll be right back."

"You should just wait here. She'll get tired of being alone and return. Then you can punish her properly. It might not yet be too late to instill some discipline. I'm sure my father spoiled her beyond belief, and with you off working at that Harvey place . . . well, the child has no doubt had to raise herself."

Ashley opened the door, forcing herself to remain silent. It would serve no purpose to explain herself or her life. Natalie was out there somewhere and the night was coming.

Lavelle turned to her sister. "You shouldn't be so critical of Ashley. She's done a wonderful job raising Natalie. The child is positively perfect."

"A perfect child wouldn't run about without consideration for her elders," Leticia replied.

Lavelle shook her head. "Letty, you have a beautiful daughter and an equally beautiful grandchild. You've pushed them away most of your life. If you aren't careful, you'll lose all opportunity to draw them close again. Because sooner or later, you're going to push hard enough that they won't come back."

Leticia's expression softened more than Lavelle had expected. "That happened a decade ago. Ashley will never forgive me."

It was the first time Lavelle had ever heard Leticia speak of needing her daughter's forgiveness. "Perhaps if she knew you desired to be forgiven, it might change things." Lavelle smiled ever so slightly. "Perhaps if you each knew how sorry you were for the lost years—for the mistakes."

Leticia shook her head and gathered up her things. "I won't make myself vulnerable in that fashion. Apologies are for weaklings." She stormed off for the stairs, not waiting for Lavelle's reply.

Lavelle watched until her sister had disappeared. She heard the bedroom door close upstairs and sighed. The day had been a defeating blow for Letty. Lavelle felt sorry for her. She had learned her fortune was in jeopardy—their father had died—and the lawyer had reminded them both in no uncertain terms that the estate of their father was forever set. Lavelle felt a bittersweet relief, whereas she knew Letty felt only fear.

"God, please help her," Lavelle prayed. "She's so very lost and alone."

E. J. could barely gather up the strength to go back to his hotel room. The work was finished; they were right on schedule and so far the problems had all been minimal—at least all his work problems had been minimal. E. J. sat at his desk, cradling his bearded chin, gazing at the chair in the same room where his wife had recently sat. How strange life had twisted this time. Up until a few weeks ago he'd thought his life would be spent alone with his images from the past. He hadn't believed it possible to get past the war and what he'd done, but now he felt God had helped him to renew his hope. Even Ashley didn't condemn him for what he'd done.

"Can I really let go, Lord? Can I let go of the past and be a better man?" he whispered. E. J. wanted desperately to believe he could. He loved Ashley—he'd never stopped. If it wouldn't have been inappropriate, he would have swept her off her feet and kissed her soundly. *But she doesn't know me,* E. J. realized. *She knows only the young man I was before I went away to war.*

He shook his head. "I don't know what to do, Lord. I don't know how to help. Natalie brought my attention back to you, but for what? How do I make this right? How can we be a family? How do I go back to being Ethan Reynolds?"

Without warning, the door flew open, slamming against the wall with a reverberating crash. Ashley came into the room like a speeding freight train. "She's gone."

"What?" He got to his feet. "Who's gone?"

"Natalie. She's gone." The look on Ashley's face was one of pure panic.

E. J. didn't think the situation so distressful. "She's probably just thinking things over. You know, just walking around town."

Ashley looked at him as though he hadn't a clue of the seriousness of the matter. And the truth was, he didn't—and it made him feel foolish for his comment.

"She's ten years old, Ethan. She has no business wandering around town or elsewhere at this hour," Ashley replied indignantly. "Besides, her pony's gone, and that can only mean that Natalie's on horseback trying to get away from all of this. That means she's planned more than just a short walk around town. We have to find her, Ethan." She burst into tears. "You have to help me."

He reached out and pulled her into his arms. It felt like the most natural thing in the world. In a rush of memories he was just twenty-one and she was his first and only love. "Of course I'll help you. She's my daughter too." He stroked her hair and tried to think about what should be done.

"I saw a couple of our friends on the way over here," Ashley said, pulling back just enough to see his face. "I told them to keep their eyes open for her—to ask around. I asked them to check around town, but Ethan, I'm sure she's not there. I just have this very bad feeling. Call it a mother's intuition."

"Does she have a good friend she might have gone to see? Someone in whom she'd confide all of this?"

"She has friends, but I don't think she would be inclined to go share this. She's hurting and scared. Her whole world has been turned upside down today. First Grandpa and now this. Oh, Ethan, what are we going to do?"

"Excuse me," a man called from the doorway.

E. J. looked up to find Marcus Greeley, the journalist who had introduced himself at the dinner with Lindbergh. "Ethan Reynolds?"

"You!" Ashley declared. She looked back at Ethan. "This man came to my door asking to talk to us. I think he's the same one who was following Natalie." She looked back at Greeley.

"You were following my daughter," Ashley said. "I know it was you. I saw you hiding and following her."

"Actually, ma'am, I was following the both of you, but your daughter just seemed to come to see Mr. Reynolds more often than not, so I found it more productive to follow her."

"Do you know where she is now?" Ashley asked, stepping away from Ethan.

"No, I can't say that I do, but I heard from some of the railroad men that she was missing. I want to help with the search."

"I don't understand why you were following Natalie," E. J. stated. "Or why you would follow either of them."

"Because unless I've missed my guess, you're Ethan Reynolds."

E. J. knew there was no sense in lying. "I am Ethan Reynolds, but I still don't understand. If you were looking for me, why bother them?"

"It's kind of a long story, but since time is of the essence here, I'll try to shorten it a bit." Marcus twisted his fedora and shrugged. "I've been looking for you since you were sent home after the Great War. See, I was on that battlefield when your act of courage saved hundreds of men. I wasn't in your company, but my company was in your division, and we were pinned down by the same machine gunner that got some of your friends. I was wounded early on and losing blood fast. There wasn't much hope of getting me out, and then you went charging through the bullets as though they were nothing more than horseflies. You saved my life."

Ethan stiffened. "I just did what had to be done."

"Yes, but no one else had been able to do that, and if you hadn't acted when you did, I wouldn't have lasted another hour. Your act of heroism allowed my buddies to get me out and back to a field hospital."

"That doesn't explain why you're here now," E. J. said, eager to get the man's focus away from battle.

"At first I just wanted to find you and thank you. I started this back in 1920," he said, laughing. "I wanted to meet you and give you a smoked ham from my folks. Sounds silly now, but it was important then. After a time when I kept running out of places to look, I thought to check with the army and see if they had any record of you.

"The army could only tell me that you had a wife, Ashley Reynolds, and where she lived. I went there, but of course she was gone. I kind of gave up the search for a while. I needed to settle on my writing. I put together a collection of stories on the war and found it well received. I wrote for several newspapers, and then one day the same publisher who'd contracted my book of stories came to me and asked me to write another book. A book about the war and the men who'd fought and where they were now that the war was ten years behind them. I immediately thought of you and what you'd done. I knew I had to try again to find you."

Ethan shook his head. "I can't imagine it being that important."

Marcus rubbed his bare chin. "Well, it was to me. My big break came one day when a friend who knew what I was trying to do with the book sent me a newspaper clipping from Winslow. It showed your daughter in a parade with some veterans. The article had stories about each of the men. He actually thought I'd want the information on the other men, but what I really found of value was the information about your daughter. I knew from reading the article that her mother's name was Ashley Reynolds—and that it had to be the same woman. I was stumped by the fact that your little girl was quoted as having lost you in the war before she was even born. I knew you were alive.

"Anyway, to make a long story short, I came here to see if I could talk to your wife and daughter and figure out why they thought you were dead. I thought maybe they were trying to hide something or maybe the newspaper writer had tried to make the story more of a heart-gripper than the truth would allow. So I decided not to approach Mrs. Reynolds and Natalie right off the bat. Instead I nosed around and asked questions here and there. Surprisingly enough, Natalie led me to you. Now I want to help find Natalie."

Ethan's mind was still reeling from the story, but he knew there'd be time to sort out the details later. "I'd appreciate the help." He turned to Ashley. "Where should we look? I really don't know the area."

Ashley shook her head. "She has several favorite places, but she isn't thinking rationally. She could have taken off to Clear Creek—she loves it there. Or she could have gone up toward the river. There are . . . some places along the . . ." Ashley broke down, burying her face in her hands.

Ethan again pulled her close, but he looked over her shoulder to Marcus Greeley. "Do you have a car?"

"No, but I'd be willing to bet money we can get one. I'll start asking around," Greeley said and quickly exited the room.

"Ashley, listen to me. You have to be strong for Natalie. You have to think clearly and help me here. I can't do this alone."

She looked into his eyes. "You aren't alone." She sniffed back her tears and regained her composure. "I'm here with you."

He nodded. "Come on. Let's see what's to be done about transportation."

They stepped from the office and into the lobby hallway to find a growing collection of people.

"We're here to help," said one man, his overalls grease-smeared along with his face.

"It's too dark to see," someone else commented. "We can look around town, but going out much farther will have to wait for first light."

"That's true," yet another person called. "Too many dangers."

Ashley grabbed E. J.'s arm. "She can't be out there all night. It's already chilly and it will get much colder. There are dangers for her as well."

E. J. looked at the men who surrounded them. "Is there no way to go searching—even with a car?"

"You can drive the roads in the dark, but you won't be able to get off across country. If she's riding that pony like she's done in the past, she ain't sticking to the roads," a balding man threw back.

E. J. looked at Ashley. "If we can get a couple of cars, we'll at least drive around and call for her. We might actually spot her. You just never know."

Ashley nodded. "I'll go find Pastor McGuire. He has a car."

"I'll run for him," the man who'd first spoken up offered. He took off before anyone could acknowledge him.

E. J. stood feeling rather helpless while several of the local men organized the collection of people into a search party. He listened to the chatter around him. People presumed Natalie was just upset because of her grandfather's death. They were sympathetic and hopeful that she'd come home before much longer, but they were also happy to look for her. Their obvious affection for his daughter warmed him through and through.

Within the hour Ethan and Ashley joined Pastor McGuire in his car, while Marcus Greeley and several other townsmen piled into an assortment of cars and flatbed trucks. They'd all agreed to meet back in one hour at the Harvey hotel. Ethan had never known when he'd been more frightened. With Ashley clinging to his hand, he knew his worry over their child was worse than anything he'd faced on the battlefield.

Lord, he prayed, *please keep her safe. Please don't allow any harm to come to her.* The prayer seemed so little—so ineffectual. Surely he could do more than pray and drive around in the dark.

But there was nothing else to be done. Just as he feared, the car lights were no real benefit against the blackness of the empty desert. After the allotted time, they turned around and headed back to town. Ashley began to sob softly against E. J.'s shoulder.

"It's going to be all right," he whispered. "We have to have faith. God wouldn't bring us all together like this just to see us separated again."

Pastor McGuire spoke up just then. "I'm having a hard time under-standing what's happening here. I heard Ashley call you Ethan earlier."

Ethan drew a deep breath. "Yes. I'm her husband."

"But you were believed to have died in France."

"I know. I was pretty close to dead, but apparently the army made a mess of things and sent her the wrong letter. We've only just learned the truth for ourselves."

"And is this the real reason for Natalie's disappearance?" McGuire asked as they pulled up in front of the Harvey hotel. He stopped the car and waited for Ethan's answer.

"She overheard her mother confront me. It's a long story, but yes, this is the reason Natalie is gone. This is why we weren't inclined to believe she'd just come back home before long. This is why we're both so scared."

The pastor shut off the engine and smiled. "Well, I'm happy to say that I know for a fact God still answers prayer. Natalie's fondest wish and deepest heartfelt prayer was for God to send her a daddy. I know because she got me in on it as well." He laughed. "Once she thinks this through, she's going to be delighted. In the meantime, we'll just pray for her safety and that she'll see the reason in coming home quickly."

E. J. nodded. He wanted to believe the pastor's words. He wanted very much to have hope so that Ashley could take courage from him. Suddenly it was very important that she see him as the man she needed him to be.

Dismissing the searchers for the night was the hardest thing E. J. ever had to do. He watched the men leave in the same spirit of dejec-tion he felt gripping his heart. Fear was a powerful opponent, and right now it seemed to be an unbeatable one.

"Why don't you go home and get some sleep?" Pastor McGuire sug-gested to Ashley. "Besides, Natalie might have already returned."

"My mother and aunt Lavelle are there," Ashley said softly. "I should go check and see if they've heard anything, but I couldn't sleep. Not in a million years."

"I'll go with you," E. J. said. He extended his hand to the pastor. "Thank you. Thank you for helping us tonight and for the prayers."

"I'll be back in the morning. I'll bring some saddle horses. We'll have a better time of it if we look for her on horseback."

E. J. nodded. "Thanks. I'll be here."

He pressed his hand against the small of Ashley's back. "Come on. Let's see if she's gone home."

They walked in silence along the city streets. Ashley didn't seem to mind that E. J. had taken hold of her hand. He wasn't entirely sure why he'd done it. They'd only just come back together, but it seemed so very right.

Ashley opened the front door and was immediately greeted by her aunt. "Have you found her?" Lavelle questioned.

Ashley looked at E. J. and bit her lower lip.

"No," E. J. replied. "We'd hoped you might have heard something."

Lavelle shook her head. Worry etched her face. "I've put on a pot of coffee." She looked at Ashley, her expression suggesting dread. "Your mother went to bed. She was quite worn-out."

"You needn't make excuses for her," Ashley replied. "She doesn't care about Natalie."

"I think she does . . . in her own way," Lavelle reasoned. "I just think she's taken this whole news of Father and the stock market quite hard. I think it's catching up with her, and Natalie was just the final straw. This very well may be a turning point in her life, Ashley. We must pray for her."

"Well, frankly, I hope she stays up there. No, actually, I wish she weren't here at all. After what she did to Natalie . . ." Ashley's words were hard and cold. "I don't need her making this worse."

"There weren't any hotel rooms available for tonight," Lavelle explained. "They've reserved her something for tomorrow. I took it upon myself to tell her to plan on staying here tonight."

"I suppose I have no choice," Ashley replied bitterly. "After all, it would hardly be the Christian thing to do. Oh, but I don't feel like being very Christian when it comes to that woman."

Her aunt patted her on the arm and turned to E. J. "Mr. Carson, isn't it?"

E. J. straightened and looked to Ashley. "I . . . uh . . ."

"Aunt Lavelle, I think we should sit down to coffee and then continue this conversation. There's something you need to know." Ashley motioned E. J. to the living room. "Just take a seat and I'll get the cups."

She and Lavelle disappeared momentarily, and when they returned she carried a tray and three cups, along with a plate of cookies. "I thought you might be hungry," she told Ethan. "Neither of us had supper."

"I could make some sandwiches," Lavelle offered, still looking curiously at the two of them. When Ashley took a seat close to E. J. on the sofa, Lavelle raised her brows in question.

Ashley poured the coffee and began the long explanation. E. J. sat in silence, knowing that it was probably better to let Ashley vent her emotions and thoughts.

"He seemed so familiar," she continued to explain, glancing at E. J. "He walked the same way Ethan walked. He even liked to whistle Ethan's favorite ragtime tune. It seemed like a silly coincidence, and in fact, I thought I was just making it up in my head. You know, because I wanted so much to remember Ethan."

"Well, this certainly is stunning news," Lavelle said. She took a long sip from her coffee, then looked E. J. in the eye. "So what happens now?"

"Now we find Natalie," E. J. replied. "Nothing else matters until we know she's safe and sound."

"I agree," Lavelle said, nodding, "but you have to be prepared for her questions. And knowing my great-niece, one of the first questions on her mind will be whether you intend to stay here in Winslow and be a father to her."

E. J. cleared his throat nervously. "I love Ashley as though the lost years between us had never happened. She's easy to love, but of course, you know that. I don't know that I'd be much good anymore as a husband or a father, but . . ." He fell silent and looked at Ashley. "I'd like a chance to try."

And in that moment, he knew it was true. Despite the past, he wanted his future. And he wanted that future to be with Ashley and Natalie—but not as E. J. Carson. He wanted his life as Ethan Reynolds back. Ethan was the man Ashley had fallen in love with, and from that love, Ethan was the man who helped create Natalie. "Ashley, I want to be Ethan again—the man you once loved and married."

The house was silent a moment before Lavelle coughed quietly and then bid them good-night. Ethan noted the time was nearing eleven. "I should go," he said softly.

Ashley had said very little since giving her explanation of who he was. She'd sat beside him on the sofa staring pensively into the fireplace.

"It's so hard to be here all safe and warm," she said as though she hadn't heard him speak, "and know that she's out there alone."

"I know," Ethan said, reaching out to take hold of her hand.

To his surprise, Ashley leaned against his shoulder. "This is like a dream and a nightmare all wrapped into one. You're here—and that's all my dreams come true. But Natalie's lost and that's all the horror a mother's heart could ever imagine."

"She's a smart girl. She's going to be all right."

"Do you really believe that?" Ashley asked, barely suppressing a yawn.

Ethan squeezed her hand. "I do. I've just spent the last few weeks in her company. She's told me stories about her life here—about her dreams. She thinks things through, and even though she acted out of emotion tonight, she'll think things through and come home."

"But what if she's not able to come home?"

"Ashley, we can't think like that. It wouldn't serve any good purpose. We have to believe that God is in control and that He's heard our prayers and will protect her."

"For so many years, I didn't believe God cared. Maybe He's punishing me."

Ethan's heart nearly broke. "No," he whispered. "God doesn't work that way. I don't know a whole lot about the Bible, but I do know that God wouldn't purposefully bring harm to an innocent child."

"But someone else might," Ashley whispered.

"God will see us through this, Ashley. I promise you, He will. She's going to be all right."

They sat in silence watching the fire, and it wasn't long before he realized that Ashley had fallen asleep. Her rhythmic breathing comforted him. Ethan eased Ashley into his arms and leaned back against the sofa and closed his eyes. It felt so right for her to be here with him.

————

He hadn't intended to sleep, but when Ethan woke up just before dawn, he realized what had happened and smiled. For the first time since the war, he hadn't been riddled with battlefield nightmares. In fact, he couldn't remember a single image haunting his sleep. Ashley had made that possible—he was certain of it. It was almost as if God had given him a sign he so desperately needed. A sign of peace and tranquility. A sign that with Ashley at his side, he could leave the past behind.

"Ashley," he whispered against her ear.

"Mmm."

"Ashley, love, wake up. It's almost light. We need to prepare for our search."

Ashley woke up slowly. She looked up into his face, her dark eyes searching his as if in a dream. "Ethan . . . you're here," she said. Apparently sleep still kept her mind from remembering the night before.

"Yes, I'm here, but we need to go look for Natalie."

She came awake instantly at the mention of their daughter's name. "She hasn't come home."

It was a statement, not a question, but Ethan felt he needed to respond nevertheless. "No, but she will. I promise you—she will."

*E*than and Ashley prepared some supplies and headed back to the Harvey hotel. The sun was barely on the horizon when to their surprise a group of men, mounted on horseback, arrived. Soon others joined them, both on horseback and in cars. True to his word, Pastor McGuire was there and with him Marcus Greeley, who looked rather uncomfortable atop the bay mount the pastor had lent him.

"I've put Brother Roberts in charge of the church and told him I needed to pastor this search." Pastor McGuire motioned to the extra horse and handed down the reins to Ethan and said, "I've brought you a good mount. Now, where do we start?"

Ethan took hold of the horse. "I think if we form a circle around the outside edge of town and keep working our way out, we'll cover more territory."

"I think that's wise," said the town marshal. "Some of my men and I will lead the teams going north and west. The rest of my men can stay here and run messages to us if needed and keep things under control. If you men will take the east and south, we'll have a good chance of covering just about everything in a ten-mile radius. I can't see her getting any farther away than that."

Ethan had no idea who had thought to let the man know of their predicament, but he was grateful for the help. In fact, he was deeply touched by the way the community had turned out to help look for his daughter.

"You stay here in case she comes home," Ethan told Ashley as he mounted the black gelding Pastor McGuire had given him.

"But I want to come and look for her too. I can't just do nothing," Ashley protested.

"But she may slip through our lines and come home. Or she may have been hiding here in town all along. We'll need to know that as soon as possible."

"But . . ."

"Mrs. Reynolds, he's right," the marshal stated rather sternly. "You need to stay here and let us do the hard work."

Ethan longed to lean down and kiss her good-bye, but instead he took the canteen she offered. "She'll be all right. Just keep praying."

"I want to believe, but my faith is weak."

Pastor McGuire overheard this and smiled. "When we're weak, then God is strong. We know for sure then that we're not operating in our own strength—but in His."

Ashley nodded and handed Ethan his pack. "Be careful."

He smiled, feeling the warmth of her concern. "I will."

Emptiness washed over Ashley as she watched the men ride away. She'd heard one of the railroad men say that the night had been warmer than usual. She prayed it was true. She had no way of knowing if Natalie had thought to take warm clothes or food.

I should have inventoried things, she thought. *That would have given me a better idea of what she might have with her.* But even as Ashley thought this, she knew it would also give her a good idea of what Natalie hadn't taken, and then she would have worried all the more.

Ashley searched around town, checking Natalie's favorite spots and talking to friends as they prepared for church. No one had seen the girl, but they assured Ashley that they were keeping an eye open for her. Ashley thanked each person for his concern, then continued her own search.

She walked down Third Street to Berry and up to Oak, then back east toward home. With every step her heart grew heavier and hope seemed out of reach. By the time she came to the wrought-iron gate of her own home, Ashley longed to break down and cry. She looked at the little two-story brick house and felt her heart overflow with grief. This used to be a home. She and Natalie had been very happy here. Would they ever be happy again?

Ashley pushed back the gate and made her way to the house. Despite her mother's claims to repossess her home and Grandpa's savings, Ashley knew she'd never give up their home—not so long as there was breath in her body. This was where she had raised Natalie. This was Natalie's home.

But what if something happened to Natalie? What if she's gotten herself killed?

The question came against her will. Ashley wiped at the tears that followed. *She can't be dead. She must be all right. Please, God, let her be all right.*

The house was quiet when Ashley entered. She checked the clock and saw that it was only nine-thirty.

"Any word?" Lavelle questioned, coming from the kitchen wearing Ashley's apron and carrying a cup of coffee.

"No. The men have formed a search party and have taken off on horseback to search the open ground."

Lavelle placed the cup and saucer on the table and pulled out a chair. "Here, sit down and have some coffee. I'll bring you some breakfast in just a minute."

"I'm not hungry," Ashley said, taking the offered seat. "The coffee sounds good, though. Thank you."

Lavelle nodded and sat down beside her. "This is the hardest part. Waiting."

Ashley took a long drink. The hot liquid warmed her chilled body. She couldn't tell if she'd grown cold because of the temperature or her own fears.

"Well, has she been found?" Ashley's mother questioned as she entered the room.

Ashley was in no mood to deal with her mother's haughty temperament, but she swallowed another sip of the coffee and shook her head. "They're still searching."

"This is certainly a fine mess. You should have been less lenient with the child. Giving her a pony was sure to lead to disaster. Why, people are killed from being thrown off of horses, and a foolish child racing out in the dead of night is sure to meet with a terrible fate."

"Mother, stop!" Ashley cried.

"Yes, please, Leticia. Try to be more encouraging."

Ashley's mother drew her chin up in defiance. "I will not be hushed or dictated to. I have a right to my opinion, and that opinion is that you've done a poor job of raising your daughter."

"Well, if I have, it's because I had a poor example to follow," Ashley retorted, her anger growing. All the frustration and fear of Natalie's disappearance quickly reordered itself into rage. "You've always concerned yourself with things that held importance only to you. You hardly gave me the time of day, much less the time I needed. Had you been able to share your time and heart as freely as you spent Grandpa's money, I might have desired to maintain a relationship with you."

"You are a vicious and cruel woman," her mother countered, "just as you were an inattentive and inconsiderate child. You never cared about the things that were important to me."

The gauntlet had been thrown down, and Ashley picked it up with great relish. "I might have cared if those things so near and dear to your heart would have included me."

"Always you. Always. You were never happy unless you were the center of attention. Your brothers doted on you. Your father doted on you. But that wasn't enough. You needed to be the center of my world as well," Leticia stated angrily. "Well, I hardly had time for spoiled little girls. There were important people to deal with, and as you grew you could have been an asset—could have helped me—but you were too self-absorbed."

Ashley opened her mouth in disbelief. "That isn't true. You had my life planned out for me, and when I refused to follow your guidelines, you dismissed me like a servant you'd caught stealing."

"You might as well have stolen from us. You took everything we offered without worrying about where it came from or how expensive it might have been."

Ashley pounded her fists on the table. "Because money never meant anything to me. I saw it only as something that occupied my father's time and consumed my mother." She got to her feet and stared her mother hard in the eye. "I have no understanding of your philosophy, because I've lived another kind of life since leaving Baltimore.

"I'll give you this much, Mother. I was selfish and inconsiderate as a child and young woman. I was . . . because I was taught to be such. I was taught that when things or people didn't meet your satisfaction, you sent them away. I was taught the price of everything and the value of nothing. It wasn't until Ethan came into my life that I understood there was something more."

"Always that man. That man coming between my plans for you— that man taking what was never his to own in the first place. I say good riddance to him. Wherever he may be, you may be sure he's amounted to nothing."

"He's out searching for our daughter," Ashley said, enjoying the look of surprise in her mother's expression. "That's right. He's here in Winslow. What you thought to destroy, God saw fit to reunite. Ethan is here, Mother, and once he finds our daughter, he's going to come home . . . and he'll deal with you."

Leticia actually paled. She gripped the back of the chair. "How can he be here? You didn't even know he was alive until I told you."

Lavelle stepped toward her sister. "God has a way of working these things out, Letty. I think you should both calm down and realize that Natalie is still out there somewhere. We should be praying and keeping our focus on her. The rest of this is just anger speaking out."

"I hate you for what you've done to us," Ashley said to her mother, her voice deadly calm. "I hate you for robbing us of eleven years of happiness. I'm glad you've lost your fortune. I hope you suffer, and suffer dearly. Furthermore, I'm glad you disdain God, because I certainly don't want to have to share eternity with the likes of you."

Ashley suddenly looked away, despising herself for her angry words. She pushed Lavelle aside and headed down the hall to Grandpa's old room and locked herself inside. Throwing herself across the bed, Ashley began to cry a torrent of tears.

Why can't I be forgiving like you wanted, Grandpa? Why can't I let go of what she did so long ago? She hurt you, too, but you loved her to the end. Why can't I just love her and forget the pain she's caused?

And then her words turned to prayer. "Oh, God, why does this have to hurt so much? Why, when Ethan has come home and hope is restored and there is a road toward a real future together in sight, does my mother have to make my life so miserable? I was happy until she came. I was happy until I learned that Grandpa was dying."

But was she? Ashley was immediately struck with her own bitterness. With an honesty that tore at her heart, she could only remember her anger and unhappiness. Loneliness and bitter regret had hardened her heart years ago. She had blamed God for taking Ethan away from her in the first place, and she had blamed her mother for trying to force her plans upon Ashley. And now she blamed her mother for keeping Ethan away for so many years.

"Being a Christian is too hard, Lord. I can't do this. I can't forgive her. She doesn't deserve to be forgiven."

"Nobody deserves forgiveness." Grandpa's words settled on her heart. *"God offered us what we didn't deserve, in order to save us from what we did deserve."*

Ashley remained very still, trying hard to remember the details of their conversation. He had been speaking to her about coming to

God—about seeking forgiveness for her own sins. Her sins were just as unforgivable as her mother's.

"But that can't be," she murmured. "I've never been like her. I've never lied like that or stolen someone's life away from them. She might as well have killed me."

Ethan's words from the night before came to her. *"I killed men—boys, really. I killed them even when I didn't have to."*

She could readily forgive what he'd done in the line of duty, even when he proclaimed himself to have acted outside of duty. Ethan's wrongs scarcely even bothered her. Why could she forgive him that and not forgive her mother?

"Because she doesn't want to be forgiven," Ashley said, sitting up. "She doesn't think she's done anything wrong. She hurts people and causes deep pain, but she doesn't care because she has no standard by which to gauge it."

Ashley considered the situation in the depth of her soul. "If she doesn't want forgiveness because she doesn't believe she's done any-thing wrong, then why should I forgive her? Why does it matter what I think or feel toward her when she's perfectly content to believe herself absolutely right in these matters?"

Forgive her for your own sake. Forgive her for the freedom that comes in letting go of the past. Forgive her because I've forgiven you.

The words seemed to come from somewhere deep within. The quickening in her spirit left Ashley no doubt where the inspiration had come from. Ashley looked to the Bible on Grandpa's nightstand. Pick-ing it up, she hugged it close.

"I don't know if I can do this," she whispered. "God, I'm only human, and I don't know how to forgive her for this. Grandpa would tell me that I should lean on you, and so that's all I have—that's all I can do. You'll have to show me how to forgive her. How to stop hating her. Please, God. Please show me."

CHAPTER TWENTY-THREE

*S*preading out across the windblown desert, the searchers looked for any sign that might give them hope that Natalie had passed that way. Ethan found himself praying continuously. Suddenly nothing in life was more important than finding that little girl.

"Lord, I know I've asked for her safety over and over during this ordeal, but I just can't keep from asking again. Help us to find her— help me to find her. I want so much just to hold her and know that she's going to be all right."

Ethan watched as the distance between himself and the other riders grew. They were like the spokes of a wheel heading out from their hub—Winslow. It seemed a responsible way to search, but the slow, methodic manner in which they conducted themselves did little to ease his concerns.

He studied the horizon with a burning desire to kick the horse into a full gallop. He wanted to reach whatever destination would prove to him that Natalie was safe and sound. He didn't even care if she was mindless of the suffering she'd caused. He didn't care if she was still as mad as a wet hornet. He just wanted to find her and bring her back safely to Ashley.

Ashley.

Even thinking of her now warmed his heart. He knew just by looking in her eyes that they had a future. She didn't care about the past. She didn't care that he'd killed men and still had nightmares. Ashley would open her home and her arms to him if that was what he wanted.

He looked at the ground for any sign Natalie might have left behind, then scanned the horizon once again. The turmoil in his heart got the better of him and a tightness rose up in his throat. *I know I'm not perfect, but I can try to be a good husband and father. I would like to try. I want to do the right thing in spite of the years that have gone by.*

Ethan looked at Pastor McGuire, who was riding toward a large collection of sandstone rocks. The reddish boulders would create the perfect hiding place.

"I'm going to check out these rocks!" McGuire called out. Ethan slowed his horse and held his breath, waiting for some sign. The pastor picked his way around the rocks, disappearing momentarily from Ethan's sight, then coming around in view again.

"She's not been here!" McGuire called out. "I don't see any tracks at all to suggest otherwise."

"Okay!" Ethan replied and waved. Disappointment welled up inside. She seemed to have vanished from the face of the earth.

Ethan studied the ground for hoof tracks that might prove the pony had passed this way, but the wind whipped up the sand and dirt, blowing it first one direction and then another. A dust devil blew up not ten feet in front of him, spooking the mount. The horse reared up a bit and the action caused Ethan to nearly lose his seat. He wasn't much of a horseman, and this added intrigue was almost more than he could handle. The gelding danced around for a moment as Ethan fought to regain control.

"Easy, fellow," he called soothingly. "Whoa, now."

The horse calmed as the windy formation spent itself and the sand fell back to earth in a new location. The animal proceeded in a cautious fashion, ears slightly back, alert to the ever-present danger that another whirlwind might threaten them. Ethan tired of the slow walk and urged the gelding forward, picking up the pace to a trot. Surely he could spot something just as easily at this speed.

After a time, Ethan could see the rock formations that edged Clear Creek. How pleasant their picnic had been here on that Sunday so long ago. He looked off in the distance. Wasn't that the direction in which Natalie planned to build her mother a house? He slowed the horse and patrolled the rock-lined creek, seeking some clue that his daughter was here and safe. He was just about to call out to Pastor McGuire when the man motioned and called to Ethan. "Look over there!"

Ethan followed the direction indicated and caught sight of Penny, Natalie's pony. His heart sank. The pony was saddled but without a rider. Ethan pressed his horse into a full gallop, but as he neared, the pony spooked and pranced away nervously. Ethan pulled back the reins and brought the gelding to a stop. "Easy, boy," he called and patted his horse's neck.

By this time Pastor McGuire and Marcus Greeley had joined him. The men had served as Ethan's right and left flank. Dismounting, he tossed his reins to McGuire and went in pursuit of Penny.

"Come on, Penny-girl." He clucked softly as he'd heard Natalie do, then reached into his pocket for the apple Ashley had given him shortly before they'd left the house. "Look what I have for you." He held up the apple and walked ever so slowly toward the spooked horse.

Penny seemed to remember him and started a slow, plodding walk toward him. Ethan took out his knife and cut a hunk of the apple and held it out. Penny picked up her pace and came to a stop only a few feet from Ethan. She eyed the offering for a moment, then apparently judged him to be a safe risk. Moving forward, she took the apple, even as Ethan took up her reins.

"Good job, Ethan," Greeley called out. "The west will make a cowboy of you yet."

Ethan smiled. "I don't recall wanting the job." He stroked Penny's nose. "I sure wish you could talk. I wish you could take me to Natalie."

"At least we know she's somewhere here in the area. The pony's not lathered or worked up." Pastor McGuire dismounted and walked to where Penny stood enjoying Ethan's attention. He forced his fingers between her saddle blanket and back. "She doesn't feel the slightest bit damp. I'd say she hasn't had this saddle on long at all. Maybe Natalie rested here for the night and when she went to saddle Penny, she got away from her."

"That could be," Ethan said, trying not to worry. "Maybe Natalie is really close," he added. "Here. I'm going on foot." He handed Penny over to McGuire. Setting off across the ground to the rocks, Ethan began calling. "Natalie! Natalie, where are you?"

Greeley did likewise, heading downstream.

Ethan felt his heart pounding at a pace he couldn't hope to calm. He scrambled onto the rock that edged the creek. The wind spit sand against his face momentarily, but once he started climbing down the creek bank, Ethan found himself more sheltered from the wind. "Natalie! Natalie, if you can hear me—answer me!"

"I'm here." Her voice sounded perturbed.

Ethan strained to listen. "Natalie, where are you?"

"I'm over here." Exasperation rang clear.

He followed the sound and spied something red sticking out just over the next ridge of rock. Scrambling over the barrier, Ethan came face-to-face with his daughter. She wore a red oblong cap that tied under her chin and a dark brown jacket that had what appeared to be a fresh tear on the sleeve. A cut on her forehead and some scratches on her face and hands were the worst of her injuries—as far as Ethan could tell. She looked otherwise unharmed but very annoyed.

Sitting there, elbows on her knees, face in her hands, as if contemplating what was to be done, Natalie looked like someone who'd rather be left alone. Ethan didn't care. He was so happy to see her safe that he acted without thinking. Picking her up, he hugged her close.

"Oh, Natalie, I thought we'd lost you for good. We found Penny, but we had no idea if you were hurt or worse." He couldn't even bring himself to suggest that she could have died.

"Penny lost her footing on the edge. It wasn't her fault. I was too close. I fell off and Penny ran away," Natalie said matter-of-factly. "Please put me down."

Ethan did as she asked. "We've been looking all over for you," he said, continuing his mental inventory. She didn't appear to have any broken bones, but the bump on her head was bleeding. "Your mother is sick with worry." Ethan reached out to touch her, but Natalie withdrew and crossed her arms.

"Is she all right?" Pastor McGuire called from where he stood with the horses.

Ethan called back, "She's fine. Would you please leave Penny and the mount you lent me and go notify the others that she's all right and that we're heading home?"

"Of course," Pastor McGuire replied. "Natalie, I'm so relieved to see you're all right. We've sure been praying for you."

"Oh, Pastor McGuire, would you also let Ashley know we're coming home?"

The man grinned down at them. "I'd be delighted."

Ethan looked down at his daughter. "You ready to head back?"

Natalie only shrugged and stared at the creek. Once the pastor and Greeley had taken off to alert the others, Natalie sat down again. The anger in her voice was apparent. "Why didn't you tell me the truth? I'm not a baby, you know." She looked at him, her brows knitted together. "I thought we were friends."

"We are friends, Natalie." Ethan sat down on the rock opposite her. "I didn't know the truth at first. You told me your father died in the war and I presumed he had. I sure didn't expect to find out that I was really your father. In fact, I didn't know the truth of it until I came face-to-face with your mother that day you introduced us outside the ice-cream store."

"You could have said something then." She looked back at the water instead of him.

"I thought it would be unfair to your mother. I figured I should tell her in private."

"But you didn't. You had lots of time to do it, but you didn't tell her. Why? Are you ashamed of us? Were you just going to leave without telling us?"

Ethan thought his heart might break at this statement. "Of course not. It had nothing to do with you and your mother. It had everything to do with me—with who I was inside."

"That doesn't make sense," Natalie said, getting to her feet. "You lied to me."

Ethan shook his head. "I didn't lie to you. You never asked me if I was your father. You made it clear you wanted a new father—a husband for your mother—but you didn't ask me if I was Ethan Reynolds." He spoke softly, trying to be honest yet careful. He wanted to calm her down, but her growing anger was apparent. "Natalie, I didn't say anything because I didn't want you to be hurt."

"Well, I am hurt, and I'm mad too." She stomped across the rocks to where the pastor had left Penny and the black mount.

Ethan followed quickly, not willing to let her get away from him again. He helped her up onto Penny, then noticing the lump on her forehead, thought better of it. "Maybe you should ride with me. You've hit your head pretty hard, and I don't want you passing out."

"I'm not going to pass out." She tossed her pigtails over her shoulder and tried hard to look older than she was. "I told you, I'm not a baby."

Ethan's heart went out to her. He stood beside Penny, holding the pony in place. "Natalie, I don't blame you for being mad at me, but please listen. I didn't mean for you to be hurt in this. I wanted to talk to your mother first—to see if there was some way we could work everything out."

"Where were you all those years? Mama said you were dead. Did she lie to me too?"

Ethan felt panicked at the question. How could he explain? He certainly couldn't tell her that her grandmother had lied to him—not without making a bad situation worse. "No. Your mother had no idea until you heard her talking to me. The army had told her I was dead. She really thought I was. And remember, I thought she was dead because someone told me she'd died from the influenza. We had no idea either one was still alive, or we would have been together.

"Furthermore, I didn't know about you at all. Your mama had never told me she was going to have a baby. You know that's true—your mama told you that much." Natalie nodded but only slightly. He continued. "When I heard you talking about your father and how he died a hero in the war, and then later when you told me what your mother's name was—I couldn't believe it. It was so shocking to me that I was almost sick from it. I couldn't believe I'd lost all those years and that I had a daughter."

"But how could Mama not know it was you?"

"I don't look like I did when we married. I have glasses and a beard now. I've had a lot of surgery on my face too. Your mama might have had suspicions about me, but she didn't know until yesterday. She saw the picture I'd sketched for you. That's why I'd asked you to keep it out of sight. I knew if she saw it, she would probably know the truth, and I hadn't had a chance to talk to her yet."

"Were you really going to talk to her?" Natalie asked. She looked down at him with an expression that betrayed all of her mistrust. "Or were you going to just leave us when you were done building the hotel?"

"Natalie, I always planned to tell your mama. That day we went to the meteorite crater, I wanted to have a long talk and tell her the truth. I knew you'd be busy, with the way you like to hike around and explore. I thought while you were playing, I could tell her who I was and see what she wanted to do about it. I thought by telling her there, she couldn't run away from me and not listen. Like you did."

Natalie's frown deepened. "Then why didn't you tell her?"

"Her friends interrupted my discussion with her and I couldn't. I really wanted her to know the truth. I wanted you to know the truth too."

"It's not fair. I wanted you for my new daddy. I don't want you to be my old daddy."

"But, Natalie, I'm the same man." And in that moment, Ethan knew the truth for himself. He was the same man. The war hadn't robbed him of everything. "Natalie, I want very much for us to be a family. I want to love you and be there for you. I want to teach you about drawing and architecture. I can't turn back the hands of time, but we can make a good try at the future."

"But it changes everything," Natalie said, her voice quivering with emotion.

"Yes. Yes, it really does. You've been living a certain way all these years, and now it will change. But I'd like to think that it will be a good change."

Natalie said nothing, and Ethan could clearly see the confusion on her face. She was wrestling with this new status—with the truth of who he was. She looked at him oddly for a moment, scrutinizing him as if seeing him for the first time.

"You aren't the way I thought you'd be. My mama told me stories about you and her. You aren't like she described."

"No, I don't imagine so. I look different . . . and I'm a different person inside," Ethan admitted.

"Now I won't get to have my picture taken with the veterans," she said, looking away.

Ethan thought he saw tears in her eyes but decided not to make any comment about them. "Natalie, you're still one very important little girl. Your mother loves you and so do I."

"But people are going to treat me different. With you alive, it changes everything."

Ethan wasn't sure he understood her comment, but he did realize the change in her life was more than a little upsetting. Natalie desperately needed to figure out how to make sense of this situation. She needed to know how she would fit in once everything was out in the open.

She looked at him, and this time he could see the tears. "People won't care about me anymore. They only loved me 'cause my daddy was a war hero."

"I seriously doubt that, Natalie." Ethan reached up to touch her cheek. "I think they love you because you're you—a sweet, wonderful little girl. Don't think them so shallow to only care about you because of what I did in the war."

"Can we go home?" she asked, wiping her nose with the back of her hand.

Ethan nodded. "Sure."

He took up the reins and mounted his horse. They rode toward Winslow in silence. How, he wondered, could he make this better for her? Should he try harder to explain? Should he stay out of the picture until Natalie and Ashley had a chance to work through the situation for themselves?

"I don't feel good," Natalie said, breaking the silence.

Ethan pulled up alongside Natalie. She looked pale. "Give me Penny's reins."

He wrapped the reins around the saddle horn, then reached out to take hold of Natalie. "I'll hold you in front of me, and then if you feel sick you won't fall off."

She nodded and willingly went to him. Ethan pulled her close and wrapped his arms around her. Every protective instinct in him took over. He wanted to shelter her from all the hurts in the world. He wanted to snap his fingers and make her feel better.

"You won't let Penny get away, will you?" she asked, leaning her head against his chest.

"Nope . . . and I won't let you get away either."

CHAPTER TWENTY-FOUR

*A*shley moved through the day in a leaden manner. Food had no taste; the air felt stale and lifeless. She could focus on nothing but Natalie. But already it was nearly three and still no word.

Lavelle had taken herself off to church after Ashley's outbursts earlier. She told Ashley she hoped to answer any questions that friends of Grandpa Whitman might have regarding the funeral and also stave off the curiosity of those who wondered why Natalie ran away.

Ashley's mother had locked herself upstairs and hadn't bothered to reappear until around noon, when she descended the stairs and partook of a cup of coffee. Her demeanor had changed. Surprisingly, she was very quiet. She asked about Natalie, then had the good graces to say nothing more when Ashley had replied that her daughter was still missing. After that, Leticia had taken herself back upstairs. Ashley had been delighted not to have to deal with her.

Lavelle checked in shortly after Leticia's appearance, then announced she was going to walk around the town and see if she could learn anything about Natalie. Ashley felt completely abandoned, yet at the same time, she knew she could bear the hours better on her own than in trying to make senseless conversation while her heart and mind were elsewhere.

Working in the kitchen, Ashley decided to bake a batch of Natalie's favorite sugar cookies. The deed made her feel more confident that Natalie would be found safe and returned home before she spent another night in the desert.

Ashley was just retrieving the first batch when her mother reappeared in the kitchen. She was dressed in her going-out suit, a dress and jacket of dark purple, trimmed in black braid. Her hat was perched to one side, her gloves were in her hands, and her pocketbook hung from her left arm.

"Are you going somewhere?" Ashley questioned, knowing it was too late for church.

"I'm moving into the Harvey House. I've arranged for them to pick up my things later this afternoon."

Ashley stared openmouthed at her mother. She couldn't help it. To hear her mother's declaration without snide comment or cruel remark was totally out of character.

"I know you're surprised," Leticia said, looking at her daughter with an expression that seemed to suggest regret. "I don't wish to further grieve you."

"Why this sudden change of heart?" Ashley asked. She went back to the task at hand and began removing the cookies from the pan. She could scarcely believe her mother's civility.

"You did make the request and it is your home," she said rather sternly. "Besides, I plan to leave immediately following Father's funeral on Wednesday. I might as well be near the train station."

Ashley couldn't stand it. She had to know why her mother was suddenly acting so genteel. She put the pan down and turned around. "Mother, why? This isn't your style. I don't understand. You had plans to fight me for this house and to change Grandpa's funeral and make a big issue out of the settlement of his estate. Now you sound as though you have accepted it all."

"I have accepted it," Leticia replied. "I know when to leave a thing alone. Father made certain provisions, and those provisions, if altered, will bring about consequences that I'm not willing to pay. Not that I'd have it to pay—not now."

Ashley still didn't know what to make of her mother's new attitude. "You aren't usually given to walking away from a fight. Why this time? Why now?"

Her mother's expression grew harsh. "It's really none of your concern what I do. You made that choice long ago."

All of Ashley's defenses rose to the occasion. "No, you made it for me," she replied. "I wasn't of a mind to never see you again. You're the one who told me to never come back—that I was dead to you. You turned your back on me when I needed you most."

"You ruined the plans your father and I had. Plans that we needed for the benefit of the family."

Ashley had never truly understood this. "Why?"

Her mother looked uncomfortable. "It's water under the bridge now and none of your business."

"It is my business," Ashley insisted. "It forever changed my life and that of my child. I feel I'm entitled to know."

Leticia looked away and cleared her throat. "We needed your marriage to the Manchester family. We had arranged it in a somewhat tentative agreement; then you up and married Ethan Reynolds." She looked back at Ashley. "Your father suffered a tremendous financial setback because of that. I had to cancel our European plans and fire two housemaids in order to trim our budget."

"I had no idea." Ashley hadn't realized her actions had made any real impact on the family.

"Your father had to sell some investments in order to keep your brothers in college. Of course, Mathias had landed a solid job with the bank, but the other two would need help in setting up their livelihoods once they finished their degrees. It wasn't an easy time, but your father forbade me to say anything to you about it." She lifted her chin defiantly. "I thought when your husband died that this was a reprieve for us. I began to immediately set plans in motion to revive the original agreement. It might have worked too, but you refused to even consider it."

"I was carrying Ethan's baby. What man of social standing was going to overlook that little bit of information?" Ashley asked matter-of-factly. Some of the bitterness faded from her heart.

"I didn't know about that. You only mentioned being unable to love again. That was nonsense in my book. Many women marry without benefit of love. I did. I saw no reason for you not to do the same."

"But had I known you were motivated out of need, rather than mere greed—"

"You would have acted no differently," her mother interrupted. "You and I both know that. You were lost in your grief and pain, and you cared nothing for mine."

Ashley knew it was true. It pricked at her conscience. *Forgive her,* that still, small voice whispered deep from within.

"I'm sorry, Mother. I truly am. You're absolutely right. I was very self-absorbed those days. When you told me you wanted nothing more to do with me, I convinced myself that I wanted nothing more to do with you as well. Grandpa always wanted me to contact you and let you know our whereabouts, but I wouldn't do it, nor would I let him. He'd told me how you'd treated him—how you'd demanded your inheritance and how he gave up trying to reason with you. I've never understood how you could have done that."

Her mother twisted her gloves. "I have no need to justify myself to you. There were reasons for my decisions. Reasons that I never expected you, a mere child, to understand."

"Maybe I'd understand them now."

"Be that as it may, I've no desire to discuss it."

Ashley shrugged. "No, I don't suppose you do." She felt her own anger stirred. *How can I forgive her when she acts like this? She doesn't feel she's done anything wrong. She just goes on and on about how things were ruined for her—never mind how she ruined things for other people.* "You've never felt you needed to explain anything you said or did. Grandpa didn't understand it, and neither did I. So we did as you demanded and took ourselves out of your life. You made your choice and it was my choice to see that you lived up to the full impact of that decision."

Leticia stiffened. "You needn't sound so smug. Your father died a broken man because of those choices."

Ashley hadn't really considered how her father might have dealt with her disappearance. She didn't like to think of him pining for her.

"He hired detectives, but the trail went cold around St. Louis."

Ashley remembered there had been some problems with her train in St. Louis. She had to change three times before she was finally sent on to Kansas City. There again, she changed trains and was given the wrong reservation for a different Mrs. Reynolds. She had ended up in Dallas, Texas, instead of Los Angeles. It hadn't been an easy trip for an expectant mother.

"You made me believe he was of the same heart and mind as you were. It was never my desire that Father should suffer."

"But it was your desire that I should suffer?" her mother questioned.

Ashley knew there was no sense in lying. "Yes. Just as it was your intention to make me suffer when you told Ethan I was dead."

Leticia nodded. "I suppose, then, we're somewhat even."

Now Ashley felt nothing but regret. Her heart ached at the thought of all those lost years. And now her daughter might be lost to her as well.

"I don't care about being even. I care about . . . ." Ashley fell silent. What did she care about? Her daughter and Ethan, of course. But what else? Did she want to mend this fence between herself and her mother?

Did she care whether her mother walked out the door to go stay at the Harvey House?

With a deep sigh, Ashley shook her head. "It isn't important." She turned back to the bowl of cookie dough. *Forgive her. Let the past go.* God nudged her conscience again. Sighing, Ashley knew what she had to do. For a moment she wrestled with the idea, then finally spoke before she could change her mind.

"You may stay here until you leave. If you want to."

Her mother said nothing for a few minutes, and Ashley refused to turn around. *That's the best I can do, God. It's the only step I can make right now. I'm trying to forgive her—I'm really trying.*

Her mother's silence was unnerving, but instead of forcing the issue, Ashley spooned the dough onto the pan and waited for some sort of response. She was ready to put the cookies in the oven before her mother finally replied.

"I'll stay here, then. Lavelle and I can visit some more, and we can be here when Natalie returns."

Ashley turned at this. She looked at her mother's expression. She had masked all emotion, lest she be too vulnerable—Ashley knew that trick very well. She tried to think of a proper response, but a knock on the front door drew her attention instead.

"Natalie!"

Ashley ran through the house and threw open the door. Pastor McGuire stood there, hat in hand. The grin on his face instantly dispelled her first fears. "Ethan has found her. She's safe and should arrive shortly. I can't stay, as I'm getting the word out to the marshal and his men."

Ashley hugged the surprised man and tears poured from her face as she stepped back. "Where was she?"

"Clear Creek, just like you suspected. You know her very well." He tipped his hat and hurried back down the sidewalk. "Ethan's bringing her home. They shouldn't be far behind."

Ashley clutched her hands together. *Natalie is safe. She will be home soon.* Putting her hand to her forehead, Ashley looked first down the street in one direction and then the other. Nothing. Just Pastor McGuire making his way at a rapid pace to the east.

Remembering her baking and fearing that it might already be burning, Ashley moved back to the kitchen. She was surprised to find her mother pulling the pan of golden sugar cookies from the oven.

"Thank you," she stated, not at all sure how to deal with her mother. Anger had been the officiator at every adult conversation up until now. The art of forgiving was an unknown factor between them.

"I couldn't see letting the house fill with smoke." Her mother's barriers were all back in place. Ashley would have smiled if not for the fact she knew it would annoy her mother. For all her life, Ashley had never seen the woman do anything this domestic.

"That was Pastor McGuire. He said that Ethan found Natalie and that she's all right. They should be here soon."

"I'm glad, Ashley," her mother said. Then after depositing the cookies, she put the potholders aside.

"Ashley!" Lavelle called. She rushed through the house to the kitchen and took hold of Ashley's arm. "I just heard that they've found Natalie."

Ashley smiled. "Yes. Yes, they did and she's safe."

"Oh, that is good news," Lavelle replied. "Is it not, sister?"

Leticia eyed Ashley and Lavelle with a blank expression. "I've already told her I was glad. Now I wish to go rest."

"Rest? But you look as if you're ready to go out," Lavelle commented.

"Nevertheless, I'm going to go rest."

Leticia pushed past them without another word. Ashley shook her head. "I've just had the strangest conversation with her. She was actually quite open for a few moments. Now she appears just as she always has. Hard and unreachable."

Lavelle patted her arm. "Give her time, Ashley. This transition will not be easy for her, and she may even decide not to make it at all."

"I just don't understand why she is suddenly willing to even consider it."

Lavelle shrugged. "It's hard to tell, and with Letty, I'm sure we won't receive an explanation. Perhaps upon losing Father, she's come to realize life is too short to act in such a cruel manner. Maybe her conscience is getting the better of her. We've prayed she might come to understand the truth—perhaps in time she will."

Ashley stared past Lavelle and through the dining area. "Even this morning, when I said what I did about her disdaining God . . . I'm ashamed to admit it but I meant the words, Lavelle. Isn't that awful? How could I say something so hideous and still expect God to love me?"

Lavelle reached out and hugged Ashley close. "Child, we all do awful things. We fail to care when we should and we worry too much when we oughtn't. Don't forget to forgive yourself as you work on learning to forgive her."

Ashley pulled away. "I'll try to remember that."

A noise at the front of the house caught her attention, and Ashley rushed to the front door and found Ethan dismounting a tall black horse. He wrapped the reins around her fence post, then took Natalie—their precious daughter—in his arms and carried her up the walkway.

"Oh, Natalie!" Ashley cried as she crossed the distance to greet them. She sobbed as she reached out to touch her daughter's face. Immediately she spied the lump on her forehead and the cuts. "Oh, you're hurt." Ashley's tears flowed in torrents.

"I'm sorry, Mama. I didn't mean to make you cry." Natalie looked as if she might burst into tears herself. "Please don't cry."

"Oh, sweetie, I can't help it. I'm so happy to have you home. Ethan, I'll take her. Would you see to Penny and send for the doctor?"

"Doctor's already on his way," Ethan replied. "I'll carry Natalie up to her bed and then tend to the horses."

Ashley nodded and opened the door for them. Ethan took the stairs quickly with Ashley right on his heels. Lavelle only smiled at them as they passed by.

Ethan gently placed Natalie on the bed and turned to leave the room. Ashley was standing only inches behind him, however, and the movement caused him to reach out to her in order to balance himself. Ashley felt an electrical charge surge through her body at his touch, but she tried to appear calm and collected.

"Sorry," he murmured.

"Don't be," Ashley said, looking deep into his eyes. "Thank you, Ethan. Thank you for finding her." She reached her arms around his neck and hugged him close. At first Ethan stood like a statue, refusing to hold her, but after she held on to him for several moments, he finally returned her embrace.

She finally let him go, but not without placing a kiss upon his bearded face. *Who was this man—her husband? Would they have a future? Could they remake their life together?* The questions overwhelmed her, threatening to steal her focus from what she needed to do for the moment.

"Let me get a basin of water and we'll clean you up," Ashley said, looking back to where her daughter lay. Natalie watched her with a worried frown, but Ashley ignored it and went quickly to work.

Returning with the basin and a washcloth and towel, Ashley began stripping away the grime and dust from her daughter's face and arms.

"I was so afraid," she said, her voice full of emotion. "I thought I might have lost you forever. I couldn't believe you were gone."

"I'm sorry. I was afraid too," Natalie admitted.

Ashley tenderly washed her daughter's cuts and scratches. "What happened to get you this lump?"

"I fell off of Penny." She came quickly to the pony's defense. "It wasn't her fault. I was riding her too close to the rocks. She misstepped and I fell and hit my head."

Ashley nodded. "I'm sure Penny was upset by the situation just as you were."

"Mama, did you know that Mr. Carson was really my daddy? I mean before you went to talk to him yesterday?"

Ashley straightened. "No, Natalie. I honestly didn't. There were things about him that reminded me of your daddy, but I thought he was forever lost to us—after all, the government said he was dead. I didn't figure they made mistakes. I never gave it a single thought that he might be alive."

Natalie bit at her lip, then questioned, "So are we going to be a family now?"

Ashley had no idea what to say, but she longed to know her daughter's heart. "What would you like?"

"I don't know." Natalie's voice sounded so frightened and lost.

Ashley hugged her daughter close. "Don't worry. You don't have to know. We'll pray and ask God to show us the right way."

"But I did pray, see," Natalie said, pulling away. "I prayed for God to send me a daddy just like my old one. Only instead of one like my old daddy . . ."

"He sent your real daddy—alive and well," Ashley filled in.

Natalie nodded. "And that changes everything."

Ashley gently laid her daughter back on the bed. "Why? Why does it change everything?" She needed desperately to understand her daughter's fears.

"Because it's not the same. I won't be the same person. Everybody's so nice to me because my daddy was a war hero."

"He's still a war hero, Natalie."

"Yes, but they thought he was dead."

Ashley shrugged. "We all did. Why does that change anything?"

Natalie shook her head. "I don't know." Exasperation filled her voice. "It's just different. I don't know what's going to happen."

Ashley was rather surprised by her daughter's reaction. "I suppose what will happen is that we'll all talk together and figure out what God has planned for us. Seems like God wouldn't have brought us all together if He hadn't meant for us to stay that way, though."

"Will they still let me decorate the graves of the veterans? Will I get to ride in the parades on Decoration Day?"

Ashley suddenly realized the heart of the situation. Her daughter's identity was at stake. "I'm sure they will, Natalie. As I said, you're still the daughter of a great war hero. Your daddy saved the lives of hundreds of men by risking his own life. But you know what?"

Natalie shook her head.

"I imagine," Ashley continued, "that the men who went out to look for you today—all those veterans who think so highly of you and took their Sunday to go out across the desert as part of the search party—won't care if your daddy is alive or not. They just love you because of who you are. They love you just for being Natalie Reynolds."

"That's what Mr. Car . . ." She frowned and drew a deep breath. "That's what Daddy said."

Ashley smiled. "He was always a very smart man."

Natalie seemed to ponder her words for a moment before adding, "He's a nice man too."

"Yes, he is. He's very nice."

The doctor came and pronounced Natalie no worse for the wear. He admonished her for giving the town a fright and suggested she just might have to share her sugar cookies with him. She in turn told her mother to be sure to share her cookies with the doctor, which Ashley did quite happily.

The doctor had gone and Ashley was tucking Natalie into bed when her mother came into the room unannounced.

"So what did the doctor say?" her mother asked rather gruffly.

Natalie eyed her grandmother with a worrisome frown while Ashley took up the plate of cookie crumbs. "He said she's fine, but she should rest."

"I see." Leticia looked as if she might like to say something more, then turned to go. Stopping just outside the door, she turned back around. "I'm glad you're all right, Natalie." She exited then as quickly as she'd come.

Ashley looked at her daughter and smiled. "I think that was Grandmother's way of saying she loves you. But don't tell her you know," she said in a whisper. "She'd rather people think her strong and capable of doing everything without having to love anybody at all." Natalie giggled and Ashley thought she'd never heard a more pleasant sound in all her life.

*W*ednesday afternoon the friends and family of Russell Whitman filed into Faith Mission Church to pay their last respects. Ashley was pleased to see such a large turnout. She'd known her grandfather was well loved, but it warmed her heart to see the proof. Grandpa wouldn't have wanted them to be maudlin and downcast, but rather he would have wanted a sense of celebration. He had gone to a better place, and therefore his last wishes had been that there would be laughter and positive stories about his life.

Ashley couldn't help getting a little teary at times, however. Pastor McGuire did a wonderful job of speaking on Grandpa's life. Several times he mentioned Grandpa's generosity to the townspeople, and Ashley glanced back slightly to see nods of affirmation.

Over and over she looked at the shiny pine casket where Grandpa's body lay. The casket remained closed, as was Grandpa's wish, but Ashley's mother and aunt had paid for a huge spray of white carnations and red roses to be placed upon it. Ashley had remembered Grandpa's wish for no flowers, so she had talked to Natalie, and they'd agreed they would purchase a plant instead and keep it alive in memory of Grandpa. Natalie asked if she could keep the plant in her room, and Ashley had agreed.

Oh, Grandpa, you'll be so missed, Ashley thought. *So many times I think of things I'd like to say to you. I'd like to have your advice about Ethan and about Mother. . . . You would be so good with explaining about forgiveness and how to keep from being bitter about the past. And you'd keep me from losing my temper with Mother. I know I can pray now and talk to God, but having you here was much more comforting.*

He's only gone from earth, Ashley reminded herself. *He's in heaven, healthy and well, with a new body.* It pained her to think of how the sickness had ravaged him. He'd wasted away to nothing, and Ashley knew he didn't want to be remembered that way. She found herself fighting to block those images. It had been hard to lose Grandpa, but it would have been harder still to see him linger with the cancer.

Ashley reached out and squeezed her daughter's hand. *Thank you, Lord, that she's here and safe. Thank you that we're not having two funerals.* The thought caused Ashley to shudder. How tragic it could have all been. She knew God had looked out for her child, but still the memories caused her grief. *But what if there's a next time?* Ashley knew they were in for a long journey together before they'd ever feel like a true family. What if Natalie could never accept Ethan as her father? What if she ran away again?

Oh, Lord, help us. It's so hard for Natalie to understand what's happened. It's hard for me to understand as well. I'm so new to this whole thing of faith. Do you love me less if I find it hard to trust you? For so many years, I'd convinced myself you didn't care. I feel like a scared child, wanting to trust and believe that it will all be well . . . but knowing from experience that bad things could still come my way.

Ashley looked past Natalie to Ethan. She wondered if he struggled with the future as much as she did. They were married. They would celebrate their twelfth anniversary in the spring. Twelve years of marriage . . . and only a few months of actually being together.

Folks probably wondered why he had joined them in the family pew. Then again, gossip had no trouble making the rounds in Winslow. By now there were bound to be many folks who knew the truth and just as many who'd embellished the truth. Sooner or later they'd know for sure what had happened. Especially if Marcus Greeley had anything to do about it. He still planned to write his book, and now more than ever, he had plans for devoting a thick chapter to Ethan and all that had happened.

Ethan. Ashley still couldn't believe Ethan was truly here. It all seemed so much like a dream. Sometimes she was completely convinced she would wake up at home and find Grandpa still alive and well and that the events of the past few months had been nothing more than her imagination working overtime.

"Russell Whitman will be sorely missed," Pastor McGuire said. His words pulled Ashley's attention away from her worries. He continued. "I myself will miss our games of checkers and chess, our walks and discussions, and the humorous way Russell had of looking at life. But most of all, I'll miss his faith. Grandpa Whitman was a man of such deep conviction and faith that he put most of us to shame."

Ashley noticed her mother shift in her seat, as if the words were entirely too much to bear. Lavelle sat beside her and reached over to pat her sister's hand as if understanding her discomfort.

"Whenever I had a problem and needed counsel, I went to Russell. One of the first things I could expect him to ask me was this: 'Sean, do you believe God can take care of this problem?' "

Ashley heard a few chuckles. No doubt more than one person had been faced with this same question. She herself had been asked that by Grandpa. Most of the time she *didn't* think God would take care of the problem. It wasn't a matter of whether or not He *could* take care of it— she just didn't believe that He would.

I'm sorry, God. I wish I'd come to know you sooner. I wish I'd listened more to Grandpa. Ashley felt tears come to her eyes and wiped at them with the hanky she'd remembered to tuck into her sleeve.

"Sometimes I told Russell I knew God *could* take care of the problem. I just didn't know if He *would.*"

Ashley startled at the pastor's words. Sean McGuire looked at her and smiled, as if knowing her thoughts. Ashley felt her face grow flushed and lowered her gaze to her gloved hands.

"Russell would just laugh and tell me I wasn't being honest with him. He'd say, 'Sean, I know you believe He will resolve the problem— you're worried, however, that He might not solve it your way.' "

Most everyone laughed, and even Ashley had to smile. Pastor Mc-Guire continued, his voice taking on a great deal of emotion. "Russell Whitman knew the right thing to say to get my eyes off myself and back on God. I think that's what he'd also ask of us today. He'd not want our focus to be on him and all that he'd done for us. Russell would want our focus on the Lord and what He did for us. Russell would want us to remember that it was only because of God that he was the man he was."

Ashley knew it was true. She listened to Pastor McGuire conclude the service and felt at peace. Grandpa was in a better place and happier than he could have ever been here on earth. She needed to remember that. She also needed to remember that Grandpa's illness and Ethan's appearance in Winslow had not taken God by surprise. God knew the way things would play out.

They were escorted from the front pews, with two elders from the church offering their support to Lavelle and Leticia. To her surprise, Ashley watched her mother dab tears from her eyes before accepting the man's offer. Maybe a little of the ice had thawed.

That day in the kitchen had been so strange to Ashley. She had never seen her mother act in such a way. At one moment she wanted to open her heart, and in the next breath she'd be angry and hostile. Still, Ashley knew her mother a little better for the telling of her tale. It didn't make things right between them, but it was a start. Perhaps it would take months or even years for her mother to figure out the truth for herself. Maybe she would never be warm and affectionate, but at least she could learn that Ashley and Natalie and even Ethan weren't the enemies in her life.

Ethan took hold of her arm and guided Ashley out to follow her mother and aunt. Natalie had stepped aside to bring up the rear and walked beside Pastor McGuire. The sunlight seemed rather diffused in the November setting. Soon Thanksgiving and Christmas would be upon them, and sometime between those two events, the Harvey hotel construction was to be completed. Ashley wondered what it would mean for Ethan and his job duties.

He'd implied that he intended to be there for them—that he wanted to be a family again. But once Mary Colter took her entourage and moved on to the next Harvey job, would Ethan feel the tug to move along as well? By his own admission, he'd never settled into one place for long since coming back from the war.

She looked up and found Ethan watching her. She fixed her gaze on him, trying to will unspoken answers from his heart. He nodded and looked away as if telling her he had no answers to give. It made her feel even more doubtful of what would happen next.

The ladies of the church had set up a meal for Ashley and her family at the house. Pastor McGuire offered to drive them home while Grandpa's coffin was being loaded in the hearse and taken to the train station. Lavelle would catch the afternoon westbound train and escort her father's body back to Los Angeles. Ashley frowned at the thought. *He'll be so far away. Why couldn't we just bury him here? At least then I could visit his grave and put flowers on the stone.*

But it was Grandpa's last wish, she chided herself, knowing she sounded more like her mother than she wanted to admit. It was Grandpa's desires—not her own or her mother's—they needed to honor. After all, he would be buried next to Grandma, and Ashley knew that was only fitting.

They crowded into the car, Ashley's mother taking a place up front with the pastor and his wife, while Ethan, Ashley, and Lavelle rode in back. Natalie sat on Ethan's lap, as it seemed the only alternative. She didn't seem bothered by the arrangement; in fact, Ashley thought Natalie looked rather content.

Ashley smiled at her daughter. Her bruised forehead wasn't quite so visible after they'd restyled her hair to give her bangs. And Natalie seemed at ease with Ethan, but there was still a hesitation in the way she interacted with him.

Time. Ashley knew it would take time. Time for Natalie to adjust her thinking and accept Ethan as her father rather than Mr. Carson the architect. Time for them to become a family.

And what about the time you need? she asked herself. *Ethan has changed. He told you so and now you've seen it for yourself.* The idea of being a wife again was both terrifying and thrilling. She could easily find herself quite content to keep house for this man—her husband.

"Do you need me to come drive you to the station this afternoon?" Pastor McGuire questioned Lavelle as they climbed out of the car a few minutes later.

"No, Ethan has offered to walk over and borrow one of the Harvey cars. He's going to drive me."

Pastor McGuire smiled. "It's been a real pleasure to get to know you, Mrs. Guzman. I hope you have a safe journey back to Los Angeles."

"Thank you, Pastor. You did a wonderful job on the eulogy. I know my father would have approved."

"Yes," Ashley added, "Grandpa would have said you did it just right." She reached out her hand. Pastor McGuire shook it vigorously.

"See you in church on Sunday?"

"Absolutely," Ashley replied. She put her arm around Natalie's shoulders and led her to the house.

"Hmmm, it smells good in here," Natalie declared, immediately going to investigate the meal.

Ethan and Ashley followed at a slowed pace while Lavelle and Ashley's mother walked behind them. Ashley wondered if her mother would comment on the service. So far she'd said very little, and Ashley couldn't help wondering if the words had made any sort of impact in her mother's heart.

The ladies from the church finished putting the food on the table just as they entered the dining room. "Look, Mama. Fried chicken," Natalie said, coming to her mother. She looked up at her mother and then at Ethan. "My mama loves fried chicken."

Ethan nodded, as if this bit of news was an important fact to remember. Ashley smiled. "I certainly do."

They took their seats and as the food was passed around, Natalie again interjected a comment. "Don't give the lima beans to Mama. She hates those." She stated this again for Ethan's benefit.

Ashley quickly realized her daughter was trying to help Ethan get to know who Ashley was. It seemed rather funny that after having Natalie play matchmaker, now she would act as guide and interpreter to help Ethan better know his own wife. Maybe in doing this little deed Natalie was also better able to adjust to the situation herself. Ashley wouldn't have put it past the child to fully comprehend what she was doing and to meticulously plan it out for everyone's benefit.

The meal soon passed and it was time to take Lavelle to the station. Ethan had gone to borrow Mary Colter's car and had just pulled up in front of the house when Lavelle came downstairs with Leticia close behind.

"Sister is going to accompany me," Lavelle told Ashley. She'd already mentioned to Ashley that she'd like to have some privacy with her sister. Ashley had agreed she'd remain behind when the time came to go to the train station.

"Oh, I'm glad. I wasn't going to be able to get away," Ashley said. "I've some things I'd like to take care of. I hope you don't mind if I stay here."

"Not at all," Lavelle replied and hugged Ashley close. "Thank you," she whispered in her niece's ear.

Ashley kissed her aunt on the cheek and bid her farewell. Natalie did likewise, then announced that she was going to go tend to Penny. Leticia, in her dark purple suit, looked at Ashley for a moment, then returned her concentration to the front door. Ashley wasn't sure if her mother had intended to say something about the pony or Natalie or if she'd wanted to comment on another matter altogether. Whatever it had been, she said nothing instead.

"Are you ready to go?" Ethan questioned as he came through the door and spied Lavelle.

"I am. If you would be so kind as to retrieve my trunk, I'd be most grateful."

Ethan nodded and bounded up the stairs, taking them two at a time. Within a moment he was heading back down, the black trunk on his shoulder. He headed out the door and Lavelle turned again to Ashley.

"I promise to visit you in the spring, and you remember your promise to come see me in the summer. Natalie will love the ocean."

Ashley could well imagine her daughter wanting to remain in Los

Angeles for that feature, if nothing else.

"I won't forget," Ashley replied. And if Ethan had no objections, Ashley fully intended to see her promise through.

———————

Ethan was glad to see that Lavelle had worked out getting Ashley and Natalie to stay home. He had plans for talking to Leticia in private and hadn't been at all sure how to go about it. He drove the two ladies to the station, listening to them comment on the future. The uncertainty of the financial world was still of grave concern to Leticia Murphy. She had little understanding of exactly how bad things might be once she returned home. He hated to see anyone suffer, but his heart was rather scarred where this woman was concerned. He didn't want to hold a grudge or treat her with indifference, but she needed to understand his position and that he would no longer allow her to interfere in his life or Ashley's and Natalie's.

They arrived at the station and Ethan made arrangements for Lavelle's luggage while Leticia bid her good-bye. Returning to where the two older women stood waiting, Ethan said, "I'm glad for the opportunity to have gotten to know you, Mrs. Guzman."

"As am I. You are a miracle. Without a doubt. I know this is all going to work out." She smiled and reached up to pat Ethan's cheek with her gloved hand. "Just give God time."

"That's the trick, isn't it?" he commented.

"To be sure."

Ethan glanced at the steam engine down the track. Wisps of steam escaped here and there, and the heady scent of oil, grease, and creosote filled the air. These were the smells of the railroad—an odor he'd gotten quite used to in his work with Mary Colter. Would he now leave that world and remain in Winslow to settle down and piece his family back together? Would they pick up and go elsewhere with him if that were the direction God led?

"I think I'll just wait in the car, Mrs. Murphy. That way you two can have some privacy," Ethan offered, knowing that the questions in his head would not be easily resolved standing there on the platform of the Winslow depot.

Leticia said nothing. Her façade of strength and fierceness held everyone at bay. Ethan didn't really care. He didn't need or desire a relationship with his mother-in-law, but he was bound and determined to have one with her daughter.

Walking back to the car, Ethan forced his thoughts to come into order. He replayed the speech he intended to make to Leticia. *If I don't make it clear now,* he reasoned, *she'll try to walk all over both of us.*

He waited nearly twenty minutes before Leticia returned. Without giving her a choice, Ethan went around to the front passenger door and opened it for her. Leticia didn't so much as glance at him. She stepped into the car and continued to stare straight ahead.

They were soon on their way, but when Ethan should have turned for home, instead he began to talk. "I have something to say to you," he began. "You may not be inclined to listen otherwise, so I'm making it so that you'll have to listen." He drove out of town and headed east.

"Where do you mean to take me?" Leticia questioned, her voice betraying fear.

"I only mean to drive out far enough that you can't just walk back, and then I mean to talk to you about Ashley and me."

Leticia looked at him for a moment. "I really have no desire . . ."

"I don't care. This is how it will be."

Ethan drove for nearly fifteen minutes before he felt comfortable pulling off to the side of the road. Once he was satisfied with their safety and the ability to see traffic coming from either direction, Ethan turned to Leticia.

"I don't trust you," he said firmly. "You lied and made Ashley and me most miserable." Leticia said nothing but continued to gaze out the windshield, as if there might be something of great interest outside.

"Your selfishness denied my wife and child a better life. Your lie left me grief stricken and hopeless for years on end. At one point, because I'd drawn away from God so completely, I even contemplated taking my life. Had you even bothered to consider that you might have contributed to the death of another human being?"

He didn't want to deal with her in anger, but her cold reserve chiseled away at his self-control.

"I won't let you cause this family any more harm," he finally said. This seemed to get her attention.

"Oh, and what will you do? Kill me here and now?"

Ethan shook his head. "No. I'm not going to cause you harm simply because that's *your* method. But I will do whatever it takes to protect my family. I have friends in high places now. Friends with money and power, just as you have. Both sets may be a little worse for wear given the crash, but I'll use whatever means I need to keep Ashley and Natalie safe."

"And you think you need to protect them from me?" she asked in disbelief.

"Absolutely. You were at the very heart of their pain. You told me Ashley was dead. And you allowed Ashley to go on believing I was dead."

"I had no way of finding her. Her own father had tried to locate her," Leticia said in her defense. "I couldn't have told her the truth even if I'd wanted to."

"But that's my point. You didn't want to. You wanted to keep us separated because you never thought I was good enough for your daughter. I'm just making sure this matter is clear once and for all. You will not interfere in our lives anymore."

"I'm Ashley's mother and I have a right to see her."

"A right you gave up a long time ago when you sent her away without a penny." He stared hard at the older woman and hoped her fidgeting was a sign of discomfort under his scrutiny. "Besides, until this moment, I've not heard you even mention wanting another chance to see her. You came to Winslow with an entirely different motive."

Leticia's shoulders rolled forward slightly. "What is it you want from me, Mr. Reynolds?"

"An understanding," Ethan said, trying to steady his temper. "I want you to be a part of Ashley and Natalie's life if that's what they desire. However, I want it on their terms." He paused and added, "And my terms." He let the words sink in for a few moments before continuing.

"If you want to spend time with them, you'll leave your fury over our marriage in the past. You'll not malign my good name, and you'll not force your opinions on my wife and child. Also, you're never to raise a hand to my child again. Do you understand?"

Leticia looked at him for a moment, her piercing eyes never so much as blinking. Then her expression seemed to soften. "I understand."

"And do you agree to those terms?"

"I suppose I must."

Ethan shook his head. "No one is forcing anything on you, Leticia. You choose to come willingly into my family or not at all. I want no moping or grudge holding. I want no false tears of martyrdom. You are the only living grandparent Natalie has. I don't know if you have other granddaughters, but she's a pretty special girl. She needs someone to look up to. What she doesn't need is someone or something else to regret."

"I understand," Leticia stated, then returned her gaze to the windshield. "I want only what I deserve."

Ethan shook his head. "No. No, you don't. Because if you were to get what you deserve, it certainly wouldn't have anything to do with Ashley and Natalie. Ashley and I were wrong to marry in the fashion we did."

This caused Leticia to turn back to him. Eyeing him with a look of disbelief, she waited for him to continue. "I know that now," he said. "I didn't then. I was young and idealistic and foolish. The war was on and it seemed that there might not be a tomorrow. I didn't think about the consequences of anything. I fell in love with Ashley and married her—and never gave a single thought to respecting your wishes. For that I'm sorry, and I do apologize. I hope that somehow you can find it in your heart to forgive me—to forgive Ashley too."

"Well . . . I . . ." Leticia shook her head. "I find this highly unexpected."

"I don't need answers today, Mrs. Murphy. I just want you to consider everything I've said, including the fact that I want your forgiveness. I brought you out here because I wasn't sure we'd have another chance to talk alone before you headed home this evening. Just think on my words, and when you feel confident of an answer from your heart, then let me know."

He maneuvered the car back onto the road, not even waiting for the older woman to answer him. He thought long and hard about the way their conversation had gone. He'd done his best, and even though there was some anger in his words, over all, Ethan felt he'd managed the situation quite well. He could only pray that Leticia would come around to seeing things their way.

———

Later that evening, Ethan, Ashley, and Natalie stood on the depot platform bidding Leticia good-bye. It was a stilted and awkward moment for all three. Natalie was still very apprehensive of her grandmother, and Ashley had no idea what to make of her mother's attitude. Ever since that day in the kitchen, she seemed less harsh but more reserved. Maybe God was truly doing a work in her heart. Ashley could only pray that it was true.

"Please let my brothers know where I am," she told her mother as the conductor called the final board. She was relieved to have finally learned that her brothers had all married and were raising families.

Mathias had two boys, Richard had three boys and a girl, and Parker had two girls and his wife was expecting. There was an entire family out there that Ashley had no knowledge of.

"I will," her mother promised. "I'm sure they'll be pleased to know. They've never understood what happened."

"Perhaps it's time to tell them," Ashley replied.

"Perhaps." Her mother's words were thoughtful. She looked at the train car and drew a deep breath. "Mr. Reynolds, Natalie, I am glad for the opportunity to have met you both. In future visits, I shall look forward to getting to know you better." She met Ethan's gaze, and Ashley thought that something unspoken was exchanged between them.

Ashley lowered her face and smiled. It wasn't much in the realm of an apology or pledge of love, but for her mother, Ashley knew it was the best she could offer. And because of how God had dealt with her own heart of late, Ashley knew that for now, it was enough.

Leticia moved toward the train, and Ashley followed her while Ethan and Natalie remained behind.

"Mother, I'm glad you came to be with Grandpa. I know it meant the world to him."

"He would have liked it better had I told him everything he wanted to hear," Leticia replied. "But I've never been given over to religious nonsense, and I'm still not convinced it has any place in my life."

Ashley nodded. "I know. But I also know how Grandpa was about planting seeds." She smiled. "After all, he found a way to cultivate a little hope in my heart. I'm sure he was able to manage at least that much with you."

Leticia lifted her chin and looked down her nose at Ashley. It was a look Ashley would always remember her mother for, as long as they lived. "Perhaps." Then quickly changing the subject, Leticia added, "I will see you in the spring. Perhaps for your new resort opening."

Ashley nodded. "It's scheduled for May, which around here is already summer, but you're more than welcome to come. Just let us know."

"Of course, it will depend on the financial status of the country and of my own personal estate. But if things do come together in proper order, maybe your brothers and their families will accompany me."

Ashley smiled. "I'd like that. I'd like that very much."

Leticia said nothing more. She allowed the porter to assist her onto the train, then stood at the top and turned only momentarily. She exchanged a glance with Ashley, offered the tiniest of waves, then disappeared into the interior.

Ashley thought of how different this departure had been from Aunt Lavelle's. Lavelle had hugged and kissed Ashley with great affection. Leticia hadn't offered a single touch. Ashley felt sad for her mother's isolation. It was the first time she'd had that feeling rather than a sense of her mother getting what she deserved. Smiling to herself, she pulled her jacket close and turned back to her family. The healing had truly begun.

"Let's go home," she said softly.

*A*fter sharing a sumptuous Thanksgiving meal with Pastor McGuire and his wife, Ashley and Ethan settled down in front of the fireplace, determined to talk about their future. Natalie stretched out on the floor at their feet and worked on a small weaving loom, making potholders for her mother.

Ethan had been waiting for this moment ever since Ashley suggested it. Thanksgiving seemed a good time to share their hopes for the future, and while Ethan was still uncertain as to what Ashley and Natalie wanted from him, he knew very well what he hoped for.

Clearing his throat nervously, Ethan picked lint off his navy blue suit coat, then looked down at his daughter. She was staring up at him—watching, waiting. She knew he wanted to talk to them, but Ethan wasn't at all sure what her response would be. He'd tried hard to get her to talk to him prior to this, but she wouldn't. She'd even stopped coming to the hotel where he was working.

"I suppose," he began rather awkwardly, "that you both know how important this is to me. How important you are to me."

Neither one said a word, making it all that much harder for Ethan. "I know we're strangers in many ways. We've spent some time together and . . . well . . . we know each other a little better than when we first met." He was making a mess of things. There just didn't seem to be words for what he wanted to convey.

How did he tell his wife and daughter that he loved them, despite the years that had separated them? How did he explain that his life would be very empty if he had to go back to living without them?

"When is the hotel scheduled to be completed?" Ashley asked.

Her soft words brought Ethan out of his thoughts. "December fifteenth is when the exterior and structure should be finished. Then we're faced with a great deal of interior work. They plan to open in May, as scheduled, in spite of the stock market problems and issues of money loss. The railroad isn't doing too badly, and they believe the money they're still putting into this creation is money and time well spent," Ethan replied.

"So what are your plans? Do you intend to see it through?"

"I'd like to," Ethan replied. "I've enjoyed working for the Harvey Company."

"As have I," Ashley stated. "In fact, I intend to start back to work as soon as possible. The Christmas season is always busy, what with folks traveling all over the countryside to be with loved ones. They'll need my help."

"But you don't have to work. I'll help with the expenses and—"

Ashley held up her hand. "No. I have plenty of money. At least for now. I plan to go to work because I like it, and I don't like sitting around here with nothing but my memories. Natalie will be in school all day, and that's when I shall work. They'll allow that schedule because I'm one of their best Harvey Girls," she said, smiling.

"Mama really is," Natalie added, as if Ethan needed convincing.

Ethan nodded. "I'm quite sure she puts them all to shame."

Natalie smiled and went back to her weaving. Ethan looked at Ashley and tried to regain control of what he had planned to say. There seemed no other way to open the discussion but to simply put his thoughts out there for everyone's scrutiny.

"I'd like for us to be a family."

Natalie and Ashley both looked at him. They seemed quite content to await his explanation on the matter. Ethan felt as if the tie around his neck were tightening. *Lord, don't let me make a mess of this.*

"I know we have a ways to go in getting to know each other, but I already love you both," Ethan said, feeling embarrassed by the words. He'd never been given over to his emotions—at least not like this. But then again, he'd never had so much at stake.

"The years that separated us weren't of our own doing—not entirely. We can't change what happened back then, but we can change what happens from this point on."

"I think we all want the same thing," Ashley said, smiling.

Ethan saw the love in her eyes and knew deep within his heart that she did indeed desire the same thing he did. Glancing at Natalie, he saw her expression was pretty much unreadable.

"I'd like to set up a design firm here in Winslow if you're both of a mind to go on living here. If not, we can easily move elsewhere. I like it here, though. The people are pleasant and good-natured, and the desert is beautiful in its own way. Still, I'll happily go to the ends of the earth if it means we can be a family."

He didn't see any change in his daughter's face. He'd so hoped she'd at least smile or give him some sign that his words met with her approval. "I'd like to teach you everything I know about drawing and design," he said to Natalie. "You are very talented and I see great promise. I believe with dedication to your dream of becoming an architect, you and I could one day have the best father-daughter team around."

Natalie perked up at this and sat up. "Would we have an office and everything? Would I have my own drawing table?"

Ethan chuckled. "Absolutely. You'd have whatever you needed to make you the very best architect."

"That would be the bee's knees," Natalie declared.

"Natalie, where in the world did you pick up that expression?" Ashley questioned.

Natalie laughed. "Jane says it all the time and so do my other friends." She glanced at the clock and gathered up her things. "I need to go give Penny her treat."

"Don't be long," Ashley said. "We've still got a lot to talk about."

Natalie nodded and slipped away, humming. Ashley turned to Ethan, her eyes wide with question. He wanted to lose himself in her dark-eyed gaze.

"Ashley, I know I'm not the same man you married. I don't even look like that man," Ethan said, stroking his well-trimmed beard. "I'm still going to struggle from time to time with nightmares from the war—and while my walk with God is growing stronger, it's still very young."

"As is mine," Ashley said, reaching out to take hold of his hand. "But at least we can share that walk."

Ethan turned toward her and gripped her hand tightly. "Ashley, I want a new life for us. I want to court you again—this time without the desperation of war looming over us, making us act irresponsibly and hastily."

"Do you regret our haste?" she asked, frowning.

"No, of course not. I wouldn't trade the time we had together for all the architectural jobs in the world. I loved you dearly, as I do now. That will only grow stronger with time."

"I love you as well," she whispered. "I never stopped. People thought me troubled because I refused to remarry or consider anyone else. But there was a part of me that couldn't let go of you—even across the years."

He nodded knowingly. "It was the same for me. I knew I couldn't bring you back from the dead, and yet you were all I wanted."

"I felt the same way," Ashley assured him.

"I want us to remarry," he said, surprising himself. "But only after we have time to get to know each other again and to help Natalie adjust. There's no need to rush this time. There's no war—no family working against us."

"I'd like that very much," Ashley said, leaning closer. She reached up and gently touched his bearded cheek. "I've dreamed of this moment for so many years. I'd cry for joy because you had come back to me. Then I'd wake up and cry in sorrow because I saw the truth of it in the morning light."

Ethan pressed her hand against his face and held it there. "You were all that kept me alive on the battlefield. I would think of you and know that I had to go on—that I had to come back. Then when I was wounded, I held on to your image and my faith that God would bring us back together."

His chest tightened and he reached out and pulled Ashley into his arms. "I cannot tell you, nor do I need to, how much it hurt to think you dead."

"I know. I know exactly."

Their faces were only inches apart, and Ethan knew he would kiss her. He only hoped that she desired it as much as he did. He leaned closer.

"Ashley?" He spoke her name as a question. He wanted permission to kiss her.

She closed the distance between them and for the first time in eleven years, they shared a kiss. The longing in Ethan's heart threatened to smother out all other thought. He pulled her closer, held her tighter. *I don't want this to ever end,* he thought.

Ashley gave herself completely—deepening their kiss, wrapping her arms tightly around his neck. Ethan had never known such joy and peace. He finally pulled back just a bit and saw the tears that streamed down her face. The sight shocked him, and he let go of her rather abruptly.

"You're crying."

She opened her eyes and smiled. "For the joy of this moment. For the way I still feel when you touch me. For the promise of our new future together."

He gently touched her wet cheek. "I've never known happiness until this moment. The past no longer seems important."

"I was reading something in the Bible. It was in the forty-third chapter of Isaiah. It said, 'Remember ye not the former things, neither consider the things of old. Behold, I will do a new thing; now it shall spring forth; shall ye not know it? I will even make a way in the wilderness, and rivers in the desert.' This is God's 'new thing,' " Ashley said softly. "I see that now. We don't need to remember the former things. They're gone. We can't reclaim the years we've lost or make my mother take back her words that so damaged us both. But we can look to the new thing God is doing."

Ethan murmured her words. "A river in the desert. How appropriate that seems."

"I thought so too. Ethan, I'm not the same girl you married in 1918. Just as your appearance is altered, so is mine. And just as the nightmares and scars of the past have damaged and wounded your heart, so my heart has suffered as well.

"We aren't children anymore. We can't be wild and impetuous. We can't run away from the world and hope it will never find us. I'm willing, however, to risk my heart with you. I want to move forward and trust God for His new creation in our lives. I will court you and I will remarry you, for I have no intention of ever letting anything come between us again. Not people or wars or time."

Ethan hugged her close and knew she could probably hear the wild beating of his heart. It didn't matter. They were together. They were home.

Ethan heard the back door open and close but remained where he was. Natalie came back into the room, pausing momentarily by the door. Ethan looked over Ashley's shoulder at his daughter, wondering if he'd see resentment on her face.

"Do I get a hug too?" she asked, looking as though she felt left out.

Ethan grinned. "You can have as many hugs as you want." He opened his arms to her and Natalie rushed to join them. She giggled as Ethan pulled her tight, smashing her between him and her mother.

Ethan knew the time had come to press his question. "Natalie, will you let me be your new daddy?"

She pulled back and shook her head. "No."

Ethan felt stricken, her stern expression forever frozen in his memory. He looked at Ashley, who appeared just as surprised as he was.

"I don't need a new daddy," Natalie said. "I've already got a real good one." She smiled and added, "I just want you for my forever daddy."

Ethan felt the tears come to his eyes, but he didn't try to hide them. "I'd like that too, Natalie." He buried his face against her neck and let the tears come. He felt Ashley and Natalie both tighten their hold on him. They were his again. As they had always been.

God had made rivers in the desert—streams of joy running through his dry and weary heart.

EPILOGUE
May 15, 1930

Ashley allowed Ethan to conduct her on a private tour of the newest of Fred Harvey's resort hotels. La Posada—the resting place—was a marvel of Spanish and Mediterranean flavoring. Surrounded by orchards and gardens, it rose up to look as though it truly had been there for years and years. Ashley almost expected to see some grand Spanish don stroll across the stone walkway to introduce himself and welcome them to his home.

"This wishing well," Ethan explained, taking her to an ornate wrought-iron creation, "was brought from Mexico."

"It's lovely," she said, completely impressed with the well and the expanse of lawn that surrounded it.

Ethan handed her a penny. "Make a wish."

She fingered the coin for a moment, then pressed it back into his hand. "I don't need to. They've all come true."

He held her gaze for a moment, then nodded and slipped the penny back into his pocket. "Guess we won't make too many walks back here."

She laughed. "Well, at least not for a while."

They pressed on, strolling the grounds as though this were their own private hacienda.

"Miss Colter tells me she received an amusing telegram this morning," Ethan said as they moved at a leisurely pace toward the doors. "It came from one of the railway officials. It offered congratulations, then stated that they hoped the income exceeds the estimates as much as the building costs did."

Ashley laughed. "They certainly went lavish and lovely for this resort. I can just imagine the people who will come here and the happiness they'll find in such a setting. It's truly more than I could have ever imagined."

"You don't know the half of it," Ethan replied. "I'm just glad it's completed. I've never been involved in such an ambitious affair, but I wouldn't have traded the experience for all the world. Miss Colter does remarkable work. Her visions are most incredible. When she first brought me here and showed me this sunken piece of land, I couldn't begin to imagine her dream. Then she started hauling in dirt and the construction company came in to work, and before I knew it the walls were up and the stucco was spread and all the rooms were finished."

He led her inside and they toured the lobby before going upstairs to the ballroom. "It's over two thousand square feet," Ethan told her.

The blend of Spanish and colonial furnishings impressed Ashley. "I can just imagine the grand dances that will be given here." She turned and grinned. "The movie stars will come and bring their rich friends and throw elaborate parties. At least that's what Glenda told me. I only hope that it's successful, for the sake of the Harvey Company."

"I pray it is as well," Ethan replied. "Over a million dollars has gone into this creation. They need to find a way to make back that money." He frowned. "But given fears for the economy, I'm not entirely sure it's sensible to believe they'll ever see a profit."

"Is it really that bad, Ethan? You aren't worried, are you?" She looked into his eyes. "We still have the money Grandpa left me—and the house, of course."

"There's really no way to determine at this point how bad things will get. I know just in talking with the railroad officials there are a good many railroads that will probably die out because of the crash. Some officials say they were anticipating something like this, although I don't know how a person could ever predict a situation where certain stocks plunge from over a thousand dollars a share to less than ten dollars a share."

"All those dreams and hopes," Ashley said, shaking her head. "I think of people like my mother, who have lived in luxury all their lives and now face poverty."

"The very wealthy probably aren't facing poverty," Ethan said. "It's probably more a matter of degree. The degree of wealth they enjoy is less. But I would be willing to believe they're still enjoying wealth, nevertheless."

"And the poor get poorer," Ashley murmured.

"Exactly."

"Mama!" Natalie came running at breakneck speed. "Grandma—I mean Grandmother Murphy—is here."

Ashley looked at Ethan and felt her entire body tense. Swallowing hard, she couldn't think of a single thing to say. Ethan stepped in for her. "Tell your grandmother we're on our way."

Natalie whirled around, the skirt of her lilac-colored dress ballooning out as always. "I'll tell her." She hurried from the ballroom and down the stairs—her shiny black shoes clattering all the way.

Ashley looked at the floor. She'd been expecting her mother's arrival, but now that the time had come, she felt like running in the opposite direction. "I hope she's changed. Her letters sound as though she's sincere in trying to be a better person. She still pries about my financial situation and about the sensibility of remaining in Winslow, but she doesn't badger and demean me."

"Then we must give her the benefit of the doubt, no?"

Ashley knew Ethan was right. Still, she had worked so hard to move away from the resentments of the past. Seeing her mother again might just force all those emotions to the foreground. "I don't want to become the woman I used to be," Ashley murmured. All around them people in various stages of animated conversation drifted past. "I didn't care about the hardness of my heart. It suited me well and kept me safe."

Ethan nodded. "I know. I used to feel the same way. But we aren't those people anymore. Just like we're not the kids we were when we first married. God's helped to bring healing to our family, and healing started with forgiveness. You forgave your mother for the past. You can't go taking it back now."

She smiled. "No, I don't suppose that would be right."

"Well, we certainly wouldn't want to have God doing the same to us." He grinned and put his arm around her waist. "Now, come on. We'll go greet Mother Murphy and see what news there is of your brothers."

Ashley knew he was right and walked along in silence, praying for the strength to deal in kindness and love. She thought of the few letters she'd shared with her mother over the last months. Her mother's financial state had been weakened by the crash, but there had remained enough money to begin laying new foundations. No one knew what the future would bring. There were both threats of depression and promises of prosperity. Only God knew the truth, and that suited Ashley just fine.

Ethan led her to the main lobby, where solid walnut swing-back benches set a regal stage with their embroidered Moorish cushions. It was here that Ashley found her mother. Sitting in a rather queenly pose, with Natalie standing before her, Leticia looked for all the world like a ruling monarch. Natalie chattered away and surprisingly enough, it appeared that Leticia was actually listening.

When her mother glanced up, Ashley managed a smile. *Help me not to be afraid, Lord. Help me not to say the wrong thing.* Their new relationship was so fragile—like one of the beautiful blue-and-white Chinese Chippendale jars that stood just to her right. One wrong move could send everything crashing to the ground.

Her mother stood as they approached. Ashley grasped Natalie's shoulders, more to steady herself than to keep Natalie from going elsewhere. "Hello, Mother. Did you have a nice trip?"

"Indeed, I did. It was far more pleasant than the last trip I made to Arizona. I was able to secure a private car. It seems one of your father's acquaintances holds a high position with the Santa Fe. Once he learned I was to make this trip, he offered his car to me."

"Grandmother said the room had velvet on the walls and that there were brocade chairs and very comfortable sofas," Natalie declared. "And she had all her meals right there at a beautiful oak table with candles and everything." It was clear to Ashley that Natalie was quite enthralled.

"Oh, and I met the most marvelous gentleman, and he tells me he knows you both," Leticia stated.

Ashley looked at Ethan then back at her mother. "Who is this man?"

"Marcus Greeley. Apparently his new book is well in the works. He's come here to interview Ethan at length. He was quite enthusiastic about it. Apparently your Ethan is quite the celebrity—a true hero of the Great War. Mr. Greeley said his story and your subsequent separation will make a . . . let's see, how did he put it? 'A feast of words.' "

"Truly?" Ashley looked at her husband. "Did you know about this?"

Ethan's face reddened. "I'd . . . ah . . . hoped he'd just forget about me." He gave a short, nervous laugh. "I'd just as soon be left to my own devices."

"But, Daddy, you're a hero and Mr. Greeley just wants to let everybody know." Natalie reached out and took hold of her father's hand. "I want everybody to know too."

Natalie's words meant a great deal to Ashley. Over the months since Natalie had first learned the truth about Ethan, she had grown closer to him and more trusting of their relationship. Now they were back to being the good friends they'd been when Ethan had first come to Winslow.

"I do hope you won't have to give this man all the details of your . . . ah . . . separation," Leticia Murphy said, looking to Ashley as if to convey her thoughts with a glance.

Ashley knew her mother was worried about her involvement—the lies she'd told Ethan about Ashley's death during the influenza epidemic. "I'm certain Ethan can think of a delicate way in which to relate the story."

Her mother grew notably more relaxed. "I'd appreciate that."

Ashley smiled, and to her surprise, her mother offered her a hint of one in return. Her face seemed softened somehow, yet she continued to bear herself in an elusive manner. Ashley thought her still the height of fashion in her two-piece dove-colored suit. The hat of matching color gave her a finishing touch of elegance.

"And what news have you brought of my brothers and their families?" Ashley asked, trying to sound lighthearted. In the months since her mother had returned to Baltimore, Ashley had received and written several letters to her brothers. They were all happy to be reunited, chiding her for letting them worry and for letting so many years pass without knowing of her whereabouts.

Her mother frowned. "They're struggling," she said matter-of-factly. "The bank isn't faring well at all. Mathias fears they might well close their doors. His wife, Victoria, is quite beside herself. Parker and Richard find that their legal services are more in demand than ever, but people haven't the financial means to pay. It's a difficult time, to be sure."

Ashley nodded. "We haven't felt the effects as much as you have back East, I'm sure. Ethan even tells me that the Santa Fe was on top of the situation and actually has come out of it in a fairly stable manner."

"It will take time," Leticia stated, sounding far less desperate than she had when she'd first learned of the crash. "But most things worth having are that way."

Ashley wondered if her mother meant to include their relationship in that statement. How strange it seemed that a mother and daughter should struggle so much to share their lives. Ashley could only pray and ask God to ease the tension between them.

"It was kind of you to let me stay at the house," Leticia said. "I arranged for someone to take my luggage there. I hope you don't mind."

Ashley smiled. "Not at all. I'm really glad you were able to come."

Leticia looked at her for a moment, then transferred her studying gaze to Ethan. "And when is this wedding to take place?"

"Sunday!" Natalie declared before either her mother or father could speak. "I get to be in the wedding with them. Isn't that wonderful, Grandmother? I have a new dress and even new shoes."

Leticia peered down her nose at the child momentarily, then offered a smile. "I imagine you'll be the prettiest girl in the room."

Natalie shook her head. "No, Mama will be. She has a new dress too, and she looks really pretty in it."

"Mother, I would imagine you're tired," Ashley interrupted, embarrassed by her daughter's comments. "Would you like me to take you back to the house? We have a car now."

"Gracious, no. I intend to tour this lovely facility. If Natalie would do the honors, I would like that very much."

Ashley was surprised that her mother was so openly friendly toward her granddaughter, but nevertheless she was glad to see it. "Natalie, would you like to show Grandmother around La Posada?"

"Sure." She went to her grandmother's side and took hold of her arm. "Come on, I'll show you my favorite room. It's the lunchroom and it has the most wonderful tiles for decoration. And there's a big hutch where they display beautiful plates. You'll really like it, Grandma."

Ashley was surprised her mother didn't correct Natalie's use of "Grandma." Instead, her mother seemed quite content to let Natalie lead the way, chattering about the contents of the room and why it was the best in the resort.

Just then, Mary Colter and Marcus Greeley walked into the room. There were several men with them—men whom Ashley didn't recognize. No doubt they were either reporters or railroad officials. Either way, the party looked very important.

"Mr. Reynolds," Mary declared as she approached them, "I don't suppose I shall ever get used to calling you that." She smiled and nodded at Ashley. "Mrs. Reynolds."

"Miss Colter, it's good to see you again. La Posada is magnificent. I'm truly amazed at what you've done here."

"Not bad for a piece of ground that used to house the roundhouse, eh?" She smiled. "Now, my boy," she said, looking at Ethan, "will you be joining us at the Grand Canyon? We're making plans for an additional hotel, and I'd love to have you working on the project."

Ashley noted that everyone seemed eager for Ethan's answer. He put his arm around Ashley and finally spoke. "I'm quite content to remain here in Winslow. There's a great deal I wish to accomplish right here, but I thank you for the offer."

"Well, the good ones—the ones who give you little trouble and do as they're told," Mary said, looking at the men beside her, "those are the ones you always lose first."

"Ashley and I are being remarried on Sunday. We'd love for you to join us," he told the group.

"I'm sure we wouldn't miss it," Mary said. Then spying someone across the room, she took her entourage, minus Marcus Greeley, and moved off in pursuit.

"So I suppose you know why I'm here," Marcus said with a grin.

"I do. I'd rather hoped you'd forgotten me," Ethan replied.

"Are you kidding? Your story is going to be the selling feature of my book. Even women will want to read a copy of *Those Who Fought.* They'll be swooning with excitement over your reunion with your wife and child."

"*Those Who Fought.* Is that the title?" Ashley questioned, hoping to take the focus off of Ethan. She knew her husband was embarrassed at the prospect of his life being poured out onto the pages of a book.

"Yes, the publisher liked the sound of it and so did I. People are quite willing to hear the tales now. And, in spite of our growing isolationist mentality, I believe the general public desires to honor those who gave so much on the battlefield."

"I'm sure you're right," Ashley replied, looking at Ethan. "If you don't mind, however, Ethan and I need to see to my mother's luggage. She was having it delivered to the house, and I don't wish to leave it sitting on the street."

"Of course," Greeley answered. "I'll look forward to seeing you for the interview tomorrow."

Ethan nodded, even as Ashley pulled him away. "I thought perhaps you'd like a reprieve," she whispered as they walked from La Posada and crossed the street on their way home.

"Thank you. I still fail to see why he needs my story. There are so many others that need telling."

"Yes, but you have to admit, our story has so many twists and turns. There probably isn't another like it. You came back from the dead. How many men can lay claim to that?"

They paused and turned back to look at the hubbub surrounding the grand resort hotel. The grounds were full of people, and a general atmosphere of festivity lent a spirit of delight to those who attended. Even if their financial world had fallen apart, the partiers seemed quite good at masking their situation. From what Ashley could tell, these beautiful people were quite content.

To her surprise, Ethan took her into his arms right there on the side of Second Street. "Ethan!" Ashley declared. "What do you think you're doing?"

"I'm going to kiss my wife," he said softly.

"But it's broad daylight and we're standing in the middle of everything. Someone might see you."

Ethan chuckled. "Let them watch. I'm not ashamed. Are you?"

Ashley looked past his gold-rimmed glasses to the dark brown eyes that studied her so intently. "I will never be ashamed of you. I still can't believe you're really here. Sometimes when I wake up in the morning, I struggle to believe that everything that has happened isn't just some sort of dream."

"Well, soon you'll have the proof beside you in your bed."

Ashley felt her face grow hot and looked past Ethan to the hotel. "We'll have to stay there someday. You know, to just be spoiled and pampered. I happen to know that the Harvey Company takes very good care of you."

Ethan laughed. "I know that to be true as well. In fact, I'm entitled to a free stay. Part of the bonus for working on the project. We could spend our honeymoon there. You know, give the house over to your mother and Natalie and have some time just to ourselves." He pulled her closer to him.

"I think I'd like that," Ashley murmured, looking back at her husband. "Oh, Ethan, I'm so very happy. Please promise me we'll always be this happy."

Ethan frowned. "You know I can't do that. There will likely be hard times—we have to accept that. To do otherwise would be unrealistic and set up expectations that would only serve to disappoint us in the future."

"I know what you say is true," Ashley replied, "and I know God will be with us no matter what. But I wish I could have some guarantees."

Ethan laughed again. "Life doesn't come with guarantees, but it does come with choices. And I choose you, now and for all time. All I want from this point forward is to enjoy the years to come with you at my side."

He kissed her tenderly, leaving Ashley breathless. How could it be that after so many years of marriage, separation, and the belief that he was dead, Ashley could still find herself so quickly stirred by his touch?

They began walking up the street, heading for home. "By the way," Ethan said, reaching out to take hold of Ashley's hand, "how do you feel about having more children?"

Ashley was taken aback for only a moment. "I suppose," she said, "we shall need to buy more ponies."

Ethan stopped abruptly before laughing out loud and pulling her close. "And build a bigger house."

"Oh, we could get by for a time," she replied. "After all, it takes several months to bring a child into the world." She flushed and looked away. Having another baby was her secret desire. How funny that he should have brought up the matter.

"So you don't mind the idea of giving Natalie a brother or sister?" he asked seriously.

Ashley looked up and saw the longing in his expression. Perhaps he had feared she'd refuse such an idea. She immediately felt sad for the time he'd missed with Natalie. *No,* she thought, *I can't live in regret. I can't keep thinking, "if only."*

Ashley reached up and gently touched Ethan's bearded cheek. "I would like very much to create new life in our new life together. I think it would be marvelous to have a whole houseful of children."

"So long as they're your children," Ethan whispered.

"So long as they're ours," Ashley corrected. "So long as they're ours."

————

The remarriage of Ethan and Ashley Reynolds was a quiet and simple affair in spite of the large number of people who turned out at Faith Mission Church that Sunday. Natalie, again everyone's darling, did a combination of sliding and hopping down the aisle in her animated fashion. Her cream-colored gown gave her a rather angelic appearance, Ethan thought.

Then Ashley came forward in her salmon-colored dress that looked quite similar to the one she'd worn the first time they'd married. Ethan's breath caught deep in his throat. A radiant glow shone from her face. *How can it be that she's mine? How is it that I should be so blessed?*

The ceremony lasted only a few minutes. They exchanged their vows; then Ethan took up the wedding ring he'd first given Ashley so many years ago and replaced it on her finger with a pledge of all that was his. His worldly goods, his heart, his very life.

And then the affair was over and they were laughing and sharing well-wishes from all their friends and family. Ashley looked rather tired by the time they were ready to put the party behind them, but Natalie seemed as fresh as ever. She came to them, her eleven-year-old gangly frame seeming almost half a foot taller than when Ethan had first met her.

Natalie wrapped her arms around them both and laughed. "Now we're really a family and nothing will ever change that."

Ethan rubbed her curls. "But we've always been a family," he said, knowing a deeper joy than he'd ever thought possible.

Natalie looked up at him and then at Ashley. "Grandpa said that family was a matter of heart. That sometimes total strangers ended up being as close as family. You were a stranger at first, but I always liked you. Guess my heart knew you were my daddy."

Ethan felt his eyes mist ever so slightly. He looked at his wife and saw the tears in her eyes. "And my heart must have known you as well," he said in a voice barely audible. "But then, how could it not? For you are my heart." He looked back at Natalie, adding, "You are both my heart, and no matter the future . . . we are family."

Beneath a Harvest Sky

"We'll never stick to schedule if you keep putting the Cadillac in the sand," Rainy Gordon teased her twin brother. She cast a glance over her shoulder at the Harvey House tourists, or "dudes," as the staff called them, who waited rather impatiently in the noon sun. Lowering her voice she asked, "How can I help?"

Gabe Gordon, better known as Sonny, looked up from beneath the brim of his ten-gallon cowboy hat and smiled. "Well, if you're done merely supervising, you could get behind the wheel and try to move this beast forward when I give you the okay. I think I've cleared as much sand as I can back here, and those rocks you brought me are bound to help give her a little more traction. But just to be safe, I'll push."

Rainy gave a salute from the brim of her uniform hat. She was grateful the Fred Harvey Company didn't require their women couriers to dress in the overexaggerated cowboy attire. Still, looking down at her Navajo tunic of dark purple velvet, silver concha belt, and squash-blossom necklace, she supposed she played the role of Indian to her brother's cowboy act.

Sliding behind the wheel of the Harvey touring car, Rainy pushed back her braided strawberry blond hair and waited for Sonny to give her the go-ahead. Getting stuck in the sand wasn't that unusual along some of the wilder stretches of New Mexico and Arizona, but they were only five miles outside of Santa Fe, and this little mishap should never have happened. Sonny hadn't had his mind on business as of late, but Rainy was hard-pressed to know what consumed his thoughts.

"Give it a try—just don't press down too hard on the accelerator. Just ease her out," Sonny called.

Rainy did as he instructed and with a jump and a lurch the Caddy reared onto solid ground, causing the dudes to cheer. Rainy giggled to herself knowing that the teenage daughters of one of their clients would surely see Sonny as their knight in shining armor. They'd positively swooned over him since first joining the tour three days ago. But that was just as the Harvey Company planned it to be.

After three years of working as a Detour courier, Rainy knew the routine better than most. She was in the entertainment business, just as surely as if she starred on the silver screen. Her job was to make people forget their problems and entice them into the wonderful, mysterious world of the Desert Southwest. As a tour guide, Rainy could direct their attention to the subtle and not-so-subtle nuances that shrouded the Indian lands and add intrigue and excitement to their otherwise dull, fearful lives.

For in 1931, there were a great many reasons to fear.

Hard times were upon them as the country was rapidly sinking into a stifled economy. Some claims led folks to believe that good times were just around the corner and that people owed it to their country to open their wallets and spend. At the same time, other predictions were far more discouraging. Doom and gloom hung over the country like an ill-tempered relative who threatened to extend his visit and take up permanent residency.

Rainy worried about her mother and father, who lived in Albuquerque. Her father worked for the university there, and while his job seemed perfectly secure, Rainy knew the economy's failings could easily change that. After all, a college education was a luxury, and many people would forego it in a flash in hopes of securing stable work in its place. If that happened often enough, her father would no longer be needed to teach history and archaeology.

"We need to move out," Sonny called, putting an end to Rainy's reflections. "Why don't you gather your dudes and let me get back in the driver's seat?"

"Only if you think you can keep us out of the sand," Rainy said, sliding from the seat. "I honestly don't know what gets into you sometimes, but maybe you could tell me about it over dinner. We can start with where your mind was when you put us in that hole."

Sonny shrugged and positioned himself behind the wheel, suddenly growing sober. "We should talk, but right now isn't the time."

His serious tone caused Rainy's imagination to run rampant. Was something wrong? Did he have some word about their jobs? Was the company about to fold? There had been all kinds of rumors suggesting major changes. Maybe Sonny had more information than she realized.

Plastering a smile on her face, Rainy went to the overweight matronly mother and her two teenage daughters. "We need to get everyone back in the touring car," she announced. The woman, red-faced and perspiring fiercely, nodded and motioned to her brood.

"Mother, tell Miss Gordon to let me sit up front with Sonny," the elder of the two girls whined. The girl had made eyes at Sonny all day long. She'd even tried to throw herself into his arms by faking a fall from a ladder, only to have her sister bear the brunt of her descent.

The woman looked to Rainy as if to comply with her daughter's request, but Rainy gave her no chance to speak. Instead she moved forward to take her place. "Let's hurry, folks. Santa Fe is just over the hill. We have supper waiting for us at La Fonda, and let me tell you, the fare there is not to be missed. Tonight they're offering a variety of choices including some wonderful Mexican dishes, broiled salmon steaks, and roast larded loin of beef with the most incredible mushroom sauce."

She positioned herself inside the front passenger door without actually taking her seat. "And for those of you who haven't yet stayed at La Fonda, you are in for a treat. The hotel has been completely renovated and offers some of the nicest rooms along the Harvey line."

The plump mother consoled her daughters and shooed them into the backseat of the touring car as an elderly couple took the seats directly behind the driver's place. Had the girl not insisted on pouting and causing a scene, the older pair might not have robbed her of at least sitting behind Sonny. Rainy fought to hide a grin as she did a final head count and climbed into the car.

"We're all here," she told her brother.

"Good thing too. We're losing the daylight." Sonny put the car into gear and headed down the road.

Rainy breathed a sigh of relief when they pulled up to La Fonda. The adobe hotel was a home away from home for her tourists, and she was only too happy to turn them over to the Harvey House for the evening.

In order to save Sonny as much grief as possible, Rainy rounded up her charges and led them into the lobby without giving them a chance for argument.

"Your luggage will be delivered to your rooms," she told them.

"I wanted to tell Sonny good-bye," the elder of the teenagers pouted. She threw Rainy a look that suggested the guide had just separated the child from her true love.

"Sonny's very busy arranging for the luggage. You may see him around the hotel later," Rainy replied.

She turned her guests over to the registrar and hurried back to the car to help Sonny with their things. "Give me your bag," she told her brother. They shared a two-room apartment at a boardinghouse very near to La Fonda. Many of the couriers and a few other drivers lived there as well. It was inexpensive and the food was good. Still, it wasn't home. Home was in Albuquerque with her mother and father. She had cherished their little adobe house for as long as she could remember. Her mother had planted a lush garden in the courtyard and Rainy loved to spend hours there just dreaming of the future and all the plans she had.

"Pedro is already taking care of the dudes' luggage," Sonny said, handing her his small bag. He pulled his cowboy hat off and used his oversized kerchief to wipe his brow and sweat-soaked auburn hair. "I thought that tour would never end," he declared.

Rainy leaned into him good-naturedly and giggled. "But you're soooooo handsome," she mimicked in the voice of the teenage tourists. "Your eyes are dreamy." She batted her lashes at her brother and both of them burst into laughter.

"You'd better behave. Seems to me you get more than your share of attention when those dudes come in the unmarried male variety."

Rainy shrugged and hoisted her own bag to balance Sonny's. "If God would just tell me which one He has in mind for me to marry, I'd happily take their attention."

Sonny sobered. "How can you be so sure your husband will come by way of the tourists?"

"I don't know that he will, but it seems as logical a conclusion as any," Rainy replied. "Should I wait to have dinner with you?"

Sonny nodded his head. "Yeah, save me a seat. I'll need to get the car to the garage and get cleaned up. How about giving me an hour?"

Rainy nodded. "Sounds good." She made her way to the two-story adobe-over-brick boardinghouse and made her way upstairs.

"You look exhausted," Maryann, one of the newer couriers, declared as she passed Rainy on the steps.

"It was a tiring group today. Lovesick girls mooning over Sonny . . . and Sonny putting us in the sand."

"I think Sonny is the bee's knees," another girl declared as she came down the oak stairs to join Maryann. "He's so sweet."

Rainy laughed. "That's pretty much how the dudes saw it. Anyway, I need to get this stuff upstairs and get over to La Fonda for dinner." The girls nodded and stepped out of her way.

"We're heading to a party over at Teresa's place," Maryann added. "You and Sonny would be welcome. It's mostly just couriers and drivers."

"I'll think about it," Rainy replied, knowing she and Sonny wouldn't be attending. Neither one was big on parties all that much—unless, of course, it was with family.

Rainy trudged down the long carpeted upstairs hall. The housekeeper, Mrs. Rivera, kept sparsely furnished but very clean quarters and Rainy appreciated it greatly. Juggling the bags, she slipped her key in the door and stepped inside with a sigh.

She deposited her bag by the door and tossed her hat to the bed. Crossing the room, she opened the door that adjoined her space to Sonny's. She left his bag on the bed and went to open the window. Sonny liked it crisp and cool at night, and the warmth and stuffiness of the room would only serve to give him a headache.

Stretching her arms overhead as she walked back to her own room, Rainy couldn't suppress a yawn. Indeed, this tour had seemed so much longer than most of the others. Rainy pulled off her silver bracelets, then removed her squash-blossom necklace of turquoise and silver. She placed the items on her dresser, noting her reflection in the standing mirror. No matter how careful she tried to be, it always seemed her fair skin managed to get burned and, in turn, add a few freckles to her already dotted nose.

"Oh, bother," she said, unfastening her braid. "If I didn't come back burned and freckled, I'd run to the doctor to see what was wrong with me."

Her long red-blond hair rippled down her back. "Why couldn't my hair be as dark as Sonny's?" Her twin brother had the most beautiful shade of auburn hair, and for some reason he tanned easily and never freckled. It was simply unfair.

Noting that time was slipping away from her, Rainy hurried to clean up and dress for dinner. Even though she was no longer required to share her dinner with the tourists as the staff had been in the early days of the Detour program, Rainy was still expected to dress nicely to represent the coveted Harvey name. "You are still an ambassador of the Harvey Company!" her supervisor would often say.

"But for how long?" Rainy murmured aloud. She pulled on a clean black skirt and tucked her frilly white blouse into the waistband. First rumor and then newspaper articles had revealed that the Harvey Company was planning to sell the Detours. In fact, it would most likely be Major Clarkson, the manager of the transportation company from its inception, who would buy the company and run it.

With the financial uncertainty of the day, everyone saw the necessity for a bit of belt tightening. Taking the train to the American Southwest and hiring the expensive Indian Detours, as the Harvey Company dubbed the guided tours, was a luxury most couldn't afford. When it came to deciding between keeping food on the table and taking a vacation, travel went way down on the priority list. Yet Clarkson knew a good thing when he saw it. He wouldn't disassociate the company too far from the Harvey reputation. The Detours would still spend their nights in Harvey hotels, eating Harvey food.

Making her way downstairs, Rainy suddenly realized how hungry she was. Her thoughts, however, didn't drift far from the question of whether or not she'd have a job in another six months. No one could be certain of work—especially women. After all, why should a single woman be given gainful employment when a man supporting a family was turned away? It was all a matter of being sensible in a time that seemed to reject all pretenses of sense and sensibility.

"Are you eating with us tonight?" Mrs. Rivera questioned as she rounded the corner with a tray of tortillas.

"No, Sonny and I will be dining at La Fonda." Rainy gave the older woman a smile and bent to inhale the aroma of the freshly fried tortillas. "Although I'm tempted to stay. You are far and away the best cook in all of Santa Fe, Mrs. Rivera."

The old woman grinned. "I'll save you some *sopapillas* on the back of the stove. You might need a late-night snack."

Rainy laughed. "I know Sonny will appreciate that."

She took her leave and walked back to La Fonda, where the bustle of tourists and workers was always a wonder to behold. The cool stone interior welcomed her with wonderful artistic drawings and the flavor of old Mexico. The hotel, rich in the furnishings and interior design of Harvey's cherished architect, Mary Colter, was the most sought-after establishment in all of Santa Fe. The rooms were lavishly furnished, the suites incomparable to anything else in the state, and the hotel food was up to the Harvey standards: huge portions and rich ingredients fashioned by the hands of some of the finest chefs in all the world.

Rainy was shown to a table for four in the back corner of the hotel restaurant. It was her favorite place to enjoy her meal. She was rarely

pestered by the tourists, and she didn't have to deal with old friends . . .
unless, of course, she wanted to. The early evening rush had cleared
out, and now there were more local diners and Harvey employees than
tourists. Rainy sighed and leaned back against the oak chair. It felt so
good to be off duty.

She'd no sooner taken her seat at the elegant table than she spied
Duncan Hartford. Her heart seemed to skip a beat as she studied his
handsome face and thick dark hair. How she wished she could get to
know him better.

Since Sonny planned to join her soon, Rainy reasoned that it
wouldn't seem out of line to invite Duncan to join them. He might as
well have been one of the Harvey employees since he worked at one of
the museums where the company arranged tours, allowing Rainy to see
him on a regular basis. He was practically family, she told herself. Never
mind that Rainy found herself attracted to this man of archaeology and
Indian research.

Her breathing quickened as she tugged on the sleeve of her Harvey
waitress. "Would you do me a favor and ask Mr. Hartford if he'd like to
join me for dinner?"

The young woman beamed Rainy a smile. "Sure thing." She wove
in and around the tables and guests to where Duncan was just about to
be led to another table. Rainy watched as the girl appeared to explain
the situation.

For one horrible moment Rainy feared he'd reject her offer. *Why
did I do that?* She'd never before gone running after a man for company.

She wanted to bury her face in her hands and pretend it had been
a mistake. *Maybe if I pretend to read the menu . . . then I won't seem so desperate.* She picked up the menu and considered her choices.

"It was very kind of you to invite me to join you this evening."

Rainy looked up to meet Duncan Hartford's deep brown eyes. She
swallowed hard. "I hope it didn't seem too . . . well . . . forward. I
mean . . . we know each other . . . pretty well, and my brother will be
watching—I mean, he'll be joining us."

He laughed and the sound was deep and throaty. He pulled back
the chair while the Harvey waitress filled their glasses with ice water.
Rainy felt rather silly. Her words seemed all jumbled, and while they
made perfect sense in her head, they didn't seem so accurate when they
came out of her mouth.

"Would you like to order now?" the Harvey Girl questioned.

"My brother should be joining us shortly," Rainy indicated. "But I'd very much like to go ahead and start with some tea."

"That sounds good to me," Duncan replied.

The waitress disappeared, leaving Rainy feeling rather uncomfortable in the silence. She'd long admired this man, but how could she make that clear without sounding like one of Sonny's young admirers?

"Oh, there you are," Sonny suddenly said, coming from behind her. "I can't stay. I need to help a friend of mine get his car running. Do you mind?" He looked from Rainy to Duncan.

Rainy swallowed hard. When she'd thought Sonny would be a part of their company, she hadn't felt quite so awkward. "You still have to eat."

"I'll grab a sandwich at home," Sonny replied. He extended his hand to Duncan. "You're Mr. Hartford from the Indian museum, right?"

Duncan shook his hand. "Yes, but please call me Duncan."

"I've seen you at the museum, but since I generally wait with the touring car, I haven't had much of a chance to get to know you." He glanced at his watch. "I'm sorry, Rainy. I really need to get over there."

Rainy nodded and unfolded her napkin to keep from having to meet Duncan's expression. "That's all right. You have a good night and I'll see you in the morning. Oh, and Mrs. Rivera is leaving you some sopapillas on the back of the stove."

"God bless that woman. She always seems to know just the right way to work herself into my heart." He gave a little wave and hurried out of the dining room.

Rainy could only think to smile and apologize. "I'm really sorry. If you feel it inappropriate to stay . . ."

"Not at all. We're both adults and we're obviously both hungry," he said with a hint of amusement in his voice.

"So is Sonny not staying?" the Harvey waitress asked as she passed their table.

"No, he had to tend to another matter," Rainy replied.

"We're ready to give you our orders if you like," Duncan added. He looked at Rainy with an expression that almost seemed sympathetic.

Maybe, she thought, *he understands how I feel. Wouldn't it be marvelous if a man could just look at the situation and comprehend the details of the matter without having to ask a lot of questions?* Rainy had often enjoyed the quiet companionship of her parents. They worked so well together and almost seemed to read each other's minds.

"And what will you have?"

Rainy broke free from her thoughts. She looked up to find both the waitress and Duncan watching her quite intently. "I'll have the beef," she murmured without bothering to look at the menu.

The waitress wrote down their orders, then went off to tend her other tables. Rainy felt the discomfort of not knowing what to say. She knew Duncan Hartford from his work at the Indian Museum and Art Gallery, but she didn't know him all that well. What she did know was that she thought him one of the most handsome men she'd ever seen and she enjoyed his kind and gentle nature when he dealt with the demanding tour groups.

She hesitated, then cleared her throat with a delicate little cough. "I hope I didn't interrupt your plans." She glanced up to find him gazing at her.

"My plans for a quick meal alone were worth interrupting. Especially when I can share the company of one as pleasant as yourself." He toyed with his necktie and smiled.

Rainy felt her stomach do a flip and reached for her water. Perhaps a drink would help to settle her nerves. "I've long admired your Scottish brogue," she said out of desperation when the water didn't do anything to calm her. "My family is also from Scotland. My father was born in Edinburgh."

"Truly?" Duncan asked, his tone revealing his surprise. "I was actually born here in the United States, but my father is a Methodist minister, and the call took him to the land of his ancestors to preach. We moved shortly after my birth and lived there for twelve years. I've refined my speech a bit since returning. I suppose an absence of nearly twenty years should alter the cadence and intonations rather completely, but . . ." he said, leaning in closer, "I can roll my *r*'s in a right bonny fashion if I've a mind to do it." He emphasized his brogue, making Rainy laugh.

The Harvey Girl again appeared, bringing them a pot of English tea. Rainy smiled when she realized Duncan had ordered tea.

"Most American men prefer coffee," she said.

"Can't say I'm not given over to drinking a cup now and again," Duncan admitted. "But for supper, I prefer tea."

Rainy thought it all marvelous. "So your parents are Scottish?" She stirred a bit of cream into her tea and noticed Duncan did likewise.

"Actually we're all American-born. My father's father was a Scot who lived in the borderlands, and his mother was English. Their families strictly forbade them to see each other, but young love refused to listen." He smiled and leaned forward. "They eloped and eventually, because both families refused to accept the marriage, they came to America. My mother's people are Scottish through and through. None of those distasteful English skeletons to hide." He pulled back and drank his tea.

Rainy sipped from her cup for a moment. They had a great deal in common—more so than she might have imagined. "My ancestors are Scottish and English as well. My uncle Sean still lives on a farm outside of Edinburgh. My parents would like to go back for a visit someday. Of course, with the economy as it is now—banks failing and the gold standard crumbling—I think they're almost afraid to hope for such a thing."

"It is a bleak time, to be sure."

The waitress arrived and in perfect Harvey fashion served their meals. "I must say, the breaded pork tenderloin is my favorite," she told Duncan as she fussed over him and made certain he had what he needed. But true to her job, she turned equal attention on Rainy as she placed the roasted loin of beef in front of her. "And this is my second favorite. I think the chef does it up better than just about any place along the Santa Fe line."

Rainy smiled. "It certainly looks good."

The Harvey Girl made certain they had everything they could possibly need, then left them to the privacy of their meal. Rainy looked up with uncertainty. "Would you like to say grace?"

Duncan threw her a look of admiration. "I would like it very much."

He murmured a prayer and blessed the food, leaving Rainy at peace for the first time in days. *How I've longed for God to send a man into my life who I could seriously consider as a husband. Not only is Duncan Hartford handsome in a rugged and understated way, but he holds to my faith and beliefs. Is he the one, God?* She looked at Duncan even as she poised the question in her mind. He sliced into his pork and extended her a piece.

"Would you like to try it?"

Rainy shook her head. "No, thank you. I've had it many times before. It's also one of my favorites."

They ate in silence for some time before Duncan braved the next round of questions. "So where do your parents live?"

"Albuquerque. My father works for the university there," Rainy added. "I used to work with him." She immediately regretted the words. Oh, how she'd tried to bury that part of her life.

"Oh? What did you do there?"

Rainy tiptoed ever so cautiously through the memories of her scarred past. No sense waking sleeping dragons. "I worked with him in the history department. He's a professor of history, and I hold a master's degree in history with a special focus on the American Indians—particularly the Hopi, Navajo, Zuni, and Pueblo."

"How marvelous. You truly are the right woman to be leading the Detour trips."

"I love the Southwest," she admitted. She forced herself to sound calm and unflustered when all the while her heart was pounding like a racehorse's hooves in the final stretch.

"As do I. My focus of study is archaeology," he admitted.

"I have a bachelor's degree in archaeology," she said, hoping he'd see how much they had in common. Instead, it led him back to troublesome waters.

"Truly? Did you utilize your degree when you worked at the university?"

Rainy felt light-headed from his question. She wasn't about to get into the details of her past. *Anything but that,* she thought. How could she possibly hope to interest Duncan Hartford in becoming her husband if she had to share the memories she longed to forget? Yet, how could she hope to move toward marriage and not share those details?

No, she thought. *Until I can clear my name, no one else needs to know what happened.*

A week later Rainy was still contemplating her supper with Duncan when Sonny came into the boardinghouse dining room and interrupted her breakfast. The look on his face prepared her for the blow of bad news, even before the words came out of his mouth. They had always been able to read each other like a book.

"You know how we planned to leave tomorrow for a week with Mom and Dad?" he questioned, plopping down in the chair opposite her. "Well, our vacation has been canceled."

She had already started to eat a hearty breakfast of scrambled eggs, potatoes, and ham, and the news didn't set well with her stomach. "What do you mean it's been canceled? We requested that time off months ago. Surely it's just a mistake."

"No mistake," Sonny said, reaching for the coffeepot.

"Good morning, Sonny," Mrs. Rivera said, coming into the room with a bowl of scrambled eggs. "Are you ready for breakfast?"

"You bet I am," he replied. "I need about a gallon of coffee, then I'll take four eggs over easy, one of those thick ham steaks, and toast." He grinned up at her and winked as she placed the bowl on the table. "That ought to get me started. I'll let you know where we go from there."

She shook her head. "I don't know where you put all that food. You're just a beanpole, and yet you eat like my uncle Gordo."

"Ah, now," Sonny said, lifting her hand to his lips, "it's just that your cooking is the best I've had, except for my mother's. If you were twenty years younger, I think I'd propose." He kissed her hand.

She giggled as if she were twenty years younger. Pulling her hand away almost reluctantly, she picked up Sonny's plate and headed to the kitchen, still chuckling to herself.

"You are such a flirt," Rainy declared. "I don't know what Mother would say if she saw you."

"She'd say I take after Dad."

Rainy laughed. "No doubt. Now explain what's going on with our vacation time."

Sonny took a long drink of coffee, then replied, "There's been a special request for our Grand Canyon trip."

"But that trip lasts over five days—and I thought that with the economy failing they were going to scale it back or eliminate it altogether."

Sonny nodded. "Well, apparently these are friends of the governor—and of the Harvey Company. It's a special group of folks who sound like they're used to getting whatever they want. Money is no object."

"Well, it must be nice," Rainy replied, pushing her eggs around. "Still, I don't know why we have to lead the tour."

"Because we were asked for—by name. We have quite a reputation for quality tours, don't ya know. They get Sonny and Rainy weather with us." He grinned at the long-standing joke. Early on, upon hearing Rainy's given name, their uncle dubbed her twin, Gabe, "Sonny." He said it didn't seem fitting to have one without the other. The nickname stuck.

"When do they want to head out?" Rainy asked.

"Tomorrow afternoon. So at least you'll get to sleep late." He grinned at his sister and then transferred the smile to Mrs. Rivera as she placed his food in front of him. "Thank you! I thought I might well waste away to nothing but teeth and bones."

"And ego," muttered Rainy under her breath.

Mrs. Rivera fawned over Sonny for another minute or two, then made certain Rainy had what she needed before moving on to the other couriers and drivers.

Rainy tried not to resent the intrusion of the Detour company on her plans. She loved what she did as it related to educating the public about the various Indian cultures and about the great American Southwest. But she didn't love the whining dudes who complained about everything—from how hot it was to the color of the touring car. She didn't love the flirtatious men who seemed to think she was just one more item on the Harvey restaurant menu. And she didn't like being told her plans had to go by the wayside because some rich friend of the governor wanted to take a vacation.

"Why didn't you just tell Sam we couldn't do it?" she asked her brother. "You could have just told him no."

Sonny tried to speak around a mouthful of toast. "I did."

Rainy waited for him to swallow before continuing. "Why didn't he reassign it?"

"He promised us two weeks off when we finished this round," Sonny said, seeming rather proud of this fact, as if he'd somehow negotiated the extra time.

"Two weeks, eh?" Rainy frowned. "You don't suppose they're cutting back even more on their trips, do you? Maybe he made the offer because he isn't going to need us much longer."

Sonny shrugged. "I can't say that it would break my heart. Sure, it's a good job with steady pay, and I'm not scoffing at that in this day and age to be sure. Still . . ." He seemed to be considering something.

Rainy waited a moment, expecting him to pick the conversation back up, but when he didn't she jumped back in.

"So we do this tour and then take two weeks off?" She sighed as Sonny nodded. "I suppose I can wait another week. Still, I was really looking forward to sleeping in my own bed."

"Well, you can tomorrow night. The tour stays over in Albuquerque and we aren't required to sleep at the hotel. We'll just go home and explain the mess to Mom and Dad and enjoy at least a short time with them."

"I suppose you're right," Rainy said, glancing at her watch. "You do realize we're supposed to take that group of older ladies around Santa Fe in fifteen minutes?"

Sonny nodded and started shoveling the food in faster than ever. Rainy gazed at the ceiling and sighed. If they could only see her brother in this, his most natural state, she seriously doubted that many women would fall all over themselves to sit beside him.

———

The officials seated in front of Duncan Hartford seemed more than a little on the serious side. The man from the Office of Indian Affairs, a Mr. Richland, seemed especially stern with his beady-eyed gaze boring holes in Duncan as though he were keeping the truth from them.

Duncan returned the man's gaze and said, "I assure you, this theft of Indian artifacts is the first problem I've heard of. We've had no trouble here at the museum."

"All of the thefts have occurred on Indian property. Reservation land," the agent told him. "We're hoping you might help us put a stop to it."

"Why me?" Duncan asked. He leaned back in his leather chair and faced the man with what he hoped was his own equally serious expression.

"You are very knowledgeable about Indian artifacts and archaeology. You also know the area. Your background has proven you to be trustworthy."

Duncan questioned, "You had me checked out?" The idea irritated him to no end. "Why would you do that?"

Richland seemed quite exasperated with Duncan's inquiries. "Because we had to know to whom we could entrust this job. We didn't want to introduce someone from our bureau because their arrival would draw undue attention to them. You, however, are already known in the area, and if you were to suddenly step into the scene, no one would be the wiser."

Duncan further braved the man's ire. "Step into what scene?"

Richland exchanged a glance with his companions. "We're afraid someone is coming onto the reservations, perhaps under the guise of the Detours, and using the tourists to cover up their jobs."

"What do I have to do with that?" Duncan questioned. "I'm not an employee of the company."

"Maybe not yet," Richland replied, "but we've made arrangements for you to become just that. We have our eye on two different teams. One is the team of," the man paused to look at his notes, "a Jeremiah Sotherby and Tamela Yates, and the other is a Rainy and Sonny Gordon. They're sister and brother."

"I know the Gordons," Duncan said thoughtfully. "Not well, but certainly better than the other couple. Tell me though, why have you singled it down to these two teams?"

At this, another man, an agent of some other federal bureau, leaned forward. "The artifacts have only gone missing after one or both of these groups have passed through the area involved. We want to put a man in with each group. Since you know these Gordon folks, we'll arrange for you to be brought in as a driver-in-training. They should be quite comfortable with your presence and would not change their plans, if they are the ones who are stealing the pieces."

Duncan considered the man's comments while the third man, a representative of the Harvey Company and good friend of Duncan's parents, who lived north in Taos, leaned forward. "Duncan, it would mean a lot to me personally if you would help in this matter. I know I can trust you not to get caught up in whatever theft ring is being run. I don't want to have this turn into an even bigger affair than it's already become. This could be bad news for the Harvey Company and the Hunter Clarkson Company. I needn't tell you that times are hard enough without additional scandal. With Major Clarkson having just agreed to purchase the Detours, it wouldn't look good to have this kind of thing go public. Perhaps Clarkson would even attempt to back out of the arrangement."

"I can understand your concern, Mr. Welch," Duncan said, toying with the cuff of his suit coat. "I suppose I could give it a try. It's not like I'm trained as a detective, however."

"But of course you are," Welch said, grinning. "You're an archaeologist. You're trained to go into a situation and ferret out the truth."

Duncan laughed. "I dig in the dirt for bits and pieces of past civilizations. That hardly makes me capable of uncovering something like this."

Welch sobered. "Duncan, it's all we have. I don't want the newspapers getting wind of this, and right now we're barely keeping it out of their hands. This could ruin us. If tourists think there is a threat of danger, they'll stop coming. Robbery is a strong personal threat. If they see the Indians being robbed, they'll figure themselves to be next. I remember many years ago when there was concern about the possibility of a jewelry thief in the midst of the staff at the Alvarado Hotel in Albuquerque. It caused all kinds of panic, and dudes requested we place them in other hotels. Nothing ever came of that rumor, but we still lost money. Now with this being an actual problem . . . can you imagine what might happen? Why, it could very well prompt the tourists to stay home altogether for fear of a widespread ring of thievery."

"So, what will I be required to do?"

"Watch the Gordons and record any suspicious activity," Richland said. "Keep an eye on everything they do. The stolen pieces have been small enough to hide in large suitcases or trunks. If you have passengers with exceptionally large baggage, you might find a way to check the contents."

"How am I supposed to do that? No one is going to want me going through their things."

Richland stared at him with a cold indifference. "I don't care how you do your job; just do it. We need to put an end to this for the sake of everyone involved."

Duncan could see the truth of it and turned to his family's friend. "I'll do it as a favor to *you*, Mr. Welch. When do you need me to start?"

"Tomorrow. We've already arranged it with your boss here at the museum. The Gordons have been hired for a five-day tour that ends at the Grand Canyon. Unless another group wishes to take the same trip in reverse, you'll board the train at the canyon and return here. The Gordons are then scheduled for a two-week vacation after that. If additional artifacts and pieces turn up missing during this trip, but then suddenly nothing goes missing in the two weeks that follow, we'll know we probably have our people."

"You shouldn't jump to any conclusions," Duncan said quietly. He couldn't imagine the beautiful redheaded Rainy stealing anything from anyone. "We'll need to check the rosters and see if the tourists who are on the Detours are the same people who've taken trips before or if they're somehow connected to those who have."

"We've given some consideration to those lists," Welch admitted.

"Yes, this is a thorough federal investigation," the Indian Affairs agent added as if Duncan had somehow questioned their professionalism.

Not wishing to make an enemy of any official, Duncan nodded. "I'm sure it is. I'm just thinking out loud."

This seemed to calm the smaller man, while the other bureau official frowned. "Please keep quiet about this matter. We don't want to scare off our people. We want to catch them red-handed, in the act."

Duncan could see the man was almost pleased with the intensity of the moment. "I'll be careful," Duncan assured them with a casual shrug. "Just remember, you came to me. I didn't ask for this. I'm glad to do what I can to help preserve the Indian relics and ruins, but I'd much rather be doing it through archaeology instead of this cloak-and-dagger intrigue."

"I assure you, Mr. Hartford, this is hardly the stuff of dime novels. We have a serious matter on our hands," Mr. Richland said, his voice rising in pitch.

Mr. Welch calmed the situation immediately. "I've known the Hartfords for some time. The family is extremely responsible and law-abiding. Duncan will not let us down."

Welch looked to Duncan with an expression that seemed to plead for assurance on this matter. With little else to do, Duncan extended his hand and shook hands with each man. "I'll give this my very best effort."

After the men had left his office, Duncan allowed himself to day-dream a bit. Rainy Gordon hadn't been far from his thoughts since she'd invited him to share her supper table the previous week. Vivacious and carefree, she seemed almost too free-spirited to be someone whom Duncan could give any serious consideration for a future relationship.

She had caught his attention on the very first day he'd met her, almost three years earlier. She'd just taken a job with the Harvey Company and was leading one of her tour groups. They'd come to the museum for a tour and an explanation of the artifacts and art pieces displayed there. When he encountered the group, he had been amused to hear Rainy denouncing the labeling of one of the ancient pieces.

Duncan had immediately made a close examination of the piece and found her to be absolutely right. The piece had clearly been mis-labeled. His admiration for her had grown from that first moment. Unfortunately, he'd been too shy to approach her about spending time together. Rainy Gordon was so full of life—she moved from person to person with an infectious smile and charm that seemed to suggest the interests of each person were her foremost concern.

"She would probably never be interested in me," Duncan muttered. "She'd never want to settle down to a life of digging in the dirt or traips-ing after someone who did such a thing for a living."

He thought of her physical beauty. Her face seemed so delicately crafted—high smooth cheeks dotted here and there with a few freckles. Her fair skin seemed sunburned when he'd last seen her, but the freck-les were endearing. Her eyes, such an icy pale blue, brought back mem-ories of cold highland lakes in Scotland.

Duncan tried to remember every detail, filling in any missing piece with his imagination. He sighed. She was athletic and obviously in great condition or she would not be able to act as a tour guide. She was used to long spells of walking and climbing as she led tourists through vari-ous ruins and wilderness lands. Yet at the same time, she cleaned up to be a most fashionable and attractive young woman.

But now there was concern over whether Rainy was a part of this ugly matter regarding the stolen artifacts. Surely she and her brother were innocent of such things. After all, she appeared to be a good Christian woman. She had asked him to pray over their meal.

He pushed back his wavy black hair and sighed. "I suppose there is nothing for me to do but pray. Father always said, 'When in doubt— pray. When not in doubt—pray.' "

He looked to the open door where the officials had exited only moments ago. Tomorrow he'd find himself in the company of Miss Rainy Gordon. They'd remain together for at least five days. Surely that would give him a very good idea as to the real quality of her character.

"It might also prove detrimental to my heart," he said, shaking his head.

CHAPTER THREE

*R*ainy rolled over in bed and yawned. Pulling the crisp white sheet over her head, she wanted nothing more than to go back to sleep. Disappointment crept in when she thought of how she might already have been at home sleeping in her own bed. It took great resolve to lower the sheet and open her eyes. She glanced at the clock and noted the lateness of the hour and moaned.

"Why do we have to do this tour now?" She had so longed to spend time with her mother and talk about the future. Her mother was the only one who would really understand her feelings—well, besides Sonny.

Sonny always seemed to understand, but at twenty-seven years old he thought himself perfectly lucky to have escaped matrimony, while at the same age, Rainy felt that life was passing her by. Her mother assured her that God had someone special for her—a man of quality and spiritual conviction.

"Sometimes," she could hear her mother say, *"he's right under your nose and you don't even realize it."*

"Well, if he's here," Rainy said, sitting up, "I sure wish God would make him more clear to me—and me to him."

After a long hot bath, Rainy sat drying her hair with a soft cotton towel. Still the thoughts of her future refused to be pushed aside. For so long she had planned to be married—to perhaps have children. She had buried herself in college studies for the early years of her adult life, but even there she thought that surely she would find a proper mate—a man who shared her passion and enthusiasm for history and archaeology. But the men who joined her in those classes only seemed intimidated by her grades and intelligence. The other women, few though they were, avoided Rainy as well. It soon became clear that Rainy made the others uncomfortable with her knowledge, and no matter how she tried to downplay her abilities and intellect, no one wanted to be her long-term friend.

"I can't help it if I'm smart," she said. Sighing, she tossed the towel aside and went to where her suitcase sat half packed.

Rainy picked up her stockings and stuffed them into a corner of the case. "I just want a husband, Lord—one who will respect me and love the things I love. Is that too much to ask for? Are compatibility and shared interests such unthinkable requirements?"

She often prayed like this. Chatting with God as though He reclined nearby in one of her chairs. Her mother had taught her early on that, while God was more than willing to listen to their petitions, people often avoided bringing the details of their lives to Him.

Rainy stuffed the rest of her things into the case and closed the lid. "I'm twenty-seven years old. I'll be twenty-eight in June, Lord. What good are my education and a good job when all I really want is a husband and family?"

But it wasn't all that she wanted. She'd had her chance at a couple of men who worked at the university. Of course, that had been before she'd been forced to resign from helping her father. The memory still left a bitter taste in her mouth.

Another glance at the clock reminded her that she'd have just enough time for lunch if she hurried. They were scheduled to leave at two and there was no arguing with those well-established timetables.

A knock and the opening of her door revealed Sonny. "I came for your luggage."

Even his good-natured smile did nothing to break Rainy from her mood. "I just finished packing. I was about to braid my hair and then get something to eat. Have you had lunch yet?"

Sonny nodded as he retrieved her suitcase. "I just finished. Mrs. Rivera suggested you were sleeping in, and I figured it was probably for the best. Go ahead and get something and meet me at the hotel." He paused at the door. "Oh, and there will be a surprise for you on this trip."

"The trip itself was a surprise," Rainy said as she set to braiding her still-damp hair.

"Well, this one will be a pleasant surprise."

"What is it?" Rainy asked, pausing to look up.

Sonny grinned. "I'm not telling. It wouldn't be a surprise then." He pulled the door closed behind him, whistling as he went on his way.

Rainy knew he always whistled when he was pleased with himself. Frowning, she only wished she knew what it was that brought him such satisfaction. Sonny had been acting strange of late, and every time she thought to question him about his mood or actions, it seemed something happened to prevent her from learning the truth. If she didn't know better, she'd think he was in love.

"Strange," she murmured. "We've always been so close, and now I feel as though I'm losing touch with him."

Rainy finished her hair and pulled on her Indian jewelry. The Detour management encouraged the girls to buy and wear as much Indian jewelry as they could. This was in hopes of promoting the very same articles in the Harvey shops. The idea was that the tourists would see the beautiful objects and rush to buy their own copies. Sales were down in the Harvey shops, however, just as they were most everywhere. Rainy thought it almost silly to encourage the purchase of an expensive silver-and-turquoise necklace when the economy was so questionable. Of course, the only people booking passage on the Indian Detours were those who had plenty of money to splurge. The common person had no hope of making such expensive sojourns.

After a quick lunch, Rainy hurried to La Fonda to find Sonny. She saw him standing behind the touring car talking to Duncan Hartford. Her stomach did a flip-flop as Duncan looked up and smiled. He wore a dark blue suit and looked quite stylish with his necktie and felt fedora.

"Here's your surprise," Sonny announced. "Duncan is coming with us. He's a new driver-in-training."

Rainy frowned. "You're working for the Detours Company? Why didn't you say something last week when we had supper together?"

Duncan looked momentarily uncomfortable. "Well . . . that is . . . I didn't know then that I would be hired."

"You could have at least told me you were considering it. We could have talked about the various tours," Rainy replied, feeling as if Duncan had somehow betrayed their friendship. She knew it was silly, but she almost felt as though he'd lied to her.

"It kind of came to me out of the clear blue," Duncan admitted. "I wasn't sure I would ever do anything like this, to be honest."

"He's going to make a great driver," Sonny threw in. "He knows this area like the back of his hand. He's a little sketchier with Arizona and he hasn't done the Puye route, but I told him we could easily teach him the ropes. He'll be mastering the tours before he knows it."

Rainy knew there was nothing to be done but welcome Duncan.

"We're glad to have you on board. We've had some real questionable recruits before, eh, Sonny?"

"That's to be sure. One man arrived all decked out in his cowboy attire not even knowing how to drive a car. I'll never know how he put that one over on the company, but he was out of here faster than a jackrabbit crossing the railroad tracks."

"Then there was the guy who kept eating all the picnic food," Rainy said with a teasing lilt to her voice. "You aren't likely to sneak around eating up all the food, are you?"

Duncan laughed and his expression revealed his genuine amusement. "I promise not to raid the picnic basket."

"Oh, and don't forget that one driver who when faced with a tire going flat called back to the shop and said, 'I have a tire going *psssst.* What do I do?' Let me tell you, he was out of a job mighty quick. You have to change a lot of tires in this business," Sonny said, shaking his head. "It's a good idea to get used to that fact up front."

"Well," Duncan began, "I not only can drive, but I can change a tire as well. I've lived in this state nearly twenty years, so I'm pretty familiar with New Mexico. My parents are pastoring a small church in Taos, but prior to that they had a church in Gallup, then one in Socorro, Magdalena, and even Las Vegas. I moved along with them until I decided to settle here in Santa Fe ten years ago."

"Sounds like you should have a good knowledge of the land, then," Rainy admitted. "Are you familiar with the height of various mountains? Can you explain various land formations and weather patterns?"

"Pretty much so. That was one of the reasons I got this job. There are a few routes Sonny was mentioning that I'm not that familiar with, but he promised to help me note the important issues on my map."

Sonny looked at his watch. "Rainy, you'd probably better go gather our tourists. They're supposed to be at the front desk by one-forty-five. It's that time now."

Rainy realized he was right and turned on her heel to go. So Duncan Hartford was going to share the next five days of her life. Could this be God's way of answering her prayer? She tried not to get too excited. After all, she was forever trying to help God arrange things. Her mother had chided her for such attitudes in the past, but Rainy always thought it a simple matter of being tuned in to what God wanted you to know. *It's not like I'm trying to be God or take His place,* she thought. *I just want to help Him out and make sure I don't miss any subtle direction change He might send my way.*

Rainy spotted the family of five waiting near the front desk in the lobby. A mustached man wearing a tan linen suit and straw hat stood beside a woman of forty-something. The woman was fussing with one of the children, a teenage girl who seemed to be having trouble with her hair ribbon.

"Good afternoon. I'm Rainy Gordon. Are you the Van Patten family?"

The man nodded. "I am Mr. Van Patten. This is my wife and our three children, Gloria, Thomas, and Richard."

Rainy smiled and shook their hands. Immediately the boys, who looked to be about sixteen or seventeen, flooded her with attention.

"Are you the one who will lead our tour?" Thomas asked.

"Will we get to sit beside you in the car?" Richard threw in.

Rainy was used to the flirtatious nature of young men. She smiled. "I am indeed your courier. I will guide you over the next five days."

"Will there be any other families joining our tour?" Mrs. Van Patten questioned.

"No, but there will be one more Detour employee aside from the driver. Mr. Hartford is training to drive for the company, so he'll be observing us and learning the routine. My brother, Sonny Gordon, will be our driver. He's very knowledgeable about the area, so feel free to ask either of us any questions you might have.

"Now, if you'll follow me, we'll be on our way. Your luggage has already been arranged for," she said as she noted Mrs. Van Patten looking behind them as they moved toward the door. "You will find it's already been loaded, in fact. The company strives to make this a most memorable and pleasant time for its guests. Part of that goal requires that we offer you the finest service available. Do not hesitate to tell us how we might make your journey more pleasant."

"My journey would be more pleasant if you sat by me in the car," Richard said, his dark eyes intense with interest.

Rainy laughed. "I'm sorry, but I have to sit up front with my brother. We can't very well lead from the back of the touring car." It was the only explanation she'd offer him, in spite of his hangdog expression.

Gloria took one look at Sonny and seemed to perk up. Then she noted Duncan and for a moment she seemed to weigh each candidate before returning her attention to Sonny. Rainy knew his rugged outfit was appealing to wealthy easterners. She wasn't sure where this family hailed from, but it was clear they were more city than country, and the cowboy attire was a novelty all its own.

"Is that our driver?" Gloria questioned Rainy as she pushed her brother aside.

"Yes. I'd like to introduce you all to Sonny Gordon. Sonny is my twin brother and the driver for our expedition." Rainy turned and reached out to touch Duncan's arm. "And this is Duncan Hartford. He's training to drive for the company, as I mentioned earlier." She turned back to Sonny and Duncan. "These are the Van Pattens. Mr. and Mrs. Van Patten and their children, Gloria, Thomas, and Richard."

Pleasantries were exchanged; then Rainy directed everyone to seats inside the touring car. Set up to hold as many as twelve, the car had more than enough room for the family to spread out and enjoy themselves. Six swiveling chairs allowed the dudes a full range of motion, while two additional bench seats were available for those who preferred a more fixed position.

The boys, disappointed to find they couldn't sit with Rainy, headed for the very back of the car while Gloria secured the swivel seat behind Sonny and beamed with pleasure when Duncan took the seat behind Rainy.

Although it was nearly April, snow could still pose a problem in the mountains. Generally the Detour trip to the Grand Canyon wasn't offered this early in the year for that very reason, and because of this the regular trip had to be altered slightly. They wouldn't be able to go high into the Sandia Mountains, but they would try to make up for it with a visit to a little native town called Placitas, which was hidden near the base of the Sandias.

Rainy began her speech about the trip and what was expected and not expected of the tourists. She explained the routine and how they should have their luggage ready prior to breakfast each morning.

"Sonny will see to it that your luggage gets on board each day. Tonight we will stay at the Alvarado Hotel in Albuquerque. The Alvarado is a marvelous hotel created in the manner of a Spanish mission. The thick stuccoed walls keep the rooms cool even in the hottest days of summer." She smiled and turned to face the tourists a bit more. "Of course, we're still experiencing very chilly nights, so you'll be pleased to know that they have steam heat to keep the rooms warm.

"While you're there, you'll be able to enjoy beautiful lawns and brick walkways. There are also marvelous verandas upon which you can sit and read. Of course, we'll only be there for the night."

Duncan endured the tour with great pleasure. He enjoyed listening as Rainy pointed out various land formations and told of the native peoples. He thought she seemed very much at home as a tour guide and wondered if she meant to make this a lifelong career.

When the group finally arrived at the Alvarado Hotel in Albuquerque, he watched with some amusement as the teenage boys told Rainy how much they'd learned and enjoyed her teaching. Rainy seemed genuinely touched, thanking them each for their special attention and feeding them tidbits of the things to come the following day.

Duncan didn't believe the boys to be half so interested in the trip and Rainy's teachings as they were with Rainy herself.

"So what are your plans for the night?" Sonny asked Duncan.

"I suppose the same as yours. Eat supper and get some rest."

"We're heading over to our parents' house after we get unloaded here. If you'd like to come with us for supper, you'd be more than welcome, and I can bring you back here for the night. We usually just sleep at home."

Duncan considered the situation for a moment. "I wouldn't want to intrude."

"It wouldn't be an intrusion at all. Our mother is a wonderful cook and always makes plenty. She extends an open invitation to our friends and co-workers, so you wouldn't be out of place at all."

Duncan knew it would be of far more comfort to join the Gordons for a home-cooked meal than to eat alone in the hotel. "I'd like very much to join you," he finally replied. If nothing else, he told himself, he'd have a great meal and be able to see Rainy in a more intimate setting. Surely if there were any strange or underhanded deeds going on between the brother and sister, they'd be more inclined to let down their guard at home.

Later that evening, Duncan pushed away from the Gordon table with a groan. "I think I overdid it," he told Rainy's mother, Edrea. She was an older version of her daughter, with a winning smile and crystal blue eyes. "It's just that it's been a while since I've been home. I miss my mother's cooking very much."

"I'm glad you enjoyed yourself," Mrs. Gordon replied. "Are you sure now that you won't have another piece of peach pie?"

"I'd surely burst if I did," Duncan replied. He watched Rainy move quickly to help her mother clear the table. The meal had been incredible, just as Sonny promised, and the company had been delightful.

Sonny yawned and stretched. "Duncan, I hate to rush you off, but if you're ready, I'll take you back to the hotel. I'm just about to drop from exhaustion."

"You're welcome to stay here with us, Mr. Hartford," Edrea Gordon said as she picked up an empty bowl.

"That you are," Raymond Gordon added.

Duncan thought for a moment about accepting, then shook his head. If he seemed too eager to stay, Rainy and Sonny might very well become suspicious. "I thank you for the invitation, but I think I should go back to the hotel. After all, my things are there and the company has already arranged a room for me." He got to his feet and noticed that Rainy had failed to return from the kitchen. He hated to leave without saying good-bye, but he didn't want to make a scene.

"I'll be out in the car," Sonny told him.

Mrs. Gordon went to Duncan as Sonny left the room. "It's always good to meet new friends. Please know you're welcome to join us any-time. Raymond would agree with me."

"Because I know better than to argue with her." His Scottish brogue hung thick in the air. Duncan relished the sound with a bit of home-sickness for the land of his childhood. "Now, if you'll excuse me," Mr. Gordon continued, "I need another cup of coffee and I see Rainy has already moved it to the kitchen."

"Good night, Mr. Gordon. I truly appreciate the meal."

"As Edrea said, you're welcome anytime." Raymond Gordon headed off in the direction of the kitchen.

"Oh, dear," Edrea suddenly said. "Your jacket is in the other room. Why don't you go tell Rainy good-bye and I'll fetch it for you."

Duncan nodded, happy for the excuse to see Rainy. He walked toward the kitchen door and paused as he overheard Rainy say some-thing to her father. Duncan glanced over his shoulder to make certain Edrea had gone. Seeing that the room was empty, he delayed his entrance long enough to eavesdrop.

"They'll never believe me. No matter what I do. No one cares what really happened or why."

"Now, daughter, God is with you. We'll be finding a way."

"But it's been three years," Rainy argued. "I don't want to take this guilt with me the rest of my life."

"I know, darling. I know."

Duncan knew he couldn't wait any longer. He pushed open the door and peeked inside. "I just wanted to tell Rainy good-bye." He smiled at the surprised woman. "Your mother told me to and I didn't want to appear the disobedient one."

Rainy smiled at this. "It's for the best. Mother would never brook any nonsense. I'll see you in the morning. If you've never slept at the Alvarado, then you're in for a treat."

Duncan nodded and headed back through the dining room just as Edrea brought his jacket. "I hope to see more of you, Mr. Hartford."

"I hope you will too."

Duncan pulled on the jacket and made his way to the car. Sonny stood outside, leaning against the driver's door, staring up into the night skies.

"Caught you daydreaming," Duncan teased.

Sonny laughed. "That isn't hard to do." He jumped into the driver's seat and started the car while Duncan took the seat Rainy had used all day.

"So what were you thinking about just then?" Duncan asked, knowing he was being more personal than their brief time together allowed for.

Sonny Gordon didn't seem to mind. "Oh, I guess my mind was in faraway lands. I have some interest in Alaska. Sometimes I contemplate taking a trip north."

"Sounds fascinating," Duncan admitted. "I hope you'll get a chance for it."

"I hope so too," Sonny said, maneuvering the car toward town.

Duncan thought of what he'd overheard Rainy saying, wishing fervently that he had the right to ask what she meant. He supposed it would just have to wait. Perhaps toward the end of the trip he and the Gordons would be much closer and then Rainy wouldn't mind such an intimate question.

*S*onny finished securing the last of the Van Pattens' ten pieces of luggage in and on the touring car. Mrs. Van Patten had been particularly difficult that morning, haranguing Sonny about the care of her matched pieces.

"This is an exceptionally expensive collection of leather luggage," she told Sonny. "See to it that you do not allow it to be scratched."

Sonny had smiled, poured on the charm, and assured her that he was used to handling such pieces. Mrs. Van Patten looked down her nose at him in an expression that suggested Sonny must surely be mistaken . . . or lying.

Once she'd gone, Sonny's thoughts drifted to the night before. He knew his sister enjoyed Duncan's company. He also suspected that his sister would probably love nothing better than to secure a more permanent position in Duncan Hartford's life.

If I could manage to get the two of them together, Sonny mused, *I wouldn't feel so bad about my own plans.* And his plans were extensive. He had just received word from two college chums who had teamed up for a government exploration trip to Alaska. The government was assessing the area to discover its potential for farming and relocating poverty-stricken families. All very new ideas, his friends assured him, but ones that held great promise—especially as drought seemed to be gripping various areas of the country. His friends droned on about the possibilities as if they needed to sell Sonny on the idea. Then they finally mentioned needing a third member for their team, a geologist, and wanted to know if he was interested.

Interested didn't begin to describe Sonny's feelings on the matter. This venture would fulfill a lifelong dream of his. Geology was a passion to him. He could only imagine the thrill of exploring the frozen north. Now his only problem was how to break the news to Rainy. Sonny knew she depended on him for companionship on the tours. She had said more than once that she might never have taken the job with the Detours if Sonny hadn't been hired on as her driver. Now his plan was to resign his position by the end of summer, and he still hadn't found a way to break the news to his sister.

Thoughts of Duncan Hartford came to mind again. With Duncan training to drive the tours, Sonny wondered if he couldn't arrange it so that Duncan could take over his place with Rainy. He wondered even more seriously if something romantic might develop between the couple. He'd seen the way Rainy had looked at Duncan—heard her talk about him too. There was no denying her high regard for him.

If Rainy and Duncan would fall in love and marry, Sonny thought, *my troubles would be over. Rainy wouldn't need me anymore. She'd have a whole new life, and her interests would lie with Duncan rather than me and Mom and Dad.*

He thought about this as he double-checked the Van Patten luggage one final time. Rainy certainly had expressed her interest in finding a husband and settling down, though Sonny knew she'd also love to be working in archaeology. Since they'd been young her heart's desire had been to work on great archaeological digs. She'd even thought for some time she might go abroad to the great pyramids of Egypt. The Middle Eastern countries were certain to be full of mystery and intrigue from the past.

Instead, he'd watched Rainy develop a deep love for the American Southwest. She had a passion for the desert and the Indians who lived there. He was amazed at the quick and easy manner in which she'd learned various Indian dialects. Furthermore, he knew she had grown to care deeply about the Indian people.

"The Van Pattens will be out shortly," Rainy called as she came from the hotel. "I left them to conclude their breakfast."

Sonny looked up and smiled. Rainy always brightened his day. They were as close as a brother and sister could be, and being twins, they felt they could very nearly read each other's minds. Given that, Sonny wondered if Rainy had any clue as to his desire to leave the Detour business. He was waiting for just the right time to tell her—praying that the timing would come neither too soon nor too late. She wouldn't be happy with him, for they always discussed major plans and changes with each other. He supposed they filled the void in each other's life where a spouse might have offered counsel. But this time he hadn't shared his plans, and he knew she'd be hurt.

"We need to head out as soon as possible if we're going to make Gallup by suppertime and still see everything in between," he replied.

Rainy straightened her serviceable brown skirt. "I know that. They were nearly finished. If they aren't out here in five minutes, I'll go get them."

"So, Rainy, I saw you eying Duncan Hartford. I think you like him," Sonny said, grinning from ear to ear.

Rainy shrugged. "He's a very nice man. Of course I like him."

"No, I mean you *like* him. As in, you're interested in him for more than friendship."

Rainy's head snapped up at this. She came to stand directly in front of him and lowered her voice considerably. "What makes you say that?"

"Rainy, don't forget I can read you better than most," Sonny replied, leaning casually against the glossy black frame of the car. "I know you want to marry and have a family, and Duncan Hartford has many of the qualities you're looking for."

"Oh, really? And how would you know what I'm looking for?" Rainy asked defensively.

Sonny laughed. "Maybe because I'm your twin brother, or maybe it's because we work together and spend a good deal of our time together, and maybe because you've told me about a million times."

Rainy gave him a sheepish smile at this. "I'm pretty bad, eh?"

"Not bad—just specific." He sobered a bit and took hold of her shoulders. "Look, sister of mine, I want you happy. I know you're putting your future to prayer, but like Mom would say, you have to be willing to leave it in God's hands in order for Him to be able to do anything with it."

"I know. But some things are harder than others to leave behind. I'm fast becoming an old maid. I don't want to spend the rest of my life regretting my earlier choices for school and an education. I don't want to come to the end of my life and find out I was wrong—maybe I can't balance pursuing my passion for archaeology with the demands of a family."

"That's not going to happen. God has been the one guiding your life. I remember how hard you prayed about college—about when to go and when to stop. Remember how much that one professor of yours wanted you to go for your doctorate, but you said no because that's what you felt God leading you to do. Have you regretted that choice?"

Rainy shrugged and Sonny dropped his hold on her. "I can't say that I regret it because I'm confident it was the right thing at the time."

"Then trust that God has this issue under control. Duncan Hartford may well have come into our lives through the Detours in order for you to know his character even better than before. You've known the man for three years, Rainy. You've seen him conduct the museum tours and have spoken to him on hundreds of occasions. He's always appeared respectable and upright—now maybe God's giving you the opportunity to spend your days with him on the tour so you'll know for sure whether or not his personality fits yours."

Rainy smiled. "And when did you figure this all out, little brother?"

"You're never going to let me live down the fact that I'm three minutes younger than you, are you?"

"Not when it serves my purpose so completely." She smiled.

"Well, it serves my purpose not to give you an answer," Sonny said, laughing. "I suggest you run ahead and get our guests. While you do that, I'll find out what's happened to Duncan, and hopefully we can get on the road within the next few minutes."

Rainy went in search of her charges, realizing that Sonny had gotten out of telling her when he'd given time to plotting a romance between her and Duncan. She had to admit he made a good point. She had prayed long and hard about all of the details regarding a man to love and spend her life with. And Duncan had been a constant in her life for the past three years. He was there for the tours she brought to the museum. He was often in La Fonda for his meals, and when she managed to be in town on Sunday, she saw him at the little community church not far from the Plaza. And now he was going to be on their trip to the Grand Canyon. Maybe God would—

Running into the rock-hard wall of another human being caused all thoughts to fly out of Rainy's mind. She felt herself falling backward. As she fought to regain her balance, she looked up to catch Duncan's stunned expression change to one of intense concern. He reached out to take hold of her but missed her by inches. Rainy smacked down hard on her backside.

"Making friends with the floor?" he questioned good-naturedly. The look of amusement changed to concern, however, as Rainy frowned. "Are you all right? I tried to catch you but . . ."

"I'm fine," Rainy said, trying to gracefully get to her feet. He reached down to help her up and kept his hold on her while she steadied herself. She rubbed her lower back.

"I'm so sorry." He gently rubbed her upper arms.

Rainy momentarily lost herself in his dark brown eyes, his tenderness her undoing. *Could he be the one, Lord? Could he be the man I'm to spend the rest of my life with?*

"It was all my fault," she said, finally finding her voice. "I wasn't watching where I was going. I was a bit preoccupied." Rainy's words sounded foreign in her ears. *What's wrong with me? I'm acting so silly.* She straightened and pulled away. With a much more serious tone, she added, "Sonny's looking for you. He's out at the car. I need to get the guests out there as well."

Duncan's manner became quite formal, almost as if she'd somehow offended him. "Very well. Mind your step."

He moved around her with little fanfare and walked toward the door. Rainy watched him momentarily. *Oh, Father, please show me what to do. Help me to be patient, because I'm not at all sure I have it within myself to keep from charging ahead.*

"Miss Gordon, I have my family rallied for the trip," Mr. Van Patten announced as he brought his entourage down the hall.

Rainy smiled. "I was just coming to find you. Looks like we'll have a beautiful day for travel. The temperature has warmed quite nicely but shouldn't get too hot. That's the luxury of traveling this time of year."

"I cannot bear the heat," Mrs. Van Patten said, her chin raised ever so slightly.

Rainy could tell the woman would most likely be a problem guest. Guests came in three varieties. Accommodating—those with easygoing personalities, who rolled with the punches and unexpected catastrophes. Confused—those who were too old, too young, or just too misplaced to enjoy themselves fully. And the problem guests—those who found fault with everything from the food to the transportation to the color of the tour guide's hair. Rainy actually had one woman refuse to take a tour with the Gordons because they had red hair and that was an omen of bad luck for her.

Rainy tried to push aside her fears of Mrs. Van Patten being just such a guest. "I shouldn't imagine it will be a problem this time of year, Mrs. Van Patten."

"And what will you do if it is hot? How will you see to our needs?"

Rainy smiled. "I shall pray for cooler temperatures and find you a fan. But right now we need to be on our way. We have a schedule to keep."

She left without waiting to hear what Mrs. Van Patten might have to say. Sometimes Rainy had a hard time keeping her sarcasm to herself. Again she sent up a petition to God for patience, only this time it was for an entirely different reason.

Along the route of their tour, Rainy told them of rock formations and rivers, of vegetation and wildlife. She pointed out a roadrunner that seemed rather intimidated by the huge touring car.

"I'm sure he's afraid we might eat him," Rainy said, laughing. She glanced at her watch. "We'll be arriving at the San Augustine Church in Isleta in about fifteen minutes. Before we get there, and because the stop is a very short one, I thought I'd give you the history of the church. Something quite unusual has taken place there, and for over one hundred years everyone from officials in Rome to the president of the United States has been rather stumped as to why these things have happened."

With that prelude into the mystery of her story, Rainy realized she had the unwavering attention of everyone in the car, with the exceptions of Sonny and Mrs. Van Patten.

"It is said," Rainy continued, "that a Franciscan friar named Brother Juan Padilla was murdered by a hostile Pueblo Indian in 1756. Now, the Pueblos are generally a very peaceful people, as they were then. The killing took place because the murderer was afraid Brother Juan might betray the Pueblos to the Spanish.

"The Pueblos were terrified at what would happen if the killing were discovered. After all, Brother Juan had been with them for some time and his healing abilities had proven to the Pueblos that he must serve a powerful god. Knowing he was of Spanish descent, they feared Brother Juan's powerful god would bring the Spanish to destroy them." Rainy loved the way the boys seemed to be perched on the edge of their seat, waiting for the rest of the story. She glanced at Duncan and saw that he, too, seemed to be thoroughly enjoying himself. He gave her a smile that warmed Rainy to the bottom of her toes.

"Ah . . . where . . . was I?" Rainy stammered, trying to regain her composure. "Oh yes. The Pueblos, fearing retribution, arranged for four of their swiftest runners to take the body of the friar to Isleta, which was nearly seventy miles to the east. There, they were to bury the friar and return.

"The runners were in a very big hurry, terrified that they'd get caught with the body and the Spanish would find out what had happened. When they arrived at Isleta, they buried the friar without any form of ceremony. They dug a six-foot-deep grave in the dirt floor of the church and buried the friar in front of the altar. They stomped down the ground so that it looked as though it had never been disturbed and fled. Their deception worked, and the tribe bore no retribution for the death of the friar.

"Fifteen years later, a caretaker noticed that there was a bulge in the floor, directly in front of the altar. He thought nothing of it, but over the years it grew and gradually began to resemble the outline of a man's body. The ground cracked and the people tried to fill it with dirt, but nothing seemed to work. Twenty years to the day after the friar's death, the people of the church came in one day to find the body of the friar lying on the ground. He looked newly dead, and his skin was soft and pliable. His robes had rotted, so they reclothed him and reburied him."

"Oh, that's awful. That poor man," Gloria Van Patten gasped. "What a horrible thing to happen."

"That wasn't the worst of it," Rainy stated. She lowered her voice for effect. The boys moved from the back of the touring car and took a seat on the midway bench. "Twenty years later the same thing happened. The friar again resurfaced and again he seemed just as freshly dead as when he'd been buried nearly forty years earlier."

"What a horrible story!" Mrs. Van Patten exclaimed.

"There's no possible way that could happen," Mr. Van Patten stated, as though Rainy had insulted his intelligence. He dutifully patted his wife's hand as if to calm her. Rainy only smiled.

"That's what many people said. So when the people grew fearful and tired of this, and after the padre had resurfaced a few more times, they called on the authorities of the church. The padre was given a proper burial with church rites in 1895. So far," she said with a smile, "Father Juan has stayed buried. But every time I bring a tour group here, I always wonder if this will be the year Father Juan reappears."

"Oh, I hope so," Thomas declared. "This is much more fun than I thought it was going to be."

"I want to be the first one in the church," Richard said, nudging his brother. "I'm the oldest and I should have the first look."

Rainy couldn't help but chuckle at their sudden interest. How disappointed they would be when they found two-inch planks on the floor as an added incentive to keep Friar Juan in the ground.

Sonny pulled up to the church and before Rainy could say another word, the Van Patten boys hurried from the car. Their parents and Gloria followed at a slower, almost apprehensive pace. Mrs. Van Patten

seemed quite pale, in fact, almost as if she had begun to worry about
what they'd find.

"That was a great bit of storytelling," Duncan said as Rainy climbed
from the car.

She straightened her skirt before meeting his gaze. "It's a fascinating story, isn't it? I've always wondered, though. If the Pueblos said
nothing about the death, then who learned the truth of what happened
to the poor friar?"

Duncan laughed. "You have a strong investigative nature. You'd
make a good archaeologist or anthropologist."

"You're kind to say so. I can't imagine anything I'd enjoy more. In
fact—"

A girl's scream filled the air, causing Duncan and Rainy to exchange
a surprised look before bolting at full speed to the open door of the
church.

Rainy couldn't imagine what had happened. She came up behind
Mr. and Mrs. Van Patten to find Gloria clinging to her mother. Mrs. Van
Patten's face was now a greenish gray, and her tight-lipped expression
suggested a true tragedy had befallen the party.

Peering inside the church, almost sure she'd find the poor old friar
had resurfaced once again, Rainy found instead that Thomas Van Patten had stretched himself out in front of the altar, hands crossed over
his chest, eyes closed. Richard stood to the side laughing hysterically.

"Oh, we scared her good, Thomas," Richard called. "You can get
up now." Thomas popped up, giggling.

Rainy shook her head while Mr. Van Patten launched into a reprimand of his sons. Leaving the scene to afford the family some privacy,
Rainy looked up to find Duncan barely containing his mirth.

"Oh, so you think that was funny too?"

"Indeed. It was perfect." He leaned toward her. "Did you see the
look on Mrs. Van Patten's face? I doubt she'll be any more trouble for
the rest of the day."

"If only it were that easy," Rainy replied. "I'm sure we'll hear an
earful before the day is done. Remember, we still have hours to go
before we reach Gallup."

CHAPTER FIVE

*D*ay three found the tour in the land of the Navajo. Rainy explained how the Navajo people had taken the dry, unyielding land and created life from it. They were able to raise crops by using ingenious manners of irrigation and raised sheep for the wool and meat they could provide. The Navajo jewelry was especially pleasing to Mrs. Van Patten. She bought several pieces before retiring for the night.

Day four brought the group into Hopi land. Here, Rainy's good friends Istaqa and his wife, Una, were happy to see her and happy to share their native stories with the tourists. Istaqa and his wife had actually allowed Rainy to live with them for several months one summer. She taught them better English, including how to read, while they taught her Hopi and lessons of their people.

Rainy had the highest admiration for both the Hopi and the Navajo. The Hopi, too, had taken the desert land and made it into fertile farms. Their ability to dry farm was a marvel that was getting more than a little attention as drought had begun to cause problems in various areas of the country. Perhaps the whites would learn that the Indian nations had something to teach them after all.

They spent the night in Tuba City, an old Mormon settlement that now acted as the western headquarters for the Navajo reservation. Their accommodations were at the Trading Post, which offered comfortable rooms and good food, although both were far simpler than seemed to please the Van Pattens. Rainy was more than a little excited to know this would be her last night of responsibility for the group. Falling asleep that night, she thought of Duncan and the fact that, while they'd been together throughout most of the trip, they'd spent very little time in private conversation. Duncan always seemed preoccupied or busy with questions for Sonny, while the Van Pattens consumed her time with everything from Mrs. Van Patten's concern about Indians growing suddenly hostile and attacking to the boys' pranks.

Finally the morning of the fifth day arrived, and Rainy knew that by evening she'd be able to eat and relax at the Harvey Hotel in Williams and be free of the Van Pattens. That promise was enough to help her endure Gloria's whining and Richard's covert love notes. At least the love notes had offered Sonny, Duncan, and Rainy a bit of amusement. The previous night Richard had accidentally slipped his note under Sonny and Duncan's door instead of Rainy's. Sonny thought the note had come from the Trading Post management and had opened it to read: *My heart is ever yours. You are the joy of all I see. Please know that I will adore you until my dying day. RVP*

Sonny had shown Duncan the note, and knowing Rainy had received similar notes from Richard Van Patten, they risked waking her to show her the missive. Rainy had chided them for being such ninnies but laughed nevertheless. She thought the boy was only toying with her, otherwise she might not have laughed. She had no desire to crush the romantic spirit of the young man. Richard, however, seemed not at all sincere in his attitude but rather appeared to be playing a game with his brother as to who could garner more of Rainy's attention.

Day five passed quickly with tours of the Painted Desert, the suspension bridge across the Little Colorado River, and the Petrified Forest. Soon they were approaching Williams, where the Van Pattens would catch the train for the Grand Canyon. Rainy had never been happier to see the familiar sights of the little town. Exhausted from the marathon trip, she sighed with relief as Sonny pulled up to the train station.

"This is the end of our journey," she announced. "I know from your itinerary that you have a week's stay planned at the Grand Canyon. I think you'll be impressed with El Tovar's service and décor. The hotel has long been admired for its beauty and quality service."

"Anything would be better than what we just endured on this trip," Mrs. Van Patten muttered.

"Now, dear, in all honesty, we knew this trip was more strenuous and less luxurious than most. We all agreed it would be fun to give it a go." Mr. Van Patten seemed to stress the latter with a stern look at his wife.

She nodded and said nothing more, and Rainy took this as her cue to exit. "I'll go inside and make sure your reservations are in order." With that, she bid the Van Pattens farewell.

————

Rainy had just finished supper and was enjoying a soothing cup of coffee when Sonny and Duncan joined her. "Where have you two been? I tried to wait to eat but got too hungry. I joined some of the other Harvey staff and ate without you."

"You know how this was supposed to be a dead-end trip?" Sonny asked. "Leave the car here, catch the train home, and so forth?"

"Yes," Rainy said, drawing the word out. "What's happened?"

Duncan took the chair opposite her, while Sonny took the one beside her and whispered, "We've been hired to do the trip in reverse."

Rainy shook her head. "But I'm tired. I don't feel like doing the trip in reverse."

"I think it will be good for all of us. I'm going to let Duncan drive part of the trip and get some practice in."

Duncan looked rather surprised at Sonny's announcement. "I beg your pardon?"

Sonny shrugged. "Everybody has to jump in sooner or later. You might as well do it now. Rainy's a great guide. She can help keep you up and running, and I'll be sleeping right behind you," he said with a grin.

"Not if I can put some pesky four-year-old in the seat beside you," Rainy said, letting her frustration get the best of her. "Or better yet, some teenage girl who thinks you are the most wonderful, most handsome man she's ever seen." She put her hands together under her chin and batted her eyelashes in imitation of the young women who fawned over her brother.

Sonny laughed and got to his feet. "You aren't that mean. Besides, it's not my fault we have to work our way back home. Just remember, we get two weeks to rest up. Look beyond the trip to the goal. Now, if you'll excuse me, I need to go down to the garage and make sure the car is in order for tomorrow."

Rainy watched him go and sighed. There was no sense trying to cover up her obvious disappointment.

"I was just going to take a walk," Duncan said softly. "Would you care to join me?"

Though rather disheartened at Sonny's news, Rainy decided to accept since she'd had so little time alone with Duncan. She smiled at him. "I probably can't stay out long, but yes, it sounds like a nice way to end the day."

Duncan came around and helped her up from her chair. "I found the trip quite fascinating. You have a real gift for dealing with the tourists."

"Sometimes I think I could trade it all," Rainy said, looking beyond Duncan to the street outside.

"But for what?"

Rainy continued walking, considering his question for a moment. "There's no easy answer to that question. There's a part of me that would walk away, without a second thought, for the right incentive." She thought of marriage or the chance to work with a company like the National Geographic Society. Her days at the university had put an end to that, however. Half the staff were members of the Society, and they knew very well why Rainy had left her position.

They walked down the stairs of the hotel and into the twilight of the Arizona skies. The temperature was much cooler than what they'd endured in the open desert lands. Rainy shivered, and before she knew it, Duncan had draped his coat around her shoulders.

"Thank you," she whispered. The golden glow of dying sun against a turquoise sky left her rather breathless and inspired. Or maybe it was just the smell of Duncan's cologne as she hugged his coat close. "I tend to forget that it gets much cooler here at times. I've even been here when there was snow on the ground." She fell silent, uncertain of what else to say.

"So what kind of incentive?" Duncan asked.

"What?" she asked. Though she knew he was referring to her earlier statement, she was hoping to stall for time to formulate an answer.

"What kind of incentive would cause you to leave the Detour business?"

She knew the answer but found it difficult to voice. "I know it might sound funny, but I've always wanted to settle down, maybe start a family."

"I wondered why you hadn't already married and done just that. I thought perhaps you didn't want to have children—or a husband."

Rainy tensed and looked to Duncan but instantly relaxed as she saw the warmth in his expression. He cared about her answer; she could see that much in his eyes. "No, it's not that. I went to school and the years just kind of slipped away. I thought I'd meet someone at school, but that never worked out."

"Why not?" Duncan asked, the breeze blowing strands of wavy black hair across his forehead.

Rainy stared at his hair momentarily. She wanted to reach up and push the tousled strands aside but instead turned back to face the narrow street, lest she give her heart away. "I seemed to intimidate the men in my classes," she finally answered. "I was a very strong student—I caught on quickly and studies were easy for me. They resented that. Especially when they added to it the fact that I was working in a field few women found of interest, much less excelled in."

Feeling uncomfortable, Rainy began to walk back toward the hotel. Duncan followed, easily coming up alongside her. "Some men are fools," he said.

Rainy looked at him, thinking perhaps he was saying more with his words than what was actually spoken. "Some women are too," she replied. Slipping from his coat, she handed it back. "I'd better go inside. I need a hot bath and a chance to get my clothes washed for the return trip. I'll see you tomorrow."

She hurried away from Duncan Hartford. Uncertainty dogged her heels. Why had she grown uncomfortable so quickly? What was it about Duncan's quiet manner that had put her so off guard?

———————

"Rainy!"

It was Sonny, and he was knocking on her door loudly enough to awaken the people in the rooms on either side of her.

"What?" she asked, opening the door.

"Are your bags ready?"

She yawned. As much as she'd tried to sleep and rest up for the day, it had been a fruitless effort. "They're ready. I just finished packing them. I washed my things out last night and had to wait until they were dry. I needed to iron out my skirt at the last minute." She motioned to the brown skirt that fell just below her knees.

Sonny looked at her hard, almost as if he were trying to figure out how to deliver some kind of horrible news. "What's wrong?" she asked. "Did I miss a spot?" She tried to twist and turn to better see her skirt.

"I need to tell you something, but you aren't going to like it."

She stilled in her actions and looked her brother in the eye. "I haven't liked much you've come to tell me these last few days."

Sonny nodded. "I understand that, but you're going to like this even less."

Rainy yawned again. "Just tell me, Sonny. You know it's the best way."

"The Driscolls are among our passengers today."

"Please tell me this is a bad joke," Rainy said, shaking her head. "You can't be serious."

"I am, I'm sorry to say, and Chester is traveling with his parents. If it's any consolation, we have a famous movie star traveling with us too. Phillip Vance. Remember? He's the one who starred in that western movie you liked so much last summer. Anyway, he's with his sister. She happens to be a writer who lives in Santa Fe."

"Why is this happening?" Rainy said, putting her hands to her head. Chester Driscoll was one of those ill-fitting pieces of her past. A piece that she had tried to force into place, only to have it pop back up.

"I'm sorry, sis. If I could do the trip without you, I would."

"Maybe I could tell them I'm sick. Surely there's another courier around here," Rainy said, desperately trying to think of how she might get out of this situation.

"I don't know. I suppose you could check into it."

Rainy doubted there would be anyone who could take her place, however. Most of the other couriers were short-run girls. They wouldn't want to drive all the way to Santa Fe and spend five days out on the road.

"No, just take my bag," Rainy said in resignation. "I'll be down shortly. I still can't believe this is happening." Sonny nodded, seeming to realize further conversation would be useless.

After Sonny had gone, Rainy sat on the edge of her bed and prayed. "Lord, I don't want to talk with those people. I don't want to be with them. I don't want to pretend to be friendly after the way they stabbed me in the back."

Rainy was momentarily taken back to Marshall Driscoll's office at the university. His position gave him a great deal of authority, and he'd had the final say on what happened to Rainy after valuable Indian artifacts were stolen and later found in her office. She could still picture the look on his face.

"If you leave quietly, the board has agreed not to press charges," Driscoll had told her.

"But I'm innocent. Someone placed those artifacts in my office. I didn't steal them." Rainy had protested her innocence for half an hour until finally Driscoll had to leave for another meeting and quickly dismissed her. He didn't care about the truth, and it was for this that Rainy faulted him.

"I'll need your answer by morning," he had stated without emotion or even the slightest hint of compassion.

Of course her answer had been to leave. She had no choice. To push the situation would have brought shame upon her family, and her father was a professor at the university. She couldn't allow him to bear any of the blame. Worse yet, Mr. Driscoll had suggested her father's position would be in jeopardy if this matter were brought to public attention.

So she left. Quietly. She left without a word to anyone—except Chester Driscoll. Chester had purported to be in love with Rainy, but all that changed when the artifacts were found in her office. He had come to say good-bye to her, promising that in time this would be behind them and they could start their love anew.

"I'm not in love with you, Chester. I have no desire to start any-thing—anew or otherwise," she had told him, even as she packed the bits and pieces of her life into a small box.

"Darling, you're just upset. Don't worry about this mess. No one really believes you stole those artifacts."

When she looked into his eyes, she suddenly knew the startling truth. Chester knew she hadn't stolen the artifacts. He knew it for a fact. His eyes betrayed the truth even as she stood there with tears flowing down her cheeks.

"What do you know about this, Chester?" she had asked angrily.

"I don't know what you're implying. I know nothing about the theft."

"Then how are you so certain of my innocence?"

He smiled. "That's easy. I know your character. I know you'd never do this thing."

"Then why didn't you tell that to the board?"

He'd had no answer, just mumbling about how no one would have taken seriously a man who was in love with the defendant.

"Why must I endure this man again, Lord?" Rainy now prayed, pushing the memories aside. "Why must I face his father and mother and the others? I've no desire to be their courier. I've no desire to make a pretense of enjoying their company for the sake of the Detours. Oh, God, please help me with this. This is so hard to deal with."

Thirty minutes later Rainy found herself face-to-face with the Dris-colls. Mrs. Driscoll, a dour little woman, had not changed much in the three years since Rainy had last seen her. Marshall Driscoll had put on at least fifty pounds, however, and Chester looked quite sporty in his top-of-the-line single-breasted coat of brown check.

"Why, Rainy Gordon," he murmured, "you look simply marvelous.

If I weren't a married man, I would definitely be in pursuit of rekindling our romance."

"We never had a romance," Rainy said, refusing to shake his hand. "I congratulate you on your marriage. I understand you married Bethel Albright, the niece of my father's good friend Professor Albright."

"I should have known you'd keep track of me," Chester said with a hint of a smirk.

"Like I would any other snake," she murmured.

"I absolutely insist on being introduced to this marvelous young woman." The voice came from a dashing blond-haired man who came up to stand at Rainy's left side.

Chester laughed. "This is Rainy Gordon, an old love of mine. Rainy, this is Phillip Vance, famed legend of the silver screen."

Phillip smiled warmly and lifted Rainy's hand to his lips. "I'm positively charmed to meet you."

"It's nice to meet you, Mr. Vance," she said, barely keeping herself from adding that she'd never been a love of Chester Driscoll's. She allowed herself a moment to study the screen star's smooth jaw, straight nose, and startling eyes.

"I'm hoping you can help me," Phillip said, his voice honey smooth.

"I'm not sure I can," Rainy replied, "but I'll certainly do my best."

Phillip beamed her a smile. "I've come to the Desert Southwest to learn more about the Indians. If you're familiar at all with my work, you'll know that most of my films are westerns. I want to make them more realistic. I'm starring in a new film called *The Mystery of Navajo Gulch.* I'm hoping to see the real Navajo people—to learn about them and better understand them. I want the movie to be as accurate as possible because I'm putting some of my own money into the making of this project."

"How very noble of you," Rainy said, not feeling at all interested in his cause.

"You think me insincere?" He looked genuinely hurt and Rainy immediately regretted her reply.

She was grateful that Chester had lost interest and had now joined his mother. He was deep in an animated conversation that included all kinds of hand gestures. *Same old Chester,* Rainy thought. Turning back to Phillip, she drew a deep breath. "I'm sorry. I'm afraid I didn't sleep well last night, but that is still no reason to be harsh with the guests. Please accept my apology. I'll do what I can to help you."

Phillip immediately perked up. "Wonderful. Now, you must come and meet my sister, Jennetta. She lives in Santa Fe and is one of those madly tortured authors who sleeps all day and writes all night. Some day she'll be famous—but right now she's just grumpy."

Phillip immediately put her at ease and Rainy couldn't help but giggle at this reference. She'd met many of the writers who frequented Santa Fe's cafes and other gathering places. Artists and writers made up a growing number of people who had embraced Santa Fe as their undisclosed place of residence. The community was branded as positively inspiring for those of an artistic nature.

Phillip led Rainy to where his sister stood talking with Marshall Driscoll. "Jennetta, dear, this is our guide, Rainy Gordon. Miss Gordon, this is my sister, Jennetta Blythe." The woman looked mousy compared to Phillip's vibrant appearance. Plain brown hair had been bobbed short and she wore a gray wool skirt and jacket that allowed only a hint of a blue blouse to peek from the top.

"Will we be leaving soon?" Jennetta questioned in a tone that suggested boredom. The look she offered Rainy seconded this emotion.

"Yes," Rainy said, forcing a smile. "If you'll all make your way down to the car, we'll head out immediately."

"Marvelous," Phillip declared. "I can hardly wait to get to know you better."

"I thought you were here for the desert and Indians," Jennetta said, scowling at Rainy. "She doesn't appear to be either one."

Rainy immediately disliked the woman but put it aside. *Five days*, she told herself. *I only have to endure them for five days.*

Duncan immediately realized that the Driscolls and the Gordons shared some kind of past. Rainy particularly avoided the younger of the Driscoll men, while conducting herself in an overly formal manner with the elder Mr. Driscoll. Duncan couldn't help but wonder what secrets the past held. Mr. Driscoll seemed to hold Rainy in some kind of contempt, while Chester appeared to go out of his way to speak in intimate whispers with her whenever the situation presented itself. Chester had put his hand on Rainy's waist only to have her elbow him sharply. But it wasn't the action so much as the look she gave him that left Duncan little doubt as to her disdain. Her glare could have frozen water at noon in the middle of the desert.

They reversed the order of their trip, spending the first night in Tuba City. Duncan, as always, helped to unload the luggage and didn't see any suspicious packages or additional suitcases. He shared a room with Sonny and saw nothing in his demeanor or actions that suggested he was about the business of stealing artifacts.

Leaving Tuba City, Sonny turned the driving over to Duncan. He hesitated, knowing that he wasn't truly interested in becoming a courier driver. Of course, he would have to at least pretend to be about the business of learning the route. The drive was a fairly easy one. They took the Kayenta Road, and because the weather had been dry, the road was decent.

"You'll want to take the lower road to the left," Sonny said, leaning over Duncan's shoulder.

"Yes, unless you want to put us in the sand, as Sonny delights in doing," Rainy teased. Duncan nodded and maneuvered the car to the left while Rainy turned to her passengers. "The body of water you see is called Sheep Dip. After we cross a sandy stretch we'll reach a lake called Red Lake. It's called this because the sand at the bottom of the lake appears red."

They passed the lake and headed on their way across the dry waste-land. At one point Rainy again turned to the guests and smiled. "This area of ruins is full of pottery and arrowheads. Little is known about the Indians who once lived here. There are several archaeologists who intend to study the area, but they feel confident the findings will prove the tribe to have been Navajo." Duncan enjoyed her comments but could tell by the way she frowned whenever she turned back to face the road that she wasn't happy at all. He couldn't help but wonder what was making her so miserable.

At midday they paused to share a picnic lunch that had been packed for them back in Tuba. Duncan felt ravenous as he settled in beside Rainy to share in the sandwiches and fresh fruit. Rainy was nearly fin-ished with her food, but helping Sonny resecure some loose luggage had delayed Duncan's lunch.

"So how do you like driving the touring car?" Rainy asked.

Duncan unwrapped a ham and cheese sandwich and shrugged. "It's an adventure, I will say that much."

"Are you sorry you gave up the museum?"

He felt a twinge of guilt. There was no way he could explain that he hadn't given up the museum. He couldn't very well tell one of the prime suspects of the investigation that he was only along to spy on her and gather information.

"I don't want to spend my life living in a museum," he finally said. "I have other plans."

"Truly? Maybe you could tell me about them sometime," Rainy said, seeming quite interested in him.

"Miss Gordon," Phillip Vance interrupted, "I wondered if you might take a walk with me and tell me about the landscape."

Rainy smiled up at the handsome man. "Of course." She quickly got to her feet and dusted off the backside of her skirt. "What would you like to know?"

They walked away with Phillip casually putting his hand on the small of Rainy's back as they ascended a slight incline. Duncan couldn't help but notice there was no sharp elbowing of Mr. Vance. On the contrary, Rainy seemed to enjoy Mr. Vance's attention very much. Duncan wanted nothing more than to run after them and insist he join the walk, but his appetite was fierce, and besides, he knew he had no business interfering in the matter.

Why does it have to be so hard to wait, Lord? I feel as though most of my life has been spent waiting for one thing or another to happen. Rainy Gordon is a beautiful and exciting woman, probably too much so for my simple life, but still I find myself drawn to her in a way I can't explain.

"You don't understand."

Duncan perked up at the statement. The voice of a man speaking in low, hushed tones carried over from the other side of the rock where Duncan ate.

"I understand better than you think," came another male voice. The second voice had to belong to Marshall Driscoll. It sounded much too refined and old to be his son's. Since Chester Driscoll was the only other man on the trip, besides Phillip Vance, the other voice must belong to him, Duncan reasoned.

"But Rainy is still determined to see the truth come out about those artifacts."

"Shut up," Driscoll told his son. "This is not a matter for discussion."

They moved away from the rock, leaving Duncan feeling rather ill. What did they know about Rainy and artifacts? The situation didn't look at all good for Rainy. First the Office of Indian Affairs believed her a possible thief, and now Driscoll's comment seemed to suggest there could be good reason to hold her accountable for the disappearing artifacts.

The sandwich settled heavily on his stomach. Swallowing hard, Duncan tried to figure out what he should do next. He could always take Chester aside and try to get the man to talk. It was doubtful he'd say anything, however. After all, the man didn't know Duncan and would have no reason to confide in him.

Maybe I should talk to Rainy and just ask her up front what his comment was about. But what if she is involved with stealing from the Indians and my questions ruin the investigation? There seemed to be no easy answer.

———

That evening, after the work of pitching tents and setting up cots had been completed, Rainy was surprised to find Phillip Vance at her side once again.

"I wondered if we might walk together?" Phillip asked. "I know I monopolized your time at lunch, but I do have more questions for you."

"Given the fact you were so willing to help us set up camp," Rainy began, "it would be uncharitable of me not to at least share a walk with you." She smiled and moved away from the gathering of tents. "So where would you like to walk? It's growing dark and we shouldn't go far. The desert is full of dangerous creatures."

"I'm sure that's wise counsel." He joined her, matching her long-legged strides with equal pacing. "I wondered if you would tell me about the Hopi people we visited today—about your friend Istaqa and his wife, Una. I liked them."

Rainy smiled. "They are wonderful people. Istaqa is one of the Indian police who keep law and order on the reservation. At first his people resented him, but they've come to discover over the years that they'd prefer to have another Hopi tell them what's right and wrong rather than have a white man do the deed. Of course, the authorities really don't hold him in very high regard, and they certainly would pull rank on him should they dislike his performance. Una is his wife of some fourteen years. They have three boys who attend the government school and do quite well."

Phillip took hold of her elbow and guided her toward an outcropping of rock. "I cannot imagine living the life they live. Do they really enjoy living in the pueblos?"

Rainy laughed. "Where else would they live? You certainly don't see any palatial mansions awaiting them, now, do you?"

Phillip appeared flushed in the fading light. Rainy realized she'd embarrassed him with her teasing. "I'm sorry," she said softly. "I shouldn't have answered in such a manner." She noticed that he continued to hold on to her arm even though they'd stopped walking.

"It's just that I feel people don't take me seriously when I say I want to learn. My sister thought me mad when I suggested this trip. She had come to visit me in Los Angeles, and when she mentioned traveling through Indian country and that souvenirs and such were available . . . well, I knew I had to see it for myself."

"And what do you think so far?" Rainy asked, warming under his intense scrutiny. The darkness robbed her of a chance to clearly see his expression, but she knew he had fixed his gaze on her.

"I'm deeply moved by the desert. It appears so harsh and lifeless, yet there is life out there. I look at the pueblos, so much like a natural outpouring of the earth, and marvel at the shapes and the sensibility of their creation. I see the people and know I shall never be as strong and worthy as they."

Rainy thought his attitude and feelings a refreshing change from so many of the tourists. His comments suggested a depth of feeling that did him honor. "The Hopi are a proud people. They can date their existence here back to A.D. 1050. They are very much as their name suggests: good, peaceful, and wise."

"I want to know everything," he said, pulling Rainy closer. He didn't even seem to notice what he'd done, yet Rainy was now only inches from him.

"Ah . . . well . . . they grow maize as a basic food. It's a type of corn. In fact, they raise over a dozen different kinds of corn—adding new varieties all the time."

"I had no idea there were so many varieties."

She found herself hesitant to speak. The words stuck in her throat. Here she was with a famous movie star. Her friends would have fainted dead away to be this close to Phillip Vance, and yet Rainy stood her ground—a bit light-headed, perhaps, but nevertheless, she was standing.

"What's it like to play a character in the movies?" she asked without thinking.

Phillip laughed. "Harder than some might think. It's mostly an endless chore of lighting and scenery details or dealing with some incompetent who has forgotten half his equipment. I actually like the acting part, but it's so different from the stage.

"But enough about me. I'm so glad you aren't like those poor girls who lose their heads at the mere mention of a celebrity name. Sometimes I begin to find a woman halfway interesting and she swoons at my feet. Terribly hard to discuss matters of importance when the other party is unconscious."

Rainy laughed out loud at this and stepped away from Phillip. "I assure you I'm not one of those women. However, you must admit no matter where you go, someone is bound to recognize you and desire to share in your glory."

He sighed and Rainy thought he sounded very sad when he replied, "Yes, it makes my life very difficult. I've often wondered if it might be possible to find friends now who are truly interested in me as a person and not me as a star."

Rainy thought about this for a moment. "You're very personable, Mr. Vance."

"Oh, please, call me Phillip," he said, moving closer to her once again.

Rainy smiled. "All right, Phillip. You have a genteel quality that I find refreshing, and yet for all your fame and fortune, you seem quite down to earth."

"Exactly!" he declared and once again took hold of her arm. As he began walking them back toward camp he added, "I knew you were different. I could see in your eyes that you understood my plight."

Rainy stumbled on a rock, but Phillip easily kept her upright. He steadied her, then stopped Rainy and turned her toward him. By the light of the campfires, Rainy could see his expression had grown very somber. She feared perhaps she'd made him overly morose.

"Rainy," he said, then paused. "May I call you by your first name?"

"Of course." She trembled slightly as he rubbed his fingers over her hands.

"Rainy, I find you the most delightful woman I've ever known. You are so very genuine and refreshing. I'd like very much to know you better, and I hope that during my stay in Santa Fe, you'll allow me to call on you."

Rainy swallowed but the desert dust left her choked. "I . . ." She cleared her throat with a little cough. "Excuse me," she apologized, then regained a bit of her composure. "I think it would be very nice to get to know you better, Mr. . . . Phillip. But after we return, I will be going to Albuquerque for two weeks. You see, my parents live there and my brother and I plan to have an extended visit with them."

"Oh, well . . . how unfortunate."

Now he really sounded sad, and Rainy could hardly bear that she'd caused it. Especially when her heart continued to suggest that perhaps this was the man who would sweep her off her feet. Perhaps this was the very man she had nagged and pleaded with God to give her for a husband.

"I could postpone my trip for a day or two," she said.

"Oh, would you?" he questioned, his voice taking on the same animation she'd heard when she'd first met him. "I think that would be absolutely delightful. We could have a chance to get to know each other that way. Perhaps to even consider something more permanent in our relationship."

Rainy felt a quiver start at her toes and work its way up her body. "Phillip, we hardly know each other well enough to think on something that serious."

"I'm sorry, but I'm used to going after what I want." He drew her hands up to his lips. "I'm not impetuous enough to rush in and say that you're what I want. . . ." He kissed her hands gently and then just held them under his chin. "But I feel fairly confident that the next few days will make up my mind for me."

Rainy realized she was getting caught up in his romantic manners. She gently disengaged her hands and smiled. "I leave my fate in God's hands. I've no doubt He will show me the way. I must retire now, Phillip. I hope you have a pleasant rest."

She moved away quickly, hoping he wouldn't follow her. He didn't and although it was what she really wanted, Rainy felt rather disappointed.

Later that night as she struggled to fall asleep, Rainy wondered if Phillip Vance was the husband God had in mind for her. *He's handsome and compassionate,* she thought. *I loved the way he treated Istaqa and Una as equals.* So many of the tourists treated the Indians as if they were merely staging and ornamentation—not real people with honest feelings.

Phillip seems to care about the Indians and their lives here in the desert. He seems to understand the complexity of their culture and to respect it. Could he be the one?

But then it dawned on Rainy that if God had sent Phillip into her life for the purpose of matrimony, she would most likely have to leave the Southwest and her desires to be a working archaeologist. Phillip would have to be in California making his movies. His lifestyle and needs were completely different from hers—much more complex.

She'd overheard Jennetta and Mrs. Driscoll talking about the lavish, newly built mansion Phillip owned in a small community outside of Los Angeles. Jennetta told of the house having over twenty-five rooms. Rainy had thought surely the woman was exaggerating, but she began naming them off with such detail that Rainy began to believe the story.

Jennetta had concluded by describing a huge swimming pool and gardens with marble statues that had come all the way from Italy. Apparently the depressed economy had not caused harm to Phillip Vance's life.

Rainy tried to imagine wearing lavish gowns and acting as hostess for Phillip. Would his friends willingly accept her because she was Phillip's wife? Or would they turn her away because she wasn't of their social class?

Lord, I don't know what you have in mind here. I don't know if you've sent Phillip to me for a purpose beyond the tour, but he does seem to like me. What do I do?

She wrestled with the thought of Duncan. Duncan understood her love of New Mexico and Arizona, and as far as she knew, he had no plans to leave the area. Still, for all the attention she'd shown Duncan, he hadn't seemed inclined to return her interest. He talked to her when they were together and he had asked her to walk with him in Williams, but that hardly constituted affection.

Why does this have to be so hard?

Just as Rainy felt her mind grow clouded and her eyes become heavy, a scream split the silence of the night.

"What in the world is happening now?" she moaned, feeling her heart race just as it had when Gloria Van Patten had been scared by her brothers.

Bolting upright, Rainy pulled on her boots and began lacing them up. The woman screamed again, and this time Rainy was positive that it had to be Jennetta Blythe.

*R*ainy wasn't the first one on the scene of Jennetta's hysterical display. Duncan stood outside with a lantern, while poor Sonny bore the brunt of the woman's tirade as she dragged him into her tent. Rainy stood back and watched with some amusement as Sonny escorted an uninvited gopher snake from Jennetta and Mrs. Driscoll's tent. The older woman stood patiently to one side while Jennetta looked as though she might kill them all as she flailed her own lantern and ranted about the conditions.

"You'd think for the price of this tour we could at least stay in a real hotel!"

"Now, now, Jennetta," Phillip said, patting her arm reassuringly. "We knew part of this trip would be spent in rustic environments. You mustn't get yourself all worked up over a little snake."

"He wasn't little," she replied angrily. "I'll not be treated as a child!" She jerked her arm away from Phillip's touch and marched into her tent. It was clear she wanted nothing to do with any of them.

Rainy smiled at her brother. "The handsome knight rescuing the lady fair," she murmured as he passed by her.

"Ha!" It was the only comment he had on the matter.

Rainy laughed and headed back to her tent.

"You hardly seemed fazed by that," Phillip declared as he came up beside her.

She looked up and smiled. "But of course not. The snake wasn't poisonous, and even if he were, there are ways to take care of the situation without resorting to hysteria."

Phillip grinned. "Perhaps she'll write a poem about it. She does that, you know."

Rainy shook her head. "I knew she was a writer of some sort, but I didn't realize Jennetta was a poet."

"Oh yes, she writes about her life. Dark, brooding, end-of-the-world kind of poetry. The more it suggests misery and torment, the more she loves it." He cast a glance back at Jennetta's tent and chuckled. "Poor Jennetta."

"Poor snake," Rainy replied.

————

Travel the next day was even more torturous than the day before. Jennetta was in a sour mood that kept the others at a distance. Phillip spent his time consoling her, which left Rainy alone until Chester Driscoll decided to seek her out.

"You know, Rainy, there's no need to play standoffish with me," he said while the others spent a bit of extra time wandering around the Navajo displays and goods. Mrs. Driscoll seemed to give her purchases little thought as she pointed to first one thing and then another.

When Rainy gave no reply, Chester reiterated, "I said that you needn't play standoffish with me."

Rainy met his gaze. "I wasn't playing."

Chester smiled. "Now, now. You owe my family too much to maintain this façade of anger."

"I *owe* your family? Neither you nor your father would defend me in the truth, and you think I owe you something for that?" Her anger was getting the better of her. She tried to remind herself that Chester was a guest of the Detour Company.

"We could have prosecuted you for the theft."

"Just because the articles turned up in my office—"

"In your desk," Chester interrupted.

Rainy scowled. "I didn't take those pieces, and you know that full well. Your father did too. One word of defense from either of you could have cleared my name with the university board. Now I'm still trying to do that on my own."

"You shouldn't waste your time. No one will ever believe you. You left quietly and didn't protest the charges so long as they were dropped. What do you suppose that meant to the board?"

Rainy tried to do a mental count to ten, but it was no use. "Exactly what I presumed they would think—that I was guilty. But I'm not."

Chester reached out to take hold of her shoulder. "Now, Rainy, you are getting upset over nothing. No one even cares about that ordeal anymore. It's already behind us. You and I, however . . . now, that's a topic that still begs discussion."

"What of your wife?" Rainy questioned, trying to pull away from his touch. He tightened his hold so that it became painful. "You're hurting me," Rainy muttered from behind clenched teeth.

"That isn't my intention, but you must hear me out. My wife would never need to know about us."

"There is no 'us.' Leave me be."

"Just hear me out for a moment," he said, eyeing her with a pleading glance.

Rainy stilled. "You have one minute and then I scream for Sonny."

Chester chuckled. "I know what you want out of life. You want a position with the National Geographic Society. You want your own dig and I can make that happen. In return, you can be my mistress and I'll buy you a wonderful house in Santa Fe. We could have a lovely life together."

"Just you, me, and the little wife, eh?"

Chester was completely unmoved. "People do it all the time. Wealthy men are allowed a level of living that other men are never given."

"Wealthy? I thought the Driscolls were more show than substance."

"That might be true for the Driscolls in general, but not for this Driscoll." He puffed out his chest and loosened his hold. "I've married into money and have no worry about the future. Oh, certainly the economy has made things more difficult. Already the cities back East are filling with unemployed beggars. But that has nothing to do with us. I can get you what you want. I can get you your dream."

"Your time is up," Rainy said, pulling away abruptly. "I have no interest in your proposition, Mr. Driscoll, and I do hope you will keep from embarrassing yourself further by refraining from future references to this conversation. If not, I'll be compelled to have a conversation of my own—with your wife."

She walked away as quickly as she could without causing a scene. Mrs. Driscoll, shopping concluded, stood patiently under an Indian-blanket awning. Jennetta Blythe stood at her side.

"Are you ladies enjoying yourselves?" Rainy asked in as pleasant a manner as she could muster.

"I won't enjoy myself again until we're in Santa Fe," Jennetta declared.

Rainy couldn't help the smile that overcame her. "My mother used to say that if you're determined to feel a certain way, you'll most likely succeed."

Phillip's sister scowled. "Whatever do you mean by that?"

"Just that if you intend to be miserable, you will be. If you decide to be happy, then you'll find a way to achieve it. You seem determined to be miserable no matter what takes place on this trip, so you are welcome to it. Just don't expect the company to love misery."

"Well! I've never encountered such rudeness."

"I guess that makes two of us," Rainy replied, matching Jennetta's hard gaze with one of her own.

Mrs. Driscoll eyed Jennetta for a moment, then turned to Rainy. "How much longer will we be detained?"

Rainy nodded. "I believe we'll be here another five or ten minutes."

"Oh, I see."

Rainy tried to think of something to say that might draw the older woman into a conversation. "Mrs. Driscoll, were you able to hold your annual Christmas party for the college faculty?"

"Yes."

Rainy had hoped she'd elaborate. "And was it a success?"

"Yes."

Mrs. Driscoll shifted her purchases from one hand to the other but otherwise showed little sign of life. Rainy thought her the most completely boring woman in all the world.

"So are you having a nice time on the tour?" Rainy questioned, trying a different angle.

"It's much too hot for this time of year," Mrs. Driscoll replied.

Rainy thought the weather had been perfect. Many times tourists came to the desert in the cooler months, hoping to avoid the piercing heat of summer. "I thought it quite lovely today."

"I'm sure someone lacking in the more refined things of life would find this day enjoyable," Jennetta chimed in. "But it really is appalling. I won't rest a moment until we're back in Santa Fe."

That evening they spent the night in Gallup, New Mexico, enjoying the hospitality of the local Harvey hotel, El Navajo. Jennetta finally seemed at peace and Mrs. Driscoll disappeared shortly after their arrival.

Rainy was glad for the reprieve but found the quiet to be short-lived when other guests began recognizing Phillip Vance and pleading for autographs and conversation. Rainy watched, with Sonny and Duncan, as the entourage of people came to pester Phillip.

"That poor man—he won't have a chance to eat his meal while it's still hot," Rainy declared, craning to the right to see past Duncan.

"He's a grown man," Duncan said. "I expect he understands by this point in his career that this is a part of the game. He'll either send them away or bask in the glory."

Rainy frowned and straightened in her chair. "What's that supposed to mean?"

Sonny laughed. "The man isn't a movie actor because he values his own company is what Duncan is saying. Mr. Vance seems pretty happy with the attention."

As if to accentuate her brother's point, Phillip let out a booming laugh that filled the air. Duncan met her gaze with raised eyebrows, as if to say, "I told you so."

Rainy lowered her gaze and poked her green beans around the plate. "He's just too sweet to send them away. He's kind to everyone."

"He's certainly been kind to you, sister dear. Maybe too kind. Maybe I need to have a private talk with Mr. Vance."

Rainy looked up at Sonny and cocked her head to one side. "I don't know what you're implying with that comment, but I assure you Mr. Vance has been nothing but a gentleman. He even treated my Indian friends with great civility and open admiration."

Sonny laughed, but it was Duncan who leaned in to say, "Your defense of Mr. Vance isn't helping your case at all."

Rainy pushed away from the table. "You're both being silly. Phillip has been very charming and, well . . . yes, he has shown me some special interest. But it's my business—not yours," she told Sonny. She then looked to Duncan and added, "Or yours."

She started across the dining room just as Phillip and his entourage rose. "Miss Gordon," Phillip called and motioned.

Rainy froze midstep. She was afraid to acknowledge him and afraid not to. Finally she looked over her shoulder to where Phillip stood alongside Chester Driscoll. "Do join us. We're retiring to the Writing Room, where Jennetta has agreed to read us a couple of her poems and I am to do a scene from my last movie. Please say you'll come."

Rainy opened her mouth to reply but found Sonny speaking instead. "Is the invitation extended to everyone?" She turned around and found that he and Duncan were only a few paces behind her.

"But of course. The more the merrier. We artists are nothing without our audience to appreciate us," Phillip replied.

His response was not what Rainy had hoped to hear. She had

thought perhaps her invitation was a summons to a private, exclusive time of privilege. There was just something about Phillip Vance that made her easily forget herself.

She followed with Sonny and Duncan as the growing party moved to the Writing Room. She took a seat toward the back, hoping it would afford her a quick getaway should the need arise. Much to her surprise, Duncan took the seat beside her, while Sonny went up closer to the impromptu stage.

Chester had been appointed the host and soon several other participants had been encouraged to join in showing off their talents.

There were several recitations of speeches that were followed by a bleak soliloquy by Jennetta Blythe entitled, "The Despair That Haunts My Soul." For Rainy, the despair was that the poem went on for twelve stanzas. Gloom and sorrow dripped from every word. The woman was clearly not a happy person.

Finally Phillip stood and gave a rousing speech from his last movie. The speech dealt with a cowboy's plea to his dying father to forgive him for past indiscretions. The audience applauded with great enthusiasm and the women rushed to plant kisses on Phillip's cheeks and lips. Rainy was rather stunned by their reaction. Phillip, in the meantime, seemed quite content with the attention. The situation confused her.

Lord, if you've brought him into my life as a potential husband, then why is he acting like that? The question surprised even Rainy. She looked at Duncan and found his gaze fixed on her, almost as if he were awaiting some response or reaction.

She got to her feet, unable to figure out her heart in the matter. Duncan had a way of making her weak in the knees, but then, so did Phillip Vance. Duncan's smile had aroused thoughts of marriage and happily ever after. But then, Phillip Vance had mastered the art of the enticing smile, too.

Suddenly she realized she was still staring at Duncan. "I suppose I'll retire for the evening."

"It's been a rather tiring day," Duncan said, getting to his feet.

Sonny came bounding toward them, shaking his head. "Have you ever seen such a fuss? I nearly had two different women sitting on my lap as they fought to get past my seat. And all for that," he said, motioning over his back.

"It was calmer back here. I didn't have any threat of ladies in my lap," Duncan replied with a grin. "But I did get a good looking over."

Rainy felt her cheeks grow hot. "I'm going to bed."

Duncan wasn't sure what to do with his feelings. He had thought of Rainy all night as he slipped in and out of sleep. And then when they gathered with the dudes at the car the next morning, he watched her with such intensity that she asked him twice if something was wrong.

He wanted to tell her about the investigation. He wanted to tell her that his feelings for her were getting . . . well, out of control. He wanted to explain everything that mattered and yet knew there was nothing he could say. At least not at this point.

"Rainy!"

Duncan looked up to find Phillip Vance making his way to where Rainy stood with Sonny. Duncan picked up a road map and ambled toward the threesome, pretending to study the route.

"When I saw the glorious sunrise, I thought of you immediately. Your hair is like the ribbons of color that unfurled across the sky," Vance said with a smile.

Rainy, who had seemed discouraged all morning, perked up at Phillip's greeting. "Well, you know what they say. Red skies in morning, sailors take warning."

"Well, there certainly aren't any sailors in this part of the world, so maybe there are others who should heed the signs," Phillip said in a teasing manner. "Anyway, I wanted to catch you before we started out for Albuquerque. We had no time to talk privately last night. Did you enjoy my performance?"

Duncan wanted to laugh out loud, but instead he touched Sonny on the shoulder and held up the map as if to suggest directions be given. Sonny darted behind the map and exchanged a grin with Duncan. Together they lowered the map just enough to watch Rainy and Phillip.

"I enjoyed it very much," Rainy told Phillip. "I remember that scene in the movie brought me to tears."

"Truly? How marvelous!" Phillip declared. "I knew you were a woman of great passion. I have a very poor relationship with my father, and I drew on that to support my character's reaction. The scene conjured all sorts of memories for me . . . but, of course, such a scene would never be allowed in real life. My father believes in grudges."

"How very sad."

Phillip sighed. "You are very understanding of my situation. So often the world leaves little room for honesty, but I find that you are a woman of not only impeccable truth but also incredible beauty."

Sonny coughed to cover a laugh. Rainy glanced their way, but it was Duncan's gaze she met. She frowned and looked back to Phillip. "Was there something else I could help you with?"

"Absolutely." Phillip oozed charm, and Duncan personally wanted to wring his neck. "I know we'll stay the night in Albuquerque. I wondered if you would be my personal escort and give me an evening tour of the city. I'd love to see all the special places—just you and me."

Rainy smiled and looked away. Duncan thought she looked rather nervous. "I'd love to," she told him.

This caused both Sonny and Duncan to drop the map. Duncan knew, from what she and Sonny had both shared, that nights in Albuquerque were always devoted to family. From the look on Sonny's face, Rainy was acting completely out of character.

"Rainy, what about Mom and Dad?" Sonny asked.

"They'll understand. Take Duncan home with you. Give them my excuses."

Sonny looked to Duncan and shook his head. "I think it's time to get on the road. You want to drive?" he asked.

Duncan nodded, although he really didn't feel like taking on the chore. At least it might help to keep his mind occupied. It might—but he doubted it.

J've really enjoyed our evening together," Phillip said as he strolled with Rainy.

"I have too," Rainy admitted. She'd known nothing but his complete attention and generosity this evening. Phillip's genuine kindness and interest in her life and the things around her proved him to be a man of integrity and consideration. Her only real frustration was that she still knew so very little about Phillip Vance, the man. He was openly delighted to talk about his life as an actor, but when it came to anything more personal, he seemed to easily avoid her questions.

"I must say, I've learned a great deal about your Indian friends. I think it marvelous that you know so much about them. You'd be a tremendous asset to the movie studio. You really should give it some thought."

"Move to California? But I don't know anyone there," Rainy said without thinking.

"You would know me," Phillip said, stopping to take hold of her hand. "And by then, well . . . who can say?"

Rainy felt a surge of frustration. These were hardly the kinds of words she wanted to hear. She wanted to know if Phillip had any real interest in deepening their relationship, of course, but she wanted to know much more. Rainy needed to know if he was like-minded—if he honored the truth, honored God. She'd always respected her mother's admonition to not get involved with nonbelievers. Rainy had worked hard, in fact, to avoid such heartaches. It was definitely something that had allowed her to keep Chester Driscoll at arm's length.

Overhead the night skies twinkled with diamondlike stars. The moon, a lazy crescent, offered little light. Rainy wanted so much to know Phillip Vance's true self, yet he never seemed able to tell her much more than who he was as an actor or public figure. Even his interests and concern about the Hopi were more related to his work than to his personality—at least that was how it seemed at times.

"Isn't it marvelous how God so intricately created the universe—so beautiful . . . so perfect?" Rainy said, hoping perhaps this line of questioning would give Phillip cause to respond and share his heart. She continued gazing into the night sky, waiting for his response.

After a moment he replied, "It's beautiful here, to be sure."

Rainy waited for him to say something more, but he seemed completely content to remain silently at her side. Frustration coursed through her veins. "Phillip, you've really said very little about yourself. I feel like I know all about Phillip Vance the actor, but what of your personal life? What did you do with yourself before getting into the movie business?" she asked, suddenly breaking the intimacy of the moment. She pulled away and continued their stroll back to the Alvarado Hotel.

Phillip quickly followed. "There really isn't much to tell. I was born and raised in New York. I went to school and developed an interest in movies from the first time I viewed a silent picture." He smiled down at her as he again claimed her arm. "I knew then that acting was for me."

"But surely you had other plans and dreams as a child."

Phillip grew momentarily thoughtful. "My mother took me to my first play when I was only five. I regularly attended after that—whenever she was to attend. My father despised the theatre, so we never told him of our destinations." He shrugged as if he'd said too much. "I suppose there was the thought to become something studious—you know, a lawyer or banker. I believe my father hoped I might follow in his footsteps and help with the family business."

"Which was?" Rainy asked, finally feeling she was getting somewhere.

"He made tools," Phillip murmured, as if ashamed. "Jennetta hated our life there and often spoke of moving from New York to California—Los Angeles, in particular. I thought it sounded marvelous. I knew it would allow me to be exposed to all that I would need to get me into movies. That's where my real passion lies."

Movies. Rainy sighed. So they were back to that topic. How was she supposed to know him better? How was she supposed to know if this was the man God intended for her to marry if he wouldn't discuss the truly important aspects of life? Still, he seemed so interested in being with her. He could have taken his pick of beautiful women, yet here he was with her. That had to mean something—didn't it?

They'd reached the hotel veranda, and Phillip stopped and pulled Rainy around to face him. "I have a surprise. I've arranged a carriage ride to take you home," he said, his expression suggesting he was quite pleased with himself.

Rainy thought the gesture very sweet. "How marvelous. It's been a long time since I've ridden in a carriage. With the Harveycars—well, I guess now that Major Clarkson has purchased the Detours they're being called courier cars—but nevertheless, with the touring cars I've had plenty of non-equestrian transportation."

"I thought this would be rather ... well ... romantic," he whispered.

"Romantic?" Rainy asked, her voice squeaking a bit. Was this the sign she'd been waiting for? Was God finally going to show her the truth about Phillip Vance?

Phillip laughed and led her toward the carriage. "I think you're absolutely marvelous."

Rainy didn't know what to make of his comment. Was he laughing at her? Did he think her naïve? *Why did I have to make that comment?* She moaned inwardly. *He probably thinks me quite immature and completely unsophisticated.*

Rainy allowed Phillip to help her into the carriage. As a young girl, her family had used horse and carriage exclusively. Her father hadn't the inclination toward nor the money to spend on an automobile. But the 1930s seemed to demand more and more attention toward change. Horses and carriages were giving way to the motorized car and quicker modes of transportation. Lindbergh had flown across the Atlantic, and air travel was rapidly becoming an acceptable alternative to the slower-paced trains. Automobiles were even more accessible with their makers desiring to produce a product that every American family could afford to buy.

Still, there was something very romantic and lovely about an evening carriage ride. Rainy settled back against the leather upholstery and sighed.

"I hope that was a sigh of contentment and not boredom," Phillip whispered.

His nearness made Rainy straighten a bit. "It was the happy kind," she replied. "I always enjoy coming home to Albuquerque. My folks ... our house ... well ... it's just very nice to be around the things and people you love. I've cherished growing up here. My mother always made our house a home. She has the most marvelous gardens in the inner courtyard. You'll have to see them sometime." Rainy found that she never quite realized how much she loved it here until after she'd been gone for a time. "I've enjoyed working with the Detours, but I also like the idea of taking time away from my job. I'm going to greatly enjoy my two weeks off."

"But you will still consider postponing for just a few days, won't you?" he asked so sweetly that Rainy couldn't do anything but nod.

"I suppose I can postpone my vacation by a day or so to show you around Santa Fe." Rainy couldn't believe she was agreeing to do such a thing. She could easily remember the disappointment she'd felt when Sonny told her of the trip to the Grand Canyon. Now, however, the idea of delaying wasn't at all unappealing. With Phillip Vance in the picture, in fact, the delay seemed quite promising.

"Phillip, may I ask you something?" Rainy decided the only way she'd get answers would be to ask very specific questions.

"Of course you may," he said, taking hold of her hand.

"What are your plans for the future? I mean, do you always intend to work as a movie star? Will you stay in California?"

He chuckled softly and turned a bit to better face her. "I see my future only getting better. I see the movie industry booming like a gold rush, and I see myself in the midst of that boom. California is a perfectly lovely place to live and my new home is marvelous. But without the right woman to share it all . . . well . . ." He looked away momentarily. "I want a wife and children. I want a closeness of family that I never experienced growing up."

"I thought from the way you spoke that you and your mother and sister were all very close," Rainy said, not giving any thought to how personal the statement might seem.

Phillip's expression seemed pained. "No, it wasn't as it might seem to an outsider. What I want is nothing like what I had growing up. I want honesty and love—compassion and open-mindedness."

Rainy thought she'd never heard anyone sound so sad. She trembled as he returned his gaze to her face and reached up to gently stroke her cheek. "I've been searching for the right woman," he murmured. "A woman who wouldn't be intimidated by the fanfare and nonsense that accompanies me. A woman who would understand the attention I'd be given by my fans. A woman who would take all of that in stride and still manage to give me the support and love I need."

Rainy felt as though time stood still as he softly spoke of his desires.

Could she be that woman? Would she want to put herself into that life—take herself away from the world she knew and loved? A tiny voice in the back of her mind questioned, *What about the support and love* you *would need?* Rainy quickly pushed the thought aside. There would be time to figure that out later.

The driver slowed the horses to a stop in front of her parents' house. The sudden lull caused Rainy to look up, almost startled. "We're here."

Phillip nodded. "I hope I didn't bore you with my talk."

"Not at all," Rainy said, more confused than ever.

"I'll walk you to the door." Phillip climbed down from the carriage and reached back up to help Rainy. As her feet touched the ground, Phillip's arms went around her and he pulled her close for a kiss.

Rainy was too surprised to really enjoy the kiss. She was so shocked that Phillip would take such a liberty with her, and yet at the same time she couldn't help but wonder if this, too, was a part of God's plan to show her the truth of His choice.

Phillip pulled away, a hesitant look on his face. "I'm sorry. I shouldn't have done that."

Rainy shook her head. "I would have preferred that you had not. We barely know each other."

He laughed. "I tend to forget myself. I have women throwing themselves at me all the time. I suppose it seemed strange not to have you respond in the same manner."

"That's who I am," Rainy defended. "I'm not like your throngs of fans."

He released her and took a step back. "Please forgive me. Don't let my ill manners spoil our evening or our future."

Rainy couldn't be angry with him. "Of course I forgive you." She smiled sweetly. "Thank you for the wonderful evening, but now I really need to get to bed. Tomorrow is the final day of our tour, and you'll want to get your money's worth."

"I think I already have," Phillip said, laughing.

———

"Where have you been?" Sonny asked as Rainy came through the door.

"You know perfectly well where I've been. I've been out with Phillip Vance." She pulled off her dress jacket and tossed it aside. "Where are Mom and Dad?" she asked, looking around the room.

"They went to bed about an hour ago. It's ten o'clock, Rainy."

"Goodness, I didn't realize it was so late."

"That much is obvious," Sonny said, trying not to allow his worry to turn to anger. "Rainy, I really was starting to worry. First you take off with Phillip instead of spending time here at home with us, and then you don't return until ten. It's not at all like you."

Rainy sat down opposite him. "No, I suppose it's not. I just felt it was something I had to do, however. I couldn't help but wonder if God had brought Phillip Vance into my life for more than just a tour."

Sonny got a sinking feeling inside. "What do you mean?"

"Well, I wonder if he's the man God will have me marry."

"What about Duncan?" Sonny questioned. He knew his sister's feelings for Duncan Hartford were more than a passing interest. How could she so easily trade one man for another?

"What about him? I've tried to show him interest and make it clear that I find his company enjoyable, but he doesn't seem to have the slightest interest in me." She leaned her elbow on the table, then shrugged. "I suppose Duncan Hartford has too many other interests to consider me."

"I wouldn't be so sure. I also wouldn't expect him to show his true feelings and compete with a movie star."

"But Phillip Vance wasn't even in the picture when I first showed Duncan my interest in him. You can't blame Phillip."

"I'm not blaming anyone," Sonny replied. "I just think you should be cautious about this. Phillip Vance seems to be the kind of man who's used to dallying with women. I'd hate to have to straighten him out over his dalliance with you."

"I'm a grown woman, little brother. I know how to handle myself."

Sonny smiled. "I'd like to believe that, but actions speak much louder than words."

"Oh, go on with you. Stop worrying about me. I'm just trying to seek out God's will for my life," Rainy replied. "God doesn't expect me to just sit around and wait for Him to drop a husband in my lap."

"Oh, He doesn't? When did He tell you this?"

Rainy squirmed a bit and shifted in her chair. She refused to meet Sonny's eyes and looked to the table instead. "I just can't imagine that He wants me to do nothing. I've prayed about it, and I just figured it was partly up to me to do something about it."

"If God wants you to marry Duncan Hartford or even Phillip Vance, don't you think He can handle the task of bringing it about, without you having to work double time to see it to fruition? It's not like you've been asked to take on an extra tour shift. We're talking about God's ability to do infinitely more than we can ask or imagine. Remember?"

"I remember."

"Besides, what if God has called you to be single?"

Rainy glared at him for this. "He hasn't. I know without a doubt that God wants me to marry and have a family. I've prayed about it. I have real peace that this is His will for my life."

"If that's the case, then why not rest in it and wait for Him to act? It's not like He's going to forget you."

She yawned. "I know all of that." Straightening a bit, she asked, "So how did you spend your evening?"

Sonny laughed. "Changing the subject, are we?"

"Yes, please. What did you do?"

Now it was Sonny's chance to grow uncomfortable. "I met with some old friends of mine. They came here to the house and we visited for a couple of hours."

"Truly? Who were they?"

"You remember Jess and Richard, my friends from college?"

Rainy nodded.

"Well, they've gotten themselves involved in an Alaskan Territory exploration group. It's a government project."

"How exciting for them. When will they head to Alaska?"

Sonny straightened, knowing he had to tell her his plans. Finalizing his departure without letting her in on it seemed almost criminal. "Part of the team is heading up at the end of August. The other part will leave in September."

"Seems like the wrong time to head up north," she said, laughing. "Don't birds usually fly south in the winter?"

He smiled. "Well, a team of thirty scientists can hardly be mistaken for birds. They're doing a winter study."

"Oh, well, that makes sense—if you like that kind of thing." She yawned again and got to her feet.

"There's more. It has to do with the team and I want to tell you about it," Sonny said, a desperate tone to his words. He knew he needed to tell her the truth of his plans. He didn't want her to accidentally learn it from someone else.

"Oh, Sonny, not now. I'm completely spent and want to go to bed. You can tell me about your friends tomorrow." She came around and kissed him atop his head. "I'm sorry I worried you."

"I just want you to be safe and happy," Sonny said as she walked from the room. She didn't reply, so he wasn't even sure she'd heard him.

Sonny felt a sense of guilt and knew it was silly. He was a grown man with every right to plan to travel to Alaska with his friends. A job as a government geologist was something he simply couldn't pass by. Rainy would understand and be happy for him, but he knew she would also be hurt that he hadn't discussed it with her early on.

"So did you talk to her?"

Sonny looked up to find his father standing in the dining room doorway. His well-worn robe was the same one Sonny had seen him wear since he and Rainy were kids. "I tried. She was tired though and wanted to get to bed."

His father nodded and joined Sonny at the table. "There will be time."

"I'm worried about her," Sonny said, shaking his head. "She's so caught up in trying to figure out whom God wants her to marry. Then there's the whole issue of wanting to figure out who framed her and got her fired at the university."

"I'd like to get to the bottom of that myself," Dad replied. "Seems senseless that a young innocent girl should be singled out like that and blamed for something everyone knew she couldn't possibly have done. I've tried to talk to Marshall Driscoll several times, but he won't even discuss it."

"He was on our tour this last trip," Sonny began. "I was stunned to see him and Mrs. Driscoll but even more surprised to find Chester with them. Rainy feels confident that Chester was somehow behind the entire incident. She said he spoke with too much familiarity regarding the matter. Yet when she's tried to talk to him about it, he turns the tables on her and reminds her that his father kept her from prosecution."

Dad nodded knowingly. "I've never understood it. Rainy was always so very conscientious about anything regarding the artifacts. I know she would never have taken them for any purpose—not even for cleaning them, as Chester suggested."

"Chester showed way too much interest in Rainy then *and* now. Even on the trip this week he was always finding ways to be alone with her. Duncan and I tried to keep that from happening very often, but it wasn't easy. Between Chester and Phillip Vance, we had our hands full."

"Well, your sister is a grown woman and times are changing. Women are able to vote and to speak their mind. Certainly they're able to choose the company they keep."

"I suppose," Sonny said, feeling rather deflated. "But I don't think at this point she knows what's good for her."

His father laughed. "I guess I could wonder if running off to the frozen north was good for you, but you'd give me some long discussion about it being your lifelong dream and how"—he got up from the table and looked down at his son—"you'd waited forever for a dream position like this to come along." His father smiled. "Hmm, on second thought, I guess we had that conversation."

"I know what you're saying, Dad." Sonny got up and stretched. "I'll try to just pray it through."

"That's the best you can do, son. Rainy knows better than to plunge into anything without taking it to God first. She'll do all right."

CHAPTER NINE

*J*can see why Jennetta loves it here," Phillip declared as he strolled the streets of Santa Fe with Rainy. "There's a feel of the ancient here. Almost as if another world existed inside this plaza center."

Rainy smiled, feeling at the moment that she'd never been happier than being on the arm of Phillip Vance. "It's a wonderful town full of Spanish and Indian influence. I love the architecture, especially—the red tile on the roofs and the courtyard gardens. I adore the adobe and wrought iron, the arched doors and windows and adobe fireplaces. It's all so very pleasant."

"And romantic," he whispered against her ear.

Rainy trembled. "Yes, definitely that."

"I feel so honored," Phillip began, "that you would agree to cancel your vacation and spend some time acting as our courier. I knew if we requested you, they would somehow find a way to persuade you."

"They didn't have to persuade me," Rainy admitted. "When the matter came up, I just felt it was the right thing to do. I prayed about it and felt even more confident of my decision."

"You put a lot of stock in prayer, don't you?"

Rainy stopped and looked up. Phillip's expression was one of curiosity laced with concern. "I do put a lot of stock in prayer. Don't you?"

Phillip shrugged and looked away. "I suppose it's never been that important to me. I didn't grow up religious, and therefore I've just never had any real use for such matters."

Rainy felt as though she had plunged from a three-story building. She might be foolish about matters of the heart, but she could never ignore the warning regarding being unequally yoked with a nonbeliever.

"But what of standards to live by?" Rainy questioned. "How do you gauge those standards?"

Phillip shoved his hands in his pockets and leaned back against the adobe face of one of the Plaza stores. "I suppose I make my own."

Rainy had heard this argument before. "Based on what?" The wind whipped her hair across her mouth as if trying to hush her.

Phillip smiled and reached out to push back her hair. "I want people to treat me well, so I treat them well."

"That's Jesus' command to 'Love thy neighbour as thyself.' " Rainy replied. "Nothing self-made in that."

Phillip laughed. "No, I don't suppose it's a new concept." He pushed off the wall and motioned to the café across the street. "Jennetta tells me the Mexican food at that café is the best in town. Why don't we have lunch there? We can sit and eat and wax theological."

Rainy allowed him to take hold of her arm but couldn't help replying, "I don't want to wax theological, Phillip. I just wondered how you—"

"Aren't you Phillip Vance?" a young woman who looked to be no more than twenty questioned. She'd come to stand directly in front of them and refused to move.

Phillip flashed her a smile and lowered his voice to match his cowboy characters. "That I am."

The girl squealed and motioned to several friends who stood in absolute awe on the opposite street corner. "It's him! It's him!"

Rainy was quickly nudged out of the way as the gaggle of giggling, screaming girls swooped in like vultures to the prey. Leaning back against the porch support, Rainy thought long and hard about the scene. *This is what it would be like to spend the rest of my life with Phillip Vance. No matter where he went, people would recognize him. Sometimes that would be good and sometimes it would be bad. But it would always be inescapable.*

She listened to Phillip talk in his soft-spoken manner. He seemed to take a genuine interest in each girl, listening as they poured out their delight in having seen him. He answered their questions and allowed their adoration—basking in the glory of it, as Sonny had suggested.

Bored with the situation, Rainy crossed the narrow street and took a seat on one of the Plaza benches. No one even seemed to notice she'd gone.

"Quite the display, isn't it?"

She looked up with dread. "Hello, Chester."

Ignoring her obvious displeasure with him, Chester took the seat beside her. He pretended to dust the pant legs of his gray suit before adding, "It's like this everywhere he goes. If there are people about, especially women, Phillip Vance doesn't wait long for a crowd."

"You speak like such an authority," Rainy said, trying hard to be civil.

"Oh, I suppose I am somewhat of one. You see, my wife has been good friends with Jennetta Blythe for some time. That's why we were out in California to begin with. Bethel's parents lived only two doors down from the Blythes. Jennetta suffered a stormy marriage to a man who never understood her. Do you want to know something really awful?"

"No!" Rainy interjected. "I don't. I have no interest in such matters."

"Ah, I suppose not," Chester said, sounding quite disappointed. "Well, where was I? Ah, yes. When Jennetta began to hear of the wonders of Santa Fe, well, she didn't wait long to make her way here. The art community has been quite rewarding for her. She found people who could understand her heart."

"I'm glad someone can understand her," Rainy murmured.

"Phillip is really quite the Casanova. He has no trouble securing a woman to keep him company. After all, look at yourself. You've cancelled a two-week furlough just to be at his side."

"I did not cancel just to be at his side," Rainy protested. "He needed a courier." She knew the excuse was lame, but she refused to have Chester suggesting she was no different from all the other silly women who flocked to Phillip Vance.

Chester laughed. "And you were the only one in the entire fleet who was available? Really, Rainy, you needn't pretend with me. Not after our past together."

"We have no past together, unless of course you count the fact that you let me be blamed for something I didn't do."

"Oh, we aren't going to talk on that tiresome subject again, are we?" He leaned closer and Rainy cringed, all the while watching the women flirt with Phillip.

Chester's breath was stale as he whispered, "Rainy, there are so many things I could do for you now. I can get you what you want. The past doesn't need to control your future. I have friends in high places, and believe me, they can move heaven and earth for me if I give them the word. You have only to agree. After all, you don't want to spend your entire life leading tourists around the desert. Why, there may not even be an Indian Detours after this year."

Rainy scooted to the far end of the bench and looked at him hard. "Why do you say that?"

Chester had the good sense to stay where he was. "I'm often privileged to overhear information. You know the financial markets have failed and that America and Europe are both suffering tremendous setbacks economically. Luxury items, such as tours and vacations, can't hope to survive. If things go as poorly as some of my friends believe they will, it would be wise to have a nest egg to bank on. I myself believe in setting up a wide reserve—diversification is the key."

"But you've not heard anything in particular to suggest the company plans to stop offering the Detours, have you?" Rainy questioned, hating to have to use Chester for information.

"Well, there is of course the obvious situation of the Harvey Company selling the Detours to Clarkson. They take their cues from the Santa Fe, and the railroad has obviously tightened its belt and wants the Harvey Company to do likewise. Clarkson may have run the transportation company, but I doubt he has the Santa Fe Railroad in his pocket as tightly as the Harvey Company does. I wouldn't be at all surprised to see him eliminate all but the most lucrative and most commonly requested tours from the rosters. As they do that, they'll obviously need fewer and fewer people."

"But people like Phillip Vance and other movie stars continue to come," Rainy protested. "Why, just last week we had three different tours with movie stars. They all raved about the tours and their plans to return and enjoy the hotels. Surely things can't be all that bad if they're willing to do that."

"They will probably be happy to share time at the resort hotels like La Posada and El Tovar, even La Fonda, but they won't want to be dragging around out in the desert for pleasure rides. And let's be realistic here—if the economy fails as my friends believe it will, even movie stars are going to be cutting way back on their spending. After all, if the general public can't afford to go to the movies, the producers of those movies certainly aren't going to have money to pay their stars. No, mark my words, the Detours won't be long for this world."

Rainy immediately thought of Sonny. It wasn't so fearful for her to be out of work. She could always live with their mother and father and no one would think less of her. An old maid living at home was perhaps pitied but never condemned. But Sonny's situation was different. Sonny was a man, and for a man to be out of work and living with his parents, well, that wouldn't be good for him. People already talked of how Sonny was approaching thirty years of age and had no steady girl. Some of the couriers had even teased him about living at home, being a "momma's boy." It was unfair and insensitive, but Sonny bore it well.

"I can see I've given you much to consider," Chester said, following Rainy to the far end of the bench. "But you needn't worry about the future. I have more power now than I did three years ago. I can keep you safe and well cared for. You don't need Phillip Vance—not that he'd give any real consideration to you when he can have his pick from important, wealthy daughters of society. Phillip is toying with you— enjoying the good time you can give him." Chester paused and got to his feet. "He does this everywhere he goes. He finds one vulnerable, needy woman and plays on her sympathy and desire."

Rainy didn't want to believe his words but was unwittingly drawn back to his gaze. Chester's sandy brown hair peeked out from beneath his straw hat, almost as if to remind him he was long overdue at the barber's shop. She would have laughed had the moment not been so serious. Chester studied her for a moment then narrowed his eyes.

"How long do you suppose you'll keep your job if the company were to find out about the university scandal?"

Rainy jumped up. "You have no call to threaten me, Chester. I did as I was asked. I left quietly. Now uphold your end of the bargain and leave me alone."

"I don't recall leaving you alone to be part of the agreement," Chester said, smiling maliciously. "But if you don't want to be a part of the National Geographic Society, suit yourself."

Just then Phillip managed to disentangle himself from the women and came bounding across the road. "I'm so sorry, Rainy. Sometimes it just can't be helped. Fans need to be pampered a bit from time to time."

"I was just explaining that to her," Chester replied. "I told her you deal with this all the time. I was just about to tell her of that poor lovesick Harvey Girl back at El Tovar. What was her name, anyway? Colleen? Collette? Co—"

"It was Caroline and is clearly not worthy of discussion," Phillip declared, not appearing too happy with Chester's comments.

"No matter. The real reason I'm here is that your sister has asked me to fetch you. Seems she has designs for heading north to Taos and needs you to join in on the plan," Chester told Phillip and added, "She told me she wouldn't accept any excuses for you not returning with me to her home."

Rainy felt only moderately disappointed to have Phillip taken from her. There was a part of her that needed time to process the events of the day. But there was also a part of her that very much wanted to sit down to a quiet lunch with Phillip Vance. She had so many questions to ask him—questions about God and faith. Maybe if she explained it better he would understand how important it was to have faith in God.

Phillip laughed. "I suppose I have no choice. But, Rainy, why don't you come along, too? Jennetta seldom allows anyone to come to her home, but if she's calling us there now, then the spirits must be favorable. She won't mind an additional person."

Rainy couldn't help but wonder what he meant by his comment about the spirits, but she had no desire to sit down to conversation with Jennetta Blythe. "I haven't had lunch yet. . . ." she began as a means to excuse herself.

"I'm sure Jennetta will have some monstrous-sized fruit platter, along with cheese and breads," Phillip countered.

Chester laughed. "Yes, indeed she does. I was there when the food arrived."

Phillip nodded as if that made all the difference in the world. "She does that on the few occasions when she has people in. We can feast there."

Rainy wasn't about to join their happy little enclave. "No, I really shouldn't. If your plans involve one of the Detour trips, just let me know."

Phillip lifted her hand to his lips. "But of course it will involve you. After you gave up your vacation for me, I must endeavor to make it worth your efforts." Rainy smiled, losing herself momentarily to his movie-star charm. He kissed her hand, then released his hold.

Feeling completely overwhelmed with her emotions, Rainy turned rather abruptly and hurried down the sidewalk. She couldn't even think of something witty or casual to say in reply. *What a mess I am. Losing control just like those silly girls I watched. They made cow eyes and fawned all over Phillip and I'm really no better.*

"There you are!" Sonny declared as he came walking out of La Fonda. "Where have you been? I looked for you at the boardinghouse, then went through La Fonda and still couldn't find you."

"I've been . . . well . . . I was showing Phillip a bit of Santa Fe," Rainy said defensively. She didn't care at all for the look of concern on her brother's face. How dare he treat her like some wayward child?

"I heard something rather disturbing and I need to know if it's true," Sonny said, the seriousness of his tone leaving little doubt that this was of utmost importance to him.

"So ask me," Rainy said, feeling annoyed.

"Is it true you've cancelled your entire vacation to take on the job of baby-sitting Phillip Vance?"

Rainy crossed her arms and lifted her chin defiantly. "And what if it is? I've been requested to courier the group. I'm being offered the two weeks at a later time and a handsome bonus as well."

"But we're generally a team," Sonny threw out. "Why didn't you talk this over with me?"

Rainy realized how inconsiderate she'd been. "I'm sorry, Gabe," she said, reverting to his given name. "I didn't think. I just figured you'd want us to take the job."

Sonny shook his head. "No, I don't want to take the job. I didn't want to take the last two jobs, but I let Sam sweet-talk me into it. I need the time away more than I need the extra money. I have plans and things to prepare for."

Rainy had no idea what could possibly be so pressing. "Look, it's just for a couple of weeks. They couldn't promise me that they could reschedule the time off immediately following this tour arrangement, but we'd get the time off before June for sure."

"I need the time now, Rainy," Sonny replied. "And I'm taking it. I already figured you'd respond exactly this way. I've asked Duncan to be your driver for what I thought was only going to be a day or two, but I'm sure he'll drive you the entire two-week period if necessary."

"You arranged it without asking me first?" Rainy questioned.

"Just like you accepted the Blythe/Vance tour without asking me."

Rainy calmed at this and saw the logic of his reasoning. She couldn't argue with the truth. "Well, I suppose Duncan is safe enough."

"I trust him to take care of you and keep you out of trouble," Sonny said, stepping forward. He took hold of Rainy and sighed. "This time off is important to me. My friends Jess and Richard are in town and . . ."

"Sonny! I hate to interrupt you, but Sam told me to talk to you before I left for the day," Duncan Hartford stated as he emerged from La Fonda. "I've been looking all over for you."

"Seems everyone is looking for someone," Rainy muttered. She noted that Duncan carried the driver uniform. Ten-gallon hat, khaki jodhpurs, plaid shirt, and silk neckerchief were neatly stacked in the bundle Duncan held. "So you're going to be my driver," Rainy added before her brother could respond.

"He told you, huh? Hope you don't mind," he said, smiling rather nervously.

Rainy laughed. "Of course I don't mind. I was surprised, but Sonny deserves to take the time off."

Duncan watched her, almost as if studying her for some further response. Rainy grew a bit uncomfortable under the scrutiny. She knew if she looked deep into his eyes, she'd probably lose herself just as she had with Phillip Vance.

Maybe I'm just in love with the idea of being in love, she reasoned and moved her gaze to Sonny, where she knew she'd be safe. But the worried expression on Sonny's face did little to settle her nerves. Why was he so upset with her? And what was it that was making him suddenly act the part of the worried brother?

CHAPTER TEN

D uncan felt rather apprehensive as he waited for the tour group to gather. He knew the route to Taos but was less familiar with the side roads of the touring sights and Indian dwellings. He studied the map Sonny had given him and read the little notes that Sonny had penciled in.

> *Watch for the turn at this point.*
> *Sand is bad on the left-hand side.*
> *Got stuck twice in this area.*

All the notes were given as little warnings to keep Duncan from putting the dudes in danger, but it all seemed a bit overwhelming. After all, he wasn't here to be a driver—he was a spy. Duncan's mind went to Rainy as he glanced over the top of the map. She stood only about ten feet away, explaining something to one of Jennetta's friends. The woman seemed quite disturbed, and Rainy was doing her best to calm the situation.

She's really a remarkable woman, he thought. *She's so good with people and tolerates their moods with ease. How could she possibly be a suspect in a crime?* It just didn't fit the woman he thought he knew.

Still, the information given him just that morning left little doubt that there was still a big chance that Rainy and her brother were responsible for at least some of the thefts. The Hopis were missing several important pieces, and the artifacts hadn't gone missing until after Rainy's tour group pulled out only days ago.

Duncan had been on that trip, but he'd had no way to watch everyone at the same time. He couldn't help but wonder how the thieves could have spirited the pieces away. They would have had to load them onto the touring car, yet Duncan had checked and rechecked the luggage and storage areas. There had been no sign of anything out of place.

The law officials had been convinced he was mistaken. They'd chided him for not being observant enough or for overlooking something. But Duncan knew how closely he'd watched Rainy and Sonny. Neither one seemed at all interested in sneaking around or keeping him from knowing their business. In fact, they seemed only too happy to have Duncan tag along and often included him.

"No, we can't do it that way," Rainy protested. Duncan again raised his eyes to peer over the map. "There are rules we have to abide by, ma'am. That's just one of the many."

"Well, I find it very inconvenient," the woman huffed, then stormed off to where Jennetta stood arguing with one of her other friends.

Duncan smiled as Rainy looked his way. She took the smile as an invitation and joined him.

"The tourists are misbehaving, I take it?"

Rainy gazed heavenward. "You have no idea how silly they're being. First, one wants to be allowed to sit up front. Then another wants to bring her parrot."

"Her what?" Duncan began folding the map, but his gaze was fixed on Rainy's rosy cheeks.

"Her parrot. Seems the woman's best friend in the world is a parrot and she never travels without him. I told her I couldn't have a parrot traveling with us, that sometimes special provisions were made for dogs—small dogs—but that a parrot was not going to be allowed." She motioned over her shoulder. "And that one wanted us to take a different route to Taos so that she could stop by her housekeeper's mother's house, where she's been promised a large bundle of herbs."

Duncan grinned. "But you've managed to keep them all in line. I'm proud of you. It couldn't have been easy."

Rainy took off her hat and fanned herself with it. "I'm really getting tired of it all. I almost wish I hadn't promised Phillip that I'd be their courier."

"Speaking of Mr. Vance, where is he?"

Rainy shrugged. "I have no idea. Jennetta said something about an herbal cleansing. I'm not at all sure what exactly that means, but I'm hoping it won't delay us past eight."

Duncan looked at his watch. "That gives him two minutes." He glanced around the gathered group. "Say, weren't there supposed to be six guests joining us?"

Rainy grinned and leaned forward. "Mrs. Dupree has her moon in the seventh house or maybe it was the fifth house and one of the planets is not aligning as it should with her . . . hmmm . . . I forget."

Duncan laughed out loud, causing the entire group to look at him momentarily. He ignored them and looked back to Rainy. "And all of this means . . ."

"She isn't coming," Rainy replied rather conspiratorially. "She's not going anywhere until her moon straightens out."

"I'm sure that's for the best." Duncan couldn't help but be amused by the entire situation. "Ah, here comes the elusive Mr. Vance. Perhaps his moons were out of order as well."

Rainy giggled. "Let's hope not, for the sake of the tour."

Duncan watched as Phillip greeted his sister and her friends, then made his way to Rainy. "I apologize if I've held the party up. My sister insisted I partake of an herbal steam bath, and I must say it did much to refresh me."

As Rainy began complimenting the color and texture of Phillip's blue cotton blazer, Duncan glanced down at his uniform and knew how ridiculous he looked. He couldn't believe the Harvey Company had ever started such a uniform. There were rumors that Clarkson planned to tone down the outfit, but it wouldn't matter to Duncan. Right now he had to wear the outlandish gear in order to fit his role as driver.

"Phillip, can you help me get everyone into the courier car?" Rainy asked sweetly. "We really need to be on our way. This isn't our usual trip to Taos, and if we're going to make it to Chimayo and then the Puye ruins by lunchtime, we're going to have to be going."

"But of course." He raised her hand to his lips and kissed her fingers.

Duncan wanted to punch him and tell him to keep his hands to himself, but he knew Rainy was enjoying the attention by the look of pleasure on her face. She followed Phillip as he went to announce to the other ladies that it was time to go, while Duncan stood stock-still and watched the entire situation.

This trip was important. If artifacts disappeared on this trip, then it would be determined that Rainy had something to do with the thefts. Still, Duncan thought, if anything of value goes missing, there's also the fact that Jennetta and Phillip are on the tour. They were on the last tour as well. Of course, he didn't suppose they'd been on the previous tours when pieces had been stolen. But it was food for thought.

Desert flowers were blooming in their bold, vibrant shades. Flowers elsewhere might well delight the landscape with pastels, but here the shades were brilliant, almost as if they were competing for attention. Overhead, the sky was a deep blue without so much as a hint of a cloud. The day couldn't have been more perfect.

As they set out, Duncan tried to keep his gaze fixed to the road, but his mind kept wandering as they made their way north to Chimayo. From time to time he couldn't help glancing at Rainy, who told the travelers tidbits and tales from her Harvey Company monologue.

The guests were less than interested. Most talked as though the area had been their home for several years, leaving Duncan to wonder why they'd bothered to pay good money for the trip via the Clarkson Detours when cheaper modes of transportation could have been found. In fact, it made him wonder a lot, but he'd known the wealthy to do even more ridiculous things than take expensive tours. When he'd lived in Las Vegas, he'd heard of a wealthy woman who had huge quantities of ice brought in by train on a daily basis during the hot summer months. It was said she had a penchant for ice baths and filled her tub several times a day with ice and water for relief from the heat.

His mother also mentioned a woman who lived in Albuquerque who paid for the upkeep of seven automobiles so that she wouldn't have to ride in any one car but once a week. He supposed the wealthy were given over to all kinds of quirks and idiosyncrasies. Maybe taking this tour was just their way of being eccentric and lavish.

They arrived at Chimayo a little before ten. The road had been perfect and Sonny's instructions proved to be accurate. Duncan allowed Rainy to direct him to where he might park the touring car.

"Just head up this road," she told him, "then turn left at the first intersection, then turn immediately to your right."

The dirt street was lined with small whitewashed homes. Long strings of chilies hung from poles on the porches, drying in the sunshine until they were needed for cooking. Here and there a dark-skinned woman sat before a loom, a riot of color woven upon its frame. The colors reminded Duncan of the desert flowers.

Warm, spicy aromas drifted through the air, causing Duncan to wish he'd eaten a more substantial breakfast. He stopped the car and secured the brake before looking to Rainy for further instruction.

"As you know, Chimayo is famous for weaving. We'll watch several weavers as they work on foot looms, and you'll have an opportunity to purchase blankets or other woven goods," Rainy announced.

She opened the car door and nodded to Duncan. "Go ahead and open their side door," she told him.

Duncan had forgotten that Sonny generally did this task. It was such a well-established routine with Sonny and Rainy that he hadn't given it much thought.

Duncan opened the door and helped the first two ladies from the car. Both were very thin and seemed intent on exploring. He stepped back to allow Phillip Vance to emerge. The man smiled at him and nodded as if they shared some special secret; then Phillip made his way to Rainy and took hold of her arm.

Duncan refused to let the situation defeat his true purpose, reminding himself that he needed to keep an eye open for anything out of the ordinary. The only problem was, he wasn't really sure what was ordinary and what wasn't.

Rainy led the group along a short cactus-lined path. Not knowing what else to do, Duncan followed. He felt rather out of place and remained silent. Perhaps he'd go wait back at the car after he found out whether or not Rainy would need him for anything else. He didn't want anyone trying to sneak something back to the car in his absence.

Rainy introduced the group of tourists to a short, plump Mexican woman named Maria, then stepped back as Maria began discussing the woolen yarn they used and the plants they procured for dying the various colors. Duncan noticed Phillip's interest in the information and took the opportunity to separate his hold on Rainy.

"If you'll excuse us for a moment," he said to Phillip, "I need to speak with Miss Gordon."

Phillip willingly stepped aside while Rainy allowed Duncan to lead her away from the group. "What's wrong?" she questioned.

"I don't know what I'm supposed to be doing," he said rather sheepishly.

Rainy laughed. "I'm sorry, Duncan. I didn't think. This is a rather special tour. Maria will have us busy for about thirty minutes. She's going to show them all about the weaving they do and then take them to another couple of weavers. After that the tour group will be ready to leave for Puye."

"Oh, I see." He glanced up the street toward a small adobe chapel. "Are we free to explore, then, or do you need to remain with the group?" Since Rainy and Sonny were the ones under suspicion, maybe he would just remain at Rainy's side and see what happened.

Rainy smiled. "I see you've spotted Santuario. Come on. Let's walk over. They usually have someone to give a tour and tell about the church."

Duncan smiled. "I'd like that."

"The ground where the church is built is said to be endowed with healing powers. People come and dig up bits of it for a kind of tea they make. It's amazing. They sometimes even take dirt to use as a charm to keep them safe from harm."

"I suppose we've both seen a great deal of superstition among the Indians and Mexicans in the area. I have to say that sometimes the cures seem worse than the curse they fear."

"As in drinking dirt tea?" Rainy asked.

Duncan laughed. "Exactly."

Santuario offered them shelter from the brilliance of the sun. Inside the air was cooler and the silence heavy.

"Welcome," an old man said in greeting. Duncan noticed his weathered brown face and toothless smile.

"We've come to see the church," Rainy explained.

"*Sí,* it is good that you do. This church was built by my ancestor Bernardo Abeyta. He was a poor farmer who had a vision to dig in the earth for his reward. As he dug here, he found a wooden cross and pieces of cloth that belonged to two martyred priests."

Duncan noted the wall niches where unusual native wood carvings made decorative offerings from artists now long gone. Below these and lining the walls on either side of the chapel were crutches and braces, cast off as proof of the healing powers of the church.

The man showed them around, talked of the miracles he'd seen, and then suggested a small offering might be in order to help with the maintenance of the shrine. Rainy produced some change and Duncan followed suit. The old man rewarded them with a gummy smile and thanked them profusely for their generosity.

"We need to get back to the car," Rainy said, noting the time. "They should be returning in about five minutes."

Duncan couldn't believe how quickly the time had passed. "I really enjoyed that," he told Rainy as they made their way back.

"This part of the country is so full of history and interesting stories. I can't imagine ever leaving it—at least not for a long period of time."

Duncan wanted to comment about Phillip Vance's interests and how she would have to leave the Southwest if she followed after him. But he didn't. Rainy was a smart woman; no doubt she had considered all of those details.

The passengers returned with their purchases, and Duncan had to admit to being surprised by the stacks of blankets purchased by Jennetta Blythe. He raised a brow in question, but she refused to make so much as a single comment. Instead, she thrust the pile into his arms and walked away. Duncan didn't like the feeling of being dismissed, but he said nothing and worked to pack the blankets in the storage area of the touring car.

Once they were all back in the car, Jennetta made an announcement. "We've talked among ourselves and have decided that rather than stopping in Puye, we'd like to go straight to Taos."

Duncan looked to Rainy, wondering what her response to this would be. Rainy didn't seem in the leastwise disturbed by this announcement.

"Since this is a custom tour and you are all in agreement, we'll proceed for Taos. Of course, we would have taken lunch at Puye."

"It's of no concern. We'll eat a late lunch in Taos," Jennetta replied.

Rainy turned. "And you are all in agreement about this?"

Duncan heard murmurs of affirmation. Rainy turned to him. "Let's go."

Heavy clouds were moving in by the time Duncan pulled up to the Don Fernando Hotel in Taos. The adobe structure seemed something of familiar territory to the group as they commented about one thing or another. He pulled to the front of the hotel and looked to Rainy once again for instruction.

"In a moment you may make your way inside. I'll go ahead and see to your reservations," Rainy instructed. She opened her door and began to step out. "Oh, and one more thing." She paused and looked back over her shoulder. "I'll speak to the manager and arrange lunch. Shall we say in half an hour?"

Again the murmurs of affirmation were thrown out between animated female chatter. Phillip Vance had been surprisingly silent, but Duncan had no doubt that would change.

Duncan made his way around the car as Rainy entered the hotel. He opened the door and helped the ladies once again from the Cadillac, remembering this time to smile and make pleasant small talk as he'd seen Sonny do.

Phillip was the last to depart from the car. He stepped from the vehicle and yawned. "Just in time for a siesta," he said, smiling at Duncan.

Duncan had to admit a nap sounded like a wonderful idea, but he said nothing. He wondered instead what Rainy planned to do with her free time. Duncan's first choice would be to make his way to his parents' house and enjoy spending as much time as possible with them. But what of Rainy? If she were involved in some sort of thieving, he would be giving her all kinds of extra time to plot and consort. He was torn about what to do.

He began unloading the luggage and his heart grew heavy. *What if she is the guilty party? Just the idea of worrying about what she'll do with her free time must suggest that deep down inside I question her innocence.*

He hated the thought. He didn't want to believe Rainy capable of any wrongdoing. She always seemed so positive—so honest. Still, the words of the law officials rang loud and clear. *"Rainy and Sonny Gordon are the only ones who have been consistently available when objects of value have disappeared from various sites. We'd like to catch them in the act, however, and see if others are involved."*

Taos was full of priceless pieces: artwork, Indian crafts, church icons. Duncan knew the possibilities were limitless.

"Well, we have lunch arranged," Rainy said as she came around the car to join Duncan. "And here's a list of the room numbers and where each person is supposed to stay. They're a bit shorthanded right now, so I'll help you get the luggage up to the rooms."

"No, that's all right. I'll carry it myself. You've worked hard enough today."

She opened her mouth to reply, but it was then that Phillip Vance made an unwelcome entry. "Rainy, we're getting together tonight for a marvelous party. One of Jennetta's friends is throwing it. He lives just a short distance from here. I'd like for you to join us."

Rainy looked to Duncan and he wanted very badly to advise her against it. Instead, he diverted his attention to the luggage and tried not to play eavesdropper.

"I'm sorry, Phillip. I really must decline. I'm tired, and tomorrow I'm to lead you and some of the others on a tour of Taos. I need my rest."

"But I promise to bring you back in plenty of time for a good night's sleep."

Duncan placed two bags directly in front of Phillip. Any closer and they'd be on the movie star's toes. Phillip stepped back a pace but said nothing.

"I can't go with you, Phillip," Rainy said. "Thank you for the invitation, but perhaps another time."

Phillip's expression was one of pure disappointment. Duncan wondered if he were merely acting or if his feelings for Rainy were such that he was truly devastated by her answer. Duncan had a hard time believing the man was capable of true feelings and decided it was all a show. He waited, however, until Phillip went inside the hotel before commenting to Rainy.

"The man is really good at what he does."

Rainy looked up, her expression betraying her confusion. "What do you mean?"

"I think he performs the part of wounded suitor," Duncan replied with a shrug. "I just think he's acting when it comes to the way he treats you."

"I take it Sonny asked you to look out for me," Rainy said, sounding slightly offended. "Well, you can tell him for me that I'm a grown woman and know very well how to take care of myself."

Duncan realized they were heading into dangerous waters and held up his hands in truce. "I don't want to fight with you. In fact, I was kind of hoping you'd agree to meet me later tonight. I'm going to go visit my parents for a time when I finish up here, but I'd like to have some time to talk with you. There are some things I need to tell you."

Rainy arched her brow. "Such as?"

"Not now. There are far too many details. Why don't we just say eight o'clock at the Plaza?"

"All right, if it's that important." Her expression remained doubtful.

"It is," Duncan promised. He had been given permission to leak a certain amount of information to Rainy. The plan was to feed her the information and see what her response might be. He hated the deception but knew of no other way to test the situation.

"Eight o'clock at the Plaza," Rainy repeated. "I'll be waiting for you."

Duncan nodded. "Thanks. I really appreciate it. And thanks, too, for the lovely day. I enjoyed our time at the church. It was a right bonny kirk," he said, exaggerating his Scottish burr.

Rainy turned to go and laughed. "Aye, 'twas indeed."

He watched her walk away. "And a right bonny lass to keep me company," he murmured. *She can't be guilty,* he told himself. *She just can't be guilty.*

Rainy walked along the Plaza corridors, enjoying the crisp cool air. There was a bit of a bite to the wind, but she hardly minded it. The smell of pine filtered down from the trees, along with the undeniable aroma of woodsmoke. It would be a perfect night to curl up in front of a fire and read a book. Even better to share that spot with someone she loved. Her thoughts went immediately to Duncan. Did she love him? Or did she just love the idea of being in love? It was a question that came back to her over and over.

Surely this longing in my heart isn't just my own doing, she reasoned. *God must have put the desire there—otherwise I would go on being content to be single, just as I have been up until now.* But love? What did she know of love?

She knew she loved her mother and father and Sonny too. She knew she'd give her life for them, just as the Bible said: " 'Greater love hath no man than this, that a man lay down his life for his friends.' " The fifteenth chapter of John had always been one of Rainy's favorites, but that thirteenth verse in particular touched her deeply. She loved her family and they were indeed her friends. Duncan Hartford made her feel weak in the knees and giddy, but so did Phillip Vance. But Phillip didn't love God and Duncan did. That fact, in and of itself, seemed to make the choice clear.

But Duncan hasn't shown any real interest in having us be anything more than friends. Surely he would have mentioned something—something to state his position if he felt that we should be more than co-workers and acquaintances.

Scanning the small adobe-lined square for any sign of Duncan, Rainy couldn't help but wonder why he'd asked to meet her here. Her mind, already cluttered with the confusion of her own thoughts regarding husbands and romance, refused to sort through any additional details. Even at supper she'd been a poor companion to those around her.

She'd wondered about Phillip and the party he'd invited her to. She'd observed the group departing for the gala and marveled at the finery and expense of their clothing. Phillip looked dazzling in his black tuxedo. He'd slicked back his blond hair, leaving only the slightest hint of a side part. His blue eyes were sparkling in the candlelight as he glanced across the room and caught sight of her. He had started to walk toward her table when Jennetta and a friend of hers named Sylvia latched on to him and practically dragged him out the front door of the Don Fernando Hotel.

Rainy thought he might have asked her again to accompany him to the party, and at that point, she probably would have said yes, although she could never have come up with an outfit to equal those of the women in Phillip's gathering. Jennetta wore a blood red gown with a deep plunging neckline. One of the other women, dressed in a full-length black velvet sheath, commented on the gown being designed by Chanel, but Rainy had little knowledge to determine whether the woman was right or not.

I've filled my mind with archaeological terms and phrases, spending hours poring over artifacts and pieces of clay while these women have made for themselves worlds of glittering jewels and fashionable attire. Rainy paused to look into the window of an art gallery. The painting displayed in the front window was of several nearly nude women lounging in a clothing-strewn dressing room. The title given was "Before the Show."

"Not exactly something you'd buy to hang in the living room," Duncan commented over her shoulder.

Rainy turned on her heel so quickly that she practically fell headlong into Duncan's arms. He reached out to take hold of her shoulders and smiled. "Glad you could meet me."

"I thought maybe you'd decided against coming," Rainy replied. "After all, it's almost quarter past the hour."

"I know and I do apologize. My mother was well into a second story of my great-aunt Tillie's birthday party when I realized how late the hour had gotten." He dropped his voice. "Do you forgive me?"

Rainy shivered, but not from the cold. She looked into his eyes and lost all rational thought. For years she'd admired Duncan from afar. It should have been so easy just to tell him that. But instead she couldn't even force her lips to form words.

"Rainy? Are you all right?"

Duncan's expression changed to one of great concern. Rainy forced herself to stop acting so childish. "I'm fine. Why did you want to see me?"

Duncan looked away and let go of his hold on her. "I've something to share with you. Something that I can't talk about in front of the guests."

"Sounds ominous. Why don't we take a seat and you can explain."

Duncan nodded. "I'm sure that would be best."

Rainy sat on one of the benches and waited while Duncan seemed to consider whether to sit close to or far away from her. He finally sat down fairly close and glanced around. With his hands affixed to his knees, Rainy longed to reach out and cover his fingers with her own. She held back, fighting her feelings. How silly she was, pining first over Duncan and then over Phillip.

Of course, she chided, *my feelings for Phillip could never go any further without him first coming to God.* The thought seemed to make clear her choice between the two men and she looked up at Duncan with a new perspective.

Maybe he'd asked her here to share his heart with her. Maybe he wanted to suggest their relationship deepen. She looked away and licked her lips. *What if he kisses me? Lord, is he the one?*

"I wanted to talk to you about something that's happened," Duncan began. "I was at the museum when I overheard talk about the theft of Indian pieces from the Hopi. In particular, some ceremonial flutes are missing."

Rainy's illusions were shattered. The memories of that long ago day when she'd stood accused of stealing from the university left a tremor in her voice. "Someone . . . stole flutes . . . from the Hopi?"

Duncan nodded. "It happened on our trip. There's some concern that one of the guests took the pieces."

Rainy cleared her throat nervously. "But you and Sonny packed and unpacked the Harvey . . . I mean courier car. You would have noticed if something were amiss."

"That's what I said."

"You mean they confronted you?" She felt a wave of nausea overcome her. It was as if the past had reared up to destroy her hope for the future. She felt light-headed and pressed her fingers to her temple.

Duncan suddenly looked very uncomfortable. Rainy couldn't help but wonder what had transpired to make him act in such a manner. "Duncan?"

He shook his head. "The thing is, I think we would do well to keep our eyes open and see if we can spot anyone in our group who might be trying the same thing here in Taos."

Rainy felt her stomach continue to churn, and she lowered her hand to comfort her midsection. "Jennetta and Phillip are the only ones with us this time who were also present on the last trip." She thought immediately of the Driscolls. Chester! He had been her bane once before. She tightened her hands into fists, wanting nothing more than to punch the arrogant little man right in the nose.

Duncan gently covered her hand with his own. "You planning to hit me?"

Rainy shook her head. "No, but I'd like to hit someone else."

"Because of the thefts?"

"That and so much more. There is one person in particular. . . ." She paused, suddenly realizing she was going too far. "I'm sorry, Duncan. I'm afraid I'm tired and not feeling very hospitable."

"Is that why you chose not to go with Phillip Vance and his friends?"

She looked at his face momentarily, then to the place where his hand still covered hers. A moment ago she was longing for such contact, and now all she wanted to do was get away. Before she could comment, however, Duncan continued.

"He's showing you a great deal of attention. Sonny is worried about it."

"Sonny should mind his own business."

"He just wants to see that you're safe—protected."

Rainy nodded. "I'm perfectly safe and protected. I have God as my shield and defense."

"Still, God doesn't want us to put ourselves in foolish situations," Duncan countered.

Rainy felt him gently stroke the side of her hand with his thumb. His touch was doing things to her mind—clouding her ability to reason. Without warning she pulled away. "I've asked God to send me a husband. If he's sent me Phillip Vance, what business is it of Sonny's . . . or yours?"

She started to walk away, but Duncan quickly joined her. "So you plan to marry Vance?"

She stopped and looked at Duncan. His eyes seemed to darken, even as his Scottish burr became more pronounced. The look he gave

her left Rainy trembling from head to toe. It seemed so consuming—
almost as if he could see inside to her soul.

"I . . . well . . . I have no plans . . . I mean, he hasn't asked me."

"But you'd like for him to?"

Rainy tried to steady her nerves and looked away. She wanted to
scream, "No, I'd much rather have you ask me." But the very thought
of that concerned her more than anything else they'd discussed. Did
she care more for Duncan than she realized? Had she grown so much
closer to him in the last few weeks that her heart was ready to accept
him as something more than a friend? Why couldn't it be a simple matter? She'd heard her friends tell tales of love at first sight—of being
certain of the man they were to marry. *Why can't I feel that way? Why can't
I know for certain that Duncan Hartford is to be my husband?* She looked up
rather startled. Why had she put Duncan's name into that question
rather than Phillip's?

Duncan still studied her, almost as if he could will the truth from
her with his stare. Rainy straightened her shoulders and drew a deep
breath. "I want to do whatever it is God wants me to do. I've prayed and
asked Him to send me a husband." She felt her cheeks grow hot. "I
don't even know why I'm telling you this."

"I think you do," Duncan said, his voice low and steady.

Rainy stepped back a pace. Being too close to Duncan Hartford just
might well be her demise. "I don't want to discuss this any further.
Some things should just be left unsaid."

"I disagree. I think there's a great deal between us that needs to be
said," Duncan replied, moving toward her.

Rainy froze. She'd long considered the possibilities that might exist
between her and Duncan. Was he the one God had sent? Would he tell
her now of his love for her—of his desire to be a part of her life?

"I know that you realize Sonny wants me to keep an eye on you,"
Duncan began. "He worries, and probably because he knows you're so
determined to find a husband, he knows that you're vulnerable to those
who might use you to their own advantage."

Rainy swallowed hard. Her mouth had taken on a cottony dryness.

"I'm trying my best to help Sonny in this situation, and I think you
really want my help. I think that's why you blurted out that revelation
regarding a husband. If you're wise, you'll listen to the counsel of those
who care."

"You?" The word came out more like a squeak than a real word.

"Of course, me. Getting to know you and Sonny, I can't help but care. I wouldn't want to see someone like Vance take advantage of you. Men like him are used to having what they want, and it doesn't really matter if what they want is a new suit or another human being. They'll take what they desire and never give the matter another thought."

Through the haze of her own confusion, Rainy was slowly but surely coming to realize that Duncan wasn't about to declare his feelings of love—but was instead proclaiming a brotherly warning of caution. The idea began to irritate Rainy. How dare he step into Sonny's role just because he'd taken on the job of driving!

"God has a plan for you," Duncan continued. "But you needn't rush it or try to manipulate it for your own desires. There shouldn't be such a sense of urgency in something that God ordains. You don't have to chase after it—He'll bring it right to you if you let Him. Maybe . . ." He paused and looked at her with such longing that Rainy almost felt startled. She edged back and he continued. "Maybe God just wants you to let go of your urgency for a mate and trust Him to be what you need."

Rainy's anger began to build. "What I don't need is for you or Sonny to lecture or preach at me. I know that God is in control, and further, I know that He has a plan for my life. I believe that plan includes a husband and children and when the time is right, God will show me the mate He has chosen. If that man is Phillip Vance, so be it. If not, then that is perfectly acceptable as well."

She walked away, surprised that Duncan didn't follow after her. Tormenting thoughts raced around inside her brain, giving her a headache and deep desire to run away from Taos and leave the whole tour group behind.

Father, I'm trying so hard to be obedient—to hear your voice rather than my own. I wouldn't choose a husband without being completely certain that he was the man you'd sent me. I don't want to do anything to displease you. I kind of figured you sent Phillip into the picture when Duncan showed no interest. Of course, I suppose I haven't really given Duncan time to show true interest. She toyed with that thought momentarily. With a heavy sigh, she sat down on a small rock wall and looked to the starry skies overhead.

Father, she continued her prayer, *I hate that Duncan treats me like a child—like a little sister—in Sonny's stead. I hate that Phillip's lifestyle leaves no room for you. I thought perhaps you'd brought Phillip into my life to be my husband. Then when I heard he wasn't interested in you, I wondered if maybe I was to help point him to you, and then he'd be ready to be my husband.*

Now Duncan suggests that I stop trying to work this out and rest in you—

to let go of worrying after a mate and let you be my husband. I know that's biblically sound advice, but still it hurts. It hurts deep inside because I'm lonely and because I see other women around me enjoying marriage and children. And, Lord, I want that so very much.

She thought of the past and how much she'd always hoped to clear her name so that she might go forward in her career. Now that thought seemed so secondary to the issues of husband and babies.

Father, I want to clear my name as well. I don't want anyone to go on in this world thinking me a thief. And now there's this situation with the missing Hopi flutes. Will I be suspected again? Will someone from the university get news of this and suggest me as a suspect? A sickening dread coursed through her. The Driscolls! They were connected to Phillip and his sister. If word got out about this, they would most definitely stir up trouble.

"Oh, God, please help me," she moaned.

CHAPTER TWELVE

*S*onny moved through his parents' house carrying a large birthday cake that read, "Happy Birthday, Gunther." Gunther Albright was his father's best friend at the university. They'd been friends from the start of Raymond Gordon's teaching career in New Mexico. Gunther, a funny sort of man, was also the uncle of Chester Driscoll's wife, Bethel. Because of this, Gunther was, of late, quite often seen in the company of the Driscolls.

Sonny thought the combination a rather strange and complicated one. The Driscolls were really no longer welcomed in his parents' circle of friends. Their refusal to help clear Rainy of the ridiculous charges against her was the main reason for the falling-out, but Sonny suspected there were other problems as well.

Entering the dining room, where tables and the sideboard stood overflowing with finger foods, Sonny was immediately set upon by Bethel Driscoll.

"Why, Sonny Gordon," she fairly purred, "I'd know you anywhere." She reached out to touch him and traced his jacketed arm down to where his hand held the cake tray. She toyed with the back of his hand for a moment, stroking her fingers over his knuckles as she smiled sweetly into his face.

She wasn't all that pretty, Sonny thought, but there was something about her manner that demanded attention. "My mother pointed you out to me. I understand you're Dr. Albright's niece and Chester Driscoll's wife."

Bethel laughed. She stepped away and raised her hands as if for emphasis. "I'm also very much my own person. Don't think to limit my identity to my uncle and husband."

Sonny nodded, rather mesmerized at the way her silver gown

shimmered. She moved again, this time twirling in front of him as an animated child might do. "I purchased this dress in Los Angeles. Do you like it?"

"It's very nice," Sonny answered, not at all sure what else to say.

"My uncle and husband hate it. They said I paid too much for it and that it's much too revealing. But, as I mentioned, I'm my own person and I make my own decisions. I think women have long been oppressed in being prohibited from choosing their own fashions. Why should our choices be dictated by men? Do you realize that all of the most famous creators of women's clothing are men?"

"No, I suppose I didn't."

She nodded. "Well, I'm sure few people realize that. If so, they probably imagine that these male masters of style are being advised by women, but it simply isn't true. They choose the fashion and design and have all the say over how it comes together. Women are stuck with wearing whatever men throw their way. It's no different for the poor woman whose husband allows her only a few dollars for a new dress and shoes or the wealthy matron who fills her closets with new clothes twice a year. We are all following along under the guidance of men."

Sonny nodded, still unsure of what she expected him to say. Sometimes conversations with strangers were easy. At those times each person seemed to have an understanding of their lines, and the conversation took place with as much ease as could be mustered between people who had no intention of intimacy.

Conversing with Bethel Driscoll wasn't that way, however. Sonny felt completely confused. Not only that, but the cake tray was starting to feel pretty heavy.

"I'm afraid," he began, "that I need to deliver the cake."

"Of course." She smiled rather coyly. "We each must do what is assigned us."

Again he nodded, but he had no idea what she meant to imply. Was she making some kind of subtle comment about clothes again?

"Oh, there you are," Sonny's mother said as he came into the living room. "I was beginning to think I'd have to hunt you down." She smiled and took the tray from him. Sonny couldn't help but wonder what his mother would have had to say about Bethel's comments. He looked at her simple navy-colored dress. She seemed simple but elegant. Bethel just looked . . . well . . . cheap.

"Look at the cake, Uncle Gunther," Bethel said as she swept into the room to stand at Sonny's side. "I'll bet they had this marvelous confectionery made at that little bakery just down the street."

Sonny's mother seemed surprised by this statement but said nothing. Sonny felt the need to rush to her defense. "Mom made the cake. She's quite remarkable in the kitchen. We never feel the need to use the bakery."

His mother flashed him a look of gratitude as she said, "We hope you are enjoying your party, Gunther. You've been such a good friend to Ray and to me."

Gunther Albright wasn't a tall man. He stood only a few inches taller than Sonny's mother's five-foot-four-inch frame. But it was the pockmarks on Gunther's face that made him seem more foreboding. Smallpox had marred him as a teenager, but he seemed hardly concerned with the scars at the age of sixty.

With his snowy hair and bushy white eyebrows, Gunther looked much older than Sonny's father, yet Sonny knew them to be rather close in age. Gunther, however, wore the weight of his years.

"I can't thank you enough for the party," Gunther said, leaning forward to kiss Sonny's mother on the cheek.

"Hey, now, what is this?" Sonny's father called out as he joined the party. "I see you kissing my best gal."

The partiers laughed and Gunther smiled. "She's the prettiest in the room and she cooks like an angel. I couldn't let her go without thanking her."

"Well, I don't know that angels cook," Ray Gordon stated, "but I do know Edrea makes the best food I've ever eaten."

"Hear, hear!" Sonny joined in. "It's one of the biggest reasons I've remained at home for this long." He wanted to take back the words as soon as they were spoken, for he'd inadvertently invited talk of his personal life.

"I wondered why you hadn't married yet," Bethel said, moving in for the kill. She lowered her voice so that only Sonny could hear her words. "Had I met you prior to meeting Chester, I might have given his proposal less consideration."

Sonny stepped back and tried not to look shocked. "Where is Chester? Is he here tonight?"

Bethel's expression took on a look of boredom. "I haven't any idea where he is. He talked of going back to Santa Fe to help my friend Jennetta with a special project."

"I thought Jennetta Blythe was going to Taos with her brother and some friends. They were hiring a courier car and my sister to guide them."

Bethel laughed. "Well, perhaps that's where he went, then."

Sonny tried not to worry about Rainy, but it was hard. He felt that he was responsible for protecting her from harm. *I should have given up my vacation and stayed with her. I shouldn't have given my responsibility over to Duncan.* He wanted to kick himself. Now he'd just worry about Rainy until he heard that she was safely back at the boardinghouse in Santa Fe.

Sonny heard his mother question Bethel about something, but he paid no attention to the words. Instead, he chose that moment to move across the room and take up conversation with another of his father's friends from the university. He wasn't about to get caught up in another conversation about fashion.

"It's an outrage if you ask me," the man declared.

Sonny looked hesitantly at the man. He didn't want to nose into the conversation and so thought maybe it would be better to leave. He turned, but the man put his hand on Sonny's shoulder.

"What are your father's plans?"

"Excuse me?" Sonny said, shaking his head. "His plans for what?"

"The university is planning to eliminate a large number of their staff. They're asking for the older faculty to retire or step down. I was just wondering what your father planned?"

Sonny looked to where his father stood talking with Gunther. "I don't know. I can't speak to the matter because he has not discussed it with me."

"I suppose I've gone and let the whole messy ordeal out of the bag," the man said, his tone apologetic.

"What mess is that?" a younger man asked.

"Oh, you know. This matter of employment in times of trial and tribulation. The university situation."

Sonny was surprised to find Gunther Albright suddenly take up the conversation. "It's ludicrous, that's what," he called from the other side of the room. Sonny's father took a step back as Gunther continued. "How dare the university ask its older, more experienced members to leave? I've worked hard to establish a good career and to benefit the school with my expertise—and this is how they reward me? By putting me out to pasture?"

Ray Gordon shook his head. "Now, Gunther, I'm sure that's not what they intended. I would imagine they're merely considering that younger men might well have families—children to provide for."

"That's no excuse. I have plenty of expenses to see to. They needn't rob me of my income and lifestyle in order to benefit another. This idea that men with families are somehow more deserving of steady work holds no credence with me."

"So you don't plan to retire, I take it," the man who'd brought up the entire matter commented in a rather lame fashion.

"I certainly do not. I will never retire for those reasons. Let someone else step down."

The somber spirit and intensity of the moment seemed to steal away the party gaiety. Sonny's mother worked quickly to retrieve the goodwill. "Let's have some cake. I happen to know that this is Gunther's favorite."

Sonny took the opportunity to slip from the room. If anyone asked where he was going, he'd tell them he was just getting a glass of water, which was exactly what he planned to do. He would not mention that he'd rather go hide in his bedroom and read the government reports on Alaska. If he tried that, his mother would just hunt him down and force his return. So, instead, he stood in the silence of the kitchen trying hard to figure out what was to be done.

"My uncle is a bit of a killjoy," Bethel announced as she came into the room. "But you have to understand. He lost a good deal of money during the crash of '29."

"I'm sure he feels quite threatened," Sonny replied, wishing Bethel would go back to the party and leave him alone. He poured himself a glass of water and drank.

"Yes, well, he needn't worry. I have enough money to keep him in cigars and brandy until he dies. He's a dear man who's cared greatly for me over the years. I could never let anything bad befall him."

Sonny toyed with the glass for a moment. "Yes, family should take care of each other. That's what the Bible says."

"Oh, so you're one of those stuffy Christians who has a list of rules and regulations a mile long," she commented, moving closer. "Don't you ever want to just have some fun?" She walked her fingers up his arm.

"I have lots of fun, Bethel, but it never conflicts with how I feel about serving God."

She feigned a pout. "But you could have so much more fun if you just pretended that God wasn't looking."

Sonny shook his head. "Nope, I don't think I could. You see, I know

God is looking. He's always with me, no matter where I go or what I do. He's in my heart because I asked Him to be there. I want His company no matter the journey."

She shook her head and moved away. "A real man wouldn't need a governess to watch over him."

Sonny chuckled. "No, indeed, but a real man can always benefit by looking to his father for direction and companionship."

———

Later that night, after the party had dispersed and the cleanup had been completed, Sonny sat alone in the living room. He thought about the evening and about his father and Gunther Albright. How terrible to have depended on a job—to have expected that job to last a lifetime—only to have it stripped from you.

"You seem deep in thought, my boy. Anything you care to discuss?"

Sonny looked up to find his father standing in the archway. "I guess I'm just concerned for you and Mom."

His father studied him momentarily before taking a seat in his favorite blue brocade chair. "And why is that?"

"Well, you heard the discussion regarding the university. Why didn't you say anything to me about this? I mean, I know you don't owe me any explanations, but I care what happens to you. Are you going to retire?"

His father seemed to consider the questions for a moment before leaning back and lacing his fingers behind his head. "I've given it a great deal of thought, and I've talked it over with your mother."

"And?" Sonny hated that his father was dragging this along at such a slow pace, but it was his father's way.

"And I believe I will retire. There are hard times coming, son. I have a bit of money saved—money that I managed not to lose when so many others lost everything. It's not a lot, but enough. I also have the property in Scotland and your Uncle Sean would like to see us come back. He'd like help with the farm. And since you're moving to Alaska to work with your friends, we've decided we might as well go."

"Scotland? Truly? What about Rainy?"

His father nodded slowly. "That has been a concern of ours, but we trust God to work out the details. Rainy is welcome to come with us. Aye, in fact, she'd be quite good company for your mother. If I know Sean, and well I do, he'll have me working from sunup to sunset, and your mother could grow quite lonely."

"I worry about Rainy. She's so vulnerable."

His father leaned forward at this. "How so?"

Sonny shrugged. "I suppose I don't even know the answer to that as well as I'd like to. She's caught up in her feelings. She thinks God is leading her to marriage, but she doesn't know which man is the one God has picked out for her. She fancies that movie star Phillip Vance. But she also likes Duncan Hartford."

"Tell me about this movie star. He must have been pretty special for her to go canceling on her mom and me."

"He's smooth, that's for sure," Sonny said. "He's too smooth. He's all glitter and glamour. Women flock to him and girls adore him. He's shown Rainy a bit of extra attention and she seems quite intrigued. I'm sure I don't understand what she's experiencing, but . . ."

"No, there aren't any 'buts' in this matter. You can't know your sister's heart. As close as you two have always been—finishing each other's sentences and always seeming to know what the other one was thinking—you can't know her heart. Rainy is a woman, and that will always stand as a mystery between you two."

"But she isn't making sense. Duncan Hartford cares for her and his interest in archaeology is exactly what Rainy desires. He's caught her attention and she finds him handsome, intelligent, and in general what she's looking for. At least she did until Phillip Vance came to town. I'm just afraid that Vance will sweet-talk her into giving up the things most dear and precious to her, and then he'll hurt her."

"Rainy is an adult. She'll have to make some of these choices for herself. She's a good woman who loves God and knows to put Him first. If she does that and seeks His will in the matter, she should be just fine."

"And if she doesn't?" Sonny hated to even voice the question, but it had to be asked.

"If she doesn't, she'll bear the consequences of her actions, just as we all do. Satan is good at deceiving people. He comes as an angel of light and offers what looks to be a good and proper path. If he came as an unattractive monster with death and destruction written clearly on his face, no one would fall prey to his schemes. It could very well be that God does intend for Duncan Hartford to be your sister's husband. Perhaps Duncan and Rainy would accomplish wonderful things for the Lord. Do you suppose Satan will sit by and allow that?"

His father got up and looked down at Sonny with great compassion. "Pray for her, son. Pray the good Lord will give her strength in adversity. She has to be able to determine what's of the Lord and what isn't. Rainy alone can make the choice, but we can support her in prayer . . . and offer advice when she allows it." He squeezed Sonny's shoulder. "Like I said, pray for her. She'll come through just fine."

"I hope so, Dad. I just don't want to see her hurt."

"Son, you can't keep that from happening. We all suffer in this world. Jesus said it would be so. That's why our faith must stand firm— otherwise we fall."

Sonny thought on his father's words long after he'd gone to bed. The next morning he was still considering them when a knock came on the front door. Opening it, Sonny found himself face-to-face with Bethel Driscoll.

"Hello, Sonny," she said, smiling in her coy manner. "I wonder if you might do me the tiniest favor."

CHAPTER THIRTEEN

After a week in Taos, the ensemble headed back to Santa Fe via the earlier forgone Puye ruins. The Puye Cliff Dwellings, carved into rock formed from compressed volcanic ash and cinders, stood as a reminder of the long heritage of New Mexican people. The Indians had built into the rock for protection, eventually stretching out to build adobe houses on the slopes and on top of the numerous mesas. The marvel of Indian pueblos fascinated Jennetta, who immediately declared upon arriving that she would write a poem devoted to the site.

Rainy directed the party to their outdoor lunch of chicken sandwiches, fruit, cheese, and coffee before taking her own lunch to a more secluded spot. Here, the scattered sage shared company with the buffalo grass and prickly-pear cactus. The varying shades of green gave a look of life to the desert land. From place to place a mouse or ground squirrel skittered across the parched ground in search of food and water.

At times this area seems so desolate and desperate, Rainy thought. The ruins gave proof to a life that had once existed. Who were the people who had carved these homes of rock? Where had they gone? Had some enemy come to snatch them away? The archaeologist in Rainy demanded answers. She longed to forget the tour and just set out on her own to study the ruins and the legacy left behind.

There was so much she desired and so little that she seemed to truly be able to grasp. *How has my life become so completely contrary to what I had planned?*

Sitting there gazing across a landscape dry and pleading for moisture, Rainy thought of her own pleadings before God. Duncan's words haunted her. So much so that she began to pray with those comments in mind.

She truly sought her heart and realized there was a great deal of truth in what Duncan had said. She knew the urgency was not of God. At first, she believed the pressure had indeed been something divinely given in order to motivate her in the direction God desired her to go. But after Duncan spoke of God's timing and there being no need to rush into a relationship, Rainy truly began to reconsider.

I don't love Phillip Vance, she told herself as she nibbled on her sandwich. *And as fond as I am of Duncan, I cannot truly say that I love him either.* Although she knew that given Duncan's love of the Southwest and of archaeology, they would have much more in common than she and Phillip would share. Plus there was the most critical situation of all: Phillip did not share her faith. Duncan did.

But my feelings are so volatile where Duncan is concerned, she thought. *He makes me feel . . .* She let her emotions surface for once. *He makes me feel cared about. He makes me feel safe.* She sucked on her lower lip and considered what such feelings might mean.

"I hope you don't mind if I join you," Phillip said, coming to sit beside Rainy.

Rainy smiled and stuffed her feelings down deep. "Not at all. Are you enjoying the ruins?"

"Very much. I had no idea such places even existed prior to coming on this trip. I think I shall miss it very much."

"When do you leave for Los Angeles?" she asked.

"Tomorrow. I'm scheduled on the afternoon train. I won't be able to get back for a while—probably not any sooner than a month, maybe two. But, Rainy, I want to come back and see you. Will you let me do that? Will you wait for me?"

Rainy felt a strange stirring as she gazed into Phillip's blue eyes. "I . . . well . . . I don't know if that's at all wise."

Phillip seemed genuinely startled by her response. He put down his lunch and looked at her for a moment as if trying to ascertain how honest she was being with him.

"Have I done something wrong?" he asked.

Rainy shook her head. "No, but I find my life turned upside down. I'm not at all sure what God would have me do."

"Don't hide behind God, Rainy."

She tensed at his words. It sounded very much like something Chester Driscoll had once said. "I'm not hiding behind God," she replied stiffly.

Phillip reached out and took hold of her hand. "I'm not insulting your faith. I'm simply trying to say that I've met people who pretended to be steeped in concern for what God wanted in their life, but rather than truly being of a spiritual mind, they were using the concept to avoid making decisions and commitments. I wouldn't want you to do that merely because the potential choices are frightening."

Rainy calmed a bit. Phillip couldn't possibly understand how she felt about her faith, but at least he wasn't trying to be harsh with her. "I don't believe I'm hiding behind God so much as hiding in Him. There's a big difference."

"Is there really?" He lowered his face but looked up at her in a manner Rainy had seen him do in the movies. It was done for effect—there was no doubt about it. She wondered if he did it consciously or if the action had been performed so many times before that by now it was a natural part of how Phillip Vance responded.

"Of course there is. The Bible is full of verses that talk about God being our shelter and refuge and about hiding in Him. He's the source of my strength and my hope. To consider any other way would never work for me." Rainy straightened and put down her sandwich. "I suppose we've all known people who didn't truly revere or honor God yet they used Him. But the Bible says God will not be mocked. I would imagine those people who have acted thusly will find a very difficult path ahead of them."

"You really believe that, don't you?" It was Phillip's turn to straighten and put aside his act.

"I do believe that, Phillip. God has too often shown himself in my life for me to believe otherwise."

"And He's never let you down? Never seemed indifferent to your pleas?"

Rainy looked away rather quickly. Phillip's words stung. Of course she had felt God rather indifferent in what had happened to her at the university. After all, He still hadn't seen fit to clear her name.

"I can tell by your reaction that you have felt God's absence at times. What happened?"

Rainy felt her breath quicken. "I'd rather not talk about it. It's rather painful."

Phillip squeezed her hand. "But perhaps we can ease that pain together."

Rainy shook her head. "Not until I find a way to right the wrong done me." She met his handsome face and offered him a weak smile. "Perhaps when that happens, then I'll share it."

"But why wait? I care deeply about you; surely you must know that," Phillip said, almost pleading.

Rainy remained unmoved. She had no desire to tell anyone what had happened. She didn't want pity or sympathy, and she certainly didn't want to be falsely judged. No, silence was the better choice.

"Look, Phillip, we have very different lives, you and me. I can't expect you to understand that, but it's true."

"There is no difference that can't be overcome," he said softly "if the parties involved desire to overcome."

"So you would give up movies and move to New Mexico in order to get to know me better?" Rainy asked, knowing the answer before he even spoke.

"A similar question might be asked of you, my dear. Would you give up New Mexico and come to California in order to better know me?"

Rainy knew in her heart that the answer was no. She couldn't see herself gallivanting off to the coast, dressing in stylish fashions and lingering until all hours at one party or another.

"Your silence tells me that you are uncertain," Phillip spoke before she could say a word. "So don't give me an answer just yet. Think about it. Think about it for a month, and when I return we can discuss this again. Then maybe you can give me an answer."

Rainy pulled away from Phillip's touch and began gathering up her lunch. "I'm not sure what the question really is."

"The question is, will you stay at my place in California and get to know me better? The house is positively huge and there are always other guests. You could come out with Jennetta, if nothing else. Please say you'll at least think about it. Please?"

Rainy felt that same sense of urgency wash over her. There was no peace in dealing with Phillip Vance. "I can't make any promises." She got to her feet and looked back down at where he sat. "I'm sure I'll be around, but I can't say that I'll be any closer to an understanding of this situation then than I am now."

She walked away feeling peace come back in little showers of hope. *God truly has this under control. Phillip Vance doesn't hold the answers to my future—God does. And furthermore, Phillip cannot understand this. It's not something he has experienced or looked at with any real depth of consideration. Perhaps I should have told him that I would consider spending more time with him if he would spend more time with God.*

But was it fair to bargain with one person's desires and force a relationship with God as a means to a more beneficial end?

She wished her mother or father or even Sonny might have been present in order to discuss the matter more thoroughly. She desperately needed guidance.

"You seem quite down in the mouth," Duncan said as he caught up with her. "Are you feeling all right?"

Rainy looked up at him ready with an angry retort, but instead she held her tongue. His expression showed genuine concern and it softened her heart. "I'm fine. Just tired."

"The days are getting warm," he offered. "The heat is enough to wear anyone out." He kicked at several rocks, and Rainy watched them dance away and settle into their new location. The desert was easily disturbed, but just as easily it readjusted itself to the disturbance. Would that human beings could do as well.

Rainy and Duncan walked back to the car in an awkward silence. Rainy wanted him to go away, but at the same time she wanted to pour her heart out to someone. "Do you ever feel confused about choices you have to make?" she finally asked. "You told me the other night that God has a plan for me—for everyone," she said, suddenly feeling rather nervous. "You also said I shouldn't feel the need to rush or manipulate the situation. But we do have to act sooner or later. We make a choice, even in deciding not to choose."

"That's true enough," Duncan said somberly. "I never suggested choices didn't have to be made. I simply said I didn't believe there should be such a sense of urgency in something so entrusted to Him." He glanced to the skies and momentarily Rainy did the same. The color was a soft turquoise with threadlike wisps of white clouds. How serene it all seemed. Rainy would have loved nothing better than to lose herself in the vast open expanse and never deal with another single problem.

"But . . ." she hesitated. She felt certain Duncan expected her to continue the conversation, but what could she say? How could she explain what she was going through? How could she explain her despair about the past at the university, her shock over the news of the missing Hopi flutes, and her desire to find a mate? How could she hope Duncan could understand that she knew Phillip Vance was a liability she couldn't afford, yet at the same time he was so very attractive and . . . *Forbidden fruit.* The thought came to her in a flash. Was that what this was about? Was God somehow testing her? Testing her desire to stay true to Him?

"But what? You never finished your thought," Duncan said softly.

Rainy caught the intensity of his gaze. It left her feeling almost breathless. My, but he was handsome. She noted how the sun had darkened his skin to a honey gold.

"Oh, goodness, look at the time," Rainy said. "We need to get back to Santa Fe." She hurried off to gather the others, leaving Duncan looking rather stunned by her exit. She couldn't explain herself to him, so she decided it was just better to walk away. *No sense in letting him get in the middle of this when God so clearly has allowed this entire situation to test my trust in Him.* She would simply devote more time in prayer for the entire matter. Once they were back in Santa Fe, she'd put in for her time off and return home for a good long think. God clearly wanted her attention, and Rainy didn't want to ignore her heavenly Father—even for a moment.

———

The next day Rainy packed her bags. She felt confident that the best thing for her to do right now was return home to Albuquerque and take some time for quiet reflection and prayer. No Phillip Vance. No Duncan Hartford. Just the peaceful sanctuary of her parents' home and their sweet company.

Her mother would help her to better understand her mixed-up feelings, and Sonny and their father would keep her from becoming too maudlin. Her father might also have some ideas about what she could do to get the Driscolls to clear her name regarding the university thefts. He seemed to be the only one who really understood that it was more than a matter of letting the issue fade away. She wanted to be vindicated. There were still people out there who believed her a thief, and Rainy could not bear this.

Making her way downstairs, she paused to speak with Mrs. Rivera. "I'm leaving now. I will be gone for two weeks, so don't be giving my room away," she teased the older woman.

"I wouldn't dream of it. You and Sonny are my best boarders."

Rainy grinned and handed her the month's rent. "Here, this will ensure it, just in case you forget us. Sonny should be back next week, unless he's made other plans that he hasn't shared with me."

"How will you get to the train station?" Mrs. Rivera asked.

"The touring company promised to send someone for me." Rainy shifted her bags and looked at her watch. "I'd better hurry. The driver is probably here already."

Rainy hurried outside, noting as she went through the door that the black touring car was waiting for her at the end of the walkway. She looked around for the driver and was taken off guard when Duncan appeared at her side. He took hold of her arm and escorted her without a word to the car.

"I was asked to drive you to the train. You're leaving in a mighty big hurry. What's the rush?" he asked as he took her bags in hand. He seemed to consider the larger of the two for a moment, then tossed both cases onto the backseat and helped Rainy into the front.

"I wanted to spend time at home. You know I was scheduled to take a two-week vacation. Sonny's time is nearly up, but I felt it was important to go anyway. Sonny can either work with another courier or he can do odd jobs for Major Clarkson until I get back."

Duncan started the car and eased it into the traffic. Rainy noticed he'd dressed rather smartly, leaving his tour-driver uniform at home. He looked quite handsome in his trousers and jacket of charcoal gray. A crisp white shirt accented with a red-and-gray striped tie made Duncan look more like a railroad owner than an employee. His fedora was the perfect touch.

"You're certainly dressed up," Rainy said before she realized the words were out of her mouth.

Duncan seemed uncomfortable with her analysis. "I was called to a meeting. It seemed appropriate attire."

"Oh." Rainy looked at him and saw that his jaw had tensed. There was the slightest tick in his cheek, suggesting he wasn't at all happy. "You seem upset."

"I am upset."

"Oh." Should she ask why? Should she try to pry into his affairs as he had done with her? Before she could question him, however, Duncan pulled the car to the side of the road and turned to her.

"Two very expensive paintings disappeared from Taos. Did you by any chance hear anything about it?"

Rainy shook her head. "No. Should I have?"

He fixed her with such an intense look that Rainy lowered her gaze to her blue cotton skirt. She trembled when he reached out and took hold of her chin. He raised her face to meet his gaze and leaned forward. For just a moment Rainy thought he might kiss her.

"If you do know something about this, you must come forward."

A sense of confusion washed over Rainy. "Why would I know anything about it?"

"Because they disappeared the day we left—or rather the night before."

Rainy shook her head. "I hadn't heard so much as a single bit of gossip suggesting it. Was that what your meeting was about?"

Duncan stiffened and dropped his hold. He gripped the steering wheel tightly. "Why are you leaving Santa Fe?"

"I told you," Rainy replied. "My work for Phillip and his sister is done, and I need a vacation. Phillip is heading back to Los Angeles this afternoon, so there is no reason to stay here."

Duncan looked at her with an expression that suggested disbelief. "No reason?"

Rainy shook her head. "No working reason. Duncan, what is this all about? I don't understand your anger. I don't know what I've done to make you feel so hostile toward me, but—"

"Rainy, I don't feel hostile toward you." Duncan took hold of her hand. "I'm worried about you."

The sinking feeling that there was something more to this than met the eye caused Rainy to pull away. "Why are you worried about me, Duncan?"

He sighed and leaned back against the car door. "There are so many reasons to worry about you. I feel like, even though we've gotten to know each other better through the Detours, I don't know you at all. I'd really like to, but you seem far more interested in other things."

"Other things or other people?" Rainy shot back in defense. "Is this about Phillip?"

Duncan clenched his jaw again. Rainy could see the muscles in his neck tense. He started the car back down the street. For several blocks he said nothing, then finally he glanced over. "I don't want to see you hurt."

"I don't want to see me hurt either. That's why I wish you'd just tell me what this is all about."

"I can't," Duncan admitted.

"Can't or won't?"

"I can't. There are things going on that I can't talk about."

Rainy watched him for a moment longer, then turned her attention to the passing scenery. She could barely contain her frustration at Duncan's riddles. Why couldn't he just speak the truth and let her be responsible for whatever needed to be addressed? She hated it when people thought they were protecting her and instead only ended up hurting her more. Chester had been that way. He had told her it was for her own good that he hadn't shared with her all that he knew about the missing artifacts.

The missing artifacts.

The words stuck in Rainy's head. Duncan talked about the theft of the Hopi flutes and now the paintings from Taos. Her stomach churned and dread settled over her like a wet blanket. *How could I have been so dense? Dear Lord, do they really think I'm responsible?*

The sudden revelation perfectly explained Duncan's attitude. "You think I stole the paintings and the flutes, don't you?"

Duncan continued to drive, his gaze fixed on the road ahead. "No. *I* don't think that."

He had emphasized the word "I," leaving Rainy even more certain of the situation. "But someone else does. Is that right?"

Duncan pulled into the station and parked the car. He sat for several moments before turning to Rainy. "I have to say I'm far more concerned about the situation with you and Phillip Vance."

Rainy shook her head. "But why? That's a matter that is clearly none of your concern."

"Maybe not directly, but since Sonny asked me to look after you while—"

"Leave Sonny out of this," Rainy said, opening her door. "If you have some reason to care about what happens to me, then stop hiding behind Sonny and tell me so. Otherwise, leave it alone."

She slammed the door, startled at the boldness of her words. She grabbed her bags off the backseat and rushed to the depot. *Oh, Lord, I'm always making a mess of things. Put a guard on my mouth and keep me from false accusations. You know I've had nothing to do with any of the missing pieces. You are the only one who can clear me of these suspicions. I don't know if someone other than Duncan considers me to be involved, but I am worried. Worried enough that I know I'll never have a moment's rest at home unless you take the matter from me and I yield it in turn.*

At the depot door she turned. Duncan remained in the car, the look on his face suggesting a bit of shock. *Good,* she thought. *Let him stew over this as I have.*

*T*he beady-eyed Indian Affairs official sat opposite Duncan's desk at the museum. "I want to know everything you did and saw while in Taos," the man said.

"I saw nothing that would help you with the recovery of the two pieces of art that disappeared from Taos," Duncan replied. "I checked and rechecked the luggage as best I could—though I obviously was not able to look inside. Not that two large oil canvases would have fit in any of the bags I loaded."

"Canvases can be rolled," the Taos deputy sheriff offered. He sat to Mr. Richland's left and seemed quite anxious about the entire matter. Duncan couldn't even remember the man's name, but his anxiety and nervous twitching made him seem an unlikely candidate for law enforcement.

"I'm sure you may not be aware of what else is going on in the world," Richland began in his condescending manner, "but this country stands on the brink of a financial disaster. People are stockpiling money and goods—at least those people who seem to understand what's happening. Someone has no doubt taken the Hopi artifacts and paintings in order to sell them to the highest bidder."

Duncan asked what seemed a logical question. "But if everyone is hoarding, who will be buying?"

"The wealthy will always find a way," Richland answered. "There are plenty of well-to-do people who intend to stay that way. They know that diversifying their holdings will be the way to stability."

Duncan shook his head. "It doesn't make any sense. There are pieces here in Santa Fe that are worth far more than those on the reservations. Why steal a few historically important artifacts that probably have very little monetary value—except to museums?"

"People have collections," Richland responded. "Collections that include all manner of items. Don't play naïve with me, Mr. Hartford. You may have no idea of the true financial status of this country, but surely you understand that there are those who would steal such artifacts to sell to museums or personal collectors."

"Of course I understand that, Mr. Richland." Duncan fought back his irritation with the man. "I'm merely suggesting that financial gain may not be the reason why those pieces are missing."

"What's your theory on the matter?" the deputy sheriff asked.

"I've given some thought to this while driving for the tours. You both realize, don't you, that the Harvey Company recently sold the Indian Detours to Major Clarkson."

"What of it?" Richland questioned.

"Suppose this isn't about the money or the Indians or even the oil paintings. What if this is about the transfer of the company? What if we're dealing with a disgruntled former employee or even someone in the Harvey Company who doesn't want to see Clarkson succeed?"

"That makes very little sense, Mr. Hartford," Richland said. The deputy nodded in agreement with him.

"I think it could make perfectly good sense. Think, gentlemen. If you were angry because you'd lost your job after the sale of the Detours business, what might you do to settle the score?"

The men stared blankly, so Duncan continued. "You'd do whatever it took to make the business look bad. You'd arrange for things to happen that could be blamed on the company. I think it's completely possible that someone has a grievance against Major Clarkson or the Harvey Company and they've set this up to create mistrust with the Indians and cities involved with the Detour business."

"But the thefts have been going on longer than Clarkson has owned the business. More information has surfaced to prove that smaller articles have disappeared from the reservations during past tours," Richland stated coolly.

"So that might help us narrow the field," Duncan replied. "Maybe we need to focus on employees who were fired from the Harvey Company before the thefts began."

"I think you're grasping at straws," the nervous deputy sheriff announced.

Duncan shrugged. "You asked me to check into this situation. I've done a great deal of thinking and observing. I saw nothing to suggest that either the employees or the guests of the Detours have stolen a single article. Of course, my experience is limited to only a handful of trips, but that's my observation."

"Then perhaps the employees or guests are arranging for the theft and then are accomplishing it through another person—someone not on the trip. This would be very easy for an employee to pull off."

Richland's determination to pin the matter on the Gordons made Duncan all the more determined to fight.

"Maybe some of your Indians are involved. After all, the United States government hasn't exactly been fair with them at times. Now that the country is in the midst of this financial downturn you mentioned, perhaps the Indians have joined together to create this mishap for their benefit."

Richland stiffened. "Mr. Hartford, that accusation is even more ludicrous than your previous suggestion."

"I'm not accusing anyone—and neither should you. I see no evidence to suggest any real culprit. That's why I want you to consider every angle before deciding who's to blame. Sonny and Rainy Gordon have no reason to steal from the Indians. They've been on good terms with them for years. In fact, Miss Gordon has close friends among both the Hopi and the Navajos."

Richland stood. "But the pieces are missing nevertheless! I need answers, Mr. Hartford. Solid, dependable answers that may be defended in a court of law."

"And I'm telling you that I have no answers for you—only speculation. I've seen nothing to offer as proof. You'll have to wait until I do before I allow you to accuse friends of mine."

"Oh, so now the Gordons are friends?"

"You can hardly work around the clock with someone and not have them become either a friend or an enemy. Sonny and Rainy Gordon are decent God-fearing people. They come from a good family. I've even shared dinner in their home. They're simple people who show no evidence of wealth—ill-gotten or otherwise."

"If they're such good people, then why have they covered up the real reason Rainy Gordon left her position with the university?" Richland asked, the sneer on his face leaving Duncan little doubt that he had already determined Rainy was guilty.

"And what would that reason be?" Duncan questioned, his Scottish brogue thickening with emotion.

"It's not on the official record, mind you, but I have a very dependable source who has told me in confidence that Rainy Gordon was responsible for the theft of several university museum pieces. They found the articles in her desk, in her locked office."

Duncan felt the wind leave him momentarily. Could it possibly be true? Was this the thing that stood between Rainy and the Driscolls? He knew Marshall Driscoll was a powerful man with the university. Perhaps this was the real reason Rainy appeared to despise the man.

"I can see I've silenced you with this news," Richland said. He pulled out his pocket watch and popped open the case. "I have to leave now or I'll never make my train. I want evidence, Hartford. We aren't paying you to ignore facts."

"I'm not ignoring anything," Duncan said, feeling sick to his stomach. Surely Rainy was innocent. "And so far," he added, "I've not been paid a cent."

Richland pushed an envelope across the top of the desk. "Here, this should satisfy you for a time. I just want to know that I'm getting my money's worth."

Duncan looked at the envelope—his thirty pieces of silver. At least that was how it felt. "I didn't accept this job for the money." Duncan pushed the envelope at Richland. "I don't want your money. I only want the stealing to stop. I was willing to help you because of the request of my family's friend, Mr. Welch. But I'm not taking your money."

"Suit yourself—so long as the job is done properly. The Gordons will be on vacation the remainder of this week. While both are gone, we can keep an account of whether or not any other artifacts or valuables disappear. Meanwhile, I will expect you to nose around and ask questions. I'll return within the week and expect to see something more concrete."

Richland hesitated a moment, then picked up the envelope. He watched Duncan the entire time, as if expecting him to change his mind. When Duncan did nothing but watch him, Richland motioned to the deputy sheriff and headed for the door. "Remember that what I've told you goes no further than these walls. There is no doubt those who are involved would sell such details to the wrong person."

Duncan nodded. Who could he possibly tell this to? Sonny? Rainy? There was no one he could share this with—except his heavenly Father. *Oh, Lord,* he began to pray, *I need clear direction on this. I need understanding.*

After spending his lunch hour in prayer and working well into the evening hours on the backlog of work he'd promised the museum, Duncan finally left for his small house on East Palace Avenue. The tiny territorial-styled house was a haven away from the busyness of his life. His one-story home had a lovely stone porch with five simple roof supports. Above this, the roof parapet was trimmed in a fired-brick crowning that gave the house a little bit of charm and personality. Inside, the furnishings were simple yet solid. He'd purchased only those pieces necessary for his comfort, despising clutter and unnecessary bric-a-brac, though at times the house seemed empty and rather lonely. He couldn't help but wonder what a woman might do with the place.

As he walked toward home Rainy's smiling face came to mind. He could almost smell the scent of her perfume. What would she suggest doing with the house? Would she want to add pieces of Indian art? Maybe she'd prefer to make it over in a manner less Southwest in nature.

But she loves the Southwest, he thought. That much he'd come to realize. She might have her secrets from the past, but she loved New Mexico and all it offered. He'd never known any woman to so thoroughly enjoy herself while sitting among ruins and desert landscape.

She can't be responsible for the thefts. Rainy isn't like that. He felt confident in his thoughts—so confident, in fact, that his only real concern was not how to prove Rainy innocent but rather how to find the guilty party.

Humming to himself as he made his way up the road to Palace Avenue, Duncan was surprised to catch sight of Jennetta Blythe. Actually, her laughter had caught his attention first. The woman had an annoying nasal laugh that set Duncan's nerves on edge.

He glanced across the street to see Jennetta in the midst of a small gathering. She seemed to be showing off some new find. Duncan couldn't really see what she held, but her circle of friends seemed more than a little impressed. He slowed his walk, hoping for a glimpse.

He paused beside a stand of honey mesquites, whose pale yellow blooms offered a sure sign that spring was upon them. The fragrance wafted on the breeze, but Duncan couldn't take time to truly enjoy it. He watched Jennetta move toward the house, her flock gathered around her as tight as could be. But then, just before she followed her friends into the house, Duncan caught a glimpse of a long cylindrical object in her hands. Laughter filled the air as the party disappeared one by one into the house.

Still uncertain of what Jennetta had held, Duncan couldn't help but wonder if it might be one of the missing Hopi flutes. From the description given him earlier, it was the right size. He wished he could have gotten a better look. With a sigh, he headed up the street as the last of Jennetta's entourage disappeared into the house.

How am I going to figure this out? I can hardly go up to that house, knock on the door, and demand to know what Jennetta was showing everyone. He gritted his teeth in frustration. There had to be an answer, but none seemed to present itself to him.

"If I don't learn the truth and do it soon," he muttered, "they'll blame Rainy and maybe even charge her with stealing. I can't let that happen."

The intensity of his feelings startled Duncan. He knew he couldn't deny the thoughts that flooded his mind—his heart. He was falling in love with Rainy Gordon.

He laughed out loud. "Falling is hardly the word for it. I've already fallen—and hard."

———

"It really was the strangest thing," Sonny told Rainy as they cleared away the breakfast dishes. "I couldn't believe Bethel Driscoll was asking me to drive her to Gallup. I mean it just didn't make sense. She offered me an enormous amount of money and told me it was vital that she get there and that she didn't trust anyone else."

"What did you do?" Rainy put the dishes in the sink and turned to face her brother.

"I told her no. I couldn't see putting myself in the position of being alone with her for several hours. It just didn't make sense. I thought the appearance of it would be damaging to her reputation and told her so. She laughed this off and insisted she absolutely had to get to Gallup to pick up something. I suggested she take the train but she refused, saying the car was the only way that would work. I have no idea what it was all about, but when she saw that I would have no part of it, she left quite angry."

"That is really strange. You don't suppose . . ." Rainy's words trailed off into thoughts. She'd always believed Chester had something to do with the university artifacts showing up in her office. Maybe Bethel and Chester were involved in the missing artifacts and oil paintings. It seemed a long shot, but Rainy thought it entirely possible.

"What were you about to say?"

Rainy shrugged. "It isn't important. Just a fleeting thought. Anyway,

I'm so glad you extended your vacation. It's been very pleasant here with you and Mom and Dad. I really hate to go back."

Sonny shifted and looked at the floor. "You wouldn't have to go back."

"Why would you say that?" Rainy questioned as she took heated water from the stove and began making herself a cup of tea. "Want some?" she asked, holding up the pot.

Sonny shook his head. "I only meant that maybe you should consider going to Scotland with Mom and Dad."

Rainy replaced the pot and eyed her brother in curiosity. "Go to Scotland?"

"Sure, why not?"

"Are you planning to go to Scotland?" Rainy noted the sudden change in Sonny's features. "You are, aren't you?"

"Now wait just a minute, Rainy. I am making plans, but . . ."

"No, I can't believe this. You're planning to leave. Why didn't you tell me you were going to go with Mom and Dad?" She felt betrayed—deserted. "I can't believe you wouldn't talk this over with me before making such a serious decision. I know we're adults, but I thought we had a closeness that allowed for such confidence."

Sonny stepped forward. "We are close, Rainy, but you're misunderstanding."

Rainy raised her hands. "Stop. I'm not going to discuss this any further." She left the kitchen and walked out into the courtyard. Here her mother's lovely garden offered comfort as the world seemed to crumble around Rainy's feet. The security she'd once counted on was seeping through the cracks a little at a time. Why was this happening? How could Sonny make plans without consulting her first?

Because he's a man and fully capable of choosing his own path, her mind suggested.

But we always talk things over. We always make certain that we get each other's advice, she argued with herself.

Oh, and that's why you consulted Sonny before getting all wrapped up in Phillip Vance? That's why you discussed putting off the vacation in order to cater to Phillip and his rich friends? Rainy immediately felt awash in guilt. Her own conscience spoke against her.

What will I do without him? She turned back to the house. "What will I do without all of them?"

Rainy knew it was silly to be so alarmed. She wasn't a child anymore. She was nearly twenty-eight years old. Maybe she wouldn't be feeling so abandoned if she had already married and had started a family of her own.

She sat down and toyed with one of her mother's rosebushes. The plant had many buds on it, and while most hinted at the rich pink color to come, some were so tightly formed they offered nothing but their green casing.

My life is just like this, she thought, gently fingering the hard green cover of one bud. *I'm wrapped up tight, so unaware of the possibility of a future outside my little shell. I've so much to learn—so much to do—and yet here I sit, afraid of what's to come, angry because my life is changing.*

She glanced up and caught sight of Sonny watching her from the kitchen window. *I should apologize, I suppose.* But she turned away rather than motioning for him to join her. No doubt he would be wounded by her actions, but she was wounded as well. And sadly, she couldn't even truly understand why.

I know he's entitled to make plans without consulting me. I know he's a grown man and well past the age of going off on his own. If he wants to live with Mom and Dad in Scotland or anywhere else, that's completely his right. She sighed. *So why do I feel so lost and empty? Why does it hurt so much to know they're all going away?*

The time following their return to Santa Fe was filled with a flurry of visitors and tourists. Apparently, just as Major Clarkson had hoped, the rich still desired diversions from their daily jobs and the ever depressing news of the economy.

Rainy sat in a meeting for the couriers and their drivers. Clarkson wanted to make certain each person was advised as to the plans for the scaled-back Detour services, and so he had arranged meetings where the supervisors would be able to convey the important details of their changes in business.

Rainy gave only halfhearted attention to one of the newer supervisors, Mrs. Lehman, as she addressed the workers. "We have several fixed routes that we will offer on a regular basis. Some of the specialty trips we offered in the past can still be had on a person-by-person basis. These customized trips will be expensive, however, as our costs are up quite drastically. There are those of you who have proven to be much requested as couriers and drivers, and of course we will continue to accommodate those requests whenever possible."

Rainy sighed and shifted uncomfortably. She caught Sonny's sympathetic gaze from across the room and looked away quickly. Sonny had attempted to discuss the family's move to Scotland several times, but Rainy refused to hear him out. The idea still disturbed her in ways she couldn't explain. Before he could get a word in, she'd told him that it was better to leave it in the past—that she was trying hard not to hold on to her anger and frustration. She'd even told him that he was entitled to do whatever he pleased with his life—yet everything she said seemed to frustrate him further.

"The Taos trip, of course, will continue to be offered," Mrs. Lehman announced. "The costs are minimal and the three days offer a well-rounded tour for most tastes. It has proven to be our most popular tour by far, and so to show that we sympathize with the American worker, we've lowered the price by ten dollars. Instead of sixty-five dollars, we'll be charging fifty-five dollars for the three-day tour and only thirty-five dollars for the two-day tour."

The mention of the Taos tour caused Rainy's mind to drift again—this time it went to Phillip Vance and his continued absence. He should have been back by now, but Rainy had heard nothing. She had only received one short letter since he left for Los Angeles. In it Phillip had maintained an ardent passion for Rainy and the fervent desire that she join him in California. Rainy never gave serious thought to the arrangement, although she did check the train schedule to Los Angeles on more than one occasion. But after that brief note in the early days of his absence, there had been no other communication. A month came and went and still there was no sign of Phillip, and Rainy had no desire to look up Jennetta Blythe to ask where her brother might be. Perhaps this was God's way of keeping Rainy from a painfully wrong decision.

Of course, the only real decision Rainy had made in her very real battle of the wills was to let go of the matter and let God take control. She still earnestly desired a husband and family and still kept her gaze on Duncan and Phillip both as potential mates; however, she wasn't feeling the same frantic desire that had haunted her not so long ago. It was difficult to trust that God had everything under control. She supposed it was more difficult for her than most because of what had happened at the university. Why would a just and fair God allow her to be blamed for things that weren't her fault? God loved her and cared about her—but He didn't seem to love and care *enough* about her to keep bad things from happening to her.

Even as she'd discussed the situation with her father, Rainy had known an odd kind of resolve. Her father said matter-of-factly that a person wasn't entitled to know why God worked things in a certain manner—that God has His ways and they are so far removed from man that they make little sense. He called it the "foolishness of God" and showed her verses of Scripture that backed up his reasoning.

Rainy could accept that God's ways were often confusing and indiscernible, but she still didn't understand why He'd allow her to lose the one thing that mattered most. She had held a wonderful position with the university. She was to have been awarded a special grant from the college to study the Hopi. She would have eventually been asked to teach a class or two and, in time, might have become a professor. It wasn't fair that she should have to lose all of that.

Then again, nothing seemed fair at the moment. Her family was leaving for Scotland. By autumn, they would be heading for the East Coast by train. From there they would take a ship to England and then take another train to Edinburgh. So it was up to her; she could either give up her driving desire to see her name cleared and go to Scotland with her family, or she could stay here in her beloved Southwest and live alone. Resignation left a bitter taste in her mouth.

"We will also offer an overnight trip," Mrs. Lehman said in a tone that seemed a bit elevated. Rainy looked up to find the woman staring directly at her.

Straightening in her seat, Rainy forced her mind to stay focused. There would be adequate time to figure out what was to be done in regard to her reputation and future.

"The overnight tour will include an itinerary that takes the dudes to the Puye Cliff Dwellings and the Santa Clara Indian Pueblo. The fare of fifteen dollars will cover three meals and one overnight stay with private bath. And, of course, the transportation itself is covered. Are there any questions?"

One young woman raised her hand and Mrs. Lehman quickly acknowledged her.

"Will the tours continue to start here in Santa Fe at La Fonda?"

"Yes, the hotel will remain the central starting point. The tours will start promptly at nine each morning. This is a convenient hour for guests coming in from the station at Lamy. The only exception will be the overnight trip, which will also leave from La Fonda but will delay until 10:30 A.M. Other questions?"

No one offered any comment, so Mrs. Lehman dismissed the group and Rainy left the room as quickly as she could. With her heels click-clacking on the stone floor of the hotel, she made her way outside. The only real interest she had was to distance herself from her friends and Sonny. She wanted to be alone, as she had so many times recently. She knew her personality seemed altered as she withdrew and sought solitude, but she couldn't help it.

I'm confused, Lord. I thought I would feel better once I got back to work and into the swing of things, but I don't. Phillip hasn't written, Duncan has been completely absent, Sonny plans to go away, and everything is changing. I want my peaceful life back—the life I had before the university incident. I need direction for my life, but I seem to be walking in circles.

She strolled along the Plaza walk, noting that at the Palace of the

Governors the Indians were beginning to pack up their wares. Every day this faithful collection of natives brought handmade jewelry and baskets to sell. They would gather here under the protection of this ancient porch and put out their wares for the tourists to purchase. Then every day, like clockwork, the evening hour would come upon them and they would gather their things and go home.

Rainy looked at her watch and realized the dinner hour was upon them. The meeting with her co-workers had taken most of the afternoon. Funny, but Rainy could barely remember anything they'd discussed.

Turning from the preoccupied Indians, Rainy glanced up again and caught sight of Duncan. He was sitting on the opposite side of the Plaza and seemed to be watching her. Not knowing what else to do, Rainy offered a little wave. She hadn't spoken to Duncan since their falling-out. She wondered if he still worried about her guilt or innocence regarding the Indian artifacts.

She waited as he got up and made his way across the Plaza to her. A trembling went through Rainy as he offered her a smile. Apparently he wasn't mad at her. Rainy took his smile as her cue and smiled in return.

"I thought maybe you weren't speaking to me after the way I acted when we were last together," she offered by way of apology. "I regret that I treated you so poorly."

"I'm the one who owes you an apology," Duncan replied. "I'd like to take you to dinner to make up for it."

Rainy nodded, trying hard not to show her surprise. "I'd like that very much. Where shall we go?"

"If you don't mind a bit of a walk, I know a marvelous place over on Alameda. It just opened up and is run by a Frenchman."

"Sounds wonderful, and I don't mind the walk at all," Rainy assured him.

They headed off in the direction of Alameda Street, and it was Duncan who once again picked up the conversation. "How have you been?"

His voice was melodic, like liquid pouring over stones. "I've been . . . well . . ." She didn't want to lie to him, but how could she explain? "I suppose the best I can say is that my life is in turmoil. I've been trying to take your advice and give it over to God, but at times that's not as easy as it sounds."

Duncan chuckled. It wasn't exactly the response Rainy had expected. "You don't have to tell me. I'm terrible at taking my own advice. It's hard for me to place my burdens at the feet of God and leave them there."

"It's a relief to hear someone else feels that way," Rainy declared. "Sometimes I feel that I must be God's biggest disappointment. I sat in church last week listening to the pastor teach on all things being possible with God, and not moments after leaving I once again felt that things seemed impossible."

Duncan nodded. "Indeed. I can relate very well, but I always rest in the fact that no matter how many times I fail, God never will. And He'll forgive my mistrust and help me to start over. He desires only that we draw near to Him—to love Him and yield our lives to Him."

"And that's what I want most of all," Rainy admitted. "I don't want my own way. . . . Not really. There are things I hope for—long for—but I won't demand them of God anymore."

"Like a husband?"

Rainy felt embarrassed by the question and looked away. "Yes," she whispered.

Duncan reached out and took hold of her arm. "You know, my father, being the preacher that he is, once gave the example of a man whose boat was capsized in a storm on the ocean. The man can't swim, but as fortune would have it, he finds himself next to a rusty old buoy. He clings to that buoy out in the middle of a stormy sea, praying and pleading that God will rescue him. He grows more weary by the minute, but still he holds on to that buoy for fear of drowning. Then, much to the man's surprise and answered prayer, a rescue boat draws up alongside and a sailor reaches out a line to rescue the man."

Rainy stopped walking and turned to look at Duncan. He continued. "The sailor throws out the rope over and over, but the man won't let go of the buoy. It's almost as if the meager safety he has as he clutches the buoy is better than the hope of what safety he might have in the ship. The sailor pleads with the man to let go of the buoy and be rescued, but the man's fears refuse to let him trust. The storm worsens and the boat moves away to safety, leaving the man to drown."

"How awful," Rainy said, forgetting momentarily that it was just a story.

"Yes, but my father said we're the same way with God. He's offering us safety and rescue and we hold on to what we have in front of us— believing that it will somehow save us instead of God."

The silence engulfed them momentarily, and then Rainy nodded slowly. She was just like that man. She was clinging with her own strength to that which she thought would be beneficial—her pride, her self-reliance. She looked to Duncan. "Yes. Yes, we are very much like that. I believe God sent you to me for the very purpose of sharing this story. I can't begin to explain it, but I almost feel as if a veil has been lifted from my eyes. I thought all along that I was clinging to God, but I have been clinging to earthly things, self-centered things, the wrong things."

"We all make that mistake from time to time. Some things look very much like they've been divinely provided, when in fact they are offering only a temporary solution. God has a complete plan, and often we settle for only part of it."

They had reached the little restaurant by this time, so Duncan ushered her inside and waited until after they'd been seated at a highly polished walnut table before commenting further.

"I'm glad I could be of help. Glad, too, that you agreed to have dinner with me. I remember what you said about hiding behind Sonny—"

"Oh, please don't hold those words against me," Rainy interrupted. "They were so awful and spoken more out of my own misery than any truth."

"I'm not holding them against you. I'm thanking you for them," Duncan said, his voice low and his gaze intense. "I do have reason to care that has nothing to do with Sonny."

The words thrilled her heart and Rainy lost herself in his gaze. She longed to reach out and touch his wavy black hair, to run her fingers along his jawline. A slight sigh escaped her and she knew by the expression on Duncan's face that he somehow understood.

"Have you decided on what you'd like for dinner?" the waiter asked.

Rainy felt enormous frustration at the interruption. She looked away. "Why don't you order for us both," she murmured to Duncan.

He ordered veal Bourguignonne and stuffed mushrooms after marveling at the enticing selection and sharing small talk with the waiter. Rainy listened to the conversation, trying hard not to make Duncan's declaration into something more than he intended.

"I really think you'll enjoy the food here," Duncan said as the waiter left them.

"I take it you've eaten here before?" Rainy questioned.

"Yes. I've come here twice now. I had the lamb on one occasion and chicken Maciel on the other. Both were absolute perfection."

Rainy picked up the linen napkin and noticed the fine silver that lined her plate. Harvey standards to be sure, she thought. She glanced around her, finding that the waiter had placed them in a most private part of the dining room. Only a few other tables were occupied, and those were at the other end of the room—well away from where she sat with Duncan. Perhaps the waiter thought them to be young lovers who were courting.

She looked back to Duncan and smiled. "I'm very impressed."

"So am I," he murmured. "That's why I asked you here tonight."

Rainy was about to ask him what he meant when a voice from her past interrupted the moment. Chester and Bethel Driscoll stood not a foot away.

"I thought that was you, Rainy. We haven't seen anything of you in weeks."

"Hello," Rainy replied, offering nothing more. She kept her focus on the candles at the center of their table.

"We couldn't help but notice that you'd just arrived," Chester continued. "I could scarcely believe my eyes. How marvelous that we're all here together."

Duncan, who had gotten to his feet, motioned to the table. "Would you care to join us?"

Rainy wanted to throw something at him for inviting them to invade her evening, but she knew it was only polite to offer. Perhaps Chester would have the good sense to realize he was unwanted and leave.

"We'd be delighted," Chester replied, pulling out a chair for his wife. As soon as he had seated Bethel he snapped his fingers for the waiter. The man rushed to his side. "We'll have our usual," he told the man.

Then seating himself, Chester turned to Rainy. "Jennetta introduced us to this wonderful place. Do you come here often?" He looked from Rainy to Duncan and back to Rainy.

Rainy toyed with her knife. "No," she answered flatly.

Duncan quickly took up the conversation. "What brings you to Santa Fe?"

"Oh, we're here to see Jennetta and Phillip," Bethel oozed.

Rainy stiffened. Phillip was in town and hadn't bothered to get in touch with her? She said nothing, but her desire to demand answers nearly overwhelmed her good manners.

Bethel leaned forward. "In fact, they were to have met us here tonight, but Phillip had friends arrive from Los Angeles, and Jennetta, after spending much time in meditation, decided to cook for them all.

She does that from time to time, don't you know."

Rainy wanted to run from the restaurant but instead gave Bethel a forced smile. "Why, no, I didn't know Mrs. Blythe could cook."

Bethel laughed like Rainy's comment was some great joke. "Oh, Jennetta is a mystery. She's an expert at a great many things but prefers to be known for her writing."

The food arrived along with a stilted silence. The couples ate and murmured comments about the quality of the meal, but little else was said until the empty plates were cleared away and strong coffee was poured. Chester immediately pulled a silver flask from his pocket and poured a generous amount of amber liquid into his coffee, then offered the flask to Bethel. Bethel did likewise, then offered the flask to Rainy.

"I don't use spirits—besides, they're illegal," Rainy said, fixing Bethel with a stare.

Bethel giggled. "Well, hopefully not for long. Uncle Gunther says that given the poor economic condition of this country, they'll have to repeal Prohibition and give folks something to live for."

"They could live for God," Rainy suggested.

Bethel's amusement faded. "What fun would that be? All those stuffy rules and dour Sunday faces. I would definitely need a drink then."

Duncan interceded before the conversation could turn ugly. "So what's the news from Albuquerque?"

Chester stirred his coffee and shrugged. "Not much that would interest anyone. I will say this, however. I had an opportunity to ride up here with one of the railroad officials. It seems those mysterious thefts of artifacts have stopped. It's been ... what did he say, dear?" He looked to Bethel. "Over a month now, right?" She nodded and sipped at her coffee. Chester smiled and looked at Rainy. "About the time you went on vacation the whole thing seemed to stop."

Rainy knew he was goading her. She knew he wanted her to feel uncomfortable. Her eyes narrowed as she met his smug expression. "Well, thank the Lord they've stopped. The Indians have suffered enough without someone stealing away important pieces of their heritage."

"The timing's strange, don't you think?" Chester questioned.

Rainy felt her stomach churn. She raised her napkin to her lips and dabbed lightly, trying hard to think of what she should say or do.

Duncan, however, came to her rescue. "Speaking of timing, it's getting late, Driscoll. I'm afraid I have a tour to drive tomorrow and Miss

Gordon also has a tour to direct. You'll have to excuse us."

Rainy could have kissed Duncan for his smooth way of dealing with Chester. He didn't need to make a scene or even acknowledge Chester's question. He merely dismissed the man.

"But we haven't even had time for dessert," Bethel said, sounding like a disappointed child.

"I'm afraid Duncan is absolutely right. I need to get ready for tomorrow. Good evening," Rainy said without meeting the expression of either Bethel or Chester. Instead, she turned to Duncan and accepted his help as she rose from her chair.

After he paid the bill, Duncan held fast to her hand, showing no sign that he desired to turn her loose. They were nearly halfway back to the Plaza before either one spoke.

"I'm sorry for the way he acted toward you," Duncan began.

"Is it true that the thefts stopped when Sonny and I were on vacation?" Rainy asked, needing to know the truth.

"They stopped after the oil paintings were taken in Taos. There haven't been any further reports of missing articles."

Rainy trembled, but this time it wasn't from Duncan's touch—it was from the fear of the obvious connection. "So will I be arrested for the thefts?"

Duncan stopped and turned her toward him. He held on to her shoulders and gazed intently into her eyes. "You aren't guilty of stealing those articles, so you have no reason to fear being arrested."

"Do you really believe that?" Rainy prayed it was true—that he truly knew her to be innocent, but her fears from the past were creeping in to haunt her.

Duncan reached up and gently touched her cheek. "I believe in you."

*R*ainy closed her eyes and leaned back into the front passenger seat of the courier car. She'd given all the regular information needed for the tour and found her dudes were barely paying attention to what she had to say. They were much too caught up with comments and concerns about the economy and the conditions of the world.

"Germany is suffering," one man began. "I have a friend who lives there. He said that banks are failing there and in Austria. Industry is suffering, and their only hope is to find some way to stabilize the economy. It's worse there than here."

Another man chimed in. "I've heard great things about that man Hitler. I heard that he blames the bankers—most of them Jews, you know. He feels they've been reckless in their business dealings. They're all in cahoots with the Bolsheviks, as I hear it."

"How can they be Bolsheviks and bankers at the same time?" the first man questioned.

"Don't be foolish; it's all a plot for world domination. Bolshevism is just a smoke screen. The Jews are using Bolshevism to hide their real intent and confuse things."

"And what is their real intent?"

Rainy couldn't help but wonder at this as well. She'd heard a great deal of anti-Jewish sentiment among the wealthy tourists who traveled with the Detours, though she had never understood the great disdain such people held for the Jews. She found herself turning around to view the two men. They gave her perusal no consideration whatsoever.

The heavier of the two men shrugged and bore an expression that suggested the answer was elementary in nature. "World domination through economic control, of course. Look at all the properties that are being foreclosed upon. The bankers are getting wealthy, even if they claim the banks themselves are failing."

"So you believe this man Hitler has all the answers for Germany?"

"He seems to have a clear understanding of what the Jews are up to—not that others haven't spoken of the same thing. In fact, I believe Hindenburg knows the truth as well, but he doesn't have the power to do anything about it. Hitler shows strength as well as courage. That alone will allow him an edge in overcoming the problem. He seems to speak for the people of Germany."

"We could sure use a man like that here in America. Hoover is a waste in the office of president."

The man nodded in agreement, but his wife reached out and patted his arm. "Now, dear, must we talk politics? This is our vacation. The first we've taken this year."

The man smiled at his wife and nodded. "But of course, you're right." He gave the other man an apologetic nod. "Forgive me if I conclude my thoughts."

The first man nodded and turned to his own wife. "So where would you like to dine tonight?"

Rainy turned back to watch the road and ignored their chatter about places to eat in Santa Fe. She couldn't help but wonder if the problems in the world would escalate to make matters in the U.S. even worse. Maybe the economy would be better in Scotland. After all, farms were very self-sufficient. Her mother and father were beginning to talk with great anticipation about the move. Rainy wanted to get caught up in their excitement, but it was difficult. She still hadn't decided what she would do.

Ever since Duncan had rescued her from Chester's accusing comments, Rainy had felt more certain of her feelings for him. He said he believed in her. He didn't think she'd taken the artifacts or the oils. He had touched her with such tenderness and said that he cared—and not because he was doing a job for Sonny.

Rainy touched her hand to her cheek. Her original longing to know Duncan better resurfaced with the memory of that night. Phillip Vance seemed a distant memory. Apparently Chester had been right on that account. Phillip seemed only to have toyed with her affections. She knew from the Driscolls that Phillip had been in town for over a week now, and still he had done nothing to get in touch with her.

Sonny maneuvered the car into a spot directly in front of La Fonda. Rainy watched him help the passengers from the car, even as she gathered her things. She needed to talk to Sonny and clear the air between them, but she didn't know what to say. Her own confusion over the problems with the Indian thefts had caused her to take out her anger on him. He was entitled to his own life and she had made such an ugly scene about it.

"Can we talk when you get back from the garage?"

Sonny seemed genuinely surprised at her question. "Why, sure. You mean at the boardinghouse?"

Rainy nodded. "I'll take our things and walk on over now. I'll wait for you there."

She walked the short distance from La Fonda to Mrs. Rivera's, all the while thinking of how silly she'd been to put Sonny at arm's length. *I'm trying to protect myself,* she reasoned. *I'm trying to keep the world at a safe distance so that I won't get hurt. But instead, I'm hurt all that much more.*

Stepping up onto the porch of the boardinghouse, Rainy nearly fell off backward when Maryann came bursting out the front door.

"I've been positively dying for you to come home. You have to come see what arrived for you!" she declared, pulling Rainy toward the lobby. "You won't believe your eyes!"

Rainy walked into the welcoming cool of the house and found an enormous bouquet of red roses waiting for her on one of the front receiving tables.

"Look! Didn't I tell you?" the girl at her side commented. "We tried counting them and lost track after the first three dozen."

Rainy shook her head. "They're for me?"

"Yes, look at the card." The girl pulled Rainy to the table and pulled a card from the bouquet.

Rainy took hold of the card and read:

Rainy, I know I've been unforgivably delayed in corresponding, but please know you've never been far from my thoughts. Please have dinner with me at La Fonda tonight at 7:30. We have much to discuss about the future. I'm more certain than ever. Phillip

She folded the card and pushed it into the pocket of her skirt. "Well, I must say, he certainly knows how to get a girl's attention."

"I'll get one of the drivers to carry these up to your room," Maryann said with giddy delight. "They weigh a ton, and you wouldn't want to risk falling and breaking this lovely vase."

Rainy noted the exotic vase. Patterned in blues and purples, the Indian-styled piece had an opening of at least twelve inches to accommodate the massive bouquet.

Maryann sighed and leaned into Rainy. "He sure must be in love with you."

Rainy thought of the girl's words and frowned. Phillip Vance was a mystery to be sure, but Rainy seriously doubted that real love was a part of the situation. Still, the flowers were beautiful and definitely caught her attention. She would join him for dinner and then maybe she'd have the chance to hear him explain his feelings.

"What if he proposes?" Maryann said, dancing around Rainy as a couple of the other couriers joined them.

"Is Rainy getting married?" one of them asked, nearly squealing the question.

"Oh, how exciting! Who are you marrying?"

"Phillip Vance, the movie star," Maryann declared.

Rainy shook her head. "I'm not marrying anyone. The flowers are from Phillip Vance—and no proposal came with them."

"But if he asks, you'll say yes, won't you?" the other courier questioned. She looked at Rainy with such an expression of anticipation that Rainy wanted to burst out laughing.

"He's not going to ask me to marry him," Rainy said matter-of-factly. She hoped her disinterested tone and firm resolve would silence the matter for good.

"But he might," Maryann murmured, delicately fingering one of the many roses.

The other girls nodded. "Yes," they said in unison. "He might."

Rainy felt a heaviness in her stomach. Maybe she should avoid dinner and just send Phillip a note explaining how she felt and why they were all wrong for each other. She could start with the fact that she loved God first and foremost and always would. Then she could ease into the fact that she didn't love Phillip—and probably never would.

———

Rainy waited for Sonny in the boardinghouse lobby for as long as she could. Hot and sweaty from her miserable day, she trudged upstairs carrying her bags—a driver behind her trying to balance the huge bouquet. Her room felt stifling, so Rainy quickly put the bags to one side and went to open the windows.

"Just put those flowers anywhere you can find a place to fit them," Rainy instructed.

"These must have cost a pretty penny," the driver said. Rainy turned from the window in time to see him create a spot for them on her tiny desk.

"Thanks, Joe. I really appreciate it. I expected Sonny to meet me after he took the car in, but he never showed up. Guess I'll catch up with him later, but in the meantime, I'm really grateful that you handled those for me."

"No problem, Rainy. And I wouldn't worry about Sonny. The garage manager was keeping all of today's drivers in for a meeting. He talked to the rest of us earlier."

"I see. Well, then, I guess I won't fret over it." She showed him out, then gathered her things in order to clean up.

After a long tepid bath, Rainy felt cooled down and much more capable of dealing with Phillip. She dressed carefully in a cotton dress of lemon yellow. Pale white flowers with tiny orange centers and lacy-leafed stems dotted the skirt of the dress.

Spending extra time, Rainy took the trouble to pin up her thick strawberry blond hair and fashion it into a stylish bun at the back of her head. She wanted to be cool as well as look attractive, yet she was determined to tell Phillip that this would be their last night together.

Her bath time had allowed time for reasonable thought and consideration of the problem. Phillip, while attractive and romantic, did not love God. In the past Rainy had put this aside, believing that it was possible that God had brought them together in order for her to lead him to salvation. But now that idea seemed silly. She knew from experience that it was much easier for her to be dragged down by someone who held no respect for God than for her to pull him up into an understanding of the Bible and God's laws. It wasn't that she couldn't share the hope of Jesus with Phillip, but she couldn't use that as a reason to see him romantically.

When Rainy had first seen the flowers and heard Maryann's excitement, she wondered seriously if her own excitement would emerge. She thought of Phillip and his gentle spirit, his kindness to her, and all that he offered. But instead of feeling something more intense, Rainy was very much aware of her lack of feeling. There was not even a glimmer of love or hope of a future that came to mind when she looked at the enormous bouquet. Phillip had been an interesting diversion, but in more ways than one, Rainy could see that he had interfered with her life in a way that could have proved to be most destructive. She needed to put an end to it tonight—to explain that his life and ways held little interest for her.

She prayed her motives would be pure. She didn't want her words to come across as sounding like punishment for Phillip's inconsiderate attitude. He needed to understand that the absence of God in his life was the true reason that she couldn't allow herself to fall in love with him. Of course, there was also Duncan.

Rainy's feelings for Duncan were stronger than ever. She tried not to focus on whether or not Duncan would return her feelings and be the man God ordained for her husband. But it was hard. Not only that, but Duncan had seen her reaction to Phillip. He might have been deeply wounded by her attitude. Her actions reminded her of something that had happened when she'd been a child. They'd had a family dog—Shep. He was more loyal than most dogs, and Rainy had loved him with all her heart. Then one day her father brought home a stray puppy. Rainy immediately gave her time and attention to the pup and completely abandoned Shep. A few weeks later the pup ran off leaving Rainy heartbroken, but Shep, ever faithful, was there to console her and lick away her tears.

She smiled at the memory. Duncan certainly wasn't to be equated with Shep, but Rainy's actions with Phillip had been the same as when that pup had come into her life. The new, exciting adventure of meeting and spending time with a movie star, a wealthy man who could give her any material thing, had temporarily distracted her. But as Rainy had told Duncan that night, a veil had been lifted. She was growing up spiritually and realized that trusting God meant something more than just saying the words. She had to live it by her actions.

Making her way to the dining room at La Fonda, Rainy gave a quick glance about the room for Phillip. It was exactly seven-thirty—he should be here. She spotted him standing by the entry. Beside him were several well-dressed men and women. Phillip was the center of attention, as usual.

Rainy made her way to the gathering, confident that these were more of his fans and that soon they could break away to discuss their relationship. She smiled when Phillip looked her way. He returned her smile and gave her an appreciative nod.

"You look wonderful," he whispered as he broke away from the crowd to take hold of her hand. "Come join us. We were just about to be seated."

Rainy tried not to look confused. "I thought it would be just you and me."

"I'm sorry," he said, looking rather chagrined. "These are some writer friends of Jennetta's. They want to talk about writing for movies and I couldn't send them away."

Rainy could think of nothing to say, so she only nodded and allowed Phillip to guide her as their table was finally ready.

Sitting beside Phillip and listening to the comments made by the ever growing party of people, Rainy felt very stupid for ever imagining that she might hold a special and solitary interest in Phillip Vance's life. She also felt more confident of her decision.

Phillip was a people pleaser. He thrived on attention and basked in the praise and devotion of his fans. Beyond that, he was eager to make himself invaluable to others, just as he was doing tonight.

"Phillip, darling, you don't mind if we squeeze in two more, do you?"

It was Jennetta, dressed in a skimpy black beaded gown that seemed overly dramatic for a quiet evening in Santa Fe.

The men quickly rose, but it was Phillip who spoke. "Of course we don't mind. We'll simply scoot in."

The waiter brought two more chairs while Jennetta took the seat on Phillip's left. Obviously he had reserved it for her, as the group surrounding them had never even attempted to take this place for themselves. Rainy felt more than a little irritation. First there had been no word from Phillip, and then he finally tried to make amends by sending her five dozen roses and inviting her to dinner—a dinner that quickly turned into a party for anyone and everyone who had an interest in Phillip Vance and the movies.

"I fail to see why it should be a problem to allow the true language of the people to be portrayed in a film," one balding man said as he leaned closer to Jennetta.

Phillip nodded. "The average person thinks nothing of swearing, but the censors will not allow that. They consider it crude and vulgar. Never mind that it is commonplace."

"But it isn't commonplace," Rainy declared. "At least not in my world."

Everyone turned their attention to her, and Rainy instantly wished she'd thought before speaking. Shifting uncomfortably, she looked to Phillip and added, "I'm sure swearing would hurt your audience numbers."

Phillip shook his head. "But must we sacrifice realism because of an oversensitive minority?"

"What makes you so sure only a minority would be offended by swearing and vulgar language?" she asked.

"Because I hear it all the time. From the common dock worker to the railroad worker to the newspaperman who interviews me to the calf-eyed schoolgirls who follow me around town, it's the common language of a people who are in despair and who find the world difficult to endure."

"So why not offer them hope instead of cursing?"

"I suppose you mean offer them God and religion."

Rainy noticed that their conversation held the attention of everyone else at the table. "Offer them God, yes. Offer them an understanding of what God desires for them—of His love for them. Offer them a way out of their despair."

"I find the entire matter of God to be a worthless pursuit," the balding man declared.

"Oh, well said, Samuel," a black-haired woman sitting opposite Phillip agreed. "I grew up in a positively hideous home where religious nonsense and piety were all the rage. My father wouldn't drink liquor, even when it was legal, and he certainly saw no use for entertainment and parties. Every Sunday," she said, leaning close as if to share a great secret, "we were all forced to attend church and then to spend the rest of the day fasting and praying for forgiveness. It was awful. As a child I would sneak out of the room on the pretense of relieving myself and would make a fast run to the kitchen, where Cook always kept me something to snack on. She always knew I would be coming and she'd have it all ready for me. It was wonderful fun to fool them all."

Rainy eyed the woman momentarily and was about to speak when Jennetta added her thoughts. "I find that a need for religiosity is stifling to the mind." The group rapidly agreed with her. "I couldn't work in my writing if I was constrained by the limitations demanded by the Christian faith. I'm sure I'm seen as the worst of sinners by our Miss Gordon here, but in truth, her beliefs will never allow her to understand the mind and soul of a true artist."

A chorus of murmured affirmation rose up from the gathering. Rainy ignored it and spoke out. "I suppose I do understand what you're saying, Mrs. Blythe. You write from the emptiness and darkness that consumes your soul. You write of despair and of hopelessness and lace it with platitudes of ambition and call it art. Because, I believe, the emptiness you feel comes from your alienation from God, then yes, a relationship with God would drastically alter and limit your art."

"I would expect that reply from the uneducated masses," a man with a pencil-thin mustache threw in.

Rainy got to her feet, unable to contain her temper if she remained in the pompous group for even a moment longer. "Sir, may I inquire as to your educational background?" she asked.

The man lifted his chin and stared down his long thin nose at Rainy. "I have a degree in literature from the University of New York." His companions nodded as if to confirm this truth.

"Anything else?" Rainy asked, knowing she shouldn't be goading the man.

"That's entirely enough," the man responded.

She nodded. "Well, given your response about uneducated masses, I presumed you might lay claim to something more. As for myself—just so that you understand I do not speak as one of the uneducated masses—I hold a bachelor's degree in history and one in archaeology. Furthermore, I hold a master's degree in history and speak four languages fluently." Most of the group straightened in unison, as if stunned by Rainy's declaration. Only Phillip and Jennetta seemed unconcerned.

"Sit down, Rainy dear. Our waiter is coming and we'll need to place our orders."

Rainy shook her head. "No, thank you, Phillip. I believe I've had my fill of this evening."

She left without another word, not surprised that Phillip remained with his friends. Making her way outside, Rainy could only shake her head at her own foolish thoughts that she might have ever fit into Phillip Vance's world.

"You look like a woman with a purpose," Sonny declared as he came alongside Rainy.

"My purpose is to get away from this place as fast and far as I can," Rainy replied, stopping her stride to take in the sad-eyed gaze of her twin. She immediately felt horrible for the anger she'd held against him. "We should talk," she said softly.

"I'd like that very much. I'm sorry about not meeting you at the boardinghouse. We had a meeting."

She nodded. "Yes, Joe told me." She motioned to one of the Plaza benches. "Why don't we go over there and sit down?"

Sonny smiled and followed her to the bench. They sat down, and Rainy breathed deeply, enjoying the cool evening air. "It was so hot at the cliff dwellings today. I'm glad Santa Fe is cooler."

Sonny yawned and leaned back against the bench. "Me too. Makes sleeping a whole lot easier."

Rainy knew it was silly to continue with mindless chitchat. "I want to clear the air between us. I know for these last few weeks we've just tolerated each other and, Sonny, I'm sorry. I should never have lost my temper when you told me about Scotland. I just panicked. I thought of all of you going away, and I didn't think of how it might make you feel for me to respond in such a manner. Please forgive me."

"You know I do," Sonny said gently. "But you really have misunderstood the entire matter."

Rainy nodded. "Then please explain and I'll hear you out."

"I did make plans without consulting you. Actually, the plans fell into place without me having much time to really consult anyone—anyone but God, that is. It's true that I plan to leave by the end of summer, but I'm not going with Mom and Dad. I plan to go to California first and then to Alaska. I'm going to work for the government on a survey party with my friends. I tried to explain this several times, but we always got into other matters or someone came to interrupt us or . . ."

"Or I got mad," Rainy said, stunned by her brother's news. At least when she'd thought of him going with their parents to Scotland, there was the possibility of her going along as well. "I'm happy for you, Sonny, but I'm also upset over the matter. You'll be miles and miles away from all of us—especially if I go to Scotland with Mom and Dad."

"I know. I've already thought a lot about that. I just feel it's the culmination of a lifelong dream. You know how I love geology. This is the perfect job for me."

Rainy took hold of his hand and patted it. "Of course it is. You'd be silly not to go. Besides, we're both a bit old to still be clinging to Mother's apron strings. I guess our homelife was just such a joy that leaving permanently never seemed like a very good idea."

"But what about you? I'll obviously be breaking up our Detour team. What will you do? Will you go to Scotland with Mom and Dad?"

Rainy dropped her hold and looked out across the Plaza. "I don't know. I've prayed and asked God to show me what the future holds—what I'm supposed to do—and I feel that He's only giving me silence in return."

"Maybe you aren't really listening," Sonny suggested.

Rainy looked at her brother and saw the compassion in his eyes. "Maybe I'm not, but I truly want to. I want to put my selfish desires aside and really heed God in this matter."

"If that's the case, Rainy, God will honor your attempt and guide you. You have to trust that to be true."

"I know."

"So what did you do about Phillip Vance?" Sonny asked, changing the subject. "I heard about the flowers. Did you have dinner with him tonight? Did he propose as Maryann hinted he might do?"

Rainy laughed. "Maryann is a hopeless romantic. She had me dressed and down the aisle before I could even consider what was happening. But to answer your question, yes, I joined him and about ten other people for dinner. I thought the dinner would be just between Phillip and me. I had planned to tell him that I couldn't see him anymore—that there was no future for us because he had no room for God in his life."

"I see. So you didn't get a chance to tell him because of the other people?"

Rainy nodded. "But I did make a statement. I'm afraid I wasn't a very good witness. I got angry and spouted off after one of the men implied that my faith in God was somehow related to my being uneducated. I told them all just exactly how well educated I truly was, then stormed out of there like a child who hadn't gotten her own way. I feel ashamed and yet at the same time I can't bring myself to go back and apologize."

"Maybe there's no need. That prideful bunch probably got no more than they deserved."

"Maybe so," Rainy said sadly, "but it was my desire to show them the love of Jesus instead of revealing my wounded pride."

"I'd imagine God understands the desire of your heart. He put it there, after all. Cheer up, Rainy. I'm sure it will be all right. Sometimes people like that won't listen to anything else."

"Yes, but my anger was an issue of pride," Rainy admitted. "All of my problems have stemmed from issues of pride. Being falsely accused of stealing, dealing with Duncan and Phillip, getting mad at you. It's just a case of prideful nature, and I must learn to control it. Otherwise, I fear that I'll end up destroying more than I manage to mend or rebuild."

Sonny chuckled softly. "Everything is changing for us. I'm going to miss these talks."

"I know some folks think it strange that a brother and sister should be so close, but, Sonny, you've always been there for me. When my girlfriends grew bored with me and left for more exciting companions, you were there to comfort me and keep me from feeling too sorry for myself."

She sighed and shifted just enough to see him better. The street-lights gave off enough of a glow to reveal the compassion in her brother's expression.

"I will always cherish what we have. You and Mom and Dad mean the world to me," Rainy declared. "I couldn't have asked for a better family, and even now that you're going so far away, I know we'll still be a family. That won't change. We'll have our memories, but we'll also have the liberty and freedom to be the individuals that God intended us to be. Sooner or later, I'll have a family of my own—you'll probably do the same. Together we'll blend that group to give Mom and Dad grandchildren, and the cycle will go on and on. I know now that I'm not losing anything—I'm gaining a great deal."

"I'm glad you feel that way," Sonny said, giving her a smile. "Because I feel that way too."

Rainy nodded knowingly. She sensed his deep commitment to her, while at the same time she knew it was well past time for them both to break from the nest and fly.

"I'll visit you in Alaska," she said, tears coming to her eyes.

"And I'll visit you wherever you end up," he said, laughing. "Even if you manage to get yourself on the moon. And given your determina-tion—that wouldn't surprise me in the least."

The following morning Sonny came to Rainy with their assignment for the day. "We're doing an overnight trip to Taos," he told her as he shoved a strip of bacon into his mouth. He reached to the serving dish for more only to have Mrs. Rivera chide him to sit and eat like a normal human being.

Rainy pushed away from her half-eaten breakfast of bacon and eggs and smiled at her brother. "That should be easy enough. Quick tour of Puye and Santa Clara. Overnight in Taos and back to La Fonda tomorrow, with the rest of the day to ourselves."

Sonny nodded. "Jennetta Blythe and Phillip Vance are going to be our passengers." He quickly finished the remaining bacon.

Rainy felt the wind go out of her. "Them? Again?" She got to her feet and motioned to Sonny. Grabbing her hat, she paused by the door only long enough to pick up her bag and hand it to Sonny. Walking to La Fonda, Rainy couldn't help but voice her concerns again. "Why are they taking this trip again?"

"I don't know, but that's not all. They're bringing a bunch of their obnoxious friends along as well."

Rainy shook her head. "I don't know why they do this. For the money they waste on these Detour trips they could buy a car and take themselves."

"I know. I thought it kind of crazy too. I thought of giving them over to Duncan and his courier, since they're making a trip to Taos as well, but they're full up."

Rainy could hardly believe that she was going to have to spend the next twenty-four hours dealing with those people. What was God up to? Why would He allow her to be forced into the company of Phillip and his sister when they and their friends so clearly despised her values?

"Look, the car's being serviced. I'll bring it around to the front in about an hour. We're supposed to be on our way by ten-thirty. That gives you plenty of time to take care of other things if you need."

"I'd like to take care of arranging another courier," Rainy admitted. "Maybe I'll talk to Mrs. Lehman. She might be able to get us off the hook."

"It's worth a try," Sonny replied.

Rainy walked into the hotel lobby and went in search of Mrs. Lehman. But the meeting gave her no reprieve. The other couriers were already on the road, nine o'clock having been their starting time. Only one other team was left in-house besides Rainy and Sonny, and they were heading to Gallup to pick up some passengers who had requested a customized tour to the Grand Canyon.

"But Sonny and I could take that tour instead," Rainy protested.

"I'm sorry," Mrs. Lehman replied, "but you and Sonny were specifically requested for this tour. You know we like to meet the request of the touring dudes whenever we can."

"Yes, I realize that," Rainy replied, knowing at that moment that she had no recourse but to follow through with the trip.

Walking back across the lobby, Rainy spotted Jennetta Blythe. She fervently hoped she might make it outdoors without Jennetta seeing her. Rainy had no desire to even acknowledge the woman, much less suffer any conversation. Not that Jennetta ever seemed interested in talking with Rainy.

Jennetta surprised Rainy, however, by moving away from her friends to greet Rainy as though the animosity at the dinner table the night before had never happened.

"Hello, Miss Gordon. I suppose you know you'll be taking my party to Taos today?"

Rainy drew a deep breath. "Yes. Although I must say it surprises me. You took this very tour not so long ago."

"Yes, well, these are friends in from the East Coast. They've never had a chance to see the ruins," Jennetta replied. "I must say, however, the real reason I've stopped you is to applaud your efforts last night."

Rainy stared at her quizzically. "What do you mean?"

"Well, I was beginning to have serious doubts about you being a suitable wife for Phillip. You seemed so mousy and weak-willed, never standing up for yourself and such. Phillip's world demands a woman who is strong and capable—one who won't shrink away from challenges. Until last night, I thought you completely incapable of such fire and endurance. I'm ready to concede that I misjudged you. You very well may make Phillip the perfect wife. It won't be easy for you to stand up to the crowds and parties required of Phillip, but at least I know you're made of something more than I previously thought."

Rainy stood speechless as Jennetta walked back to her friends. She supposed Jennetta somehow believed herself to have paid Rainy a compliment, but Rainy certainly didn't see it that way.

How dare she assume that I plan to marry Phillip. What in the world has he said to her to bring her to such a conclusion? Rainy walked outside the hotel and paced the strip of sidewalk in front.

Jennetta certainly didn't apologize for her attitude last night. In fact, she apparently saw nothing wrong with the way she and her friends acted, Rainy seethed. *They insult me and think nothing of it—certainly not enough to warrant an apology.*

Then, as if that weren't bad enough, Jennetta presumes upon the kind of life I would have if I married her brother. She has it all figured out in her mind. She probably has the wedding planned and the caterers hired and . . . Rainy forced herself to calm down. She drew a deep breath and leaned back against the cool stone wall.

Why am I so upset? Those people have proven themselves to be rude and insensitive. They have their world and ways and I have mine. The two do not mix, but I already knew that. So why should I be so upset just because Jennetta wants to presume upon a relationship that will never be?

Rainy smoothed down her purple velvet tunic and straightened her silver concha belt. Calm was gradually returning. *I'm just being silly. I'll find a chance to talk to Phillip later, and then I'll set everything straight.*

An hour later they were on their way north. Phillip had tried briefly to get Rainy away from the crowd, but she refused. She also encouraged the seating so that Phillip would be at the far back and she'd be free of him during the trip. She wasn't about to try to explain herself to him in this crowd.

They left a trail of dust behind them as they headed out across the desert land. Rainy talked of the history of the area, giving her standard speech. She spoke of the Indians who had lived in the area for hundreds and hundreds of years, and while her guests didn't interrupt or try to talk over her, Rainy could see they were bored and indifferent.

They stopped first at the Santa Clara Pueblo, where the Tewas, a gentle Indian people, were going about their affairs. Rainy explained that for the brief visit they should be mindful of their manners. Rainy remembered that it hadn't been so long ago that one of the other tours had a mishap that found some of the dudes climbing on the pueblos. Rainy quickly explained the houses were off limits and rounded her people up after only fifteen minutes. Not long afterward they stopped for lunch and exploration at the Puye Cliff Dwellings, and after a couple of hours there they were on their way once again.

The heat of the day made Rainy wish she could wear a lightweight cotton blouse instead of her tunic. Even Sonny had it better, as his shirt was cotton and his white hat tended to reflect the sun rather than absorb it. She fanned herself lightly as the temperature inside the black Cadillac climbed.

By the time they pulled into Taos, Jennetta was already instructing her friends about their evening.

"Have a nice cold bath first and then we can gather for dinner. I know some marvelous places to eat, and we can get anything we want to drink," she advised. "The only place in town that doesn't sell some form of liquor is the church." Her friends laughed and commented on the sensibility of the town ignoring the laws that robbed them of a pleasant time.

Rainy helped Sonny to pull out the luggage and recognized Phillip's touch the moment he reached out to tap her shoulder. She looked up and met his somber expression.

"Are you angry with me?" His tone sounded concerned.

"I don't really have the time to discuss it right now," Rainy said softly, almost shyly. It was almost like the first day they'd met—all awkward and uneven, not quite knowing how to treat the situation. She didn't want to say things in front of Sonny or the others who still lingered near the car. Humiliating Phillip wasn't her desire. "We could talk later this evening."

"I'm afraid Jennetta has the night completely planned out. Could we meet at breakfast?"

Rainy shook her head. "Don't worry about it. It really isn't that important. I'll catch up with you sometime." She reached in to pull out the suitcase she'd often seen Jennetta carry. It felt incredibly light. In fact, if Rainy didn't know better, she would have thought it was empty.

"Please don't be angry with me," Phillip pleaded. "I didn't mean for last night to turn ugly. I was very upset that you got hurt."

Rainy put the case on the ground and looked into Phillip's warm expression. "You could have been more supportive," she said, though she had not intended to be drawn into a conversation.

"I know and I'm sorry."

Rainy nodded. "You're forgiven. I hope you have a wonderful time this evening."

"Come with us."

Rainy saw Sonny give her a raised eyebrow, but he remained silent as he pulled the last of the bags from the car. "I'm busy, Phillip. You know how it is. Now if you'll excuse me, I have to make sure everyone got checked in without any trouble."

She left him looking rather dumbstruck. Maybe he thought this was just a game she was playing, but Rainy had little interest in such forms of entertainment. A game was more Jennetta's speed. Jennetta—who was already planning for Rainy and Phillip to marry.

Jennetta.

Rainy's thoughts went back to the empty suitcase. Was it really empty, and if so, why? The idea of the missing artifacts came to mind. Rainy felt her breath catch in the back of her throat. She stopped mid-step and looked back through the doorway at the touring car. She felt as if she held all the clues to a great mystery, but they were out of order and, as such, made no sense.

"Hello, Rainy."

She whirled around to find Duncan. "What are you doing here?"

He smiled and it seemed to light up his whole face. His wavy black hair looked windblown and his dark eyes seemed to assess her with extreme interest.

"I had a tour," he explained. "I wondered if you'd like to join me for dinner tonight. My mother is a great cook, and she's promised wonderful beef roast and fresh bread."

Rainy lost her thoughts of Jennetta and nodded. "That sounds wonderful. Do I have time to freshen up?"

He grinned. "You look fresh enough, but of course. Dinner isn't for another hour."

Sonny trudged into the lobby with the last of the luggage. Duncan immediately offered his help, but Sonny waved him off.

"I've got these things stacked just so," Sonny said. "I'm going to deliver them, take a bath, and go to bed. I'm bushed."

Sonny mastered the stairs in short order, and only after he'd disappeared from sight did Rainy turn her attention back to Duncan. Before she could speak, however, a woman's shrill laughter filled the air. Phillip Vance came in from the street with a woman on each arm. Both of his companions wore heavy makeup and tight dresses that seemed to accentuate their every curve. Phillip leaned first one way and then the other as the women whispered in his ears. He laughed at their comments, then ushered the women upstairs.

Rainy had no idea where they were headed or why. The entire scene just made her glad she had determined to remove herself from Phillip's influence. Looking to Duncan, she found him with an expression that suggested sympathy.

"Oh, Duncan. Why can't more men be like you?"

————

Duncan watched Rainy with intense interest as his mother asked her question after question about her work for the touring company.

"I've loved being able to share history with people who generally have no clue about the Southwest. The tourists, or 'dudes,' as we call them, often come out here with this image of the Wild West and of Indians and cowboys shooting it out over the next hill. I've heard women worry over having the windows of the cars down for fear an Indian arrow might come through and kill them all."

"Oh my," Joanna Hartford declared. "You would think they would know better."

Rainy smiled. "You would think so, but I'm always amazed at the general lack of knowledge and understanding. One woman tourist we had stood in the midst of several Indian children and asked me if they would bite her if she were to stroke their black hair." Rainy's facial expression changed to one that showed sadness over the memory. "I told the woman they were children, not wild animals, and she reprimanded me, saying that everyone with even the tiniest bit of education knew they were savages."

Duncan's father nodded. "I've encountered that attitude many a time. It's the same mentality that says the Indian cannot be saved for eternity because they have no soul."

Rainy shook her head. "How can people be so blind? I truly had hoped that the Detours would help people better understand the Indians. I have friendships that span across several tribes and those have been hard made—simply because of attitudes like that."

"Father has endured the same problems gaining the trust of the Indians as he works to share his faith with them," Duncan threw in.

"I admire what you do here," Rainy said, pushing around a piece of roast with her fork, "but do you ever feel it's much too little—too late?"

Lamont Hartford laughed in a deep hearty manner. Duncan knew his father had been asked this question many a time. He watched his father's dark eyes narrow slightly as he sobered. "Do you believe," he asked, "that God's timing is ever too late?"

Rainy smiled. "I've wondered that very thing from time to time, but I don't really think His timing is ever too late." She glanced at Duncan, her cheeks reddening slightly. Duncan immediately thought of her desire for a husband and family. "I often feel that God is delayed in answering my prayers," she continued, "but from my own upbringing and growing faith, I know that isn't the case. Sometimes, however, I wish He would hurry things along for my sake."

Duncan's father smiled and nodded. "I've wished it often myself. I can't blame you for your desires, but I would encourage you to trust that He has your best interest in mind."

––––––

The weeks passed by and then a month and then nearly two, and still Duncan found himself remembering the details of the dinner at his parents' house. Rainy had come dressed in a simple dress of pale lavender. She'd pinned her hair up and Duncan thought it looked very fetching, but he longed to see it down, flowing across her shoulders to her waist. Rainy had treated his parents as though she'd known them for years.

After he'd returned home from walking Rainy to her hotel, Duncan's mother had commented that Rainy seemed to be a very special young woman and that God clearly had His mark on her. Duncan's father had also noted his complete approval of such company for Duncan. Both of his parents encouraged Duncan to share his feelings about Rainy, but he wasn't yet ready to speak on the matter.

Now, as the summer months melted away, Duncan felt a sense of frustration in that he hadn't seen much of Rainy. She and Sonny had been quite caught up with their courier duties, and rumor had it that both planned to resign their positions at the end of the month. Duncan worried that Rainy planned to move to Scotland with her parents. He wanted very much to talk to her and let her know his feelings, but it seemed they were never in Santa Fe together. Today he'd been told over the lunch hour that Rainy would be in town that night. She was to have the next day off and Duncan decided he would use the time to his advantage.

He knocked on the front door of Rainy's boardinghouse and waited, with card in hand. He had decided he would leave an invitation for Rainy to join him for dinner. He knew her routine would bring her home before she headed off for supper. Rainy had mentioned more than once that she absolutely had to wash off the day's dust before sitting down to enjoy a meal.

"Sí?" the heavyset Mexican woman who answered the door questioned.

"I'd like to leave this note for Rainy Gordon. Would you please see that she gets it?"

The woman nodded and took the envelope. "You are Mr. Vance, the movie star who sent the flowers?" Her words stabbed at Duncan even while her smile stretched from ear to ear.

"No, I'm not Mr. Vance. I'm Duncan Hartford. We work together—sort of."

The woman's smile faded. "Sí, I will give her the letter."

"Thank you." Duncan desired nothing more than to get away from the woman and avoid any more questions. He tried to console himself with the fact that at least Phillip hadn't come calling here at the boardinghouse—at least Duncan figured he hadn't. Wouldn't the woman have known he wasn't Vance otherwise? Still, just the thought of her delighted expression when she thought he was Vance gave Duncan cause for worry.

Hours later, Duncan was not at all pleased to find himself once again face-to-face with Mr. Richland from the Office of Indian Affairs. The matter of stolen artifacts was definitely not the kind of thing he wanted to give his attention to when the supper hour was so close at hand and visions of Rainy in her lavender dress kept coming to mind. No, he'd much rather go find Rainy and share a meal than sit here and listen to Richland tell him how guilty the Gordons were.

"Three important brass statues disappeared from Taos while the Gordons were there with their tourists," Richland began.

"But the time you've outlined proved to have other tours there as well. My tour group was there and so was at least one other group that I know of," Duncan offered. "Could have been more."

"Be that as it may, there were no thefts for over two months—including the two weeks Miss Gordon was on vacation."

"So you're still determined to blame the Gordons for this?"

Richland looked down his nose at Duncan. His expression seemed pinched, almost pained. "I'm determined to arrest the guilty parties and put a stop to this nonsense. The other driver and courier we were considering prior to this have both resigned and gone elsewhere to work. The Gordons remain, and now the stealing has begun again."

Duncan had hoped Richland's recent lack of communication meant that the matter was resolved or at least put aside for lack of evidence, but he supposed he should have known that the problem was not resolved since he was still driving for the Detours. "As I mentioned to you before, you might want also to consider the fact that in each of the tours where articles have disappeared over the last few months, the Detour passengers in the Gordons' care have been the same. Or they have been connected in some way."

"We considered it but find that it's not relevant."

Duncan pushed down his anger. "Of course it's relevant. You have chosen to blame the Gordons because they had the opportunity to perform the thefts. I'm saying they weren't the only ones who have had the opportunity. You can hardly rush in accusing and arresting with nothing more than this."

"I think perhaps you've gotten too close to this, Mr. Hartford. You don't seem to be willing to look at the facts. Perhaps your usefulness has reached its limits."

"I never set out to be a part of this to begin with. You came to me. The Gordons are my friends, and I won't see them falsely accused." Duncan raised his hand. "Hear me out. I've seen some strange things, things that suggest that perhaps Jennetta Blythe and her brother, Phillip Vance, are to blame for the disappearance of the artifacts."

Richland leaned forward. "Why do you say this?"

"I saw Jennetta showing off a piece that very well could have been one of the ceremonial flutes. I couldn't get a good look at the item, however. Then I overheard Phillip Vance comment on the original oils he took back to Los Angeles. It seems very likely that the missing Taos paintings could be the very oils to which he was referring."

Richland suddenly looked interested. Leaning back in his chair, he rubbed his chin. "All right. So let's say that's a possibility. What do you suggest we do about it? You can hardly expect me to rush ahead and have Phillip Vance arrested. The man is famous. It would be in all the newspapers before we could even determine if the paintings were the ones we were looking for. We have been good about cooperating with the various companies involved to keep this quiet. Charging Vance would eliminate any hope of continuing that silence."

"I realize that," Duncan admitted. "That's why I propose to set a trap for them. I've talked to my superiors here, and they have agreed to cooperate. I suggest I talk privately with Jennetta Blythe. I'll talk to her brother as well if he's in town. I will tell them that I have a variety of articles here at the museum that I would be willing to sell to the highest bidder. I could even make something up about the history of the pieces and such."

"The museum would put actual artifacts at risk?"

"No, the pieces would be insignificant pieces made to look like the real thing. I can replicate them well enough that Mr. Vance and his sister won't be any wiser. If they take the bait, then you can let the charade play out. I'll sell them the pieces and you can arrest them with the items in hand."

Richland shook his head. "But that wouldn't work. The pieces wouldn't be authentic, and proving the intent to purchase stolen goods would be difficult. They could just as easily say that they knew the pieces were of no significance and that you had assured them they were legally for sale—perhaps even out of your own private collection. No, if you can get the museum to agree to put genuine artifacts at risk, then perhaps it might work, but otherwise I cannot agree to this."

"But you have to admit that these circumstances do raise questions. When I was with the Gordons, I watched them every step of the way—I barely slept in order to keep a continuous eye on them. Jennetta Blythe and her brother have had every opportunity to slip around unnoticed. If found in areas where they shouldn't be, they could easily have feigned ignorance or being lost. I think the situation is such that you should have someone follow them and keep track of their activities."

"Perhaps you're right. Maybe I'll take you off of watching the Gordons and have you watch this Blythe woman instead."

Duncan breathed a sigh of relief. At least Richland was being reasonable about the matter. With his eyes narrowed, Richland studied Duncan a moment in silence, then nodded. "Go ahead and set your trap. Approach them if you can get the museum to allow you to use real artifacts. I'll get someone to watch them and see what they do. You send word to me as soon as you have word from them one way or another."

"Of course," Duncan said, getting to his feet as Mr. Richland did likewise. "I can't help but believe we're on to something here. I wouldn't have suggested it otherwise."

"I hope, for your sake, you're right. I would hate to be made the laughingstock of New Mexico. It wouldn't sit well with me, Mr. Hartford."

"Nor with me."

As soon as Richland departed, Duncan immediately went to his superiors. It took some convincing, but they finally agreed that Duncan could offer three pieces of museum art. One was an intricately detailed squash blossom necklace. Another piece was a wooden statuette of the Madonna and Child. Last was a beautifully designed silver tray. All three pieces were chosen because of their durability. Duncan knew that even if he had to go forward with some sort of exchange, the pieces would probably remain unharmed in the process.

With that matter taken care of, Duncan then began to consider how he might approach Jennetta and Phillip. He would have to handle the matter delicately. If they were to blame, then a bold approach might scare them off. But if Duncan was too subtle in the matter, they might not take the bait. It was also possible that if they were completely innocent, they might run to the legal authorities and expose the investigation, and that was the last thing he needed.

He thought of Rainy and wondered if she could get him an audience with either Jennetta or Phillip. Surely there was a way. He pulled on his coat and hat and set out to find Rainy. With any luck at all he could avoid explaining himself and still accomplish what was needed. Once he managed to prove Rainy's innocence, then maybe he could tell her about his feelings for her. Maybe he'd even let it be known that he'd worked hard to keep Richland from jumping to conclusions and having her arrested. If she knew how much he cared, how he'd tried to protect her from the law officials, how he'd even set aside the job he'd worked so hard to get, then maybe she'd understand how deeply he'd come to love her.

He smiled to himself. Yes, it would be best to wait until her name was cleared, and then they'd both be at liberty to reveal their true feelings.

He glanced at his watch and headed for La Fonda, knowing Rainy would probably be there checking her dudes in. If not, he'd head back to the boardinghouse and wait for her there.

The bustle of the crowd in the lobby of La Fonda made Duncan worry that he'd missed Rainy. He asked several of the couriers he knew if they had any idea where Rainy might be. No one had seen her since she'd dropped her travelers off at the registration desk nearly thirty minutes earlier.

Duncan was just about to give up when he rounded the corner to find a young couple in a tight embrace. They were kissing rather passionately, but all at once the woman pushed the man away. Duncan quickly ducked into the shadows.

The woman was Rainy and the man was Phillip Vance.

Y ou had no right to do that!" Rainy broke from Phillip's embrace and headed for the hotel door.

Phillip followed and took hold of her before she could rush outside. "I only kissed you."

Rainy nodded. "Yes, but you had no right."

"But you're the woman I love . . . the woman who loves me."

"Oh, half the world loves you, Phillip Vance," Rainy said, then stormed out of the hotel. She could hear Phillip hot on her heels. Once outside, Rainy turned around and met Phillip head on. "But I'm not one of them."

"Not one of what?"

"I'm not one of the masses who love you."

She could see his expression contort. It was almost as if he couldn't comprehend what she was saying. He'd been adored for so long, Rainy figured he probably had no idea how to deal with rejection.

"But I thought you would marry me. I thought it was understood. You seemed quite happy in my company."

Rainy sighed. How could she make it any clearer to him? "Phillip, we've hardly seen each other in the last two months. I presumed you'd put aside any interest in me because I didn't have so much as a letter in that time."

"I wanted to write, but I was busy with my work. Surely you can understand that. You travel all the time and know there is hardly a chance for lengthy communications."

"I think if I were of a mind to marry someone, I would have made the time for 'lengthy communications,' as you put it."

Phillip's expression contorted. "But I thought you cared for me. You seemed so happy in my company."

Rainy wanted to roll her eyes. How very self-centered this man could be. Even now he seemed to have no idea that more than once she'd been miserable sharing his companionship.

"To be honest, Phillip, at first I thought you were the type of man I could love. I'll admit I was definitely enamored by your movie-star charm and handsome features." She smiled and reached out to touch Phillip's arm. "But we're too different. I've had a lot of time to think about this. We're from two different worlds. You have a lifestyle I could never hope to be happy in."

"You don't know that," he protested.

"Oh, but I do." She squeezed his arm and felt her heart ache at the pleading in his voice. "At the end of August, I plan to go to Scotland with my parents." She hated the thought of leaving New Mexico, but there didn't seem to be a better answer.

"Please don't say these things, Rainy. Please."

Rainy began to walk toward the Plaza. She hoped that by doing so she might clear her mind. She hadn't been prepared for Phillip's emotions, and now she felt guilty for the way she'd just blurted out her thoughts. She supposed it was because, after weeks and weeks of not seeing him, she just wanted to get the message across before he was called back unexpectedly to California.

"Rainy, you're just afraid of the unknown," Phillip argued as he followed behind her.

"No, it isn't that. I can't make you understand this, but my first allegiance, my first love, is to God. You have no desire for God in your life, and we would always be at odds over this. I thought maybe you'd come into my life so that I could share the joy I have in Jesus Christ. But you want no part of that—in fact, you scoff at such things."

His expression grew more desperate. He took hold of her and shook her ever so gently. His blond hair fell forward, making him look more like a little boy pleading for his own way than a man in love. "But I would never deny you the right to worship your God in any fashion you desired."

"But my faith is the foundation of who I am. Everything about me—everything you claim to love—is a product of that foundation. So long as it was just a matter of 'my God' versus 'your god'—never to be 'our God'—we couldn't be happy."

"But I have no god . . . so there would be no conflict."

Rainy felt tears come to her eyes. "Oh, Phillip, you've made for yourself a god of fame and fortune. You have a god, but you simply refuse to understand the hold it has on you. I'm sorry, but I know deep in my heart I could never fully love or respect any man who didn't love and respect God first."

"Then it's truly over?"

Rainy smiled as a tear glistened in her eye. "It never really began, Phillip."

Phillip cast his gaze to the ground. "Then I suppose I should go."

"Yes," Rainy said softly. "I'm sure that would be best."

Phillip turned to go, then stopped. He looked around in true movie-star fashion, dropped his gaze to the ground, then slowly looked up. "I really do love you."

Rainy had a vague recollection of this scene from a movie, but instead of rushing into his arms as the screen heroine had done, she shook her head. "Good-bye, Phillip."

He walked away, leaving Rainy with her sorrow. She wasn't sad for what they might have had, but rather she was grieved by the fact that Phillip cared nothing for God. She walked along the Plaza, ignoring the couples that surrounded her, wishing she could sort through her feelings.

Should I have tried harder to help him understand, Lord? Should I have worked more diligently to bring him to an understanding of the Bible? The more she questioned her actions, the worse she felt. So much of her life was in turmoil, and this scene with Phillip, although necessary and overdue, was more than she wanted to deal with. Maybe he really did love her. Maybe it wasn't just a game to him.

She sat down on one of the benches not far from the obelisk that stood in honor of the fallen dead from various battles. The memorial only served to remind Rainy that life was fleeting and the choices you made were ones that often changed the course of your life forever. Would Scotland be one of those choices? Was there a strong, God-fearing Scotsman who waited in her future? Did she even care anymore?

Putting her hands to her face, Rainy tried to fight back her tears, but it was no use.

"Rainy?"

It was Duncan, but she couldn't bring herself to look at him. "What do you want?"

"Are you all right?"

She wiped at her tears and steadied her voice. "I'm fine."

"You don't look fine. You look like you're crying."

"Well, that's because I am crying."

Duncan sat down beside her. "Why?"

Rainy bit at her lower lip as a sob broke from her voice. "Because I've just hurt Phillip deeply. I didn't want to hurt him, but I did."

"How did you hurt him?"

She finally met his gaze. "I refused his proposal of marriage." She broke down and cried in earnest. "I just don't know what to do anymore."

Duncan surprised her by pulling her into his arms. "Just cry if it makes you feel better."

"But it doesn't. It doesn't help at all," she sobbed. "I'm confused and frustrated and I don't know what God wants of me. I try to do what I'm supposed to. I pray and get a peace about things, then something comes along to wreak havoc with my life." She cried even harder.

"Shhh, it'll be all right—you'll see."

"I try to make the right decisions, Duncan, really I do. But I'm no good at it. I just keep making the wrong decisions and everyone always thinks the worst of me."

"I don't understand. Who thinks badly of you?"

Rainy pulled away just enough to see his face. "Everyone. Just think of it. You yourself were concerned about whether or not I'd stolen Indian artifacts and oil paintings. When I worked at the university I was falsely accused of stealing artifacts too. It's like a bad dream repeating itself again.

"I've never stolen anything in my life, but because someone put artifacts in my desk and locked my office tight, I was blamed for the theft. Now I fear it's happening all over again and I'm being blamed for something I didn't do. And every time I try to figure a way to clear my name, something happens to keep me from succeeding. I'm so weary. I don't know what to do anymore."

Duncan pulled her back against him. "Just have a good cry and you'll feel better."

Rainy warmed to his embrace but stated, "No, I won't. You don't understand. I love God, but I don't seem to be able to let go of my fears and let Him control my destiny. I'm always pushing and pulling and trying to make things go my way. Even now, even telling you all of this, in the back of my mind I'm still trying to figure out who really took the artifacts. I think Chester Driscoll had a hand in my being blamed at the university, so I can't help but wonder if he isn't involved in the thefts on the trip. After all, he has either accompanied us on those trips or he's had friends who have. Then I think to myself, just forget the whole thing and move to Scotland, where no one knows you."

She reached up and wiped her eyes, then just rested against Duncan's shoulder. "Why can't life be simple?"

Duncan chuckled. "I've asked myself that many a time. But seriously, Rainy, if you think there's some good reason to believe Driscoll has had a hand in the thefts, you should let someone know."

She rose up and pushed away. "No one would believe me. They'd just think I'm trying to take the focus off of myself. Until I have some real evidence or can get Chester to admit whatever role he played, I suppose I'll just have to bear the misery. And since it's already been three years, I doubt clues and evidence are just going to pop up for the taking. No . . . I think getting as far away from here as possible is the answer." But her tone said otherwise, and she knew she was far from convincing.

With regret, she eased out of his arms, immediately missing their comfort. Duncan had proven himself to be quite kind and considerate, but she didn't want to take advantage of that.

"I'm sorry for all of this. I shouldn't have told you that stuff about the university and Chester. I've never told anyone outside of my family. Please promise me you'll keep it between us."

Duncan nodded. "Of course. I would never do anything to hurt you."

They sat in silence for several minutes. Rainy drew a deep breath as she sat back against the park bench, feeling foolish for breaking down and crying. *Duncan must think me a real ninny. He's probably sitting there right now trying to figure out a way to leave gracefully.*

Then, as if to prove her wrong, Duncan asked, "What did you mean that day when you asked why more men couldn't be like me?"

CHAPTER NINETEEN

*R*ainy was taken aback by Duncan's question. "What?"

Duncan grinned. "You heard me. Why did you make that state-ment about wishing more men were like me? It was the night we were in Taos and Phillip Vance came into the hotel with a couple of floozies hanging all over him."

"I remember." Rainy had already spilled the truth about her deep-est, darkest secret. Why not tell him the real reason for her words? "I suppose . . . well . . . because you've always been kind to me. Even when you hardly knew me. In fact, I see you being kind to everyone."

"What do you mean by 'kind'?"

Rainy stretched her legs out in front of her. "Do you mind if we walk while we talk? I'm weary from sitting."

Duncan nodded and followed her as she got to her feet. Rainy crossed the street and walked past the Palace of the Governors and on up to Washington Street. The summer skies overhead were fading in the twilight. The air held a definite flavor of red chilies and other spices. Rainy felt the gnawing in her stomach and wished she'd taken time to eat supper.

"You're a kind and gentle man, Duncan. I saw that right from the start. When I brought my first group of tourists to see the museum you were very attentive and . . . kind." She smiled. "There's really no other word for it."

"You pointed out the museum's mistake on the label of an artifact, as I recall," he said with a smirk.

"Yes, but you handled it very graciously. You didn't just dismiss me because I was female or because your pride wouldn't allow you to believe the museum capable of mistakes. You listened to me, observed the item, and agreed to further research the matter. I appreciated that. It was prideful of me to point that error out in the middle of a group of dudes, but you handled it with great ease and . . .''

"And kindness?" he asked.

Rainy nodded and after walking three blocks north on Washington, she crossed the street to head back to the Plaza. She didn't want to get too far away from the safety of her room at the boardinghouse. Should the situation with Duncan prove to become uncomfortable, she wanted the option to flee. As childish as that sounded, she simply couldn't bear to deal with another embarrassing or painful encounter. Hopefully Duncan would understand her situation and keep his distance.

"You've been kind in many ways over the years. I remember the extra care you gave the tour groups. I remember once when I had dropped a stack of boxed lunches, you appeared out of nowhere and helped me pick them up—then you carried them for me. We hardly even knew each other except for the museum and tours."

"I remember that," Duncan said thoughtfully. "I never thought of it as an act of kindness—but merely a gentleman's response to a lady in trouble."

They were back to the Plaza and their pace had slowed considerably. Rainy paused in the shadows of a shop portico. "You are a kind man in so many ways, Duncan Hartford. You rescued me at dinner when Chester was making his little innuendos about the stolen relics, and you were kind just now to offer me a friendly shoulder to cry on." She met his gaze and lost herself for a moment in the depths of his brown eyes. She longed to reach up and touch his cheek, to put her hands in his hair, to hold him close.

Duncan appeared just as captivated. He turned to speak, but he remained silent, almost as if understanding her feelings—her need.

Rainy felt the skin on her arms tingle as Duncan closed the inches between them. "Would you like me to be kind to you right now?" he murmured, gently reaching out to touch her arms and then her shoulders.

Rainy could bear her longing no more. She reached up to touch his hair, just as she'd wanted to do. "Oh, yes, Duncan," she breathed. "Be kind to me."

Duncan's mouth came down on hers in a passionate kiss that took Rainy's breath away. She wrapped her arms around him tightly, fearful that if she didn't, she might very well melt right into the ground. Duncan made her feel at peace—and at the same time he had her heart racing. He seemed to reach inside her and pull out all the bits of doubt and hopelessness. She felt her strength return as his kiss deepened. Now there was no doubt in her mind—the infatuation, the silly school-girl crush . . . had turned into something much more persuasive. Dared she call it love?

Duncan pulled away, his hands lingering on her face. Rainy opened her eyes to find the questioning look in his expression. She wanted to speak, but the words wouldn't come. Surely he couldn't doubt how she felt about him. Scotland seemed a remote possibility now.

"I'm sure sorry to interrupt this, ah, moment," Sonny said. He cleared his throat nervously. Duncan let go of Rainy rather quickly and stepped away while Rainy met her brother's amused look.

"What's the matter?" she questioned.

"I just got a bit of news and I knew you'd want to know about it right away. We've been booked to do a one-way tour to the Grand Canyon. We're to leave tomorrow morning, take a customized route through the reservations so that the dudes can see the Hopi Snake Dance, then head down to Flagstaff and finally over to Williams, where they'll take the train to the canyon."

Rainy nodded, but Duncan seemed confused. "I thought they'd cancelled all the longer drives."

"Anything can be bought for a price," Rainy replied. "You know how people are. Major Clarkson said so long as the dudes were willing to pay, we'd take them where they wanted to go. We just don't openly advertise the longer trips." She looked at him strangely. "Didn't they tell you this in the drivers' meeting?"

"I guess I forgot," Duncan replied. "How long will you be gone, Sonny?"

"We leave tomorrow morning, and it will take us five days to get to Williams. But there's something else to this. Something Rainy needs to know." His expression grew sympathetic. "Jennetta Blythe is the one who set up the tour. She wants to take some friends on the ultimate Wild West trip. She's also bringing Chester and Bethel along."

Rainy felt the wind go out of her. She swallowed hard and shook her head. "No. I won't do it. I'll go talk to Mrs. Lehman right now, but I will not lead that tour group."

"Don't bother. I've already argued the point. She said we were specifically requested and the clients are willing to pay double the usual price for us. They would take no substitutes, and Mrs. Lehman and Major Clarkson said it was of the utmost importance that we please the customer."

"Well, I'll resign my position now instead of waiting until the end of the month," Rainy said in anger. "I'm not traveling another mile with that collection of ninnies."

Duncan reached out and touched her arm. "You might get the answers you're looking for—especially if Chester is on the trip."

"What are you talking about?" Sonny questioned.

Duncan held her gaze, and Rainy realized he was absolutely right. She might very well uncover the clues to her vindication. It was a long shot—none of the other trips had borne fruit—but it was always possible. She shrugged in defeat and sighed.

Rainy turned to Sonny. "He knows about the past. I told him about the university and how I have always believed Chester had something to do with what happened."

"So now you figure going on this trip is somehow going to give you the answers?" Sonny looked first to Rainy and then to Duncan. "Why now?"

Duncan shrugged. "I'm just suggesting it might be beneficial. It might offer her nothing but frustration too."

Rainy felt trapped, and yet a part of her was eager to see if this trip would somehow be different. Maybe Duncan's intuition was God-given. Maybe it was a sign that she would be able to learn the truth once and for all. Defeated, she said, "I guess there's no real choice but to go."

Sonny gave her an apologetic smile. "I tried, sis. Really I did."

Rainy knew he spoke the truth. "I'll be all right. After all, you'll be there to help me." Her stomach rumbled loud enough for everyone to hear. "Right now, I think I'd do well to get some supper. I'm famished."

"I haven't eaten either," Sonny admitted, then looked to Duncan. "Want to join us?"

"No, I have some business to take care of," Duncan murmured. He let go of Rainy and touched his hand to his hat. "I'll catch up with both of you when you get back from the tour."

———

Duncan watched Rainy and her brother walk past La Fonda and disappear down the street before trying to decide what to do next. He wanted very much to locate Phillip and his sister and tell them about his museum artifacts. The timing was critical. If they were involved, perhaps his offer of artifacts would keep them from stealing anything on the Grand Canyon trip and Rainy wouldn't look so bad.

Going in to the hotel registration desk, Duncan asked for Phillip

Vance's room number. He knew Phillip always stayed at La Fonda when in town. He'd checked out that much. He wasn't sure why, however. With Jennetta situated not far from the Plaza and the main thrust of activities, he couldn't imagine why she would send her brother to a hotel.

Bounding up the stairs, Duncan tried to think how he might approach Phillip. He didn't want to appear too eager. After all, if they weren't guilty of stealing, they might well believe him to be out of his head and report him to the police. The last thing Duncan needed was that kind of interference. Worse still, they might tell their friends what had happened and ruin the entire investigation.

He paused outside the door, whispered a prayer, then knocked loudly. He could only hope that Phillip was inside. It wasn't quite the hour for parties to begin their entertainment. To his relief, he heard voices coming from the other side of the door. In a moment, Phillip Vance opened the door. He stood there wearing a red satin smoking jacket, a cigarette in hand.

"Oh, hello . . . Mr. . . . Hartson?" Phillip said hesitantly.

"Hartford. I wondered if you had a moment to talk to me."

"Well, my sister is here," Phillip began, "but I'm sure she won't mind. We're making an early evening of it because she's heading to the Grand Canyon tomorrow."

Duncan nodded. "Yes, I'd heard that. What I have to say won't take long, and I'd be happy to share the information with your sister as well."

Phillip nodded. "Then please come in."

Duncan entered the lion's den—at least that's what it felt like to him. He tried to appear as though this were something he did on an everyday basis. Jennetta Blythe slinked into view. She was dressed in a rather dowdy manner, just as she'd been the first time Duncan had met her. Her hair had recently been cut and seemed not to have adjusted well to the trim. She looked nothing like the socialite he'd seen before.

"I'm glad I could find you both," Duncan said, smiling. "I must say, however, I thought it rather odd that Phillip would have a suite here at the hotel while you live right in town, Mrs. Blythe."

Jennetta seemed indifferent to his observation. "My home is my sanctuary where I create. I can't have a lot of people running about. It would cause problems for the spirits. They would be disturbed," she said matter-of-factly.

"The spirits?"

Phillip chuckled. "Jennetta fancies her house is haunted."

"It *is* haunted, and the spirits help me to write. I have absolutely no one in unless I'm convinced the spirits would approve. Often they do approve, but not for overnight—I never have guests sleep over. I know the spirits would find that much too disruptive."

Duncan nodded as if he'd heard this before.

"So what brings you here, Mr. Hartford?"

Duncan coughed, trying to cover his sudden case of nerves. "Well, the truth is, I remember Mrs. Blythe purchasing some Indian trinkets and thought perhaps you were both connoisseurs of the Indian culture and their artwork."

"I suppose we are," Phillip replied. "I, of course, first came here to better my understanding of the American West. I wanted to utilize it for my movies. Jennetta came here to write. You do know that Santa Fe is a writer's community, don't you?"

Duncan nodded. "I'm very familiar with that aspect of this town. I also know it to have a strong community of painters. The stories surrounding the Cinco Pintores are notorious."

Jennetta gave a scoffing laugh. "The Five Painters, indeed. Writers are much more of an influence here. Painters go to Taos—at least painters of any real repute. My dear friend Mary Austin lives on the Camino del Monte Sol. She's been published many times. She's even working right now on a book that deals with the Indians and some of their 'trinkets,' as you called them. There are far more writers than you would guess. We're a quiet bunch overall and prefer not to be disturbed."

"I stand corrected," Duncan said, smiling. "I do recall several years ago that Willa Cather came to the museum for information on the Archbishop of Santa Fe. Seems she was putting together a fiction book."

Jennetta nodded enthusiastically. "Yes, exactly! That's what I'm speaking of. You cannot discredit the strong influence of writers."

Duncan nodded. "Well, I should get back to what I originally came for. The truth is, I've seen your interest in Indian artifacts and I wondered if you would be interested in purchasing some pieces that will not be offered to the general public."

Jennetta moved closer, her eyes widening, while Phillip sat down and took a long drag on the cigarette. "What kind of pieces?" she asked.

Duncan felt his heart begin to race. He described the three pieces and their value and meaning. He hinted at the fact that they were museum-owned and were soon to be changed out from their exhibit and put into storage.

"They probably won't be missed for years," he added.

Neither Jennetta nor Phillip acted in any way distressed by the idea of Duncan selling stolen merchandise. Their reaction, or lack of it, gave Duncan hope that he was definitely on the right trail. "I could have the pieces right away."

"I'm particularly interested in the squash blossom necklace," Jennetta said, her eyes gleaming. "I don't suppose you have set a price?"

Duncan shook his head and shrugged. "I know what the pieces are worth from working with them; however, given the circumstances, we both know that negotiating the price will benefit us both."

Jennetta stared him down like a hunter going in for the kill. "I think we could probably come to some arrangement. You'll have to wait until I get back from our trip, however. I positively cannot do any business until I consult . . . the spirits."

*R*ainy was uncertain as to how she'd deal with Phillip Vance when she saw him, but when the dudes showed up with Jennetta, Phillip was strangely absent. Jennetta offered no explanation, and she seemed rather moody and silent. Her friends chided her for her misery and teased that no doubt great poems would be born out of such bleak moments. Still Jennetta said little.

The trip was to be different than most. The route was customized, starting with an early morning departure from Santa Fe and no stops, except for food and gasoline, until they stopped for the night in Gallup. The dudes in this tour had already seen the little side ventures and were more focused on making it in time for the annual Hopi Snake Dance.

Rainy endured the first twenty-four hours with as much grace and consideration as she could. Chester made a nuisance of himself, commenting that he'd heard Rainy was resigning at the end of the month and wondering about the reason for the sudden departure. Rainy ignored him as much as she could, but as they arrived at the Hopi reservation, he seemed to be in prime form.

"I don't suppose the fact that you're leaving for Scotland has anything to do with the missing artifacts, would it?" he asked, coming up from behind Rainy.

She turned around to face him with a grimace. "Chester, you have continued to annoy me on this trip. Why not give us both a rest? I have no interest in hearing anything you have to say, and frankly, although my resignation was going to be turned in at the end of this month, I wouldn't hesitate to up the date and quit early if it meant I would be free of listening to you."

"But you must admit it seems strange."

"Why should it seem strange? The university has asked my father to take an early retirement. The economy of the country is failing fast and hard. My father owns property in Scotland, we have family there, and it seems the logical place to go. I have no reason to remain behind."

"I thought you and Vance had some sort of understanding."

"Well, you thought wrong," Rainy replied and turned back to her paper work.

"Look, you're always misunderstanding my motives," Chester whispered as he leaned close to her ear.

Rainy moved away. "I don't believe I've misunderstood anything you've said or done. When I was falsely accused of stealing the artifacts at the university, I knew you had the information I needed to clear my name."

Chester looked rather shocked. His face paled. "I . . . had nothing of the kind."

"Your words are far from convincing. I asked you one night prior to the university's final decision why you didn't go in there and fight for me. You said it would result in your own dismissal. Why was that, Chester, if not for the fact that you had more information than you were allowing anyone to know? Wasn't it you who took the artifacts and placed them in my office? After all, you had a key."

Chester seemed to regain his composure. "You can't pin this on me. My family is well respected."

"So was mine until you and yours did us wrong."

Noting the time, Rainy gathered her things. "We leave for the snake dance in ten minutes. I suggest you be ready unless you plan to miss it, which is just as fine by me." She could barely contain her anger. She knew by the look on his face that she'd hit pay dirt with her suspicions, but Chester wasn't about to jeopardize everything by admitting his participation.

Lord, help me in this. I know he holds the key to the past.

To Rainy's disappointment, ten minutes later Chester was present, along with his wife. Bethel and Jennetta looked positively miserable and Rainy could only suppose it was due to the heat. Someone told her it might well reach one hundred degrees. She didn't mind the warmth, but these poor creatures of luxury and ease seemed unable to endure the sun's intensity for long.

Hiding behind her huge straw hat, Jennetta dabbed herself with a cloth and remained silent while Rainy ushered her clients into the car so that they could drive to the mesa where the dance would be held.

Rainy gave the same speech she gave every year. "You need to understand how very important this ritual is to the Hopi. The government once tried to put an end to the celebration back in 1923. They said time could be better used by working instead of celebrating. They wanted the Hopi to move the event to the winter, not understanding that the snakes would be hibernating then.

"The dance has its basis in the myths and legends of the Hopi people. It's said that Ti-yo, a hero god who is often seen in Hopi legends, wanted to follow the river at the bottom of the Grand Canyon and see where it would take him. His father helped him build a boat and made gifts for the people he would meet along the way.

"The first place he came to was a small hole in the ground where he knew Spider Woman lived. Spider Woman welcomed him and because of his gift, she offered to go along with him and advise him as he made his journey. She took along magic potions that would calm the snakes and other wild animals so that Ti-yo would not be harmed.

"The journey continued and Ti-yo went even deeper into the canyon, where he met other beings. He offered his gifts and was given gifts in return. When he reached the Woman of Hard Substance, he found she lived in a kiva of turquoise and coral. As they sat talking, the Sun came in and landed on the kiva roof. Ti-yo gave him gifts, and the Sun told Ti-yo to take hold of his girdle and Sun would take him around the earth.

"When Ti-yo's journey ended, he spent time in the Snake House and learned what songs to sing and how to paint his body so that the rain would come. He was then given two maidens. One to be his own wife and one for his brother. Spider Woman made a special basket for him and the women to bring back to his home. Later, Ti-yo and his brother married the women.

"After this, the village had trouble with snakes coming in to eat their corn. The legend says the maidens reverted to snakelike beings that bore small snakes that attacked and killed the children of the village. The mothers of these children forced their men to migrate, and in migrating they taught the snake ritual to their Hopi brothers and sisters as they traveled."

"What a marvelous story," Bethel declared. "I love Indian lore."

Others quickly agreed with her. Rainy let them chatter a bit more while Sonny drove on. Finally she interrupted. "We will not be allowed to see the entire ceremony of the snake dance. Prior to our arrival there is a gathering of rattlesnakes by the priests. The snakes are then brought into the kiva and dumped on the floor. The priests will take their choice of snakes, although it is said the snakes actually choose their men. Each priest takes his snakes home and washes them in cold water and yellow root medicine. Then the priest throws away his clothing and washes himself. He must then fast a day and dance all night. He will feed the rattlesnakes before even feeding himself, and when the time for the dance comes, he will gather his snakes, one in his mouth and one in each hand."

"Oh, that sounds absolutely vile," Jennetta said, actually looking a bit green.

"You will see for yourself that the actual dance has its vile moments," Rainy declared. "There have been times when the snakes have bitten the men and yet still they dance and pay little attention to their wounds. They appear to suffer no harm from the venom."

"How does that work?" one man questioned. "Have they pulled the fangs out of the little beasts first?"

Rainy shook her head. "No, you can clearly see the rattlesnakes still maintain their fangs. No one is really certain why the Hopi survive unaffected. During the dance you'll see the men tickle the head, neck, and mouth of the snakes with a ceremonial wand. This seems to stupefy the snake. Some observers claim that the wand must have some sort of potion or herb that sedates the animal, but I cannot say this is true."

They finally arrived at the mesa, where a great many other tourists had gathered as well. The Hopi Snake Dance was not to be missed.

Rainy positioned her people and reminded them to remain silent and do nothing to interfere with the dance. As the ceremony played itself out, she couldn't help but think of how this would be the last time she'd see the snake dance. The thought saddened her, but no more so than the thought of leaving Duncan.

Now that he's kissed me, perhaps I should delay my plans. Maybe things will come together for us, she thought. Rainy glanced to the skies overhead. There were clouds in the west. The dance was said to bring rain and often the dancers finished in the midst of a downpour. Rainy couldn't help but wonder if it would be that way today.

The dancers went through their routine, and at the conclusion the priests offered a prayer and the snake dancers took up bundles of snakes and ran back to level ground below the mesa. Here they let the snakes go in four different directions. This was so that the snakes could deliver their prayers to the underworld and the rain gods would hear and answer.

A purification ritual took place afterward and ended with the Hopi men taking an emetic and vomiting over the side of the mesa. At this point, Jennetta and Bethel both blanched and moved back to the car. Other dudes were not so fortunate and soon joined in the purging ritual without intending to.

Rainy smiled to herself and made her way to the touring car with her stunned dudes. Sonny helped everyone load up and they headed back to their lodging in near silence. It generally went this way, so Rainy didn't offer much chatter. She told them they would remain at the reservation for an extra day before heading to Flagstaff and that the Hopi had agreed to share more information about their culture and beliefs. If anyone wanted to talk to them, Rainy could arrange a private meeting. No one took her up on the offer, much to her surprise.

That evening Rainy went to have dinner with her friends Istaqa and Una. When they first met, both had welcomed Rainy with open arms when she had demonstrated her desire to understand and know them better. In turn, Rainy had shared her faith in God, and Istaqa and Una had accepted Jesus as their Savior.

"We're so glad you could eat with us," Una said, embracing Rainy. "Where is your brother?"

"He was having some trouble with the car and needed to check on it. He said to give you his apologies."

Una nodded. "He will be missed."

They gathered and prayed, and Rainy didn't know when she'd enjoyed herself more. For a time she actually stopped worrying about Chester and the artifacts. She chose instead to listen to Una talk about their boys and how well they were doing in school.

"I don't think I'll have a chance to see you again anytime soon," Rainy explained as dinner concluded and they sat sipping coffee. "I'm resigning my job at the end of the month and will probably move to Scotland with my parents."

Una and Istaqa exchanged a strange look, and Rainy couldn't help but ask them what was wrong. Istaqa looked at his cup, refusing to meet Rainy's eyes. She studied the man and his blunt features. His hair was cut in Hopi fashion, straight and just below the ear. He wore a band around his head as many of his people did. He generally was very straightforward with Rainy, but now he suddenly seemed uncomfortable.

"What is it? Have I done something to offend you?"

Una reached out and patted Rainy's hand. "It is not you. There have been problems and Istaqa worries."

Rainy thought of the thefts. "Yes, I know about the problems."

Istaqa looked up. His dark eyes seemed to scrutinize her with more interest. Rainy felt uneasy and continued. "I've been told there were thefts and that the Detours trips seemed to correspond with those thefts." Outside, thunder rumbled as the rains moved in. The snake dance had apparently done its job.

Una nodded. "It hasn't been good."

"I actually came here not only to share supper," Rainy admitted, "but in hopes that you'd help me in this very matter. There are people out there who want to blame me for these thefts."

Una looked to Istaqa. For a moment neither one spoke, then Una nodded and gave her husband a nudge. Istaqa finally spoke. "There has been trouble and your name has been given many times."

"But why? You know me. You know I wouldn't steal from you. You know I respect the Hopi."

"We know," Una said, looking to her husband. He nodded as well.

"I did not believe their words," Istaqa stated. "But the Indian agent and his people have been quite convinced of your guilt."

Rainy slumped back in defeat. "I'm trying so hard to find the real culprit, but if everyone else is determined to blame me, I'll be working all alone and never get anywhere."

"You won't work alone," Una said. "You'll work with God."

"He seems to be my only friend."

"No," Istaqa said. "We are your friends. You have been a blessing to us, and we will not believe these lies against you. That is what I told Mr. Richland when he suggested you were to blame. You and Sonny."

"Who is this Mr. Richland?"

"He is the man from the Office of Indian Affairs. He has been so convinced of your guilt he has hired someone to watch you—to get close to you so that they can know the truth."

"Hired someone? Who? What's the name of this person?" Rainy asked, feeling angry at the thought that her every move was being watched.

"I shouldn't tell you this," Istaqa said. "But I am supposed to watch you too." He smiled and shook his head. "It's all worthless to me. I know you are not guilty."

"I appreciate the fact that you believe in me," Rainy said, reaching out to touch both Istaqa and Una. "You have been dear friends. But now I need to know who Mr. Richland has hired to watch me."

Istaqa sighed. "Very well. His name is Hartford. Duncan Hartford."

———————

Rainy left shortly after this declaration. She felt that if she didn't leave, she might very well repeat the vomiting ritual viewed earlier that day. She felt a cold numbness creep over her body. Duncan was nothing more than a spy sent to keep track of her comings and goings. No wonder he always seemed to turn up when she was alone. No wonder he invited her to dinner—walked with her—kissed her.

Rainy felt sick. "Oh, God, how can this be? I knew he was aware of the situation. He shared with me that others thought me guilty. Now I can see he only did that hoping I'd talk." She moaned as she remembered that she'd told Duncan about the situation at the university.

The hopelessness of her dilemma washed over her in waves. "Oh, God, where are you?"

*T*hings went from bad to worse for Rainy. First was the declaration from Istaqa regarding Duncan's involvement in the investigation; then Sonny arrived while Rainy was eating breakfast to tell her that Jennetta Blythe had disappeared. The latter didn't really surprise Rainy—the woman had been moody and unresponsive since the trip first began. All sorts of images ran through her head. Had Jennetta fallen into harm? Had she run off with some new love?

"What do you mean, disappeared?" Rainy asked, forcing herself to remain calm. Maybe it wasn't as bad as she thought.

"I mean she left the hotel shortly after the snake dance and no one has seen her since."

Rainy sighed. "She didn't return to her room last night?"

"No, apparently not. Bethel is beside herself and wonders if we can delay the trip until Jennetta's return."

"I suppose we could consider it, since Jennetta arranged this trip, but we are expected to keep to our schedule. Perhaps I should talk to Jennetta's friends and see if anyone knows what's become of her."

Sonny shook his head and gave his hat a twirl. "I did that as soon as Bethel came to me. No one has seen her. They all admit that some-thing was bothering her, but no one has a clue as to what it might be."

Rainy pushed back from the table. "I suppose I'll go talk to Istaqa and see if he can nose around and find her. She couldn't have gotten that far."

"No, I don't suppose so. You don't think it has anything to do with the missing artifacts, do you?"

Rainy startled at this. She'd talked very little to Sonny about the situation and it seemed strange that he should comment on it now. "How much do you know?"

Sonny shrugged. "Quite a bit. I've talked some to Duncan and I've also talked to several other people. I've wondered about Jennetta and Phillip because of their continued trips. It just doesn't make sense that they would take trip after trip. The Detours are costly and, while entertaining and fun, I don't see those two as benefiting from it."

Rainy couldn't agree more with her brother. "Let's walk around a bit. You can go with me to Istaqa's and tell him what you know."

They walked along together and Rainy felt an overwhelming sorrow as she thought of Duncan. How could he do this to her? How could he kiss her and comfort her, then use her for information? Her hurt went beyond anything Rainy could explain to Sonny.

They didn't go far before they ran into Istaqa. He waved as they approached and listened to their concerns about Jennetta.

"I'll see what I can find out," he told Rainy.

"We need to leave tomorrow morning," she said. "But obviously I can't ignore the fact that one of my dudes is missing."

Istaqa nodded. "I'll talk to you this evening. You can both come to dinner. Una will be happy."

Throughout the day there was no word of Jennetta and by evening's dinner with Una and Istaqa, they were no closer to knowing her whereabouts than they had been that morning. Jennetta's disappearance made Rainy even more suspicious of her involvement with the missing artifacts. Rainy could only imagine that Jennetta had latched onto goods that she couldn't hide in the touring car and perhaps was making provision for their return to Santa Fe by some other means.

"Is anything missing—has anyone reported missing artifacts?" she asked Istaqa.

"No. Nothing has been mentioned."

Rainy shook her head. "It's possible that Jennetta is secreting something out of the reservation. She has enough money to pay people off and get pretty much whatever she wants."

"I've asked around about her. One woman mentioned having seen someone who fit her description, but she couldn't be sure it was Mrs. Blythe."

"I'm still willing to bet she's up to no good. I think Jennetta has something up her sleeve and this little disappearing act of hers is to cover it up or take care of business."

By the next morning, Rainy was even more convinced as they pulled out of the Hopi village without Jennetta. Istaqa promised to continue looking for the missing woman and to get her to the train once found. It was all they could do.

It wasn't until they left the car in Williams and prepared to return by train to Santa Fe, while their dudes went to the Grand Canyon with Chester and Bethel, that Rainy learned the truth. Istaqa wired the depot to say word had come that Jennetta had gotten sick and had arranged for someone to take her to the train in Winslow. She had ridden the rails back to Santa Fe so she could see her doctor.

Rainy was relieved to know the truth but was still suspicious. It could all be a ruse after all. Just a plot to keep the others from knowing what Jennetta was truly up to. Besides, why hadn't she at least explained the truth to Bethel?

Taking her seat on the train, Rainy immediately pretended to sleep. She figured Sonny would want to discuss Duncan after the kiss he'd witnessed, but she didn't want to talk about him or the missing pieces. She'd already decided enough was enough. She wasn't going to wait until the end of the month to resign her position. She would do it as soon as she returned. Maybe then she could avoid ever having to see Duncan again.

I can't bear to think of him kissing me . . . that it was part of a scheme to spy on me. I can't believe I've lost my heart to him and he's played me for a fool.

The thoughts churned in her head, leaving her with a tight pain in her chest. How could she have been so taken in by him? His kindness was her undoing. When people treated her poorly as Chester and his father had, she could handle it. She could deal with the unruly guests who joined the tours. She could bear up under irritated travelers, surly supervisors, and irrational hotel management, but just let someone be nice to her and . . . well, the effect was obvious.

Rainy dozed off and on, but she was very much aware of her pain, even in her sleep. Her dreams were laced with accusations and ugly scenes of confrontation. She would question Duncan only to have him kiss her again and tell her that he was taking her to jail or that he knew she was innocent but that he had to get evidence against her. The thoughts were jumbled and confusing, and Rainy always woke with a start, sweaty and hot from the close confines of the train. Her head ached from a throbbing pain that had started when they were some-where around Holbrook.

By the time they arrived in Albuquerque, Rainy had decided to stay overnight with her folks. "I don't feel well, Sonny. Take me home. I want to see Mom and Dad."

"What's wrong?" he asked, his tone revealing his concern.

"I don't know exactly. I have a horrible headache, though, and I don't think I can sit another minute on this train. Please just take me home so that I can take a cold bath and sleep."

Sonny did just that. When they arrived, their mother greeted them in surprise but quickly escorted her daughter upstairs. "Take your bath and I'll bring you something for your headache," her mother promised before drawing the drapes.

Rainy went through the paces, feeling no real relief from the tepid water. She sank into the tub and tried to push aside the thoughts that raced through her head.

When done, Rainy quickly dressed in a nightgown of lightweight cotton. She threw herself across her bed and pleaded with God for answers. Clinging to her pillow, Rainy let loose the tears that had threatened to flow all day. She didn't want her mother to find her crying, but the tears were impossible to stop. Her emotions demanded the purging.

"Oh, God," she whispered, "how could this happen? Why should I be accused? You know my innocence. Why can't I be free of this? I love Duncan, but now I learn that he's only been interested in me because of the investigation."

She buried her face in the pillow and cried in earnest.

"Rainy?"

Her mother gently touched her shoulder. Rainy raised her face and shrugged. "I'm sorry."

Her mother put a glass on Rainy's nightstand and sat down beside her daughter. "What's wrong? What has happened to cause these tears?"

"Oh, Mama, it's terrible. I feel so silly and so used." She struggled to sit up and accepted the glass of water from her mother.

"I've put some headache powders in the water, so drink it down," her mother instructed.

Rainy did as she was told, then wiped her eyes. "I've fallen in love, but I've done so with the wrong man."

Her mother's gentle nature immediately calmed her. "Why don't you tell me all about it?"

Rainy nodded. Her mother's graying red hair and careworn face reminded Rainy that the years were passing by much too quickly. She took hold of her mother's hand and held it to her face. "I fell in love with Duncan Hartford."

"Why, he's a very pleasant young man. Why do you say he's the wrong man?"

"Because he's only kept company with me in order to watch me. He was hired to keep track of me and see if I was the one responsible for the missing Indian artifacts."

She dropped her hold on her mother's hand and shook her head. "I can't believe the way this is all happening again. I didn't take those pieces. I've done nothing wrong, and yet, once again, I find myself in the middle of the same type of controversy. How can this be God's will for my life?"

Her mother smiled. "We don't always know what God is doing. We have to trust that He sees the injustice of this moment, however."

"Well, I'm finished with Duncan and everyone else in Santa Fe. I'm going to stay here until I feel better, then I'm going to Santa Fe to resign early. I know they expected me to finish out the month, but I can't. I don't want to ever see Duncan again."

"You aren't going to confront him with this new information? Let him explain it himself?"

Her mother's words were like a slap in the face. "Why should I?"

"You don't like being falsely accused without people seeking the truth. Shouldn't you seek the truth from Duncan?"

Rainy didn't like hearing her mother's suggestion, but it pierced her conscience immediately and she knew without any question that her mother was right. "But it hurts so much. Seeing him will only compound the pain."

"But it might also ease it," her mother declared. "If you learn the truth, it might very well change everything."

"But what if this is the truth? How do I deal with it then? How do I face up to falling in love with Duncan if he's only been nice to me in order to pry into my past?"

"God will give you grace to deal with whatever comes your way. Trust Him, Rainy. That's all I can say. There is nothing I can do or tell you that will ease your misery. Only the truth can do that for you—but you won't learn the truth if you don't ask."

"I'll think about it," Rainy promised.

The next day Sonny went back to Santa Fe while Rainy stayed in Albuquerque. She continued to consider her mother's words. Perhaps she was right. Maybe talking to Duncan would help her to understand his position. But did she want to understand his position? What if he apologized and told her he was indeed sent to spy on her? What if his kiss meant nothing?

"Will you pack some dishes for me while I run to the market?" Rainy's mother asked as Rainy sat moping in the living room.

Rainy looked up to find her mother adjusting a small straw hat. Her mother's inner contentment gave her a more youthful and radiant appearance this morning. Rainy wondered how her mother managed to bear up under the stress of life.

"Rainy, did you hear me?"

Rainy startled as if she'd been in a dream. "Oh, sorry. Sure. I think I can do that without causing too much damage."

"I've no doubt you can handle the job admirably. Just use the crates on the far wall. They have packing materials already in them. I've been wrapping things in newspaper first, however, and then I put them in the packing."

Rainy nodded. "If you're picking up food for supper, I heard Dad say he was hungry for mashed neeps."

"I heard him say it, too, so turnips are on my list."

Her mother had been gone no more than ten minutes when a knock came at the door. Rainy, in no mood for company, seriously considered not answering. After all, she wasn't usually in residence and no one would know that she was there. But the knocking was so persistent that Rainy worried it might be some kind of emergency with her father or mother, so she opened the door to find a rather rumpled-looking Gunther Albright smiling back at her.

"I didn't know you were in town," he said.

Rainy smiled and opened the door wider. "I've only been here a day. I'm afraid you've missed both of my parents. Dad is at the university dealing with last-minute details, and my mother has just gone out to the market."

"I knew your father was away. I tried to catch up with him at the school. I have a few things I need to discuss with him and thought perhaps he'd already arrived home. If not, I can wait for him." He leaned down and lowered his voice. "I also want to discuss a going-away party for your father. I want to send him into retirement on a good note. Perhaps you and I can conspire on this?"

Rainy immediately felt at ease. Planning a party for her father would be a great deal of fun and perhaps just the thing to bring her out of her self-pitying mood. "That's so kind of you, Gunther. I think it would bless Dad's heart to have such a party. Why don't you come in? We can discuss the details and I'll give the information to Mom."

"That sounds just fine." He handed his hat to Rainy.

Rainy placed his hat on the receiving table and moved toward the front room. "Can I get you some refreshments?"

Gunther joined her in the living room. "No, I'm just fine. Oh, I see the packing has already begun."

"Yes. I'm afraid they aren't taking much. They've given a great deal away and sold off other pieces. Mom said they were taking only what they couldn't bear to leave behind."

"Probably wise, given the distance of the journey. I understand you're thinking about going with them."

"Yes. It wasn't an easy decision. I love New Mexico and the thought of leaving makes me quite sad." She sighed and forced a smile. "But I felt it would be for the best in the long run. I'm going to resign my position with the touring company tomorrow and help them prepare."

"I wonder if you might have time for another adventure or two before you leave. The departure is still set for September first, correct?" Gunther said, surprising Rainy. He toyed at smoothing a wrinkle in his well-worn tan trousers. "I would really appreciate your help in a matter. We should be able to work it in prior to your leaving."

Rainy sat down and urged Gunther to do the same. "I never consider propositions standing," she teased. In truth, Gunther looked quite tired and Rainy wanted him to relax and rest.

Gunther did as she suggested, then leaned forward, hands on his knees. "I want to organize a dig in a remote area of the Hopi reservation northwest of Winslow. The area shows great promise according to some old manuscripts I've located. I was hoping you could help me negotiate the terms of the dig and help me get permission."

Rainy felt rather awkward, for Gunther's request had taken her totally off guard. "What would the purpose of the dig be?"

"Education, of course."

Rainy considered the matter for a moment. "Well, there are all the rules and paper work to be dealt with, of course. It won't be easy, but I think if we explained the purpose isn't for selling the pieces but to substantiate history, it would probably be better received. And we cannot, in any manner, disturb burial sites."

Gunther nodded. "No, of course not. I knew you'd understand. I'd actually like to write a book about the area and the people. You can also help me in that matter. Set me up with your friends and such. They'd probably be more willing to tell me their legends and histories if they knew I was a friend of yours. And since you'll be gone, I can't very well seek out your help in the future."

"Yes, that's true. The Hopi are generally suspicious of most whites. They've suffered much at the hands of our race. I would hate for them to endure any more. You would have to agree to be as unobtrusive as possible, but of course you know all of that."

"Indeed I do. What say we agree to meet on Friday? We can take the train to Winslow, where I'll arrange a car for us. I'll take care of all the expenses," Gunther stated. "And I'll be happy to pay you for your time."

"That won't be necessary. I'm happy to help—you know my passion for educating people about the Southwest."

Just then her mother returned and to Rainy's surprise her father followed in close on her heels.

"Look who's here, Mom . . . Dad. Gunther was just telling me about a book he wants to write about the Hopi. Isn't that marvelous?"

"I'm sure if anyone can do the Hopi justice, it would be Gunther," her father said.

"I was also hoping to talk to you," Gunther stated, getting up from the sofa. "I tried to catch you at the university as I heard you were there sorting through some of your books and such, but alas, I missed you. There are a couple of details I need to go over with you before you leave the country."

Rainy's father nodded. "Why don't we head into my study, then? We can talk and maybe Edrea will bring us some tea and cookies."

Rainy's mother nodded. "I'd be happy to do just that."

Gunther lifted Rainy's hand to his lips as she'd seen him do with her mother. "Until Friday?"

"Yes, that will be fine."

The two men went off down the hall while Rainy slipped over to her mother. "Gunther wanted to talk to you about a retirement party for Dad as well. I didn't have a chance to get much information out of him. We had just started to talk when you came in."

Her mother laughed. "Gunther is usually all business. His birthday party must have softened his edges. I'll be sure and speak to him when the chance presents itself. Maybe when they've finished talking you could pull your father into the courtyard on the pretense of needing to talk to him about something, and then I could talk privately with Gunther. Would that work?"

Rainy giggled. "Our great conspiracy. Of course we'll make it work."

Finally Rainy knew she could no longer put off her trip to Santa Fe. She had to resign and collect her things, and after two more talks with her mother, she was almost convinced that she should speak to Duncan. On the train ride, she considered how she might approach him on the topic.

I could just blurt out what I know and confront him, she mused. *Or . . . I could tell him that I love him and see what his reaction is.* Both seemed impossible to do.

Rainy poured over the details of the matter all the way to Santa Fe. When she resigned her position she wasn't at all regretful of or sorrowed by her action because she was still thinking about how she might confront Duncan. By now her curiosity drove her on. *Let him explain himself,* she thought as she climbed the stairs at the boardinghouse. *Let him tell me why he thought his actions were worthy of a Christian man. I should just tell him how much he's hurt me—make it clear that my heart is broken. That will show him.*

But revenge wasn't really what she wanted. She wanted Duncan.

She entered her room, knowing that she had to get ready for her departure the next morning. There really was a lot to tend to and very little time. Glancing around the room she would soon be leaving for the last time, Rainy had never felt more alone. Unable to bear it, she left her packing and knocked on the adjoining room door to see if Sonny was in.

When he didn't answer, she presumed he was working. If anyone could understand her plight, it would be Sonny. She thought maybe he could offer her some advice. She hadn't told him about Duncan's connection with the law officials, but she knew Sonny liked Duncan and he might very well have some idea of how she could deal with the matter. Discouraged, Rainy went back to her packing.

Sitting alone, Rainy tried to pray for wisdom but felt as though her petitions were bouncing off the ceiling. When she tired of packing, she took a long bath to clear her mind, but even that didn't help much. She curled up in front of the open window and combed out her long hair.

Gunther's request came to mind, and Rainy tried to focus on his plans instead of Duncan. She hoped the old man would be fair and kind to the Hopi as he wrote about them. Gunther seemed an even-handed sort. He'd never questioned her as to why she'd quit the university to go to work for the Harvey Company, and he'd always been very good to her family.

With her hair nearly dry, Rainy decided to send a note to Istaqa via one of the touring groups. She wanted to explain Gunther's plans ahead of time and give him a chance to discuss the matter with the tribal elders. She briefly considered trying to get through by phone, but knew it would be difficult at best and very expensive. Of course, she had no idea if any of the couriers were scheduled for a customized trip through the Hopi village, but she had heard that one was headed for Canyon de Chelly. That wasn't so terribly far from the Hopi reservation. Perhaps someone could arrange to get the note to Istaqa from there. It would just offer him a little advance warning before she showed up with Gunther. It might even allow for him to have all the terms and conditions in order and save them time.

Taking out a piece of paper and a pen, Rainy was suddenly overwhelmed by a feeling of nostalgia. She'd had this room as her own for nearly two years now. She'd been born and raised in America and now faced the possibility of living in Scotland for the remainder of her life. What would that be like?

She pushed the thoughts aside and addressed her letter to Istaqa and Una, but seeing their names on the paper brought tears to her eyes. *How can I leave New Mexico and the Southwest? How can I take myself away from the people and places I love? Scotland is a world away. Will I find a museum to work in—a dig site to join?* The situation discouraged her more than ever.

A knock on the door startled her momentarily. She glanced at her watch. It was nearly five-thirty. Perhaps it was Sonny. She crossed the room and opened the door to find Duncan Hartford standing in front of her.

Duncan's mouth dropped open as Rainy grabbed hold of his arm and dragged him down the hall of the boardinghouse. Her hair was flying in wild strawberry-blond ribbons behind her as she led him into the street.

She continued to pull him along until they reached the Plaza. They crossed to the opposite side and were halfway across the park when Rainy stopped just as quickly as she'd started. When she turned abruptly, Duncan wasn't sure what to expect.

"We need to talk."

He nodded, still mesmerized by the way the wind whipped at her hair. He'd never seen her wear it loose. He felt entranced and wanted only to reach out and touch the strands, but the fiery look in her expression caused him to stand stone still.

"I've heard something very troubling, and rather than misjudge the situation and make matters worse, I feel it only appropriate to ask you about it."

"All right," Duncan replied, finally feeling able to speak.

Rainy pushed back her hair and drew a deep breath. "Were you hired to keep track of me—to spy on me and get close to me—so that you could learn whether or not I was stealing Indian art pieces?"

Duncan felt his breath catch. His mouth went dry. "I . . . well . . . I was hired to investigate the thefts . . . yes."

Rainy narrowed her icy blue eyes. "That's not what I asked. Were you hired specifically to watch me?"

Duncan knew that he had to be honest, but at the same time he knew without a doubt it would forever change their relationship. "I . . . uh . . ."

Tears came to Rainy's eyes. "So it is true. I can't believe it. You led me to believe . . . Oh, I won't even say it. I can't believe this is happening. I wanted to give you the benefit of the doubt as my mother said I should do, but now . . ."

"Wait," he said, taking hold of her arms. "It's not as it seems."

"Of course not," she said snidely. "It never is. You were just doing a job."

"I was trying to get to the truth. They wanted me to watch you and Sonny and to prove you were the ones stealing the artifacts. I wanted to prove you were innocent. I was trying to figure out what was going on."

"Oh, really? And just what was it you were trying to figure out when you kissed me?" She lifted her chin defiantly, tears coursing down her cheeks. "I don't want to hear any more. Whether you believe me or not, I did not take those artifacts. I would never do that. I didn't steal the pieces at the university and I'm not responsible for the thefts of the last few months. I really don't care what you think or believe, but it's the truth!" She jerked away from him and ran back across the park.

Duncan sighed and sat down on a nearby bench. Betrayal was the only word for what he knew she must feel. He had no idea how she'd found out about his involvement, but her reaction definitely didn't bode well for their future—unless he could get her to listen to his explanation.

Duncan sighed again. How could things have gotten so out of hand? All he wanted to do was support her, to clear her name. Hadn't he fought for her over and over? Hadn't he worked hard to convince Richland that he couldn't just storm in and arrest the Gordons?

It didn't make sense that she wouldn't listen to him. He knew she cared about him—she would never have kissed him the way she did if she didn't have feelings for him. *So what can I do about it now? How do I make her listen to me when she clearly isn't willing to hear anything I have to say? If I went after her, she'd only think I was making things up to excuse my actions.*

Duncan wished fervently he'd never been asked to look into the Indian thefts. He thought of Jennetta's promise to look him up when she got back to town, but the tour had returned yesterday by train and still there had been no word from Jennetta. He'd thought to ask Chester Driscoll if he had seen her when he'd run into him at La Fonda, but the opportunity never arose and Duncan let it go for the time.

The entire matter was much messier than he'd ever believed it would be. Maybe the only way to prove to Rainy that he believed in her innocence, however, was to prove Jennetta guilty.

He leaned back against the bench and tried to reason out his next step. He thought of his father's counsel to trust God to make the truth known. He also understood Rainy's frustration, however, when she'd mentioned the length of time she'd waited to clear her name.

"God's timing is never too early or too late," his father had often said.

As a child, Duncan had tried to disprove this with logic and reasoning. He could still hear his conversations with his dad. "But if God is never too late or too early, then why didn't God keep Jesus from having to die on the cross? If Jesus was willing to be a sacrifice for our sins, why wasn't that enough? Why would God make Him go through all that pain and suffering? Why not just say, 'Poof—it's done. You have taken on the sins of the world and now everyone who comes to me through you will be forgiven'?"

Duncan's father had been patient with his tenderhearted son. "Suffering has always been with man since the fall in the Garden of Eden. When people stepped out of God's will for them and decided to take matters in their own hands, there had to be consequences. The consequence of sin was pain and suffering."

"But Jesus didn't sin. He only took the sin on in order to see that we could have forgiveness," Duncan had argued with all his fifteen-year-old authority.

"Jesus had to become the sacrifice for our sins. It wasn't enough that He took on the guilt of the world—there had to be a consequence for it. If there was no sacrifice, it would make God unjust. Jesus couldn't just take on the sins and not suffer the punishment. It wasn't a matter of God's timing being off, Duncan, it was a matter of God remaining sovereign and just."

Duncan had considered his father's words for a long time. He could see the truth of them, but the timing issue still bothered him, and it didn't seem fair. In the events of human lives, God's timing often seemed skewed.

His father then said, "Duncan, we can't know the mind of God. We can't always understand the result or reason of the things that take place in our lives. The fifty-fifth chapter of Isaiah says, 'For my thoughts are not your thoughts, neither are your ways my ways, saith the Lord. For as the heavens are higher than the earth, so are my ways higher than your ways, and my thoughts than your thoughts.' Sometimes God allows things that make no sense to you or me. We may never know why, but we have to trust that He does and that it's the right way for things to be."

Duncan knew he would have to do the same now. He would have to trust that God had the matter under control. He'd done nothing wrong. His motives were pure. He had set out on a mission to do nothing more than find out who was stealing from the Indians. Rainy just happened to get in the middle of it.

———

In Albuquerque, Rainy tried to help her mother with a glad heart. She forced herself to get enthusiastic about plans for her father's party, but no matter what she did, Duncan was always in her thoughts. Even as she planned to help Gunther with his project, Rainy thought of Duncan and wondered if he'd just see her as doing whatever she could in order to steal more artifacts.

By Thursday evening Rainy had spent a great deal of time in prayer and felt almost ready to let go of the past, when Sonny surprised them with a visit. The look on his face told Rainy it wasn't good news.

"What's happened?" she asked, hanging her colorful apron to one side.

"It's Jennetta Blythe," Sonny said, pulling out a dining room chair to sit down.

Their parents came into the room, both wearing broad smiles. "Sonny, it's so good to see you again so soon," their mother said and kissed him atop his head.

Rainy saw his frustration. "Sonny has come with news of one of our tourists, who disappeared while traveling in Arizona with us. Remember I told you how Mrs. Blythe couldn't be found and then we had to leave without her?"

Their parents nodded in unison, and Sonny picked up the conversation. "Well, it seems the reason she disappeared was to visit some old Indian medicine woman. She wanted to . . . end her pregnancy."

"I didn't even know she *was* pregnant," Rainy said in surprise.

"No one did. Not even Phillip," Sonny admitted.

Rainy thought of the situation and shook her head. "Why would she want to kill her baby? I mean, I know Jennetta was divorcing her husband, but they might have worked things out for the sake of the child."

"I don't know about that, but Jennetta's in the hospital. She nearly died from whatever medicines that old woman gave her. She lost the baby, but she could still lose her life as well. Phillip is beside himself. I asked him if he wanted me to bring you to talk to Jennetta, but he said no. He said he couldn't bear to see you just now, but I thought maybe you should go anyway."

Rainy felt torn. She had plans to travel with Gunther in the morning. She hadn't told anyone because she didn't want to be lectured about it. No doubt her father wouldn't like her going off across the desert with only an old man for protection and help in case their automobile broke down. Her mother would no doubt worry about it as well.

"I don't know that it would be such a wise idea for Rainy to go," her father said thoughtfully. "If Phillip has asked that she not come, then we should honor his wishes."

Sonny shrugged. "I just thought she could share Jesus with Jennetta and Phillip."

"Phillip needs a man to guide him in these spiritual matters," Rainy finally said. "I tried to talk to him about God, but I don't think he heard much of what I had to say." She ached for Phillip. It was her fervent wish that he might find salvation—not so that he might be eligible husband material, but rather so that he might find the peace that he desired.

"Why don't you go to Phillip and share the Gospel, son?" their father questioned.

Rainy quickly agreed. "I think he might very well listen to another man. Phillip's life was seemingly perfect when I tried to talk to him. Maybe hearing God's truth would mean much more now."

"But I don't really know him like you do. Maybe we could go together."

Rainy felt a twinge of guilt. "I really feel I would do more harm than good, given our past. I might just end up hurting him even more. Please do this for me, Sonny. It's God he needs, not me."

Their father put his hand on Sonny's shoulder. "Your sister is right. He doesn't need to be clouding his thoughts right now. Seeing Rainy again might make matters all the more difficult. The important thing is to support him while he awaits word on his sister."

"Well, when you put it that way it does make sense. Sure, I'll go back and stay with him at the hospital," Sonny offered.

Rainy reached out and squeezed his hand. "Tell him that I'm praying for Jennetta and for him as well. If he wants me to visit, I will."

Sonny started to get up, but his mother said, "Stay where you are. You can't go back until you have some supper. I still have some tamales on the back of the stove."

Rainy moved away as her father began talking with Sonny about how to handle the situation with Phillip. The evening air felt refreshing as she moved into the courtyard, yet guilt became her companion. There was a part of her that wanted nothing more than to go back to Santa Fe and comfort Phillip, but at the same time she wanted to run as far away as possible. She was actually glad Phillip had asked that she not come.

Lord, I need you to help me through this, she prayed. *I need to be strong in my resolve and I need to trust that you are in control. Please be with Jennetta and heal her body. Heal her on the inside as well.*

The thought of Jennetta taking the life of her own baby angered Rainy. Slipping into a chair, she tried to reason it all out. She knew Jennetta's way of living was self-centered and spoiled, but she couldn't imagine how anyone could reach such a decision.

"Rainy, are you all right?" her mother asked softly.

Rainy turned and nodded. "I was just trying to pray for Jennetta and Phillip, but . . ."

"But what?"

"But why would she kill her baby? Just imagine it."

"I can't because I've always loved being a mother. From the first moment I knew I was expecting you two, I rejoiced." She came and sat beside Rainy in the garden. "Don't be angry with Jennetta. She must have been very scared."

"I know that in my heart and I do feel bad for her. But I can't help but be convinced that she also did this because the baby was an inconvenience to her. Jennetta is an arrogant, self-absorbed woman. A baby wouldn't fit into her lifestyle."

Her mother reached over and patted Rainy's hand. "She needs God. The things of God make no sense to her. She can't understand the value of her child's life because she doesn't understand the value of her own life. You've said yourself that she seems to be miserable most of the time."

Rainy realized her mother was right. "Yes, she is. She's always writing the most depressing stuff—at least to hear Phillip tell it."

"Well, when your soul is lost in sorrow, it's hard to write anything uplifting. My guess is that Jennetta's life is in shambles. There is a great deal of ugliness involved in any divorce. She very well may be overwhelmed with her emotions over that. The baby was probably too much for her to even consider. Be compassionate, Rainy. We cannot approve of what she's done, but we can pray for her and show her love. That's what being a woman of God is all about."

Rainy nodded. "I'll keep praying about it. I know I have so much to do in my own life that I have no right to look at another's person's life with expectations of perfection."

"Sometimes the hardest thing is to deal with the log in our own eye," her mother said sympathetically. "If you look to God, He'll help you to put your own heart in order, Rainy. Then you'll be better equipped to pray and understand the lives of those around you."

"But you said nothing about this," Rainy's mother argued as Rainy tried to explain her mission with Gunther.

Rainy had purposefully waited until her father and Sonny had both gone before springing the news on her mother. "Gunther just needs my help in arranging matters with the Hopi. He has a couple of dig sites that he wants to research to see if the finds will confirm other findings or offer new evidence."

"I understand the purpose of the trip, but I don't like the idea of my daughter going off across the desert without proper help. If you broke down, Gunther would never be able to make repairs to the car or even change a tire."

"Mother, I know that very well. I can change a tire if need be," Rainy protested. "Look, I promised him I'd help. He'll be here any minute and he's already purchased train tickets."

"So you'll go by train most of the way?"

Rainy shoved another blouse into her bag. "Yes. We'll take the train to Winslow."

"Well, I suppose there's nothing I can say to change your mind. I don't like the idea, however." Her mother pushed back an unruly strand of graying red hair and sighed. "Why can't you wait until Sonny has time to go with you?"

"Because Gunther, knowing that we planned to leave on the first of September, wanted to work through this now. He may not even be able to accomplish it all before we leave, but at least I can help him have a good start." Rainy stopped what she was doing and took her mother's hands in her own. "I promise to be careful. We'll take extra food and water when we go into the desert, and I'll make sure that everyone knows our route."

Her mother nodded. "All right. Look, I've made a batch of cinnamon cookies. I'll wrap some up for you."

Rainy grinned. "Thanks, Mom. I know Gunther and I will enjoy them."

Rainy finished her packing and had just brought down her bag when Gunther arrived. "Come on in." She shoved her thick braid up under a wide-brimmed straw hat.

He shook his head. "There's no time. I'm afraid I was delayed this morning. We'll have to hurry if we're to make our train."

Rainy turned to her mother and kissed her on the cheek. "I should be back in a few days. Don't worry about me."

"You take good care of her, Gunther. I don't like the idea of you two setting off on your own. She's just a young woman and you are not capable of running marathons anymore."

Gunther laughed awkwardly. "I don't intend to run any marathons, my dear woman." He kissed her hand, then reached for Rainy's bag. "We'll take it slow and easy. You'll see. Everything will work out just fine."

Rainy's mother thrust the cookies into her daughter's hands, then kissed her soundly. "You send word if you have any trouble at all."

"I will, Mom."

———

Sonny didn't know how to deal with Phillip Vance. The man was used to people adoring him and falling at his feet. How would he respond to Sonny's words? People generally didn't like hearing that they were living in a manner that was less than acceptable to God. How could Sonny approach the situation, tell Phillip about Jesus, and not offend him?

He found Phillip sitting alone, much to Sonny's surprise. He looked haggard and rumpled. He'd obviously slept in his linen suit, as the wrinkles bore evidence. It made Sonny less self-conscious about his own casual attire.

"Hello," Sonny said, coming into the waiting room.

"Oh, hello." Phillip started to get up but Sonny waved him off.

"Please don't get up. You look like you've had a bad time of it. How's your sister?"

Phillip sighed. "It looks like she's going to make it through, but she had to have surgery. The doctor said she'll never be able to have children."

"I'm glad she's going to make it ... but sorry for the situation," Sonny offered.

"I don't know why she did it. I would have helped her in any way I could."

"Sometimes people do things that make no sense to us. They're desperate and needy and they just don't give it much thought."

Phillip stared off into space as though the answer to all his questions might materialize before him. Sonny wished he could ease his pain, but there was nothing he could do but pray. Pray. The thought struck him.

"You know, I took the train to Albuquerque yesterday and I told my family, including Rainy, what had happened. They're all praying for you and for Jennetta. They started last night."

"The doctor said she'd lost so much blood that she probably should have died. She was very weak by the time he operated, but she made a turn for the better early this morning." Phillip rubbed his eyes for a moment and shook his head. "Is Rainy here?"

"No," Sonny said softly. "You said you didn't want her here, so she stayed home. She did send her wishes and prayers that Jennetta would recover and that you would be strengthened."

"It's for the best." Disappointment rang clear in his voice. "I thought she might have married me," Phillip said, again staring off into space. "I thought being with her—having her for my wife—would make everything better ... different."

Sonny sat down beside Phillip. "How so?"

Phillip shook his head. "I don't know." He seemed so out of place in the sterile confines of the waiting room. He looked to where a crucifix was nailed to the wall opposite them. Sonny's gaze followed suit as Phillip continued. "She trusts God and she couldn't be with me because I don't."

"Why don't you trust God?" Sonny asked.

"I don't know. I suppose because it never seemed necessary to me. Then, too, I've heard the uproar from the religious masses about how movies are sinful and people are going to hell because of what I provide them. I make my living as an actor, and I'm condemned because of it." He seemed so lost and hopeless. "Rainy was the first woman to really make me feel alive. She didn't care about my status as an actor and didn't care about my money." He sighed. "She didn't care about me, period."

"That's not true. I probably shouldn't say this, but Rainy was pretty taken with you at first."

Phillip looked up. "She was?"

Sonny didn't know how much he should say. He didn't want the conversation to be about Rainy, but rather about God's love. "Rainy thought you were very charming. She's taken with men who show manners and consideration for other people. You were like that and so she thought highly of you."

"Then why . . ."

"You know the reason, Phillip. Rainy has given her life to God. She trusts Him for direction and she desires to serve Him as best she can. If that's through her work for the Detours or through archaeology, then so be it. If it's as a wife and mother, then she's just as glad to do that too. But God must come first, and Rainy knew you'd never play second fiddle to anyone."

Phillip leaned back and stared at the cross on the wall. "She's a wise woman. I wouldn't have liked being second to anyone, not even God. Religion has so many rules and regulations, and I'm sure I'd never have been able to stand up to that kind of perfection. I'm a disciplined man, but not in that way. I like my fun."

"So do I, but I also like the peace that comes from holding myself accountable to God."

Sonny watched as Phillip got up and walked to the cross, then reached out and traced the wooden image of Christ. "How can peace come out of something so violent as this?"

"The peace doesn't come from the act of killing Jesus. It comes from His willingness to take the blame and burden of sin in our place. My peace comes daily in knowing that He rose from the dead and that He's interceding for me with the Father. It comes because I know that even if death takes this body, my soul has eternal life in heaven, where all things old will pass away. All things here will fade to dust. Nothing here will matter. Not what I do as a geologist—not what you do as an actor. What will matter then is what we did for God."

"If that's true," Phillip said, turning to face Sonny, "then I've nothing to show for my life."

"But you can change all of that. See the error of your way and repent of it. Turn to God and seek His will for your life. He wants to welcome you into His care—He wants to be there for you."

"How can you be so sure of that? How can you trust that He listens and truly cares?"

Sonny got up and went to where Phillip stood. He reached out and touched Phillip. "You said yourself that the doctor figured your sister would die. But she didn't. I believe our prayers to God were heard and answered."

"But would God demand that I give up my acting? Would He take from me the very things I love?"

"If you loved them more than Him, He might well ask you to give them up."

Phillip shook his head. "I just don't know that I could ever do that."

Sonny felt a deep sadness for the man. It reminded him of the story of the rich young ruler. The man had come to Jesus proclaiming to do everything taught by scriptural law. Jesus told him then to sell everything he had and follow Him. The man couldn't do it because too much was at stake. He was very wealthy—how could he give it all up? Now Phillip was up against the same thing. Sonny had no idea if God would call him to give up acting, but he did know that God required one hundred percent of your heart. Phillip clearly couldn't or wouldn't give that up just yet.

"Think about it, Phillip. Just think on it. Let God speak to your heart and tell you what's true and necessary and what isn't. You might be surprised at the outcome."

"I will think about it," Phillip replied. "After all, it gives you and Rainy a great deal of peace and confidence. It must not be all bad." He smiled weakly.

"I need to go," Sonny said, noting the time. "But I'll come back this afternoon before I leave for Albuquerque."

Phillip nodded and reached out his hand. "Thank you for coming and give Rainy my . . . my best."

Sonny shook Phillip's hand. "I will."

That afternoon, Sonny concluded his business as quickly as possible. He turned in his resignation, packed his things, and made arrangements to head home. He was just about to head to the hospital again when Duncan Hartford caught up with him.

"Sonny, I'd hoped to run into you. Well, actually I was hoping to run into Rainy. I've looked all over for her, but they told me she'd resigned and moved out of the boardinghouse. Is that true?"

It seemed the day for desperate men. Duncan looked almost frantic in his search. "She's in Albuquerque. She did resign early and now she's helping Mom pack for the trip to Scotland."

"So she really plans to leave America?"

"I suppose so," Sonny said rather thoughtfully. "I know her heart isn't in it, but there aren't a whole lot of options for her."

"I desperately need to talk to her. I don't want her to leave. . . ." He paused and looked away. "At least not without explaining the truth."

"Did you two have another falling-out?"

Duncan pushed back his hat. "You could say that."

"Why don't you walk over to the hospital with me and tell me about it? I wanted to check in on Jennetta Blythe."

"Sure, I'll walk with you. It'd probably do me good to explain the situation, but I hope you'll hear me out before you judge me."

Sonny raised a brow. "Sounds really serious."

"It is."

————

Three hours later, Duncan sat beside Sonny on the train to Albuquerque. Sonny had listened to Duncan and, instead of reacting in the emotional way Rainy had, had understood and accepted Duncan's explanation. He'd also believed Duncan when he spoke of how much he loved Rainy.

"You need to tell her yourself," Sonny had said. "Come back with me to Albuquerque and spend the night with us. With you under the same roof, she'll have to listen. Besides, Dad would never allow her to go on pouting and refusing to hear you out."

To Duncan it seemed the reprieve he'd prayed for. He only hoped that Rainy saw it the same way.

"I tried to lay a trap for Jennetta Blythe and her brother," Duncan admitted. "I promised Mr. Richland I'd try to bait them with museum pieces and see if they were willing to buy them."

Sonny seemed interested. "What happened?"

"Jennetta told me she'd be in touch after the trip," Duncan replied. "But now I suppose we'll never know if she was the one who was arranging to steal the missing pieces."

Sonny grew thoughtful. "Given everything you've said, I just can't help but wonder if Rainy wasn't right. Maybe it is Chester Driscoll. He's had plenty of opportunity, and even if Jennetta had one of the missing Hopi flutes, she just might have gotten it from Driscoll."

"It's worth considering," Duncan agreed. "I just don't know how we go about proving it one way or another. Chester's no fool."

"Let's talk to Rainy about it. She may have an idea since she's thought him guilty—or at least involved—from the very start."

"All right," Duncan said. "I just hope she doesn't slam the door in my face."

Sonny laughed. "Well, just in case, maybe I'd better go in first."

ainy and Gunther planned to spend the night at La Posada, the magnificent Harvey hotel in Winslow, Arizona. Rainy always enjoyed coming to La Posada. The gardens were refreshing and beautifully set against orchards and fountains. No expense had been spared on the marvelous creation.

Bordered on one side by railroad tracks and by Highway 66 on the other, the hotel had been created to look like an ancient hacienda. The stone floors and arched entryways gave the hotel a Spanish look. Rainy had to admit the architects and builders had done their jobs well.

"Rainy Gordon!" a thin, dark-haired woman declared as Rainy entered the dining room. "When did you get here?"

Rainy embraced the Harvey Girl and laughed. "Daisy! I didn't know you were working at La Posada. I just got here. I arrived with my father's good friend Gunther Albright. He's that older man just across the hall." She motioned and the younger woman craned her neck to see. Rainy had first met Daisy Kincaid at La Fonda, where she worked as a Harvey waitress. Nearly a year earlier, Daisy had transferred to Chicago but now, apparently, she was back in the Southwest.

"I was going to ask if he might be a younger, single friend of your father's, but I can see for myself he's not," Daisy giggled.

"No, definitely not. So when did you come to La Posada? I thought you were up Chicago way."

Daisy directed her to the counter. "Sit here and I'll bring you something to eat. You are hungry, aren't you?"

"Famished. Gunther had to look into a problem with the car he requested, so he told me I might as well get a bite. We're going up to the Hopi villages, where we plan to discuss an archaeological dig that

Gunther wants to begin. I have friends up there who just might be able to help him get the permission he needs. But enough about me. Tell me everything you've been doing."

"Well, it's hard to tell everything," Daisy teased. She placed a glass of lemonade in front of Rainy and laughed. "I almost got married."

"No," Rainy said, leaning in. "Why only almost?"

Daisy rolled her gaze to the ceiling and laughed. "He was flighty, as my mother put it, and he was a vacuum cleaner salesman. Mother said you just couldn't trust a man who's always working in dirt."

Rainy grinned. "I suppose that leaves archaeologists out as well." Determined to have a pleasant visit with Daisy, she tried not to think of Duncan. "So is that why you're back in the desert? Baking your brain in order to forget your failed encounter with love?"

Daisy shook her head. "Goodness, no. I found myself pining for the desert as much as anything. Crazy as it sounds for this Michigan girl, I just couldn't stay away."

After an hour of chatter and a pleasant lunch of chicken salad and cantaloupe, Rainy got up to leave. "I never fail to be amazed at these lovely blue-and-yellow Spanish tiles," she said, running her hand along the counter top. "What a wonder. The entire hotel is like an oasis in the desert."

"It is," Daisy agreed. "We've had so many movie stars come here. You'd be very impressed. We even had Phillip Vance."

Rainy smiled and nodded. She didn't even begin to feel like explaining Phillip to Daisy. "Well, look, I should continue to make preparations for our trip. We plan to head out early in the morning."

"I'll be working the breakfast shift. Come see me before you go. You'll want to take some sandwiches and fruit. I'll pack you something special."

Rainy hugged her friend and thanked her for the kind offer and the conversation. Making her way upstairs, Rainy saw nothing of Gunther. She hoped he was able to figure out what had become of the car. He'd certainly been angry when he'd learned it wasn't waiting for him as requested.

Rainy's room was simple but charming. The windows had been opened to let in the evening breeze and there was a pitcher of water and a small bowl of fruit on the wooden desk beside the window. Rainy sat down and began undoing her bootlaces. Again, feelings of nostalgia washed over her as her gaze fixed on the handwoven Indian rug beneath her feet.

"Oh, Lord, this is so hard for so many reasons," she murmured and pulled off her boot. She couldn't help but think of Duncan and wonder what he was doing. She visualized his wavy black hair and brown eyes, his firm jawline and gentle lips. She touched her hand to her mouth, remembering the feel of his kiss.

"I don't want to stay mad at Duncan Hartford. I want to forgive him and rush back to Santa Fe and tell him that I will love him forever." She sighed. "But I can't. He would never believe me. Not after I acted like a spoiled child. Someday I may learn to keep my mouth shut and not jump to conclusions, but I fear it's too late for Duncan and me."

She pulled off the other boot, then went to unpack her belongings. Spying her Bible, she began to read through a few psalms. They were always comforting to her, but today she couldn't concentrate long enough to feel anything but confusion and frustration.

"Lord," she prayed aloud, "I've tried hard to let this go. I know I've done a poor job in many ways. I know I should never have let matters get out of hand. I thought I understood your will for my life and I thought you'd given me a clear and easy path to attain that will. But none of this has been easy, and I feel rather beaten and depleted."

She put the Bible aside and stretched out on the bed. On her back with her hands beneath her head, Rainy stared at the ceiling and tried not to imagine Duncan's face or his touch. She tried not to hear his voice or see his eyes. She thought she'd almost managed the matter as she began to doze off to sleep, but her dreams betrayed her.

In her mind, she saw herself Duncan's wife. They were happy. They were working together on a dig and she had found something of great interest to show her husband. Duncan had nodded approvingly and had lifted her in the air to whirl her round and round. The action took her breath away and Rainy awoke with a start, gasping for air.

The silence of the room reminded her that she was all alone. The dream had been a pleasurable moment and now, in its absence, Rainy felt only empty loneliness in its place.

Tossing and turning in her bed, Rainy argued with herself and then with God. "I can forgive him, Lord. I can forgive the fact that he wormed his way into my heart in order to spy on me. I really can. But if he's the man for me, then why did he not believe me innocent? Why did he get involved with the investigation and try to prove me guilty?"

Or was he trying to prove you innocent? A voice from deep within seemed to challenge her.

That thought had never come to mind. Maybe Duncan had put

himself into the position of assisting the authorities because he didn't believe her guilty, just as he'd said. Rainy sat straight up in bed at this thought. *Have I misjudged him?* Were his actions meant to save me instead of condemn me? Just then she remembered Duncan's words that day in Santa Fe. *"I wanted to prove you were innocent."*

Rainy suddenly felt ill. *Have I ruined everything, Lord? Have I put an end to my one chance at happiness with Duncan?* She got up and began to pace. "Oh, God, please take this misery from me. I long to do whatever it is you want me to do. I can't bear the way I feel." She pressed her hand against the soft folds of her skirt. "Deep inside, I want to do the right thing. I just don't know what it is."

She threw herself to her knees. In the middle of the room, she prayed as she'd never prayed before. "I know I've not always listened for your voice. I know that I've often tried to take control of situations and work them out in my own way. I see how I did that with Duncan and even with Phillip. I charged into those situations without allowing you to work. But, God, in all honesty, I love Duncan. Please forgive me and show me that I haven't ruined my only chance for love with him. Please give me a sign—show me a verse—something, Lord."

She prayed for what seemed an eternity, begging and pleading for God's forgiveness and direction. By the time Rainy fell back into bed, she was exhausted—wearied from struggling to understand God's will for her life. Would it always be this hard?

———

"She went where?" Sonny questioned, more than a little upset.

"Calm down, son. I wasn't any happier than you to hear what she did," his father stated, "but you know your sister and her headstrong ways."

"But this goes even beyond her usual nonsense. To go out on a trip like this with no one but your friend for a companion is . . . Why didn't you insist she have someone else go along? Why didn't she wait for me? I would have been happy to help."

Sonny paced back and forth as Duncan watched and waited for someone to answer. He wanted to know the same things. He felt more than a little frustrated that he wouldn't be able to talk to Rainy and explain his actions. He didn't want even one more day to pass between them without her hearing the truth.

"I tried to suggest that she wait for you," Sonny's mother said. "But Gunther needed to get the cooperation of the Hopi as soon as possible, and I had no idea you would return so quickly. I guess she just felt she needed to do Gunther this favor on behalf of us."

"But she won't be able to dig them out if they get stuck. Those roads up from Winslow can be really bad at times. What if she's in a sandstorm? She could forget about the arroyos and get caught in a flash flood. After all, this is the rainy season and they've already had several heavy rains over that way."

Sonny's father held up his hands. "You're only serving to worry your mother. If it's all that much of a concern, why don't you take the train out tomorrow and go after her?"

"That's it!" Duncan declared, getting to his feet. "Let's go after her. Let's help them. Two vehicles would be better than one. If one gets stuck the other one can pull it out."

"Rather like the verses in Ecclesiastes, eh?" Ray Gordon said with a smile. " 'Two are better than one; because they have a good reward for their labour. For if they fall, the one will lift up his fellow: but woe to him that is alone when he falleth; for he hath not another to help him up. Again, if two lie together, then they have heat: but how can one be warm alone? And if one prevail against him, two shall withstand him; and a threefold cord is not quickly broken.' Together, you two will make Rainy a threefold cord and she's sure to be safe."

"I can arrange a car in Winslow with Clarkson's company. I might even be able to get us free passage on the train," Sonny said with a grin.

"If not, I'll pay for it," Duncan replied. He turned to Ray and grew rather embarrassed. "You might as well know that I plan to marry your daughter—if it meets with your approval."

Ray looked to his wife and both exchanged broad smiles. "It's more important that it meets with Rainy's approval. Perhaps," Ray said, putting his arm around Duncan, "we need to have a little talk."

———

Duncan had never known more frustration than waiting for the morning train. He had longed to leave the night before, but there was no way to get passage to Winslow. Sonny had even tried to get them on a freight train, but that hadn't worked at all.

Now as they stood waiting to board their train, he could hardly force coherent thought. *What if she's in danger? What if they've gotten stuck in the desert and had to spend the night?* He paced on the platform while Sonny sat nearby, hat in hand.

"Well, Sonny Gordon," Bethel Driscoll announced as she approached them. "What brings you here?"

"Catching a train," Sonny said rather sarcastically.

Duncan immediately suspected that Sonny wanted to keep their mission under wraps. He gave Bethel a tentative smile and tipped his hat. "Good morning."

"Mr. Hartford, isn't it?" She smiled rather coyly.

"Yes, ma'am."

"Are you two traveling together?"

"Yes," Sonny said matter-of-factly, getting to his feet. "What are you doing here? I thought given Jennetta's medical condition you'd be at her side in Santa Fe."

"I was with Jennetta until yesterday. She told me to leave her alone and demanded I go, so I did." She shrugged as though the incident meant nothing to her. "I'm to meet some friends coming in from Santa Fe. They're going to stay with me while Chester is away."

Sonny didn't seem to have the time or interest to get into Bethel's affairs with Jennetta, so he chose to keep the subject on Chester's travels. "And where has he gotten off to this time?" Sonny asked.

Bethel laughed. "Oh, he's on some fool expedition with my uncle."

Duncan forced himself not to react. He held his breath momentarily for fear of making a scene. Sonny seemed to be taking the same track.

"Chester and Gunther are working together?" Sonny asked.

"Oh, mercy, yes," Bethel said. "They've been involved in several projects these last months. I've never seen a man so enthusiastic about working with Indian artifacts as Chester. Sometimes I think he might be part Indian. We have the silly things all over the house."

Sonny and Duncan exchanged a look. Duncan knew exactly what Sonny was thinking. Duncan would love to see the pieces in Bethel's house, but in order to do so, even if she were willing, they'd miss their train.

As if on cue, the train whistle sounded from a mile down the track. "Here she comes," Sonny murmured.

Duncan nodded. "I guess we'll be saying good-bye, Mrs. Driscoll."

She laughed. "Well, you could both delay your trip and have breakfast with my party. We're quite a lively bunch, don't you know."

"Thank you, no. We have some pretty urgent business," Sonny replied for them.

Duncan thought it an understatement. To him, the business had just become a matter of life and death. Especially with Chester Driscoll involved.

*M*ore coffee?'' Daisy asked as she picked up leftover breakfast dishes from the places on either side of Rainy.

"No, I figure Gunther will be here any minute. He's not one to be delayed when he's ready to go. He was livid that we had to spend the extra day here as it was. He expected the car to be at his beck and call and when it wasn't, well, he was very unpleasant.''

"I can believe that. He seemed angry when he came down for breakfast. Just shoveled his food in and left," Daisy said, leaning forward. "And he didn't leave a tip.''

Rainy shook her head. "Sounds like him. Anyway, he's probably just preoccupied with the car situation. When they didn't have a car here when we arrived—or yesterday—he had to make calls and get things taken care of, and he's not at all happy about that. Then I had the audacity to suggest that I was going to drive. You would have thought I'd told him he would be hog-tied to the hood for the duration of the trip.''

Daisy giggled and Rainy laughed. "He assured me that either he would drive or he'd hire a driver whom I could direct." Rainy finished the last of her toast. "I figure the latter would be better. At least I know it would put my mother's mind at ease. She worries that we'll break down and not be able to fend for ourselves.''

Daisy reached under the counter. "I have a lunch packed for you. Sandwiches, fruit, cheese, and some pie. Oh, and I have a jug of ice water.''

Rainy reached down to the pack at her feet. "Would you mind filling my canteen as well? No sense taking it empty." While Daisy was gone, she slipped a quarter under her plate. *That should make up for Gunther's lack of tipping.*

Daisy returned just as Rainy got to her feet. "Thanks, Daisy," she said, tucking the canteen in her bag. "I should be back tomorrow, the next day at the latest. I can't imagine our work taking much longer than that."

Daisy nodded. "Are you going up to Polacca?"

"Well, that was the original plan, but Gunther actually talked last night of taking the cutoff just north of Egloffstein Butte. I don't know if he means to head to Keems Canyon, however, or Oraibi. Frankly, I'd rather just stick with the main road. It can be perilous enough if you aren't careful."

Daisy cleared away her dishes as they said their good-byes. "Be careful. You know the weather has been rather unpredictable. We've had some bad rains and more are no doubt coming our way. There were even a couple of the smaller bridges that washed out."

"I'm sure we'll be just fine, especially if Gunther hired a local driver."

Rainy took up her bag and found room for the lunch Daisy had packed. With this arranged, she made her way to the lobby. Gunther had apparently just settled their bill and was tucking his wallet into his pocket when he spied Rainy.

"Oh, there you are. Good. I was afraid if we waited much longer to start, we'd be in a bad way."

Rainy couldn't imagine why he was so concerned with the time. "Well, I'm here and ready. Did you get the car situation settled?"

"Yes, but it wasn't easy," Gunther said rather brusquely. His face contorted as if the entire matter were an uncomfortable memory. "We should be set now."

He headed for the door that would lead them away from the tracks and out into a small circular drive on the Route 66 side of the hotel. Rainy noted he wore the same crumpled linen suit that he'd worn on the train. She ventured a guess that he'd probably slept in the thing as well.

She, on the other hand, felt very fresh and smart in her tan-colored skirt and white cotton blouse. She'd worn long sleeves to keep from burning in the sun, but the weight of the material was light enough to let the air blow through and keep her cool.

Gunther took her bags and threw them onto the backseat while Rainy secured her straw hat. She tied it loosely so that she could push it back off her head if she chose. Most likely she'd wear it even in the car because it shielded her eyes from the sun and kept her from getting a headache, something she'd learned early on in her years in New Mexico.

To her amazement, Gunther motioned her to the back. "You'll be more comfortable there." He held the door for her.

"Oh, did you manage to get a driver?" she questioned.

"Yes, in a manner of speaking."

He didn't wait long at all before closing the door behind her and getting into the front seat. Rainy adjusted her bags, then looked up to find Chester Driscoll staring back at her.

"Hello, Rainy."

"What is he doing here?" she asked Gunther.

"My niece was worried that I was too old to be traipsing out across the desert alone," he replied as Chester started the car. "She talked to your parents and they all thought it would be a good idea if Chester drove for us."

Rainy found it difficult to believe that her parents would suggest Chester for any activity that involved her. They knew how she felt about him. As Chester eased the car onto Highway 66 and headed east, Rainy knew she'd have to make a scene in order to get him to stop and let her out. And that would certainly ruin Gunther's plans.

Settling back against the seat, she folded her arms against her chest. Something didn't seem quite right, but she couldn't put her finger on it.

Chester glanced back at her and smiled. "You don't really mind, now, do you? I mean, we're old friends."

"I don't suppose I really have a choice in the matter," Rainy replied.

They drove in silence for a time, but when Gunther motioned Chester to take the turn-off from the highway and head north, Rainy felt her uneasiness grow. It was one thing to be stuck in the desert with Gunther, but it was an entirely different thing to have to stomach Chester's company.

Rainy watched the dry desert landscape for some sign that all would be well. The early morning light was already sending the night hunters and scavengers into hiding. A coyote paused in his lope to look back at their car, almost as if he were checking to see if the noise had scared up something to eat. Seeing that the car was much too large a beast to take on his own, the coyote continued into the rocks and disappeared.

Rainy wished she could disappear. In the front, Gunther and Chester had begun to discuss Gunther's autumn classes. He planned to teach about the Civil War, including the lesser-known battles such as the

Battle of Glorieta, which took place some thirty miles east of Santa Fe. He also would be teaching classes on the Crimean War and pre–Civil War England and presenting a session of lectures on New Mexico.

"The university will finally have a rich selection of quality classes," Gunther said, seeming to forget that Rainy's father had had an active part in choosing which classes would be offered. "I believe your father and the board will be pleased with the changes. By eliminating some of the less experienced men, we should have a vast improvement in the history department."

"Yes, it took some convincing to get the board to listen to Father's suggestion that they fire those newer employees, but he shared with them the concerns you had."

Rainy could hardly believe her ears. Had Gunther really found a way to manipulate Marshall Driscoll? Maybe she should have enlisted his help in trying to clear her name.

"I'm concerned that further dismissals will be in order," Gunther said, "but of course, we can deal with that at a later date. The important thing is that I will be in charge."

Rainy felt that Gunther was betraying her father. After all, her father had been in charge of the department prior to this. For Gunther to insult the selection of classes, he might as well insult her father. But that was ludicrous. Gunther treated her father like a brother.

Rainy leaned back and closed her eyes. They had a long way to go, and given the fact that Chester was driving, they might well be even longer than was typical. She tried not to think of his comments about the university or of him as guilty of the Indian artifact thefts, but the suspicion kept resonating in her mind. *I know he has something to do with it. He's been on the tours or has had friends on the tours. What if he's paying them to smuggle the goods to him when he can't be on the trips as one of the dudes?*

"So did you manage to secure that crate?" Chester questioned.

"Shut up, you imbecile," Gunther hissed.

Rainy was momentarily startled but forced herself to feign sleep. They might well go on discussing whatever it was Gunther wanted hushed up if they thought she was asleep.

"Sorry," Chester apologized. "I figured with her sleeping it wouldn't do any harm to discuss business."

"But she could just as easily have woken up," Gunther replied. "Let's leave it be and discuss business at a later time."

Rainy, although disappointed, tried hard to remain still. The heat was steadily growing, however, and her forehead was beginning to drip with sweat in spite of the fact that Gunther had his window down.

She shifted restlessly, hoping the men would be no wiser to her ruse. They went on talking quietly, in hushed voices that Rainy couldn't make out. With the droning rhythm of the car, Rainy managed to doze. She again dreamed of Duncan, but the images weren't as pleasant. She was saying good-bye at the railroad station—leaving Duncan behind. She tried to hear what he was saying, but a loud noise kept her from understanding. Suddenly Rainy felt herself falling. She awoke to find the car swerving madly to the right.

"Hold her steady, you fool!" Gunther yelled. "Do you want to flip us over?"

Rainy sat up just as Chester managed to put the car into deep sand. The engine died as they came to rest. Yawning, she straightened her hat and looked around. She recognized their location immediately. She hadn't slept long at all, because they were not far from Winslow— maybe fifteen miles.

"Now look what you've done!"

"Gunther, I didn't cause the tire to blow," Chester said defensively.

Gunther was already getting out the car. Rainy had never seen the man so angry. He slammed the door and kicked sand at the car. "Well, don't just sit there! Get out here and change the tire."

Chester looked to Rainy. "I don't know how to change a tire. I have people to do those kind of things."

"I can change a tire, Chester," Rainy said, pushing her bag back in place.

She eased out of the car. The vehicle slumped hopelessly to the right side. Not far from them the rocky outline of red sandstone threw short gray shadows across the desert floor. Rainy shielded her eyes.

Sighing, she turned back to where Gunther and Chester stood. "Well, where's the spare tire?"

"We seem to be without a spare," Gunther declared.

Rainy raised a brow. Looking at Chester she said, "You came into the desert without a spare tire? Next I suppose you'll tell me you didn't bring extra water either."

Chester looked rather embarrassed. "Well . . . I didn't think . . ."

"No, you certainly didn't," Gunther answered angrily. Banging his fist against the back of the car, Gunther paced to the front of the vehicle. "So now what do you propose we do?"

"We could wait awhile and see if anyone comes along," Rainy

offered. "It's always a possibility that the Indian agent for the Hopi villages will need to make a trip back or forth."

"It's going to be at least one hundred and ten degrees this afternoon. Do you really want to stand around here and wait to see if someone chances to come along?" Chester said, taking out his anger on Rainy.

Rainy put her hands to her hips. "Do you have a better plan?"

"We should probably walk to where we can get help."

Rainy laughed. "And where would that be? It's at least fifteen miles back to Winslow, and that's the closest place we'll get a tire repaired or replaced. You didn't even think to pack water. Good thing I brought a jug, or we'd all die of thirst."

"You have water?" Gunther questioned. "Why didn't you say so? I'm absolutely parched."

Rainy smiled and walked back toward the car. "I'm sorry, Gunther. You should have said something sooner." She passed by the older man and patted him on the arm. "Why don't you take it easy over there in the shade. I'll bring you the water."

Gunther ignored her kindness. "I just want a drink; I'm not an invalid."

"Of course not," she said, understanding his frustration was with Chester and not with her.

Rainy reached into the backseat and pulled out her bag. She didn't bother to bring out her own canteen but rather brought the jug Daisy had packed for them. Leaving the food as well, Rainy came to where Gunther stood, still fuming over their situation.

"Look," Rainy said softly, "the heat of the day is going to be upon us soon and we really should do what we can to make ourselves more comfortable. Last night you mentioned bringing a tent. Maybe we can use it, along with the car, to make some shade before the heat gets too intense. Then we can just ration out the water and take it easy. Come nightfall, we can all hike back to Winslow—or I'll hike it on my own. I know the way and I can probably cover the distance in half the time."

Gunther's expression registered contempt. "I need to get to the Hopi village—not to Winslow."

Rainy shrugged. "Well, I can't help you there. However, I can walk back to Winslow, borrow a spare from the Clarkson Company, and get someone to bring me back in the morning."

"Oh, this is hopeless!" Chester declared.

"Be quiet," Rainy and Gunther answered in unison.

Rainy saw Chester take a step back. Without warning, the wind lifted his fedora and sent it sailing across the road. Rainy almost laughed at the willy-nilly manner in which he ran to catch the wayward hat.

Ignoring Chester's curses and Gunther's growling disapproval, Rainy went to the trunk that was lashed on the back of the car. Opening it, she frowned. It was empty except for a small satchel. She turned, shaking her head.

"Where's the tent? Where are the tools?"

By this time Chester had come back, hat plastered firmly on his head. "I left them all back in Winslow. I didn't figure we'd need them."

Rainy had lost her patience. "Are you crazy? This is the kind of thing that gets people killed." She looked at Gunther, who was already wiping his face and neck with his handkerchief.

"Gunther wanted the space. . . ."

"Shut up, Driscoll. I've had enough of your lip. You were stupidly irresponsible. I specifically told you to pack the tent on top of the car if no other place. Instead you strip the car down, leave the spare tire, the water, the tools, and the only hope we had for any decent shelter from the sun."

"We have the car."

Rainy shook her head. The situation was going from bad to worse. "Look, the car is going to heat up, but maybe if we use it sparingly for shade we'll be all right."

"Well, that's just great," he muttered.

Realizing there was little to do except ask for God's intervention, Rainy whispered a silent prayer. After a moment she turned back to Gunther. "We'll need to watch out for snakes and the like."

"I'm walking back," Chester said, slapping the lid down on the trunk.

"You're hardly in any condition for such a thing. You'll be dead in a matter of hours," Rainy said without emotion.

"By all means, let him go," Gunther muttered.

Rainy shrugged. "Do as you will, but we'll be better off staying right here."

Gunther agreed and reluctantly Chester finally settled down. Rainy took a drink and sat down in the backseat to think. Gunther sat in the front passenger seat. He leaned over the seat and shook his head.

"My niece has married an incompetent fool."

"He's just not trained," Rainy said, trying to be kind. "Are you hungry, Gunther? I picked up some lunch for us this morning."

He smiled. "Always keeping one step ahead of the need, eh? Too bad you didn't think to pack a spare tire as well." He shook his head as if still in disbelief over Chester's actions. Finally he looked at her and nodded. "Yes, I'm quite hungry."

"Good," Rainy said. "We need to ration the food out, so I'll only offer you a sandwich for now." She dug into the bag and pulled out the packet Daisy had made. "I have roast beef or ham and cheese."

"Ham and cheese will do nicely."

She handed him the wax-wrapped sandwich. "I guess I should call Chester and feed him too." Gunther said nothing so Rainy took up another sandwich. Precious Daisy. Bless her for packing a hearty lunch.

"I have a roast beef sandwich for you," Rainy announced as she approached Chester, who was pacing. "You really should try to conserve your energy and stay cool."

He snatched the sandwich from her hand. "There isn't any place out here that's cool." He unwrapped the offering and looked back to Rainy. "Where'd you get this?"

"A friend packed a lunch for me to bring along."

"What else do you have?"

"Nothing for now. We need to ration our food." Chester grumbled but started munching on the sandwich.

Rainy worried as she made her way back to the car. *Maybe I should separate the food and hide some away.* Chester wouldn't be likely to listen to her should she protest his actions. She quickly shifted a few things around and left the bulk of the food, including most of her mother's cookies, inside her bag. She placed the rest of the packet given her by Daisy atop her bag.

"Gunther, would you care for one of my mother's cookies? I think we can splurge and have a cookie with our sandwich."

"Perhaps later. I assure you, I understand only too clearly the need to ration our meager fare."

Rainy leaned back in the seat and felt the heat drain away her energy. She lowered the straw hat down over her eyes and slept.

It seemed like it had only been minutes when she awoke to hear Gunther and Chester arguing behind the car. Groggy from the over-heated car, she strained to make sense of their words.

"You are without a doubt the reason we're stranded here," Gunther declared. "You're stupid, Driscoll. You have no common sense and you don't think any further than what interests you at the moment. How completely foolish to leave basic survival items back in Winslow."

"I resent you calling me stupid. I'm not stupid. I just thought you wanted as much space as possible for those articles. Have you forgotten our real mission here? Under the circumstances, I believe I've shown far more sense and intelligence than you have. After all, you brought Rainy Gordon along."

Rainy's brows knit together as she pushed back her hat. She tried to remain still as she edged closer to the open door. She had to catch everything they were saying.

"Rainy will keep the Hopi from asking too many questions. They respect her. She'll be our ticket to success."

"She certainly wasn't our ticket to success at the university."

"You were the fool who put the stolen artifacts in her desk. You were supposed to put them in her father's desk, but no. You ruined a perfectly good plan to get rid of Raymond Gordon once and for all, but you had to do things your way."

"I thought I could press her into marrying me. Lucky for your niece my plan failed."

"I hardly see it as luck that you and Bethel have married. . . . What in the world?"

Rainy was barely aware she'd climbed from the car until she found the duo looking at her with as much surprise registered in their expressions as she felt must surely be in her own. She stared open-mouthed at Gunther and Chester.

"How could you have betrayed my father like that?" she asked Gunther. "He's cared for you like a brother."

"Oh, this is rich," Gunther said, slamming his fist against the car. "Now do you see what you've done?"

"Me?" Chester protested, pointing at the middle of his sweat-soaked shirt. He'd long ago discarded his jacket, but not Gunther.

Now Rainy saw the reason why. Gunther pulled out a revolver he had been hiding under his coat and waved it in the air. "You, my dear, have stumbled into something you should not know about."

"You're stealing from the Hopi. You've been stealing from the Indians all along—haven't you?" She backed up a pace and tried to swallow down the dust in her dry throat.

"This is a messy affair," Gunther said, shaking his head. "I had hoped to spare you the details. You've always been kind to me, even if your father did steal my job with the university."

"How can you say that?"

Gunther's face contorted. "I say it because it's true. He took the position that was rightfully mine. I was left with whatever I could get. Begging leaves a bad taste in my mouth.''

Rainy felt light-headed at the thought of what Gunther was saying. "So you just pretended to be a friend to my family? For what purpose?"

"For the purpose of getting rich," he declared. "Chester immediately understood my goals because his desire was also to get rich. Now with the economy falling apart in bits and shreds, we have to hurry to secure our future.''

"By stealing?"

"By whatever means are necessary.''

Rainy felt sick. She clutched at her stomach as nausea overwhelmed her. "You let me be blamed for the university situation. You ruined my career, my dreams. Chester threatened me several times, then turned around and promised me the moon—including a position with National Geographic—all if I became his mistress."

Gunther scowled at Chester but said nothing. Chester, however, appeared eager to stay on Gunther's good side.

"She's lying, Gunther. I wouldn't do anything to hurt Bethel.''

"I don't trust you any farther than I can throw you, Driscoll. You'd been nothing but a greedy pain in the neck since I took you on. I'm sorry you ever married my niece. Miss Gordon may be naïve and overly simplistic in her religious notions, but she isn't a liar.''

"But I'm telling you—''

"I don't want to hear it," Gunther said, holding up his hand. "We have a bad situation here and I need to decide how to resolve it.''

Chester moved away to the edge of the road while Rainy tried to process all that she'd just been told. How could this be? How could her family have so clearly misjudged Gunther's character?

Chester began to shout. "Look! I see a car!''

Rainy could only pray the vehicle would take them to safety and get her away from Gunther and his gun. She felt weak in the knees. *Maybe the heat has done more to me than I thought.*

She moved toward the car. "I need a drink of water.''

Gunther didn't try to stop her. He went instead to stand beside Chester. The gun was cleverly concealed behind his back. Rainy had the water jug midway to her lips when it dawned on her that Gunther would probably force the people in the other car to give up their vehicle. *What can I do to keep them from being harmed?* Her mind raced as what looked like a black touring car drew nearer.

Oh, God, please help me, she prayed. She quickly drank from the jug and replaced it as the touring car came within a few hundred yards. Rainy made up her mind then and there to warn the people in the car.

Racing across the short distance, she yelped in pain when Gunther reached out and yanked her back. Her ankle burned from the violent twist Gunther gave her. "Where do you think you're going?"

"I won't let you hurt them." She tried to fight him, but by now the car had stopped in front of them and Gunther had raised his gun to her head.

She grew still and looked across to find a shocked Sonny and Duncan staring back at her from inside the car.

*D*uncan wanted only to remove Rainy from harm. Seeing her there, blue eyes wide with fear, gun to her head, made him less than a patient man. He got out of the car without even waiting to see if Sonny had some kind of plan.

"What do you think you're doing?" he asked Gunther.

"Stay back. You don't want to hurt her, do you?"

Rainy tried to pull away, but Gunther held her tight. Seeing her struggle made Duncan desperate to free her. "Let her go."

"I don't believe you're in a position to give orders, Mr. Hartford," Chester Driscoll declared.

Duncan waited for Sonny to come around the car. With a smile the auburn-haired man shoved his hands in his pockets and struck a non-threatening pose. "What's this all about, Gunther? Get too much sun today?"

"He's the one who's been taking the artifacts," Rainy declared, trying to balance on one foot. Duncan could see that she favored her left side. He wondered how badly she was hurt and whether or not she could run for cover if need be. "He and Chester are the ones who planted those Indian pieces in my desk and then blamed me."

Sonny frowned. "Why would you do that, Gunther? You're like an uncle to us. I thought you were our friend."

Gunther laughed and his pockmarked face contorted. "I did what I had to do to earn your father's trust. I never intended to cause Rainy harm. Chester took matters into his own hands and ruined my plans to see your father dismissed or, better yet, jailed. But that's not important. Right now I'm hot and tired and I want to leave. And you, Sonny, are going to take me where I want to go."

"Sure, we can all pile in the touring car."

Gunther shook his head. "No. Not all of us. Just you and me and Chester." He shoved Rainy into Duncan's waiting arms.

Duncan quickly shielded her with his body as Rainy cried out in pain. He didn't know what to think of the strange matter of Gunther Albright being responsible for the thefts. He really didn't even know the man, although he'd had a couple of minor encounters with him through the university.

Duncan looked to Sonny, who seemed to think the arrangement acceptable. "That's fine, Gunther. We can leave Duncan and Rainy here. I can come back for them later."

Gunther raised his gun again and pointed it straight at Duncan. "I can't have witnesses. I'll have to leave the state now as it is. But I won't be pursued. Your sister knows too much, and while I've always liked her, I can't have her sending the police after me."

"Ah, Rainy won't say anything," Sonny assured in his very matter-of-fact manner. "Will you, Rainy?"

"I'll do whatever it takes to keep you from hurting Sonny," Rainy declared from behind Duncan. She tried to pop around in order to see Gunther, but Duncan refused to let her and held her fast.

"See?" Sonny continued. "She'll be a good gal because she doesn't want you to hurt me. That's an even trade."

"Hardly," Gunther said. He seemed to consider the matter momentarily. "She said we're about fifteen miles from Winslow. Is that a fair assessment?"

Sonny nodded. "Easy fifteen."

Gunther sighed. "Very well. Take us to Winslow. We'll deal with things from there." He moved closer to Duncan while Chester went to the car. "If you say one word of this to anyone—if you walk out of here and send the authorities after me—I'll not hesitate to kill Sonny. Do you understand?"

Rainy peered around Duncan and this time he didn't attempt to stop her. "We understand. We won't do anything to endanger Sonny's life. Please don't hurt him."

"Sonny will be my insurance against problems. If either one of you does anything to cause me grief, Sonny will pay the price. Just remember that." Gunther gathered his things and then, on what seemed to be a whim, picked up the water jug and took a long drink before emptying the rest of the contents onto the parched ground. He shrugged at Duncan as if offering an apology, then made his way to the car. "Let that be added incentive."

Duncan wanted nothing more than to run to the car and knock the man to the ground. The rage inside him threatened to interfere with rational thought. Only having Rainy at his side kept him from risking everything.

"Sonny will accompany me back to my home," he said from the car window. "He will go with me as long as I feel there's a threat from either of you. Knowing what's in store for me if I'm caught, I won't care one whit about adding his murder to my list."

Rainy ripped away from Duncan. She tried to rush for Gunther but fell to her knees when her left leg collapsed beneath her. "But, Gunther, the theft of a few articles—articles that you may still have in your possession—well . . . that's hardly as bad as murder."

"My dear," he said as Sonny put the car into gear, "you don't know the half of it. It wouldn't be my first murder."

Duncan saw Rainy pale as she tried to get to her feet. "Gunther, please."

The old man ignored her and motioned Sonny into action.

Sonny turned the car around and headed back to Winslow while Rainy and Duncan watched in despair. Duncan went to her as soon as the car headed south. He slowly helped her to her feet and opened his arms to her. Rainy fell against him in tears. "Oh, Duncan, what are we to do?" Her sobs pierced his heart and broke the anger he felt.

Duncan pushed back her straw hat and dabbed at her sweat-soaked brow with his handkerchief. "We will pray first, and then we'll assess the situation and see what action might best suit our purpose."

"I can't even think clearly. I doubt I can pray with any real eloquence."

Duncan smiled. "God doesn't much care how we sound." He let his Scottish brogue thicken. "He loves us with an everlastin' love—no matter how eloquently we pray. Good thing too. I've always been better with ancient artifacts than with words."

Rainy nodded. "I've been praying and I'll keep praying, but I'm so afraid." She paused and her expression grew thoughtful. "You could walk out in a few hours, when it's not so hot," Rainy continued, wiping at her tears with the back of her hand. "That was my original plan, but now my ankle is twisted and I know I can't walk far."

"Are you all right otherwise? They didn't hurt you, did they?"

Rainy shook her head. "Chester worried me, but he didn't touch me. I didn't even twist my ankle until you showed up with Sonny. Though it hurts a great deal, I have to admit my pride smarts, too, from being so foolish and not recognizing Gunther's involvement."

"Ah, anyone could have missed that. He was just an old man."

"And he seemed to actually love my mother and father," Rainy said, looking dumbfounded. "I just can't believe this. How could he have deceived people so completely?"

"It's easy to deceive the ones who trust you and love you," Duncan said. "They aren't looking for any reason to be suspicious. I'm sure if Gunther only offered kindness and a congenial manner that your parents probably believed him to be a good friend."

"They did," Rainy agreed. "That's what hurts so much."

"Well, don't give it another thought. Gunther will get what's coming to him. Mr. Richland isn't about to let this situation go unpunished. Sonny and I learned from Bethel Driscoll that Chester was headed out here to work with his uncle. We put the pieces together then and there, and I wired Mr. Richland with the information. My guess is that even now, Richland has alerted the law enforcement officials and will have a plan in place to deal with Gunther and Chester."

"But what about Sonny? If they go charging in there with the police, Sonny may get killed."

"Sonny's a smart man. Give him credit, Rainy. He can deal with this. He did exactly what he wanted to do—he got Gunther and Chester away from us and headed back to Winslow, where he knows there's bound to be help."

"I suppose so," she said reluctantly.

"I know so," Duncan said encouragingly. "Right now we need to figure out how we can help Sonny—and ourselves. It's too bad Gunther poured out the last of the water."

"Oh, he didn't!" Rainy declared. She pushed away from Duncan's side and hobbled to the car. Opening the door, she pulled out her canteen. "I had a feeling Chester would try to pilfer our meager supplies. Little did I know it'd turn out this way."

"No, you couldn't have known," Duncan said, coming to stand beside her. "No one suspected Gunther. Chester seemed suspicious, but he appears to be nothing more than Albright's lackey. That's why you can't blame yourself in any of this. Even I had it figured to be Jennetta or Phillip—never you."

It was as if those two little words changed everything between them. Duncan caught the expression on Rainy's face, then watched as she tucked the canteen back inside the car. "We have some food too. One of the Harvey Girls packed fruit and cheese and pie, along with sandwiches. So if you get hungry we have plenty. Oh, and my mother sent cookies."

She moved away from him in her awkward manner, but Duncan wasn't about to let it go at that. "Rainy, I never thought you were guilty. I have to admit there were times when the evidence seemed completely against you, but I still held on to the belief that you had nothing to do with it. Even when the Indian Affairs man told me about your mishap at the university, I never believed you were responsible."

"You knew about the university? Even before I told you?" She searched his face for the truth.

He reached out and touched her cheek. "I knew."

Rainy shook her head. "I can't believe all of this is happening. What if Gunther tries to hurt Sonny? I can't bear the thought of it." She stepped away from Duncan and struggled to the road again. She looked to the south for several minutes, shading her eyes with her hand. "Sonny's just about to get everything he's ever wanted. He's been given his dream job—a geologist position with the government." She turned back to Duncan. "Did you know that?"

Duncan nodded, feeling terrible for the trembling in her voice. If he didn't take her mind from Sonny, he feared she might well begin another onslaught of tears.

"I wanted to tell you the truth about what happened with the investigation," he said softly, "but it wasn't the only reason I came here with Sonny."

Rainy lowered her hand and looked at Duncan. "What other reason was there?"

"I wanted you to know how I feel about you."

He crossed the distance between them, and before he could give Rainy a chance to protest he took her in his arms. "I don't care what else happens—I have to tell you how I feel."

Rainy nodded. "I'm listening."

At least she didn't fight him. The fact that she allowed him to embrace her gave Duncan hope. "I was a complete idiot not to make my feelings known to you that first night you asked me to share your supper table at La Fonda. I had cared about you from afar, and those feelings only grew more intense up close. I love you, Rainy. I know that without any doubt or hesitation. I love you and I want you to be my wife."

Rainy cocked her head to one side. Her expression suggested she was waiting for something more, but Duncan had no idea what it could be. He'd already spilled out his guts—told her what was in his heart.

"Please just tell me I haven't totally ruined my chances with you. Please tell me there's still a chance for us. I need to have hope."

Rainy raised her head and looked from side to side. "Hope doesn't seem to grow in abundance out here in the desert. We're stuck out here, my ankle is swelling as we speak, and Sonny is traveling with a madman who holds a gun. And in the middle of all of this, you proclaim your love and devotion."

Duncan grinned. "It'll make a great story to tell our children and grandchildren."

"Duncan, we have to make it out of here before we can talk about getting married, much less the rest of your plans."

"We'll make it out of here all right. Especially if you say yes to my proposal."

"Oh, and why's that?" Rainy questioned. "How does my saying yes help us get out of here?"

Duncan tightened his grip on her. "Because then I'll definitely have something to live for."

Rainy shook her head. "Your timing is the worst."

"I know."

"I mean, I plan to leave for Scotland in a few days."

Duncan shook his head this time. "I wouldn't have let you go."

"I'd already convinced myself I could never have you," Rainy admitted. "You know how I was praying for a husband."

He shrugged. "And here I am."

She looked at him for a moment and sighed. "I don't know what to do with you. You drive me positively mad. One minute I understand you—the next you seem like a stranger."

"Spend the rest of your life getting to know me," he encouraged.

"If we don't get out of here, it may well be a short lifetime." She grimaced and tried to shift her weight.

"Look, we need to get you off your ankle." He scooped her into his arms and carried her back to the car. "I know it's hot, but you need to rest. I'll put you in the backseat and then help you elevate your foot."

The look on her face was one of pain and worry. Pausing as he placed her inside the car, Duncan bent down to meet her gaze. "We're going to make it out of this, you'll see. I know God didn't bring us this far to let us die here."

"And just where did God bring us?" Rainy questioned.

"He brought us to the truth." Duncan kissed her lightly on the forehead. "The truth about the missing artifacts, the university thefts—and the truth about how we feel about each other. That is, unless you've changed your mind."

Rainy shook her head. "I didn't change it—I tried to change it and Phillip Vance tried to help me change it, but there was always something about you. Something in the middle of all my thoughts and feelings. There were times I wanted to run up to you and tell you everything and beg you to marry me."

"You wouldn't have had to beg, sweetheart. I would have willingly complied."

He touched his lips to hers ever so gently. He wanted nothing more than to kiss her for a long, long time, but there was work to do and he knew their survival depended on it. Pulling away, he whispered in her ear.

"Marry me, please."

She opened her eyes and looked up. "If we get out of here alive, I'll gladly marry you."

He grinned and backed away from the car. "You've given me a challenge to be sure, but now I have a reason to fight. You'll see how stubborn we Scots can be."

"I'm Scottish myself, or have you forgotten?"

He laughed. "Nay, I've not forgotten it, lassie. I'm countin' on it."

Rainy thought about his words as she watched him walk away from the car. He was counting on her stubbornness. For what? To survive? To make it through the pain? She knew her tenacious behavior had gotten her into trouble on many an occasion.

She watched Duncan scrounge for materials to build a fire. He hoped someone would see the smoke and come in search of the problem. She could only pray his plan worked.

Oh, Father, everything seems wrong. She grinned at the sight of Duncan. *Well, not everything,* she admitted. *I'm quite happy with your choice of a husband for me, but everything else seems quite hopeless. Please, Father, help us to right these wrongs. Save us, Lord. Save us from the desert isolation and heat. Send the cooling breeze of the evening. Help us get to safety.*

She prayed over and over while Duncan worked. He paused only long enough to take the tiniest of drinks and then he was back to work.

"He's a good man, Lord." She whispered the words as Duncan tried to set fire to the odd pile of fuel he'd collected. Her suitcase and clothes were among the sacrificed articles, as well as the trunk that had been on the back of the car.

At first the fire seemed unwilling to take, but then, much to Rainy's relief, the flame caught and began to consume some of the smaller, drier pieces of brush. Thick billowing smoke from the clothes and trunk filled the air.

"Well, at least that much has worked," she said with a sigh. "Now, if someone will just see it and come to help."

*R*ainy shifted uncomfortably in the backseat of the car. She'd tried to sleep through the chill of the desert night, but it seemed impossible. Her dreams were laced with wild images of Gunther and the desert. At one point she found herself in a dry field of overripe corn. The full moon overhead shone down nearly as bright as the sun and the corn withered on the stalk. Rainy tried to save the corn by watering it but found her water ran out after only a few stalks. Then, in frustration, she tried to pick the corn but instead the pieces turned to Indian treasures and Rainy stood holding first a piece of jewelry and then an intricate pot. People pointed at her, some accused her, and with a start, Rainy awoke to feel her hips sore and her ankle swollen and stiff. Realizing her situation, she wanted only to have a good cry.

Sitting up, she tried not to disturb her aching leg any more than she had to. What a rotten twist to her situation. *If I could have kept myself from injury, we might have walked to safety.*

Opening the car door, Rainy eased to the edge of the seat and looked out at the night sky. The stars were soothing to her. In the midst of such madness, they seemed to offer her something stable and consistent. She recognized several constellations, remembering how she and Sonny would sit until late into the night as children, watching the skies, talking about God and what they would do when they grew up.

"Oh, Sonny," Rainy whispered so as not to wake Duncan in the front seat, "I pray you're safe."

Thoughts of Sonny refused to leave her mind. She wondered where he was and whether or not Gunther had given up on the idea of forcing Sonny to travel with him. She thought of Sonny's dreams and plans for Alaska and tears came to her eyes.

I thought I was strong, Lord. I thought I could handle just about any test or trial. I thought the only real problems I had were finding a husband and clearing my name—both very selfish ambitions.

Now I sit here, unable to help anyone or to do anything, and I've never been more frustrated. I've always relied on my education and wits. I've always felt ever so self-sufficient and capable. But I'm not, Lord. I'm not. Please show us what to do. Please help us to get out of this mess without harm coming to anyone.

She worked her way back into her sleeping place and tried to get comfortable. Just when she thought it impossible to fall asleep, Rainy was once again dreaming of the dry desert lands.

Hours later Rainy woke again, this time with the distinct feeling that something was happening. She feared for a moment that Gunther had returned, but after craning her neck to see, Rainy was relieved to find their campsite still deserted.

"It's nearly sunrise," Duncan murmured from the front seat.

Rainy could see a hint of light and color on the eastern horizon. "What are we going to do? Our signal fire hasn't brought any help, and the roads have been deserted all night."

"Someone's bound to come through here," Duncan offered. "Aren't the harvests going on in the area? Aren't people bringing crops in for sale? Moving cattle or sheep—that kind of thing?"

"We can't count on that. This isn't exactly the main road." Rainy straightened up and leaned against the car door to ease the tension in her back. "We've used almost all the water in the canteen. I still can't hope to walk very far, but you could get to Winslow and—"

"I'm not leaving you here," he said, sitting up to look over the seat at her.

"But we don't have any water."

"We can drain the radiator and use what's there. I don't know what it will taste like, but we can try to filter it with a piece of cloth."

Rainy realized it was a good idea. "That would give you enough to take in the canteen."

Duncan's jaw tightened. "I said . . ."

Rainy reached out and touched his hand. "I know what you said, Duncan, but if you don't go for help, we may die out here just as Gunther planned." She looked out the window to the horizon. "It'll be fully light before long and the heat may become unbearable. If you leave now, you could get to Winslow before the worst of it and get back here with help before the afternoon heat becomes too stifling."

Duncan sighed and gripped her hand tightly. "There has to be another way."

Rainy shook her head. "But there's not. We've only got a bit of the food left. Enough for one meager meal, but that's it. Look, if we're going to survive this, we both need to make sacrifices."

"But if Sonny manages to ditch Gunther and Chester, he'll know where to come to find us. I really think we should stay here with the car."

"But Gunther and Chester know where to come too," Rainy reasoned. "You have to see that there's no other way. Right now you're in good shape. You've had food and water and rest." She smiled and added, "What little rest could be had." Sobering again, she continued. "But, Duncan, hours from now that won't be the case, and if no one shows up and Sonny still can't get to us, we'll gradually grow weak and sick from the lack of water."

She saw Duncan's look of resignation and knew he finally agreed. "All right," he said. "I'll go."

"Good. You'll be back before you know it and then we can help Sonny. I only hope we're not too late," Rainy said, feeling her emotions go topsy-turvy on her again. "I just hope he's all right. We used to be close enough to sense when the other one was in danger, but I can't sense anything at all. You don't suppose that means . . ."

"Don't even say it," Duncan said. "You know better. Sonny is a survivor. He's not going to be defeated by the likes of Gunther Albright and Chester Driscoll. You'll see. He's probably already figured a way to get himself out of this. Remember, we sent word to Richland and told him where we were headed and what you were doing. Did you let any of your Hopi friends know that you were coming?"

"Yes, I sent a message with a courier. The group was only going as far as Canyon de Chelly, but she promised to take it over after the tour was completed. I'm sure Istaqa knew we were on our way to see him."

"Good. When you didn't show up, he probably began to check what happened. Maybe he would have even called La Posada."

"It's possible—if the phone lines are working. The system isn't always the best out here."

"I understand," Duncan said, nodding. "But between Istaqa knowing and Richland being apprised of the situation, someone is bound to come to our rescue and to Sonny's."

"I hope so. I couldn't bear it if . . ."

Duncan smiled reassuringly. "Nothing bad will happen. Trust God to have this under control. It'll work out. You'll see."

Rainy wanted to see. She wanted to have hope, but even as Duncan bustled around outside the car, preparing for his walk to Winslow, she was losing faith. Soon she'd be alone, and though she couldn't tell Duncan, she was terrified. What if Chester Driscoll came back for her? Once Duncan was gone, she'd be defenseless.

She couldn't tell Duncan her fears. He'd just insist on staying at her side, and Rainy knew their only hope was in his walking to Winslow. She sighed and reached for one of her mother's cookies.

"Oh, Mother, I wish I'd listened to your apprehensions. I know I'm in this fix because of my pride and determination to control everything. I should have listened to you and given thought to what you had to say." She took a bite of the cookie to ease the rumblings in her stomach, but the dry texture only made her more thirsty. Funny how water didn't seem all that important when there was plenty of it.

She heard Duncan working to drain the radiator and wondered how awful the water would taste. It would be better than dying of thirst, but the thought still caused her to shudder.

I should never have tried to keep this from Dad. He wouldn't have allowed me to leave with Gunther. Had I not tried to sneak around, I would be safe at home and Sonny wouldn't be in danger. Her regret threatened to eat her alive. This must have been what her father had tried to teach her so long ago about obedience. If Rainy had obeyed, she'd be safe now. Instead, she'd endangered the lives of not only herself but Sonny and Duncan as well.

Glancing up, Rainy noticed a hint of dust on the horizon. She strained her eyes to make out the forms of several riders on horse and mule.

"Duncan!" she cried. "Riders are coming."

Duncan came around to where she sat. "Where?"

Rainy pointed to the north. "I think they may be Hopi." Struggling, she got out of the car and hopped around to the front. Duncan came up to support her. "Yes! I think it's Istaqa."

Rainy began to wave wildly while bouncing on her right foot. "Istaqa!"

The man at the front of the entourage waved and Rainy relaxed against Duncan. "He sees us. We're going to be all right."

"I already knew that," Duncan said with a grin. He pulled Rainy close. "I couldn't possibly lose you now."

Rainy looked deep into his eyes. Without hesitation she stretched up on her tiptoes and kissed him on the mouth. "I never knew what an optimist I was marrying."

"You didn't know you were even marrying me until yesterday."

"Hmmm. Well, maybe my heart knew."

"And maybe it was just the seductive spell of the desert and the harvest sky," Duncan whispered.

She grinned. "Or maybe the spell woven over me by one very handsome Scot."

"Hmmm," he said against her ear, "maybe."

She stood in Duncan's supportive embrace as Istaqa and six other Hopi riders and two extra mules came to a halt in front of the brokendown car.

"Una sent me out. She said you must be in trouble, otherwise you would have let us know why you didn't come to us yesterday."

"You don't know the half of it," Rainy said. "My brother is in real danger. The man I was bringing to you turned out to be the very man who's been behind the artifact thefts. Gunther Albright was a good friend of my family, but apparently he's been stealing what he could for some time."

Istaqa eyed Duncan suspiciously. He nodded as if in greeting, then turned his attention back to Rainy. "This Albright man, he has your brother?"

"Yes. Sonny and Duncan showed up yesterday, and Gunther forced Sonny to take him and his partner, a man named Chester Driscoll, back to Winslow. I twisted my ankle; otherwise Duncan and I would have walked to Winslow last night."

"Would you have any water you could spare?" Duncan suddenly asked. "I'm afraid Albright dumped most of ours, and the prospect of drinking radiator water isn't very appealing."

Istaqa signaled to one of his companions and a waterskin was handed down. Duncan helped Rainy drink first and then drank his fill before handing the bag back to Istaqa.

"I don't know when anything has ever tasted so good," Rainy commented. She grimaced at the throbbing pain in her ankle. "Can you get us to Winslow?"

"I'll take you there," Istaqa replied. He turned to the man at his left and gave instructions in Hopi. The man immediately brought up the two extra mules, then motioned for three of the other men to follow.

"I'll send my companions back to alert our people. If this man you speak of is waiting for you in Winslow, or if he's on the trail up ahead, we will need to know that others can get the word out." Istaqa's square-cut black hair blew gently in the breeze as his dark eyes narrowed. "I will make sure this man is stopped. I will see your brother safe."

Rainy felt a deep love for her friend. The compassion he felt for her and Sonny was very evident. "I know you will."

————

"This is ridiculous!" Gunther Albright paced back and forth as Sonny worked to dig out the car.

"I can't help it, Gunther. Those patches of sand get me every time—just ask my sister."

Sonny hid his grin as he bent over the log he was using to try to free the tire from the sand. He wasn't trying too hard, however. After spending the previous afternoon driving in circles, Sonny had managed to get them stuck in the sand. He calculated they were only about five miles from Winslow, but Gunther had no idea where they were and neither did Chester.

"We'll die out here if you don't dig us out," Chester said, his voice in a panic.

"We aren't going to die, Chester," Sonny answered as he eased up and pretended to reassess the situation.

"Some of us may if you don't figure a way out of this mess," Gunther declared. "I didn't come all this way to spend the night in the middle of nowhere, yet that's what you've forced upon me. Now that it's getting light, I expect you to dig us out of this hole and get us to Winslow."

"I'm working on it, Gunther. I don't want to be out here any more than the rest of you," Sonny said in a serious manner. He stared Gunther in the eye. "After all, you've left my sister and friend to die. I want out of here every bit as much as you do." He saw that the older man was exhausted. Gunther had refused to sleep, fearful that Sonny might somehow free the car and leave without him knowing it. The old man wouldn't even leave the car unless Chester was sitting in it for insurance. Now Sonny knew they were both ready to drop, and he planned to use that to his advantage.

"I don't much care what you want. Get back to work. I don't intend to spend even another hour here."

Sonny went back to the pretense of digging out. He walked to the edge of the road and picked up a few stones and put them in front of the car tire. Seeing that he was working, Gunther went back to where Chester sat in the shade of some scraggly mesquite.

"This is a fine mess you've gotten me into," Sonny heard Gunther say. He lowered his voice then, however, and Sonny couldn't hear any further comments. He watched from the corner of his eye as Gunther eased onto the ground and leaned back to rest. He pointed to Sonny and said something to Chester. Sonny could only imagine that he was instructing the man to keep watch. Chester nodded while Gunther pulled his hat down over his eyes. With great reluctance, Chester got up and walked to the car.

"Don't try anything stupid, Gordon. I'll be sitting here in the car watching you the whole time."

"You do that, Driscoll. I'll feel a whole lot safer just knowing you're on guard."

Chester frowned but nevertheless crawled in behind the wheel of Sonny's touring car.

Sonny grinned again and got down on the ground. He dug around the wheel and glanced every so often over to where Gunther dozed. It wasn't long until he heard snores coming from the front seat of the vehicle as well. When he was certain that both men were asleep, he jumped to his feet and hiked out across the desert toward Winslow.

At a good lope, Sonny knew he could make the distance in a little over an hour. He was in good shape and had an ample supply of water in the canteen he wore on his hip. He also felt confident that God had provided this moment for him. He was rested and alert, having slept through most of the night. He could do this. He would do this and he would rescue Rainy and Duncan before it was too late.

The day was still rather pleasant by the time Sonny walked into Winslow. He went immediately to the town marshal and explained the situation.

"We've already had word from some Indian Bureau man named Richland," the marshal told Sonny. "I've had my men out searching the area, but they were told over at the hotel that Albright had already left the area."

"Yes, he'd taken my sister and headed north to Hopi country. Albright and Driscoll are stuck just northeast of town. I can lead you there. My sister and friend, however, are stranded about fifteen miles north, just off the main road. They've been there all night and they don't have water."

"Everything's going to be all right," the man said without emotion. His calm was maddening to Sonny, who could think of nothing but his sister dying from heatstroke.

The marshal rounded up two cars and a deputy and motioned Sonny to the front seat of his own car. "We'll take Albright and Driscoll into custody first, then go on ahead and find your sister."

Sonny hated the delay. "Isn't there another car I could borrow? I hate to leave her there any longer."

"Try not to worry. This won't take long."

"But Albright has a gun. He may not come willingly."

The marshal shrugged and smiled. "Gun or no gun, he doesn't have much of a choice. I can leave him to the desert until he's more cooperative."

Sonny nodded. "Let's get to it, then."

To Sonny's amusement, Gunther and Chester were still asleep when he returned with the marshal. The men were so confused and disoriented as they awoke that they were easily taken into custody.

"If I could get a hand from your deputy," Sonny said after the men were secured in the backseat of the marshal's car, "I could get this car out of the sand." The marshal nodded and motioned his deputy to give Sonny assistance.

Sonny maneuvered a long pole into a position that would give them the best advantage. He and the deputy worked for several minutes until Sonny was confident that the car was about to be freed. "Okay, just give it a little gas."

"You know," a familiar voice called out, "we're never going to stick to our schedule if you keep getting us stuck in the sand."

Sonny dropped the pole and whirled around. Spying Rainy and Duncan on muleback with Istaqa at their side, he felt the world suddenly go right. "You're safe—you're here!"

Rainy laughed. "Of course, silly. And you're stuck in the sand as usual. Why the Harvey Company ever hired you to drive for them is beyond me."

"I guess they hired me because of my dashing good looks and dreamy eyes. Remember, the part about the eyes was particularly important."

Duncan got down from the mule and came to where Sonny stood. "Can I give you a hand with this?"

Sonny breathed a sigh of relief and slapped his friend on the back. "Yup, then you can buy me breakfast and we'll talk about your wedding plans."

Duncan looked surprised and glanced back at Rainy. "Wedding plans?"

Sonny nodded, giving Duncan a most serious expression. "You spent the night in the desert with my sister. Now you have to marry her."

Duncan shook his head. "No, I don't *have* to marry her. I *want* to marry her. And she said yes when I asked her to do just that."

Sonny met Rainy's pleased expression. "She had her hat set on getting a husband—she prayed night and day about it. You didn't stand a chance, you know."

Duncan sighed and shrugged. "Life is hard." He grinned up at Rainy and winked. "Might as well suffer it with someone who's as pretty and sweet as your sister."

"My sister—sweet? Haven't you learned about her temper yet?" Sonny questioned. "Then there's her—"

"That's enough, Sonny," Rainy interjected. She threw him a cautionary glance, then turned a sweet smile on Duncan. "He doesn't care about my flaws. He loves me."

Sonny nudged Duncan with his elbow. "We'll talk later."

Duncan nodded. "To be sure."

———————

In Albuquerque, Rainy recovered from her twisted ankle and planned her wedding. Her parents decided to delay the trip to Scotland long enough to see their only daughter wed and to help the university out of a terrible bind for their fall schedule.

"The board was rather stunned to learn that Gunther Albright was behind this mess. They thought him to be the most mild mannered and even tempered of any of their professors," Rainy's father told her as they gathered around the breakfast table.

"He certainly had us fooled," her mother stated as she deposited a plate of scrambled eggs smothered in salsa.

Rainy still shuddered at the memory of Gunther's gun at her head. "I still can't believe he could be so cruel to us—especially you and Dad. You treated him like a brother."

Her father nodded and took up the Bible for family devotions. "He was a wolf in sheep's clothing. The Word warns us of people like that. People who come claiming to be one thing when they're really something else."

"But don't you feel as though all your kindness to him was a wasted effort?" Rainy asked. She took the plate of eggs and served her father a generous portion before serving herself. Handing the bowl to her mother, she waited for her father's answer.

"I guess I don't feel it was wasted. Gunther will remember that we were kind to him. He'll remember that I came to him in jail and forgave him for everything—including the fact that he threatened your life and that of Sonny's. That was probably the hardest part of all."

"Yes, to be sure," her mother replied. "But it was what God would have us do. I wouldn't trust Gunther again or allow him another opportunity to repeat his actions, but I can forgive him."

"I feel I have so much to learn," Rainy said with a sigh. "I've been so angry with Chester and Gunther. I've tried to just let go of my feelings, but it's hard."

Her father covered her hand with his own. "It will probably take time."

"But it didn't take you all that much time. It's only been a week and a half and you're willing to forgive."

Her father nodded. "I've learned from past experience that the sooner I deal with a grievance, the sooner I recover my life. The longer I let the matter remain in turmoil and bitterness, the more time I lose. It's a part of maturity and growth. It'll come to you in time—with each situation like this that you have to work through and forgive. The important part is that you be willing to let God work through you and use you in this. He can help you—if you really want to forgive Chester and Gunther."

Rainy nodded. "I know that you're right."

"Well, I have the last of my things loaded in the car," Sonny announced as he bounded into the dining room.

"Then come have breakfast before it gets cold," their mother chided.

Rainy looked to her brother and grinned. "So the great adventure begins."

"A little later than I planned, but instead of stopping in California, I'll go right on up to Juneau, where I'll meet up with my friends."

They joined hands as Rainy's father led them in a blessing. "Father, we thank you for the food on our table and the bounty we enjoy. We praise you for the many blessings we've been given—for Rainy's name being cleared and her safe return and for Sonny's safe return and the realization of his dream in Alaska. We thank you for these things and so many more. Amen."

"Amen," the family murmured in unison.

Rainy was reluctant to let go of her brother's and father's hands.

"I'm going to miss you both so much." Her eyes misted with tears. "But at the same time, I'm so excited about the future God has shown each of us. I just want you all to know how much I love you."

She met her mother's gaze from across the table and knew deep within her heart that if anyone understood, her mother did. After all, she had married and, as a young bride, had left her homeland and family to come to America. She knew what it was to be separated from those she held most dear.

Sonny leaned over and kissed her on the cheek. "I love you too. Now stop being all sappy. I'm starving."

They all laughed, including Rainy. Somehow in that one silly moment, she knew everything would be just fine. They were a family—and no matter the distance in miles, their love would always keep them close.

———

"So tell me the truth, Mom. What do you think of Duncan?"

"He's a wonderful man," her mother said as she put in the last stitches on the hem of Rainy's wedding dress.

Rainy toyed with her veil and hugged it close. "He is wonderful. Oh, Mom, I'm so happy. I thought this day would never come."

Her mother smiled. "I know. I feared you'd grow impatient and take whatever you could just to get married and have a family. It's always best, however, when we hold out for what God has in mind. You never would have been happy married to a movie actor."

"I know," Rainy said thoughtfully. "I thought about that the other day. I tried to imagine the parties and the travel—the big house and servants. I know I would have been miserable. I think Phillip definitely cared about me, but I don't know that he could hope to understand me. Duncan understands me."

"That's because he shares your love of God and your passion for the Southwest. You both love archaeology and digging for pieces of history. When you can share those kinds of things and understand each other's needs, it can't help but make for a good marriage."

Rainy nodded and exclaimed in joy as her mother held up the ivory dress for her inspection. "Oh, Mom, it's beautiful!"

Rainy's mother had worn the gown when she'd married Raymond Gordon in 1895, and it had been the height of fashion. Edrea had taken the dress and restyled it in a manner better fitting to the 1930s.

Rainy fingered the satin and marveled at the changes. Her mother had taken the pinafore lace from the bodice and worked the high neck-line into a soft, molded scoop. The full muttonchop sleeves were cut down to make a sleeker line.

"I can't believe it's even the same dress," Rainy said as her mother turned the gown to reveal the back.

"The lace for your veil was taken from the train," her mother explained. "I think it looks quite nice, if I do say so myself."

Rainy embraced her mother, careful not to crush the gown. "It's wonderful. I love it so much—especially knowing that it was first worn by you."

Her mother held her tight for a moment. "All of your life you'll remember this. When times are good, you'll remember it with a fond-ness and joy that just blends naturally into everything around you. When times are bad, your thoughts will be uplifted by the memory of your wedding day and the anticipation you held for your future."

Her mother pulled away and put the dress aside. She motioned Rainy to sit with her on the bed. "Darling, I want you to know how proud I am of you. I know how hard it was for you to face the accusa-tions at the college and not hate your adversaries. I know, too, it was equally difficult to deal with Gunther and Chester's actions."

"It isn't easy," Rainy said softly. "But just as Dad said, it's a process. I'm trying to work through it a little at a time. Day by day."

"That's the wisest thing to do. After all, Jesus told us to take up our cross *daily*. There's a reason for that. Some people try to take care of life's struggles in bigger chunks and some people never try at all. But I'm a firm believer that you should take everything one step at a time— even forgiveness. You'll need to remember to do likewise when Duncan upsets you or changes your plans. It isn't always easy to live with another human being, but the situations that develop between husband and wife are even more difficult than those that develop with parents or sib-lings."

Rainy knew her mother spoke with great wisdom, but in all honesty she couldn't imagine her mom and dad ever arguing or feeling strife toward each other. "But you and Dad never fought—did you?"

Her mother laughed softly. "Oh, mercy, but did we fight. I didn't know how to be patient back then and, well, this may come as a surprise to you, but when I first met your father, I wasn't interested in God. I didn't know anything about the love of Jesus or His sacrifice for me."

"I guess I didn't realize that," Rainy said, trying to remember if she'd ever heard her mother speak of her coming to salvation. She'd just always imagined that her mother had loved God from childhood, just as Rainy had.

"I wasn't the best of souls to share time with," her mother continued. "Ray was such a sweet boy—so mild mannered and giving. He worked with his father on their sheep farm outside of Edinburgh. He loved working with the sheep, loved spending long hours in the fields. I, on the other hand, preferred the parties and fun that could be had with my friends."

"It doesn't seem at all like you."

"I've changed. The love of God changed my heart. I fell in love with your father because he was the only person who truly loved me for myself. He didn't care if I was dressed up in satins and lace. He only cared that I belong to him—and to God. He talked to me long and hard about the Bible and why we needed a savior. But my family was well-to-do, and while we hadn't really turned our noses up at the idea of church and such things, we were hardly a God-fearing people."

"Why have I never heard this before?" Rainy questioned. "I remember you talking about Grandma and Grandpa both being powerful witnesses for Jesus."

"And they were, in their old age. Your father helped us all to find Jesus for ourselves, but even after I prayed to be saved from hell, I still had a great deal to do to work on my personality and attitude. I had to learn that there was more to life and relationships than money. It wasn't easy. I was used to buying what I needed, and sometimes that included my friends."

"I can't imagine you like that." Rainy reached out and grasped her mother's hand.

"Where did you imagine your temper came from?" her mother teased. She hugged Rainy close and smoothed back a stray piece of red-blond hair. "When the doctor told me he was certain I was to have twins, I prayed that you'd both be boys. I feared having a daughter. I was afraid she'd be just like me—ill-tempered, rushing to conclusions, spoiled. Then when you were born, I was overjoyed. I had a son and a daughter. Because the delivery had been so difficult, I knew you were all I would ever have. But you know what? You were enough."

"Was I that much trouble?" Rainy asked, sitting up. She looked quite seriously into her mother's tender expression.

"No, you were that much love. You were wonderful, Rainy. I could never have hoped for anything better. You'll always hold a special place in my heart. I just want you to know how complete you made my life."

Tears came to Rainy's eyes. "I love you so much—Daddy too. I don't know what I'll ever do without you two."

"You'll come and visit us. Who knows? You might even fall in love with Scotland."

Rainy nodded. "I've come to believe in these last few months that anything is possible."

———

A month later, Rainy smoothed the satin of her mother's gown and prepared to become the wife of Duncan Hartford. The butterflies in her stomach told her that she was not nearly as brave as she presumed. Licking her dry lips, Rainy whispered a silent prayer for strength and peace.

"I know I'm doing the right thing, Lord," she whispered as she caught her reflection in the mirror. "I just need you to stay with me every step of the way—I don't want to mess this up."

Her father soon came for her, and before she knew it she was walking down the aisle.

Lamont Hartford smiled at his son and soon-to-be daughter-in-law. "Dearly beloved, we are gathered together . . ."

How special, Rainy thought, *to have Duncan's father officiate our wedding.* She could see how much it pleased Duncan. If only Sonny could have delayed his trip to be at her wedding, the day would have been perfect—but it was perfect enough. Sonny had his own life, and she was happy he was in the interior of Alaska with his friends and a new job. She knew she held his love—even from three thousand miles away.

"Who giveth this woman to be wed?"

"Her mother and I," Rainy's father answered. He leaned over and kissed Rainy soundly on the cheek. "We love you so much," he whispered, then left her in Duncan's care—for the rest of her life.

Rainy felt a lump form in the back of her throat. The seriousness of the moment seemed to weigh down on her. *I know I'm doing the right thing.* She drew in a deep breath. *I've never been more sure of anything.*

"Rainy Gordon, wilt thou have this man . . ."

Rainy's eyes filled with tears as she corralled her thoughts and looked at Duncan's questioning gaze. She felt his reassurance as he squeezed her hand. "I will." *I will have this man for my husband and I will love him for all of my days.*

Duncan gently pushed the ring onto her finger, then kissed her sweetly as Duncan's father declared them man and wife. Rainy thought she might faint dead away from the intensity of the moment, but before she knew it she was being whisked away for a picture.

"You're beautiful," Duncan whispered in her ear as they allowed the photographer to pose them. Rainy was arranged in a high-backed chair while Duncan stood directly behind her.

The photographer fussed with her dress, positioning the folds of the material first one way and then another. Rainy leaned her head up to catch sight of her husband. "You don't look so bad yourself."

Duncan lightly fingered the lapel of his dark suit. "Anything to please you."

Rainy giggled. "I'm going to remember you said that."

"Miss Gordon—I mean, Mrs. Hartford, I wondered if I could speak to you for just a moment."

Rainy looked up to find Marshall Driscoll standing just beyond the photographer. She stiffened but felt Duncan's comforting touch as he gently rubbed her shoulder.

"What can I do for you? I'm rather busy."

"One more moment and we'll be finished," the photographer promised. He went to his camera and Rainy waited in silence for the moment to be forever captured.

All the while, Mr. Driscoll stood to one side watching. It rather unnerved her, but Rainy knew there was nothing she could do. To her relief her father and mother soon joined them. Her father held out his hand and shook Marshall Driscoll's hand and smiled. Rainy couldn't help but feel a sense of curiosity and even frustration. What was this man doing at her wedding, and why was her father welcoming him?

The pictures were taken and the photographer soon gathered his things and left. Rainy remained seated, uncertain of what else to do. She watched her parents with Driscoll and wondered how they could possibly be so accommodating to this man.

Seeing that Rainy was watching him, Driscoll left her parents and crossed the room. "I'm sorry for the intrusion," he said, "but I had to come."

"Why?" Rainy asked.

"Because I wanted to apologize." Suddenly his expression suggested defeat. He lowered his gaze. "I'm sorry for what Chester . . . what he put you through. I knew about some things and presumed others. I knew you weren't guilty of the thefts at the university, but I couldn't bring myself to get to the bottom of it and expose Chester. He never confided in me—at least not to the extent that I knew what he was up to these last months."

Driscoll seemed most contrite for what had happened and Rainy's anger faded. "It was kind of you to come and apologize."

"That's not all," her father said, joining them. "Marshall has asked me to stay on with the university permanently."

Rainy perked up at this. "And what did you tell him?"

"I declined," her father said. "I told him that my plans were set for Scotland and we would only delay long enough to get teachers in position for the classes Gunther's dismissal left open. Then I told him that I had a very qualified daughter who would probably love to work at the university—especially in the areas of archaeology and Indian history."

Rainy looked at Duncan, who beamed her a smile. She shook her head in disbelief and looked to Marshall Driscoll. "And what did you have to say about that, Mr. Driscoll?"

"I thought it a wonderful idea. I've already released a letter to the board exonerating you of all guilt and accusations. I've made it quite clear that my son was to blame for the mishap three years ago. My son and Gunther Albright." He paused and drew a deep breath. "We're prepared to offer you a position."

Rainy nodded. A part of her wanted to jump for joy and immediately accept whatever position Driscoll might offer but another part couldn't have cared less. She turned to Duncan and reached for his hand. "My husband and I will discuss it and I'll let you know."

Marshall Driscoll nodded. "I hope very much you'll join us."

With that said, he allowed Rainy's parents to lead him from the room. Rainy got to her feet and turned to face Duncan. "So . . . what do you think?"

"I think I love you more and more by the minute," he said, pulling her close.

"No, I already know that part. What do you think about Mr. Driscoll's offer?"

Duncan's expression grew thoughtful. "Is that what you want?"

Rainy studied her husband for a moment. She thought of all the time she'd spent fretting over the university and what might have been. She thought of how desperately she'd longed to clear her name. God had worked out all of the details—freeing her from the stigma of being a thief, giving her a husband to love her. Without a doubt, everything seemed much clearer now.

She slowly shook her head. "No. No, it isn't what I want at all. I want to have your children and spend my life enjoying your company."

He slowly grinned. "I think I can arrange both."

She laughed. "I've seen your determination when you set your mind to a thing. I've no doubt you can accomplish whatever you decide is worthy."

He nuzzled her neck. "So you won't mind terribly that I've talked to the National Geographic Society about a husband-and-wife team who can provide them extensive research on the Hopi and Navajo Indians?"

Rainy's eyes widened. "Truly? What did they say?"

"They were very interested."

"Oh!" She couldn't help pulling away to give a little jump and clap her hands. "I can't believe you did that. This is wonderful!"

Duncan picked her up and whirled her in a circle. "I always want you to be this happy."

Rainy reached up and ran her fingers through his wavy black hair. "I love you, Duncan Hartford." She heard his sigh and joined it with her own.

Later that night, long after everyone else was asleep, Rainy and Duncan strolled in the garden together. Rainy wore a flowing nightgown and robe of white lawn, her strawberry blond hair flowing down to her waist. She felt like a princess in a fairy tale and Duncan was her prince.

Looking to him, she smiled warmly at the sight of him in his loose open shirt and gray trousers. They held hands as they walked. Words seemed unnecessary. He was everything she'd ever wanted—loving, giving, and kind. *What a wonder it is to be wife to this man,* Rainy thought.

She smelled the fragrant scent of her mother's honeysuckle—so sweet and delicate. A friend had brought her the plant from California and her mother had babied the bush until it grew strong and supple. There were other flowers—some in pots, some planted around the courtyard walk and walls. There was so much of her mother here in this garden. So much of Rainy's past was here as well. The garden had always been a comfort to her.

"I'll miss this place," Rainy told Duncan. "Even when I was in Santa Fe working for the Harvey Company, I knew I could come here anytime I wanted. Mother worked absolute wonders with this garden, and now she'll go away and the new owner will never know how much effort she put into it."

Overhead a full moon shone down on them, lighting the path as if it were day. Duncan put his arm around her shoulders and whispered in Rainy's ear, "I have a surprise for you. I worked out the details with your father and . . . well . . . I bought this place."

"What!" Rainy pulled away and caught the amused expression on his face. "You honestly did?"

He shrugged. "You seemed to like it so much, and I figured we'd need a place to come when we were not out on a dig. Does it please you?"

She laughed and hugged him tight. "You know it does. Oh, thank you, Duncan. I don't know what to say."

"You've already said it. You told me that you love me, and that's all I'll ever need."

"I agree," she said, stretching on tiptoe to kiss him, "and I intend to say it often."

"Just so long as you mean it each time."

Beneath the harvest skies God blessed their union with a deep abiding peace and satisfaction. Rainy believed that nothing would ever be more wonderful than these first moments with her husband. *Sometimes,* she thought, *to have the very best, you must let go of the mediocre that you hold to so tightly.* She'd let go of her desire to control her life—she'd let go of her plans for helping God answer her prayers and she was learning to let go of her doubts and insecurities. Together, Rainy knew that she and Duncan would be able to face most anything. And with God at their side, Rainy knew there was nothing they couldn't accomplish.

It was a new beginning.

A starting place for all the dreams they would share.

Snuggling against her husband, Rainy had no room for doubt. The future was much too promising.

Looking for More
Good Books to Read?

Penguins

Liz Pichon

Orchard Books · New York

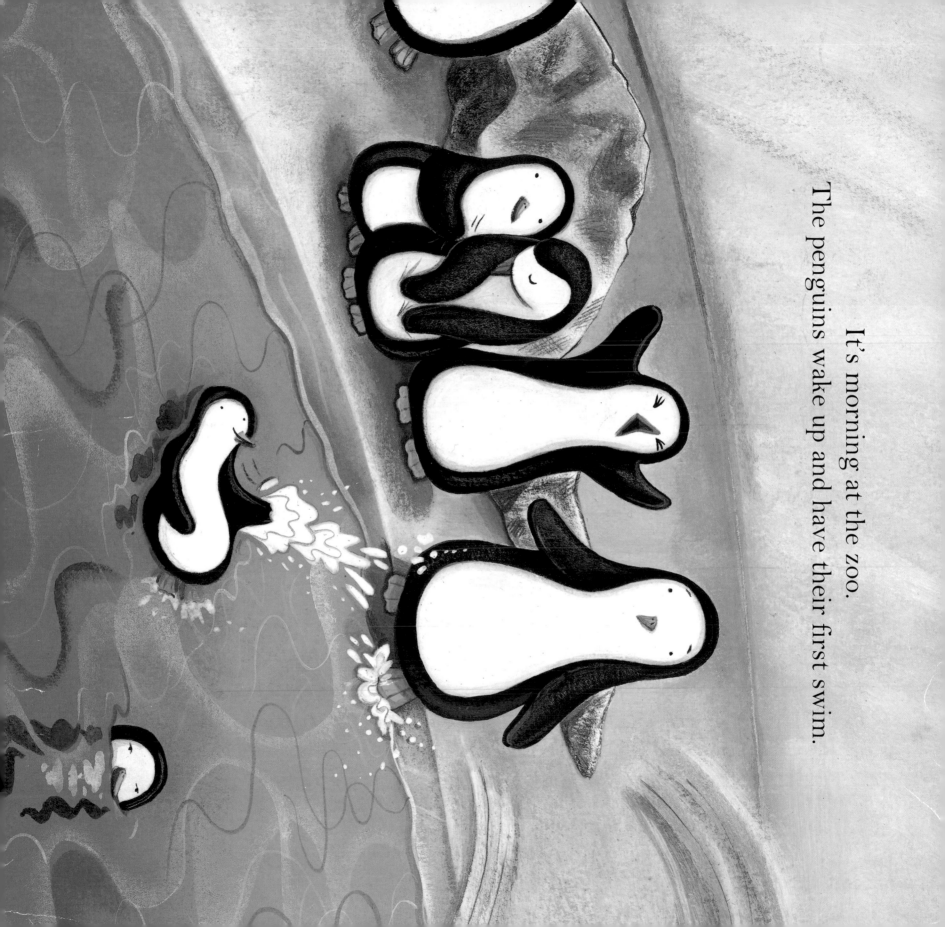

It's morning at the zoo.
The penguins wake up and have their first swim.

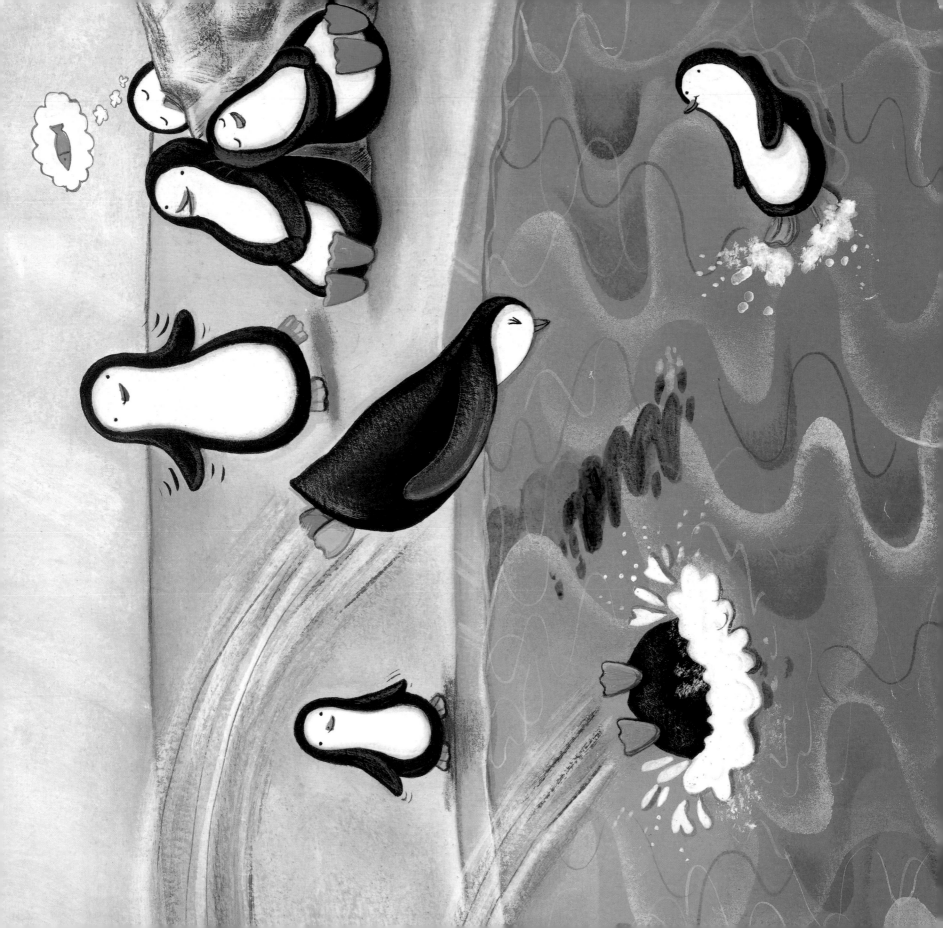

EVERYDAY PENGUIN ACTIVITIES

1. Swim.

2. Eat fish.

3. Play penguin games.

4. Sleep standing up.

5. Look at people.

6. Look at more people.

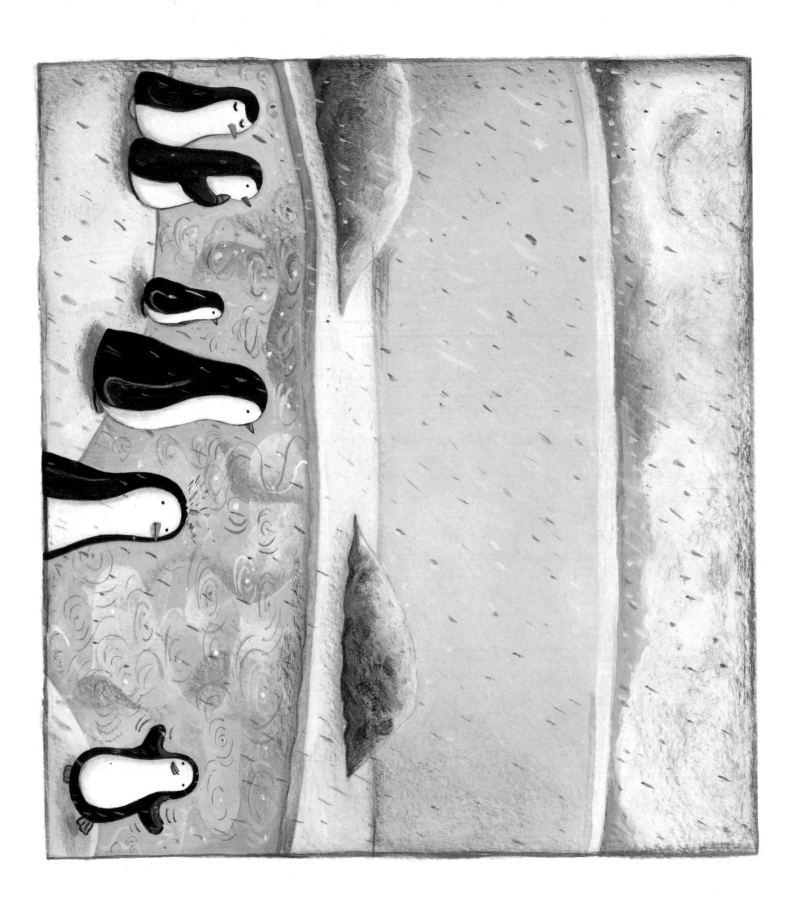

On rainy days, the penguins don't do much at all.

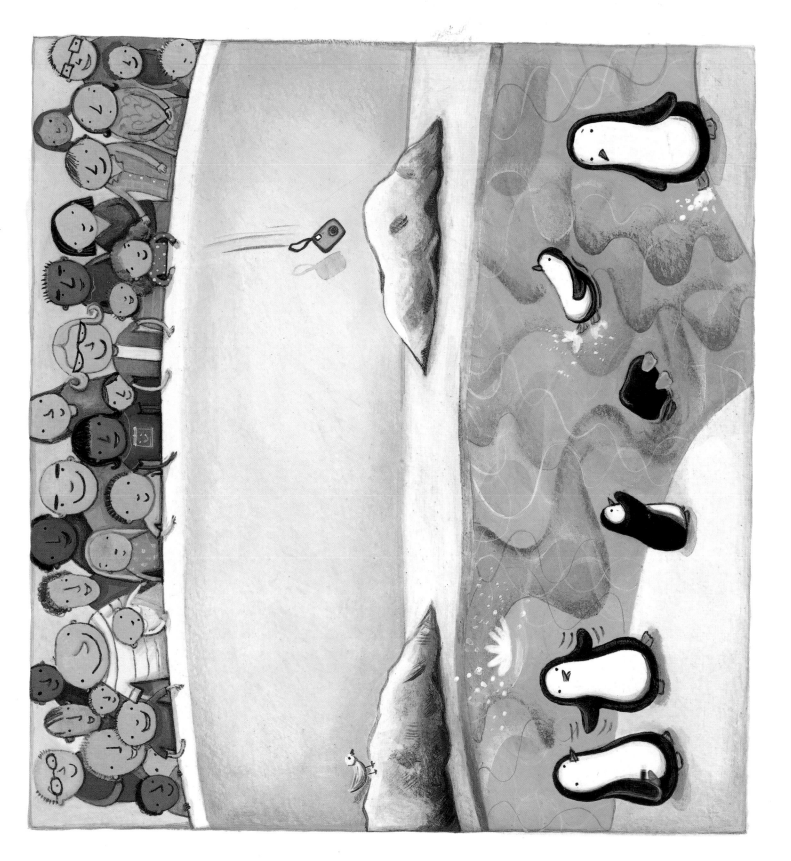

But when the sun shines and the people come, it's fun, fun, fun!

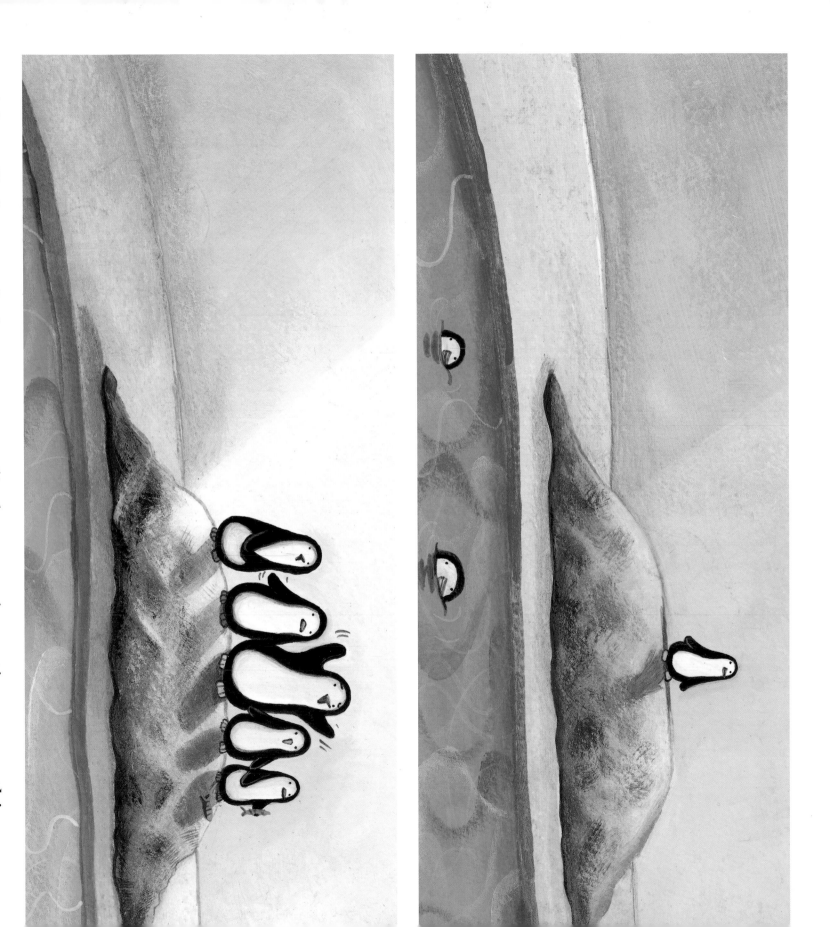

After all the people have gone, a little penguin notices something. "DON'T TOUCH IT!" says his mother. "Somebody will be back for it."

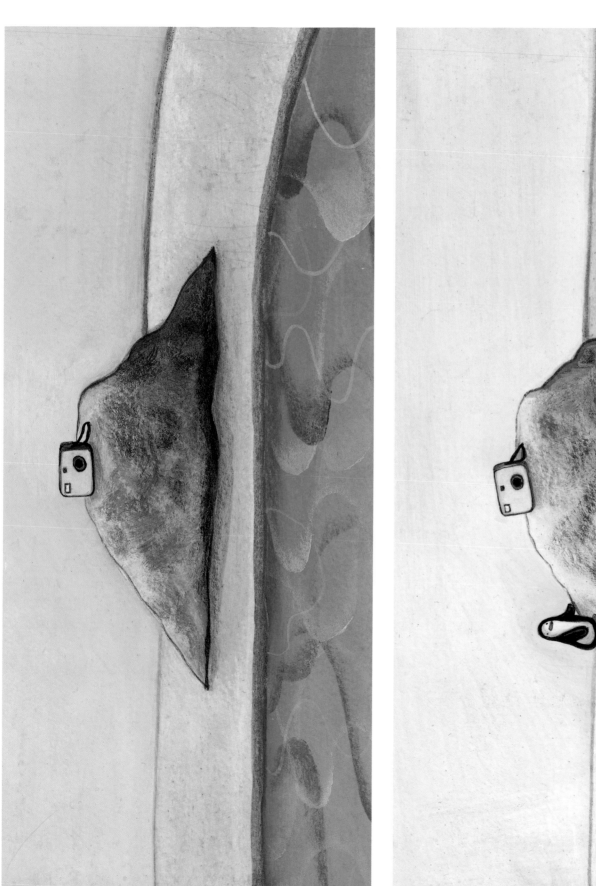

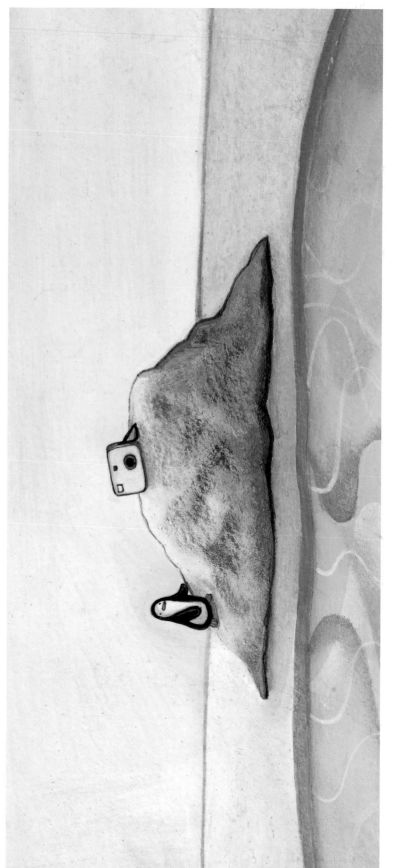

But nobody comes back.

The little penguin moves closer for a better look.

He goes over and picks it up.

"It's a camera!" says the little penguin.

"What do you do with a camera?" the other penguins ask.

"You smile at it!" says the little penguin, grinning.

"Are you sure you can't eat it?"
asks a hungry penguin.

A baby penguin
jumps on the
camera and says,
"Let's press ALL
the buttons!"

FLASH!

They all get bug eyes.

"Everyone waddle over
there and line up," says
the little penguin.

"Okay," they reply.

The little penguin looks through
the camera lens.

"What do we do?"
shout all the other penguins.

The little penguin puts his flipper
on the button and says,
"Everyone look at me and say FISH!"

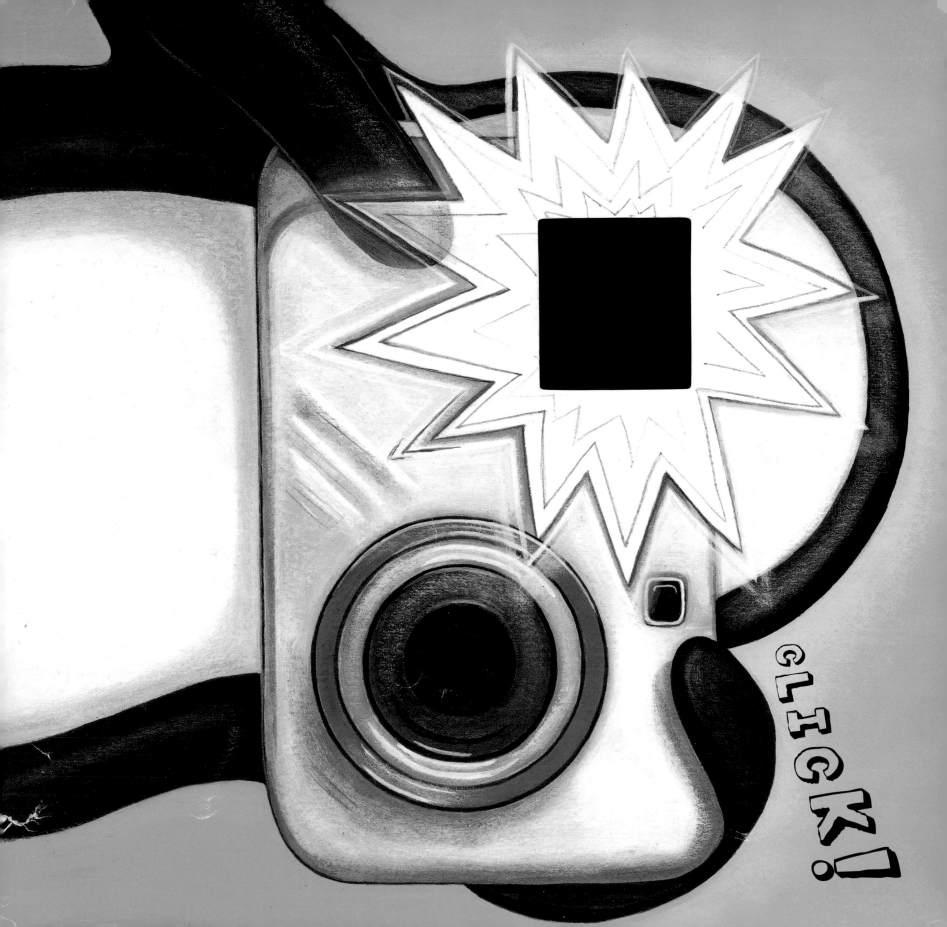

"FISH!"

The little penguin takes the picture.

CLICK!

Now all the penguins
want to use the camera.

CLICK!

They take lots and lots
of amazing pictures.

flash!

But suddenly…

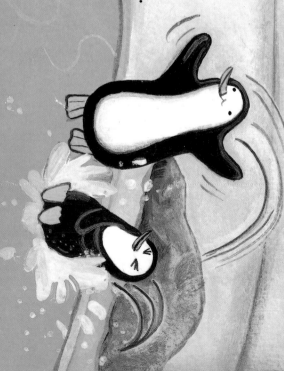

. . . the camera stops working!

"Oh, dear," says the mother penguin, "you'd better put it back now."

So the little penguin puts the camera back on the rock where he found it.

The next morning the zookeeper sees the camera. "What's this doing here?" he says. "I'd better take it to lost and found."

Soon the camera is returned to the little girl who dropped it.

"Your camera is not broken," says the zookeeper, "but the penguins seem to have pecked it a bit."

"That's okay!" the little girl replies. "I love penguins!"

A few days later the pictures are developed. There are pictures of monkeys, lions, tigers, and elephants. And, strangely, there are quite a few pictures of penguins, too!